THE
SEVENTH
SCROLL

THE
SEVENTH
SCROLL

Wilbur Smith

Thorndike Press • **Chivers Press**
Thorndike, Maine USA   Bath, Avon, England

This Large Print edition is published by Thorndike Press, USA and by Chivers Press, England.

Published in 1995 in the U.S. by arrangement with St. Martin's Press, Inc.

Published in 1995 in the U.K. by arrangement with Macmillan General Books.

U.S. Hardcover   0-7862-0482-6   (Basic Series Edition)
U.K. Hardcover   0-7451-7893-6   (Windsor Large Print)
U.K. Softcover   0-7451-3718-0   (Paragon Large Print)

The text of this Large Print edition is unabridged.
Other aspects of the book may vary from the original edition.

Set in 16 pt. News Plantin by Rick Gundberg.

Printed in the United States on permanent paper.

British Library Cataloguing in Publication Data available

Library of Congress Cataloging in Publication Data

Smith, Wilbur A.
   The seventh scroll / Wilbur Smith.
     p.   cm.
   ISBN 0-7862-0482-6 (lg. print : hc)
   1. Large type books. I. Title.
  [PR9405.9.S5S48 1995b]
  823—dc20   95-8532

Once more this book is for
my wife Danielle.
Despite all the happy loving years we have
spent together I feel that we are
only just beginning.
There is so much more to come.

The dusk crept in from the desert, and shaded the dunes with purple. Like a thick velvet cloak it muted all sounds, so that the evening was tranquil and hushed.

From where they stood on the crest of the dune they looked out over the oasis and the complex of small villages that surrounded it. The buildings were white with flat roofs and the date palms stood higher than any of them except the Islamic mosque and the Coptic Christian church. These bastions of faith opposed each other across the lake.

The waters of the lake were darkling. A flight of duck slanted down on quick wings to land with a small splash of white close in against the reed banks.

The man and the woman made a disparate couple. He was tall, though slightly bowed, his silvering hair catching the last of the sunlight. She was young, in her early thirties, slim, alert and vibrant. Her hair was thick and curling, restrained now by a thong at the nape of her neck.

'Time to go down now. Alia will be waiting.' He smiled down at her fondly. She was his second wife. When his first wife died he thought that she had taken the sunlight with her. He had not expected this last period of happiness in his life. Now he had her and his work. He was a man happy and contented.

Suddenly she broke away from him, and pulled the thong from her hair. She shook it out, dense and dark, and she laughed. It was a pretty sound. Then she plunged down the steep slip-face of the dune, her long skirts billowing around her flying legs. They were shapely and brown. She kept her balance until halfway down, when gravity overwhelmed her and she tumbled.

From the top he smiled down on her indulgently. Sometimes she was still a child. At others she was a grave and dignified woman. He was not certain which he preferred, but he loved her in both moods. She rolled to a halt at the bottom of the dune and sat up, still laughing, shaking the sand out of her hair.

'Your turn!' she called up at him. He followed her down sedately, moving with the slight stiffness of advancing age, keeping his balance until he reached the bottom. He lifted her to her feet. He did not kiss her, although the temptation to do so was strong. It was not the Arab way to show public affection, even to a beloved wife.

She straightened her clothing and retied her hair before they set off towards the village. They skirted the reed beds of the oasis, crossing the rickety bridges over the irrigation canals. As they passed, the peasants returning from the fields greeted him with deep respect.

'*Salaam aleikum, Doktari!* Peace be with you,

8

doctor.' They honoured all men of learning, but him especially for his kindness to them and their families over the years. Many of them had worked for his father before him. It mattered little that most of them were Moslem, while he was a Christian.

When they reached the villa, Alia, the old housekeeper, greeted them with mumbles and scowls. 'You are late. You are always late. Why do you not keep regular hours, like decent folk? We have a position to maintain.'

'Old mother, you are always right,' he teased her gently. 'What would we do without you to care for us?' He sent her away, still scowling to cover her love and concern for him.

They ate the simple meal on the terrace together, dates and olives and unleavened bread and goat's milk cheese. It was dark when they finished, but the desert stars were bright as candles.

'Royan, my flower.' He reached across the table and touched her hand. 'It is time to begin work.' He stood up from the table and led the way to his study that opened out on to the terrace.

Royan Al Simma went directly to the tall steel safe against the far wall and tumbled the combination. The safe was out of place in this room, amongst the old books and scrolls, amongst the ancient statues and artefacts and grave goods that were the collection of his lifetime.

When the heavy steel door swung open, Royan

stood back for a moment. She always felt this prickle of awe whenever she first looked upon this relic of the ages, even after an interval of only a few short hours.

'The seventh scroll,' she whispered, and steeled herself to touch it. It was nearly four thousand years old, written by a genius out of time with history, a man who had been dust for all these millennia, but whom she had come to know and respect as she did her own husband. His words were eternal, and they spoke to her clearly from beyond the grave, from the fields of paradise, from the presence of the great trinity, Osiris and Isis and Horus, in whom he had believed so devoutly. As devoutly as she believed in another more recent Trinity.

She carried the scroll to the long table at which Duraid, her husband, was already at work. He looked up as she laid it on the tabletop before him, and for a moment she saw the same mystical mood in his eyes that had affected her. He always wanted the scroll there on the table, even when there was no real call for it. He had the photographs and the microfilm to work with. It was as though he needed the unseen presence of the ancient author close to him as he studied the texts.

Then he threw off the mood and was the dispassionate scientist once more. 'Your eyes are better than mine, my flower,' he said. 'What do you make of this character?'

She leaned over his shoulder and studied the

hieroglyph on the photograph of the scroll that he pointed out to her. She puzzled over the character for a moment before she took the magnifying glass from Duraid's hand and peered through it again.

'It looks as though Taita has thrown in another cryptogram of his own creation just to bedevil us.' She spoke of the ancient author as though he were a dear, but sometimes exasperating, friend who still lived and breathed, and played tricks upon them.

'We'll just have to puzzle it out, then,' Duraid declared with obvious relish. He loved the ancient game. It was his life's work.

The two of them laboured on into the cool of the night. This was when they did their best work. Sometimes they spoke Arabic and sometimes English; for them the two languages were as one. Less often they used French, which was their third common language. They had both received their education at universities in England and the United States, so far from this very Egypt of theirs. Royan loved the expression 'This very Egypt' that Taita used so often in the scrolls.

She felt a peculiar affinity in so many ways with this ancient Egyptian. After all, she was his direct descendant. She was a Coptic Christian, not of the Arab line that had so recently conquered Egypt, less than fourteen centuries ago. The Arabs were newcomers in this very Egypt of hers, while her own blood line ran

11

back to the time of the pharaohs and the great pyramids.

At ten o'clock Royan made coffee for them, heating it on the charcoal stove that Alia had lit for them before she went off to her own family in the village. They drank the sweet, strong brew from thin cups that were half-filled with the heavy grounds. While they sipped, they talked as old friends.

For Royan that was their relationship, old friends. She had known Duraid ever since she had returned from England with her doctorate in archaeology and won her job with the Department of Antiquities, of which he was the director.

She had been his assistant when he had opened the tomb in the Valley of the Nobles, the tomb of Queen Lostris, the tomb that dated from about 1780 BC.

She had shared his disappointment when they had discovered that the tomb had been robbed in ancient times and all its treasures plundered. All that remained were the marvellous murals that covered the walls and the ceilings of the tomb.

It was Royan herself who had been working at the wall behind the plinth on which the sarcophagus had once stood, photographing the murals, when a section of the plaster had fallen away to reveal in their niche the ten alabaster jars. Each of the jars had contained a papyrus scroll. Every one of them had been written and placed there by Taita, the slave of the queen.

Since then their lives, Duraid's and her own, seemed to have revolved around those scraps of papyrus. Although there was some damage and deterioration, in the main they had survived nearly four thousand years remarkably intact.

What a fascinating story they contained, of a nation attacked by a superior enemy, armed with horse and chariot that were still alien to the Egyptians of that time. Crushed by the Hyksos hordes, the people of the Nile were forced to flee. Led by their queen, Lostris of the tomb, they followed the great river southwards almost to its source amongst the brutal mountains of the Ethiopian highlands. Here amongst those forbidding mountains, Lostris had entombed the mummified body of her husband, the Pharaoh Mamose, who had been slain in battle against the Hyksos.

Long afterwards Queen Lostris had led her people back northwards to this very Egypt. Armed now with their own horses and chariots, forged into hard warriors in the African wilderness, they had come storming back down the cataracts of the great river to challenge once more the Hyksos invader, and in the end to triumph over him and wrest the double crown of upper and lower Egypt from his grasp.

It was a story that appealed to every fibre of her being, and that had fascinated her as they had unravelled each hieroglyph that the old slave had penned on the papyrus.

It had taken them all these years, working at night here in the villa on the oasis after their daily routine work at the museum in Cairo was done, but at last the ten scrolls had been deciphered — all except the seventh scroll. This was the one that was the enigma, the one which the author had cloaked in layers of esoteric shorthand and allusions so obscure that they were unfathomable at this remove of time. Some of the symbols he used had never figured before in all the thousands of texts that they had studied in their combined working lives. It was obvious to them both that Taita had not intended that the scrolls should be read by any eyes other than those of his beloved queen. These were his last gift for her to take with her beyond the grave.

It had taken all their combined skills, all their imagination and ingenuity, but at last they were approaching the conclusion of the task. There were still many gaps in the translation and many areas where they were uncertain whether or not they had captured the true meaning, but they had laid out the bones of the manuscript in such order that they were able to discern the outline of the creature it represented.

Now Duraid sipped his coffee and shook his head as he had done so often before. 'It frightens me,' he said. 'The responsibility. What to do with this knowledge we have gleaned. If it should fall into the wrong hands . . .' He sipped and sighed before he spoke again. 'Even if we take it to the right people, will they believe this material that is nearly four thousand years old?'

'Why must we bring in others?' Royan asked with an edge of exasperation in her voice. 'Why can we not do alone what has to be done?' At times like these the differences between them were most apparent. His was the caution of age, while hers was the impetuosity of youth.

'You do not understand,' he said. It always annoyed her when he said that, when he treated her as the Arabs treated their women in a totally masculine world. She had known the other world where women demanded and received the right to be treated as equals. She was a creature caught between those worlds, the Western world and the Arab world.

Royan's mother was an Englishwoman who had worked at the British Embassy in Cairo in the troubled times after World War II. She had met and married Royan's father, who had been a young Egyptian officer on the staff of Colonel Nasser. It was an unlikely union and had not persisted into Royan's adolescence.

Her mother had insisted upon returning to England, to her home town of York, for Royan's birth. She wanted her child to have British citizenship. After her parents had separated, Royan, again at her mother's insistence, had been sent back to England for her schooling, but all her holidays had been spent with her father in Cairo. Her father's career had prospered exceedingly, and in the end he had at-

15

tained ministerial rank in the Mubarak government. Through her love for him she came to look upon herself as more Egyptian than English.

It was her father who had arranged her marriage to Duraid Al Simma. It was the last thing that he had done for her before his death. She had known he was dying at the time, and she had not found it in her heart to defy him. All her modern training made her want to resist the old-fashioned Coptic tradition of the arranged marriage, but her breeding and her family and her Church were against her. She had acquiesced.

Her marriage to Duraid had not proved as insufferable as she had dreaded it might be. It might even have been entirely comfortable and satisfying if she had never been introduced to romantic love. However, there had been her liaison with David while she was up at university. He had swept her up in the hurly-burly, in the heady delirium, and, in the end, the heartache, when he had left her to marry a blonde English rose approved of by his parents.

She respected and liked Duraid, but sometimes in the night she still burned for the feel of a body as firm and young as her own on top of hers.

Duraid was still speaking and she had not been listening to him. She gave him her full attention once more. 'I have spoken to the minister again, but I do not think he believes in me. I think that Nahoot has convinced him that

16

I am a little mad.' He smiled sadly. Nahoot Guddabi was his ambitious and well-connected deputy. 'At any rate the minister says that there are no government funds available, and that I will have to seek outside finance. So, I have been over the list of possible sponsors again, and have narrowed it down to four. There is the Getty Museum, of course, but I never like to work with a big impersonal institution. I prefer to have a single man to answer to. Decisions are always easier to reach.' None of this was new to her, but she listened dutifully.

'Then there is Herr von Schiller. He has the money and the interest in the subject, but I do not know him well enough to trust him entirely.' He paused, and Royan had listened to these musings so often before that she could anticipate him.

'What about the American? He is a famous collector,' she forestalled him.

'Peter Walsh is a difficult man to work with. His passion to accumulate makes him unscrupulous. He frightens me a little.'

'So who does that leave?' she asked.

He did not reply, for they both knew the answer to her question. Instead, he turned his attention back to the material that littered the work table.

'It looks so innocent, so mundane. An old papyrus scroll, a few photographs and notebooks, a computer printout. It is difficult to believe how dangerous these might be in the wrong hands.' He sighed again. 'You might almost say that they are deadly dangerous.'

Then he laughed. 'I am being fanciful. Perhaps it is the late hour. Shall we get back to work? We can worry about these other matters once we have worked out all the conundrums set for us by this old rogue, Taita, and completed the translation.'

He picked up the top photograph from the pile in front of him. It was an extract from the central section of the scroll. 'It is the worst luck that the damaged piece of papyrus falls where it does.' He picked up his reading glasses and placed them on his nose before he read aloud.

' "*There are many steps to ascend on the staircase to the abode of Hapi. With much hardship and endeavour we reached the second step and proceeded no further, for it was here that the prince received a divine revelation. In a dream his father, the dead god pharaoh, visited him and commanded him, 'I have travelled far and I am grown weary. It is here that I will rest for all eternity.' "* ' Duraid removed his glasses and looked across at Royan, ' "*The second step*". It is a very precise description for once. Taita is not being his usual devious self.'

'Let's go back to the satellite photographs,' Royan suggested, and drew the glossy sheet towards her. Duraid came around the table to stand behind her.

'To me it seems most logical that the natural

18

feature that would obstruct them in the gorge would be something like a set of rapids or a waterfall. If it were the second waterfall, that would put them here —' Royan placed her finger on a spot on the satellite photograph where the narrow snake of the river threaded itself through the dark massifs of the mountains on either hand.

At that moment she was distracted and she lifted her head. 'Listen!' Her voice changed, sharpening with alarm.

'What is it?' Duraid looked up also.

'The dog,' she answered.

'That damn mongrel,' he agreed. 'It is always making the night hideous with its yapping. I have promised myself to get rid of him.'

At that moment the lights went out.

They froze with surprise in the darkness. The soft thudding of the decrepit diesel generator in its shed at the back of the palm grove had ceased. It was so much a part of the oasis night that they noticed it only when it was silent.

Their eyes adjusted to the faint starlight that came in through the terrace doors. Duraid crossed the room and took the oil lamp down from the shelf beside the door where it waited for just such a contingency. He lit it, and looked across at Royan with an expression of comical resignation.

'I will have to go down —'

'Duraid,' she interrupted him, 'the dog!'

He listened for a moment, and his expression changed to mild concern. The dog was silent

19

out there in the night.

'I am sure it is nothing to be alarmed about.' He went to the door, and for no good reason she suddenly called after him.

'Duraid, be careful!' He shrugged dismissively and stepped out on to the terrace.

She thought for an instant that it was the shadow of the vine over the trellis moving in the night breeze off the desert, but the night was still. Then she realized that it was a human figure crossing the flagstones silently and swiftly, coming in behind Duraid as he skirted the fish-pond in the centre of the paved terrace.

'Duraid!' She screamed a warning and he spun round, lifting the lamp high.

'Who are you?' he shouted. 'What do you want here?'

The intruder closed with him silently. The traditional full-length *dishdasha* robe swirled around his legs, and the white *ghutrah* headcloth covered his head. In the light of the lamp Duraid saw that he had drawn the corner of the head-cloth over his face to mask his features.

The intruder's back was turned towards her so Royan did not see the knife in his right hand, but she could not mistake the upward stabbing motion that he aimed at Duraid's stomach. Duraid grunted with pain and doubled up at the blow, and his attacker drew the blade free and stabbed again, but this time Duraid dropped the lamp and seized the knife arm.

The flame of the fallen oil lamp was guttering

and flaring. The two men struggled in the gloom, but Royan saw a dark stain spreading over her husband's white shirt front.

'Run!' he bellowed at her. 'Go! Fetch help! I cannot hold him!' The Duraid she knew was a gentle person, a soft man of books and learning. She could see that he was outmatched by his assailant.

'Go! Please! Save yourself, my flower!' She could hear by his tone that he was weakening, but he still clung desperately to his attacker's knife arm.

She had been paralysed with shock and indecision these few fatal seconds, but now she broke free of the spell and ran to the door. Spurred by her terror and her need to bring help to Duraid she crossed the terrace, swift as a cat, and he held the intruder from blocking her way.

She vaulted over the low stone wall into the grove, and almost into the arms of the second man. She screamed and twisted away from him as his outstretched fingers raked across her face, and almost broke free, but his fingers hooked in the thin cotton stuff of her blouse.

This time she saw the knife in his hand, a long silvery flash in the starlight, and it goaded her to fresh effort. The cotton tore in his grip and she was free, but not quickly enough to escape the blade. She felt the sting of it across her upper arm, and she kicked out at him with all the strength of panic and her hard young

21

body behind it. She felt her foot slam into the softness of his lower body with a shock that jarred her knee and ankle, and her attacker cried out and fell to his knees.

Then she was away and running through the palm grove. At first she ran without purpose or direction. She ran simply to get as far from them as her flying legs would carry her. Then gradually she brought her panic under control. She glanced back, but saw nobody following her. As she reached the edge of the lake she slowed her run to conserve her strength, and she became aware of the warm trickle of her own blood down her arm and then dripping from her fingertips.

She stopped and rested her back against the rough bole of one of the palms while she tore a strip of cloth from her ripped blouse and hurriedly bound up her arm. She was shaking so much from shock and exertion that even her uninjured hand was fumbling and clumsy. She knotted the crude bandage with her teeth and left hand, and the bleeding slowed.

She was uncertain of which way to run, and then she saw the dim lamplight in the window of Alia's shack across the nearest irrigation canal. She pushed herself away from the palm trunk and started towards it. She had covered less than a hundred paces when a voice called from the grove behind her, speaking in Arabic, 'Yusuf, has the woman come your way?'

Immediately an electric torch flashed from the

darkness ahead of her and another voice called back, 'No, I have not seen her.'

Another few seconds and Royan would have run full into him. She crouched down and looked around her desperately. There was another torch coming through the grove behind her, following the path she had taken. It must be the man she had kicked, but she could tell by the motion of the torchbeam that he had recovered and was moving swiftly and easily again.

She was blocked on two sides, so she turned back along the edge of the lake. The road lay that way. She might be able to meet a late vehicle travelling on it. She lost her footing on the rough ground and went down, bruising and scraping her knees, but she jumped up again and hurried on. The second time she stumbled, her out-thrust left hand landed on a round, smooth stone the size of an orange. When she went on she carried the stone with her; as a weapon it gave her a glimmer of comfort.

Her wounded arm was beginning to hurt, and she was driven by worry for Duraid. She knew he was badly wounded, for she had seen the direction and force of the knife thrust. She had to find help for him. Behind her the two men with torches were sweeping the grove and she could not keep her lead ahead of them. They were gaining on her — she could hear them calling to each other.

She reached the road at last, and with a small whimper of relief climbed out of the drainage ditch on to the pale gravel surface. Her legs were shaking under her so that they could hardly carry her weight, but she turned in the direction of the village.

She had not reached the first bend before she saw a set of headlights coming slowly towards her, flickering through the palm trees. She broke into a run down the centre of the road.

'Help me!' she screamed in Arabic. 'Please help me!'

The car came through the bend and before the headlights dazzled her she saw that it was a small, dark-coloured Fiat. She stood in the centre of the road waving her arms to halt the driver, lit by the headlights as though she were on a theatre stage.

The Fiat stopped in front of her, and she ran round to the driver's door and tugged at the handle. 'Please, you must help me —'

The door was opened from within, and then was thrown back with such force that she staggered off-balance. The driver leapt out into the roadway and caught her by the wrist of the injured arm. He dragged her to the Fiat and pulled open the back door.

'Yusuf! Bacheet!' he shouted into the dark grove. 'I have her.' And she heard the answering cries and saw the torches turn in their direction. The driver was forcing her head down and trying to push her into the back seat, but she realized then that she still had the stone in her good hand. She turned slightly and braced herself, and then swung her fist with the stone still clenched in it against the side of his head. It caught him squarely on the temple. Without another sound he dropped to the gravel surface and lay motionless.

Royan dropped the stone and pelted away down the road, but she found that she was running straight down the path of the headlights, and they lit her every movement. The two men in the grove shouted again and came up on to the gravel roadway behind her, almost shoulder to shoulder.

Glancing back, she saw them gaining on her swiftly, and she realized that her only chance was to get off the road and back into the darkness. She turned and plunged down the bank. Immediately she found herself waist-deep in the waters of the lake.

In the darkness and the confusion she had become disorientated. She had not realized that she had reached the point where the road skirted the embankment at the water's edge. She knew that she did not have time to climb back on to the road, and she knew also that there were thick clumps of papyrus and reeds ahead of her, that might give her shelter.

She waded out until the bottom sloped away steeply under her feet, and she found herself forced to swim. She broke into an awkward breaststroke, hampered by her skirts and her injured arm. However, her slow and stealthy movements created almost no disturbance on the surface, and before the men on the road had reached the point where she had descended the bank, she reached a dense stand of reeds.

She eased her way into the thick of them and let herself sink. Before the water covered her nostrils she felt her toes touch the soft ooze of the lake bottom. She stood there quietly, with just the top of her head above the surface and her face turned away from the bank. She knew her dark hair would not reflect the light of a probing torch.

Though the water covered her ears, she could make out the excited voices of the men on the road. They had turned their torches down towards the water and were shining them into the reeds, searching for her. For a moment one of the beams played full on her head, and she drew a deep breath ready to submerge, but the beam moved on and she realized that they had not picked her out.

The fact that she had not been seen even in the direct torchlight emboldened her to raise her head slightly until one ear was clear and she could make out their voices.

They were speaking Arabic, and she recognized the voice of the one named Bacheet. He appeared to be the leader, for he was giving the orders.

'Go in there, Yusuf, and bring the whore out.'

She heard Yusuf slipping and sliding down the bank and the splash as he hit the water.

'Further out,' Bacheet ordered him. 'In those

reeds there, where I am shining the torch.'

'It is too deep. You know well I cannot swim. It will be over my head.'

'There! Right in front of you. In those reeds. I can see her head.' Bacheet encouraged him, and Royan dreaded that they had spotted her. She sank down as far as she could below the surface.

Yusuf splashed around heavily, moving towards where she cowered in the reeds, when suddenly there was a thunderous commotion that startled even Yusuf, so that he shouted aloud, 'Djinns! God protect me!' as the flock of roosting duck exploded from the water and launched into the dark sky on noisy wings.

Yusuf started back to the bank and not any of Bacheet's threats could persuade him to continue the hunt.

'The woman is not as important as the scroll,' he protested, as he climbed back on to the roadway. 'Without the scroll there will be no money. We always know where to find her later.'

Turning her head slightly, Royan saw the torches move back down the road towards the parked Fiat whose headlights still burned. She heard the doors of the car slam, and then the engine revved and pulled away towards the villa.

She was too shaken and terrified to make any attempt to leave her hiding-place. She feared that they had left one of their number on the road to wait for her to show herself. She stood on tiptoe with the water lapping her lips, shivering more with shock than with cold, determined to wait for the safety of the sunrise before she moved.

It was only much later when she saw the glow of the fire lighting the sky, and the flames flickering through the trunks of the palm trees, that she forgot her own safety and dragged herself back to the bank.

She knelt in the mud at the water's edge, shuddering and shaking and gasping, weak with loss of blood and shock and the reaction from fear, and peered at the flames through the veil of her wet hair and the lake water that streamed into her eyes.

'The villa!' she whispered. 'Duraid! Oh please God, no! No!'

She pushed herself to her feet and began to stagger towards her burning home.

Bacheet switched off both the headlights and the engine of the Fiat before they reached the turning into the driveway of the villa and let the car coast down and stop below the terrace.

All three of them left the Fiat and climbed the stone steps to the flagged terrace. Duraid's body still lay where Bacheet had left it beside the fishpond. They passed him without a glance and went into the dark study.

Bacheet placed the cheap nylon tote bag he

carried on the tabletop.

'We have wasted too much time already. We must work quickly now.'

'It is Yusuf's fault,' protested the driver of the Fiat. 'He let the woman escape.'

'You had a chance on the road,' Yusuf snarled at him, 'and you did no better.'

'Enough!' Bacheet told them both. 'If you want to get paid, then there had better be no more mistakes.'

With the torchbeam Bacheet picked out the scroll that still lay on the tabletop. 'That is the one.' He was certain, for he had been shown a photograph of it so that there would be no mistake. 'They want everything — the maps and photographs. Also the books and papers, everything on the table that they were using in their work. Leave nothing.'

Quickly they bundled everything into the tote bag and Bacheet zipped it closed.

'Now the *Doktari*. Bring him in here.'

The other two went out on to the terrace and stooped over the body. Each of them seized an ankle and dragged Duraid back across the terrace and into the study. The back of Duraid's head bounced loosely on the stone step at the threshold and his blood painted a long wet skid mark across the tiles that glistened in the torch-light.

'Get the lamp!' Bacheet ordered, and Yusuf went back to the terrace and fetched the oil lamp from where Duraid had dropped it. The flame was extinguished. Bacheet held the lamp to his ear and shook it.

'Full,' he said with satisfaction, and unscrewed the filler cap. 'All right,' he told the other two, 'take the bag out to the car.'

As they hurried out Bacheet sprinkled paraffin from the lamp over Duraid's shirt and trousers, and then he went to the shelves and splashed the remainder of the fuel over the books and manuscripts that crowded them.

He dropped the empty lamp and reached under the skirts of his *dishdasha* for a box of matches. He struck one of them and held it to the wet run of paraffin oil down the bookcase. It caught immediately, and flames spread upwards and curled and blackened the edges of the manuscripts. He turned away and went back to where Duraid lay. He struck another match and dropped it on to his blood- and paraffin-drenched shirt.

A mantle of blue flames danced over Duraid's chest. The flames changed colour as they burned into the cotton material and the flesh beneath it. They turned orange, and sooty smoke spiralled up from their flickering crests.

Bacheet ran to the door, across the terrace and down the steps. As he clambered into the rear seat of the Fiat, the driver gunned the engine and pulled away down the driveway.

The pain roused Duraid. It had to be that intense to bring him back from that far place on the very edge of life to which he had drifted.

He groaned. The first thing he was aware of as he regained consciousness was the smell of his own flesh burning, and then the agony struck him with full force. A violent tremor shook his whole body and he opened his eyes and looked down at himself.

His clothing was blackening and smouldering, and the pain was as nothing he had ever experienced in his entire life. He realized in a vague way that the room was on fire all around him. Smoke and waves of heat washed over him so that he could barely make out the shape of the doorway through them.

The pain was so terrible that he wanted it to end. He wanted to die then and not to have to endure it further. Then he remembered Royan. He tried to say her name through his scorched and blackened lips, but no sound came. Only the thought of her gave him the strength to move. He rolled over once, and the heat attacked his back that up until that moment had been shielded. He groaned aloud and rolled again, just a little nearer to the doorway.

Each movement was a mighty effort and evoked fresh paroxysms of agony, but when he rolled on to his back again he realized that a

31

gale of fresh air was being sucked through the open doorway to feed the flames. A lungful of the sweet desert air revived him and gave him just sufficient strength to lunge down the step on to the cool stones of the terrace.

His clothes and his body were still on fire. He beat feebly at his chest to try to extinguish the flames, but his hands were black burning claws.

Then he remembered the fishpond. The thought of plunging his tortured body into that cold water spurred him to one last effort, and he wriggled and wormed his way across the flags like a snake with a crushed spine.

The pungent smoke from his still cremating flesh choked him and he coughed weakly, but kept doggedly on. He left slabs of his own grilled skin on the stone coping as he rolled across it and flopped into the pond. There was a hiss of steam, and a pale cloud of it obscured his vision so that for a moment he thought he was blinded. The agony of cold water on his raw burned flesh was so intense that he slid back over the edge of consciousness.

When he came back to reality through the dark clouds he raised his dripping head and saw a figure staggering up the steps at the far end of the terrace, coming from the garden.

For a moment he thought it was a phantom of his agony, but when the light of the burning villa fell full upon her, he recognized Royan. Her wet hair hung in tangled disarray over her face, and her clothing was torn and running with lake water and stained with mud and green algae. Her right arm was wrapped in muddy rags and her blood oozed through, diluted pink by the dirty water.

She did not see him. She stopped in the centre of the terrace and stared in horror into the burning room. Was Duraid in there? She started forward, but the heat was like a solid wall and it stopped her dead. At that moment the roof collapsed, sending a roaring column of sparks and flames high into the night sky. She backed away from it, shielding her face with a raised arm.

Duraid tried to call to her, but no sound issued from his smoke-scorched throat. Royan turned away and started down the steps. He realized that she must be going to call for help. Duraid made a supreme effort and a crow-like croak came out between his black and blistered lips.

Royan spun round and stared at him, and then she screamed. His head was not human. His hair was gone, frizzled away, and his skin hung in tatters from his cheeks and chin. Patches of raw meat showed through the black crusted mask. She backed away from him as though he were some hideous monster.

'Royan,' he croaked, and his voice was just recognizable. He lifted one hand towards her in appeal, and she ran to the pond and seized the outstretched hand.

'In the name of the Virgin, what have they

done to you?' she sobbed, but when she tried to pull him from the pond the skin of his hand came away in hers in a single piece, like some horrible surgical rubber glove, leaving the bleeding claw naked and raw.

Royan fell on her knees beside the coping and leaned over the pond to take him in her arms. She knew that she did not have the strength to lift him out without doing him further dreadful injury. All she could do was hold him and try to comfort him. She realized that he was dying — no man could survive such fearsome injury.

'They will come soon to help us,' she whispered to him in Arabic. 'Someone must see the flames. Be brave, my husband, help will come very soon.'

He was twitching and convulsing in her arms, tortured by his mortal injuries and racked by the effort to speak.

'The scroll?' His voice was barely intelligible. Royan looked up at the holocaust that enveloped their home, and she shook her head.

'It's gone,' she said. 'Burned or stolen.'

'Don't give it up,' he mumbled. 'All our work —'

'It's gone,' she repeated. 'No one will believe us without —'

'No!' His voice was faint but fierce. 'For me, my last —'

'Don't say that,' she pleaded. 'You will be all right.'

'Promise,' he demanded. 'Promise me!'

'We have no sponsor. I am alone. I cannot do it alone.'

'Harper!' he said. Royan leaned closer so that her ear touched his fire-ravaged lips. 'Harper,' he repeated. 'Strong — hard — clever man —' and she understood then. Harper, of course, was the fourth and last name on the list of sponsors that he had drawn up. Although he was the last on the list, somehow she had always known that Duraid's order of preference was inverted. Nicholas Quenton-Harper was his first choice. He had spoken so often of this man with respect and warmth, and sometimes even with awe.

'But what do I tell him? He does not know me. How will I convince him? The seventh scroll is gone.'

'Trust him,' he whispered. 'Good man. Trust him —' There was a terrible appeal in his 'Promise me!'

Then she remembered the notebook in their flat at Giza in the Cairo suburbs, and the Taita material on the hard drive on her PC. Not everything was gone. 'Yes,' she agreed, 'I promise you, my husband, I promise you.'

Though those mutilated features could show no human expression there was a faint echo of satisfaction in his voice as he whispered, 'My flower!' Then his head dropped forward, and he died in her arms.

The peasants from the village found Royan still kneeling beside the pond, holding him, whispering to him. By that time the flames were abating, and the faint light of dawn was stronger than their fading glow.

All the senior staff from the museum and the Department of Antiquities were at the funeral service in the church of the oasis. Even Atalan Abou Sin, the Minister of Culture and Tourism and Duraid's superior, had come out from Cairo in his official black air-conditioned Mercedes.

He stood behind Royan and, though he was a Moslem, joined in the responses. Nahoot Guddabi stood beside his uncle. Nahoot's mother was the minister's youngest sister, which, as Duraid had sarcastically pointed out, fully made up for the nephew's lack of qualifications and experience in archaeology and for his ineptitude as an administrator.

The day was sweltering. Outside, the temperature stood at over thirty degrees, and even in the dim cloisters of the Coptic church it was oppressive. In the thick clouds of incense smoke and the drone of the black-clad priest intoning the ancient order of service Royan felt herself suffocating. The stitches in her right arm pulled and burned, and every time she looked at the long black coffin that stood in front of the ornate and gilded altar, the dreadful vision of Duraid's bald and scorched head rose before her eyes and she swayed in her seat and had to catch herself before she fell.

At last it was over and she could escape into the open air and the desert sunlight. Even then her duties were not at an end. As principal mourner, her place was directly behind the coffin as they walked in procession to the cemetery amongst the palm groves, where Duraid's relatives awaited him in the family mausoleum.

Before he returned to Cairo, Atalan Abou Sin came to shake her hand and offer her a few words of condolence. 'What a terrible business, Royan. I have personally spoken to the Minister of the Interior. They will catch the animals responsible for this outrage, believe me. Please take as long as you need before you return to the museum,' he told her.

'I will be in my office again on Monday,' she replied, and he drew a pocket diary from inside the jacket of his dark double-breasted suit. He consulted it and made a note, before he looked up at her again.

'Then come to see me at the Ministry in the afternoon. Four o'clock,' he told her. He went to the waiting Mercedes, while Nahoot Guddabi came forward to shake hands. Though his skin was sallow and there were coffee-coloured stains beneath his dark eyes, he was tall and elegant with thick wavy hair and very white teeth. His suit was impeccably tailored and he smelt faintly of an expensive cologne. His expression was grave and sad.

'He was a good man. I held Duraid in the highest esteem,' he told Royan, and she nodded without replying to this blatant untruth. There had been little affection between Duraid and his deputy. He had never allowed Nahoot to work on the Taita scrolls; in particular he had never given him access to the seventh scroll, and this had been a point of bitter antagonism between them.

'I hope you will be applying for the post of director, Royan,' he told her. 'You are well qualified for the job.'

'Thank you, Nahoot, you are very kind. I haven't had a chance to think about the future yet, but won't you be applying?'

'Of course,' he nodded. 'But that doesn't mean that no one else should. Perhaps you will take the job out from in front of my nose.' His smile was complacent. She was a woman in an Arab world, and he was the nephew of the minister. Nahoot knew just how heavily the odds favoured him. 'Friendly rivals?' he asked.

Royan smiled sadly. 'Friends, at least. I will need all of those I can find in the future.'

'You know you have many friends. Everyone in the department likes you, Royan.' That at least was true, she supposed. He went on smoothly, 'May I offer you a lift back to Cairo? I am certain my uncle will not object.'

'Thank you, Nahoot, but I have my own car here, and I must stay over at the oasis tonight to see to some of Duraid's affairs.' This was

38

not true. Royan planned to travel back to the flat in Giza that evening but, for reasons that she was not very sure of herself, she did not want Nahoot to know of her plans.

'Then we shall see you at the museum on Monday.'

Royan left the oasis as soon as she was able to escape from the relations and family friends and peasants, so many of whom had worked for Duraid's family most of their lives. She felt numbed and isolated, so that all their condolences and pious exhortations were meaningless and without comfort.

Even at this late hour the tarmac road back through the desert was busy, with files of vehicles moving steadily in both directions, for tomorrow was Friday and the sabbath. She slipped her injured right arm out of the sling, and it did not hamper her driving too much. She was able to make reasonably good time. Nevertheless, it was after five in the afternoon when she made out the green line against the tawny desolation of the desert that marked the start of the narrow strip of irrigated and cultivated land along the Nile which was the great artery of Egypt.

As always the traffic became denser the nearer she came to the capital, and it was almost fully dark by the time she reached the apartment block in Giza that overlooked both the river and those great monuments of stone which stood so tall and massive against the evening sky, and which for her epitomized the heart and history of her land.

She left Duraid's old green Renault in the underground garage of the building and rode up in the elevator to the top floor.

She let herself into the flat and then froze in the doorway. The sitting room had been ransacked — even the rugs had been pulled up and the paintings ripped from the walls. In a daze she picked her way through the litter of broken furniture and smashed ornaments. She glanced into the bedroom as she went down the passage, and saw that it had not escaped. Her clothes and those of Duraid were strewn over the floor, and the doors of the cupboards stood ajar. One of these was smashed off its hinges. The bed was overturned, and the sheets and bolsters had been flung about.

She could smell the reek of broken cosmetic and perfume bottles from the bathroom, but she could not yet bring herself to go in there. She knew what she would find. Instead she continued down the passage to the large room that they had used as a study and workshop.

In the chaos the first thing that she noticed and mourned was the antique chess set that Duraid had given her as a wedding present. The board of jet and ivory squares was broken in half and the pieces had been thrown about the room with vindictive and unnecessary violence. She stooped and picked up the white queen. Her head had been snapped off.

Holding the queen in her good hand she moved like a sleepwalker to her desk below the window. Her PC was wrecked. They had shattered the screen and hacked the mainframe with what must have been an axe. She could tell at a glance that there was no information left on the hard drive; it was beyond repair.

She glanced down at the drawer in which she kept her floppy disks. That and all the other drawers had been pulled out and thrown on the floor. They were empty, of course; along with the disks, all her notebooks and photographs were missing. Her last connections with the seventh scroll were lost. After three years of work, gone was the proof that it had ever existed.

She slumped down on the floor, feeling beaten and exhausted. Her arm started to ache again, and she was alone and vulnerable as she had never been in her life before. She had never thought that she would miss Duraid so desperately. Her shoulders began to shake and she felt the tears welling up from deep within her. She tried to hold them back, but they scalded her eyelids and she let them flow. She sat amongst the wreckage of her life and wept until there was nothing more left within her, and then she curled up on the littered carpet and fell into the sleep of exhaustion and despair.

By the Monday morning she had managed to restore some order into her life. The police had come to the flat and taken her statement, and she had tidied up most of the disarray. She had even glued the head back on her white queen. When she left the flat and climbed into the green Renault her arm was feeling easier, and, if not cheerful, she was at least a great deal more optimistic, and sure of what she had to do.

When she reached the museum she went first to Duraid's office and was annoyed to find that Nahoot was there before her. He was supervising two of the security guards as they cleared out all Duraid's personal effects.

'You might have had the consideration to let me do that,' she told him coldly, and he gave her his most winning smile.

'I am sorry, Royan. I thought I would help.' He was smoking one of his fat Turkish cigarettes. She loathed the heavy, musky odour.

She crossed to Duraid's desk, and opened the top right-hand drawer. 'My husband's day book was in here. It's gone now. Have you seen it?'

'No, there was nothing in that drawer.' Nahoot looked at the two guards for confirmation, and they shuffled their feet and shook their heads. It did not really matter, she thought. The book had not contained much of vital interest. Duraid had always relied on her to record and store all data of importance, and most of it had been on her PC.

'Thank you, Nahoot,' she dismissed him. 'I will do whatever remains to be done. I don't want to keep you from your work.'

'Any help you need, Royan, please let me know.' He bowed slightly as he left her.

It did not take her long to finish in Duraid's office. She had the guards take the boxes of his possessions down the corridor to her own office and pile them against the wall. She worked through the lunch-hour tidying up all her own affairs, and when she had finished there was still an hour until her appointment with Atalan Abou Sin.

If she was to make good her promise to Duraid, then she was going to be absent for some time. Wanting to take leave of all her favourite treasures, she went down into the public section of the huge building.

Monday was a busy day, and the exhibition halls of the museum were thronged with groups of tourists. They flocked behind their guides, sheep following the shepherd. They crowded around the most famous of the displays. They listened to the guides reciting their well-rehearsed spiels in all the tongues of Babel.

Those rooms on the second floor that contained the treasures of Tutankhamen were so crowded that she spent little time there. She managed to reach the display cabinet that con-

43

tained the great golden death-mask of the child pharaoh. As always, the splendour and the romance of it quickened her breathing and made her heart beat faster. Yet as she stood before it, jostled by a pair of big-busted and sweaty middle-aged female tourists, she pondered, as she had so often before, that if an insignificant weakling king could have gone to his tomb with such a miraculous creation covering his mummified features, in what state must the great Ramessids have lain in their funeral temples. Ramesses II, the greatest of them all, had reigned sixty-seven years and had spent those decades accumulating his funerary treasure from all the vast territories that he had conquered.

Royan went next to pay her respects to the old king. After thirty centuries Ramesses II slept on with a rapt and serene expression on his gaunt features. His skin had a light, marble-like sheen to it. The sparse strands of his hair were blond and dyed with henna. His hands, dyed with the same stuff, were long and thin and elegant. However, he was clad only in a rag of linen. The grave robbers had even unwrapped his mummy to reach the amulets and scarabs beneath the linen bandages, so that his body was almost naked. When these remains had been discovered in 1881 in the cache of royal mummies in the cliff cave at Deir El Bahari, only a scrap of papyrus parchment attached to his breast had proclaimed his lineage.

There was a moral in that, she supposed, but

as she stood before these pathetic remains she wondered again, as she and Duraid had done so often before, whether Taita the scribe had told the truth, whether somewhere in the far-off, savage mountains of Africa another great pharaoh slept on undisturbed with all his treasures intact about him. The very thought of it made her shiver with excitement, and goose pimples prickled her skin and raised the fine dark hair at the nape of her neck.

'I have given you my promise, my husband,' she whispered in Arabic. 'This will be for you and your memory, for it was you who led the way.'

She glanced at her wrist-watch as she went down the main staircase. She had fifteen minutes before she must leave for her appointment with the minister, and she knew exactly how she would spend that time. What she was going to visit was in one of the less-frequented side halls. The tour guides very seldom led their charges this way, except as a short-cut to see the statue of Amenhotep.

Royan stopped in front of the glass-fronted display case that reached from floor to ceiling of the narrow room. It was packed with small artefacts, tools and weapons, amulets and vessels and utensils, the latest of them dating from the twentieth dynasty of the New Kingdom, 1100 BC, whilst the oldest survived from the dim ages of the Old Kingdom almost five thousand years ago. The cataloguing of this accumulation was only rudimentary. Many of the items were not described.

At the furthest end, on the bottom shelf, was a display of jewellery and finger rings and seals. Beside each of the seals was a wax impression made from it.

Royan went down on her knees to examine one of these artefacts more closely. The tiny blue seal of lapis lazuli in the centre of the display was beautifully carved. Lapis was a rare and precious material for the ancients, as it had not occurred naturally in the Egyptian Empire. The wax imprint cut from it depicted a hawk with a broken wing, and the simple legend beneath it was clear for Royan to read: 'TAITA, THE SCRIBE OF THE GREAT QUEEN'.

She knew it was the same man, for he had used the maimed hawk as his autograph in the scrolls. She wondered who had found this trifle and where. Perhaps some peasant had plundered it from the lost tomb of the old slave and scribe, but she would never know.

'Are you teasing me, Taita? Is it all some elaborate hoax? Are you laughing at me even now from your tomb, wherever it may be?' She leaned even closer, until her forehead touched the cool glass. 'Are you my friend, Taita, or are you my implacable adversary?' She stood up and dusted off the front of her skirt. 'We shall see. I will play the game with you, and we shall see who outwits whom,' she promised.

The minister kept her waiting only a few minutes before his male secretary ushered her into his presence. Atalan Abou Sin wore a dark, shiny silk suit and sat at his desk, although Royan knew that he preferred a more comfortable robe and a cushion on the rugs of the floor. He noticed her glance and smiled deprecatingly. 'I have a meeting with some Americans this afternoon.'

She liked him. He had always been kind to her, and she owed him her job at the museum. Most other men in his position would have refused Duraid's request for a female assistant, especially his own wife.

He asked after her health and she showed him her bandaged arm. 'The stitches will come out in ten days.'

They chatted for a while in a polite manner. Only Westerners would have the gaucherie to come directly to the main business to be discussed. However, to save him embarrassment Royan took the first opportunity he gave her to tell him, 'I feel that I need some time to myself. I need to recover from my loss and to decide what I am to do with the rest of my life, now that I am a widow. I would be grateful if you would consider my request for at least six months' unpaid leave of absence. I want to go to stay with my mother in England.'

Atalan showed real concern and urged her, 'Please do not leave us for too long. The work you have done has been invaluable. We need you to help carry on from where Duraid left off.' But he could not entirely conceal his relief. She knew that he had expected her to put before him her application for the directorship. He must have discussed it with his nephew. However, he was too kind a man to relish having to tell her that she would not be selected for the job. Things in Egypt were changing, women were emerging from their traditional roles, but not that much or that swiftly. They both knew that the directorship must go to Nahoot Guddabi.

Atalan walked with her to the door of his office and shook her hand in parting, and as she rode down in the lift she felt a sense of release and freedom.

She had left the Renault standing in the sun in the Ministry car park. When she opened the door the interior was hot enough to bake bread. She opened all the windows and fanned the driver's door to force out the heated air, but still the surface of the driver's seat burned the backs of her thighs when she slid in behind the wheel.

As soon as she drove through the gates she was engulfed in the swarm of Cairo traffic. She crawled along behind an overloaded bus that belched a steady blue cloud of diesel fumes over the Renault. The traffic problem was one that seemed to have no solution. There was so little parking available that vehicles lined the verge of the road three and four deep, choking the flow in the centre to a trickle.

As the bus in front of her braked and forced her to a halt, Royan smiled as she recalled the old joke that some drivers who had parked at the kerb had to abandon their cars there, for they were never able to extricate them from the tangle. Perhaps there was a little truth in this, for some of those vehicles she could see had not been moved for weeks. Their windscreens were completely obscured with dust and many of them had flat tyres.

She glanced in the rear-view mirror. There was a taxi stopped only inches from her back bumper, and behind that the traffic was backed up solidly. Only the motorcyclists had freedom of movement. As she watched in the mirror, one of these came weaving through the congestion with suicidal abandon. It was a battered red 200 cc Honda so covered with dust that the colour was hardly recognizable. There was a passenger perched on the pillion, and both he and the driver had covered the lower half of their faces with the corners of their white headcloths as protection against the exhaust fumes and dust.

Passing on the wrong side, the Honda skimmed through the narrow gap between the taxi and the cars parked at the kerb with nothing to spare on either side. The taxi-driver made an obscene gesture with thumb and forefinger,

49

and called on Allah to witness that the driver was both mad and stupid.

The Honda slowed slightly as it drew level with Royan's Renault, and the pillion passenger leaned out and dropped something through the open window on to the passenger seat beside her. Immediately the driver accelerated so abruptly that for a moment the front wheel was lifted off the ground. He put the motorcycle over into a tight turn and sped away down the narrow alleyway that opened off the main thoroughfare, narrowly avoiding hitting an old woman in his path.

As the pillion passenger looked back at her the wind blew the fold of white cotton from his face, and with a shock she recognized the man she had last seen in the headlights of the Fiat on the road beside the oasis.

'Yusuf!' As the Honda disappeared she looked down at the object that he had dropped on to the seat beside her. It was egg-shaped and the segmented metallic surface was painted military green. She had seen the same thing so often on old TV war movies that she recognized it instantly as a fragmentation grenade, and at the same moment she realized that the priming handle had flown off and the weapon was set to explode within seconds.

Without thinking, she grabbed the door handle beside her and flung all her weight against the door. It burst open and she tumbled out in the road. Her foot slipped off the clutch and the Renault bounded forward and crashed into the back of the stationary bus.

As Royan sprawled in the road under the wheels of the following taxi, the grenade exploded. Through the open driver's door blew a sheet of flame and smoke and debris. The back window burst outwards and sprayed her with diamond chips of glass, and the detonation drove painfully into her eardrums.

A stunned silence followed the shock of the explosion, broken only by the tinkle of falling glass shards, and then immediately there was a hubbub of groans and screams. Royan sat up and clasped her injured arm to her chest. She had fallen heavily upon it and the stitches were agony.

The Renault was wrecked, but she saw that her leather sling bag had been blown out of the door and lay in the street close at hand. She pushed herself unsteadily to her feet and hobbled over to pick it up. All around her was confusion. A few of the passengers in the bus had been injured, and a piece of shrapnel or wreckage had wounded a little girl on the sidewalk. Her mother was screaming and mopping at the child's bloody face with her scarf. The girl struggled in her mother's grip, wailing pitifully.

Nobody was taking any notice of Royan, but she knew the police would arrive within minutes. They were geared up to respond swiftly to fundamentalist terror attacks. She knew that if they found her here she would be tied up in days of interrogation. She slung the bag over her shoulder and walked as swiftly as her bruised leg would allow her to the alleyway down which the Honda had disappeared.

At the end of the street was a public lavatory. She locked herself in one of the cubicles and leaned against the door with her eyes closed, trying to recover from the shock and to get her confused thoughts in order.

In the horror and desolation of Duraid's murder she had not until now considered her own safety. The realization of danger had been forced upon her in the most savage manner. She remembered the words of one of the assassins spoken in the darkness beside the oasis, 'We always know where to find her later!'

The attempt on her life had failed only narrowly. She had to believe that there would be another.

'I can't go back to the flat,' she realized. 'The villa is gone, and anyway they would look for me there.'

Despite the unsavoury atmosphere she remained locked in the cubicle for over an hour while she thought out her next movements. At last she left the toilet and went to the row of stained and cracked washbasins. She splashed her face under the tap. Then in the mirror she combed her hair, touched up her make-up, and straightened and tidied her clothing as best she was able.

She walked a few blocks, doubling back on her tracks and watching behind her to make sure she was not being followed, before she hailed a taxi in the street.

She made the driver drop her in the street behind her bank, and walked the rest of the way. It was only minutes before closing time when she was shown into the cubicle office of one of the sub-accountants. She withdrew what money was in her account, which amounted to less than five thousand Egyptian pounds. It was not a great sum, but she had a little more in her Lloyds Bank account in York, and then she had her Mastercard.

'You should have given us notice to withdraw an article from safe deposit,' the bank official told her severely. She apologized meekly and played the helpless little-girl-lost so convincingly that he relented. He handed over to her the package that contained her British passport and her Lloyds banking papers.

Duraid had numerous relatives and friends who would have been pleased to have her to stay with them, but she wanted to remain out of sight, away from her usual haunts. She chose one of the two-star tourist hotels away from the river where she hoped she could remain anonymous amongst the multitudes of the tour groups. At this type of hotel there was a high turnover of guests, for most of them stayed only for a few nights before moving on up to Luxor and Aswan to view the monuments.

As soon as she was alone in her single room she phoned British Airways reservations. There was a flight to Heathrow the following morning at ten o'clock. She booked a one-way economy seat and gave them the number of her Mastercard.

It was after six o'clock by then, but the time difference between Egypt and the UK meant that it would still be office hours there. She looked up the number in her notebook. Leeds University was where she had completed her studies. Her call was answered on the third ring.

'Archaeology Department. Professor Dixon's office,' said a prim English school-marm voice.

'Is that you, Miss Higgins?'

'Yes, it is. To whom am I speaking?'

'It's Royan. Royan Al Simma, who used to be Royan Said.'

'Royan! We haven't heard from you for an absolute age. How are you?'

They chatted for a short while, but Royan was aware of the cost of the call. 'Is the Prof in?' she cut it short.

Professor Percival Dixon was over seventy and should have retired years ago. 'Royan, is it really you? My favourite student.' She smiled. Even at his age he was still the randy old goat. All the pretty ones were his favourite students.

'This is an international call, Prof. I just want to know if the offer is still open.'

'My goodness, I thought you said that you couldn't fit us in, what?'

54

'Change of circumstances. I'll tell you about it when I see you, if I see you.'

'Of course, we'd love to have you come and talk to us. When can you manage to get away?'

'I'll be in England tomorrow.'

'My goodness, that's a bit sudden. Don't know if we can arrange it that quickly.'

'I will be staying with my mother near York. Put me back to Miss Higgins and I will give her the telephone number.' He was one of the most brilliant men she knew, but she didn't trust him to write down a telephone number correctly. 'I'll call you in a few days' time.'

She hung up and lay back on the bed. She was exhausted and her arm was still hurting, but she tried to lay her plans to cover all eventualities.

Two months ago Prof Dixon had invited her to lecture on the discovery and excavation of the tomb of Queen Lostris, and the discovery of the scrolls. It was that book, of course, and more especially the footnote at the end of it, that had alerted him. Its publication had caused a great deal of interest. They had received enquiries from Egyptologists, both amateur and professional, all around the world, some from as far afield as Tokyo and Nairobi, all of them questioning the authenticity of the novel and the factual basis behind it.

At the time she had opposed letting a writer of fiction have access to the transcriptions, especially as they had not been completed. She felt that the whole thing had reduced what should have been an important and serious academic subject to the level of popular entertainment, rather like what Spielberg had done to palaeontology with his park full of dinosaurs.

In the end her voice had been over-ruled. Even Duraid had sided against her. It had been the money, of course. The department was always short of funds to conduct its less spectacular work. When it came to some grandiose scheme like moving the entire Temple of Abu Simbel to a new site above the flood waters of the Aswan High Dam, then the nations of the world had poured in tens of millions of dollars. However, the day-to-day operational expenses of the department attracted no such support.

Their half share of the royalties from *River God*, for that was the book's title, had financed almost a year of research and exploration, but that was not enough to allay Royan's personal misgivings. The author had taken too many liberties with the facts contained in the scrolls, and had embroidered historical characters with personalities and foibles for which there was not the least evidence. In particular she felt he had portrayed Taita, the ancient scribe, as a braggart and a vainglorious poseur. She resented that.

In fairness she was forced to concede that the author's brief had been to make the facts as palatable and readable as possible to a wide lay public, and she reluctantly agreed that he had succeeded in doing so. However, all her scientific training revolted against such a popularization of something so unique and wonderful.

But she sighed and put these thoughts out of her head. The damage was done, and thinking about it only served to irritate her.

She turned her thoughts to more pressing problems. If she was to do the lecture that the Prof had invited her to deliver, then she would need her slides and these were still at her office in the museum. While she was still working out the best way to get hold of them without fetching them in person, exhaustion overtook her and she fell asleep, still fully clothed, on top of the bed.

In the end the solution to her problem was simplicity itself. She merely phoned the administration office and arranged for them to collect the box of slides from her office and send it out to the airport in a taxi with one of the secretaries.

When the secretary handed them over to her at the British Airways check-in desk, he told her, 'The police were at the museum when we opened this morning. They wanted to speak to you, Doctor.'

Obviously they had traced the registration of the wrecked Renault. She was pleased that she had her British passport. If she had tried to leave the country with her Egyptian papers she might have run into delays: the police would probably have placed a restriction order on all passport control points. As it was, she passed through the checkpoint with no difficulty and, once she was in the final departure lounge, she went to the news-stand and studied the array of newspapers.

All the local newspapers carried the story of the bombing of her car, and most of them had resurrected the story of Duraid's murder and linked the two events. One of them hinted at fundamentalist religious involvement. *El Arab* had a front-page photograph of herself and Duraid, which had been taken the previous month at a reception for a group of visiting French tour operators.

It gave her a pang to see the photograph of her husband looking so handsome and distinguished, with herself on his arm smiling up at him. She purchased copies of all the papers and took them on board the British Airways flight.

During the flight she passed the time by writing down in her notebook everything she could remember from what Duraid had told her of the man that she was going to find. She headed the page: 'Sir Nicholas Quenton-Harper (Bart).' Duraid had told her that Nicholas's great-grandfather had been awarded the title of baronet for his work as a career officer in the British colonial service. For three generations the family had maintained the strongest of ties with Africa, and especially with the British colonies and spheres of influence in North Africa: Egypt and the Sudan, Uganda and Kenya.

According to Duraid, Sir Nicholas himself had served in Africa and the Gulf States with the British army. He was a fluent Arabic and Swahili speaker and a noted amateur archaeologist and zoologist. Like his father, grandfather and great-grandfather before him, he had made numerous expeditions to North Africa to collect specimens and to explore the more remote regions. He had written a number of articles for various scientific journals and had even lectured at the Royal Geographical Society.

When his elder brother died childless, Sir Nicholas had inherited the title and the family estate at Quenton Park. He had resigned from the army to run the estate, but more especially to supervise the family museum that had been started in 1885 by his great-grandfather, the first baronet. It housed one of the largest collections of African fauna in private hands, and its ancient Egyptian and Middle Eastern collection of artefacts was equally famous.

However, from Duraid's accounts she concluded that there must be a wild, and even lawless, streak in Sir Nicholas's nature. It was obvious that he was not afraid to take some extraordinary risks to add to the collection at Quenton Park.

Duraid had first met him a number of years previously, when Sir Nicholas had recruited him to act as an intelligence officer for an illicit expedition to 'liberate' a number of Punic bronze castings from Gadaffi's Libya. Sir Nicholas had sold some of these to defray the expenses of the expedition, but had kept the best of them for his private collection.

More recently there had been another expedition, this time involving an illegal crossing of the Iraqi border to bring out a pair of stone bas-relief friezes from under Saddam Hussein's nose. Duraid had told her that Sir Nicholas had sold one of the pair for a huge amount of money; he had mentioned the sum of five million US dollars. Duraid said that he had used the money for the running of the museum, but that the second frieze, the finest of the pair, was still in Sir Nicholas's possession.

Both these expeditions had taken place years before Royan had met Duraid, and she wondered idly at Duraid's readiness to commit himself to the Englishman in this way. Sir Nicholas must have had unique powers of persuasion, for if they had been apprehended in the act there was no doubt that it would have meant summary execution for both of them.

As Duraid had explained to her, on each occasion it was only Nicholas's resourcefulness and his network of friends and admirers across the Middle East and North Africa, which he had been able to call on for help, that had seen them through.

'He is a bit of a devil,' Duraid had shaken

his head with evident nostalgia at the memory, 'but the man to have with you when things are tough. Those days were all very exciting, but when I look back on it now I shudder at the risks we took.'

She had often pondered on the risks that a true in-the-blood collector was prepared to take to slake his passion. The risk seemed to be out of proportion to the reward, when it came to adding to his accumulations; and then she smiled at her own pious sentiments. The venture that she hoped to lead Sir Nicholas into was not exactly without risk, and she supposed that a circumlocution of lawyers might debate the legality of it endlessly.

Still smiling, she fell asleep, for the strain of these last few days had taken their toll. The air hostess woke her with an admonition to fasten her seat-belt for the landing at Heathrow.

Royan phoned her mother from the airport. 'Hello, Mummy. It's me.'

'Yes, I know that. Where are you, love?' Her mother sounded as unflappable as ever.

'At Heathrow. I am coming up to stay with you for a while. Is that all right?'

'Lumley's B and B,' her mother chuckled. 'I'll go and make your bed. What train will you be coming up on?'

'I had a look at the timetable. There is one

from King's Cross that will get me into York at seven this evening.'

'I'll meet you at the station. What happened? Did you and Duraid have a tiff? Old enough to be your father. I said it wouldn't work.'

Royan was silent for a moment. This was hardly the time for explanations. 'I'll tell you all about it when I see you this evening.'

Georgina Lumley, her mother, was waiting on the platform in the gloom and cold of the November evening, bulky and solid in her old green Barbour coat with Magic, her cocker spaniel, sitting obediently at her feet. The two of them made an inseparable pair, even when they were not winning field trials cups. For Royan they painted a comforting and familiar picture of the English side of her lineage.

Georgina kissed Royan's cheek in a perfunctory manner. 'Never was one for all that sentimental fiddle-faddle,' she often said with satisfaction, and she took one of Royan's bags and led the way to the old mud-splattered Land Rover in the car park.

Magic sniffed Royan's hand and wagged his tail in recognition. Then in a dignified and condescending manner he allowed her to pat his head, but like his mistress he was no great sentimentalist either.

They drove in silence for a while and Georgina lit a cigarette. 'So what happened to Duraid, then?'

For a minute Royan could not reply, and then

the floodgates within her burst and she let it all come pouring out. It was a twenty-minute drive north of York to the little village of Brandsbury, and Royan talked all the way. Her mother made only small sounds of encouragement and comfort, and when Royan wept as she related the details of Duraid's death and funeral, Georgina reached across and patted her daughter's hand.

It was all over by the time they reached her mother's cottage in the village. Royan had cried it out and was dry-eyed and rational again as they ate the dinner that her mother had prepared and left in the oven for them. Royan could not remember when last she had tasted steak and kidney pie.

'So what are you going to do now?' Georgina asked as she poured what remained in the black bottle of Guinness into her own glass.

'To tell the truth, I don't know.' As she said it, Royan wondered ruefully why so many people used that particular phrase to introduce a lie. 'I have six months' leave from the museum, and Prof Dixon has arranged for me to give a lecture at the university. That is as far as it goes for the moment.'

'Well,' said Georgina as she stood up, 'there is a hot-water bottle in your bed and your room is there for as long as you wish to stay.' From her that was as good as a passionate declaration of maternal love.

Over the next few days Royan arranged her

slides and notes for the lectures, and each afternoon she accompanied Georgina and Magic on their long walks over the surrounding countryside.

'Do you know Quenton Park?' she asked her mother during one of these rambles.

'Rather,' Georgina replied enthusiastically. 'Magic and I pick up there four or five times a season. First-class shoot. Some of the best pheasant and woodcock in Yorkshire. One drive there called the High Larches which is notorious. Birds so high they baffle the best shots in England.'

'Do you know the owner, Sir Nicholas Quenton-Harper?' Royan asked.

'Seen him at the shoots. Don't know him. Good shot, though,' Georgina replied. 'Knew his papa in the old days before I married your father.' She smiled in a suggestive way that startled Royan. 'Good dancer. We danced a few jigs together, not only on the dance floor.'

'Mummy, you are outrageous!' Royan laughed.

'Used to be,' Georgina agreed readily. 'Don't get many opportunities these days.'

'When are you and Magic going to Quenton Park again?'

'Two weeks' time.'

'May I come with you?'

'Of course — the keeper is always looking for beaters. Twenty quid and lunch with a bottle of beer for the day.' She stopped and looked at her daughter quizzically. 'What is all this about, then?'

'I hear there is a private museum on the estate. They have a world-renowned Egyptian collection. I wanted to get a look at it.'

'Not open to the public any more. Invitation only. Sir Nicholas is an odd chap, secretive and all that.'

'Couldn't you get an invitation for me?' Royan asked, but Georgina shook her head.

'Why don't you ask Prof Dixon? He is often one of the guns at Quenton Park. Great chum of Quenton-Harper.'

It was ten days before Prof Dixon was ready for her. She borrowed her mother's Land Rover and drove to Leeds. The Prof folded her in a bear hug and then took her through to his office for tea.

It was nostalgic of her days as a student to be back in the cluttered room filled with books and papers and ancient artefacts. Royan told him about Duraid's murder, and Dixon was shocked and distressed, but she quickly changed the subject to the slides that she had prepared for the lecture. He was fascinated by everything she had to show him.

It was almost time for her to leave before she had an opportunity to broach the subject of the Quenton Park museum, but he responded immediately.

'I am amazed that you never visited it while you were a student here. It's a very impressive collection. The family has been at it for over a hundred years. As a matter of fact, I am shooting on the estate next Thursday. I'll have a word with Nicholas. However, the poor chap isn't up to much at the moment. Last year he suffered a terrible personal tragedy. Lost his wife and two little girls in a motor accident on the M1.' He shook his head. 'Awful business. Nicholas was driving. I think he blames himself.' He walked her out to the Land Rover.

'So we will see you on the twenty-third,' he told Royan as they parted. 'I expect that you will have an audience of at least a hundred, and I have even had a reporter from the *Yorkshire Post* on to me. They have heard about your lectures and they want to do an interview with you. Jolly good publicity for the department. You'll do it, of course. Could you come a couple of hours early to speak to them?'

'Actually I will probably see you before the twenty-third,' she told him. 'Mummy and her dog are picking up at Quenton Park on Thursday, and she has got me a job as a beater for the day.'

'I'll keep an eye open for you,' he promised, and waved to her as she pulled away in a cloud of exhaust smoke.

The wind was searing cold out of the north. The clouds tumbled over each other, heavy and blue and grey, so close to earth that they brushed the crests of the hills as they hurried ahead of the gale.

Royan wore three layers of clothing under the old green Barbour jacket that Georgina had lent her, but still she shivered as they came up over the brow of the hills in the line of beaters. Her blood had thinned in the heat of the Nile valley. Two pairs of fisherman's socks were not enough to save her toes from turning numb.

For this drive, the last of the day, the head keeper had moved Georgina from her usual position behind the line of guns, where she and Magic were expected to pick up the crippled birds that came through to them, into the line of beaters.

Keeping the best for last, they were beating the High Larches. The keeper needed every man and woman he could get into the line to bring in the pheasant from the huge piece of ground on top of the hills and to push them off the brow, out over the valley where the guns waited at their pegs far below.

It seemed to Royan a supreme piece of illogical behaviour to rear and nurture the pheasants from chicks, and then, when they were mature, go to such lengths to make them as difficult to shoot as the keeper could devise. However, Georgina had explained to her that the higher and harder to hit the birds passed over the guns, the more pleased the sportsmen were, and the more they were willing to pay for the privilege of firing at them.

'You cannot believe what they will pay for a day's shooting,' Georgina had told her. 'Today will bring in almost £14,000 to the estate. They will shoot twenty days this season. Work that out and you will see that the shoot is a major part of the estate's income. Quite apart from the fun of working the dogs and beating, it gives a lot of us local people a very useful bit of extra money.'

At this stage of the day, Royan was not too certain just how much fun there was to be had from the job of beating. The walking was difficult in the thick brambles, and Royan had slipped more than once. There was mud on her knees and elbows. The ditch ahead of her was half-filled with water and there was a thin skin of ice across the surface. She approached it gingerly, using her walking-stick to balance herself. She was tired, for there had already been five drives, all as onerous as this one. She glanced across at her mother and marvelled at how she seemed to be enjoying this torture. Georgina strode along happily, controlling Magic with her whistle and hand signals.

She grinned at Royan now, 'Last lap, love. Nearly over.'

Royan was humiliated that her distress had been so obvious, and she used her stick to help her vault the muddy ditch. However, she miscalculated the width and fell short of the far bank. She landed knee-deep in the frozen water and it poured in over the top of her wellington boots.

Georgina laughed at her and offered her the end of her own stick to pull her out of the glutinous mud. Royan could not hold up the line by stopping to empty her flooded boots, so she went on, squelching loudly with each pace.

'Steady on the left!' the order from the head keeper was relayed over the walkie-talkie radio, and the line halted obediently.

The art and skill of the keeper was to flush the birds from the tangled undergrowth, not in one massed covey, but in a steady trickle that would pass over the waiting guns in singles and pairs, giving them the chance, after they had fired two barrels, to take their second gun from the loader and be ready for the next bird to appear in the sky high above them. The size of the keeper's tip and his reputation depended on the way he 'showed' the birds to the waiting guns.

During this respite Royan was able to regain her breath, and to look around her. Through a break in the grove of larches that gave the drive its name, she could see down into the valley.

There was an open meadow at the foot of

the hills, the expanse of smooth green grass broken up by patches of dirty grey snow from the previous week's fall. Down this meadow the keeper had set a line of numbered pegs. At the beginning of the day's sport the guns had drawn lots to decide the peg number from which each of them would shoot.

Now each man stood at his allotted peg, with his loader holding his second gun ready behind him, ready to pass it over when the first gun was empty. They were all looking up expectantly to the high ground from which the pheasant would appear.

'Which is Sir Nicholas?' Royan called to her mother, and Georgina pointed to the far end of the line of guns.

'The tall one,' she said, and at that moment the keeper's voice on the radio ordered, 'Gently on the left. Start tapping again.' Obediently the beaters tapped their sticks. There was no shouting or hallooing in this delicate and strictly controlled operation.

'Forward slowly. Halt to the flush of birds.'

A step at a time the line moved ahead, and in the brambles and bracken in front of her Royan could hear the stealthy scuffle of a number of pheasants moving forward, reluctant to take to the air until they were forced to do so.

There was another ditch in their path, this one choked with an almost impenetrable thicket of brambles. Some of the larger dogs, like the

Labradors, balked at entering such a thorny barrier. Georgina whistled sharply and Magic's ears went up. He was soaked and his coat was a matted mess of mud and burrs and thorns. His pink tongue lolled from the corner of his grinning mouth and the sodden stump of his tail was wagging merrily. At that moment he was the happiest dog in England. He was doing the work that he had been bred for.

'Come on, Magic,' Georgina ordered. 'Get in there. Get them out.'

Magic dived into the thickest and thorniest patch, and disappeared completely from view. There was a minute of snuffling and rooting around in the depths of the ditch, and then a fierce cackle and flurry of wings.

A pair of birds exploded out of the bushes. The hen led the way. She was a drab, nondescript creature the size of a domestic fowl, but the cock bird that followed her closely was magnificent. His head was capped with iridescent green and his cheeks and wattles were scarlet. His tail, barred in cinnamon and black, was almost as long again as his body and the rest of his plumage was a riot of gorgeous colour.

As he climbed he sparkled against the lowering grey sky like a priceless jewel thrown from an emperor's hand. Royan gasped with the beauty of the sight.

'Just look at them go!' Georgina's voice was thick with excitement. 'What a pair of crackerjacks. The best pair today. My bet is that not one of the guns will touch a feather on either of them.'

Up, and then on up, the two birds climbed, the hen drawing the cock after her, until suddenly the wind boiling over the hills like overheated milk caught them both and flung them away, out over the valley.

The line of beaters enjoyed the moment. They had worked hard for it. Their voices were tiny and faint on the wind as they urged the birds on. They loved to see a pheasant so high and fast that it could beat the guns.

'Forward!' they exulted. 'Over!' and this time the line came involuntarily to a halt as they followed the flight of the pair that were twisting away on the wind.

In the valley bottom the faces of the guns were turned upwards, pale specks against the green background. Their trepidation was almost palpable as they watched the pheasant reach their maximum speed, so that they could no longer beat their wings, but locked them into a backswept profile as they began to drop down into the valley.

This was the most difficult shot that any gun would face. A high pair of pheasant with a half gale quartering from behind, dropping into the shot at their terminal rate of flight, set to pass over the line at the extreme effective range of a twelve-bore shotgun. For the men below it was a calculation of speed and lead in all three dimensions of space. The best of shots might hope to take one of them, but who would dare to think of both?

'A pound on it!' Georgina called. 'A pound that they both get through.' But none of the beaters who heard her accepted the wager.

The wind was pushing the birds gently sideways. They started off aimed at the centre of the line, but they were drifting towards the far end. As the angle changed, Royan could see the men at the pegs below her brace themselves in turn as the birds appeared to be heading straight for them, and then relax as the wind moved them on. Their relief was evident as, one after the other, each of them was absolved from the challenge of having to make such an impossible shot with all eyes fastened upon him.

In the end only the tall figure at the extreme end of the line stood in their flight path.

'Your bird, sir,' one of the other guns called mockingly, and Royan found that instinctively she was holding her breath with anticipation.

Nicholas Quenton-Harper seemed unaware of the approach of the pair of pheasant. He stood completely relaxed, his tall frame slouching slightly, his shotgun tucked under his right arm with the muzzles pointing at the ground.

At the moment that the leading hen bird reached a point in the sky sixty degrees out ahead of him he moved for the first time. With casual grace he swung the shotgun up in a sweeping arc. At the instant that the butt touched his cheek and shoulder he fired, but the gun never stopped moving and went on to describe the rest of the arc.

The distance delayed the sound of the shot reaching Royan. She saw the barrels kick with the recoil, and a pale spurt of blue smoke from the muzzle. Then Nicholas lowered the gun as the hen suddenly threw back her head and closed her wings. There was no burst of feathers from her body, for she had been hit cleanly in the head and killed instantly. As she began the long plummet to earth Royan heard the thud of the shot.

By then the cock was high over Nicholas's head. This time as he mounted the gun in that casual sweeping gesture he arched his back to point upwards, his long frame bending from the waist like a drawn bow. Once again at the apex of the swing the weapon kicked in his grasp.

'He has missed!' Royan thought with a mixture of satisfaction and disappointment, as the cock sailed on seemingly unscathed. Part of her wanted the beautiful bird to escape, while part of her wanted the man to succeed. Gradually the profile of the high cock altered as the wings folded back and it rolled over in flight. Royan had no way of knowing that his heart had been struck through, until seconds later he died in mid-air and the locked wings lost their rigid set.

As the cock tumbled to earth, a spontaneous chorus of cheers ran down the line of beaters, faint but enthusiastic on the icy north wind. Even the other guns added their voices with cries of, 'Oh, good shot, sir!'

Royan did not join in the cheering, but for the moment her fatigue and cold were forgotten. She could only vaguely appreciate the skill that those two shots had called for, but she was impressed, even a little awed. Her very first glimpse of the man had fulfilled all the expectations that Duraid's stories about him had raised in her.

By the time the last drive ended it was almost dark. An old army truck came rumbling down the track through the forest along which the tired beaters and their dogs waited. As it slowed they scrambled up into the back. Georgina gave Royan a boost from behind before she and Magic followed her up. They settled thankfully on one of the long hard benches, and Georgina lit a cigarette as she joined in the chat and banter of the under-keepers and beaters around her.

Royan sat silently at the end of the bench, enjoying the sense of achievement at having come through such a strenuous day. She felt tired and relaxed, and strangely contented. For one whole day she had not thought either of the theft of the scroll or of Duraid's murder and the unknown and unseen enemy who threatened her with a violent death.

The truck ground down the hill and slowed as it reached the bottom, pulling in to the verge to let a green Range Rover pass. As the two

75

vehicles drew level, Royan turned her head and looked down into the open driver's window of the expensive estate car, and into the eyes of Nicholas Quenton-Harper at the wheel.

This was the first time she had been close enough to him to see his features. She was surprised at how young he was. She had expected him to be a man of Duraid's age. She saw now that he was no older than forty, for there were only the first strands of silver in the wings of his thick, rumpled hair. His features were tanned and weatherbeaten, those of an outdoors man. His eyes were green and penetrating under dark, beetling brows. His mouth was wide and expressive, and he was smiling now at some witticism that the driver of the truck called to him in a thick Yorkshire accent, but there was a sense of sadness and tragedy in the eyes. Royan remembered what the Prof had told her of his recent bereavement, and she felt her heart go out to him. She was not alone in her loss and her mourning.

He looked directly into her eyes and she saw his expression change. She was an attractive woman, and she could tell when a man recognized that. She had made an impression on him, but she did not enjoy the fact. Her sorrow for Duraid was still too raw and painful. She looked away and the Range Rover drove on.

Her lecture at the university went off extremely well. Royan was a good speaker and she knew her subject intimately. She held them fascinated with her account of the opening of the tomb of Queen Lostris and of the subsequent discovery of the scrolls. Many of her audience had read the book, and during question time they pestered her to know how much of it was the truth. She had to tread very carefully here, so as not to deal too harshly with the author.

Afterwards Prof Dixon took Royan and Georgina to dinner. He was delighted with her success, and ordered the most expensive bottle of claret on the wine list to celebrate. He was only mildly disconcerted when she refused a glass of it.

'Oh, dear me, I forgot that you were a Moslem,' he apologised.

'A Copt,' she corrected him, 'and it's not on religious grounds. I just don't like the taste.'

'Don't worry,' Georgina counselled him, 'I don't have the same odd compulsion to masochism as my daughter. She must get it from her father's side. I'll give you a hand to finish the good stuff.'

Under the benign influence of the claret the Prof became expansive, and entertained them with the accounts of the archaeological digs he had been on over the decades. It was only over the coffee that he turned to Royan.

'Goodness me, I almost forgot to tell you. I have arranged for you to visit the museum at Quenton Park any afternoon this week. Just ring Mrs Street the day before, and she will be waiting to let you in. She is Nicholas's PA.'

Royan remembered the way to Quenton Park from when Georgina had driven them to the shoot, but now she was alone in the Land Rover. The massive main gates to the estate were made of ornate cast iron. A little further on, the road divided and a cluster of road signs pointed the way to the various destinations: 'Quenton Hall. Private', 'Estate Office' and 'Museum'.

The road to the museum curved through the deer park where herds of fallow deer grazed under the winter-bare oaks. Through the misty landscape she had glimpses of the big house. According to the guidebook that the Prof had given her, Sir Christopher Wren had designed the house in 1693, and the master landscapist, Capability Brown, had created the gardens sixty years later. The results were perfection.

The museum was set in a grove of copper beech trees half a mile beyond the house. It was a sprawling building that had obviously been added to more than once over the years. Mrs

Street was waiting for her at the side door, and introduced herself as she let Royan in. She was middle-aged, grey-haired and self-assured. 'I was at your lecture on Monday evening. Fascinating! I have a guidebook for you, but you will find the exhibits well catalogued and described. I have spent almost twenty years at the job. There are no other visitors today. You will have the place to yourself. You must just wander around and please yourself. I shall not leave until five this evening, so you have all afternoon. If I can help you in any way my office is at the end of the passage. Please don't hesitate.'

From the first moment that Royan walked into the display of African mammals she was enthralled. The primate room housed a complete collection of every single species of ape and monkey from that continent: from the great silver-backed male gorilla to the delicate colobus in his long flowing mantle of black and white fur, they were all represented.

Although some of the exhibits were over a hundred years old, they were beautifully preserved and presented, set in painted dioramas of their natural habitat. It was obvious that the museum must employ a staff of skilled artists and taxidermists. She could guess what this must have cost. Wryly she decided that the five million dollars from the sale of the plundered frieze had been well spent.

She went through to the antelope room and

stared around her in wonder at the magnificent beasts preserved here. She stopped before a diorama of a family group of the giant sable antelope of the now extinct Angolan variety, *Hippotragus niger variani*. While she admired the jet black and snowy-chested bull with his long, back-swept horns, she mourned his death at the hand of one of the Quenton-Harper family. Then she checked herself. Without the strange dedication and passion of the hunter-collector who had killed him, future generations might never have been able to look upon this regal presence.

She passed on into the next hall which was given over to displays of the African elephant, and paused in the centre of the room before a pair of ivory tusks so large that she could not believe they had ever been carried by a living animal. They seemed more like the marble columns of some Hellenic temple to Diana, the goddess of the chase. She stooped to read the printed catalogue card:

Tusks of the African Elephant, Loxodonta africana. *Shot in the Lado Enclave in 1899 by Sir Jonathan Quenton-Harper. Left tusk 289 lb. Right tusk 301 lb. Length of larger tusk 11'4". Girth 32". The largest pair of tusks ever taken by a European hunter.*

They stood twice as high as she was tall, and they were half as thick again as her waist. As she passed on into the Egyptian room she mar-

80

velled at the size and strength of the creature that had carried them.

She came up short as her eyes fell upon the figure in the centre of the room. It was a fifteen-foot-high figure of Ramesses II, depicted as the god Osiris in polished red granite. The god-emperor strode out on muscular legs, wearing only sandals on his feet and a short kilt. In his left hand he carried the remains of a war-bow, with both the upper and lower limbs of the weapon broken off. This was the only damage that the statue had suffered in all those thousands of years. The rest of it was perfect — the plinth even bore the marks of the mason's chisel. In his right fist Pharaoh carried a seal embossed with his royal cartouche. Upon his majestic head he wore the tall double crown of the upper and lower kingdoms. His expression was calm and enigmatic.

Royan recognized the statue instantly, for its twin stood in the grand hall of the Cairo museum. She passed it every day on her way to her office.

She felt anger rising in her. This was one of the major treasures of her very Egypt. It had been plundered and stolen from one of her country's sacred sites. It did not belong here. It belonged on the banks of the great river Nile. She felt herself shaking with the strength of her emotion as she went forward to examine the statue more closely and to read the hieroglyphic inscription on the base.

The royal cartouche stood out in the centre of the arrogant warning: '*I am the divine Ramesses, master of ten thousand chariots. Fear me, O ye enemies of Egypt.*'

Royan had not read the translation aloud; it was a soft, deep voice close behind her that spoke, startling her. She had not heard anyone approaching. She spun round to find him standing close enough to touch.

His hands were thrust into the pockets of a shapeless blue cardigan. There was a hole in one elbow. He wore faded denim jeans over well-worn but monogrammed velvet carpet slippers — the type of genteel shabbiness that certain Englishmen often cultivate, for it would never do to seem too concerned with one's appearance

'Sorry. Didn't mean to startle you.' He smiled a lazy smile of apology, and his teeth were very white but slightly crooked. Suddenly his expression changed as he recognized her.

'Oh, it's you.' She should have been flattered that he remembered her from so fleeting a contact, but there was that flash of something in his eyes again that offended her. Nevertheless, she could not refuse the hand he offered her. 'Nick Quenton-Harper,' he introduced himself. 'You must be Percival Dixon's old student. I think I saw you at the shoot last Thursday. Weren't you beating for us?'

His manner was friendly and forthright, so she felt her hackles subsiding as she responded,

'Yes. I am Royan Al Simma. I think you knew my husband, Duraid Al Simma.'

'Duraid! Of course, I know him. Grand old fellow. We spent a lot of time in the desert together. One of the very best. How is he?'

'He's dead.' She had not meant it to sound so bald and heartless, but then there was no other reply she could think of.

'I am so terribly sorry. I didn't know. When and how did it happen?'

'Very recently, three weeks ago. He was murdered.'

'Oh, my God.' She saw the sympathy in his eyes, and she remembered that he also had suffered. 'I telephoned him in Cairo not more than four months ago. He was his old charming self. Have they found the person who did it?'

She shook her head and looked around the hall to avoid having to face him and let him see that her eyes were wet. 'You have an extraordinary collection here.'

He accepted the change of subject at once. 'Thanks mostly to my grandfather. He was on the staff of Evelyn Baring — Over Bearing, as his numerous enemies called him. He was the British man in Cairo during —'

She cut him short. 'Yes, I have heard of Evelyn Baring, the first Earl of Cromer, British Consul-General of Egypt from 1883 to 1907. With his plenipotentiary powers he was the unchallenged dictator of my country for all that period. Numerous enemies, as you say.'

Nicholas's eyes narrowed slightly. 'Percival warned me you were one of his best students. He didn't, however, warn me of your strong nationalistic feelings. It is clear that you didn't need me to translate the Ramesses inscription for you.'

'My own father was on the staff of Gamal Abdel Nasser,' she murmured. Nasser was the man who had toppled the puppet King Farouk and finally broken the British power in Egypt. As president he had nationalized the Suez Canal in the face of British outrage.

'Ha!' he chuckled. 'Different sides of the track. But things have changed. I hope we don't have to be enemies?'

'Not at all,' she agreed. 'Duraid held you in the highest esteem.'

'As I did him.' He changed the subject again. 'We are very proud of our collection of royal *ushabti*. Examples from the tomb of every pharaoh from the old Kingdom onwards, right up to the last of the Ptolemys. Please let me show it to you.' She followed him to the huge display case that occupied one complete wall of the hall. It was lined with shelf after shelf of the doll-like figures which had been placed in the tombs to act as servants and slaves for the dead kings in the shadow world.

With his own key Nicholas opened the glazed doors of the case and reached up to bring down the most interesting of the exhibits. 'This is the *ushabti* of Maya who served under three pharaohs, Tutankhamen, Ay and Horemheb. It is from the tomb of Ay who died in 1343 BC.'

He handed the doll to her and she read aloud the three thousand-year-old hieroglyphics as easily as though they had been the headlines of that morning's newspaper. 'I am Maya, Treasurer of the two Kingdoms. I will answer for the divine Pharaoh Ay. May he live for ever!' She spoke in Arabic to test him, and his reply in the same language was fluent and colloquial.

'It seems that Percival Dixon told me the truth. You must have been an exceptional student.'

Engrossed now in their common interest, speaking alternately Arabic and English, the initial sharp prickles of antagonism between them were dulled. They moved slowly round the hall, lingering before each display case to handle and examine minutely each object that it contained.

It was as though they were transported back over the millennia. Hours and days seemed of no consequence in the face of such antiquity, and so it startled both of them when Mrs Street returned to interrupt them, 'I am off now, Sir Nicholas. Can I leave it to you to lock up and set the alarm? The security guards are on duty already.'

'What time is it?' Nicholas answered his own question by glancing at the stainless steel Rolex Submariner on his wrist. 'Five-forty already, what on earth happened to the day?' He sighed theatrically. 'Off you go, Mrs Street. Sorry we kept you so long.'

'Don't forget to set the alarm,' she warned him, and then to Royan, 'He can be so absent-minded when he is off on one of his hobbyhorses.' Her fondness towards her employer was obviously that of an indulgent aunt.

'You've given me enough orders for one day. Off you go,' Nicholas grinned, as he turned back to Royan. 'Can't let you go without showing you something that Duraid was in on with me. Can you stay for a few minutes longer?' She nodded and he reached out as if to take her arm, and then dropped his hand. In the Arab world it is insulting to touch a woman, even in such a casual manner. She was aware of the courtesy, and she warmed to his good manners and easy style a little more.

He led her out of the exhibition halls through a door marked 'Private. Staff Only', and down a long corridor to the room at the end.

'The inner sanctum.' He ushered her in. 'Excuse the mess. I must really get around to tidying up in here one of these years. My wife used to —' He broke off abruptly, and he glanced at the silver-framed photograph of a family group on his desk. Nicholas and a beautiful darkhaired woman sat on a picnic rug under the spreading branches of an oak. There were two little girls with them and the family resemblance to the mother was strong in both of them. The youngest child sat on Nicholas's lap while the elder girl stood behind them, holding the reins of her Shetland pony. Royan glanced sideways at him and saw the devastating sorrow in his eyes.

So as not to embarrass him she looked around the rest of the room, which was obviously his study and workshop. It was spacious and comfortable, a man's room, but it illustrated the contradictions of his character — the bookish scholar set against the man of action. Amongst the muddle of books and museum specimens lay fishing reels and a Hardy split cane salmon rod. On a row of wall hooks hung a Barbour jacket, a canvas shotgun slip and a leather cartridge bag embossed with the initials N.Q.-H.

She recognized some of the framed pictures on the walls. They were original nineteenth-century watercolours by the Scottish traveller David Roberts, and others by Vivant Denon who had accompanied Napoleon's *L'armée de l'Orient* to Egypt. They were fascinating views of the monuments drawn before the excavations and restorations of more modern times.

Nicholas went to the fireplace and threw a log on the fading coals. He kicked it until it flared up brightly and then beckoned her to stand in front of the floor-to-ceiling curtains that covered half of one wall. With a conjuror's flourish he pulled the tasselled cord that opened the curtains and exclaimed with satisfaction, 'What do you make of that, then?'

She studied the magnificent bas-relief frieze

that was mounted on the wall. The detail was beautiful and the rendition magnificent, but she did not let her admiration show. Instead she gave her opinion in offhand tones.

'Sixth King of the Amorite dynasty, Hammurabi, about 1780 BC,' she said, pretending to study the finely chiselled features of the ancient monarch before she went on, 'Yes, probably from his palace site southwest of the ziggurat at Ashur. There should have been a pair of these friezes. They are worth in the region of five million US dollars each. My guess is that they were stolen from the saintly ruler of modern Mesopotamia, Saddam Hussein, by two unprincipled rogues. I hear that the other one of the pair is at present in the collection of a certain Mr Peter Walsh in Texas.'

He stared at her in astonishment, and then burst out laughing. 'Damn it! I swore Duraid to secrecy but he must have told you about our naughty little escapade.' It was the first time she had heard him laugh. It seemed to come naturally to his lips and she liked the sound of it, hearty and unaffected.

'You are right about the present owner of the second frieze,' he told her, still laughing. 'But the price was six million, not five.'

'Duraid also told me about your visit to the Tibesti Massif in Chad and southern Libya,' she remarked, and he shook his head in mock contrition.

'It seems I have no secrets from you.' He

went to a tall *armoire* against the opposite wall. It was a magnificent piece of marquetry furniture, probably seventeenth-century French. He opened the double doors and said, 'This is what Duraid and I brought back from Libya, without the consent of Colonel Muammar al Gadaffi.' He took down one of the exquisite little bronzes and handed it to her. It was the figure of a mother nursing her infant, and it had a green patina of age.

'Hannibal, son of Hamilcar Barca,' he said, 'about 203 BC. These were found by a band of Tuareg at one of his old camps on the Bagradas river in North Africa. Hannibal must have cached them there before his defeat by the Roman general Scipio. There were over two hundred bronzes in the hoard, and I still have fifty of the best of them.'

'You sold the rest of them?' she asked, as she admired the statuette. There was disapproval in her tone as she went on, 'How could you bear to part with something so beautiful?'

He sighed unhappily, 'Had to, I am afraid. Very sad, but the expedition to retrieve them cost me a fortune. Had to cover expenses by selling some of the booty.'

He went to his desk and brought out a bottle of Laphroaig malt whisky from the bottom drawer. He placed the bottle on the desk top and set two glasses beside it. 'Can I tempt you?' he asked, but she shook her head.

'Don't blame you. Even the Scots themselves

admit that this brew should only be drunk in sub-zero weather on The Hill, in a forty-knot gale, after stalking and shooting a ten-point stag. May I offer you something a little more lady-like?'

'Do you have a Coke?' she suggested.

'Yes, but that is really bad for you, even worse than Laphroaig. It's all that sugar. Absolute poison.'

She took the glass he brought to her and returned his toast with it.

'To life!' she agreed, and then she went on, 'You are right. Duraid did tell me about these.' She replaced the Punic bronze in the *armoire,* then came to face him at the desk. 'It was also Duraid who sent me to see you. It was his dying instruction to me.'

'Aha! So none of this is coincidence then. It seems I am the unwitting pawn in some deep and nefarious plot.' He pointed to the chair facing his desk. 'Sit!' he ordered. 'Tell!'

He perched above her on the corner of the desk, with the whisky glass in his right hand and with one long, denim-clad leg swinging lazily as the tail of a resting leopard. Though he was smiling quizzically, he watched her face with a penetrating green gaze. She thought that it would be difficult to lie to this man.

She took a deep breath, 'Have you heard of an ancient Egyptian queen called Lostris, of the second intermediate period, co-existent with the first Hyksos invasions?'

90

He laughed a little derisively and stood up, 'Oh! Now we are talking about the book *River God*, are we?' He went to the bookcase and brought down a copy. Although well thumbed, it was still in its dust-jacket, and the cover illustration was a dreamy surrealistic view in pastel shades of green and rose purple of the pyramids seen over water. He dropped it on the desk in front of her.

'Have you read it?' she asked.

'Yes,' he nodded. 'I read most of Wilbur Smith's stuff. He amuses me. He has shot here at Quenton Park a couple of times.'

'You like lots of sex and violence in your reading, obviously?' She pulled a face. 'What did you think of this particular book?'

'I must admit that he had me fooled. Whilst I was reading it, I sort of wished that it might be based on fact. That was why I phoned Duraid.' Nicholas picked up the book again and flipped to the end of it. 'The author's note was convincing, but what I couldn't get out of my mind was the last sentence.' He read it aloud. ' *"Somewhere in the Abyssinian mountains near the source of the Blue Nile, the mummy of Tenus still lies in the unviolated tomb of Pharaoh Mamose."* '

Almost angrily Nicholas threw the book down on the desk. 'My God! You will never know how much I wanted it to be true. You will never know how much I wanted a shot at Pharaoh Mamose's tomb. I had to speak to Duraid.

When he assured me it was all a load of bunkum, I felt cheated. I had built up my expectations so high that I was bitterly disappointed.'

'It's not bunkum,' she contradicted him, and then corrected herself quickly, 'well, at least not all of it.'

'I see. Duraid was lying to me, was he?'

'Not lying,' she defended him hotly. 'Just delaying the truth a little. He wasn't ready to tell you the whole story then. He didn't have the answers to all the questions that he knew you would ask. He was going to come to you when he was ready. Your name was at the top of the list of potential sponsors that he had drawn up.'

'Duraid did not have the answers, but I suppose you do?' He was smiling sceptically. 'I was caught once. I am not likely to fall for the same cock and bull a second time.'

'The scrolls exist. Nine of them are still in the vaults at the Cairo museum. I was the one who discovered them in the tomb of Queen Lostris.' Royan opened her leather sling bag and rummaged around in it until she brought out a thin sheaf of glossy 6 x 4 colour photographs. She selected one and passed it to him. 'That is a shot of the rear wall of the tomb. You can just make out the alabaster jars in the niche. That was taken before we removed them.'

'Nice picture, but it could have been taken anywhere.'

She ignored the remark and passed him another photograph. 'The ten scrolls in Duraid's workroom at the museum. You recognize the two men standing behind the bench?'

He nodded. 'Duraid and Wilbur Smith.' His sceptical expression had turned to one of doubt and bemusement. 'What the hell are you trying to tell me?'

'What the *hell* I am trying to tell you is that, apart from a wide poetic licence that the author took unto himself, all that he wrote in the book has at least some foundation in the truth. However, the scroll that most concerns us is the seventh, the one that was stolen by the men who murdered my husband.'

Nicholas stood up and went to the fireplace. He threw on another log and bashed it viciously with the poker, as if to give release to his emotions. He spoke without turning around, 'What was the significance of that particular scroll as opposed to the other nine?'

'It was the one that contained the account of Pharaoh Mamose's burial and, we believe, directions that might enable us to find the site of the tomb.'

'You believe, but you aren't certain?' He swung around to face her with the poker gripped like a weapon. In this mood he was frightening. His mouth was set in a tight hard line and his eyes glittered.

'Large parts of the seventh scroll are written in some sort of code, a series of cryptic verses. Duraid and I were in the process of deciphering these when —' she broke off and drew a long breath, 'when he was murdered.'

'You must have a copy of something so valuable?' He glared at her, so that she felt intimidated. She shook her head.

'All the microfilm, all our notes, all of it was stolen along with the original scroll. Then whoever killed Duraid went back to our flat in Cairo and destroyed my PC on to which I had transposed all our research.'

He threw the poker into the coal scuttle with a clatter, and came back to the desk. 'So you have no evidence at all? Nothing to prove that any of this is true?'

'Nothing,' she agreed, 'except what I have here.' With a long slim forefinger she tapped her forehead. 'I have a good memory.'

He frowned and ran his fingers through his thick curling hair. 'And so why did you come to me?'

'I have come to give you a shot at the tomb of Pharaoh Mamose,' she told him simply. 'Do you want it?'

Suddenly his mood changed. He grinned like a naughty schoolboy. 'At this moment I cannot think of anything I want more.'

'Then you and I will have to draw up some sort of working agreement,' she told him, and she leaned forward in a businesslike manner. 'First, let me tell you what I want, and then you can do the same.'

It was hard bargaining, and it was one in

the morning when Royan admitted her exhaustion. 'I can't think straight any more. Can we start again tomorrow morning?' They still had not reached an agreement.

'It's tomorrow morning already,' he told her. 'But you are right. Thoughtless of me. You can sleep here. After all, we do have twenty-seven bedrooms here.'

'No, thanks.' She stood up. 'I'll go on home.'

'The road will be icy,' he warned her. Then he saw her determined expression and held up his hands in capitulation. 'All right, I won't insist. What time tomorrow? I have a meeting with my lawyers at ten, but we should be finished by noon. Why don't you and I have a working lunch here? I was supposed to be shooting at Ganton in the afternoon, but I will cancel that. That way I will have the afternoon and evening clear for you.'

Nicholas's meeting with the lawyers took place the next morning in the library of Quenton Park. It was not an easy nor a pleasant session, but then he never expected it to be. This had been the year in which his world began to fall to pieces around his head. He gritted his teeth as he remembered how the year had opened with that fatal moment of fatigue and inattention at midnight on the icy motorway, and the blinding headlights of the truck bearing down on them.

He had not recovered from that before the next brutal blow had fallen. This was the financial report of the Lloyd's insurance syndicate on which Nicholas, like his father and grandfather before him, was a 'Name'. For half a century the family had enjoyed a regular and substantial income from their share of the syndicate profits. Of course, Nicholas had been aware that liability for his share of any losses that the syndicate suffered was unlimited. The enormity of that responsibility had weighed lightly; for there had never been serious losses to account for, not for fifty years, not until this year.

With the California earthquake and environmental pollution claims awarded against one of the multinational chemical companies, the syndicate's losses had amounted to over twenty-six million pounds sterling. Nicholas's share of that loss was two and a half million pounds — some of which had been settled, but the rest was due for payment in a little over eight months' time — together with whatever nasty surprises next year might hold.

Almost immediately after that the Quenton Park estate's crop of sugar beet, almost a thousand acres in total, had been hit by *rhizomania*, the mad root disease. They had lost the lot.

'We will need to find at least two and a half million,' said one of the lawyers. 'That should be no problem — the Hall is filled with valuable items, and what about the museum? What could we reasonably expect from the sale of some of the exhibits?'

Nicholas winced at the thought of selling the Ramesses statue, the bronzes, the Hammurabi frieze or any item of his cherished collection at the Hall or the museum. He acknowledged that their sale would cover his debts, but he doubted that he could live without them. Almost anything was preferable to parting with them.

'Hell, no,' Nicholas cut in, and the lawyer looked across at him coldly.

'Well, let's see what else we've got,' he continued remorselessly. 'There's the dairy herd.'

'That will bring in a hundred thousand, if we are lucky,' Nicholas grunted. 'Leaves only two point four million to find.'

'And your racing stud,' the accountant came into the conversation.

'I have only six horses in training. Another two hundred grand.' Nicholas smiled without humour, 'Brings us down to two point two. We are getting there slowly.'

'The yacht,' suggested the youngest lawyer.

'It's older than I am,' Nicholas shook his head, 'belonged to my father, for heaven's sake. You probably wouldn't be able to give it away. Sentimental is the only value it has. My shotguns would be worth more.'

Both lawyers bent their heads over their lists, 'Ah, yes! We have those. A pair of Purdey side-lock ejectors in good condition. Estimate forty thousand.'

'I also have some secondhand socks and underpants,' Nicholas admitted. 'Why don't you list those also?'

They ignored the jibe. 'Then there is the London house,' the elder lawyer went on unperturbed, inured to human suffering. 'Good address. Value one point five million.'

'Not in this financial climate,' Nicholas contradicted him. 'A million is more realistic.' The lawyer made a note in the margin of his document before going on, 'Of course we want to avoid, if at all possible, putting the entire estate up for sale.'

It was a hard and difficult meeting which ended with nothing definitely decided, and Nicholas feeling angry and frustrated.

He saw the lawyers off, and then went up to the family quarters to take a quick shower and change his shirt. As an afterthought, and for no good reason, he shaved and splashed aftershave on his cheeks.

He drove across the park and left the Range Rover in the museum car park. The snow had turned to sleet, and his bare head was sprinkled with cold droplets by the time he had crossed the car park.

Royan was waiting in Mrs Street's office. The two of them seemed to be getting along well together. He stopped outside the door to listen to her laughter. It made him feel a little better.

The cook had sent across a hot lunch from the main house. She seemed to believe that a substantial meal would keep this foul weather at bay. There was a tureen of thick, rich minestrone and a Lancashire hotpot, with a half bottle of red Burgundy for him and a jug of freshly squeezed orange juice for her. They ate in front of the fire, while the rain whipped against the windowpanes.

While they ate he asked her to give him the details of Duraid's murder. She left out nothing, including her own injuries, and drew back her sleeve to show him the dressing over the knife wound. He listened intently as she told him of the second attempt on her life in the streets of Cairo.

'Any suspicions?' he asked, when she had finished. 'Anybody you can think of who might be responsible?' But she shook her head.

'There was no warning of any kind,' she said.

They finished the meal in silence, each of them thinking their own thoughts. Over the coffee he suggested, 'All right, then. What about our agreement?'

They argued back and forth for nearly an hour.

'It's difficult to agree on your share of the booty, until I know just what your contribution is going to be,' Nicholas protested as he topped up their coffee cups. 'After all, I am going to be called on to finance and conduct the expedition —'

'You will just have to trust that my contribution will be worthwhile, otherwise there will simply be no booty, as you call it. Anyway you can be certain I am not going to tell you one thing more until we have an agreement, and have shaken hands on it.'

'A bit harsh?' he asked, and she gave him a wicked smile.

'If you don't like my terms, there are three other names on Duraid's list of possible sponsors,' she threatened.

'All right,' he cut in with a contrived look of martyrdom, 'I agree to your proposal. But how do we calculate equal shares?'

'I shall choose the first item of any archaeological artefacts we are able to retrieve, and you the next, and so on, turn about.'

'How about I choose first?' He raised an eyebrow at her.

'Let's spin for it,' she suggested, and he fished a pound coin from his pocket.

'Call!' He flipped the coin, and while it was in the air she called, 'Heads.'

'Damn!' he exclaimed, as he retrieved the coin and shoved it back into his pocket. 'So, you get first choice of the booty, if there ever is any.' He held out his hand across the lunch table. 'It will be yours to do exactly what you want to do with it. You can even donate it to the Cairo museum, if that is still your particular aberration. Deal?' he asked, and she took his hand.

'Deal!' she agreed, and then added, 'Partner.'

'Now let's get down to it. No more secrets between us. Tell me every detail that you have been holding back.'

'Bring that book,' she pointed to the copy of *River God*, and while he fetched it she pushed the dirty dishes aside. 'The first thing we should go over is the sections of the book that Duraid edited.' She turned to the last pages. 'Here. This is where Duraid's obfuscation begins.'

'Good word,' Nicholas smiled, 'but let's keep it simple. You have obfuscated me enough already.'

She did not even smile. 'You know the story to this point. Queen Lostris and her people are driven out of Egypt by the Hyksos and their superior chariots. They journey south up the Nile until they reach the confluence of the White and Blue Niles. In other words, present-day Khartoum. All this is reasonably faithful to the scrolls.'

'I recall. Go on.'

'In the holds of their river galleys they are carrying the mummified body of Queen Lostris's husband, Pharaoh Mamose the Eighth. Twelve years previously she has sworn to him as he lay dying of a Hyksos arrow through his lung that she would find a secure burial site for him, and that she would lay him in it with all his vast treasure. When they reach Khartoum she determines that the time has at last come for her to make good her promise to him. She sends out her son, the fourteen-year-old Prince Memnon, with a squadron of chariots to find the burial site. Memnon is accompanied by his mentor, the narrator of the history, the indefatigable Taita.'

'Okay, I remember this section. Memnon and Taita consult the black Shilluk slaves they have captured, and on their advice decide to follow the left-hand fork of the river, or what we know as the Blue Nile.'

Royan nodded and continued the story. 'They travelled eastwards and were confronted by formidable mountains, so high that they were described as a blue rampart. So far what you read in the book is a fairly faithful rendition of the scrolls, but at this point,' she tapped the open page, 'we come to Duraid's red herring. In his description of the foothills —'

Before she could continue, Nicholas interjected, 'I remember thinking when I originally read it that it didn't accurately describe the area where the Blue Nile emerges from the Ethiopian highlands. There are no foothills. There is only the sheer western escarpment of the massif. The river comes out of it like a snake out of its hole. Whoever wrote that description doesn't know the course of the Blue Nile.'

'Do you know the area?' Royan asked, and he laughed and nodded.

'When I was younger and even more stupid than I am now, I conceived the grandiose plan of boating the Abbay gorge from Lake Tana down to the dam at Roseires in the Sudan. The Abbay is the Ethiopian name for the Blue Nile.'

'Why did you want to do that?'

'Because it had never been done before. Major Cheesman, the British consul, had a shot at it in 1932, and nearly drowned himself. I thought I could make a film, and write a book about the voyage and earn myself a fortune from the royalties. I talked my father into financing the expedition. It was the kind of mad escapade that appealed to him. He even wanted to join the expedition. I studied the whole course of the Abbay river, not only on maps. I also bought myself an old Cessna 180 and flew down the gorge, five hundred miles from Lake Tana to the dam. As I said, I was twenty-one years old and crazy.'

'What happened?' She was fascinated. Duraid had never told her about this, but it was the type of adventure that she would have expected this man to launch into.

'I recruited eight of my friends from Sandhurst, and we devoted our Christmas holidays to the attempt. It was a fiasco. We lasted two days on those wild waters. The gorge is the most hellish corner of this earth that I know of. It's almost twice as deep and as rugged as the Grand Canyon of the Colorado river in Arizona. It smashed up our kayaks before we had covered twenty miles out of the five hundred. We had to abandon all our equipment and climb the walls of the gorge to reach civilization again.'

He looked serious for a moment, 'I lost two members of our party. Bobby Palmer was drowned, and Tim Marshall fell on the cliffs. We were not even able to recover their bodies. They are still down there somewhere. I had to tell their parents —' he broke off as he remembered the agony of it.

'Has anybody ever succeeded in navigating the Blue Nile gorge?' she asked, to distract him.

'Yes. I went back a few years later. This time not as leader, but as a very junior member of the official British Armed Forces Expedition. It took the army, the navy and the air force to beat that river.'

She stared at him with a feeling of awe. He had actually rafted the Abbay. It was as though she had been led to him by some strange fate. Duraid was right. There was probably no man in the world better qualified for the work in hand.

'So you know as much as anybody about the real nature of the gorge. I will try to give you a general indication of what Taita actually set down in the seventh scroll. Unfortunately this section of the scroll had suffered some damage and Duraid and I were obliged to extrapolate from parts of the text. You will have to tell me how this agrees with your own knowledge of the terrain.'

'Go ahead,' he invited her.

'Taita described the escarpment very much the way you did, as a sheer wall from which the river emerged. They were forced to leave their chariots, which were unable to cover the steep and rugged terrain of the canyon. They were forced to go forward on foot, leading the pack horses. Soon the gorge grew so steep and dangerous that they lost some of these animals, which fell from the wild goat tracks they were following and plunged into the river far below. This did not deter them and they pressed on at the orders of Prince Memnon.'

'I can see it exactly as he describes it. It's a fearsome bit of countryside.'

'Taita then describes coming to a series of obstacles, which he describes as "steps". Duraid and I could not decide with certainty what these were. But our best guess was that they were waterfalls.'

'No shortage of those in the Abbay gorge, either,' Nicholas nodded.

'This is the important part of his testimony. Taita tells us that after twenty days' travel up the gorge they came upon the "second step". It was here that the prince received a fortuitous message from his dead father, in the form of a dream, in which he chose this as the site of his own tomb. Taita tells us that they travelled no further. If we are able to determine what it was that stopped them, that would give us an accurate measurement of just how far into the gorge they penetrated.'

'Before we can go any further we will need maps and satellite photographs of the mountains,

105

and I will have to go over my expedition notes and diary,' Nicholas decided. 'I try to keep my reference library up-to-date, and so we should have satellite photographs and the most recent maps on file here in the museum. If they are Mrs Street is the one to find them.'

He stood up and stretched, 'I will dig out my diaries this evening and read over them. My great-grandfather also hunted and collected in Ethiopia in the last century. I know he crossed the Blue Nile near Debra Markos in 1890-something. I'll get out his notes as well. They are preserved in our archives. The old boy may have written something there that could help us.'

He walked with her to the old green Land Rover in the car park, and as she started the engine he told her through the open window, 'I still think that you should stay over here at the Hall. It must be an hour-and-a-half's drive across to Brandsbury — each way that's three hours a day. We are going to have a lot of work to do before we can even think of leaving for Africa.'

'What would people think?' she asked, as she let out the clutch.

'I have never given a damn about people,' he called after her. 'What time will I see you tomorrow?'

'I have to stop off to see the doctor in York. He is going to take the stitches out of my arm. I won't be here before eleven,' she stuck her head out of the window to yell back at him.

The wind tossed her dark hair around her face. His fancy had always run towards dark-haired women. Rosalind had had that mysterious Eastern look. He felt guilty and disloyal making the comparison, but the memory of Royan was hard to shake off.

She was the first woman who had interested him since Rosalind had gone. The admixture of her blood drew him. She was exotic enough to pique his taste for the oriental, but English enough to speak his language and understand his sense of humour. She was educated and knowledgeable about those things that interested him, and he admired her spirit. Usually Eastern women were trained from birth to be self-effacing and compliant. This one was different.

Georgina had phoned her doctor in York to make an appointment to have the stitches removed from Royan's arm. They left after breakfast from the cottage in Brandsbury. Georgina was driving and Magic sat between them on the bench seat.

As they turned into the village street, Royan noticed a large MAN truck parked down near the post office, but she thought no more about it.

Once they were out in the countryside they found there were patches of heavy fog that in places reduced visibility to thirty yards, but Georgina made no concessions to the weather, and sent the Land Rover rattling and whining through it at the top of its speed, which Royan reflected thankfully was on the right side of sixty miles an hour.

She glanced over her shoulder to check the road behind them, and saw that the MAN truck was following them. Only the cab rose above the sea of low mist that surrounded it like the conning tower of a submarine. Even as she watched it, a bank of fog intervened and swallowed it up. She turned back to listen to her mother.

'This government is a troop of incompetent nincompoops.' Georgina squinted her eyes against the smoke from the cigarette that dangled from her lips. She drove single-handed, stroking Magic's flowing silken ear with her free hand, 'I don't mind ministers boffing themselves into a stupor, but when they start fiddling around with my pension I get really mad.' Her mother's pension from the foreign service was her sole source of income, and it wasn't much.

'You don't truly want a Labour government, now tell the truth, Mummy,' Royan teased her. Her mother had always been the arch Conservative.

Georgina wavered, and then avoided the choice, 'All I say is, bring back Maggie.'

Royan turned slightly in her seat and glanced through the dirty rear window again. The truck was still behind them, looming out of the fog and the trail of blue exhaust smoke that Georgina was laying behind her like the vapour trail of a jet aircraft. Up until now it had hung back, but suddenly it accelerated up behind them.

'I think he wants to pass you,' Royan told Georgina mildly.

The massive bonnet of the truck was only twenty feet from their rear bumper. The radiator was emblazoned with the chrome logo 'MAN' and stood taller than the cab of the Land Rover, so that she could not see the face of the driver from where she sat.

'Everybody wants to pass me,' lamented Georgina. 'Story of my life.' She held the centre of the narrow road doggedly.

Royan glanced back again, and saw that the truck was creeping still closer. It filled the rear window completely. The driver declutched and revved the gigantic engine menacingly.

'You'd better give over. I think he means business.'

'Let him wait,' Georgina grunted around her cigarette butt. 'Patience is a virtue. Anyway, can't let him through here. There is a narrow stone bridge ahead of us. Know this stretch of road like the way to my own bathroom.'

At that moment the truck-driver sounded his klaxon so close that it was deafening. Magic jumped up on the rear seat and barked in outrage.

'Stupid bastard,' Georgina swore bitterly.

'What does he think he is playing at? Write down his number plate. I am going to report him to the York police.'

'His plates are covered with mud. Can't make it out, but it looks like a continental registration. German, I think.'

As if the driver had heard her protest he slowed slightly and fell back until a gap of twenty yards opened between the two vehicles. Royan had swivelled right round in the seat to watch him.

'That's better,' Georgina said smugly. 'Ruddy Hun learning some manners.' She peered ahead through the fog, 'There is the bridge —'

For the first time Royan was able to see up into the driver's cab of the truck. The driver wore a balaclava helmet that covered all but his eyes and nose with dark blue wool. It gave him a sinister and evil aspect.

'Look out!' Royan screamed suddenly. 'He is coming straight at us!' The engine beat of the great truck rose to a bellow that engulfed them like the sound of a gale-driven sea. For a moment Royan saw nothing but glittering steel and then the front of the truck smashed into them from behind.

She was thrown half over the back of her seat by the impact. She dragged herself up and saw that the truck had picked them up like a fox with a bird in its jaws. It carried the Land Rover forward on the steel bull bars that protected the shining chromed radiator.

Georgina wrestled with the wheel, trying to maintain control, but the effort was futile. 'Can't hold her. The bridge! Try and get clear —'

Royan hit the quick-release buckle on her safety-belt and reached for the door handle. The stone walls of the bridge were racing towards them at a terrifying pace. The Land Rover was slewing across the road, completely out of control.

The door burst open in Royan's grip, but she could not push it all the way before the Land Rover was flung into the solid stonework columns that guarded the approaches to the bridge.

The two women screamed in unison as the vehicle crumpled, and the impact hurled them forward. The windscreen shattered as they bounced off the stone columns, and the body of the Land Rover flipped over as it went down the embankment and began to roll.

Royan was catapulted through the open door and flung clear. The slope of the bank broke her fall, but it knocked the wind out of her. She bounced and rolled down the incline and then dropped into the icy waters of the stream below the bridge.

Just before her head went under, she found herself looking up at the sky and the bridge above her. She caught one last glimpse of the truck before it roared away. It was towing two huge cargo trailers. The tall bodywork of the trailers stood higher than the guard rail of the bridge.

Both of the trailers were covered by a heavy green nylon tarpaulin roped down to the lugs on the body. She had only a subliminal glimpse of a large red trademark and company name painted on the side of the nearest trailer, but before she could register the name she was plunged below the surface of the stream and the cold and the force of her fall drove the air from her lungs.

She fought her way to the surface of the river, and found she had been washed some way downstream. Impeded by her sodden clothing, she floundered to the bank and used the branch of a tree to haul herself out.

She knelt in the mud, coughing up the water she had swallowed and trying to assess what injury she had suffered in the collision. Then her own plight was forgotten as she heard the terrible sounds of her mother's agony from the overturned wreck of the Land Rover.

In frantic haste she clawed herself to her feet and stumbled through the wet and frosted grass to where the Land Rover lay on its back at the foot of the embankment. The bodywork was crumpled and torn, and the bright silver aluminium metal shone through where the dark green paint had been stripped away. The engine had stalled, and the front wheels were still spinning aimlessly as she reached it.

'Mummy! Where are you?' she cried, and the terrible sounds never checked. She used the metal body of the vehicle to steady herself as she dragged herself towards the sound, dreading what she might find.

Georgina sat on the wet earth with her back against the side of the car. Her legs were thrust out straight ahead of her. The left one was twisted so that the toe of the booted foot was pointed down into the mud at an unnatural angle. The leg was obviously broken at the knee or very close to it.

This was not the cause of Georgina's distress. She held Magic in her lap, and was bowed over him in an attitude of abandoned grief; the sound of it bubbled up unchecked from deep inside her. The spaniel's chest had been crushed between metal and earth. His tongue lolled from the corner of his mouth in his last smile, but the blood dripped steadily from the pink tip and Georgina was using her scarf to wipe it away.

Royan sank down beside her mother and placed one arm around her shoulders. She had never before seen her mother weep. She hugged her hard and tried by main strength to quell the sound of her sorrow, but it went on and on.

She never knew how long they sat together like that. But at last the sight of her mother's maimed leg, and an awakening fear that the driver of the truck might return to finish the job, roused her. She crawled up the bank and tottered into the centre of the road to stop the next car that arrived on the scene.

Not until Royan was two hours late for their meeting did Nicholas become sufficiently worried to phone the police in York. Fortunately he had noticed the licence plate of the Land Rover. It was an easy one for him to remember. The registration number was his mother's initials combined with an unlucky 13.

There was a delay while the woman constable checked her computer, and then she came back. 'I am sorry to have to tell you, sir, that Land Rover was involved in an accident this morning.'

'What happened to the driver?' Nicholas demanded brusquely.

'The driver and one passenger have been taken to the York Minster Hospital.'

'Are they all right?'

'I am sorry, sir. I don't have that information.'

It took Nicholas forty minutes to reach the hospital and almost as long again to trace Royan. She was in the women's surgical ward, sitting beside her mother's bed. Her mother had not yet come round from the anaesthetic.

She looked up when Nicholas stood over her. 'Are you all right? What the hell happened?'

'My mother — her leg is badly smashed up. The surgeon had to put a pin in her thigh — the femur.'

'How are you?'

'A few bruises and scrapes. Nothing serious.'

'How did it happen?'

'A truck — it pushed us off the road.'

'Not deliberate?' Nicholas felt something inside him quail as he remembered another truck on another road on another night.

'I think so. The driver wore a mask, a balaclava. He crashed into us from behind. It must have been deliberate.'

'Did you tell the police?'

She nodded. 'Apparently the truck was reported stolen early this morning, long before the accident, while the driver was stopped at one of those Little Chef cafés. He is German. Speaks no English.'

'That is the third time they have tried to kill you,' Nicholas told her grimly. 'So I am taking over now.'

He went out into the hospital waiting room and used the telephone there. The chief constable of the county was a personal friend, as was the hospital administator.

By the time he returned, Georgina had come round from the anaesthetic. Although still woozy she was comfortable as they wheeled her off to the private ward that Nicholas had arranged. The orthopaedic surgeon arrived a few minutes later.

'Hello, Nick, what are you doing here?' he greeted Nicholas. Royan was surprised how many people knew him.

Then he turned his attention to Georgina. 'How are you feeling? We have got ourselves a nice little compound fracture. Looks like confetti in there. We've managed to put it all together again, but you're going to be with us for ten days at the very least.'

'Right you are, young lady,' Nicholas told Royan as they left Georgina sleeping. 'What more do you need to convince you? My housekeeper has made up a room for you at the Hall. I am not letting you wander around on your own any more. Otherwise, next time they try to cull you they may have a little more luck.'

She was still too shaken and upset to argue, and she climbed meekly into the front seat of the Range Rover and let him drive her first to have her stitches removed and then back to Quenton Park. As soon as they arrived, he sent her up to her bedroom.

'The cook will send dinner up to you. Make sure you take the sleeping pill that the doc gave you. Somebody will fetch your gear from Brandsbury if you give the key to your mother's cottage to Mrs Street. In the meantime my housekeeper has set out some nightclothes and a toothbrush in your room for you. I don't want to hear from you again before tomorrow morning.'

It was good to have him take control of her life. For the first time since that terrible night at the oasis she felt secure and safe. Still, she made one last gesture of independence and self-reliance; she flushed the Mogadon sleeping tablet down the toilet.

The nightdress that was laid on her pillow was full-length sheer silk with finest Cambrai lace at the cuffs and throat. She had never worn anything so luxurious and sensual against her skin before. She realized that it must have belonged to his wife, and the knowledge stirred mixed emotions in her. She climbed up into the four-poster bed, but even that lonely expanse of over-soft mattress and her unfamiliar surroundings did not keep her too long from sleep.

In the morning a young housemaid woke her with a copy of *The Times* and a pot of Earl Grey tea, then returned a few minutes later with her holdall.

'Sir Nicholas would like you to take breakfast with him in the dining room at eight-thirty.'

While she showered Royan inspected her naked body in the full-length mirror that covered one wall of the bathroom. Apart from the knife wound on her arm, which was still livid and only partially healed, there was a dark bruise on her thigh and another down her left flank and buttock, legacies of the car crash. Her shin was scraped raw, and gingerly she pulled a pair of slacks over the injury. She limped a little as she went down the main staircase to find the dining room.

'Please help yourself.' Nicholas looked up from his newspaper to greet her as she hesitated in the doorway. He waved at the display of breakfast dishes on the sideboard. As she spooned scrambled eggs on to her plate, she recognized the landscape on the wall in front of her as a Constable.

'Did you sleep well?' He didn't wait for an answer, but went on, 'I have heard from the police. They found the MAN truck abandoned in a lay-by near Harrogate. They are going over it now but they don't expect to find much. We seem to be dealing with someone who knows what he is doing.'

'I must phone the hospital,' she said.

'I have already done so. Your mother had an easy night. I left a message that you would visit her this evening.'

'This evening?' She looked around sharply. 'Why so late?'

'I intend to keep you busy until then. I want to get my money's worth out of you.'

He stood as she came to the table, and drew back her chair to seat her. She found the courtesy made her feel slightly uncomfortable, but she made no comment.

'The first attack on you and Duraid at your villa in the oasis — we can draw no conclusions from that, apart from the fact that the assassins knew exactly what they were after, and where to look for it.' She found the abrupt change of subject disconcerting. 'However, let's give some thought to the second attempt in Cairo. The hand grenade. Who knew you were going to the Ministry that afternoon, apart from the minister himself?'

She reflected as she chewed and swallowed a mouthful of egg. 'I am not sure. I think I told Duraid's secretary, maybe one of the other research assistants.'

He frowned and shook his head. 'So half the museum staff knew about your appointment?'

'That is about it, yes. Sorry.'

He pondered a moment, 'All right. Who knew you were leaving Cairo? Who knew you were staying at your mother's cottage?'

'One of the clerks from administration brought my slides out to the airport.'

'Did you tell him what flight you were leaving on?'

'No, definitely not.'

'Did you tell anybody at all?'

'No. That is —' she hesitated.

'Yes?'

'I told the minister himself during our interview, when I asked for leave of absence. Not him — surely not?' her expression reflected her horror at the thought.

Nicholas shrugged, 'Some funny things happen. Of course, the minister knew all about the work that you and Duraid were doing on the seventh scroll?'

'Not all the details, but — yes — in general terms he knew what we were up to.'

'All right. Next question, tea or coffee?' He poured coffee into her cup, and then went on,

119

'You said that Duraid had a list of possible sponsors for an expedition. Might give us some ideas as to a short-list of suspects?'

'The Getty Museum,' she said, and he smiled.

'Cross one from the list. They don't go around tossing grenades in the streets of Cairo. Who else was there on the list?'

'Gotthold Ernst von Schiller.'

'Hamburg. Heavy industry. Metal and alloy refineries. Base mineral production.' Nicholas nodded. 'Who was the third name on the list?'

'Peter Walsh,' she said. 'The Texan.'

'That's the one,' he nodded. 'Lives in Fort Worth. Fast-food franchising. Mail order retail.' There were very few collectors with the substance to compete with the major institutions when it came to making significant acquisitions of antiquities or to financing archaeological exploration. Nicholas knew them all, for it was a mutually antagonistic circle of no more than a couple of dozen men. He had competed with each of them at one time or another on the auction floors of Sotheby's and Christie's, not to mention other less salubrious venues where 'fresh' antiquities were sold. The adjective 'fresh' was used in the context of 'fresh out of the ground'.

'Those are two beady-eyed bandits. They would probably eat their own children if they felt peckish. What would they do if they thought you stood in their way to the tomb of Mamose? Do you know if either of them contacted Duraid after the book was published, the way I did?'

'I don't know. They may have.'

'I cannot imagine that either of those beauties would have missed such an easy trick. We must believe that they both know that Duraid had something going on. We will put their names on our list of suspects.' Then he inspected her plate. 'Enough? Another spoonful of egg? No? Very well, let's go down to the museum and see what Mrs Street has found for us to work on.'

When they walked into his study, she was impressed by the amount of organization that he had accomplished in such a short time. He must have been busy at it all last night, turning the room into a military-type headquarters. In the centre of the room stood a large easel and blackboard on which were pinned a set of overlapping satellite photographs. She went across to study them, and then glanced at the other material pinned on the board.

Along with a large-scale map covering the same area of south-western Ethiopia as the satellite photographs there were lists of names and addresses, lists of equipment and stores which he had obviously used on previous African expeditions, sheets of calculations of distance and what looked like a preliminary financial budget. At the top of the board was a schedule headed 'Ethiopia — General Information'. There were five closely typed foolscap sheets, so she did not read through the entire schedule, but she

121

was impressed by his thoroughness in preparation.

Royan determined to study all this material at the earliest opportunity, but now she crossed to one of the two chairs he had set up at a table facing the board. He stood at the board and picked up a silver-topped swagger stick from the table, brandishing it like a schoolmaster's pointer.

'Class will come to order.' He rapped on the board. 'The first thing you have to do is convince me that we will be able to pick up the spoor of Taita again after it has had several thousand years to cool. Let us first consider the geographical features of the Abbay gorge.'

Nicholas described the course of the river on the satellite photograph with his pointer. 'Along this section the river has cut its way through the flood basalt plateaux. In places the cliffs of the sub-gorge are sheer, as high as four or five hundred feet on each side. Where there are intrusive strata of harder igneous schists the river has not been able to erode them. They form a series of gigantic steps in the course of the river. I think you are correct in your assumption that Taita's "steps" are actually waterfalls.'

He came to the table and picked out a photograph from amongst the bundles of papers that covered it. 'I took this in the gorge during the Armed Forces Expedition in 1976. It will give you an idea of what some of those falls are like.'

He passed her a black and white riverscape of towering cliffs on either hand and a cascade of water that seemed to fall from the heavens to dwarf the tiny figures of half-naked men and boats in the foreground.

'I had no idea it was like that!' She stared at it in awe.

'Doesn't do justice to the splendid desolation down there in the gorge,' he told her. 'From a photographer's point of view there is no place to stand from which you can get it all into perspective. But at least you can see how that waterfall would halt a party of Egyptians coming upriver on foot, or at least with pack horses. There is usually some sort of path alongside the cataracts made by elephant and other wild game over the ages. However, there is simply no way to bypass waterfalls such as this one, and to get around those cliffs.'

She nodded, and he went on, 'Even coming downstream we had to lower the boats and all our equipment down each set of waterfalls on ropes. It wasn't easy.'

'Let us agree that it was a waterfall that stopped them going further — the second waterfall from the westerly approaches,' she conceded.

Nicholas picked up the swagger stick and on the satellite photograph traced the course of the river up from the dark wedge shape of the Roseires dam in central Sudan. 'The escarpment rises on the Ethiopian side of the border, that is where the gorge proper begins. No roads or towns in there, and only two bridges far up-stream. Nothing for five hundred miles except racing Nile waters and savage black basalt rock.' He paused to let that sink in.

'It is one of the last true wildernesses on earth, with an evil reputation as the haunt of wild animals and even wilder men. I have marked the main falls that show in the gut of the gorge here on the satellite photo.' With the pointer he picked them out, each circled neatly in red marker pen.

'Here is waterfall number two, about a hundred and twenty miles upstream from the Sudanese border. However, there are a number of factors we have to consider, not least the fact that the river may have altered its course during the last four thousand years since our friend, Taita, visited it.'

'Surely it could not have escaped from such a deep canyon, four thousand feet,' she protested. 'Even the Nile must be held captive by that?'

'Yes, but it would certainly have altered the existing bed. In the flood season the volume and force of the river exceeds my ability to describe it to you. The river rises twenty metres up the side walls and bores through at speeds of ten knots or more.'

'You navigated that?' she asked doubtfully.

'Not in the flood season. Nothing could survive that.'

They both stared at the photograph in silence

for a minute, imagining the terrors of that mighty stretch of water in its full fury.

Then she reminded him, 'The second waterfall?'

'Here it is, where one of the tributary rivers enters the main flow of the Abbay. The tributary is the Dandera river and it rises at twelve thousand feet altitude, below the peak of Sancai Mountain in the Choke range, here about a hundred miles north of the gorge.'

'Do you remember the spot where it joins the Abbay from when you were there?'

'It was over twenty years ago, and even then we had been almost a month down there in the gorge, so it all seemed to merge into a single nightmare. The memory blurred with the monotonous surroundings of the cliffs and the dense jungle of the walls, and our senses were dulled by the heat and the insects and the roar of water and the repetitive, unremitting toil at the oars. But, strangely, I do remember the confluence of the Dandera and the Abbay for two reasons.'

'Yes?' She sat forward eagerly, but he shook his head.

'We lost a man there. The only casualty on the second expedition. Rope parted and he fell a hundred feet. Landed on his back across a spur of rock.'

'I am sorry. But what was the other reason you remember the spot.'

'There is a Coptic Christian monastery there, built into the rock face about four hundred feet above the surface of the river.'

'Down there in the depths of the gorge?' She sounded incredulous. 'Why would they build a monastery there?'

'Ethiopia is one of the oldest Christian countries on earth. It has over nine thousand churches and monasteries, a great many of them in similarly remote and almost inaccessible places in the mountains. This one at the Dandera river is the reputed burial site of St Frumentius, the saint who introduced Christianity to Ethiopia from the Byzantine Empire in Constantinople in the early third century. Legend has it that he was shipwrecked on the Red Sea shore and taken to Aksum, where he converted the Emperor Ezana.'

'Did you visit the monastery?'

'Hell, no!' he laughed. 'We were too busy just surviving, too eager to escape from the hell of the gorge to have any time for sightseeing. We descended the falls and kept on downriver. All I remember of the monastery are the excavations in the cliff face high above the pool of the river, and the distant figures of the troglodytic monks in their white robes lining the parapet of the caves to watch impassively as we passed. Some of us waved up to them, and felt quite rebuffed when they made no response.'

'How would we ever reach that spot again, without a full-scale river expedition?' she wondered aloud, staring disconsolately at the board.

'Discouraged already?' He grinned at her.

126

'Wait until you meet some of the mosquitoes that live down there. They pick you up and fly with you to their lairs before they eat you.'

'Be serious,' she entreated him. 'How would we ever get down there?'

'The monks are fed by the villagers who live up on the highlands above the gorge. Apparently, there is a goat track down the wall. They told us that it takes three days to get down that track into the gut of the gorge from the rim.'

'Could you find your way down?'

'No, but I have a few ideas on the subject. We will come to that later. Firstly, we must decide what we expect to find down there after four thousand years.' He looked at her expectantly. 'Your turn now. Convince me.' He handed her the silver-headed pointer, dropped into the chair beside her and folded his arms.

'First you have to go back to the book.' She exchanged the pointer for the copy of *River God*. 'You remember the character of Tanus from the story?'

'Of course. He was the commander of the Egyptian armies under Queen Lostris, with the title of Great Lion of Egypt. He led the exodus from Egypt, when they were driven out by the Hyksos.'

'He was also the Queen's secret lover and, if we are to believe Taita, the father of Prince Memnon, her eldest son,' she agreed.

'Tanus was killed during a punitive expedition

against an Ethiopian chief named Arkoun in the high mountains, and his body was mummified and brought back to the Queen by Taita,' Nicholas expanded the story.

'Precisely.' She nodded. 'This leads me on to the other clue that Duraid and I winkled out.'

'From the seventh scroll?' He unfolded his arms and sat forward in his seat.

'No, not from the scrolls, but from the inscriptions in the tomb of Queen Lostris.' She reached into her bag and brought out another photograph. 'This is an enlargement of a section of the murals from the burial chamber, that part of the wall that later fell away and was lost when the alabaster jars were revealed. Duraid and I believe that the fact that Taita placed this inscription in the place of honour, over the hiding-place of the scrolls, was significant.' She passed the photograph to him, and he picked up a magnifying glass from the table to study it.

While he puzzled over the hieroglyphics Royan went on, 'You will recall from the book how Taita loved riddles and word games, how he boasts so often that he is the greatest of all bao players?'

Nicholas looked up from the magnifying glass, 'I remember that. I go along with the theory that bao was the forerunner of the game of chess. I have a dozen or so boards in the museum collection, some from Egypt and others from further south in Africa.'

'Yes, I would also subscribe to that theory. Both games have many of the same objects and rules, but bao is a more rudimentary form of the game. It is played with coloured stones of different rank, instead of chess men. Well, I believe that Taita was not able to resist the temptation to display his riddling skills and his cleverness to posterity. I believe that he was so conceited that he deliberately left clues to the location of the Pharaoh's tomb, both in the scrolls and amongst the murals that he tells us he painted with his own hands in the tomb of his beloved Queen.'

'You think that this is one of those clues?' Nicholas tapped the photograph with the glass.

'Read it,' she instructed him. 'It's in classical hieroglyphics — not too difficult compared to his cryptic codes.'

' "*The father of the Prince who is not the father, the giver of the blue that killed him,*" ' he translated haltingly, ' "*guards eternally hand in hand with Hapi the stone testament of the pathway to the father of the Prince who is not the father, the giver of blood and ashes.*" '

Nicholas shook his head, 'No, it doesn't make sense,' he protested, 'I must have made an error in the translation.'

'Don't despair. You are making your first acquaintance with Taita, the champion bao player and consummate riddler. Duraid and I puzzled over it for weeks,' she reassured him. 'To work it out, let's go back to the book. Tanus was not the father of Prince Memnon in name, but, as the Queen's lover, was his biological father. On his deathbed, he gave Memnon the blue sword that had inflicted his own mortal wound during the battle with the native Ethiopian chief. There is a full description of the battle in the book.'

'Yes, when I first read that section, I remember thinking that the blue sword was probably one of the very earliest iron weapons, and in an age of bronze would have been a marvel of the armourer's art. A gift fit for a prince,' Nicholas mused, and went on, 'So *the father of the prince who is not the father* is Tanus?' He sighed with resignation. 'For the moment I accept your interpretation.'

'Thank you for your trust and confidence in me,' she said sarcastically. 'But to proceed with Taita's riddle — Pharaoh Mamose was Memnon's father in name only, but not his blood father. Again the father who was not the father. Mamose passed down to the prince the double crown of Egypt, the red and white crowns of Upper and Lower Kingdoms — the blood and the ashes.'

'I am able to swallow that more easily. What about the rest of the inscription?' Nicholas was clearly intrigued.

'The expression "hand in hand" is ambiguous in ancient Egyptian. It could just as well mean very close to, or within sight of, something.'

'Go on. At last you have me sitting up and taking notice,' Nicholas encouraged her.

'Hapi is the hermaphroditic god or goddess of the Nile, depending on the gender he or she adopts at any particular moment. Throughout the scrolls Taita uses Hapi as an alternative name for the river.'

'So if we put the seventh scroll and the inscription from the Queen's tomb together, what then is your full interpretation?' he insisted.

'Simply this: Tanus is buried within sight of, or very close to, the river at the second waterfall. There is a stone monument or inscription on, or in, his tomb that points the way to the tomb of Pharaoh.'

He exhaled through his teeth. 'I am exhausted from all this jumping to conclusions. What other clues have you ferreted out for me?'

'That's it,' she said, and he looked at her with disbelief.

'That's it? Nothing else?' he demanded, and she shook her head.

'Just suppose that you are correct so far. Let us suppose that the river is recognizably the same in shape and configuration as it was nearly four thousand years ago. Let us further suppose that Taita was indeed pointing us towards the second waterfall at the Dandera river. Just what do we look for when we get there? If there is a rock inscription, will it still be intact or will it be eroded away by weather and the action of the river?'

131

'Howard Carter had an equally slender lead to the tomb of Tutankhamen,' she pointed out mildly. 'A single piece of papyrus, of dubious authenticity.'

'Howard Carter had only the area of the Valley of the Kings to search. It still took him ten years,' he replied. 'You have given me Ethiopia, a country twice the size of France. How long will that take us, do you think?'

She stood up abruptly, 'Excuse me, I think I should go and visit my mother in hospital. It's fairly obvious that I am wasting my time here.'

'It is not yet visiting hours,' he told her.

'She has a private room.' Royan made for the door.

'I will drive you to the hospital,' he offered.

'Don't bother. I will call a taxi,' she replied in a tone that crackled with ice.

'A taxi will take an hour to get here,' he warned, and she relented just enough to let him lead her to the Range Rover. They drove in silence for fifteen minutes, before he spoke.

'I am not very good at apologies. Not much practice, I am afraid, but I am sorry. I was abrupt. I didn't mean to be. Carried away by the excitement of the moment.'

She did not reply, and after a minute he added, 'You will have to talk to me, unless we are to correspond only by note. It will be a bit awkward down in the Abbay gorge.'

'I had the distinct impression that you were

no longer interested in going down there.' She stared ahead through the windscreen.

'I am a brute,' he agreed, and she glanced sideways at him. It was her undoing. His grin was irresistible, and she laughed.

'I suppose I will just have to come to terms with that fact. You are a brute.'

'Still partners?' he asked.

'At the moment you are the only brute I have. I suppose that I am stuck with you.'

He dropped her off at the main hospital entrance. 'I will pick you up here at three o'clock,' he told her and drove on into the centre of York.

From his university days Nicholas had kept a small flat in one of the narrow alleys behind York Minster. The entire building was registered in the name of a Cayman Island company, and the unlisted telephone there did not route through an internal switchboard. No ownership could be traced to him personally. Before he had met Rosalind the flat had played an important part in his social life. But nowadays Nicholas only used it for confidential and clandestine business. Both the Libyan and the Iraqi expeditions had been planned and organized from here.

He hadn't used the flat for months, and it was cold and musty-smelling and uninviting. He put a match to the gas fire in the grate and filled the kettle. With a mug of steaming tea in front of him he placed a call to a bank in

Jersey, followed immediately by another to a bank in the Cayman Islands.

'A wise rat has more than one exit from its burrow.' This was a family maxim, passed down through the generations. There should always be a little something tucked away for the day the heavens opened. He was going to need funds for the expedition, and the lawyers had most of those locked up already.

He gave the passwords and account numbers to each of the bank managers and instructed them to make certain transfers. It always amazed him how easily matters could be arranged, as long as you had money.

He checked his watch. It was still early morning in Florida, but Alison picked up the phone on the second ring. She was the blonde feminine dynamo who ran Global Safaris, a company that arranged hunting and fishing expeditions to remote areas around the world.

'Hello, Nick. We haven't heard from you in over a year. We thought you didn't love us any more.'

'I have been out of it for a while,' he admitted. How do you tell people that your wife and two little girls had died?

'Ethiopia?' She did not sound at all disconcerted by the request. 'When did you want to go?'

'How about next week?'

'You have to be joking. We only work with one hunter there, Nassous Roussos, and he is booked two years in advance.'

'Is there nobody else?' he insisted. 'I have to be in and out again before the big rains.'

'What trophies are you after?' she hedged. 'Mountain nyala? Menelik's bushbuck?'

'I am planning a collecting trip for the museum, down the Abbay river.' It was as much as he was prepared to tell her.

She hedged a little longer and then told him reluctantly, 'This is without our recommendation, do you understand. There is only one hunter who may take you on at such short notice, but I don't even know if he has a camp on the Blue Nile. He is a Russian, and we have had mixed reports about him. Some people say he is ex-KGB and was one of Mengistu's bunch of thugs.'

Mengistu was the 'Black Stalin' who had deposed and then murdered the old Emperor Haile Selassie, and in sixteen years of despotic Marxist rule had driven Ethiopia to its knees. When his sponsor, the Soviet Empire, had collapsed, Mengistu had been overthrown and fled the country.

'I am desperate enough to go to bed with the devil,' he told her. 'I promise I won't come back to you with any complaints.'

'Okay, then, no come-backs —' and she gave him a name and a telephone number in Addis Ababa.

'I love you, Alison darling,' Nicholas told her.

'I wish,' she said, and hung up on him.

He didn't expect that it would be easy to telephone Addis, and he wasn't disappointed in his expectations. But at last he got through. A woman with a sweet lisping Ethiopian accent answered and switched to fluent English when he asked for Boris Brusilov.

'He is out on safari at present,' she told him. 'I am Woizero Tessay, his wife.' In Ethiopia a wife did not take on her husband's name. Nicholas remembered enough of the language to know that the name meant Lady Sun, a pretty name.

'But if it is in connection with safari business I can help you,' said Lady Sun.

Nicholas picked Royan up outside the hospital entrance.

'How is your mother?'

'Her leg is doing well, but she is still distraught about Magic — about her dog.'

'You will have to get her a puppy. One of my keepers breeds first-class springers. I can arrange it.' He paused and then asked delicately, 'Will you be able to leave your mother? I mean, if we are going out to Africa?'

'I spoke to her about that. There is a woman from her church group who will stay with her until she is well enough to fend for herself again.'

Royan turned fully around in her seat to examine his face. 'You have been up to something since I last saw you,' she accused him. 'I can

136

see it in your face.'

He made the Arabic sign against the evil eye, 'Allah save me from witches!'

'Come on!' He could make her laugh so readily, she was not sure if that was a good thing or not. 'Tell me what you have up your sleeve.'

'Wait until we get back to the museum.' He would not be moved, and she had to bridle her impatience.

As soon as they entered the building he led her through the Egyptian room to the hall of African mammals, and then stopped her in front of a diorama of mounted antelope. These were some of the smaller and medium-sized varieties — impala, Thompson's and Grant's gazelle, gerenuk and the like.

'*Madoqua harperii.*' He pointed to a tiny creature in one corner of the display. 'Harper's dikdik, also known as the striped dik-dik.'

It was a nondescript little animal, not much bigger than a large hare. The brown pelt was striped in chocolate over the shoulders and back, and the nose was elongated into a prehensile proboscis.

'A bit tatty,' she gave her opinion carefully, unwilling to offend him, for he seemed inordinately proud of this specimen. 'Is there anything special about it?'

'Special?' he asked with wonder in his voice. 'The woman asks if it is special.' He rolled his eyes heavenward and she had to laugh again at his histrionics. 'It is the only known specimen in existence. It is one of the rarest creatures on earth. So rare that it is probably extinct by now. So rare that many zoologists believe that it is apocryphal, that it never really existed. They think that my sainted great-grandfather, after whom it is named, actually invented it. One learned reference hinted that he may have taken the skin of the striped mongoose and stretched it over the form of a common dik-dik. Can you imagine a more heinous accusation?'

'I am truly appalled by such injustice,' she laughed.

'Darned right, you should be. Because we are going to Africa to hunt for another specimen of *Madoqua harperii,* to vindicate the honour of the family.'

'I don't understand.'

'Come with me and all will be explained.' He led her back to his study, and from the jumble on the tabletop picked out a notebook bound in red Morocco leather. The cover was faded and stained with water marks and tropical sunlight, while the corners and the spine were frayed and battered.

'Old Sir Jonathan's game book,' he explained, and opened it. Pressed between the pages were faded wild flowers and leaves that must have been there for almost a century. The text was illuminated by line drawings in faded yellow ink of men and animals and wild landscapes. Nicholas read the date at the top of one page.

2nd of February 1902. In camp on the Abbay river. All day following the spoor of two large bull elephants. Unable to come up with them. Heat very intense. My men played out. Abandoned the chase and returned to camp. On the return march spied a small antelope grazing on the river-bank, which I brought down with one shot from the little Rigby rifle. On close examination it proved to be a member of the genus Madoqa. *However, it was of a species that I had never seen before, larger than the common dik-dik and possessing a striped body. I believe that this specimen may be new to science.*

He looked up from the diary. 'Old great-grandpa Jonathan has given us the perfect excuse for going down into the Abbay gorge.' He closed the book, and went on, 'As you pointed out, to cater for our own expedition would require months of planning and organization, not to mention the expense. It would mean having to obtain approval and permission from the Ethiopian government. In Africa that can take months, if not years.'

'I don't imagine that the Ethiopian government would be too cooperative if they suspected our real intentions,' she agreed.

'On the other hand, there are a number of legitimate hunting safari companies operating throughout the country. They have all the necessary permits, governmental contacts, vehicles, camping equipment and logistic back-up necessary to travel and stay in even the remotest areas. The authorities are quite accustomed to foreign hunters arriving and leaving with these companies, whereas a couple of *ferengi* nosing around on their own would have the local military and everybody else down on them like a herd of angry buffalo.'

'So we are going to travel as a pair of dik-dik hunters?'

'I have already made the booking with a safari operator in Addis Ababa, the capital. My plan is to look upon the whole of our project in three distinct and separate stages. The first stage will be this reconnaissance. If we find the lead we are hoping for, then we will go back again with our own men and equipment. That will be stage two. Stage three, of course, will be getting the booty out of Ethiopia, and that I assure you from past experience will not be the easiest part of the operation.'

'How will you do that —' she began, but he held up his hands.

'Don't ask, because at this stage I don't have even the vaguest idea how we will do it. One stage at a time.'

'When do we leave?'

'Before I tell you when, let me ask you one more question. Your interpretation of the Taita riddle — did you explain that in the notes that were stolen from you at the oasis?'

'Yes, everything was either in those notes or

on the microfilm. I am sorry.'

'So the uglies will have it all neatly laid out for them, just the way you laid it out for me.'

'I am afraid they will, yes.'

'Then to reply to your question as to when, the answer is *tout de suite*, and the tooter the sweeter! We must get into the Abbay gorge before the competition beats us to it. They have had your conclusions and suppositions for almost a month. For all we know they are on their way already.'

'When?' she repeated eagerly.

'I have booked two seats on the British Airways flight to Nairobi this Saturday — that is, in two days' time. We will connect there with an Air Kenya flight to Addis that will get us in on Monday at around midday. We will drive down to London this evening and stay over at my digs there. Are your yellow fever and hepatitis shots up to date?'

'Yes, but I have no equipment and hardly any clothing with me. I left Cairo in rather a hurry.'

'We will see to that in London. Trouble with Ethiopia is it's cold enough to emasculate a brass monkey in the highlands, and like a sauna bath down in the gorge.'

He crossed to the board and began to check off the items on his list. 'We will both start malarial prophylactics immediately. We are going into an area of chloroquine-resistant *P. falciparum* mosquitoes, so I will put you on

141

Mefloquine —' He worked swiftly through the list.

'Of course all your travel documents are in order, or you wouldn't be here. We will both need visas for Ethiopia, but I have a contact who can arrange that in twenty-four hours.'

As soon as he completed the list he sent her up to her room to pack the few personal items she had brought with her from Cairo.

By the time they were ready to leave Quenton Hall it was dark outside, but still he stopped for an hour at the York Minster Hospital to allow her to say goodbye to her mother. He waited in the Red Lion pub across the road, and he smelt of Theakston's Old Peculier when she climbed back into the Range Rover beside him. It was a pleasant, yeasty aroma, and she felt so much at ease in his company that she lay back in the seat and fell asleep.

His London house was in Knightsbridge, but despite the fashionable address it was much less grand than Quenton Hall, and she felt more at home there, even if it was only for two days. During that time she saw little of Nicholas, for he was busy with all the last-minute arrangements, which included a number of visits to government offices in Whitehall. He returned with wads of letters of introduction to high officials and British Embassies and High Commissions throughout East Africa.

'Ask any Englishman,' she smiled to herself. 'There is no such thing as upper-class privilege any longer, nor is there an old-boy network that runs the country.'

While he was away, she went off with the shopping list he had given her. Even walking the streets of the safest capital city in the world she found herself looking back over her shoulder, and ducking in and out of ladies' rooms and tube stations to make certain that she was not being followed.

'You are acting like a terrified child without its daddy,' she scolded herself.

However, she felt a quite disproportionate sense of relief each evening when she heard his key in the street door of the empty house where she waited, and she had to control herself so as not to rush down the stairs to welcome him.

On Saturday morning, when a taxi cab deposited them at the departures level of Heathrow Terminal Four, Nicholas surveyed their combined luggage with approval. She had only a single soft canvas bag, no larger than his, and her sling bag over her shoulder. His hunting rifle was cased in travel-worn leather, with his initials embossed on the lid. A hundred rounds of ammunition was packed in a separate brass-bound magazine and he carried a leather briefcase that looked like a Victorian antique.

'Travelling light is one of the great virtues. Lord save us from women with mountains of luggage,' he told her, refusing the services of a porter and throwing it all on to a trolley, which he pushed himself.

She had to step out to keep up with him as he strode through the crowded departures hall. Miraculously the throng opened before him. He tilted the brim of his panama hat over one eye and grinned at the girl at the check-in counter, so that she came over all girlish and flustered.

It was the same once they were aboard the aircraft. The two stewardesses giggled at everything he said, plied him with champagne and fussed over him outrageously, to the obvious irritation of the other passengers, including Royan herself. But she ignored him and them and settled back to enjoy the unaccustomed luxury of the reclining first-class seat and her own miniature video screen. She tried to concentrate on the screen images of Richard Gere, but found her attention wandering to other images of wild canyons and ancient stelae.

Only when Nicholas nudged her did she look around at him a little haughtily. He had set up a tiny travelling chessboard on the arm of the seat between them, and now he lifted an eyebrow at her and inclined his head in invitation.

When they landed at Jomo Kenyatta airport in Kenya they were still locked in combat. They were level at two games each, but she was a bishop and two pawns up in the final deciding game. She felt quite pleased with herself.

At the Norfolk Hotel in Nairobi he had booked a pair of garden bungalows, one for each of them. Within ten minutes of her flopping down on the bed, he called her from next door on the house phone.

'We are going to dinner with the British High Commissioner tonight. He is an old chum. Dress informal. Can you be ready at eight?'

One did not have to rough it too onerously when travelling around the world in this man's company, she thought.

It was a relatively short haul from Nairobi up to Addis Ababa, and the landscape below them unfolded in fascinating sequences that kept her glued to the cabin window of the Air Kenya flight. The hoary summit of Mount Kenya was for once free of cloud, and the snow-clad double peaks glistened in the high sunlight.

The bleak brown deserts of the Northern Frontier District were relieved only by the green hills that surrounded the oasis of Marsabit and, far out on the port side, the flashing waters of Lake Turkana, formerly Lake Rudolf. The desert finally gave way to the highlands of the great central plateau of the ancient land of Ethiopia.

'In Africa only the Egyptians go back further than this civilization,' Nicholas remarked as they watched it together. 'They were a cultured race when we peoples of northern climes were still dressing in untanned skins and living in caves. They were Christians when Europeans were still pagans, worshipping the old gods, Pan and Diana.'

'They were a civilized people when Taita passed this way nearly four thousand years ago,' she agreed. 'In his scrolls he writes of them as almost his cultural equals, which was rare for him. He disparaged all the other nations of the old world as his inferiors in every way.'

From the air Addis was like so many other African cities, a mixture of the old and the new, of traditional and exotic architectural styles, thatched roofs alongside galvanized iron and baked tiles. The rounded walls of the old *tukul*s built with mud and wattle contrasted with the rectangular shapes and geometrical planes of the brick-built multi-storeyed buildings, the blocks of flats and the villas of the affluent, the government buildings and the grandiose, flag-bedecked headquarters of the Organization of African Unity.

The distinguishing features of the surrounding countryside were the plantations of tall eucalyptus trees, the ubiquitous blue gums that provided firewood. It was the only fuel available to so many in this poor and war-torn land, which over the centuries had been ravaged by marauding armies and, more recently, by alien political doctrines.

After Nairobi the high-altitude air was cool and sweet when Royan and Nicholas left the aircraft and walked across the tarmac to the terminal building. As they entered, before they had even approached the row of waiting immigration officers someone called his name.

'Sir Nicholas!' They both turned to the tall young woman who glided towards them with all the grace of a dancer, her dark and delicate features lit by a welcoming smile. She wore full-length traditional skirts which enhanced her movements.

'Welcome to my country of Ethiopia. I am Woizero Tessay.' She looked at Royan with interest, 'And you must be Woizero Royan.' She held out her hand to her and Nicholas saw that the two women liked each other immediately.

'If you will let me have your passports, I will see to the formalities while you relax in the VIP lounge. There is a man from your British Embassy waiting there to greet you, Sir Nicholas. I don't know how he knew that you were arriving.'

There was only one person waiting in the VIP lounge. He was dressed in a well-cut tropical suit and wore the orange, yellow and blue diagonally striped old Sandhurst tie. He stood up and came to greet Nicholas immediately, 'Nicky, how are you? It's good to see you again. Must be all of twelve years, isn't it?'

'Hello, Geoffrey. I had no idea they had stuck you out here.'

'Military attaché. His Excellency sent me down to meet you as soon as he heard that you and I had been at Sandhurst together.' Geoffrey looked at Royan with marked interest, and with a resigned air Nicholas introduced them.

'Geoffrey Tennant. Be careful of him. Biggest ram north of the equator. No girl safe within half a mile of him.'

'I say, steady on,' Geoffrey protested, looking pleased with the reference that Nicholas had given him. 'Please don't believe a word the man says, Dr Al Simma. Notorious prevaricator.'

Geoffrey drew Nicholas aside and quickly gave him a résumé of conditions in the country, particularly in the outlying areas. 'HE is a little worried. He doesn't like the idea of you swanning around out there on your own. Lots of nasty men down there in the Gojam. I told him that you knew how to look after yourself.'

In a remarkably short time Woizero Tessay was back. 'I have cleared all your luggage, including the firearm and ammunition. This is your temporary permit. You must keep it with you at all times whilst you are in Ethiopia. Here are your passports — the visas are stamped and in order. Our flight to Lake Tana leaves in an hour, so we have plenty of time to check in.'

'Any time you need a job, come and see me,' Nicholas commended her efficiency.

Geoffrey Tennant walked with them as far as the departures gate, where he shook hands, 'Anything I can do, it goes without saying.

148

"*Serve to Lead*", Nicky.'
' "*Serve to lead*"?' Royan asked, as they walked out to the waiting aircraft.
'Sandhurst's motto,' he explained.
'How nice, Nicky,' she murmured.
'I have always considered Nicholas to be more dignified and appropriate,' he said.
'Yes, but Nicky is so sweet.'

In the high, thin air the Twin Otter aircraft that took them on the last, northern, leg pitched and yawed in the updraughts from the mountains below.

Although they were at fifteen thousand feet above sea level, the ground was close enough for them to make out the villages and the sparse areas of cultivation around them. Subjected for so many centuries to primitive agricultural methods and to the uncontrolled grazing of domestic herds, the land had a thin, impoverished look, and the bones of rock showed through the thin red fleshing of earth.

Abruptly ahead of them the plateau over which they were flying was rent through by a monstrous chasm. It was as though the earth had received a mighty sword-stroke that struck through to her very bowels.

'The Abbay river!' Tessay leaned forward in her seat to tap Royan's shoulder.

The rim of the gorge was clear-cut, and then

149

the slope dropped away at an angle of over thirty degrees. The bare plains of the plateau gave way immediately to the heavily forested walls of the gorge. They could make out the candelabra shapes of giant euphorbia rising above the dense jungle. In places the walls had collapsed in scree slopes of loose rock, and in others they were up-thrust into bluffs and needles that erosion had sculpted with a monstrous artistry into the figures of towering humanoids and other fantastic creatures of stone.

Down and down it plunged, and they winged out over the void until they could look directly down, a mile and more, on to the glittering snake of the river in the depths. The funnel shape of the upper walls formed a secondary rim as they reached the sheer cliffs of the sub-gorge five hundred feet above the Nile water. Deep down there between its terrible cliffs the river gouged dark pools and long slithering runs through the red sandstone. In places the gorge was forty miles across, in others it narrowed to under ten, but through all its length the grandeur and the desolation were infinite and eternal. Man had made no impression upon it.

'You will soon be down there,' Tessay told them in a voice so awed that it was almost a whisper, and they were both silent. Words seemed superfluous in the face of such raw and savage nature.

Almost with relief they watched the northern wall rise to meet them, and the high mountains of the Choke range stood up against the tall blue African sky, higher than their fragile little craft was flying.

The aircraft banked into its descent and Tessay pointed over the starboard wingtip.

'Lake Tana,' she told them. It was a wide and lovely body of water, over fifty miles long, studded with islands on each of which stood a monastery or an ancient church. As they dropped in over the water on the final approach, they could make out the white-robed priests plying between the islands on their traditional little boats made from bundles of papyrus.

The Otter touched down on the dirt strip beside the lake and rolled out in a long trailing cloud of dust. It swung in and stopped engines beside the run-down terminal building of thatch and daub.

The sunlight was so bright that Nicholas pulled a pair of sunglasses from the breast pocket of his khaki jacket and placed them on his nose as he stood at the top of the boarding ladder. He took in the pock-marks of bullets and shrapnel on the dirty white walls of the terminal, and the burnt-out hull of a Russian T35 battle tank standing in the grass on the verge of the runway. The barrel of its turret gun pointed earthwards, and grass had grown up between the rusted tracks.

The other passengers pushed forward impatiently behind him, jostling him and jabbering with excitement as they saw friends and relatives waiting to greet them under the eucalyptus trees that shaded the building. There was only one vehicle parked out there, a sand-coloured Toyota Land Cruiser. The roundel on the driver's door had at its centre the painted head of a mountain nyala, with long corkscrew horns, and in a ribbon below it the title 'Wild Chase Safaris'. A white man lounged behind the wheel.

As Nicholas came down the ladder behind the two women, the driver slipped out of the truck and strode out on to the strip to meet them. He was dressed in a faded khaki bush suit, and he was tall and lean and walked with a spring to his step.

'Fortyish,' Nicholas judged his age from the grizzling in his short beard. 'One of the hard men,' Nicholas thought. His ginger hair was cropped short, his eyes were pale killer blue. There was a puckered white scar that ran across one cheek and up to twist and deform his nose.

Tessay introduced Royan to him first, and he made a short, choppy bow as he shook her hand. *'Enchanté,'* he told her in an execrable French accent and then looked at Nicholas.

'This is my husband, Alto Boris,' Tessay introduced him. 'Boris, this is Alto Nicholas.'

'My English is bad,' Boris said. 'My French is better.'

'Not much to choose between them,' Nicholas thought, but he smiled easily and said, 'So we will speak French then. *Bonjour,* Monsieur Brusilov. I am delighted to make your acquaintance.' He offered the Russian his hand.

Boris's grip was hard — too hard. He was making a contest out of the greeting, but Nicholas had expected it. He knew this type of old, and he had taken a deep grip so Boris could not crush his fingers. Nicholas held him without allowing any strain or effort to show on his lazy smile. Boris was the first to break the handshake, and there was just the trace of respect in those pale eyes.

'So you have come for a dik-dik?' he asked, just short of a sneer. 'Most of my clients come for big elephant, or at least for mountain nyala.'

'Bit rich for my nerves,' Nicholas grinned, 'all that big stuff. Dik-dik will suit me fine.'

'Have you ever been down in the gorge?' Boris demanded. His Russian accent overpowered the French words and made them difficult to follow.

'Sir Nicholas was one of the leaders of the 1976 river expedition,' Royan intervened sweetly, and Nicholas was amused by her unexpected intervention. She had picked up the antagonism between them very quickly, and come to his rescue.

Boris grunted, and turned to his wife. 'Have you got all the stores I ordered?' he demanded.

'Yes, Boris,' she answered meekly. 'They are all on board the aircraft.' She is afraid of him, Nicholas decided, probably with good reason.

'Let's get loaded up, then. We have a long journey ahead of us.'

The two men rode in the front seats of the

Toyota, and the women sat behind them with many of the packages of stores packed in around them. Good African protocol, Nicholas smiled to himself: men first, women fend for themselves.

'You don't want to do the tourist run, do you?' Boris made it sound like a threat.

'The tourist run?'

'The outlet from the lake, and the power station,' he explained. 'The Portuguese bridge over the gorge and the point where the Blue Nile begins,' he added. But before they could accept he warned them, 'If you do, we won't get into camp until long after dark.'

'Thanks for the suggestion,' Nicholas told him politely, 'but I have seen it all before.'

'Good.' Boris made his approval evident. 'Let's get out of here.'

The road swung away into the west, below the high mountains. This was the Gojam, the land of the aloof mountaineers. It was well-populated country, and they passed many tall, thin men along the roadside as they strode along behind their herds of goats and sheep, with their long staffs held crossways over their shoulders. Both men and women wore *shammas*, woollen shawls, and baggy white jodhpur pants, with their feet in open sandals.

They were people with proud and handsome features, their hair dressed out into thick, bushy halos, and their eyes fierce as those of eagles. Some of the younger women in the villages they passed through were truly beautiful. Most of the men were heavily armed. They carried two-handed swords in chased silver scabbards, and AK-47 assault rifles.

'Makes them feel like big men,' Boris chuckled. 'Very brave, very macho.'

The huts in the villages were circular walled *tukuls,* surrounded by plantations of eucalyptus and spiky-headed sisal.

Bruised purple storm clouds boiled over the high peaks of the Choke and swept them with squalls of rain. Like silver coins, the huge drops rattled against the windscreen of the Land Cruiser and turned the road to a running river of mud under their wheels.

The condition of the road surface was appalling; in places it deteriorated into a rocky gully which even the four-wheel drive Toyota could not negotiate, and Boris was forced to make his own track across the rocky hillside. Often reduced to walking speed, they were nevertheless tossed about in their seats as the wheels bounced over the rough terrain.

'These damn blacks don't even think to repair the roads,' Boris grunted. 'They are happy to live like animals.' None of them replied, but Nicholas glanced up into the rear-view mirror at the faces of the two women. They were closed and neutral, hiding any hurt that either of them might have felt at the remark.

As they went on, the road, bad as it had been originally, became even worse. From here onwards the soft muddy surface had been torn up by the tyres and tracks of heavy traffic.

'Military traffic?' Nicholas raised his voice above the buffeting rain squalls, and Boris grunted.

'Some of it. There is a lot of *shufta* activity along the gorge — bandits and dissident warlords. However, most of this traffic is mineral-prospecting. One of the big mining companies has got concessions in Gojam and they are moving in to begin drilling.'

'We have passed no civilian vehicles,' Royan remarked, 'not even public buses.'

'We have just come through a terrible period in our long and troubled history,' Tessay explained to her. 'We are an agrarian-based economy. Once we were known as the bread basket of Africa, but when Mengistu seized power he drove us right over the edge of poverty. He used starvation as a political weapon. We are still suffering terribly. Very few of our people can afford the luxury of a motor vehicle. Most of them are worried how they will be able to afford food for their children.'

'Tessay has an economics degree from Addis University,' Boris chuckled. 'She is very clever. She knows everything. You ask her, she will tell you. History, religion, economics — just ask her.' Tessay relapsed into silence at the rebuff.

In the middle of the afternoon the rain at last eased and a timid sun peered through the

156

cloud banks. Boris stopped the Toyota in a deserted stretch of countryside. 'Pinkel pause,' he announced. 'Wee-wee stop. Pee-pee time.'

The two girls left the truck and wandered away amongst the rocks. When they returned to the vehicle they had changed their clothing. Both of them now wore the *shammas* and the jodhpur trousers of the country.

'Tessay has made me a gift of a traditional Tigrean costume,' said Royan, pirouetting for Nicholas's approval.

'Looks good, too,' he gave his opinion. 'You will be a lot more comfortable in pants.'

The sun was lowering as the road dropped into another rocky valley, down the length of which ran a river with steep, eroded banks. Above the river nestled a circular, white-walled church with a wooden Coptic cross set high on its reed-thatched roof. The village of *tukul*s huddled around the church.

'Debra Maryam,' Boris announced with satisfaction, 'the hill of the Virgin Mary, and the river is the Dandera. I sent my men on ahead in the big truck. They will have the camp ready and be waiting for us. We will sleep here tonight, and tomorrow we will follow the river downstream until we reach the rim of the gorge.'

Boris's camp staff had set up the tents in a eucalyptus grove just beyond the village.

'The second tent is yours,' Boris pointed it out.

'That will do fine for Royan,' Nicholas agreed.

157

'I will need a tent on my own.'

'Dik-dik and separate tents,' Boris looked at him with a flat, pale stare. 'A hell of a man. You impress me.'

He shouted for his men to erect Nicholas's tent alongside the other, the side walls almost touching.

'You may get up your courage during the night,' he leered at Nicholas. 'Don't want you to have too far to walk.'

The shower under which they bathed was a drum hung in the lower branches of one of the blue gum trees, with a roofless canvas screen set up around it. Royan used it first and came back looking cheerful and refreshed, and with a damp towel wrapped around her hair.

'Your turn, Nicky!' she called to Nicholas as she passed his tent. 'The water is beautifully hot.'

It was dark by the time Nicholas had showered and changed. He walked across to the dining tent where the rest of the party were already seated in camp chairs around the fire. The two women sat a little to one side, talking quietly, and Boris had his feet propped on the low table as he leaned back in his chair with a glass in one hand.

He indicated the vodka bottle on the table, as Nicholas stepped into the circle of firelight, 'Get yourself a drink. Ice in the bucket.'

'I prefer a beer,' Nicholas told him. 'Thirsty drive.' Boris shrugged and bellowed for his camp butler to bring a brown bottle from the portable gas refrigerator.

'Let me tell you something, a little secret.' He grinned at Nicholas as he poured himself another vodka. 'There is no such animal as a striped dik-dik these days, even if there ever was one. You are wasting your time and your money.'

'Fine,' Nicholas agreed mildly. 'It's my time and my money.'

'Just because some old fart shot one back in the Dark Ages, doesn't mean you are going to find another now. We could go up into the tea plantations for elephant. I saw three bulls there only ten days ago. All with tusks over a hundred pounds a side.'

As they argued, the level in Boris's vodka bottle fell like the Nile at the end of the inundation. When Tessay told them that the meal was ready, Boris carried the bottle with him; he stumbled on his way to the table. During the meal his only contribution to the conversation was to snarl at Tessay.

'The lamb is raw. Why don't you see to it that the cook does it properly? Damn monkeys, you have to watch everything they do.'

'Is your lamb undercooked, Alto Nicholas?' Tessay asked without looking at her husband. 'I can have them cook it longer.'

'It's perfect,' he assured her. 'I like mine pink.'

By the end of dinner the vodka bottle at

Boris's elbow was empty, and his face was flushed and swollen. He got up from the table without a word and disappeared into the darkness in the direction of his tent, swaying on his feet and occasionally catching his balance with a two-step jig.

'I apologize,' Tessay told them quietly. 'It is only in the evenings. In the day he is fine. It is a Russian tradition, the vodka.' She smiled brightly; only her eyes stayed sad.

'It is a lovely night, and too early yet for bed. Would you like to walk up to the church? It is very old and famous. I will have one of the servants bring a lantern, so that you may admire the murals.'

The servant walked ahead of them, lighting their way, and an ancient priest waited to welcome them on the portico of the circular building. He was thin and so very black that only his teeth flashed in the gloom. He carried a magnificent Coptic cross in massive native silver, set with carnelians and other semi-precious stones.

Both Royan and Tessay dropped on their knees in front of him to ask for his blessing. He slapped their cheeks lightly with the cross and genuflected over them, mumbling his benediction in Amharic. Then he ushered them into the interior.

The walls were covered with a magnificent display of paintings in brilliant primary colours. In the lantern light they blazed like gemstones.

There was a strong Byzantine flavour to the style: the saints' eyes were huge and slanted, with great golden halos over their heads. Above the altar, with its tinsel and brass furnishing, the Virgin cradled her infant while the three wise men and a host of angels knelt in adoration. Nicholas slipped his Polaroid camera from the pocket of his jacket and adjusted the flash. He wandered around the church photographing these murals, while Tessay and Royan knelt before the altar side by side.

Once he had finished his photography Nicholas found a seat on the hand-hewn wooden pews and sat quietly watching their intent faces which the candlelight touched with golden highlights, and he was moved by the beauty of the moment.

'I wish I had that kind of faith,' he thought, as he had so often before. 'It must be a comfort in the hard times. I wish I were able to pray like that for Rosalind and the girls.' He could not stay longer, and he went out and sat on the church portico where he watched the night sky.

In these high altitudes, in the thin unpolluted air, the stars were such a dazzling blaze that it was difficult to pick out the individual constellations. After a while his sadness abated. It was good to be back in Africa.

When the two women emerged at last from the dark interior, Nicholas gave the old priest a one hundred birr note and a Polaroid photograph of himself which the old man clearly valued above the money. Then the three of them walked back down the hill together in companionable silence.

'Nicky!' Royan shook him awake. When he sat up and switched on his torch, he saw that she had thrown the woollen shawl over a pair of men's striped pyjamas before she had come into his tent.

'What is it?' he asked, but before she could answer he heard the sound of a hoarse and angry voice shouting invective in the night, and then the unmistakable thud of a clenched fist striking flesh and bone.

'He's beating her.' Royan's voice was tight with outrage. 'You have to make him stop.'

There was a cry of pain after the blow, and then sobs.

Nicholas hesitated. Only a fool interferes between a man and his wife, and his reward usually is to have them unite and turn savagely upon him.

'You must do something, Nicky, please.'

Reluctantly he swung his legs out of the cot and stood up. He slept in boxer shorts, and he did not bother to find his shoes. She followed him, also on bare feet, to the end of the grove where Boris's tent stood beyond the dining tent. There was a lantern still burning within, and it threw magnified shadows on the canvas walls. He saw that Boris had his wife by the hair and was dragging her across the floor, roaring at her in Russian.

'Boris!' Nicholas had to shout his name three times to get his attention, and then they saw the shadow play on the canvas as he dropped Tessay and flung open the tent flap.

He was dressed only in a pair of underpants. His torso was lean and muscular, the chest flat and hard-looking, covered with coppery curls. On the floor behind him Tessay lay face down, sobbing into her cupped hands. She was naked, and the planes of her body were sleek as those of a panther.

'What the hell is going on here?' Nicholas demanded, his anger only just beginning to stir as he witnessed the gracious, gentle woman's distress and humiliation.

'I am giving this black whore a lesson in good manners,' Boris gloated, his face still swollen and flushed with drink and passion. 'It's none of your business, English, unless you want to pay some money and have a bit of pork for yourself.' He laughed, an ugly sound.

'Are you all right, Woizero Tessay?' Nicholas looked directly into Boris's face, sparing the woman the further humiliation of another man's eyes on her nudity.

Tessay sat up, lifted her knees against her chest, and hugged them with both arms to cover her body.

'It's all right, Alto Nicholas. Please go away before there is real trouble.' Blood was trickling from one nostril into her mouth, and dyeing her teeth pink.

'You heard my wife, English bastard. Go away! Mind your own business. Go away, before I give you a little lesson in good manners also.'

Boris staggered forward and thrust his open hand against Nicholas's chest. Nicholas moved as smoothly and as effortlessly as a matador avoiding the first wild charge of the bull. He swayed to one side, and used Boris's own momentum to send him on in the direction in which he was already committed. Completely off balance, the Russian reeled across the open ground in front of the tent until he collided with one of the camp chairs and went down in a sprawling heap.

'Royan, take Tessay to your tent!' he ordered softly. Royan ran into the tent and pulled a sheet from the nearest cot. She spread it over Tessay's shoulders and lifted her to her feet.

'Please, don't do this,' Tessay sobbed. 'You don't know him when he gets like this. He will hurt somebody.'

Royan dragged her, still protesting and weeping, out of the tent, but by now Boris was on his feet again. He bellowed with rage and picked up the camp chair that had tripped him. With a single jerk he tore off one of the legs and hefted it in his bunched fist.

'You want to play games, English? All right,

we play!' He rushed at Nicholas, swinging the chair leg like a Ninja baton, so that it hissed with the force with which he aimed it at his head. As Nicholas ducked under it Boris reversed the swing, going for the side of his chest, under his upraised arm. It would have staved in his ribs if it had landed, but again Nicholas twisted away.

They circled each other warily, and then Boris charged again. If it had not been for the effect of the vodka on the Russian's reflexes Nicholas would never have taken a chance with an adversary of this calibre, but Boris was just loose enough in his control to allow him to duck in under the swinging chair leg. He straightened, with all his weight rolling into the punch, and his fist slogged into the pit of Boris's belly just under the sternum. The Russian's breath was driven out of him in a great gusty belch.

The chair leg flew from his grip, and he doubled over and collapsed. Clasping his middle, and heaving and wheezing for breath, Boris lay curled in the dust. Nicholas stooped over him and told him softly in English, 'This sort of behaviour simply isn't good enough, old chap. We don't bully girls. Please don't let it happen again.'

He straightened up and spoke to Royan, 'Get her to your tent and keep her there.' He combed his hair back from his face with his fingers. 'And now, if you have no serious objections, may we get a little sleep?'

It rained again during the early hours. The heavy drops drummed down on the canvas and the lightning lit the interior of the tents with an eerie brilliance. However, by the time that Nicholas went through to the dining tent for breakfast the next morning, the clouds had cleared and the sunshine was bright and cheering. The sweet mountain air smelt of wet earth and mushrooms.

Boris greeted Nicholas with hearty good fellowship. 'Good morning, English. We had some fun last night. I still laugh to remember it. Very good jokes. One day soon we will have some more vodka, then we will make some more good jokes.' And he bellowed through to the kitchen tent, 'Hey! Lady Sun, bring your new boyfriend something to eat. He is hungry from all the sport last night.'

Tessay was quiet and withdrawn as she supervised the servants handing round breakfast. One eye was swollen almost closed, and her lip was cut. She did not look at Nicholas once during the meal.

'We will go on ahead,' Boris explained jovially as they drank coffee. 'My servants will break camp, and follow us in my big truck. With luck, we will be able to camp tonight on the rim above the gorge, and tomorrow we will begin the descent.'

As they were climbing into the truck, Tessay was able to speak to him softly for a moment, without danger of Boris overhearing her. 'Thank you, Alto Nicholas. But it was not wise. You don't know him. You must be careful now. He does not forget, nor does he forgive.'

From the village of Debra Maryam Boris took a branch road that ran alongside the Dandera river directly southwards. The road they had followed the previous day from Lake Tana was shown on the map as a major highway. It had been bad enough. But this track that they were now on was marked as a secondary road 'not passable in all weather'. To compound matters, it seemed that most of the heavy traffic that had torn up the main road had followed this same track. They came to a place where some huge vehicle had become bogged down in the rain-saturated earth, and the efforts to free it had left areas of ploughed land and an excavation like a bomb crater that resembled an old photograph of the battlefields of First World War Flanders.

Twice during the day the Toyota too became stuck in this foul ground. Each time this happened, the big truck that was following them came up and all the servants swarmed down from the cargo body to push and heave the Toyota through. Even Nicholas stripped to the waist to work with them in the mud to free it.

'If you had only listened to my advice,' Boris

grumbled, 'we would not be here. There is no game where you want to go, and there are no roads worth the name either.'

In the early afternoon they stopped beside the river for an alfresco lunch. Nicholas went down to the pool beside the road to wash off the mud and filth of the morning's labours. He had been in the forefront of the efforts to keep the truck moving. Royan followed him down the slope and perched on a rock above the pool while he stripped off his shirt and knelt at the verge to splash himself with the cold mountain water. The river was muddy yellow and swollen from the rainstorms.

'I don't think Boris believes your story about the striped dik-dik,' she warned him. 'Tessay tells me that he is suspicious of what we are up to.' She watched with interest as he sluiced his chest and upper arms. Where the sun had not touched it, his skin was very white and unblemished. His chest hair was thick and dark. She decided that his body was good to look at.

'He is the type that would go through our luggage if he gets a chance,' Nicholas agreed. 'You didn't bring anything with you that has any clues for him? No papers or notes?'

'Only the satellite photograph, and my note-books are all in my own shorthand. He won't be able to make anything of them.'

'Be very careful of what you discuss with Tessay.'

'She is a dear. There is nothing underhand about her.' Heatedly Royan came to the defence of her new friend.

'She may be all right, but she's married to my chum Boris. Her first allegiance lies there. No matter what your feelings towards her, don't trust either of them.' He dried himself on his shirt, slipped it on and then buttoned it over his chest. 'Let's go and get something to eat.'

Back at the parked truck Boris was pulling the cork from a bottle of South African white wine. He poured a tumblerful for Nicholas. Chilled in the river, it was crisp and fruity. Tessay offered them cold roast chicken and *injera* bread, the flat, thin sheets of stone-ground unleavened bread of the country. The trials and labours of the morning's travels faded into insignificance as Royan lay beside Nicholas in the grass and they watched a bearded vulture sailing high against the blue. It saw them and drifted overhead curiously, twisting its head to look down at them. Its eyes were masked in black like those of a highwayman, and the distinctive wedge-shaped tail feathers flirted with the wind the way the fingers of a concert pianist would stroke the ivories of the keyboard.

When it was time to go on, Nicholas gave her his hand to lift her to her feet. It was one of their rare moments of physical contact, and she held on to his fingers for just a second or two longer than was strictly necessary.

There was no improvement in the surface of

the track as they drew nearer to the rim of the gorge, and the hours passed in this bone-jarring, teeth-rattling progress. The track snaked over a rise and then dog-legged down the far slope. Halfway down Boris swore in Russian as they came round the hairpin bend of a high earthen bank to find a huge diesel truck slewed across the track, almost blocking it.

Even though they had been following the tracks of this convoy of vehicles since the previous day, this was the first of them that they had encountered, and it took Boris by surprise. He hit his brakes so suddenly that his passengers were almost catapulted from their seats, but on the steep incline in the mud the brakes did not bring them to a complete halt. Boris was forced to change down into his lowest gear and steer for the narrow gap between the bank and the truck.

From the back seat Royan looked out of the window beside her, up the high side of the diesel truck. There was a company name and logo emblazoned in scarlet on the green background.

A strong feeling of *déjà vu* overcame her as she stared at the image. She had seen this sign recently, but her memory cheated her: she could not recall the time or the place. She only knew that it was of vital importance that she should remember.

The side of the Toyota scraped against the metal of the truck, and then they were past it. Boris leaned out of his window and shook his fist at the driver of the larger vehicle.

He was a local man, probably recruited in Addis by the owner of the truck. Grinning at Boris's antics, he leaned out of his own cab to return the clenched fist salute, adding a nice little touch by jerking a raised forefinger upwards.

'Dung-eater!' Boris roated with outrage at being bested in the exchange, but he did not stop. 'No use even talking to them. What do they know? Black chimps!'

For the rest of the wearisome journey Royan remained silent and withdrawn, shaken and troubled by the conviction that she had seen the trademark of the winged red horse before, with, set above it in a pennant, the name of the company: 'PEGASUS EXPLORATION'.

As they approached the end of the day's journey at last they passed a signpost beside the track. The supporting legs of the sign were solidly set in concrete, and the artwork was of such high quality that it could only have been that of a professional signwriter.

Across the top of the board an arrow indicated a newly bulldozed road that headed off to the right, and the directions read:

PEGASUS EXPLORATION
BASE CAMP — ONE KILOMETRE
PRIVATE ROAD
NO ENTRY TO
UNAUTHORIZED TRAFFIC

171

The scarlet horse reared in the centre of the board with its wings spread wide, on the point of flight.

Now she gasped aloud as the elusive memory came upon her with stunning clarity. She remembered where she had last seen the flying red horse. In an instant she was transported back into the icy waters of an English salmon river, flung from the rolling body of the Land Rover, the huge MAN truck roaring over the bridge above her, and, for a subliminal pulse of time, the prancing red horse upon its side.

'It's the same!' she almost shouted aloud, but controlled herself. The terror of the moment returned to her with full force, and she found herself breathing hard and her heart racing as though she had run a long way.

'It cannot be a coincidence,' she assured herself silently, 'and I am not mistaken. It is the same company. Pegasus Exploration.'

She was withdrawn and distracted for the last few miles of the journey, until the track they were following ended abruptly on the brink of the sheer cliffs of the escarpment. Here Boris pulled on to the grassy verge and stopped the engine.

'This is as far as we ride. We camp here tonight. My big truck is not far behind. They will make camp as soon as they arrive. Tomorrow we will go down into the gorge on foot.'

As they dismounted, Royan tugged at Nicholas's arm, 'I must speak to you,' she whispered urgently, and she followed him as he led her along the bank of the river.

He found a place for them to sit side by side, with their legs dangling over the drop. Beside them the swollen yellow river seemed to sense what lay ahead of it. The cold mountain waters speeded up, swirled amongst the rocks, and gathered themselves for that dizzying leap out into empty space. The cliff below them was a sheer wall of rock almost a thousand feet deep. It was so high that in the evening light the abyss far below was a dark, mysterious place, its bottom hidden from them by shadow and spray from the falls. As Royan looked down into it her sense of balance swirled with vertigo. She cringed back from the edge and found herself instinctively leaning against Nicholas's shoulder to steady herself. Only when they touched did she realize what she was doing, and she pulled away from him self-consciously.

The muddied waters of the Dandera river leaped from the brink, and were miraculously transformed into curtains of ethereal lacework as they fell. Like the skirts of a waltzing bride they shimmered and swirled, and rainbows of light played through them as though from an embroidery of seed pearls. Still falling, the columns of white spray twisted and changed into lovely but ephemeral shapes, until they struck the lower ledges of glistening black rock and exploded outwards into fresh clouds of white that at last screened the dark depths of the abyss with an opalescent veil.

It was with a conscious effort that Royan pulled her mind away from the awe-inspiring scene and back to the troubled present.

'Nicky, do you remember I told you about the truck that forced my mother and me over the bridge in the Land Rover?'

'Of course.' His expression was mystified as he studied her face. 'You are upset. What is it, Royan?'

'The truck had signwriting down the sides of the trailers that it was towing.'

'You told me, yes. Green and red. You told me that you didn't get a good enough look to read the sign.'

'It was the same as the truck we passed this afternoon. I saw the sign at the same angle as before and it came back to me. The red Pegasus, the flying horse.'

He studied her face for a while, 'Are you absolutely certain?'

'Absolutely!' She nodded vehemently.

Nicholas stared out over the magnificent panorama of the gorge spread below them. It was forty miles to the far wall of the canyon, but in the brilliant rain-washed air it seemed so close that he could reach across and touch it.

'A coincidence?' he wondered at last.

'Do you think so? A very strange and wonderful coincidence, then. Pegasus in both Yorkshire and Gojam? Do you accept that?'

'It doesn't make sense. The truck that hit you was stolen —'

'Was it?' she demanded. 'Are we sure of that?'

'If it wasn't, then let's hear your ideas.'

'If you were planning an assassination, would you rely on stealing a truck conveniently left at a Little Chef for you?'

He shook his head, 'Go on.'

'Suppose you arranged for your own truck to be placed there for you, and for your driver to report it stolen only after you had a good head start on the police.'

'It's possible,' he agreed without enthusiasm.

'Whoever murdered Duraid, and made two further attempts to kill me, obviously has considerable resources at his disposal. He is able to make arrangements in Egypt and England. On top of that, he has the seventh scroll in his possession. He has our notes and all our workings and translations which point him clearly to this spot on the Abbay river. Just suppose that he has control of a company like Pegasus — is there any reason why he can't be here in Ethiopia, just as we are, right at this moment?'

Nicholas was silent for a while. He picked up a stone from the ledge beside him and tossed it out over the cliff. They both watched it drop away, dwindling in size until it vanished in the veils of spray far below where they sat.

Abruptly Nicholas stood up and reached for her hand to pull her to her feet beside him.

175

'Come on,' he said.

'Where are we going?'

'Pegasus base camp. Let's go and have a chat to the site foreman.'

Boris protested angrily and hurried to intervene when Nicholas climbed into the Toyota and started the engine, 'Where the hell do you think you are going?'

'Sight-seeing.' Nicholas let in the clutch. 'Back in an hour.'

'Hey, English, my truck!' He ran to catch up with them, but Nicholas accelerated away.

'Charge me for the hire.' He grinned back at Boris in the rear-view mirror.

They reached the signposted turn-off and followed the side track over the ridge. The Pegasus camp lay on the far side. Nicholas braked to a halt on the crest of the rise and they studied it in silence.

An area of about ten acres had been cleared and levelled. It was surrounded by a barbed-wire security fence, with a single closed gate. Three of the massive diesel trucks in their green and red livery were parked in a rank inside the fence. There were also several smaller vehicles and a tall mobile drilling rig in the line. The rest of the yard was filled with prospecting equipment and stores. There were stacks of drilling rods and steel core boxes, wooden crates of spares, and several hundred forty-four-gallon drums of diesel and oil and drilling mud. The drums and the stores were stacked with a neat-ness and sense of good order that was startling in this wild and rocky landscape. Just inside the gate stood a small village of a dozen buildings made of corrugated sheet sections, of the Quonset type. They too were set out in a street of military precision.

'A big, well-organized outfit,' Nicholas commented. 'Let's go down and see who is in charge.'

There were two armed guards on the gate, dressed in the camouflage uniform of the Ethiopian army. They were clearly surprised by the arrival at the gate of the strange Land Cruiser, and when Nicholas sounded his horn one of them came forward suspiciously with his AK-47 rifle at the ready.

'I want to speak to the manager here,' Nicholas told him in Arabic, with enough haughty authority to make the sentry uncertain and uneasy.

The soldier grunted, went back and consulted his colleague, then lifted the handset of the two-way radio and spoke earnestly into the mouthpiece. There was a five-minute delay after he finished speaking, and then the door of the nearest Quonset building opened and a white man came out.

He was dressed in khaki coveralls and a soft bush cap. His eyes, covered by mirrored sunglasses, were set in a deeply tanned, leathery face. His physique was short and chunky, and his sleeves were rolled up over hairy, workthickened arms. After speaking a few words to the guards at the gate he came out to the Toyota.

'Yeah? What's going down here?' he demanded in a Texan drawl, speaking around the stub of an unlit cigar.

'The name is Quenton-Harper.' Nicholas dismounted from the truck to greet him, and held out his hand. 'Nicholas Quenton-Harper. How do you do?'

The American hesitated, and then took the hand as though he had been offered an electric eel to squeeze.

'Helm,' he said. 'Jake Helm, from Abilene, Texas. I am the foreman here.' His hand was that of an artisan, with calloused palms and lumpy scar tissue over the knuckles, and half moons of black grease under the fingernails.

'Terribly sorry to worry you. I am having some trouble with my truck. I wondered if you had a mechanic who could have a look at it for me.' Nicholas smiled winningly, but received no encouragement from the man.

'Not company policy.' He shook his head.

'I am prepared to pay for any —'

'Listen, buddy, I said no.' Jake removed the cigar from his mouth and examined it minutely.

'Your company — Pegasus. Can you tell me where your head office is situated? Who is your managing director?'

'I am a busy man. You are wasting my time.' Helm returned the cigar to his mouth and began to turn away.

'I will be hunting in this area over the next few weeks. I would not like to endanger any of your employees with a stray shot. Can you give me some idea of where you will be working?'

'I am running a prospecting outfit here, mister. I don't give out news flashes on my movements. Beat it!'

He turned and walked to the gate and gave brusque orders to the guards before marching back to his office building.

'Satellite disc on the roof,' Nicholas remarked. 'I wonder who our lad Jake is speaking to at this very moment.'

'Somebody in Texas?' Royan hazarded.

'Doesn't follow, necessarily,' Nicholas demurred. 'Pegasus is probably a multinational. Just because Jake is one, doesn't mean his boss is Texan also. Not a very instructive conversation, I am afraid.' He started the engine and U-turned the Toyota. 'But if someone at Pegasus is the ugly mixed up in this, he will recognize my name. We have given them notice of our arrival. Let's see what we have flushed out of the bushes.'

When they got back to the Dandera river falls, they found that Boris's truck had arrived, the tents had been erected, and the chef had brewed tea for them. Boris was less welcoming than his chef, and maintained a sullen silence while Nicholas tried to placate him for commandeering his truck. It was only after his first vodka of the evening that he mellowed sufficiently to speak again.

'The mules were supposed to be waiting for us here. Time means nothing to these people. We cannot start down into the gorge until they arrive.'

'Well, at least while we are waiting for them I will have a chance to sight in my rifle,' Nicholas remarked with resignation. 'In Africa it never pays to be in a hurry. Too wearing on the nerves.'

After a leisurely breakfast the next morning, when there was still no sign of the mules, Nicholas fetched his rifle case.

When Nicholas lifted the weapon out of its nest of green baize, Boris took it from him and examined it minutely.

'An old rifle?'

'Made in 1926,' Nicholas nodded. 'My grandfather had it made for himself.'

'They knew how to make them in those days. Not like the mass-produced crap they turn out today.' Boris pursed his lips critically. 'Short Mauser Oberndorf double square-bridge action, beautiful! But it has been rebarrelled, no?'

'The original barrel was shot out. I had it replaced with a Shilen match barrel. It will shoot the wings off a mosquito at a hundred paces.'

'Calibre 7 x 57, is it?' Boris asked.

'275 Rigby, as a matter of fact,' Nicholas corrected him, but Boris snorted.

'It is exactly the same cartridge — just your English bloodiness must call it something else.' He grinned. 'It will push a 150 grain bullet out there at 2800 feet per second. It is a good rifle, one of the best.'

'You will never know, my dear fellow, how much your approval means to me,' Nicholas murmured in English, and Boris chuckled as he handed the rifle back to him.

'English jokes! I love your English jokes.'

When Nicholas left camp carrying the little rifle in its slip case, Royan followed him down to the river and helped him fill two small canvas bags with white river sand. He laid them on top of a convenient rock and they formed a firm but malleable rest for the rifle as he settled it over them.

Using the open hillside as a safe back-stop, he stepped out two hundred yards and at that range set up a cardboard carton on which he had taped a Bisley-type target. He came back to where Royan waited and then settled down behind the rock on which the weapon lay.

Royan was unprepared for the report of the first shot from the dainty, almost feminine-looking rifle. She jumped involuntarily, and her ears sang.

'What a horrible, vicious thing!' she exclaimed. 'How can you bring yourself to kill lovely animals with a high-powered gun like that?' she demanded.

'Rifle,' he corrected her, as he noted the strike of the shot through his binoculars. 'Would it make you feel better if I used a low-powered rifle, or beat them to death with a stick?'

The shot had struck three inches right and two inches low. As he adjusted the telescopic sight he attempted to explain. 'An ethical hunter does everything in his power to kill as swiftly and as cleanly as is possible, and that means stalking in as close as he is able to do, using a weapon of adequate power and sighting it the best way he knows how.'

His next shot struck exactly on line but only an inch above the bullseye. He wanted it to shoot three inches high at that range. He worked on the sight again.

'Gun or rifle, but I don't understand why you would want to deliberately kill any of God's creatures,' she protested.

'That I can never explain to you.' He aimed deliberately and fired once. Even through the lower magnification of the sight lens he could see that the bullet had struck exactly three inches high.

'It is something to do with an atavistic urge that few men, no matter how cultured and civilized they deem themselves, can deny completely.' He fired a second time. 'Some of them work it out in the board room, others on the golf course or the tennis court, and some of us on a salmon river, in the ocean deeps or in the hunting field.'

He fired a third shot, merely to confirm the previous two, and then went on, 'As for God's creatures, he gave them to us. You are the believer. Quote me Acts 10, verses 12 and 13.'

'Sorry.' She shook her head. 'You tell me.'

' ". . . *all manner of fourfooted beasts of the earth, and wild beasts, and creeping things, and fowls of the air*," ' Nicholas obliged her. ' "*And there came a voice to him, Rise, Peter; kill, and eat.*" '

'You should have been a lawyer,' she moaned in mock despair.

'Or a priest,' he suggested, and went forward to retrieve the target. He found that his last three shots had punched a tiny symmetrical rosette three inches above the bull, all three bullet holes just touching each other.

He patted the butt stock of the little rifle, 'That's my lovely darling, Lucrezia Borgia.' He had named the rifle for her beauty and for her murderous potential.

He slid the rifle back into its leather slip case and they walked back together. As they came in sight of the camp, Nicholas pulled up short.

'Visitors,' he said, and raised his binoculars. 'Aha! We have flushed something out of the undergrowth. That is a Pegasus truck parked there and, unless I am much mistaken, one of our visitors is the charming laddie from Abilene. Let's go down and find out what is going on.'

As they drew closer to camp, they realized

that there were a dozen or more heavily armed, uniformed soldiers clustered around the red and green Pegasus truck, and that Jake Helm and an Ethiopian army officer were seated under the awning of the dining tent in serious and intent conversation with Boris.

As soon as Nicholas entered the tent, Boris introduced him to the bespectacled Ethiopian officer. 'This is Colonel Tuma Nogo, the military commander of the southern Gojam region.'

'How do you do?' Nicholas greeted him, but the colonel ignored the pleasantry.

'I want to see your passport, and your firearms licence,' he ordered arrogantly, while Jake Helm chewed complacently on the evil-smelling butt of an extinguished cigar.

'Yes, of course,' Nicholas agreed, and went to his own tent to fetch his briefcase. He opened it on the dining table, and smiled at the officer. 'I am sure you will also want to see my letter of introduction from the British Foreign Secretary in London, and this one from the British Ambassador in Addis Ababa. Here is another from the Ethiopian Ambassador to the Court of St James, and this *firman* is from your own Minister of Defence, General Siye Abraha.'

The colonel stared in consternation at this fruit salad of ornate official letterheads and scarlet beribboned seals. Behind the gold-rimmed glasses his eyes were bemused and confused.

'Sir!' He jumped to his feet and saluted. 'You are a friend of General Abraha? I did not know.

Nobody informed me. I beg your pardon for this intrusion.'

He saluted again, and his embarrassment made him awkward and ungainly. 'I came to warn you only that the Pegasus Company is conducting drilling and blasting operations. There may be some danger. Please be alert. Also there are many bandits and outlaws, *shufta*, operating in this area.' Colonel Nogo was flustered and barely coherent. He stopped and drew a deep breath to steady himself. 'You see, I have been ordered to provide an escort for the employees of the Pegasus Company. If you yourself experience any trouble while you are here, or if you need assistance for any reason you have only to call on me, sir.'

'That is extremely civil of you, colonel.'

'I will detain you no longer, sir.' He saluted a third time and backed off towards the Pegasus truck, taking the Texan foreman along with him. Jake Helm had not uttered a word since their arrival, and now he left without a farewell.

Colonel Nogo gave Nicholas his fourth and final salute through the cab window as the truck pulled away.

'Deuce!' Nicholas told Royan, as he acknowledged the salute with a nonchalant wave. 'I think that point was definitely ours. Now at least we know that, for whatever reason, Mr Pegasus definitely does not want us in his hair. I think we can expect his next service fairly promptly.'

They walked back to where Boris sat in the

185

dining tent and Nicholas told him, 'All we need now are your mules.'

'I have sent three of my men to the village to find them. They should have been here yesterday.'

The mules arrived early the next morning, six big sturdy animals, each accompanied by a driver dressed in the ubiquitous jodhpurs and shawl. By mid-morning they were loaded and ready to begin the descent into the gorge.

Boris paused at the head of the pathway, and looked out over that valley. For once even he seemed to be subdued and awed by the immensity of the drop and the rugged splendour of the gorge.

'You will be passing into another land in another age,' he warned them in an uncharacteristically philosophical mood. 'They say that this trail is two thousand years old, as old as Christ.' He spread his hands in a deprecating gesture. 'The old black priest in the church at Debra Maryam will tell you that the Virgin Mary passed this way when she fled from Israel after the crucifixion.' He shook his head. 'But then these people will believe anything.' And he stepped out on to the pathway.

It clung to the cliff, descending at such an angle that each pace was down a rock step so deep that it stretched the tendons and the sinews in their groins and knees, and jarred their spines.

They were forced to use their hands to scramble the rougher and steeper sections, where it was almost as though they were descending a ladder.

It seemed impossible that the mules under their heavy packs could follow them down. The plucky beasts lunged down each of the rock steps, landing heavily on their forelegs, then gathered themselves for the next drop. The trail was so narrow that the bulky packs scraped against the rock wall on one hand, while on the other hand the drop sucked at them giddily.

When the path dog-legged and changed direction, the mules could not make the turn in one attempt. They were forced to back and fill, edging their way round the narrow trail, sweating with terror and their eyes rolling until the whites flashed. The drivers urged them on with wild cries and busy whips.

At places the pathway entered the body of the mountain, passing behind butts and needles of rock that time and erosion had prised away from the cliff face. These rocky gateways were so narrow that the mules had to be unloaded and the packs carried through by the drivers, and then the mules were reloaded on the far side.

'Look!' Royan cried in astonishment and pointed out into the void. A black vulture rose up out of the depths on widespread pinions and floated past them almost within arm's length, turning its gruesome naked head of pink lappeted skin to stare at them with inscrutable black eyes before sailing away.

'He is using the thermals of heated air from the valley for lift,' Nicholas explained to her. He pointed out along the cliff to an overhanging buttress on the same level as themselves. 'There is one of their nests.' It was a shaggy mound of sticks piled on an inaccessible ledge. The excrement of the birds that had inhabited it over the ages had painted the cliff face below with streaks of brilliant white, and even at this distance they could catch whiffs of rotting offal and decaying flesh.

All that day they clung to the precipitous track as they eased their way down that terrible wall. It was late afternoon, and they were only halfway down, when the trail turned back upon itself once more and they heard the rumble of the falls ahead. The sound grew louder and became a thunderous roar as they moved around the corner of another buttress and came in full sight of the falls.

The wind created by the torrent tugged at them and forced them to clutch for handholds. The spray blew around them and wetted their upturned faces, but the Ethiopian guide led them straight on until it seemed that they must be washed away into the valley still hundreds of feet below.

Then, miraculously, the waters parted and they stepped behind the great translucent curtain into a deep recess of moss-covered and gleaming wet rock, carved from the cliff by the force of water over the aeons. The only light in this gloomy place was filtered through the waterfall, green and mysterious like some undersea cavern.

'This is where we sleep tonight,' Boris announced, obviously enjoying their astonishment. He pointed to bundles of firewood piled at the rear of the cave, and the smoke-blackened wall above the stone hearth. 'The muleteers carrying food and supplies down to the priests in the monastery have used this place for centuries.'

As they moved deeper into the cavern, the sound of falling water became muted to a dull background rumble and the rock underfoot was dry. Once the servants had lit the fire, it became a warm and comfortable, not to say romantic, lodging.

With an old soldier's eye for the most comfortable spot, Nicholas laid out his sleeping bag in a corner at the back of the cave, and quite naturally Royan unrolled hers beside his. They were both tired out by the unusual exertion of climbing down the cliff wall, and after supper they stretched out in their sleeping bags in companionable silence and watched the firelight playing on the roof of the cave.

'Just think!' Royan whispered. 'Tomorrow we will be retracing the footsteps of old Taita himself.'

'To say nothing of the Virgin Mary,' Nicholas smiled.

'You are a horrid old cynic,' she sighed. 'And what is more, you probably snore.'

'You are about to find out the hard way,'

he told her, but she was asleep before him. Her breathing was gentle and even, and he could just hear it above the sound of the water. It was a long time since he had had a lovely woman lying at his side. When he was sure she was deeply under, he reached across and touched her cheek gently.

'Pleasant dreams, little one,' he whispered tenderly. 'You have had a busy day.' That was the way he had often bid his younger daughter sleep.

The muleteers were stirring long before the dawn, and the whole party was on the pathway again as soon as the light was strong enough to reveal their footing. When the early sun struck the upper walls of the cliff face, they were still high enough above the valley floor to have an aerial view of the terrain. Nicholas drew Royan aside and they let the rest of the caravan go on down ahead of them.

He found a place to sit and unrolled the satellite photograph between them. Picking out the major peaks and features of the scene, they orientated themselves and began to make some order out of the cataclysmic landscape that rioted below them.

'We can't see the Abbay river from here,' Nicholas pointed out. 'It's still deep in the subgorge. We will probably only get our first glimpse of it from almost directly above.'

'If we have identified our present position accurately, then the river will make two ox-bow bends around that bluff over there.'

'Yes, and the confluence of the Dandera river with the Abbay is over there, below those cliffs.' He used his thumb knuckle as a rough scale measure. 'About fifteen miles from here.'

'It looks as though the Dandera has changed its course many times over the centuries. I can see at least two gullies that look like ancient river beds.' She pointed down: 'There, and there. They are all choked with jungle now.' She looked crestfallen, 'Oh, Nicholas, it is such a huge and confused area. How are we ever going to find the single entrance to a tomb hidden in all that?'

'Tomb? What tomb is this?' Boris demanded with interest. He had come back up the trail to find them. They had not heard his approach, and now he stood over them. 'What tomb are you talking about?'

'Why, the tomb of St Frumentius, of course,' Nicholas told him smoothly, showing no concern at having been overheard.

'Isn't the monastery dedicated to the saint?' Royan asked as smoothly, as she rolled up the photograph.

'*Da.*' He nodded, looking disappointed, as though he expected something of more interest. 'Yes, St Frumentius. But they will not let you visit the tomb. They will not let you into the inner part of the monastery. Only the priests are allowed in there.'

He removed his cap and scratched the short, stiff bristles that covered his scalp. They rasped like wire under his fingernails. 'This week is the ceremony of Timkat, the Blessing of the Tabot. There will be a great deal of excitement down there. You will find it very interesting, but you will not be able to enter the Holy of Holies, nor will you be able to see the actual tomb. I have never met any white man who has seen it.'

He squinted up at the sun. 'We must get on. It looks close, but it will take us two more days to reach the Abbay. It is bad ground down there. A long march, even for a famous dik-dik hunter.' He laughed delightedly at his own joke, and turned away down the path.

As they approached the bottom of the cliff, the gradient of the trail smoothed out and the steps became shallower and further apart. The going became easier and their progress swifter, but the air had changed in quality and taste. It was no longer cool, bracing mountain air but the languid, enervating air of the equator, with the smell and taste of the encroaching jungle.

'Hot!' said Royan, shrugging out of the woollen shawl.

'Ten degrees hotter, at least,' Nicholas agreed. He pulled his old army jersey over his head, leaving his hair in curly disarray. 'And we can expect it to get hotter before we reach the

Abbay. We still have to descend another three thousand feet.'

Now the path followed the Dandera river for a while. Sometimes they were several hundred feet above it, and shortly afterwards they splashed waist-deep through a ford, hanging on to the panniers of the mules to keep themselves from being swept away on the flood.

Then the gorge of the Dandera river was too deep and steep to follow any longer, as sheer cliffs dropped into dark pools. So they left the river and followed the track that squirmed like a dying snake amongst eroded hills and tall red stone bluffs.

A mile or two further downstream they rejoined the river in a different mood as it rippled through dense forest. The dangling lianas swept the surface and tree moss brushed their heads as they passed, straggling and unkempt as the beard of the old priest at Debra Maryam. Vervet monkeys chattered at them from the treetops and ducked their heads in wide-eyed outrage at the human intrusion into these secret places. Once a large animal crashed away through the undergrowth, and Nicholas glanced across at Boris.

The Russian shook his head, laughing. 'No, English, not dik-dik. Only kudu.'

On the hillside above them the kudu paused to look back. He was a large bull with full twists to his wide corkscrew horns, a magnificent beast with a maned dewlap and pricked ears shaped like trumpets. He stared at them with huge, startled eyes. Boris whistled softly and his attitude changed abruptly.

'Those horns are over fifty inches. They would get a place right at the top of *Rowland Ward*.' He was referring to the register of big game which was the Bible of the trophy hunter. 'Don't you want to take him, English?' He ran to the nearest mule and pulled the Rigby rifle from its slip case, then ran back and offered it to Nicholas.

'Let him go.' Nicholas shook his head. 'Only dik-dik for me.'

With a flirt of his white powder-puff tail, the bull was gone over the ridge. Boris shook his head disgustedly and spat into the river.

'Why did he try to insist that you kill it?' Royan demanded as they went on.

'A photograph of a record pair of horns like that would look good on his advertising brochure. Suck in more clients.'

All day they followed the winding trail, and in the late afternoon they camped in a clearing above the river where it was evident that other caravans had camped many times before them. It seemed obvious that this road was divided into time-honoured stages: every traveller took three full days from the top of the falls to reach the monastery, and they all camped at the same sites.

'Sorry. No shower here,' Boris told his clients. 'If you want to wash, there is a safe pool around

194

the first bend upstream.'

Royan looked appealingly at Nicholas, 'I am so hot and sweaty. Please won't you stand guard for me, where you can hear me call if I need you?'

So he lay on the mossy bank just below the bend, out of sight but close enough to hear her splash and squeal at the cold embrace of the water. Once when he turned his head he realized that the current must have drifted her downstream, for through the trees he caught a flash of a naked back, and the curve of a buttock, creamy and glistening wet with water. He looked away again guiltily, but he was startled by the intensity of his physical arousal brought on by that brief glimpse of lambent skin dappled with the late sunlight through the trees.

When she came downstream along the bank, singing softly, towelling her wet hair, she called to him, 'Your turn. Do you want me to stand guard for you?'

'I am a big boy now.' He shook his head, but as she passed him he noticed the saucy glint in her eye, and he wondered suddenly if she had been fully aware of just how far downstream she had swum, and how much he had seen. He was titillated by the thought.

He went upstream to the pool alone, and as he stripped he looked down at himself and felt guilty when he saw how she had moved him. Since Rosalind, no other woman had had this effect on him.

'A nice cold plunge won't do you any harm, my lad.' He threw his jeans over a bush, and dived into the pool.

As they sat at the campfire after the evening meal, Nicholas looked up suddenly and cocked his head.

'Am I hearing things?' he wondered.

'No,' Tessay laughed. 'That is singing you hear. The priests from the monastery are coming to welcome us.'

They saw the torches then, winding up the hillside in procession, flickering through the trees as they approached the camp. The muleteers and the servants crowded forward, singing and clapping rhythmically to greet the deputation from the monastery.

The deep male voices soared and then dropped away, almost to a whisper, then rose again in descant, haunting and beautiful, the sound of Africa in the night. It drove icy thrills down Nicholas's spine, so that he shivered involuntarily.

Then they saw the white robes of the priests, flitting like moths in the torchlight as they wound along the trail. The camp servants fell on their knees as the first of the holy men entered the perimeter of the camp. They were young acolytes, bare-headed and bare-footed. They were followed by the monks, wearing long robes

196

and tall turbans. Their ranks wheeled aside and opened up, an honour guard for the phalanx of deacons and fully ordained priests in their gaudy embroidered robes and vestments.

Each of them carried a heavy Coptic cross, set on a tall staff and intricately chased and worked in native silver. They in turn opened into two ranks, still chanting, and allowed the canopied palanquin to be carried forward by four hefty young acolytes and placed in the centre of the camp. The crimson and yellow silk curtains shimmered in the light of the camp lanterns and the torches of the procession.

'We must go forward to welcome the abbot,' Boris told Nicholas in a stage whisper. 'His name is Jali Hora.' As they stepped up to the litter, the curtains were drawn dramatically aside and a tall figure stepped down to earth.

Both Tessay and Royan sank to their knees respectfully, and clasped their hands at the breast. However, Nicholas and Boris remained on their feet, and Nicholas inspected the abbot with interest.

Jali Hora was skeletally thin. Beneath the skirts of his robe his legs were like sticks of cured tobacco, tar-black and twisted, with desiccated sinew and stringy muscle. His robe was green and gold, worked with gold thread that glittered in the firelight. On his head he wore a tall hat with a flat top embroidered with a pattern of crosses and stars.

The abbot's face was dead sooty black, the

skin wrinkled and riven with the deep etchings of age. There were few teeth behind his puckered lips, and even those were yellowed and askew. His beard was startling silver white, breaking like storm surf on the old bones of his jaw. One eye was opaque blue and blinded with tropical ophthalmia, but the other eye glistened like that of a hunting leopard.

He began to speak in a high, quavering voice. 'A blessing,' Boris warned Nicholas, and they both bowed their heads respectfully. The assembled priests came in with the chanted response each time the old man paused.

When at last he had finished giving his blessing Jali Hora made the sign of the cross in four directions, rotating slowly towards each point of the compass, while two altar boys swung their silver censers vigorously, deluging the night with pungent clouds of incense smoke.

After the blessing the two women came forward to kneel before the abbot. He stooped over them and struck them lightly on each cheek with his silver cross, chanting a falsetto blessing over them.

'They say the old man is over a hundred years old,' Boris whispered to Nicholas.

Two white-robed *debteras* brought forward a stool of African ebony, so beautifully carved that Nicholas eyed it acquisitively. He guessed that it was probably centuries old, and would have made a handsome addition to the museum collection. The two *debteras* took Jali Hora's elbows and gently seated him on the stool. Then the rest of the company sank to the earth in a congregation around him, their black faces lifted towards him attentively.

Tessay sat at his feet, and when her husband spoke she translated quietly for him into Amharic. 'It is a great pleasure and an honour for me to greet you again, Holy Father.'

The old man nodded, and Boris went on, 'I have brought an English nobleman of royal blood to visit the monastery of St Frumentius.'

'I say, steady on, old boy!' Nicholas protested, but all the congregation studied him with expectant interest.

'What do I do now?' he asked Boris out of the corner of his mouth.

'What do you think he came all this way for?' Boris grinned maliciously. 'He wants a gift. Money.'

'Maria Theresa dollars?' he enquired, referring to the centuries-old traditional currency of Ethiopia.

'Not necessarily. Times have changed. Jali Hora will be happy to take Yankee green-backs.'

'How much?'

'You are a nobleman of royal blood. You will be hunting in his valley. Five hundred dollars at least.'

Nicholas winced and went to fetch his bag from one of the mule panniers. When he came back he bowed to the abbot and placed the sheaf of currency in his outstretched, pink-palmed claw. The abbot smiled, exposing the yellow stumps of his teeth, and spoke briefly.

Tessay translated for him, 'He says, "Welcome to the monastery of St Frumentius and the season of Timkat." He wishes you good hunting on the banks of the Abbay river.'

Immediately the solemn mood of the devout company changed. They broke out in smiles and laughter, and the abbot looked expectantly at Boris.

'The holy abbot says it has been a thirsty journey,' Tessay translated.

'The old devil loves his brandy,' Boris explained, and shouted to the camp butler. With some ceremony a bottle of brandy was brought and placed on the camp table in front of the abbot, shoulder to shoulder with the bottle of vodka in front of Boris. They toasted each other, and the abbot tossed back a dram that made his good eye weep with tears, and his voice husky as he directed a question at Royan.

'He asks you, Woizero Royan, where do you come from, daughter, that you follow the true path of Christ the Saviour of man?'

'I am an Egyptian, of the old religion,' Royan replied. The abbot and all his priests nodded and beamed with approval.

'We are all brothers and sisters in Christ, the Egyptians and the Ethiopians,' the abbot told her. 'Even the word Coptic derives from the Greek for Egyptian. For over sixteen hundred years the Abuna, the bishop, of Ethiopia was

200

always appointed by the Patriarch in Cairo. Only the Emperor Haile Selassie changed that in 1959, but we still follow the true road to Christ. You are welcome, my daughter.'

His *debtera* poured another dram of brandy and the old man swallowed it at a gulp. Even Boris looked impressed, 'Where does the skinny old black tortoise put it?' he wondered aloud. Tessay did not translate, but she lowered her eyes and the hurt she felt for the insult to the holy man showed on her madonna features.

Jali Hora turned to Nicholas. 'He wants to know what animals you have come to hunt here in his valley,' Tessay told him.

Nicholas steeled himself and then replied carefully. There was a long moment of disbelief, then the abbot cackled happily and the assembled priests shouted with incredulous mirth.

'A dik-dik! You have come to hunt a dik-dik! But there is no meat on an animal that size.'

Nicholas let them get over the first shock, and then produced a photograph of the mounted specimen of *Madoqua harperii* from the museum. He placed it on the table in front of Jali Hora.

'This is no ordinary dik-dik. It is a holy dik-dik,' he told them in portentous tones, nodding at Tessay for the translation. 'Let me recount the legend.' They were silenced by the prospect of a good story with religious overtones. Even the abbot arrested the glass on its way to his lips and replaced it on the table. His one eye swivelled from the photograph to Nicholas's face.

'When John the Baptist was dying of starvation in the desert,' Nicholas began, and a few of the priests crossed themselves at the mention of the saint's name, 'he had been thirty days and thirty nights without a morsel passing his lips —' Nicholas spun out the yarn for a while, dwelling on the extremities of hunger endured by the saint, details savoured by his audience who liked their holy men to suffer in the name of righteousness.

'In the end the Lord took mercy on his servant and placed a small antelope in a thicket of acacia, held fast by the thorns. He said unto the saint: "I have prepared a meal for you that you shall not die. Take of this meat and eat." Where John the Baptist touched the small creature, the marks of his thumb and fingers were imprinted upon its back for all time, and all generations to come.' They were silent and impressed.

Nicholas passed the photograph to the abbot. 'See the prints of the saint's fingers upon it.'

The old man studied the print avidly, holding it up to his single eye, and at last he exclaimed, 'It is true. The marks of the saint's fingers are clear to see.'

He passed it to his deacons. Encouraged by the abbot's endorsement, they exclaimed and wondered over the picture of the insignificant creature in its coat of striped fur.

'Have any of your men ever laid eyes upon

202

one of these animals?' Nicholas demanded, and one after the other they shook their heads. The photograph completed the circle and was passed to the rank of squatting acolytes.

Suddenly one of them leaped to his feet prancing, brandishing the photograph and gibbering with excitement.

'I have seen this holy creature! With my very own eyes, I have seen it.' He was a young boy, barely adolescent.

There were cries of derision and disbelief from the others. One of them snatched the print from the boy's grasp and waved it out of his reach, taunting him with it.

'The child is soft in the head, and often possessed by demons and fits,' Jali Hora explained sorrowfully. 'Take no notice of him, poor Tamre!'

Tamre's eyes were wild as he ran down the rank of acolytes, trying desperately to recapture the photograph. But they passed it back and forth, keeping it just out of his reach, teasing him and jeering at his antics.

Nicholas rose to his feet to intervene. He found this taunting of a weak-minded lad offensive, but at that moment something tripped in the boy's mind, and he fell to the ground as though struck down by a club. His back arched and his limbs twitched and jerked uncontrollably, his eyes rolled back into his skull until only the whites showed, and white froth creamed on his lips that were drawn back in a grinning rictus.

Before Nicholas could go to him, four of his peers picked him up bodily and carried him away. Their laughter dwindled into the night. The others acted as though this was nothing out of the ordinary, and Jali Hora nodded to his *debtera* to refill his glass.

It was late when at last Jali Hora took his leave and was helped into the palanquin by his deacons. He took the remains of the brandy with him, clutching the half-empty bottle in one clawed hand and tossing out benedictions with the other.

'You made a good impression, Milord English,' Boris told him. 'He liked your story of John the Baptist, but he liked your money even more.'

When they set out the next morning, the path followed the river for a while. But within a mile the waters quickened their pace, and then raced through the narrow opening between high red cliffs and plunged over another waterfall.

Nicholas left the well-trodden trail and went down to the brink of the falls. He looked down two hundred feet into a deep cleft in the rock, only just wide enough to allow the angry river to squeeze through. He could have thrown a stone across the gap. There was no path nor foothold in that chasm, and he turned back and rejoined the rest of the caravan as it detoured away from the river and into another thickly wooded valley.

'This was probably once the course of the Dandera river, before it cut a fresh bed for itself through the chasm.' Royan pointed to the high ground on each side of the path, and then to the water-worn boulders that littered the trail.

'I think you are right,' Nicholas agreed. 'These cliffs seem to be an intrusion of limestone through the basalt and sandstone. The whole area has been severely faulted and cut up by erosion and the ever-changing river. You can be certain that those limestone cliffs are riddled with caves and springs.'

Now the trail descended rapidly towards the Blue Nile, falling away almost fifteen hundred feet in altitude in the last few miles. The sides of the valley were heavily covered with vegetation and at many places small springs of water oozed from the limestone and trickled down the old river bed.

The heat built up steadily as they went down, and soon even Royan's khaki shirt was stained with dark patches of sweat between her shoulder blades.

At one stage a freshet of clear water gushed from an area of dense bush high up the hillside and swelled the stream into a small river. Then they turned a corner of the valley and found that they and the stream had rejoined the main flow of the Dandera river. Looking back up the gorge, they could see where the river had emerged from the chasm through a narrow archway in the cliff. The rock surrounding the cleft was a peculiar pink in colour, smooth and polished, folded back upon itself so that it resembled the mucous membrane on the inside of a pair of human lips.

The rock was of such an unusual colour and texture that they were both struck by it. They turned aside to study it while the mules went on downwards, the clatter of their receding hoofbeats and the voices of the men echoing and reverberating weirdly in this confined and unearthly place.

'It looks like some monstrous gargoyle, gushing water through its mouth,' Royan whispered, looking up at the cleft and at those strange rock formations. 'I can imagine how the ancient Egyptians, led by Taita and Prince Memnon, would have been moved if they had ever reached this place. What mystical connotations would they have attributed to such a natural phenomenon.'

Nicholas was silent, studying her face. Her eyes were dark with awe, and her expression solemn. In this setting she reminded him strongly of a portrait that he had in his collection at Quenton Park. It was a fragment of a fresco from the Valley of the Kings, depicting a Ramessidian princess.

'Why should that surprise you?' he asked himself. 'The very same blood runs in her veins.'

She turned to face him, 'Give me hope, Nicky. Tell me that I have not dreamed all this. Tell me that we are going to find what we are looking for, and that we are going to vindicate Duraid's death.'

Her face was up-turned to his, and it seemed to glow under the light dew of perspiration and the strength of her commitment. He was seized by an almost overwhelming urge to take her up in his arms and kiss those moistly parted lips, but instead he turned away and started down the trail.

He dared not look back at her until he had himself fully under control. After a while he heard her quick, light tread on the rock behind him. They went on down in silence, and he was so preoccupied that he was unprepared for the sudden stunning vista that opened abruptly before them.

They stood high on a ledge above the sub-gorge of the Nile. Below them was a mighty cauldron of red rock five hundred feet deep. The main flow of the legendary river plunged in a green torrent into the shadowy abyss. It was so deep that the sunlight did not reach down into it. Beside them the sparser waters of the Dandera river took the same leap, falling white as an egret's feather, twisting and blowing in the false wind of the gorge. In the depths the waters mingled, churning and roiling together in a welter of foam, turning upon themselves like a great wheel, weighty and viscous as oil, until at last they found the exit gorge and tore away down it with irresistible force and power.

'You sailed through that in a boat?' Royan asked, with awe in her voice.

'We were young and foolish, then,' Nicholas said with a sad little smile that was haunted by old memories.

They were silent for a long while. Then Royan said softly, 'One can see how this would have stopped Taita and his prince as they came up-stream.' She looked about her, and then pointed down the gorge towards the west. 'They certainly could never have come up the sub-gorge itself. They must have followed the line of the top of the cliffs, right along here where we are standing.' Her voice took on an edge of excitement at the thought.

'Unless they came up the other side of the river,' Nicholas suggested to tease her, and her face fell.

'I hadn't thought of that. Of course it's possible. How would we ever cross over, if we find no evidence on this side?'

'Let's consider that only when it's forced upon us. We have enough to contend with as it is, without looking for more hardships.'

Again they were silent, both of them considering the magnitude and uncertainty of the task that they had taken on. Then Royan roused herself.

'Where is the monastery? I can see no sign of it.'

'It's in the cliff right under our feet.'

'Will we camp down there?'

'I doubt it. Let's catch up with Boris and find out what he intends to do.'

They followed the trail along the edge of the cauldron, and came up with the mule caravan at a spot where the track forked. One branch turned away from the river into a wooded depression, while the other still hugged the rimrock.

Boris was waiting for them, and he indicated the track that led away from the river. 'There is a good campsite up there in the trees where I stayed last time I hunted down here.'

There were several tall wild fig trees throwing shade across this glade, and a spring of fresh water at the head. To minimize the loads, Boris had not carried tents down into the gorge. So as soon as the mules were unloaded he set his men to building three small thatched huts for their accommodation, and to digging a pit latrine well away from the spring.

While this work was going on, Nicholas beckoned to Royan and Tessay, and the three of them set off to explore the monastery. Where the trail forked, Tessay led them along the path that skirted the cliff top, and soon they came to a broad rock staircase that descended the cliff face.

There was a party of white-robed monks coming up the stone stairway, and Tessay stopped briefly to chat to them. As they went on she told Nicholas and Royan, 'Today is Katera, the eve of the festival of Timkat, which begins tomorrow. They are very excited. It is one of the major events of the religious year.'

'What does the festival celebrate?' Royan asked. 'It is not part of the Church calendar in Egypt.'

'It's the Ethiopian Epiphany, celebrating the baptism of Christ,' Tessay explained. 'During the ceremony the *tabot* will be taken down to the river to be rededicated and revitalized, and the acolytes will receive baptism, as did Jesus Christ at the hand of the Baptist.'

They followed the staircase down the sheer cliff face. The treads of the steps had been dished by the passage of bare feet over the centuries. Down they went, with the great cauldron of the Nile boiling and hissing and steaming with spray hundreds of feet below them.

Suddenly they came out on to a wide terrace that had been hewn by man's hand from the living rock. The red rock overhung it, forming a roof to the cloister with arches of stone left in place by the ancient builders to support it. The interior wall of the long covered terrace was riddled with the entrances to the catacombs beyond. Over the ages the cliff face had been mined and burrowed to form the halls and cells, the vestibules, churches and shrines of the monastic community which had inhabited them for well over a thousand years.

There were groups of monks seated along the

length of the terrace. Some of them were listening to one of the deacons reading aloud from an illuminated copy of the scriptures.

'So many of them are illiterate,' Tessay sighed. 'The Bible must be read and explained to even the monks, for most of them are unable to read it for themselves.'

'This was what the Church of Constantine was like, the Church of Byzantium,' Nicholas pointed out quietly. 'It remains the Church of cross and book, of elaborate and sumptuous ritual in a predominantly illiterate world today.'

As they wandered slowly down the cloister they passed other seated groups who, under the direction of a precentor, were chanting and singing the Amharic psalms and hymns. From the interior of the cells and caves there came the hum of voices raised in prayer or supplication, and the air was thick with the smell of human occupation that had taken place over hundreds of years.

It was the smell of wood smoke and incense, of stale food and excrement, of sweat and piety, of suffering and of sickness. Amongst the groups of monks were the pilgrims who had made the journey, or been carried by their relatives, down into the gorge to make petition to the saint, or to seek from him a cure for their disease and suffering.

There were blind children weeping in their mothers' arms, and lepers with the flesh rotting and falling from their bones, and still others

211

in the coma of sleeping sickness or some other terrible tropical affliction. Their whines and moans of agony blended with the chanting of the monks, and with the distant clamour of the Nile as it cascaded into the cauldron.

They came at last to the entrance to the cavern cathedral of St Frumentius. It was a circular opening like the mouth of a fish, but the surrounds of the portals were painted with a dense border of stars and crosses, and of saintly heads. The portraits were primitive, and rendered in ochre and soft earthy tones that were all the more appealing for their childlike simplicity. The eyes of the saints were huge and outlined in charcoal, their expressions tranquil and benign.

A deacon in a grubby green velvet robe guarded the entrance, but when Tessay spoke to him he smiled and nodded and gestured for them to enter. The lintel was low and Nicholas had to duck his head to pass under it, but on the far side he raised it again to look about him in amazement.

The roof of the cavern was so high that it was lost in the gloom. The rock walls were covered with murals, a celestial host of angels and archangels who flickered and wavered in the light of the candles and oil lamps. They were partially obscured by the long tapestry banners that hung down the walls, grimy with incense soot, their fringes frayed and tattered. On one of these St Michael rode a prancing white horse, on another the Virgin knelt at the foot of the cross, while above her the pale body of Christ bled from the wound of the Roman spear in his side.

This was the outer nave of the church. In the far wall the doorway to the middle chamber was guarded by a massive pair of wooden doors that stood open. The three of them crossed the stone floor, picking their way between the kneeling petitioners and pilgrims in their rags and tatters, in their misery and their religious ecstasy. In the feeble light of the lamps and the blue haze of incense smoke they seemed lost souls languishing eternally in the outer darkness of purgatory.

The visitors reached the set of three stone steps that led up to the inner doors, but their way was blocked at the threshold by two robed deacons in tall, flat-topped hats. One of these addressed Tessay sternly.

'They will not even let us enter the *qiddist,* the middle chamber,' Tessay told them regretfully. 'Beyond that lies the *maqdas,* the Holy of Holies.'

They peered past the guards, and in the gloom of the *qiddist* could just make out the door to the inner sanctum.

'Only the ordained priests are allowed to enter the *maqdas,* for it contains the *tabot* and the entrance to the tomb of the saint.'

Disappointed and frustrated, they made their way out of the cavern and back along the terrace.

They ate their dinner under a sky full of stars. The air was still stiflingly hot, and clouds of mosquitoes hovered just out of range of the repellents with which they had all smeared their exposed skin.

'And so, English, I have got you where you wanted to be. Now, how are you going to find this animal that you have come so far to hunt?' The vodka was making Boris belligerent again.

'At first light I want you to send out your trackers to work the country downstream from here,' Nicholas told him. 'Dik-dik are usually active in the early morning, and again late in the afternoon.'

'You are teaching your grandpapa to skin a cat,' said Boris, mangling the metaphor. He poured himself another vodka.

'Tell them to check for spoor.' Nicholas deliberately laboured his point. 'I imagine that the tracks of the striped variety will look very similar to those of the common dik-dik. If they find indications, then they must sit quietly along the edge of the thickest patches of bush and watch for any movement of the animals. Dik-dik are very territorial. They won't stray far from their own turf.'

'*Da! Da!* I will tell them. But what will you do? Will you spend the day in camp with the ladies, English?' He grinned slyly. 'If you are

lucky, you may soon not need separate huts?'
He guffawed at his own wit, and Tessay looked
distressed and stood up with the excuse that
she was going to the kitchen hut to supervise
the chef.

Nicholas ignored the boorish pleasantry.
'Royan and I will work the riverine bush along
the banks of the Dandera river. It looked very
promising habitat for dik-dik. Warn your people
to keep clear of the river. I don't want the
game disturbed.'

They left camp the next morning in the glimmer of the dawn. Nicholas carried the Rigby
rifle and a light day pack, and led Royan along
the bank of the Dandera. They moved slowly,
stopping every dozen paces to look and listen.
The thickets were alive with the sounds and
movements of the small mammals and birds.

'The Ethiopians do not have a hunting tradition, and I imagine the monks never disturb
the wildlife here in the gorge.' He pointed to
the tracks of a small antelope in the moist earth
of the bank. 'Bushbuck,' he told her. 'Menelik's
bushbuck. Unique to this part of the world.
A much sought-after trophy.'

'Do you really expect to find your great-
grandfather's dik-dik?' she asked. 'You seemed
so determined when you discussed it with Boris.'

'Of course not,' he grinned. 'I think the old
man made it up. It should rather have been
named Harper's chimera. It probably was the
skin of a striped mongoose that he used after

215

all. We Harpers didn't get on in the world by always sticking to the literal truth.'

They paused to watch a Tacazze sunbird fluttering over a bunch of yellow blossoms on a creeper high above them in the canopy of the riverine forest. The tiny bird's plumage sparkled like a tiara of emeralds.

'Still, it gives us a wonderful excuse to fossick about in the bushes.' He glanced back to make certain that they were well clear of the camp, and then gestured for her to sit beside him on a fallen treetrunk. 'So, let's get it clear in our minds what we are looking for. You tell me.'

'We are looking for the remains of a funerary temple, or the ruins of the necropolis where the workers lived while they were excavating Pharaoh Mamose's tomb.'

'Any sort of masonry or stonework,' he agreed, 'especially some sort of column or monument.'

'Taita's stone testament,' she nodded. 'It should be engraved or chiselled with hieroglyphics. Probably badly weathered, fallen over, covered with vegetation — I don't know. Anything at all. We are fishing blind in dark waters.'

'Well, why are we still sitting here? Let's start fishing.'

In the middle of the morning Nicholas found the tracks of a dik-dik along the river bank. They took up a position against the bole of one of the big trees and sat quietly for a while in the shadows of the forest, until at last they were rewarded by a glimpse of one of the tiny creatures. It passed close to where they sat, wriggling its trunklike proboscis, stepping daintily on elfin hooves, nipping a leaf from a low-hanging branch, and munching it busily. However, its coat was a uniform drab grey, unrelieved by stripes of any kind.

When it disappeared into the undergrowth, Nicholas stood up. 'No luck. Common variety,' he whispered. 'Let's get on.'

A little after noon they reached the spot where the river issued from between the pink flesh-coloured cliffs of the chasm. They explored these as far as they were able before their way was blocked by the cliffs. The rock fell straight into the flood, and there was no foothold at the water's edge that would allow them to penetrate further.

They retreated downstream, and crossed to the far bank over a primitive suspension bridge of lianas and hairy flax rope that Nicholas guessed had been built by the monks from the monastery. Once again they tried to push on into the chasm. Nicholas even attempted to wade around the first buttress of pink rock that barred the way, but the current was too strong and threatened to sweep him off his feet. He was forced to abandon the attempt.

'If we can't get through there, then it's highly unlikely that Taita and his workmen would have done so.'

They went back as far as the hanging bridge

and found a shady place close to the water to eat the lunch that Tessay had packed for them. The heat in the middle of the day was stupefying. Royan wet her cotton neckerchief in the river and dabbed at her face as she lay beside him.

Nicholas lay on his back and studied every inch of the pink cliffs through his binoculars. He was looking for any cleft or opening in their smooth polished surfaces.

He spoke without lowering the binoculars. 'Reading *River God*, it looks as if Taita actually enlisted help to switch the bodies of Tanus, Great Lion of Egypt, and the Pharaoh himself.' He lowered the glasses and looked at Royan. 'I find that puzzling, for it would have been an outrageous thing to do in terms of his period and belief. Is that a fair translation of the scrolls? Did Taita truly switch the bodies?'

She laughed and rolled over to face him. 'Your old chum Wilbur has an overheated imagination. The only basis for that whole bit of story-telling is a single line in the scrolls. *"To me he was more a king than ever Pharaoh had been."*' She rolled on to her back again. 'That is a good example of my objection to the book. He mixes fact and fantasy into an inextricable stew. As far as I know and believe, Tanus rests in his own tomb and the Pharaoh in his.'

'Pity!' Nicholas sighed and stuffed the book back in his pack. 'It was a romantic little touch that I enjoyed.' He glanced at his wrist-watch and stood up. 'Come on, I want to do a recce down the other spur of the valley. I spotted some interesting ground up there whilst we were on the approach march yesterday.'

It was late afternoon when they arrived back at the camp, and Tessay hurried out of her kitchen hut to greet them.

'I have been waiting for you to return. We have had an interesting invitation from Jali Hora, the abbot. He has invited us to a banquet in the monastery to celebrate Katera, the eve of Timkat. The servants have set up your shower, and the water is hot. There is just time for you to change before we go down to the monastery.'

The abbot sent a party of young acolytes to escort them to the banqueting hall. These young men arrived in the short African twilight, carrying torches to light the way.

Royan recognized one of these as Tamre, the epileptic boy. When she singled him out for her warmest smile, he came forward shyly and offered her a bouquet of wild flowers that he had picked from beside the river. She was unprepared for this courtesy, and without thinking she thanked him in Arabic.

'Shukran.'

'Taffadali,' the boy replied immediately, using the correct gender of the response, and in an accent that told her instantly that he was fluent in her language.

'How do you speak Arabic so well?' she asked, intrigued.

The boy hung his head with embarrassment and mumbled, 'My mother is from Massawa, on the Red Sea. It is the language of my childhood.'

When they set off for the monastery, the boy monk followed Royan like a puppy.

Once more they descended the stairway down the cliff and came out on to the torchlit terrace. The narrow cloisters were packed with humanity, and as they made their way through the press, with the honour guard of acolytes clearing a way for them, black faces called Amharic greetings and black hands reached out to touch them.

They stooped through the low entrance to the outer nave of the cathedral. The chamber was lit with oil lamps and torches, so that the murals of saints and angels danced in the uncertain light. The stone floor was covered with a carpet of freshly cut reeds and rushes, their sweet herbal perfume leavening the heavy, smoky air. It seemed that the entire brotherhood of monks were seated cross-legged on this spongy carpet. They greeted the entrance of the little party of *ferengi* with cries of welcome and shouts of benediction. Beside each seated figure stood a flask of *tej*, the honey mead of the country. It was clear from the happy, sweaty faces that the flasks had already done good service.

The visitors were led forward to a spot that had been left clear for them directly in front of the wooden doors to the *qiddist*, the middle chamber. Their escort urged them to sit and make themselves comfortable in this space. As soon as they were settled, another party of acolytes came in from the terrace bearing flasks of *tej*, and knelt to place a separate pottery flask in front of each of them.

Tessay leaned across to whisper, 'Better you let me sample this *tej* before you try it. The strength and colour and taste vary in every place that it is served, and some of it is ferocious.' She raised her flask and drank directly from the elongated neck. When she lowered the flask she smiled, 'This is a good brew. If you are careful, you will be all right with it.'

The monks seated around them were urging them to drink, and Nicholas raised his flask. The monks clapped and laughed as he tasted the liquor. It was light and pleasant, with a strong bouquet of wild honey. 'Not bad!' he gave his opinion, but Tessay warned him, 'Later they will almost certainly offer you *katikala*. Be very careful of that! It is distilled from fermented grain and it will take your head off at the shoulders.'

The monks were concentrating their hospitality on Royan now. The fact that she was a Coptic Christian, a true believer, had impressed them. It was obvious also that her beauty had not gone entirely unremarked by this company of holy and celibate men.

Nicholas leaned close to her, and whispered, 'You will have to fake it for their benefit. Hold it up to your lips and pretend to swallow, or they will not leave you in peace.'

As she lifted the flask the monks hooted with delight and saluted her with their own upraised flasks. She lowered the flask again, and whispered to Nicholas.

'It's delicious. It tastes of honey.'

'You broke your vow of abstinence!' he chided her laughing. 'Did you?'

'Just a drop,' she admitted, 'and anyway I never made any vows.'

The acolytes knelt in turn in front of each guest, offering them a bowl of hot water in which to wash their right hands in preparation for the feast.

Suddenly there was the sound of music and drums, and a band of musicians filed through the open doors of the *qiddist*. They took up their positions along the side walls of the chamber, while the congregation craned expectantly to peer into its dim interior.

At last Jali Hora, the ancient abbot, appeared at the head of the steps. He wore a full-length robe of crimson satin, with a gold thread-embroidered stole around his shoulders. On his head was a massive crown. Though it glittered like gold, Nicholas knew that it was gilt brass, and the multi-coloured stones with which it was set were just as certainly glass and paste.

Jali Hora raised his crook, which was surmounted by an ornate silver cross, and a weighty silence fell upon the company.

'Now he will say the grace,' Tessay told them, and bowed her head.

Jali Hora's grace was fervent and lengthy, his reedy falsetto punctuated by devout responses from the monks. When at last he came to the end, two splendidly robed *debteras* helped Jali Hora down the stairs and seated him on his carved *jimmera* stool at the head of the circle of senior deacons and priests.

The religious mood of the monks changed to one of festive bonhomie as a procession of acolytes entered from the terrace, each of them bearing upon his head a flat woven reed basket the size of a wagon wheel. They placed one of these in the centre of each circle of guests.

Then at a signal from Jali Hora, acting in unison they whipped the lid off each basket. A jovial cheer went up from the monks, for each basket contained a shallow brass bowl that was filled from rim to rim with round sheets of the flat grey unleavened *injera* bread.

Two acolytes staggered in from the terrace, barely able to carry between them a steaming brass pot filled with gallons of *wat,* a spicy stew of fat mutton. Over each of the bowls of *injera* bread they tipped the great pot and slopped gouts of the runny red-brown *wat,* the surface glistening with hot grease.

The assembly fell on the food voraciously.

They tore off wads of *injera* and scooped up the mess of *wat* with it, and then stuffed the parcel into their open mouths, which remained open as they chewed. They washed it down with long swallows from the *tej* flasks, before wrapping themselves another parcel of running *wat*. Soon every one of them was greasy to the elbow and their chins were smeared thickly, as they chewed and drank and shouted with laughter.

The serving acolytes dumped thick cakes of another type of *injera* beside each guest. These were stiffer and less yeasty in taste, friable and crumbling, unlike the latex rubber consistency of the thin grey sheets of the first kind.

Nicholas and Royan tried to show their appreciation of the food without coating themselves with layers of it as the others were doing. Despite its appearance the *wat* was really rather tasty, and the dry yellow *injera* helped to cut the grease.

The communal brass bowls were emptied in remarkably short order. Only the churned up mess of bread and grease remained when the acolytes came tottering in under the weight of another set of pots, this time filled to overflowing with curried chicken *wat*. This was splashed into the bowls on top of the remains of the mutton, and again the monks had at it.

While they gobbled up the chicken, the *tej* flasks were replenished and the monks became more raucous.

'I don't think I can take much more of this,'

Royan told Nicholas queasily.

'Close your eyes and think of England,' he advised her. 'You are the star of the evening. They aren't going to let you escape.'

As soon as the chicken was eaten, the servers were back with fresh pots, this time brimming with fiery beef *wat*. They dumped this on the remnants of both the mutton and the chicken.

The monk in the circle opposite Royan emptied his flask, and when an acolyte tried to refill it, he waved the lad away with a shout of, '*Katikala!*'

The cry was taken up by the other monks. '*Katikala! Katikala!*'

The acolytes hurried out and returned with dozens of bottles of the gin-clear liquor and brass bowls the size of tea cups.

'This is the stuff to be careful of,' Tessay told them. Surreptitiously both Nicholas and Royan were able to dribble the contents of their bowls into the mat of reeds on which they were sitting, but the monks guzzled theirs down greedily.

'Boris is getting his share,' Nicholas remarked to Royan. The Russian was red-faced and sweating, grinning like an idiot as he downed another bowlful.

Enlivened by the *katikala* the monks started playing a game. One of them would wrap a packet of beef *wat* with a sheet of *injera*, and then, as it dripped fat from his poised right hand, he would turn to the monk beside. The

225

victim would open his mouth until his jaws were at full stretch, and the packet would be stuffed into it by his considerate neighbour. The morsel was, of course, as large as a human gape could possibly accommodate, and in order to engulf it the victim had to risk death by asphyxiation.

The rules of the game seemed to be that he was not allowed to use his hands to get it into his own mouth, neither should he dribble down the front of his robe, nor splutter gravy over those seated near to him. His contortions, together with his gulping and choking and gasping for air, were the source of uncontrollable hilarity. When at last he succeeded in getting it down, a brass bowl of *katikala* was held to his lips as a reward. He was expected to send the contents in the same direction as the parcel of *injera*.

Jali Hora, by now warmed with *tej* and *katikala,* lurched to his feet. In his right hand he held aloft a streaming parcel of *injera*. As he began an unsteady progress across the chamber, with his shiny crown awry, they did not at first realize his intentions. The entire company watched him with interest.

Then suddenly Royan stiffened and whispered with horror, 'No! Please, no. Save me, Nicky. Don't let this happen to me.'

'This is the price you pay for being the leading lady,' he told her. Jali Hora was making his rather erratic way towards where she sat. The gravy from the morsel he carried for her was trickling down his forearm and dripping from his elbow.

The band standing along the side wall struck up a lively air. As the abbot came to a halt in front of Royan, rocking on his suspension like an ancient carriage, they fiddled and fifed and the drummers broke out in a frenzy.

The abbot presented his gift, and with one last despairing glance at Nicholas Royan faced the inevitable. She closed her eyes and opened her mouth.

To roars of encouragement and the urgings of fife and drum, she struggled and chewed. Her face turned rosy and her eyes watered. At one point Nicholas thought she would have to admit defeat and spit it out on to the reed-covered floor. But slowly and courageously, a bit at a time, she forced it down and then fell back exhausted.

Her audience, clapping and hooting, loved every moment of it. The abbot sank stiffly to his knees in front of her and embraced her, almost losing his crown in the process. Then without relinquishing his embrace, he made himself a place beside her.

'It looks as though you have made another conquest,' Nicholas told her dryly. 'I think he will be on your lap at any moment, if you don't duck and run.'

Royan reacted swiftly. She reached across and grabbed a bottle of *katikala*, and a bowl which she filled to the brim.

'Drink it up, Pops!' she told him, and held the bowl to his lips. Jali Hora accepted the challenge, but he had to release her to drink from her hand.

Suddenly Royan started so violently that she spilled what was left in the bowl down the old man's robe. The blood drained from her face and she began to tremble as though in a high fever as she stared at Jali Hora's crown, which had slipped forward over his eyes.

'What is it?' Nicholas demanded quietly but urgently, and he reached across to steady her with a hand on her arm. Nobody else in the chamber had noticed her distress, but he was fully attuned to her moods by now.

Still staring ashen-faced at the crown, she dropped the bowl and reached down and grasped his wrist. He was startled by her strength. Her grip was painful, and he saw that she had driven her nails into his flesh so hard that she had broken the skin.

'Look at his crown! The jewel! The blue jewel!' she gasped.

He saw it then, amongst the gaudy shards of glass and pebbles of semi-precious garnets and rock crystal. The size of a silver dollar, it was a seal of blue ceramic, perfectly round, and baked to a hard, impervious finish. In the centre of the disc was an etching of an Egyptian war chariot, and above it the distinctive and unmistakable outline of the hawk with the broken wing. Around the circumference was a legend engraved in hieroglyphics. It took him only a few moments to read it to himself:

I COMMAND TEN THOUSAND CHARIOTS.
I AM TAITA, MASTER OF THE ROYAL HORSE.

Royan desperately wanted to escape from the oppressive atmosphere of the cavern. The parcel of *wat* that the abbot had forced upon her had mixed heavily with the few mouthfuls of *tej* she had swallowed, and this feeling in turn was aggravated by the smell of the dirty food bowls thick with congealing grease and the fumes of raw *katikala*. Already some of the monks were puking drunk, and the smell of vomit added to the cloying miasma of incense smoke within the chamber.

However, she was still the centre of the abbot's attention. He sat beside her stroking her bare arm and reciting garbled extracts from the Amharic scriptures; Tessay had long ago given up translating for her. Royan looked hopefully at Nicholas but he was withdrawn and silent, seeming oblivious of his surroundings. She knew that he was thinking about the ceramic seal in the abbot's crown, for his eyes kept returning thoughtfully to it.

She wanted to be alone with him to discuss this extraordinary discovery. Her excitement outweighed the distress of her overloaded stomach. She felt her cheeks flushed with it. Every time she looked up at the old man's crown her heart fluttered, and she had to make an effort to stop herself reaching up, seizing the shiny blue seal and ripping it from its setting to examine it more closely.

She knew how unwise it was to draw attention to the scrap of ceramic, but when she glanced across the circle she saw that Boris was far past noticing anything other than the bowl of *katikala* in his hand. In the end it was Boris who gave her the excuse for which she had been seeking. He tried to get to his feet, but his legs collapsed under him. He sagged forward quite gracefully, and his face dropped into the bowl of grease-sodden *injera* bread. He lay there snoring noisily, and Tessay appealed to Nicholas.

'Alto Nicholas, what am I to do?'

Nicholas considered the unlovely spectacle of the prostrate hunter. There were scraps of bread and beef stew sticking like confetti in his cropped ginger hair.

'I rather suspect Prince Charming has had enough for one night,' he murmured.

He stood up, stooped over Boris and gripped one wrist. With a sudden jerk he lifted him into a sitting position, and then heaved him upright and over his shoulder in a fireman's lift.

'Good night, all!' he told the assembled monks, very few of whom were in any condition to respond. Then he carried Boris away, draped over his shoulders with head and feet dangling.

The two women had to hurry to keep up with Nicholas as he strode down the terrace and then up the stone stairway without a pause.

'I did not realize Alto Nicholas was so strong,' Tessay panted, for the stairs were steep and the pace was hard.

'I didn't either,' Royan admitted. She experienced a ridiculous proprietary pride in his feat, and smiled at herself in the darkness as they approached the camp.

'Don't be silly,' she admonished herself. 'He isn't yours to boast about.'

Nicholas threw his burden down on Boris's own bed in the thatched hut and stood back panting heavily, the sweat trickling down his cheeks.

'That's a pretty good recipe for a heart attack,' he gasped.

Boris groaned, rolled over and vomited copiously over his pillows and bedlinen.

'On that pleasant note I will bid you all goodnight and sweet dreams,' Nicholas told Tessay, stepping out of the hut into the warm African night.

He breathed in the smell of the forest and the river with relief, and then turned to Royan as she gripped his arm.

'Did you see —' she burst out excitedly, but he laid his fingers on her lips to silence her, and with a cautionary frown in the direction of Boris's hut led her away to her own hut.

'Did you see it?' she demanded, unable to

contain herself longer. 'Could you read it?'

' "*I command ten thousand chariots,*" ' he recited.

' "*I am Taita, master of the royal horse,*" ' she completed it for him. 'He was here. Oh, Nicky! He was here. Taita was here. That's the proof we wanted. Now we know that we are not wasting our time.'

She flopped down on her camp bed and hugged herself ecstatically. 'Do you think the abbot will let us examine the seal?'

He shook his head, 'My guess is no. The crown is one of the monastery treasures. Even for you, his favourite lady, I don't think he would do it. Anyway, it would not be wise to show any great interest in it. Jali Hora obviously does not have any idea of its significance. Apart from that, we don't want to alert Boris.'

'I suppose you are right.' She moved over on the bed to make room for him. 'Sit down.'

He sat down beside her, and she asked, 'Where do you suppose the seal came from? Who found it? Where, and when?'

'Steady on, dear girl. That's four questions in one, and I don't have an answer to any of them.'

'Guess!' she invited him. 'Speculate! Throw some ideas around!'

'Very well,' he agreed. 'The seal was manufactured in Hong Kong. There is a little factory there that turns them out by the thousands. Jali Hora bought it from a souvenir store in

Luxor when he was on holiday in Egypt last month.'

She punched his arm, hard. 'Be serious,' she ordered.

'Let's hear if you can do better,' he invited her, rubbing his arm.

'Okay, here I go. Taita dropped the seal here in the gorge while he was working on the construction of Pharaoh's tomb. Three thousand years later an old monk, one of the very first to live here at the monastery, picked it up. Of course, he could not read the hieroglyphics. He took it to the abbot, who declared it to be a relic of St Frumentius, and had it set in the crown.'

'And they all lived happily ever after,' Nicholas agreed. 'Not a bad shot.'

'Can you find any holes?' she demanded, and he shook his head. 'Then you agree that this proves that Taita really was here, and that it proves our theories are correct?'

' "*Proves*" is too strong a word. Let's just say that it points in that direction,' he demurred.

She wriggled around on the bed to face him squarely. 'Oh, Nicky, I am so excited. I swear I will not be able to sleep a wink tonight. I just can't wait for tomorrow, to get out there and start searching again.'

Her eyes were bright, and her cheeks flushed a warm rosy brown. Her lips were parted, and he could see the pink tip of her tongue between them. This time he could not stop himself. He

233

leaned very slowly towards her, treating her gently, giving her every opportunity to pull away if she wished to avoid him. She did not move, but her shining expression turned slowly to one of apprehension. She stared into his eyes, as if seeking something, some reassurance. When their lips were an inch apart, Nicholas stopped, and it was she who made the last movement. She brought their mouths together.

At first it was soft, just a light mingling of their breath, and then it became harsher, more urgent. For a long, heart-stopping moment they devoured each other, and her mouth tasted soft and sweet as ripe fruit. Then suddenly she whimpered, and with a huge effort of will tore herself out of his arms. They stared at each other, both of them shaken and confused.

'No,' she whispered. 'Please, Nicky, not yet. I am not ready yet.'

He picked up her hand and turned it between his palms. Then lightly he kissed the tips of her fingers, savouring the smell and the taste of her skin.

'I'll see you in the morning.' He dropped her hand and stood up. 'Early. Be ready!' he said, and stooped out through the doorway of the hut.

As he was dressing the next morning he heard her moving around in her hut, and when he whistled softly at her door she stepped out to meet him, dressed and eager to start.

'Boris is not awake yet,' Tessay told them as she served their breakfast.

'Now that is a great surprise to me,' Nicholas said, without looking up from his plate. He and Royan were still slightly awkward in each other's presence, remembering the circumstances in which they had parted the previous evening. However, as Nicholas slung the rifle and the pack over his shoulder and they set off up the valley, their mood changed to one of anticipation.

They had been going for an hour when Nicholas glanced over his shoulder and then cautioned her with a frown. 'We are being followed.'

Taking her wrist, he drew her behind a slab of sandstone. He flattened himself against the rock and gestured at her to do the same. Then he poised himself, and suddenly leaped forward to seize the lanky figure in a dirty white *shamma* who was sneaking up the valley behind them. With a howl the creature fell to his knees, and began gibbering with terror.

Nicholas hauled him to his feet. 'Tamre! What are you doing following us? Who sent you?' he demanded in Arabic.

The boy rolled his eyes towards Royan. 'No, please, *effendi*, do not hurt me. I meant no harm.'

'Leave the child, Nicky. You will precipitate another fit,' Royan intervened. Tamre scurried behind her and clung to her hand for protection, peering out around her shoulder at Nicholas as though his life were in danger.

'Peace, Tamre,' Nicholas soothed him. 'I will not hurt you, unless you lie to me. If you do, then I will thrash you until there is no skin on your back. Who sent you to follow us?'

'I came alone. Nobody sent me,' blubbered the boy. 'I came to show you where I saw the holy animal with the fingermarks of the Baptist on his skin.'

Nicholas stared at him for a moment, before he began to laugh softly. 'I'll be damned if the boy doesn't really believe he saw great-grandfather's dik-dik.' Then he scowled ferociously. 'Remember what will happen to you, if you are lying.'

'It is true, *effendi*,' Tamre sobbed, and Royan came to his defence.

'Don't badger him. He is harmless. Leave the poor child.'

'All right, Tamre. I will give you a chance. Take us to where you saw the holy animal.'

Tamre would not relinquish his grip on Royan's hand. He clung to it as he danced beside her, leading her along, and within a hundred yards his terror had faded and he was smiling and giggling at her shyly.

For an hour he led them away from the Dandera river and up over the high ground above the valley, into an area of thick scrub and upthrust ridges of weathered limestone. The thorny branches of the bush were densely intertwined, and grew so close to the ground that there

236

seemed to be no way through them. However, Tamre led them on to a narrow twisting path, just wide enough for them to avoid the red-tipped hook thorns on each side of them. Then abruptly he stopped and pulled Royan to a halt beside him. He pointed down, almost at his own toes.

'The river!' he announced importantly. Nicholas came up beside them and whistled softly with surprise. Tamre had led them around in a wide circle to the west, and then brought them back to the Dandera river at a point where it still ran in the bed of the deep ravine.

Now they stood on the very edge of the chasm. He saw at once that, although the top of the rocky ravine was less than a hundred feet wide, the chasm opened out below the rim. From the surface of the water far below, the rock wall belled out in the shape of one of the pottery *tej* flasks. It narrowed again as it neared the top where they stood.

'I saw the holy thing over there.' Tamre pointed to the far side of the chasm where a small feeder spring meandered out of the thorny bush. Streamers of bright green moss, nourished by the spring, hung from the lip of the concave rock wall, and the water trickled down them and dripped from the tips into the river two hundred feet below.

'If you saw it there, why did you bring us to this side of the river?' Nicholas demanded.

Tamre looked as though he were on the point

of tears. 'This side is easier. There is no path through the bush on the other side. The thorns would hurt Woizero Royan.'

'Don't be a bully,' Royan told him, and put her arm around the boy's shoulder.

Nicholas shrugged, 'It looks like the two of you are ganging up on me. Well, seeing that we are here, we might as well sit a while and see if great-grandpa's dik-dik puts in an appearance.'

He picked out a spot in the shade of one of the stunted trees that hung on the lip of the chasm, and with his hat swept the ground clear of fallen thorns until there was a place for them to sit. He placed his back against the trunk of the thorn tree and laid the Rigby rifle across his lap.

By this time it was past noon, and the heat was stifling. He passed the water bottle to Royan and, while she drank, glanced at Tamre and suggested to her in English, 'This might be a good time to find out what, if anything, the lad knows about the Taita ceramic in the crown. He is besotted with you. He will tell you anything you want to know. Question him.'

She began gently, chatting softly to the boy. Occasionally she stroked his head and petted him as though he were a puppy. She spoke to him of the previous night's banquet, the beauty of the underground church, and the antiquity of the murals and the tapestries, and then at last mentioned the abbot's crown.

'Yes. Yes. That is the stone of the saint,' he agreed readily. 'The blue stone of St Frumentius.'

'Where did it come from?' she asked. 'Do you know?'

The boy looked embarrassed, 'I do not know. It is very old, perhaps as old as Christ the Saviour. That is what the priests say.'

'You do not know where it was found?'

He shook his head, but then, eager to please her, he suggested, 'Perhaps it fell from heaven.'

'Perhaps.' Royan glanced at Nicholas, who rolled his eyes upwards and then pushed his hat forward to cover his face.

'Perhaps St Frumentius gave it to the first abbot when he died.' Tamre warmed to the subject. 'Or perhaps it was in his coffin with him when he was placed in his tomb.'

'All these things are possible, Tamre,' Royan agreed. 'Have you seen the tomb of St Frumentius?'

He looked around him guiltily. 'Only the ordained priests are allowed into the *maqdas*, the Holy of Holies,' he hung his head and whispered.

'You have seen it, Tamre,' she accused him gently, stroking his head. She was intrigued by the boy's guilt. 'You can tell me. I will not tell the priests.'

'Only once,' he admitted. 'The other boys. They sent me to touch the *tabot* stone. They would have beaten me if I had not. All the new acolytes are made to do this.' He began to babble with the horror of the memory of his initiation ordeal. 'I was alone. I was very afraid. It was after midnight when the priests were asleep. Dark. The *maqdas* is haunted by the ghost of the saint. They told me that if I was unworthy the saint would strike me down with lightning.'

Nicholas removed the hat from his face and straightened up slowly. 'My word, the child is telling the truth,' he said softly. 'He *has* been into the Holy of Holies.' Then he looked across at Royan, 'Keep questioning him. He may just give us something useful. Ask him about the tomb of St Frumentius.'

'Did you see the tomb of the saint?' she asked, and the boy nodded vigorously. 'Did you go into the tomb?' This time he shook his head.

'No. There are bars across the entrance. Only the abbot is allowed into the tomb, on the birthday of the saint.'

'Did you look through the bars?'

'Yes, but it is very dark. I saw the coffin of the saint. It is wood and there is painting on it, the face of the saint.'

'Is he a black man?'

'No — a white man with a red beard. The painting is very old. The picture is faded, and the wood of the coffin is rotting and crumbling.'

'Is it lying on the floor of the tomb?'

Tamre screwed up his face in thought, then after careful consideration shook his head. 'No, it is on a shelf of stone in the wall.'

'Is there anything else you remember about the tomb of the saint?' Royan tried to prod his memory, but Tamre shook his head.

'It was very dark, and the opening in the bars is small,' he apologized.

'It does not matter. Is the tomb in the back wall of the *maqdas?*'

'Yes, it is behind the altar and the *tabot* stone.'

'What is the altar made of — stone?'

'No. It is wood, cedarwood. There are candles, and a big cross, and the many crowns of the abbot, and the chalice and staff.'

'Is it painted?'

'No, it is carved with pictures. But they are different from the pictures inside the tomb of the saint.'

'What is different? Tell me, Tamre.'

'I don't know. The faces are funny. They wear different clothes. There are horses.' He looked puzzled. 'They are different.'

Royan tried for a while to get a clearer description from him, but he became more and more confused and contradictory when she pushed him, so she changed tack.

'Tell me about the *tabot*,' she suggested, but Nicholas forestalled her.

'No, you tell me about the *tabot*,' he demanded of her. 'Is it similar to the Jewish Tabernacle?'

She turned to him, 'Yes, at least in the Egyptian Church it is. It is usually kept in a jewelled box and wrapped in an embroidered cloth of

241

gold. The only difference is that the Jewish Tabernacle is carved with the ten commandments, but in our Church it is carved with the words of dedication of the particular church that houses it. It is the living heart of the Church.'

'What is the *tabot* stone?' Nicholas frowned with concentration.

'I don't know,' she admitted. 'Our Church does not have a *tabot* stone.'

'Ask him!'

'Tell me about the *tabot* stone, Tamre.'

'It is so high, and so square.' He indicated a height of a little above his own shoulder, and the width of his spread hands.

'And the *tabot* stands on top of this stone?' Royan guessed.

Tamre nodded.

'Why did they send you to touch the stone and not the *tabot* itself?' Nicholas demanded, but Royan shook her head to silence him.

'Let me do the talking. You are too harsh with him.' She turned back to the boy. 'Why the stone, rather than the Ark of the *tabot* that stands on top of it?'

Tamre shrugged helplessly. 'I don't know. They just did.'

'What does the stone look like? Are there paintings on it also?'

'I don't know.' He looked distraught at not being able to satisfy her. He wanted desperately to please her. 'I don't know. The stone is wrapped with cloth.'

Nicholas and Royan exchanged startled glances, and then Royan turned back to the boy.

'Covered?' Royan leaned closer to him. 'The stone is covered?'

'They say that it is only uncovered by the abbot on the birthday of St Frumentius.'

Again Nicholas and Royan stared at each other, and then he smiled thoughtfully. 'I would rather like to have a look at the tomb of the saint, and the stone in its uncovered state.'

'You'd have to wait for the saint's birthday,' she said, 'and have yourself ordained. Only the priests —' she broke off and stared at him again. 'You aren't thinking of — no, you wouldn't, would you?'

'Who, me?' he grinned. 'Perish the thought.'

'If they caught you in the *maqdas*, they would tear you to little pieces.'

'The answer, then, would be not to let them catch me.'

'If you go, I am going with you. How are we going to manage it?'

'Throttle back, dear girl. The thought only occurred to me ten seconds ago. Even on my good days, I need at least ten minutes to come up with a brilliant plan of action.'

They both stared out across the chasm in silence, until Royan whispered softly, 'The covered stone. Taita's stone testament?'

'Don't say it aloud,' he pleaded, and made the sign against the evil eye. 'Don't even think it aloud. The Devil is listening.'

243

They were silent again, both of them thinking furiously. Then Royan started, 'Nicky, what if —' she broke off. 'No, that won't work.' She relapsed into frowning silence again.

Tamre broke the quiet with a sudden squeak of excitement, 'There it is. Look!'

They were both startled by the interruption. 'What is it?' Royan turned to him.

Tamre seized her arm and shook it. He was trembling with emotion. 'There it is. I told you.' With his other hand he was pointing out across the river, 'There at the edge of the thorn bushes. Can't you see it?'

'What is it? What can you see?'

'The animal of John the Baptist. The holy marked creature.'

Following the direction of his outflung arm, she picked out a soft, brownish blur of movement at the edge of the thicket on the far bank. 'I don't know. It is too far —'

Nicholas scrabbled in his pack and brought out his binoculars. He lifted and focused them, and then he began to chuckle.

'Hallelujah! Great-grandpa's reputation is safe at last.' He passed the binoculars to Royan. She focused them and found the little creature in the field. It was three hundred yards away, but through the ten-power lens she could make it out in detail.

It was almost half as large again as the common dik-dik that they had seen the previous day, and instead of drab grey its coat was a rich red brown. Its most striking feature, however, was the distinct dark bars of chocolate colour across its shoulders and back — five evenly spaced markings that did indeed look like the imprint of fingers and thumb.

'*Madoqua harperii*, no less,' Nicholas whispered to her. 'Sorry, great-grandfather, for doubting you.'

The dik-dik stood half in shadow, wriggling its nose as it snuffled the air. Its head was held high, suspicious and alert. The soft breeze was quartering between them and the animal, but every so often a wayward eddy gave it the faint whiff of humanity that had alarmed it.

Royan heard the snick of the rifle action as Nicholas worked the bolt and chambered a round. Hurriedly she lowered the glasses, and glanced at him. 'You aren't going to shoot it?' she demanded.

'No, not at that range. Over three hundred yards, and a small target. I'll wait for it to get closer.'

'How can you bring yourself to do it?'

'How can I not? That's what I came here to do, amongst other things.'

'But it's so beautiful.'

'I take it, then, that it would be perfectly all right to whack it if it were ugly?'

She said nothing, but raised the binoculars again. The eddy of the wind must have changed, for the dik-dik lowered its head to nibble at a tuft of coarse brown grass. Then lifted its head again and came on down the clearing in the thorn scrub, stepping daintily, pausing every few paces to feed again.

'Go back!' She tried to will it into safety, but it kept on coming, meandering towards the edge of the chasm.

Nicholas rolled on to his stomach and settled himself behind the root of the tree. He screwed up his hat into a soft pad on which to rest the rifle.

'Two hundred yards,' he muttered to himself. 'That's a fair shot. No further.' Resting the cushioned rifle on the twisted root, he aimed through the telescopic sight. Then he lifted his head, waiting to let it come within certain range.

Abruptly the dik-dik lifted its head again and came to a halt, quivering with tension.

'Something he doesn't like. Dammit all, wind must have changed again,' Nicholas growled. At that moment the little antelope bolted. It streaked across the clearing, back the way it had come, and disappeared into the thorn scrub.

'Go, dik-dik, go!' said Royan smugly, and Nicholas sat up and grunted with disgust.

'I can't make out what frightened him.' Then his expression changed and he cocked his head. There was an alien sound on the air, growing each second — a harsh, rising clatter and a shrill, whining whistle.

'Chopper! What the hell!' Nicholas recognized the sound immediately. He took the binoculars from Royan's hand and turned them to the sky, sweeping the cloudless blue emptiness above the crenellated tops of the escarpment.

'There it is,' he said grimly, adding, 'Bell Jet Ranger,' as he recognized the profile. 'Coming this way, by the looks of it. No point in drawing attention to ourselves. Let's get under cover.'

He shepherded Royan and the boy under the spread branches of the thorn tree. 'Sit tight,' he told her. 'No chance they will spot us under here.'

He watched the approaching helicopter through the binoculars. 'Probably Ethiopian air force,' he said softly. 'Anti-*shufta* patrol, most likely. Both Boris and Colonel Nogo warned us that there are a lot of rebels and bandits operating down here in the gorge —' he broke off abruptly. 'No. Hold on. That's not military. Green and red fuselage, and the red horse emblem. None other than your old friends from Pegasus Exploration.'

The sound of the rotors crescendoed, and now with her naked eye Royan could make out the flying horse on the fuselage of the helicopter as it flew low across their front, half a mile out, headed down towards the Nile.

Neither of them paid any attention to Tamre as he crouched behind Royan, trying to hide behind her body. His teeth were chattering with terror and his eyes rolled until the whites showed.

'It looks as if our friend Jake Helm has got

himself some fancy transport. If Pegasus is in any way connected with Duraid's murder and the other attempts on your life, then we can expect them to be breathing heavily down our necks from now on. They are now in a position to overlook us at will.' Nicholas was still watching the aircraft through the binoculars.

'When your enemy is up in the air, it gives you a helpless feeling.' Royan edged instinctively closer to him, staring up.

The green and scarlet machine disappeared over the hump of the sub-gorge, down towards the monastery.

'Unless he's just on a joy-ride, he's probably looking for our camp,' Nicholas guessed. 'Under orders from the main man to keep tabs on us.'

'He will have no trouble finding it. Boris made no attempt to conceal the huts,' Royan said uneasily. 'Let's get out of here, then.' She stood up.

'Good plan.' Nicholas was about to follow her, when suddenly he caught her hand and drew her down again. 'Hold it. They are coming back this way.'

The engine beat was rising again. Then they caught a glimpse of the helicopter through the canopy of leaves and thorn branches overhead.

'Now he is following the river. Still searching for something, by the looks of it.'

'Us?' Royan asked nervously.

'If they are under orders from the head man, could be,' Nicholas agreed. The machine was very close now, and the shrill whine of the engine was deafening.

At that moment Tamre's nerve broke. He let out a wail of terror, 'It is the Devil, come to take me. Save me, Jesus Christ the Saviour, save me!'

Nicholas put out a hand to restrain him, but he was not quick enough. Tamre broke free and leaped to his feet. Still howling with fear of the pit and the flames of hell, he darted away down the path into the thorn scrub, the skirts of his *shamma* swirling about his skinny legs and his shiny black face swivelled back over his shoulder to watch the approaching machine.

The pilot spotted him immediately, and the nose of the helicopter sank in their direction. It came directly towards them, slowing as it approached the lip of the chasm. They could make out the heads of the two occupants behind the windscreen of the forward cabin. Still decelerating, the aircraft hung suspended over the river, pivoting on the spinning disc of its rotor, while Royan and Nicholas crouched down in the scrub, trying to avoid detection.

'That's the American from the prospecting camp.' Royan recognized Jake Helm, despite the bulky radio earphones and the mirrored dark glasses. He and the black pilot were craning their necks to search the river banks.

'They haven't spotted us —' But even as Nicholas said it, Jake Helm looked directly at them across the open void. Although his expression did not change, he tapped the pilot's shoulder and pointed down at them.

The pilot let the helicopter sink lower until it hovered in the opening of the chasm, almost on the same level as they were. Only a hundred feet separated them now. No longer making any attempt at concealment, Nicholas leaned back against the bole of the thorn tree. He tipped his panama hat forward over one eye and gave Jake Helm a laconic wave.

The foreman made no response to the greeting. He regarded Nicholas with a flat, baleful stare, then struck a match and held the flame to the tip of the half-smoked cigar between his lips. He flipped the dead match away and blew a feather of smoke in Nicholas's direction. Still without change of expression, he said something to the pilot out of the corner of his mouth.

Immediately the helicopter rose vertically and banked away to the north, heading back directly towards the wall of the escarpment and the base camp on its summit.

'Mission accomplished. He found what he was looking for.' Royan sat up. 'Us!'

'And he must have spotted the camp. He knows where to find us again,' Nicholas agreed.

Royan shivered and hugged herself briefly. 'He gives me the creeps, that one. He looks like a toad.'

'Oh, come on!' Nicholas chided her. 'What have you got against toads?' He stood up. 'I don't think we are going to see great-grand-

250

father's dik-dik again today. He has been thoroughly shaken up by the chopper. I'll come back for another try tomorrow.'

'We should go and look for Tamre. He has probably had another fit, the poor little fellow.'

She was wrong. They found the boy beside the path. He was still shivering and weeping, but had not suffered another seizure. He calmed down quickly when Royan soothed him, and followed them back towards the camp. However, when they neared the grove he slipped away in the direction of the monastery.

That evening, while it was still light, Nicholas took Royan back to the monastery.

'I believe that the criminal fraternity refer to a reconnaissance of this nature as "casing the joint",' he remarked, as they stooped through the entrance of the rock cathedral and joined the throng of worshippers in the outer chamber.

'From what Tamre says, it sounds as though the novices wait until they know that the priests on duty are ones that will nod off during their watch,' Royan told him softly, as they paused to gaze through the doors into the middle chamber.

'We don't have that sort of insider knowledge,' Nicholas pointed out.

There were priests passing backwards and forwards through the doors as they watched.

'There doesn't seem to be any sort of procedure,' Nicholas noted. 'No password or ritual to allow them through.'

'On the other hand, they greeted the guards at the door by name. It's a small community. They must all know each other intimately.'

'There doesn't seem any chance at all that I could dress up like a monk and brazen my way through,' Nicholas agreed. 'I wonder what they do to intruders in the sacred areas?'

'Throw them off the terrace to the crocodiles in the cauldron of the Nile?' she suggested maliciously. 'Anyway, you are not going in there without me.'

This was not the time to argue, he decided, and instead he tried to see as much as possible through the open doors of the *qiddist*. The middle chamber seemed much smaller than the outer chamber in which they stood. He could just make out the shadowy murals that covered the portions of the inner walls that he could see. In the facing wall was another doorway. From Tamre's description, he realized that this must be the entrance to the *maqdas*. The opening was barred by a heavy grille gate of dark wooden beams, the joints of the cross-pieces reinforced with gussets of hand-hammered native iron.

On each side of the doorway, from rock ceiling to floor, hung long embroidered tapestries depicting scenes from the life of St Frumentius. In one he was preaching to a kneeling congregation, with the Bible in one hand and his right hand raised in benediction. In the other tapestry he was baptizing an emperor. The king wore a high golden crown like that of Jali Hora, and the saint's head was surrounded by a halo. The saint's face was white, while the emperor's was black.

'Politically correct?' Nicholas asked himself, with a smile.

'What is amusing you?' Royan asked. 'Have you thought of a way of getting in there?'

'No, I was thinking of dinner. Let's go!'

At dinner Boris showed no ill effects from the previous night's debauch. During the day he had taken out his shotgun and shot a bunch of green pigeons. Tessay had marinated these and barbecued them over the coals.

'Tell me, English, how was the hunting today? Did you get attacked by the deadly striped dik-dik? Hey? Hey?' He bellowed with laughter.

'Did your trackers have any success?' Nicholas asked mildly.

'*Da! Da!* They found kudu and bushbuck and buffalo. They even found dik-dik, but no stripes. Sorry, no stripes.'

Royan leaned forward and opened her mouth to intervene, but Nicholas cautioned her with a shake of the head. She shut her mouth again and looked down at her plate, slicing a morsel from the breast of a pigeon.

'We don't really need company tomorrow,' Nicholas explained mildly in Arabic. 'If he knew, he would insist on coming with us.'

253

'Did your Mummy never teach you no manners, English? It's rude to talk in a language
that others can't understand. Have a vodka.'

'You have my share,' Nicholas invited him.
'I know when I am outclassed.'

During the rest of the meal Tessay replied
only in low monosyllables when Royan tried
to draw her into the conversation. She looked
tragic and defeated. She never looked at her
husband, even when he was at his loudest and
most overbearing. When the meal ended, they
left her sitting with Boris at the fire. Boris had
a fresh bottle of vodka on the table beside him.

'The way he is pumping the liquor, it looks
as if I might be called out on another midnight
rescue mission,' Nicholas remarked as they made
their way to their own huts.

'Tessay has been in camp all day with him.
There has been more trouble between them.
She told me that as soon as they get back to
Addis Ababa she is going to leave him. She
can't take any more of this.'

'The only thing I find surprising is that she
ever got mixed up with an animal like Boris
in the first place. She is a lovely woman. She
could pick and choose.'

'Some women are drawn to animals,' Royan
shrugged. 'I suppose it must be the thrill of
danger. Anyway, Tessay has asked me if she
can come with us tomorrow. She cannot stand
another day in camp with Boris on her own.
I think she is really afraid of him now. She

says that she has never seen him drink like this before.'

'Tell her to come along,' Nicholas said resignedly. 'The more of us the merrier. Perhaps we will be able to frighten the dik-dik to death by sheer weight of numbers. Save me wasting ammunition.'

It was still dark when the three of them left camp the next morning. There was no sign of Boris and, when Nicholas asked about him, Tessay said simply, 'After you went to bed last night he finished the bottle. He won't be out of his hut before noon. He won't miss me.'

Carrying the Rigby, Nicholas led them up into the weathered limestone hills, retracing the path along which Tamre had taken them the previous day. As they walked, Nicholas heard the two women talking behind him. Royan was explaining to Tessay how they had sighted the striped dik-dik, and what they planned.

The sun was well up by the time they again reached the spot under the thorn tree on the lip of the chasm, and settled down to wait in ambush.

'How will you retrieve the carcass, if you do manage to shoot the poor little creature?' Royan asked.

'I made certain of that before we left camp,' he explained. 'I spoke to the head tracker. If he hears a shot he will bring up the ropes and help me get across to the other side.'

'I wouldn't like to make the journey across

255

there.' Tessay eyed the drop below them.

'They teach you some useful things in the army, along with all the rubbish,' Nicholas replied. He made himself comfortable against the thorn tree, the rifle ready in his lap.

The women lay close by him, talking together softly. It was unlikely that the sound of their low voices would carry across the ravine, Nicholas decided, so he did not try to hush them.

He expected that if it came at all, the dik-dik would show itself early. But he was wrong. By noon there was still no sign of it. The valley sweltered in the midday sun. The distant wall of the escarpment, veiled in the blue heat haze, looked like jagged blue glass, and the mirage danced across the rocky ridges and shimmered like the waters of a silver lake above the tops of the thorn thickets.

The women had long ago given up talking, and they lay somnolent in the heat. The whole world was silent and heat-struck. Only a bush dove broke the silence with its mournful lament, 'My wife is dead, my children are dead, Oh, me! Oh, my! Oh, me!' Nicholas found his own eyelids becoming leaden. His head nodded involuntarily, and he jerked it up only to have it flop forward again. On the very edge of sleep he heard a sound, close by in the thorn scrub behind him.

It was a tiny sound, but one that he knew so well. A sound that whiplashed across his nerve endings and jerked him back to full consciousness, with his pulse racing and the coppery taste of fear in the back of his throat. It was the metallic sound of the safety-catch on an AK-47 assault rifle being slipped forward into the 'Fire' position.

In one fluid movement he lifted the rifle out of his lap and rolled twice, twisting his body to cover the two women who lay beside him. At the same time he brought the Rigby into his shoulder, aimed into the scrub behind him from where the sound had come.

'Down!' he hissed at his companions. 'Keep your heads down!'

His finger was on the trigger and, even though it was a puny weapon with which to take on a Kalashnikov, he was ready to return fire. He picked up his target immediately, and swung on to it.

There was a man crouched twenty paces away, the assault rifle he carried aimed into Nicholas's face. He was black, dressed in worn and tattered camouflage fatigues and a soft cap of the same material. His webbing held a bushknife and grenades, water bottle and all the other accoutrements of a guerrilla fighter.

'*Shufta!*' thought Nicholas. 'A real pro. Don't take chances with this one.' Yet at the same time he realized that if the intention had been to kill him, then he would be dead already.

He aimed the Rigby an inch over the muzzle of the assault rifle, into the bloodshot right eye of the *shufta* behind it. The man acknowledged the stand-off with a narrowing of his eyes, and then gave an order in Arabic.

'Salim, cover the women. Shoot them if he moves.'

Nicholas heard movement on his flank and glanced in that direction, still keeping the *shufta* in his peripheral vision.

Another guerrilla stepped out of the scrub. He was similarly dressed, but he carried a Soviet RPD light machine gun on his hip. The barrel was sawn off short to make the weapon more handy for bush fighting, and there was a loop of ammunition belt draped around his neck. He came forward carefully, the RPD aimed point-blank at the two women. Nicholas knew that, with a touch on the trigger, he could chop them both to mincemeat.

There were other stealthy rustling sounds in the bush all around them. These two were not the only ones, Nicholas realized. This was a large war party. He might be able to get off one shot with the Rigby, but by then Royan and Tessay would be dead. And he would not be far behind them.

Very slowly and deliberately he lowered the muzzle of the rifle until it was pointing at the ground. Then he laid the weapon down and raised his hands.

'Get your hands up,' he told the women. 'Do exactly what they tell you.'

The guerrilla leader acknowledged his surrender by coming to his full height and speaking rapidly to his men, still in Arabic.

'Get the rifle and his pack.'

'We are British subjects,' Nicholas told him loudly, and the guerrilla looked surprised by his use of Arabic. 'We are simple tourists. We are not military. We are not government people.'

'Be quiet. Shut your face!' he ordered, as the rest of the guerrilla patrol emerged from cover. Nicholas counted five of them all told, though he knew there were probably others who had not come forward. They were very professional as they rounded up their prisoners. They never blocked each other's field of fire, nor offered an opportunity of escape. Quickly they searched them for weapons, then closed in around them and hustled them on to the path.

'Where are you taking us?' Nicholas demanded.

'No questions!' The butt of an AK-47 smashed between his shoulder blades and almost knocked him off his feet.

'Steady on, chaps,' he murmured mildly in English. 'That wasn't really called for.'

They were forced to keep marching through the heat of the afternoon. Nicholas kept a check on the position of the sun and the distant glimpses of the escarpment wall. He realized that they were heading westwards, following the course of the Nile towards the Sudanese border. It was late afternoon, and Nicholas estimated that they had covered some ten miles, before they came upon a side shoot of the main valley.

The slopes were heavily wooded, and the three prisoners were herded into a patch of this forest.

They were actually within the perimeter of the guerrilla camp before they were aware of its existence. Cunningly camouflaged, it consisted merely of a few crude lean-to shelters and a ring of weapons emplacements. The sentries were well placed, and all the light machine guns in the foxholes were manned.

They were led to one of the shelters in the centre of the camp, where three men were squatting around a map spread on a low camp table. These were obviously officers, and there was no mistaking which of the three was the commander. The leader of the patrol which had captured them went to this man, saluted him deferentially and then spoke to him urgently, pointing at his captives.

The guerrilla commander straightened up from the table, and came out into the sunlight. He was of medium height, but was imbued with such an air of authority that he seemed taller. His shoulders were broad and his body square and chunky, with the beginning of a dignified spread around the waist. He wore a short curly beard which contained a few strands of grey, and his features were refined and handsome. His skin tones were amber and copper. His dark eyes were intelligent, his gaze quick and restless.

'My men tell me that you speak Arabic,' he said to Nicholas.

'Better than you do, Mek Nimmur,' Nicholas

told him. 'So now you are the leader of a bunch of bandits and kidnappers? I always told you that you would never get to heaven, you old reprobate.'

Mek Nimmur stared at him in astonishment, and then began to smile. 'Nicholas! I did not recognize you. You are older. Look at the grey on your head!'

He opened his arms wide and folded Nicholas into a bear hug.

'Nicholas! Nicholas!' He kissed him once on each cheek. Then he held him at arm's length and looked at the two women, who were standing amazed.

'He saved my life,' he explained to them.

'You make me blush, Mek.'

Mek kissed him again, 'He saved my life twice.'

'Once,' Nicholas contradicted him. 'The second time was a mistake. I should have let them shoot you.'

Mek laughed delightedly. 'How long ago was it, Nicholas?'

'It doesn't bear thinking about.'

'Fifteen years ago at least,' Mek said. 'Are you still in the British army? What is your rank? You must be a general by now!'

'Reserves only,' Nicholas shook his head. 'I have been back in civvy street a long time now.'

Still hugging Nicholas, Mek Nimmur looked at the women with interest. 'Nicholas taught me most of what I know about soldiering,' he told them. His eyes flicked from Royan to Tessay, and then stayed on the Ethiopian girl's dark and lovely face.

'I know you,' he said. 'I saw you in Addis, years ago. You were a young girl then. Your father was Alto Zemen, a great and good man. He was murdered by the tyrant Mengistu.'

'I know you also, Alto Mek. My father held you in high esteem. There are many of us who believe that you should be the president of this Ethiopia of ours, in place of that other one.' She dropped him a graceful little curtsey, hanging her head in a shy but appealing gesture of respect.

'I am flattered by your opinion of me.' He took her hand and lifted her to her full height. Then he turned back to Nicholas, 'I am sorry for the rough welcome. Some of my men are over-enthusiastic. I knew that there were *ferengi* asking questions at the monastery. But enough, you are with friends here. I bid you welcome.'

Mek Nimmur led them to his shelter, where one of his men brought a soot-blackened kettle from the fire and poured viscous black coffee into mugs for them.

He and Nicholas plunged into reminiscences of the days prior to the Falklands war when they had fought side by side, Nicholas as a covert military adviser, and Mek as a young freedom fighter opposing the tyranny of Mengistu.

'But the war is over now, Mek,' Nicholas remonstrated at last. 'The battle is won. Why are you still out in the bush with your men? Why aren't you getting rich and fat in Addis, like all the others?'

'In the interim government in Addis there are enemies of mine, men like Mengistu. When we have got rid of them, then I will come out of the bush.'

He and Nicholas embarked into a spirited discussion of African politics, so deep and complicated that Royan knew very few of the personalities whom they were discussing. Nor could she follow the nuances and the subtlety of religious and tribal prejudices and intolerance that had persisted for a thousand years. She was, however, impressed by Nicholas's knowledge and understanding of the situation, and the way in which a man like Mek Nimmur asked his opinion and listened to his advice.

In the end Nicholas asked him, 'So now you have carried the war beyond the borders of Ethiopia itself? You are operating in Sudan, as well?'

'The war in the Sudan has been raging for twenty years,' Mek confirmed. 'The Christians in the south fighting against the persecution of the Moslem north —'

'I am well aware of that, Mek. But that is not Ethiopia. It's not your war.'

'They are Christians, and they suffer injustice. I am a soldier and a Christian. Of course it is my war.' Tessay had been listening avidly to every word that Mek spoke, and now she nodded her head in agreement, her eyes dark and solemn with hero worship.

'Alto Mek is a crusader for Christ and the

263

rights of the common man,' Tessay told Nicholas in awed tones.

'And he dearly loves a good fight,' Nicholas laughed, punching his shoulder affectionately. It was a familiar gesture which could easily have given offence, but Mek accepted it readily and laughed back at him.

'What are you doing here yourself, Nicholas, if you are no longer a soldier? There was a time when you also loved a good fight.'

'I am completely reformed. No more fighting. I have come to the Abbay gorge to hunt dik-dik.'

'Dik-dik?' Mek Nimmur stared at him with disbelief, and then he roared with laughter. 'I don't believe it. Not you. Not dik-dik. You are up to something.'

'It is the truth.'

'You are lying, Nicholas. You never could lie to me. I know you too well. You are up to something. You will tell me about it when you need my help.'

'And you will still give me your help?'

'Of course. You saved my life twice.'

'Once,' said Nicholas.

'Even once is enough,' said Mek Nimmur.

While they talked, the sun slanted down the sky.

'You are my guests for tonight,' Mek Nimmur told them formally. 'In the morning I will escort you back to your camp at the monastery of St Frumentius. That is also my destination. My men and I are going to the monastery to celebrate the festival of Timkat. The abbot, Jali Hora, is a friend and an ally.'

'And the monastery is probably your deep cover base. You use it and the monks for re-supply and intelligence. Am I right?'

'You know me too well, Nicholas.' Mek Nimmur shook his head ruefully. 'You taught me much of what I know, so why should you not be able to guess my strategy? The monastery makes a perfect base of operations. It's close enough to the border —' he broke off, smiling. 'But there is no need to explain it to you, of all people.'

Mek had his men build a night shelter for Nicholas and Royan, and cut a mattress of grass to cushion their sleep. They lay close together under the flimsy roof. The night was sultry, and they did not miss their blankets. Nicholas had a tube of insect repellent in his pack to keep the mosquitoes at bay.

After they had settled down on the grass mattress, their heads were close enough together to allow them to converse in quiet tones. When he turned his head Nicholas could see the dark silhouettes of Mek Nimmur and Tessay still sitting close together by the fire.

'Ethiopian girls are different from the Arabs, and from most other African women.' Royan too was watching the other couple. 'No Arab girl would dare be alone with a man like that. Especially if she were a married woman.'

'Any way you cut it, they make a damned fine pair,' he gave his opinion. 'Good luck to them. Tessay hasn't had much of that lately — she is overdue.'

He turned his head and looked into her face, 'What about you, Royan, what are you? Are you a decorous, submissive Arab, or an independent, assertive Western girl?'

'It's both a little early and much too late for intimate questions of that nature,' she told him, and turned over, presenting him with her back.

'Ah, we are standing on ceremony this evening! Goodnight, Woizero Royan.'

'Goodnight, Alto Nicholas,' she replied, keeping her face turned away from him so that he could not see her smile.

The guerrilla column moved out before dawn the next morning. They marched in full battle order, with scouts moving ahead and flankers covering each side of the path.

'The army come down here into the gorge very seldom, but we are always ready for them when they do come,' Mek Nimmur explained. 'We try to give them a hearty welcome.'

Tessay was watching Mek Nimmur as he spoke; indeed, she had seldom taken her eyes off him that morning. Now she murmured to Royan, 'He is a truly great man, a man who could unite our land, perhaps for the first time in a thousand years. I feel humble in his presence, and yet I also feel like a young girl again, filled with joy and hope.'

The march back to the monastery took the entire morning. When they came in sight of the Dandera river, Mek Nimmur drew his men back off the path into thick bush, while sending only one scout forward. After an hour's wait, a party of acolytes came up from the monastery, each carrying a large bundle balanced upon his head.

They greeted Mek with deep reverence, and handed over their bundles to his men before returning down the pathway into the gorge of the Abbay.

The bundles contained priestly *shammas*, head-cloths and sandals. Mek's men changed out of their camouflage fatigues into these garments, all of which were well worn and unwashed for the sake of authenticity. They wore only their sidearms under the robes. All their other weapons and equipment they cached in one of the caves in the limestone cliffs, and left a detachment to guard them.

Now as a party of monks they covered the last few miles to the monastery, to be welcomed joyously by the community there. Here Nicholas and the women left Mek, and climbed the steep path up into the grove of wild fig trees. Boris was waiting for them, pacing about the camp, angry and frustrated.

"Where the hell have you been, woman?' he snarled at Tessay. 'Been whoring around all night, have you?'

'We lost our way yesterday evening.' Nicholas fed him the cover story that they had agreed with Mek Nimmur, to maintain his security. Boris was hardly the man to trust. 'And we were picked up by a party of monks from the monastery this morning. They brought us back.'

'You are the big hunter and tracker, are you?' Boris sneered at him. 'You didn't need me to guide you, hey? You got yourself lost, did you, English? I see now why you want only to shoot dik-dik.' He guffawed without humour, and looked at Tessay with those pale dead eyes. 'I will talk to you later, woman. Go and see to the food.'

Despite the heat, both Nicholas and Royan were hungry. In short order, Tessay was able to serve a tasty cold lunch under the shady branches of the fig trees. Nicholas refused the wine that Boris offered him.

'I want to go out hunting again this afternoon. I have lost almost a whole day.'

'You want me to hold your hand this time, English? Make sure you don't lose yourself again?'

'Thanks, old chap, but I think I can manage without you.'

While they ate Nicholas nudged Royan and

told her, 'Your admirer has arrived.'

He jerked his head at the lanky, ungainly figure of Tamre, who had sneaked up quietly and was now sitting near the kitchen hut. As soon as Royan looked at him his face split into a doting idiotic grin, and he bobbed his head and squirmed with ecstatic shyness.

'I will not come with you this afternoon,' Royan told Nicholas quietly, when Boris was not listening. 'I think there is going to be trouble between him and Tessay. I want to stay here with her. Take Tamre with you.'

'My word, what an attractive alternative. All my life I have waited for this moment.' But when he had picked up his rifle and pack, he beckoned the boy to follow him. Tamre looked around eagerly for Royan, but she was in her hut. At last, dragging his feet, he followed Nicholas up the valley.

'Take me to the other side of the river,' he told the boy. 'Show me how to reach the side where the holy creature lives.' Tamre perked up at the prospect, and broke into a shambling trot as he led Nicholas over the suspension bridge below the pink cliffs.

For an hour they followed the path, but gradually it petered out until it ended in bad and broken ground amongst the erosion-carved hills. Undeterred, Tamre plunged into the thorny scrub, and for another two hours they scrambled over rocky ridges and through thorn-choked valleys.

'I can see why you didn't want to bring Royan

this way round,' Nicholas grunted. His bare arms were scored by thorn, and the legs of his trousers were ripped in half a dozen places. However, he was memorizing the route and knew that he could find his way back again without difficulty.

At last they topped another ridge and Tamre stopped and pointed down over the far side. Below them Nicholas could make out the cleft of the chasm, and the small open glade from which the dik-dik spring issued. He could even recognize the thorn tree on the far bank of the Dandera river under which they had been sitting when Mek's men had surprised them.

He rested a few minutes and swallowed a few mouthfuls from the water bottle before passing it to Tamre. 'He's a monk, for goodness' sake,' he consoled himself. 'The little devil is not going to have AIDS, now, is he?' But he wiped the mouth of the bottle carefully when Tamre handed it back to him.

Before starting down the slope he checked the Rigby rifle again, blowing dust off the lens of the scope. Then he sighted through it at a dik-dik-sized rock at the foot of the slope, whilst he twisted the ring on the telescope down to its lowest magnification. He was now ready for a quick shot at close range in thick bush. Satisfied at last, he chambered a round, set the safety-catch and stood up.

'Keep behind me,' he told the boy. 'And do what I do.'

He drifted down the slope, pausing after every few slow steps to check the thorn scrub ahead and on both sides. When he reached the spring head, the earth was damp and soft. A number of animals and birds had been drinking here. He recognized the spoor of both kudu and bushbuck, but amongst these were the tiny, heart-shaped prints of his quarry.

He moved on quietly and at the edge of the scrub he found a midden, a boundary post which the dik-dik had used to mark out its chosen territory. The pile of buckshot-sized pellets of dung would be added to each time the little antelope returned to defecate at this spot.

By now Nicholas was totally absorbed in the hunt. His earlier failures had merely served to pique his fascination. He brought as much concentration to bear as if it had been a man-eating lion he was following. He crept forward a pace at a time, checking the ground before he let his foot fall on a dry twig or patch of rustling leaves, his eyes moving more swiftly than his feet, picking out any movement or touch of colour in the thorny palisade.

It was a flicker of an ear that gave the creature away. It was standing half in shadow, its ruddy coat blending into the backdrop of dried branches, still as if carved from mahogany. Only that small movement betrayed it. It was so close that Nicholas could see the reflection of light from one eye bright as polished onyx, and then the elongated nose wriggled with agitation. It

271

was aware of danger, but uncertain from what quarter it was to come.

Achingly slowly, Nicholas lifted the Rigby to his shoulder. Through the lens he could make out every hair in the tuft between the pricked ears and the little black needle horns. He moved the cross hairs down on to the junction between neck and head. He wanted to restrict the damage to the pelt, so as to make the mounting and taxidermy easier.

'It is the holy creature. Praise God and St John the Baptist!' cried Tamre in a loud voice at his elbow, and he fell to his knees with his hands clasped in front of his eyes.

The dik-dik dissolved like a puff of brown smoke out of the field of the lens, and there was only a soft rustle in the scrub as it fled. Nicholas lowered the rifle slowly and looked down at the boy. He was still on his knees, gabbling out praises and prayers.

'Nice work. I think Woizero Royan must have you in her pay,' he said in English. He reached down, hauled the boy to his feet and switched into Arabic. 'You will stay here. You will not move. You will not speak. You will even breathe very, very quietly, until I come back to fetch you. If you utter even one little prayer before I return, I will personally start you on your journey to meet St Peter at the gates of heaven. Do you understand me?'

He went forward alone, but the little antelope was thoroughly alarmed by now. Nicholas saw it twice more, but he only had fleeting glimpses of ruddy brown movement almost entirely screened by bush. He stood directing bitter imprecations towards the boy monk and listening to the tick of small hooves on dry earth as it raced away, deeper into the thickets. In the end he was forced to give up the hunt for that day.

It was after dark when he and Tamre got back to camp. As soon as Nicholas stepped into the circle of firelight, Royan came to meet him.

'What happened?' she asked. 'Did you see the dik-dik again?'

'Don't ask me. Ask your accomplice. He scared it off. It is probably still running.'

'Tamre, you are a fine young man, and I am very proud of you,' she told him. The boy wriggled like a puppy, giggling and hugging himself with the joy of her approval as he scurried away down the path to the monastery.

Royan was so pleased with the outcome of the hunt that she poured Nicholas a whisky with her own hand and brought it to him as he sagged wearily by the fire.

He tasted it and shuddered, 'Never let a teetotaller pour for you. With a heavy hand like that you should take up tossing the caber or blacksmithing.' Despite the complaint, he took another tentative sip.

She sat close to him, fidgeting with excitement, but it was a while before he became aware of her agitation.

'What is it? Something is eating you alive.'

She threw a cautionary glance in the direction of where Boris sat on the opposite side of the fire, and then dropped her voice, leaned close to him and spoke in Arabic.

'Tessay and I went down to the monastery this afternoon to see Mek Nimmur. Tessay asked me to go with her, just in case Boris — well, you know what I mean.'

'I have a vague idea. You were playing chaperone.' Nicholas took another sip of the whisky and gasped. He exhaled sharply and his voice was husky. 'Go on,' he invited her.

'At one stage, before I left them alone together, we were discussing the festival of Timkat. On the fifth day the abbot takes the *tabot* down to the Abbay. Mek tells us there is a path down the cliff to the water's edge.'

'Yes, we know that.'

'This is the interesting part — this you didn't know. Everybody joins the procession down to the river. Everybody. The abbot, all the priests, the acolytes, every true believer, even Mek and all his men, they all go down to the river and stay there overnight. For one whole day and night the monastery is deserted. Empty. Nobody there at all.'

He stared at her over the rim of his glass, and then slowly he began to smile, 'Now that is very interesting indeed,' he admitted.

'Don't forget, I am coming with you,' she told him severely. 'Don't you dare to even think of leaving me behind.'

Nicholas went to her hut again that evening after dinner. This was the only place in camp where they could be sure of privacy, and where they were safe from eavesdropping. However, this time he did not make the mistake of sitting on her bed. While she perched on the end of it, he took the stool opposite her.

'Before we start planning this thing, let me ask you one question. Have you considered the possible consequences?'

'You mean, what happens if the monks catch us at it?' Royan asked.

'At the very least we can expect them to run us out of the valley. The abbot has a tremendous amount of power. At the worst we can be physically attacked,' Nicholas told her. 'This is one of the most sacred sites in their religion, and don't underestimate that fact. There is a great deal of danger involved. It could go as far as a knife between the ribs, or something nasty in our food.'

'We would also alienate Tessay. She is a deeply religious woman,' Royan added.

'Even more importantly, we would probably outrage Mek Nimmur as well.' Nicholas looked distressed at the thought. 'I don't know what he would do, but I don't think our friendship would stand the test.'

They were both quiet for a while, considering the cost that they might have to pay. Nicholas broke the silence.

'Then again, have you considered your own position? After all, it is your own Church that we will be desecrating. You are a committed Christian. Can you justify this to yourself?'

'I have thought about it,' she admitted. 'And I am not altogether happy about it, but it isn't really my Church. It's a different branch of the Coptic Church.'

'Splitting hairs, aren't we?'

'The Egyptian Church does not deny anyone access to even the most sacred precincts of its church building. I do not feel myself bound by the abbot's prohibition. I feel that as a believing Christian I have the right to enter any part of the cathedral that I wish.'

He whistled softly, 'And you are the one who once said that I should have been a lawyer.'

'Please don't, Nicky. It's not something you should joke about. All I know is that, no matter what, I have to go in there. Even if I give offence to Tessay and Mek and all the priesthood, I have to do it.'

'You could let me do it for you,' he suggested. 'After all, I am an old heathen. It would not spoil my chances of salvation. I don't have any.'

'No.' She shook her head firmly. 'If there is an inscription or something of that nature, I need to see it. You read hieroglyphics quite well, but not as well as I do, and you don't know the hieratic script. I am the expert — you are just a gifted amateur. You need me.

276

I am going in there with you.'

'All right. That is settled, then,' he said with finality. 'Let's start planning. We had better draw up a list of equipment that we may need. Flashlight, knife, Polaroid camera, spare film —'

'Art paper and soft pencils to lift an impression of any inscriptions,' she added to the list.

'Hell!' He snapped his fingers with chagrin. 'I didn't think to bring any.'

'See what I mean? Amateur. I did.'

They talked on until late, and at last Nicholas glanced at his wrist-watch and stood up.

'Long after midnight. I am scheduled to turn into a pumpkin at any moment. Goodnight.'

'There are still two days of the festival before the *tabot* is taken down to the river. Nothing we can do until then. What are your plans?'

'Tomorrow I am going back after that damned little Bambi. It has made a fool of me twice already.'

'I am coming with you,' she said firmly, and that simple declaration gave him a disproportionate amount of pleasure.

'Just as long as you leave Tamre at home,' he warned her as he stooped out through the door.

The tiny antelope stepped out from the deep shadow of the thorn thicket, and the early morning sunlight gleamed on the silky pelt. It kept walking steadily across the narrow clearing.

277

Nicholas's breathing quickened with excitement as he followed it with the telescopic sight. It was ridiculous that he should feel so wrought up with the hunting of such a humble little animal, but his previous failures had sharpened his anticipation. Added to that was the peculiar passion that drives the true collector. Since he had lost Rosalind and the girls, he had thrown all his energy into the building up of the collection at Quenton Park. Now, suddenly, procuring this specimen for it had become a matter of supreme importance to him.

His forefinger rested lightly on the side of the trigger guard. He would not fire until the dik-dik came to a standstill. Even that walking pace would make the shot uncertain. He had to place his bullet precisely, to kill swiftly but at the same time to inflict the least possible damage to the skin.

To this end he had loaded the Rigby with full metal jacket bullets — ones that would not expand on impact and open a wide wound channel, nor rip out a gaping hole in the coat as they exited. These solid bullets would punch a tiny hole the size of a pencil that the taxidermist at the museum would be able to repair invisibly.

He felt his nerves screwing up as he realized that the dik-dik was not going to stop in the open. It made steadily for the thick scrub on the far side of the clearing. This might be his last chance. He fought the temptation to take the shot at the moving target, and it required an effort of will to lift his finger off the trigger again.

The antelope reached the wall of thorn scrub and, the moment before it disappeared, stopped abruptly and thrust its tiny head into the depths of one of the low bushes. Standing broadside to Nicholas, it began to nibble at the pale green tufts of new leaves. The head was screened, so he had to abandon his intention of going for that shot. However, the shoulder was exposed. He could make out the clear outline of the blade beneath the glossy red-brown skin. The dik-dik was angled slightly away from him, in the perfect position for the heart shot, tucked in low behind the shoulder.

Unhurriedly he settled the reticule of the scope on the precise spot, and squeezed the trigger.

The shot whip-cracked in the heavy heated air and the tiny antelope bounded high, coming down to touch the earth already at a full run. Like a rapier rather than a cutlass, the solid bullet had not struck with sufficient shock to knock the dik-dik over. Head down, the dik-dik dashed away in the typical frantic reaction to a bullet through the heart. It was dead already, running only on the last dregs of oxygen in its bloodstream.

'Oh, no! Not that way,' Nicholas cried as he jumped to his feet. The tiny creature was racing straight towards the lip of the cliff. Blindly it leaped out into empty space and flipped into a somersault as it fell, dropping from their sight, down almost two hundred feet into the chasm of the Dandera river.

'That was a filthy bit of luck.' Nicholas jumped over the bush that had hidden them and ran to the rim of the chasm. Royan followed him and the two of them stood peering down into the giddy void.

'There it is!' She pointed, and he nodded. 'Yes, I can see it.'

The carcass lay directly below them, caught on an islet of rock in the middle of the stream.

'What are you going to do?' she asked.

'I'll have to go down and get it.' He straightened up and stepped back from the brink. 'Fortunately it's still early. We have plenty of time to get the job done before dark. I'll have to go back to camp to fetch the rope and to get some help.'

It was afternoon before they returned, accompanied by Boris, both his trackers and two of the skinners. They brought with them four coils of nylon rope.

Nicholas leaned out over the cliff and grunted with relief. 'Well, the carcass is still down there. I had visions of it being washed away.' He supervised the trackers as they uncoiled the rope and laid it out down the length of the clearing.

'We will need two coils of it to get down to the bottom,' he estimated and joined them, painstakingly tying and checking the knot himself. Then he plumbed the drop, lowering the end of the rope down the cliff until it touched the surface of the water, and then hauling it back and measuring it between the spread of his arms.

'Thirty fathoms. One hundred and eighty feet. I won't be able to climb back that high,' he told Boris. 'You and your gang will have to haul me back up.'

He anchored the rope end with a bowline to the bole of one of the wiry thorn trees. Then he again tested it meticulously, getting all four of the trackers and skinners to heave on it with their combined weight.

'That should do it,' he gave his opinion as he stripped to his shirt and khaki shorts and pulled off his chukka boots. On the lip of the cliff he leaned out backwards with the rope draped over his shoulder and the tail brought back between his legs in the classic abseil style.

'Coming in on a wing and a prayer!' he said, and jumped out backwards into the chasm. He controlled his fall by allowing the rope to pay out over his shoulder, braking with the turn over his thigh, swinging like a pendulum and kicking himself off the rock wall with both feet. He went down swiftly until his feet dangled into the rush of water, and the current pushed him into a spin on the end of the rope. He was a few yards short of the spur of rock on which the dead dik-dik lay, and he was forced to let himself drop into the river. With the end of the rope held between his teeth he swam the last short distance with a furious overarm crawl, just beating the current's attempt to sweep him away downstream.

He dragged himself up on to the island and took a few moments to catch his breath, before he could admire the beautiful little creature he had killed. He felt the familiar melancholy and guilt as he stroked the glossy hide and examined the perfect head with the extraordinary proboscis. However, there was no time now for regrets, nor for the searching of his hunter's conscience.

He trussed up the dik-dik, tying all four of its legs together securely, then he stepped back and looked up. He could see Boris's face peering down at him.

'Haul it up!' he shouted, and gave three yanks on the rope as the agreed signal. The trackers were hidden from his view, but the slack in the rope was taken up and then the dik-dik lifted clear of the island and rose jerkily up the wall of the chasm. Nicholas watched it anxiously. There was a moment when the rope seemed to snag when the carcass was two-thirds of the way to the top, but then it freed itself and snaked on up the cliff.

Eventually the dik-dik disappeared from his sight, and there was a long delay until the rope end dropped back over the lip. Boris had been sensible enough to weight it with a round stone the size of a man's head, and he was hanging over the top of the cliff, watching its progress and signalling to his men to control the descent.

When the end of the weighted line touched the surface of the water it was just out of Nicholas's reach. From the top of the cliff Boris began to swing the line until the end of it pendulumed close enough for Nicholas to grab it. With a bowline knot Nicholas tied a loop in the end of the line and slipped it under his armpits. Then he looked up at Boris.

'Heave away!' he yelled, and tugged the dangling rope three times. The slack tightened and then he was lifted off his feet. He began to ascend in a series of spiralling jerks and heaves. As he rose, the belled wall of the chasm arched in to meet him, until he could fend off from the rock with his bare feet and stop himself spiralling at the end of the rope. He was fifty feet from the top of the cliff when suddenly he stopped abruptly, dangling helplessly against the rock face.

'What's going on?' he shouted up at Boris.

'Bloody rope has jammed,' Boris yelled back. 'Can you see where it is stuck?'

Nicholas peered up and realized that the rope had rolled into a vertical crack in the face, probably the same one that had almost stopped the dik-dik reaching the top. However, his own weight was almost five times that of the little antelope, and had forced the rope much more deeply into the crack.

He was suspended high in the air, with a drop of almost a hundred feet under him.

'Try and swing yourself loose!' Boris shouted down at him. Obediently, Nicholas kicked himself back and twisted on the rope to try and roll it clear. He worked until the sweat streamed down into his eyes and the rope had rubbed him raw under the arms.

'No use,' he shouted back at Boris. 'Try to haul it out with brute force!'

There was a pause, and then he saw the rope above the crack tighten like a bar of iron as five strong men hauled on the top end with all their strength. He could hear the trackers chanting their working chorus as they threw all their combined weight on the line.

His end of the line did not budge. It was a solid jam, and he knew then that they were not going to clear it. He looked down. The surface of the water seemed much further than a hundred feet below.

'The terminal velocity of the human body is one hundred and fifty miles an hour,' he reminded himself. At that speed the water would be like concrete. 'I won't be going that fast when I hit, will I?' he tried to reassure himself.

He looked up again. The men on the top of the cliff were still hauling with all their weight and strength. At that moment one of the strands of the nylon rope sheared against the cutting edge of the rock crack, and began to uncurl like a long green worm.

'Stop pulling!' Nicholas screamed. 'Vast heaving!' But Boris was no longer in sight. He was helping his trackers, adding his weight to the pull.

The second strand of the rope parted and unravelled. There was only a single strand holding him now.

It was going to go at any moment, he realized. 'Boris, you ham-fisted bastard, stop pulling!' But his voice never reached the Russian, and with a pop like a champagne cork the third and final strand of the rope parted.

He plunged downwards, with the loose end of the severed rope fluttering above his head. Flinging both arms straight upwards over his head to stabilize his flight, he straightened his legs, arrowing his body to hit feet first.

He thought about the island under him. Would he miss its red rock fangs or would he smash into it and shatter every bone in his lower body? He dared not look down to judge it in case he destabilized his fall and tumbled in mid-air. If he hit the water flat it would crush his ribs or snap his spine.

His guts seemed to be forced into his throat by the speed of his fall, and he drew one last breath as he hit the surface feet first. The force of it was stunning. It was transmitted up his spine into the back of his skull, so that his teeth cracked against each other and bright lights starred his vision. The river swallowed him under. He went down deep, but he was still moving so fast when he hit the rocky bottom that his legs were jarred to the hips. He felt his knees buckle under the strain, and he thought that both his legs had been broken.

The impact drove the air out of his lungs, and it was only when he kicked off the bottom, desperate for air, that he realized with a rush of relief that both his legs were still intact. He broke out through the surface, wheezing and coughing, and realized that he must have missed the island by only the length of his body. However, by now the current had carried him well clear of it.

He trod water on the racing stream, shook the water from his eyes and looked around him swiftly. The walls of the chasm were streaming past him, and he estimated his speed at around ten knots — fast enough to break bone if he hit a rock. As he thought it, another small island flashed past him almost close enough to touch. He rolled on to his back and thrust both feet out ahead of him, ready to fend off should he be thrown on to another outcrop.

'You are in for the whole ride,' he told himself grimly. 'There is only one way out, and that is to ride it to the bottom.'

He was trying to calculate how far he was above the point where the river debouched from the chasm through the pink stone archway, how far he still had to swim.

'Three or four miles, at the least, and the

river falls almost a thousand feet. There are bound to be rapids and probably waterfalls ahead,' he decided. 'From here it does not look good. I'd say the betting is three to one against getting through without leaving some skin and meat on the rocks behind you.'

He looked up. The walls canted in from each side, so that at places they almost met directly over his head. There was only a narrow strip of blue sky showing, and the depths were gloomy and dank. Over the ages the river had scoured the rock as it cut its way through.

'Damned lucky this is the dry season. What is it like down in here in the rainy season?' he wondered. He looked up at the high-water mark etched on the rock fifteen or twenty feet above his head.

Shuddering at the image he looked down again, concentrating on the river ahead. He had his breath back by now, and he checked his body for any damage. With relief he decided that, apart from some bruising and what felt like a sprained knee, he was unhurt. All his limbs were responding, and when he swam a few strokes to one side to avoid another spur of rock, even the sore knee worked well enough to get him out of trouble.

Gradually he became aware of a new sound in the canyon. It was a dull roar, growing stronger as he sped onwards. The walls of the chasm converged upon each other, the gut of rock narrowed and the flood seemed to accelerate as it was squeezed in and confined. The sound of water built up rapidly into a thunder that reverberated in the canyon.

Nicholas rolled over and swam with all his strength across the current until he reached the nearest rock wall. He tried to find a handhold, a place where he could anchor himself, but the rock was polished smooth by the river. It slipped past under his desperately grasping hands, and the river bellowed in his head. He saw the surface around him flatten out and smooth like solid glass. Like a horse laying back its ears as it gathers itself for a jump, the river had sensed what lay ahead.

Nicholas pushed himself away from the rock wall to try and give himself room in which to manoeuvre, and pointed his feet once more downriver. Abruptly the air opened under him and he was launched out into space. All around him white spuming water filled the air, and he was swirled off balance and tossed like a leaf in the torrent. The drop seemed to last for ever, and his stomach swooped against his ribs. Then once more he struck with all his weight and was driven far below the surface.

He fought his way up and abruptly burst out through the surface with his breathing whistling up his throat. Through streaming eyes he saw that he was caught up in the bowl of swirling water below the falls. The waters revolved and eddied, turning in a stately minuet upon themselves.

As he turned, he saw first the high sheet of white water of the falls down which he had tumbled, and then, still turning, the narrow exit from the basin through which the river resumed its mad career downstream. But for the moment he was safe and quiet here in the back-eddy below the falls. The current pushed him against the side of the basin, close in beneath the chute of the falls. He reached out and found a handhold on a clump of mossy fern growing out of a crack in the wall.

Here, at last, he had a chance to rest and consider his position. It did not take him long, however, to realize that his only way out of the chasm was to follow the course of the river and to take his chances with whatever lay downstream. He could expect rapids, if not another set of falls like this one that thundered away close beside him.

If only there were some way up the wall! He looked up, but his spirits quailed as he considered the overhang that formed a cathedral roof high above him.

While he still stared upwards, something caught his eye. Something too regular and regimented to be natural. There was a double row of dark marks running vertically up the wall of rock, beginning at the surface of the water and climbing up the wall to the rim almost two hundred feet overhead. He relinquished his hold on the clump of fern and dog-paddled slowly down to where these marks reached the water.

As he reached them he realized that they were niches, cut about four inches square into the wall. The two rows were twice the spread of his arms apart, and the niche in one row lined up in the horizontal plane exactly with its neighbour in the second row.

Thrusting his hand into the nearest opening, he found that it was deep enough to accommodate his arm to the elbow. This opening, being below the flood level of the waters, was smoothed and worn, but when he looked to those higher up the wall, above the water mark, he saw that they had retained their shape much more clearly. The edges were sharp and square.

'My word, how old are they to have been worn like that?' he marvelled. 'And how the hell did anybody get down here to cut them?'

He hung on to the niche nearest him and studied the pattern in the cliff face. 'Why would anybody go to all that amount of trouble?' He could think of no reason nor purpose. 'Who did this work? What would they want down here?' It was an intriguing mystery.

Then suddenly something else caught his eye. It was a circular indentation in the rock, precisely between the two rows of niches and above the high-water mark. From so far below it looked to be perfectly round — another shape that was not natural.

He paddled further around, trying to reach a position from which he would have a clearer view of it. It seemed to be some sort of rock engraving, a plaque that reminded him strongly of those marks in the black boulders that flank the Nile below the first cataract at Aswan, placed there in antiquity to measure the flood levels of the river waters. But the light was too poor and the angle too acute for him to be certain that it was man-made, let alone to recognize or read any script or lettering that might have been incorporated in the design.

Hoping to devise some way of climbing closer, he tried to use the stone niches as aids. With a great deal of effort, using them as foot and hand-holds, he managed to lift himself out of the water. But the distances between holds were too great and he fell back with a splash, swallowing more water.

'Take it easy, my lad — you still have to swim out of here. No profit in exhausting yourself. You will just have to come back another day to get a closer look at whatever it is up there.'

Only then did he realize how close he was to total exhaustion. This water coming down from the Choke mountains was still cold with the memories of the high snows. He was shivering until his teeth chattered.

'Not far from hypothermia. Have to get out of here now, while you still have the strength.'

Reluctantly he pushed himself away from the wall of rock and paddled towards the narrow opening through which the Dandera river resumed the headlong rush to join her mother

Nile. He felt the current pick him up and bear him forward, and he stopped swimming and let it take him.

'The Devil's roller-coaster!' he told himself. 'Down and down she goes, and where she stops nobody knows.'

The first set of rapids battered him. They seemed endless, but at last he was spewed out into the run of slower water below them. He floated on his back, taking full advantage of this respite, and looked upwards. There was very little light showing above him, for the rock almost met overhead. The air was dank and dark and stank of bats. However, there was little time to examine his surroundings, for once again the river began to roar ahead of him. He braced himself mentally for the assault of turbulent waters, and went cascading down the next steep slide.

After a while he lost track of how far he had been carried, and how many cataracts he had survived. It was a constant battle against the cold and the pain of sodden lungs and strained muscle and overtaxed sinew. The river mauled him.

Suddenly the light changed. After the gloom at the bottom of the high cliffs it was as though a searchlight had been shone directly into his eyes, and he felt the force and ferocity of the river abating. He squinted up into bright sunlight, and then looked back and saw that he had passed out below the archway of pink rock into that familiar part of the river which he had explored with Royan. Coming up ahead of him was the rope suspension bridge, and he had just sufficient strength remaining to paddle feebly towards the small beach of white sand below it.

One of the hairy tattered ropes dangled to the surface of the water, and he managed to catch hold of it as he drifted past and swing himself in towards the beach. He tried to crawl fully ashore, but he collapsed with his face in the sand and vomited out the water he had swallowed. It felt so good just to be able to lie without effort and rest. His lower body still hung into the river, but he had neither the strength nor the inclination to drag himself fully ashore.

'I am alive,' he marvelled, and fell into a state halfway between sleep and unconsciousness.

He never knew how long he had been lying like that, but when he felt a hand shaking his shoulder, and a voice calling softly to him, he was annoyed that his rest had been disturbed.

'*Effendi*, wake up! They seek you. The beautiful Woizero seeks you.'

With a huge effort Nicholas roused himself and sat up slowly. Tamre knelt over him, grinning and waggling his head.

'Please, *effendi*, come with me. The Woizero is searching the river bank on the far side. She is weeping and calling your name,' Tamre told him. He was the only person Nicholas had ever met who contrived to look worried and to grin at the same time. Nicholas looked beyond him and saw that it must be late afternoon, for the sun sat fat and red on the lip of the escarpment.

While still sitting in the sand Nicholas checked his body, making an inventory of his injuries. He ached in every muscle, and his legs and arms were scraped and bruised, but he could detect no broken bones. And although there was a tender lump on the side of his head where he had glanced off a rock, his mind was clear.

'Help me up!' he ordered Tamre. The boy put his shoulder under Nicholas's armpit, where the rope had burnt him, and hoisted him to his feet. The two of them struggled up to the bank and on to the path, and then hobbled slowly across the swinging bridge.

He had hardly reached the other bank when there was a joyous shout from close at hand.

'Nicky! Oh, dear God! You are safe.' Royan ran down the path and threw her arms around him. 'I have been frantic. I thought that —' she broke off, and held him at arm's length to look at him. 'Are you all right? I was expecting to find your broken body —'

'You know me,' he grinned at her and tried not to limp. 'Ten feet tall and bullet-proof. You don't get rid of me that easily. I only did it just to get a hug from you.'

She released him hurriedly. 'Don't read anything into that. I am kind to all beaten puppies, and other dumb animals.' But her smile belied the words. 'Nevertheless, it's good to have you back in one piece, Nicky.'

'Where is Boris?' he asked.

'He and the trackers are searching the banks lower down the river. I think he is looking forward to finding your corpse.'

'What has he done with my dik-dik?'

'There is certainly nothing too much the matter with you if you can worry about that. The skinners have taken it down to the camp.'

'Damn it to hell! I must supervise the skinning and preparation of the trophy myself. They will ruin it!' He put his arm around Tamre's shoulder. 'Come on, my lad! Let's see if I can break into a trot.'

Nicholas knew that in this heat the carcass of the little antelope would decompose swiftly, and the hair would slough from the hide if it were not treated immediately. It was imperative to skin it out immediately. Already it had been left too long, and the preparation of a hide for a full body mount was a skilled and painstaking procedure.

It was already dark as they limped into the camp. Nicholas shouted for the skinners in Arabic.

'Ya, Kif! Ya, Salin!' and when they came run-

295

ning from their living huts he asked anxiously, 'Have you begun?'

'Not yet, *effendi*. We were having our dinner first.'

'For once gluttony is a virtue. Do not touch the creature until I come. While you are waiting for me, fetch one of the gas lights!' He limped to his own hut as fast as his aches would allow. There he stripped and anointed all his visible scrapes and abrasions with mercurochrome, flung on fresh dry clothes, rummaged in his bag until he found the canvas roll which contained his knives, and hurried down to the skinning hut.

By the brilliant white glare of the butane gas lantern he had only just completed the initial skin incisions down the inside of the dik-dik's legs and belly when Boris pushed open the door of the hut.

'Did you have a good swim, English?'

'Bracing, thank you.' Nicholas smiled. 'I don't expect you want to eat your words about my striped dik-dik, do you?' he asked mildly. 'No such bloody animal, I think you said.'

'It is like a rat. A true hunter would not bother himself with such rubbish,' Boris replied haughtily. 'Now that you have your rat, perhaps we can go back to Addis, English?'

'I paid you for three weeks. It is my safari. We go when I say so,' Nicholas told him. Boris grunted and backed out of the hut.

Nicholas worked swiftly. His knives were of

a special design to facilitate the fine work, and he stropped them at regular intervals on a ceramic sharpening rod until he could shave the hairs from his forearm with just the lightest touch.

The legs had to be skinned out with the tiny hooves still attached. Before he had completed this part of the work, another figure stooped into the hut. He was dressed in a priest's *shamma* and headcloth, and until he spoke Nicholas did not recognize Mek Nimmur.

'I hear that you have been looking for trouble again, Nicholas. I came to make sure that you were still alive. There was a rumour at the monastery that you had drowned yourself, though I knew it was not possible. You will not die so easily.'

'I hope you are right, Mek,' Nicholas laughed at him.

Mek squatted opposite him. 'Give me one of your knives and I will finish the hooves. It will go quicker if I help you.'

Without comment Nicholas passed him one of the knives. He knew that Mek could skin out the hooves, for years before he had taught him the art. With two of them working on the pelt, it would go that much faster. The sooner the skin was off, the less chance there would be of deterioration.

He turned his attention to the head. This was the most delicate part of the process. The skin had to be peeled off like a glove, and the eyelids and lips and nostrils must be worked from the inside. The ears were perhaps the most difficult to lift away from the gristle in one piece. They worked in companionable silence for a while, which Mek broke at last.

'How well do you know your Russian, Boris Brusilov?' he asked.

'I met him for the first time when I stepped off the plane. He was recommended by a friend.'

'Not a very good friend.' Mek looked up at him and his expression was grim. 'I came to warn you about him, Nicholas.'

'I am listening,' said Nicholas quietly.

'In '85 I was captured by Mengistu's thugs. They kept me in the Karl Marx prison camp near Addis. Brusilov was one of the interrogators there. He was KGB in those days. His favourite trick was to stick the pressure hose from a compressor up the anus of the man or woman he was questioning and turn on the tap. They blew up like a balloon, until the gut burst.' He stopped speaking while he moved around to work on the other hoof of the antelope. 'I escaped before he got around to questioning me. He retired when Mengistu fled, and went hunting. I don't know how he persuaded Woizero Tessay to marry him, but knowing what I do of the man, I expect she did not have much choice in the matter.'

'Of course, I had my suspicions about him,' Nicholas admitted.

They were quiet after that until Mek whispered, 'I came to tell you that I may have to kill him.'

Neither of them spoke again until Mek had finished working on all four hooves. Then he stood up. 'These days, life is uncertain, Nicholas. If I have to leave here in a hurry, and I do not have a chance to say goodbye to you, then there is somebody in Addis who will pass a message to me if you ever need me. His name is Colonel Maryam Kidane in the Ministry of Defence. He is a friend. My code name is the Swallow. He will know who you are talking about.'

They embraced briefly. 'Go with God!' said Mek, and left the hut quietly. The night swallowed his robed figure and Nicholas stood for a long time at the door, until at last he turned back to finish the work.

It was late by the time he had rubbed every inch of the skin with a mixture of rock salt and Kabra dip to cure it and protect it from the ravages of the bacon beetle and other insects and bacteria. At last he laid it out on the floor of the hut with the wet side uppermost and packed more rock salt on the raw areas.

The walls of the hut were reinforced with mesh netting to keep out hyenas. One of these foul creatures could gobble down the pelt in a few seconds. He made certain the door was wired shut before he carried the lantern up to the dining hut. The others had all eaten and gone to bed hours earlier, but Tessay had left his dinner in the charge of the Ethiopian chef. He had not realized how hungry he was until he smelt it.

The next morning Nicholas was so stiff that he hobbled down to the skinning hut like an old man. First he checked the pelt and poured fresh salt over it, then he ordered Kif and Salin to bury the skull of the dik-dik in an ant heap to allow the insects to remove the surplus flesh and scour the brain pan. He preferred this method to boiling the skull.

Satisfied that the trophy was in good condition, he went on down to the dining hut, where Boris greeted him jovially.

'And so, English. We leave for Addis now, *da?* Nothing more to do here.'

'We will stay to photograph the ceremony of Timkat at the monastery,' Nicholas told him. 'And after that I may want to hunt a Menelik's bushbuck. Who knows? I've told you before. We go when I say so.'

Boris looked disgruntled. 'You are crazy, English. Why do you want to stay in this heat to watch these people and their mumbo-jumbo?'

'Today I will go fishing, and tomorrow we will watch Timkat.'

'You do not have a fishing rod,' Boris protested, but Nicholas opened the small canvas roll no larger than a woman's handbag and showed him the four-piece Hardy Smuggler rod nestling in it.

He looked across the table at Royan, 'Are you coming along to ghillie for me?' he asked.

They went upstream to the suspension bridge where Nicholas set up the rod and tied a fly on to his leader.

'Royal Coachman.' He held it up for her appraisal. 'Fish love them anywhere in the world, from Patagonia to Alaska. We shall soon find out if they are as popular here in Ethiopia, as well.'

She watched from the top of the bank as he shot out line, rolling it upon itself in flight, sailing the weightless fly out to midstream, and then laying it gently on the surface of the water so that it floated lightly on the ripples. On his second cast there was a swirl under the fly. The rod tip arced over sharply, the reel whined and Nicholas let out a whoop.

'Gotcha, my beauty!'

She watched him indulgently from the top of the bank. In his excitement and enthusiasm he was like a small boy. She smiled when she noticed how his injuries had miraculously healed themselves, and how he no longer limped as he ran back and forth along the water's edge, playing the fish. Ten minutes later he slid it, gleaming like a bar of freshly minted gold as long as his arm, flopping and flapping up on to the beach.

'Yellow fish,' he told her triumphantly.

'Scrumptious. Breakfast for tomorrow morning.'

He came up the bank and dropped down in the grass beside her. 'The fishing was really just an excuse to get away from Boris. I brought you here to tell you about what I found up there yesterday.' He pointed up through the archway of pink stone above the bridge. She came up on her elbow and watched him with her full attention.

'Of course, I have no way of telling if it has anything to do with our search, but somebody has been working in there.' He described the niches that he had found carved into the canyon wall. 'They reach from the lip right down to the water's edge. Those below the high-water mark have been severely eroded by the floods. I could not reach those higher up, but from what I could see they have been protected from wind and rain by the dished shape of the cliff; it has formed a veranda roof over them. They appear to be in pristine condition, very much in contrast to those lower down.'

'What do we deduce from that?' she asked.

'That they are very old,' he answered. 'Certainly the basalt is pretty hard. It has taken a long, long time for water to wear it down the way it has.'

'What do you think was the purpose of those holes?'

'I am not sure,' he admitted.

'Could it be that they were the anchor points for some sort of scaffolding?' she asked, and he looked impressed.

'Good thinking. They could be,' he agreed. 'What other ideas occur to you?'

'Ritual designs,' he suggested. 'A religious motif.' He smiled as he saw her expression of doubt. 'Not very convincing, I agree.'

'All right, let's consider the idea of scaffolding. Why would anybody want to erect scaffolding in a place like that?' She lay back in the grass and picked a straw which she nibbled reflectively.

He shrugged. 'To anchor a ladder or a gantry, to gain access to the bottom of the chasm?'

'What other reason?'

'I can't think of any other.'

After a while she shook her head. 'Nor can I.' She spat out the piece of grass. 'If that is the motive, then they were fairly committed to the project. From your description it must have been a substantial structure, designed to support the weight of a lot of men or heavy material.'

'In North America the Red Indians built fishing platforms over waterfalls like that from which they netted the salmon.'

'Have there ever been great runs of fish through these waters?' she asked, and he shrugged again.

'Nobody can answer that. Perhaps long ago — who knows.'

'Was that all you saw down there?'

'High up the wall, aligned with mathematical precision between the two lines of stone niches, there was something that looked like a bas-relief carving.'

She sat up with a jerk and stared at him avidly. 'Could you see it clearly? Was it script, or was it a design? What was the style of the carving?'

'No such luck. It was too high, and the light is very poor down there. I am not even certain that it wasn't a natural flaw in the rock.'

Her disappointment was palpable, but after a pause she asked, 'Was there anything else?'

'Yes,' he grinned. 'Lots and lots of water moving very very fast.'

'What are we going to do about this putative bas-relief of yours?' she asked.

'I don't like the idea in the least, but I will have to go back in there and have another look.'

'When?'

'Timkat tomorrow. Our one chance to get into the *maqdas* of the cathedral. After that we will make a plan to explore the gorge.'

'We are running out of time, Nicky, just when things are getting really interesting.'

'You can say that again!' he murmured. She felt his breath on her lips, for their faces were as close together as those of conspirators or of lovers, and she realized the double meaning of her own words. She jumped to her feet and slapped the dust and loose straw from her jodhpurs.

'You only have one fish to feed the multitude. Either you have a very high opinion of yourself, or you had better get fishing.'

Two *debteras* who had been detailed by the bishop to escort them tried to force a way for them through the crowds. However, they had not reached the foot of the staircase before the escort itself was swallowed up and lost. Nicholas and Royan became separated from the other couple.

'Keep close,' Nicholas told Royan, and maintained a firm grip on her upper arm as he used his shoulder to open a path for them. He drew her along with him. Naturally, he had deliberately contrived to lose Boris and Tessay in the crush, and it had worked out nicely the way he had planned it.

At last they reached a position where Nicholas could set his back firmly against one of the stone columns of the terrace, to prevent the crowd jostling him. He also had a good view of the entrance to the cavern cathedral. Royan was not tall enough to see over the heads of the men in front of her, so Nicholas lifted her up on to the balustrade of the staircase and anchored her firmly against the column. She clung to his shoulder for support, for the drop into the Nile opened behind her.

The worshippers kept up a low monotonous chant, while a dozen separate bands of musicians tapped their drums and rattled their sistrums. Each band surrounded its own patron, a chieftain in splendid robes, sheltering under a huge gaudy umbrella.

There was an air of excitement and expectation almost as fierce as the heat and the stink. It built up steadily and, as the singing increased in pitch and volume, the crowd began to sway and undulate like a single organism, some grotesque amoeba, pulsing with life.

Suddenly from within the precincts of the cathedral there came the chiming of brass bells, and immediately a hundred horns and trumpets answered. From the head of the stairway there was a fusillade of gunfire as the bodyguards of the chieftains fired their weapons in the air.

Some of them were armed with automatic rifles, and the clatter of AK-47 fire blended with the thunder of ancient black powder muzzleloaders. Clouds of blue gunsmoke blew over the congregation, and bullets ricocheted from the cliff and sang away over the gorge. Women shrieked and ululated, an eerie, blood-chilling sound. The men's faces were alight with the fires of religious fervour. They fell to their knees and lifted their hands high in adoration, chanting and crying out to God for blessing. The women held their infants aloft, and tears of religious frenzy streaked their dark cheeks.

From the gateway of the underground church emerged a procession of priests and monks. First came the *debtera*s in long white robes, and then the acolytes who were to be baptized at the riverside. Royan recognized Tamre, his long

306

gangling frame standing a head above the boys around him. She waved over the crowd and he saw her and grinned shyly before he followed the *debteras* on to the pathway to the river.

By this time night was falling. The depths of the cauldron were obscured by shadows, and hanging over it the sky was a purple canopy pricked by the first bright stars. At the head of the pathway burned a brass brazier. As each of the priests passed it he thrust his unlit torch into the flames and, as soon as it flared, he held it aloft.

Like a stream of molten lava the torchlit procession began to uncoil down the cliff face, the priests chanting dolefully and the drums booming and echoing from the cliffs across the river.

Following the baptism candidates through the stone gateway came the ordained priests in their tawdry robes, bearing the processional crosses of silver and glittering brass, and the banners of embroidered silk, with their depictions of the saints in the agony of martyrdom and the ecstasy of adoration. They clanged their bells and blew their fifes, and sweated and chanted until their eyes rolled white in dark faces.

Behind them, borne by two priests in the most sumptuous robes and tall, jewel-encrusted headdresses, came the *tabot*. The Ark of the Tabernacle was covered with a crimson cloth that hung to the ground, for it was too holy to be desecrated by the gaze of the profane.

The worshippers threw themselves down upon

the ground in fresh paroxysms of adoration. Even the chiefs prostrated themselves upon the soiled pavement of the terrace, and some of them wept with the fervour of their belief.

Last in the procession came Jali Hora, wearing not the crown with the blue stone, but another even more splendid creation, the Epiphany crown, a mass of gleaming metal and flashing *faux* jewels which seemed too heavy for his ancient scrawny neck to support. Two *debtera*s held his elbows and guided his uncertain footsteps on to the stairway that led down to the Nile.

As the procession descended, so those worshippers nearest to the head of the stairs rose to their feet, lit their torches at the brazier and followed the abbot down. There was a general movement along the terrace to join the flow, and as it began to empty, Nicholas lifted Royan down from her perch on the balustrade.

'We must get into the church while there are still enough people around to cover us,' he whispered. Leading her by the hand, with his other hand hanging on to the strap of his camera bag, he joined the movement down the terrace. He allowed them to be carried forward, but all the time he was edging across the stream of humanity towards the entrance to the church. He saw Boris and Tessay in the crush ahead of him, but they had not seen him, and he crouched lower so as to screen himself from them.

As he and Royan reached the gateway to the

outer chamber of the church, he eased them out of the throng of humanity and drew her gently through the low entrance into the dim, deserted interior. With a quick glance he made certain that they were alone, and that the guards were no longer at their stations beside the inner gates. Then he moved quickly along the side wall, to where one of the soot-grimed tapestries hung from the ceiling to the stone floor. He lifted the folds of heavy woven wool and drew Royan behind them, letting them fall back into place, concealing them both.

They were only just in time, for hardly had they flattened their backs against the wall and let the tapestry settle when they heard footsteps approaching from the *qiddist*. Nicholas peeked around the corner of the tapestry and saw four white-robed priests cross the outer chamber and swing the main doors closed as they left the church. There was a weighty thud from outside as they dropped the locking beam into place, and then a profound silence pervaded the cavern.

'I didn't reckon on that,' Nicholas whispered. 'They have locked us in for the night.'

'At least it means that we won't be disturbed,' Royan replied briskly. 'We can get to work right away.'

Stealthily they emerged from their hiding-place, and moved across the outer chamber to the doorway of the *qiddist*. Here Nicholas paused and cautioned her with a hand on her arm. 'From here on we are in forbidden territory. Better let me go ahead and scout the lie of the land.'

She shook her head firmly. 'You are not leaving me here. I am coming with you all the way.' He knew better than to argue.

'Come on, then.' He led her up the steps and into the middle chamber.

It was smaller and lower than the room they had left. The wall hangings were richer and in a better state of repair. The floor was bare, except for a pyramid-shaped framework of hand-hewn native timber upon which stood rows of brass lamps, each with the wick floating in a puddle of melted oil. The meagre light they provided was all that there was, and it left the ceiling and the recesses of the chamber in shadow.

As they crossed the floor towards the gates that closed off the *maqdas,* Nicholas took two electric torches from his camera bag and handed one to her. 'New batteries,' he told her, 'but don't waste them. We may be here all night.'

They stopped in front of the doors to the Holy of Holies. Quickly Nicholas examined them. There were engravings of St Frumentius on each panel, his head enclosed in a nimbus of celestial radiance and his right hand lifted in the act of benediction.

'Primitive lock,' he murmured, 'must be hundreds of years old. You could throw your hat through the gap between the hasp and the tongue.' He slipped his hand into the bag and brought out a Leatherman tool.

'Clever little job, this is. With it you do anything from digging the stones out of a horse's hoof, to opening the lock on a chastity belt.'

He knelt in front of the massive iron lock and unfolded one of the multiple blades of the tool. She watched anxiously as he worked, and then gave a little start as with a satisfying clunk the tongue of the lock slid back.

'Mis-spent youth?' she asked. 'Burglary amongst your many talents?'

'You don't really want to know.' He stood up and put his shoulder to one leaf of the door. It gave with a groan of unlubricated hinges, and he pushed it open only just wide enough for them to squeeze through, then immediately shut it behind them.

They stood side by side on the threshold of the *maqdas* and gazed about them in silent awe.

The Holy of Holies was a small chamber, much smaller than either of them had expected. Nicholas could have crossed it in a dozen strides. The vaulted roof was so low that by standing on tiptoe he could have touched it with his outstretched fingertips.

From the floor upwards the walls were lined with shelves upon which stood the gifts and offerings of the faithful, icons of the Trinity and the Virgin rendered in Byzantine style, framed in ornate silver. There were ranks of statuettes of saints and emperors, medallions and wreaths made of polished metal, pots and bowls and jewelled boxes, candelabra with many

311

branches, on each of which the votive candles burned providing an uncertain wavering light. It was an extraordinary collection of junk and treasures, of objects of virtue and garish bric-à-brac, offered as articles of faith by the emperors and chieftains of Ethiopia over the centuries.

In the centre of the floor stood the altar of cedarwood, the panels carved with visionary scenes of revelation and creation, of the temptation and the fall from Eden, and of the Last Judgement. The altar cloth was crocheted raw silk, and the cross and the chalice were in massive worked silver. The abbot's crown gleamed in the candlelight, with the blue ceramic seal of Taita in the centre of its brow.

Royan crossed the floor and knelt in front of the altar. She bowed her head in prayer. Nicholas waited respectfully at the threshold until she rose to her feet again, and then he went to join her.

'The *tabot* stone!' He pointed beyond the altar, and they went forward side by side. At the back of the *maqdas* stood an object covered with a heavy damask cloth encrusted with embroidered thread of silver and gold. From the outline beneath the covering they could see that it was of elegant and pleasing proportions, as tall as a man, but slender with a pedestal topping.

They both circled it, studying the cloaked shape avidly, but reluctant to touch it or to uncover it, fearful that their expectations might prove unwarranted, and that their hopes would be dashed like the turbulent river waters plunging into the cauldron of the Nile. Nicholas broke the tension that gripped them by turning away from the *tabot* stone to the barred gate in the back wall of the sanctuary.

'The tomb of St Frumentius!' he said, and went to the grille. She came to his side, and together they peered through the square openings in the woodwork that was black with age. The interior was in darkness. Nicholas prodded his torch through one of the openings and pressed the switch.

The tomb lit up in a rainbow of colour so bright in the beam of the torch that their eyes took a few moments to adjust and then Royan gasped aloud.

'Oh, sweet heaven!' She began to tremble as if in high fever, and her face went creamy pale as all the blood drained from it.

The coffin was set into a stone shelf in the rear wall of the cell-like tomb. On the exterior was painted the likeness of the man within. Although it was badly faded and most of the paint had flaked away, the pale face and reddish beard of the dead man were still discernible.

This was not the only reason for Royan's amazement. She was staring at the walls above and on either side of the shelf on which the coffin lay. They were a riot of colour, every inch of them covered with the most intricate and elaborate paintings that had miraculously weathered the passage of the millennia.

Nicholas played his torchbeam over them in awestruck silence, and Royan clung to his arm as if to save herself from falling. She dug her sharp nails into his flesh, but he was heedless of the pain.

There were scenes of great battles, fighting galleys locked in terrible combat upon the blue eternal waters of the river. There were scenes of the hunt, the pursuit of the river horse and of great elephants with long tusks of gleaming ivory. There were battle scenes of regiments plumed and armoured, raging in their fury and blood lust. Squadrons of chariots wheeled and charged each other across these narrow walls, half obscured by the dust of their own mad career.

The foreground of each mural was dominated by the same tall heroic figure. In one scene he drew the bow to full stretch, in another he swung high the blade of bronze. His enemies quailed before him, he trod them underfoot or gathered together their severed heads like a bouquet of flowers.

Nicholas played the beam over all this splendid array of art, and brought it to a stop upon the central panel that covered the entire main wall above the shelf on which the rotting coffin lay. Here the same godlike figure rode the footplate of his chariot. In one hand he held the bow and in the other a bundle of javelins. His head was bare of any helmet, and his hair flowed out behind him in the wind of his passage, a thick golden braid like the tail of a lion. His features were noble and proud, his gaze direct and indomitable.

Below him was a legend in classical Egyptian hieroglyphics. In a sepulchral whisper Royan translated them aloud:

> Great Lion of Egypt.
> Best of One Hundred Thousand
> Holder of the Gold of Valour
> Pharaoh's Sole Companion
> Warrior of all the Gods
> May you live for ever!

Her hand shook upon his arm, and her voice choked and died away, stifled with emotion. She gave a little sob, and then shook herself as she brought herself back under control.

'I know this artist,' she said softly. 'I have spent five years studying his work. I would know it anywhere.' She drew a breath. 'I know with utter certainty that nearly four thousand years ago Taita the slave decorated these walls and designed this tomb.'

She pointed to the name of the dead man carved into the stone above the shelf on which his coffin lay.

'This is not the tomb of a Christian saint. Centuries ago some old priest must have stumbled upon it and, in his ignorance, usurped it for his own religion.' She drew another shaky breath. 'Look there! That is the seal of Tanus, Lord Harreb, the commander of all the armies of Egypt, lover of Queen Lostris and the natural father of Prince Memnon, who became the Pharaoh Tamose.'

They were both silent then, lost in the wonder of their discovery. Nicholas broke the silence at last.

'It's all true, then. The secrets of the seventh scroll are all here for us, if we can find the key to them.'

'Yes,' she said softly. 'The key. Taita's stone testament.' She turned back towards the *tabot* stone and approached it slowly, almost fearfully.

'I can't bring myself to look, Nicky. I am terrified that it's not what we hope it is. You do it!'

He went directly to the column, and with a magician's flourish jerked away the damask cloth that covered it. They stared at the pillar of pink mottled granite that he had revealed. It was about six feet high and a foot square at the base, tapering up to half that width at the flat pedestal of the summit. The granite had been polished, and then engraved.

Royan stepped forward and touched the cold stone, running her fingers lingeringly over the hieroglyphic script in the way a blind man reads Braille.

'Taita's letter to us,' she whispered, picking out the symbol of the hawk with a broken wing from the mass of close-chiselled script, tracing the outline with a long, slim forefinger that trembled softly. 'Written almost four thousand years ago, waiting all these ages for us to read and understand it. See how he has signed it.' Slowly she circled the granite pillar, studying each of the four sides in turn, smiling and nodding, frowning and shaking her head, then smiling again as if it were a love letter.

'Read it to me,' Nicholas invited. 'It's too complicated for me — I understand the characters, but I cannot follow the sense or the meaning. Explain it to me.'

'It's pure Taita.' She laughed, her awe and wonder at last giving way to excitement. 'He is being his usual obscure and capricious self.' It was as though she were talking of a beloved but infuriating old friend. 'It's all in verse and is probably some esoteric code of his own.' She picked out a line of hieroglyphics, and followed them with her finger as she read aloud, ' *"The vulture rises on mighty pinions to greet the sun. The jackal howls and turns upon his tail. The river flows towards the earth. Beware, you violators of the sacred places, lest the wrath of all the gods descend upon you!"* '

'It's nonsense jargon. It does not make sense,' he protested.

'Oh, yes, it makes sense all right. Taita always makes sense, once you follow the way his oblique mind is working.' She turned to face him squarely. 'Don't look so glum, Nicky. You can't expect to read Taita like an editorial in *The*

Times. He has set us a riddle that may take weeks and months of work to unravel.'

'Well, one thing is certain. We can't stay here in the *maqdas* for weeks and months while we puzzle it out. Let's get to work.'

'Photographs first.' She became brisk and businesslike. 'Then we can lift impressions from the stone.'

He set down the camera bag and knelt over it to open the flap. 'I will shoot two rolls of colour first, and then use the Polaroid. That will give us something to work on until we can have the colour developed.'

She stood out of his way as he circled the pillar on his knees, keeping the angle correct so as not to distort the perspective. He took a series of shots of each of the four sides, using different shutter speeds and exposures.

'Don't use up all your film,' she warned him. 'We need some shots of the walls of the tomb itself.'

Obediently he went to the grille gates and studied the locking system. 'This is a bit more complicated than the outer gate. If I try to get in here, I might do some damage. I don't think it will be worth the risk of being discovered.'

'All right,' she agreed. 'Work through the openings in the grille.'

He filmed as best he was able, extending the camera through the openings at the full stretch of his arms, and estimating his focus.

'That's the lot,' he told her at last. 'Now

for the Polaroids.' He changed cameras and repeated the entire process, but this time Royan
held a small tape measure against the pillar to
give the scale.

As he exposed each plate he handed it to her
to check the development. Once or twice when
the flash setting on the camera had either over-
exposed or rendered the subject too dull, or
for some other reason she was not satisfied, she
asked him to repeat the shot.

After almost two hours' work they had a complete set of Polaroids, and Nicholas packed his
cameras away and brought out the roll of art
paper. Working together, they stretched it over
one face of the pillar and secured it in place
with masking tape. Then he started at the top
and she at the bottom. Each with a black art
crayon, they rubbed the precise shape and form
of the engravings on to the sheet of blank paper.

'I have learned how important this is when
dealing with Taita. If you are not able to work
with the original, then you must have an exact
copy. Sometimes the most minute detail of the
engraving may change the entire sense and
meaning of the script. He layers everything with
hidden depths. You have read in *River God* how
he considers himself to be the riddler and pun-
ster *par excellence* and the greatest exponent of
the game of bao that ever lived. Well, that much
of the book is accurate. Wherever he is now,
he knows the game is on and he is revelling
in every move we make. I can just imagine him

giggling and rubbing his hands together with glee.'

'Bit fanciful, dear girl.' He settled back to work. 'But I know what you mean.'

The task of transferring the outline of the designs on to the blank sheets of art paper was painstaking and monotonous, and the hours passed as they laboured on hands and knees or crouched over the granite pillar. At last Nicholas stepped back and massaged his aching back.

'That does it, then. All finished.'

She stood up beside him. 'What time is it?' she asked, and he checked his wrist-watch.

'Four in the morning. We had better tidy up in here. Make certain we leave no sign of our visit.'

'One last thing,' Royan said, tearing a corner off one of the sheets of art paper. With it she went to the altar where the abbot's crown lay. Quickly she taped the scrap of paper over the blue ceramic seal in the centre of the crown, and filled it with a rubbing of the design of the hawk with a broken wing.

'Just for luck,' she explained to him, as she came back to help him fold the long sheets of paper and pack them back in the bag. Then they gathered up the shreds of discarded masking tape and the empty film wrappers that he had strewn on the stone slabs.

Before they covered the granite stele with the damask cloth, Royan caressed the stone panels of script as if to take leave of them for ever.

Then she nodded at Nicholas.

He spread the cloth over the pillar and they adjusted the folds to hang as they had found them. From the threshold of the brass-bound door they surveyed the *maqdas* for the last time, then he opened the door a crack.

'Let's go!' She squeezed through and he followed her out into the *qiddist* of the church. It took him only a few minutes to slide the tongue of the lock back into place.

'How will we get out through the main doors?' she asked.

'I don't think that will be necessary. The priests obviously have another entrance from their quarters directly into the *qiddist*. You very seldom see them using the main gates.' He stood in the centre of the floor, and looked around carefully. 'It must be on this side if it leads directly into the monks' living quarters —' he broke off with a grunt of satisfaction. 'Aha! You can see where all their feet have actually worn a pathway over the centuries.' He pointed out a smooth area of dished and worn stone near the side wall. 'And look at the marks of grubby fingers on the tapestry over there.' He crossed quickly to the hanging and drew a fold aside. 'I thought as much.' There was a narrow doorway concealed behind the hanging. 'Follow me.'

They found themselves in a dark passageway through the living rock. Nicholas flashed his torch down its length, but he masked the bulb with his hand to show only as much light as

321

they needed. 'This way.'

The passage turned at right-angles and ahead they could make out a dull illumination. Nicholas switched off the torch and led her on.

Now there was the smell of stale food and humanity, and they passed the doorless entrance to a monk's rock cell. Nicholas flashed his torch into it. It was deserted and bare. A wooden cross hung on the wall with a truckle bed below it. There were no other furnishings. They went on past a dozen others which were almost identical.

At the next turning of the passage Nicholas paused. He felt a tiny draught on his cheek, and the taste of fresh air on his tongue. 'This way,' he whispered.

They hurried on, until suddenly Royan grabbed his shoulder from behind and forced him to stop.

'What —' he began, but she squeezed his shoulder to silence him. He heard it then, the sound of a human voice, echoing eerily through the labyrinth of passageways.

Then came a weird haunting cry, that of a soul in agony, wailing and sobbing. They crept forward, trying to make their escape before they were discovered, but the sounds grew stronger as they went on.

'Dead ahead,' Nicholas warned her in a whisper. 'We are going to have to sneak past.'

Now they saw soft yellow lamplight spilling from the doorway of one of the cells into the passage. There came another heart-rending female cry that echoed down the passage and froze them in their tracks.

'That's a woman's voice. What is happening?' Royan breathed, but he shook his head for silence and led her on.

They had to pass the open door of the lit cell. Nicholas edged towards it with his back flattened to the opposite wall. She followed him, keeping close and clinging to his arm for comfort.

As they looked into the cell the woman cried out again, but this time her voice blended with that of a man. It was a duet without words, but racked with all the feral agony of a passion too fierce to be borne in silence.

In their full view a couple lay naked upon the truckle bed. The woman lay spread-eagled, holding the man's hips between her uplifted knees. Her arms wound hard around his back, upon which each separate muscle stood out proudly and gleamed with sweat. He thrust down into her savagely, his buttocks bunching and pounding with the force of a great black battering ram.

She rolled her head from side to side as another incoherent cry was torn from her straining throat. It seemed too much for the man above her to bear, and he reared back like a flaring cobra, his pelvis still locked to hers, but his back arched like a war bow. Spasm after spasm gripped him. The sinews in the back of his legs were stretched to snapping point, and the muscles in his back fluttered and jumped like separate living creatures.

The woman opened her eyes and looked directly at them as they stood transfixed in the doorway, but she was blinded with the strength of her passion. Her eyes were sightless, as she cried aloud to the man above her.

Nicholas drew Royan away, and they slipped down the passageway and out on to the deserted terrace. They stopped at the foot of the staircase, and breathed the sweet cool night air that was perfumed by the waters of the Nile.

'Tessay has gone to him,' Royan whispered softly.

'For tonight at least,' Nicholas agreed.

'No,' Royan denied. 'You saw her face, Nicky. She belongs to Mek Nimmur now.'

The dawn was flushing the serrated crests of the escarpment to the colours of port wine and roses when they reached camp and separated at the door to Royan's hut.

'I am bushed,' she told Nicholas. 'The excitement has been too much for me. You won't see me again before noon.'

'Good thinking! Sleep as long as you wish. I want you scintillating and perceptive when we start going over the material which we gathered last night.'

It was long before noon, however, when Nicholas was woken from a deep sleep by the harsh and intrusive bellows of Boris as he stormed into the hut.

'English, wake up! I must talk to you. Wake up, man, wake up.'

Nicholas rolled over and thrust one arm out from under the mosquito net as he groped for his wrist-watch. 'Damn you, Brusilov! What the hell do you want?'

'My wife! Have you seen my wife?'

'Now what has your wife got to do with me?'

'She has gone! I have not seen her since last night.'

'The way you treat her, that comes as no stunning surprise. Now go away and leave me to sleep.'

'The whore has run off with that black bastard, Mek Nimmur. I know all about them. Don't try and protect her, English. I know everything that goes on around here. You are trying to cover for her — admit it!'

'Get out of here, Boris. Don't try and involve me in your sordid private life.'

'I saw you and that *shufta* bastard talking in the skinning hut the other night. Don't try to deny it, English. You are in this thing with them.'

Nicholas flung back the mosquito net and jumped out of his bed. 'Kindly moderate your language when you talk to me, you great oaf.'

Boris backed off towards the door. 'I know

that she has run away with him. I searched for them all last night at the river. They have gone, and most of his men with them.'

'Good for Tessay. She is showing some taste in men for a change.'

'You think I will let the whore get away with this? You are wrong, very wrong. I am going to follow them and kill them both. I know which way they are headed. You think I am a fool. I know all about Mek Nimmur. I was head of intelligence —' He broke off as he realized what he had said. 'I will shoot him in the belly and let that whore Tessay watch him die.'

'If you are going after Mek Nimmur, then my bet is that you won't be coming back.'

'You don't know me, English. You beat me up one night when I had a bottle of vodka in my belly, so you think I am easy, *da?* Well, Mek Nimmur will see now how easy I am.'

Boris flung out of the hut. Nicholas pulled on a shirt over his shorts and followed him.

Back in his own hut, Boris had flung a few essential items into a light pack. Now he was stuffing cartridges into the magazine of his 30/06 hunting rifle.

'Let them go, Boris,' Nicholas advised him in a more reasonable tone of voice. 'Mek is a tough lad — they don't come tougher — and he has a war party of fifty men with him. You are old enough to know that you can never hold on to a woman by force. Let her go!'

'I do not want to hold on to her. I want to

kill her. The safari is over, English.' He flung a pair of keys on a leather tag on the floor at Nicholas's feet. 'There are the keys of the Land Cruiser. You can make your own way back to Addis from here. I will leave four of my best men to look after you, and hold your hand. Leave the big truck for me to use. When you get to Addis, leave the keys of the Land Cruiser with my tracker, Aly. I will know where to find him later. I will send you the money I owe you for cancellation. Don't worry — I am a man of principles.'

'How could I ever doubt it?' Nicholas smiled. 'Goodbye, old chum. I wish you luck. You'll need plenty of that if you are going up against Mek Nimmur.'

Boris was several hours behind his quarry, and as soon as he had left the camp he broke into a jog trot that carried him down the pathway to join the main track to the west, towards the Sudanese border. He ran like a scout, with an easy swinging gait that ate up the ground.

'Looks as though he is still in good shape, even with the vodka.' Despite himself Nicholas was impressed as he watched him go. 'But I wonder how long he will be able to keep up that pace?'

He turned back to his own quarters to get a little more sleep, but as he passed her hut Royan popped her head out. 'What was all the shouting about? I thought that you and Boris were having another little difference of opinion.'

'Tessay has done a bunk. Boris has guessed that she has gone off with Mek, and he is chasing after them.'

'Oh, Nicky! Can't we warn them?'

'No chance of that, but unless Mek has gone soft he will be expecting Boris to come after him. In fact, now that I come to think of it, he is probably hoping for just that chance to even the score. No, Mek doesn't need any more help from us. Go back to sleep!'

'I can't possibly sleep now. I am so worked up. I have been looking at the Polaroids that we took last night. Taita has given us an overflowing cup. Come and have a look at this.'

'Just one hour's sleep more?' He made a mock plea.

'Immediately, if not sooner.' She laughed at him.

In her hut she had the Polaroids and the rubbings spread out on the camp table, and she beckoned him to take the seat beside her.

'While you were snoring your head off, I made some progress.' She laid four Polaroids side by side, and placed her large magnifying glass over them. It was a professional land surveyor's model on folding legs, and under it every detail of the photographs was revealed. 'Taita has headed each of the sides of the stele with the name of one of the seasons of the year — spring, summer, autumn and winter. What do you think he was getting at?'

'Page numbers?'

'Exactly my own thought,' she agreed. 'The Egyptians considered spring as the beginning of all new life. He is telling us in which order to read the panels. This one is spring.' She selected one of the photographs.

'It starts with four standard quotations from the *Book of the Dead*.' She quoted the first few lines of the opening section: ' *"I am the first breeze blowing softly over the dark ocean of eternity. I am the first sunrise. The first glimmer of light. A white feather blowing in the dawn wind. I am Ra. I am the beginning of all things. I will live for ever. I shall never perish."* ' Still holding the glass poised, she looked up at him. 'As far as I can see, they do not differ substantially from the original. My instinct is to set these aside for the time being. We can always come back to them later.'

'Let's go with your instinct,' he suggested. 'Read the next section.'

She held the glass to the Polaroid. 'I am not going to look at you while I read this. Taita can be as earthy as Rabelais when he is in the mood. Anyway, here goes. *"The daughter of the goddess pines for her dam. She roars like a lioness as she hurries to meet her. She leaps from the mountain, and her fangs are white. She is the harlot of all the world. Her vagina pisseth out great torrents. Her vagina has swallowed an army of men. Her sex eateth up the masons and the workers of stone. Her vagina is an octopus that has swallowed up a king."* '

329

'Whoa there!' Nicholas chuckled. 'Pretty fruity stuff, don't you think?' He leaned forward to study her face, for it was still turned away from him. 'Och, lassie, you have roses in your bonny cheeks. Not a blush, surely not?'

'Your Scots accent is not in the least convincing,' she told him coldly, still not looking at him. 'When you have finished being clever at my expense, what do you think of what I have just read?'

'Apart from the obvious, I haven't any idea.'

'I want to show you something.' She stood up and packed the photographs and the rolls of art paper back into the haversack. 'You'll need to get your boots on. I am taking you on a little walk.'

An hour later they stood in the centre of the suspension bridge, swaying gently high above the swift waters of the Dandera river.

'Hapi is the goddess of the Nile. Is this river not then her daughter, pining to meet her, leaping from the mountain top, roaring like a lioness, her fangs white with spume?' she asked him.

They stared in silence at the archway of pink stone through which the river poured, and suddenly Nicholas grinned lasciviously. 'I think that I know what you are going to say next. That's what I first thought of when I looked at that cleft. You said it was like a gargoyle's mouth, but I had another image.'

'All I can say is that you must have some

extraordinary lady friends,' she said, and then covered her mouth. 'Ooops! I didn't mean to say that. I am being as disgusting as either you or Taita.'

'The workmen swallowed up in there!' His voice became more excited. 'The masons and the workers in stone!'

'Pharaoh Mamose was a god. The river has swallowed up a god with her — with her stone archway.' She was equally excited. 'I must admit that I would not have made the association if you hadn't explored the interior of the cavern, and found those niches in the wall.' She shook his arm. 'Nicky, we have to get in there again. We have to get a clearer look at that bas-relief you found on the cavern wall.'

'It will take some preparation,' he said dubiously. 'I will have to splice the ropes and make some sort of pulley system, and I will have to drill Aly and the other men to avoid a repetition of my last little fiasco. We won't be ready to make the attempt until tomorrow morning at the very earliest.'

'You get on with it. I will have plenty to keep me occupied with the translation of the stele.' Then she stopped and looked up at the sky. 'Listen!' she whispered.

He cocked his head and above the sound of the river, heard the whining flutter of rotors in the air.

'Dammit!' he snapped. 'I thought we had lost the Pegasus presence. Come on!' He grabbed her arm and hustled her off the bridge. When they reached the land he jumped down on to the beach, and she followed him. The two of them crept under the hanging eaves of the bridge.

They sat quietly on the white sandy beach and listened to the Jet Ranger helicopter approaching swiftly, and then circling back over the hills beyond the pink cliffs. This time the pilot had not spotted them, for he turned away and began to patrol up and down the line of the chasm. Suddenly the engine-beat changed dramatically as the pitch altered and the pilot pulled up the collective.

'Sounds as if he is going in for a landing up there in the hills,' Nicholas said as he crawled out from under the bridge. 'I would feel a lot easier without them snooping around.'

'I don't think we have too much to worry about,' Royan disagreed. 'Even if they are connected with Duraid's killers, we are still way out ahead of them. Obviously they have not tumbled to the importance of the monastery, and the stele.'

'I hope you are right. Let's get back to camp. We must not let them see us in the vicinity of the chasm again. It will be too much of a coincidence for them to find us hanging around here every time they come this way.'

While Royan went to her hut and pored over her photographs and etchings, Nicholas worked with the trackers and skinners. He spliced the unravelled end of the nylon rope to the second hank, to make a single length five hundred feet long. Then he cannibalized the canvas fly of the cooking hut, cutting it up and whipping the raw edges to make a sling seat. He fashioned the ends of the rope into a harness which he spliced into the four corners of the canvas seat.

He had no block and tackle, so he put together a crude gantry of poles which could be extended out over the cliff edge to keep the rope clear of the rock. The rope would run through the groove that he drilled in the end of the central beam with a red-hot iron. He lubricated it with cooking lard.

It was the middle of the afternoon by the time he had completed his preparations. Then, leaving Royan in camp, he led his men, burdened with the coils of rope and the pole sections of the gantry, back up the pathway to the spot where he had abseiled down into the ravine to retrieve the carcass of the dik-dik. From there they worked their way downstream, following the rim of the cliff. It was heavy going for thorn scrub grew right up to the edge, and in many places they were forced to use their machetes to hack their way through.

The sound of the waterfall guided him. As they moved downriver it grew louder, until the rock seemed to quiver under his feet with the roar of falling waters. Finally, by leaning out over the edge and peering downwards, Nicholas could make out the flash of spray in the depths below.

'This is the spot.' He grunted with satisfaction, and explained to Aly in Arabic what he wanted done.

In order to determine the exact position in which to set up the gantry, Nicholas climbed into the canvas sling seat and had them lower him twenty feet down the cliff face, just as far as the beginning of the overhang. Up to that point he was able to keep the nylon rope from abrading on the rock, but he was also able to see around the bulge of the face.

Hanging backwards over the falls and the rocky bowl of the river one hundred and fifty feet below him, he was able at last to see the double row of niches in the rock face. However, the bas-relief engraving was still hidden from view by the tumblehome of the cliff. He gave Aly the signal and they hauled him up.

'We must set up the gantry a little further down,' he told him, and directed them as they hacked away the dense shrubbery that choked the rim. Then suddenly he exclaimed, 'I'll be damned!' He went down on one knee to examine the rim rock that the thorns had concealed.

'There are more excavations here.'

Exposed to the elements, unlike those works further down that had been protected by the overhang, these were badly eroded. There were just vague traces remaining in the rim rock, but he was certain that these indentations were the upper anchor points for the ancient scaffolding. They set up their own gantry on the same levelled area, and extended the long pole out over the drop. Then they rigged and secured it with a crude cantilever system of ropes and lighter poles.

When they were finished, Nicholas crawled out to the end to test the structure and to run the end of the rope through the slot he had prepared for it. The whole structure seemed solid and firm. Nevertheless, it was with relief that he crawled back to solid ground.

He stood up and looked over the tops of the thorn scrub to where the lowering sun was fuming red and angry on the horizon.

'Enough for one day,' he decided. 'The rest can wait for tomorrow.'

The next morning Nicholas and Royan were both up and drinking coffee at the campfire while it was still dark. Aly and his men were squatting at their own fire near by, talking quietly and coughing over the first cigarettes of the day. The project seemed to have caught their imagination. They had no inkling of the reason for this second descent into the chasm, but the enthusiasm of the two *ferengi* was infectious.

As soon as it was light enough to see the path, Nicholas led them back up into the hills. The men chatted cheerfully amongst themselves in Amharic as they hurried through the thorn scrub, and they came out on the rim rock just as the sun broke out over the eastern escarpment of the valley. Nicholas had drilled the men the previous day, and he and Royan had sat half the night going over the plans, so each of them knew their part and they lost little time in setting themselves up for the descent.

Nicholas had stripped to shorts and tennis shoes, but this time he had brought along an old Barbarians rugby jersey for warmth. While he pulled this over his head he pointed out to Royan the platform that had been dug out from the solid rock.

She examined it carefully. 'It's very hard to be sure, but I think you are right. This probably is man-made.'

'When you get further down you will have no doubts. There is very little weathering of the face under the overhang, and the niches are almost perfectly preserved — until they reach the high-water mark, that is,' he told her, as he took his seat in the sling and swung out over the cliff. Dangling from the end of the gantry he gave Aly the sign, and the men lowered him down into the gorge. The rope ran smoothly through the lubricated slot.

He saw at once that he had judged it correctly, and that he was descending in line with the double row of niches. He came level with the enigmatic circle on the cliff face, but it was fifty feet from him, and a growth of gaudy-coloured lichens had streaked and discoloured the rock, partially obscuring the details, so that he still could not be certain that it was not a natural flaw. He passed it and went on down as Aly and his team paid out the rope from above.

When he reached the surface of the water he slipped out of the sling and dropped in. The water was very cold. He trod water, gasping, until his body became acclimatized. Then he gave Aly three tugs on the signal rope. While the canvas seat was hauled up he swam to the side of the pool and held on to one of the carved stone niches for support. He had forgotten how gloomy and cold and lonely it was here in the bottom of the chasm.

After a long delay he craned his head backwards and watched Royan come into sight around the bulge of the overhang, dangling in the sling seat and revolving slowly at the end of the nylon rope. She looked down and waved at him cheerfully.

'Full marks to that girl,' he grinned. 'Not much puts the wind up her.' He wanted to shout encouragement, but he knew it was futile because the thunder of the falls smothered all other sound. So he contented himself with returning her wave.

Halfway down he saw her tugging frantically on the signal rope. Aly had been warned to expect this, and her descent was halted immediately. Then she leaned back in the sling, hanging on with only her left hand, as she groped for Nicholas's binoculars which hung from their strap on to her chest. She was twisted at an awkward angle as she held the glasses to her eyes and tried to manipulate the focus wheel with one hand. He saw that she was obviously having difficulty picking up the round mark on the wall and keeping it in the field of the lens, for the sling was swinging from side to side and at the same time revolving slowly.

She struggled at the end of the rope for what seemed to Nicholas a very long time, but probably was no more than a few minutes. Then abruptly she dropped the binoculars on to her chest, threw back her head and let out a scream that, despite the roar of falling water, carried clearly to Nicholas a hundred feet beneath her. She was kicking her legs joyfully and waving her free hand at him, wild with excitement, as Aly began paying out the rope once more. Still screaming incoherently, she was looking down at him with a face that seemed to light up the cathedral gloom of the gorge.

'I can't hear you,' he yelled back, but the falls defeated both their efforts to communicate.

Royan was wriggling about in her seat, shouting and gesticulating wildly, and now she let go the harness with her other hand and leaned further out to keep him in sight as the sling revolved. She was still twenty feet above the water when she almost lost her balance entirely, and very nearly toppled backwards out of the sling.

'Careful there,' he yelled up at her. 'Those glasses are Zeiss. Two thousand quid at the Zurich duty-free!'

This time his voice must have carried, for she stuck her tongue out at him in a schoolgirlish gesture. But her movements became more circumspect. When her feet were almost touching the water she signalled on the rope to stop her descent and hung there, fifty feet across the pool from him.

'What did you find?' he shouted across.

'You were right, you wonderful man!'

'Is it man-made? Is it an inscription? Could you read it?'

'Yes, yes and yes to all three of your questions!' She grinned triumphantly as she teased him.

'Don't be infuriating. Tell me.'

'Taita's ego got the better of him once again. He couldn't resist signing his work.' She laughed. 'He has left us his autograph — the hawk with a broken wing!'

'Marvellous! Plain bloody marvellous!' he exalted.

'Proof that Taita was here, Nicky. To carve that cartouche, he must have been standing on a scaffolding. Our first guess was right. That niche you are holding on to is part of his ladder to the bottom of the gorge.'

'Yes, but why, Royan?' he yelled back at her. 'Why was Taita down here? There is no evidence of any excavation or building work.'

They both looked around the gloomy cavern. Apart from the tiny rows of niches, the walls were unbroken, smooth and inscrutable until they plunged into the dark water.

'Under the falls?' she shouted across. 'Is there a cutback in the rock? Can you get across there?'

He pushed off from the cliff, and swam towards the thundering chute of water. Halfway across, the current caught him and he had to swim with all his strength to make any headway against it. Thrashing the water with flailing arms and kicking out strongly, he managed to reach a spur of polished, algae-slick rock at the nearest end of the falls.

The water crashed over his head, but he edged his way along under the rock step into the heart of the cascade. Halfway across, the water overwhelmed him. It tore him off his precarious perch, hurled him back into the basin below and swirled him end over end. He surfaced in the middle of the pool, and once again had to swim with all his strength to break free of the grip of the current and to reach the slack water below the wall again. He clung to his handhold in the stone niche, and panted like a bellows.

'Nothing?' she called.

He shook his head, unable to answer until he had finally regained his breath. Finally he managed: 'Nothing. It's a solid rock wall behind the falls.' He gasped another breath, and then invited sarcastically, 'Next bright idea, madam?'

She was silent and he was glad of the respite. Then she called again, 'Nicky, how far do those niches go down?'

'You can see,' he told her, 'right to the one I am holding on to.'

'What about below the surface?'

'Don't be silly, woman.' He was getting cold and irritable. 'How the hell could there be cuttings below the surface?'

'Try!' she yelled almost as irritably. He shook his head pityingly, and drew a deep breath. Still clinging to his handhold, he extended his limbs and body to their full stretch. Then his head went under the dark surface as he groped down as far as he could reach with his toes.

Suddenly he shot back, snorting for air with a startled look on his face. 'By Jove!' he shouted. 'You are right! There is another niche down there!'

'I hate to say I told you so.' Even at that range he could see the smug expression on her face.

'What are you? Some kind of witch?' Then he broke off and rolled his eyes heavenward in despair. 'I know what you are going to ask me to do next.'

'How far do the niches go down?' she called in honeyed tones. 'Will you dive down for me, dear Nicky?'

'That's it,' he said. 'I knew it. I am going to speak to my shop steward. This is slave labour. From now onwards I am on strike.'

'Please, Nicky!'

He hung in the water, pumping air in and out of his lungs, hyperventilating, flushing his bloodstream with oxygen to increase his underwater endurance to its limits. In the end he expelled the contents of his lungs completely, squeezing out the last breath until his chest ached with the effort, and then he sucked in again, filling his lungs to their capacity with fresh air. Finally, with his chest fully expanded, he duck-dived, standing on his head with his legs high out of the water and letting their weight drive him under.

Sliding head-first down the submerged wall, he reached down, groping for the next niche below the surface. He found it, and used it to accelerate his dive, pulling himself on downwards.

He found the second niche below that, and pulled himself on downwards. The niches were about six feet apart — a nautical fathom. Using them as a measure, he was able to calculate his progress accurately.

Swimming on downwards, he found another

niche, then another. Four rows of niches, twenty-four feet below the surface. His ears were popping and squeaking as the pressure squeezed the air out of his Eustachian tubes.

He kept on downwards and found the fifth row of niches. Now the air in his lungs was compressing to almost half its surface volume, and as his buoyancy decreased so his descent became easier and more rapid.

His eyes were wide open, but the waters below him were dark and turbid. He could make out only the surface of the wall directly in front of his face. He saw the sixth niche appear ahead of him and he grasped it, then hesitated.

'Thirty-six feet of depth already, and no sign yet of bottom,' he thought. There had been a time, when he was spearfishing competitively with the army team, that he could free-dive to sixty feet and stay at that depth for a full minute. But he had been younger then and in peak physical condition.

'Just one more niche,' he promised himself, 'and then back up to the surface.' His chest was beginning to throb and burn with the need to breathe, but he pulled hard on his handhold and shot down. He saw the vague shape of the seventh niche appear out of the murk below him.

'They go right to the bottom,' he realized with amazement. 'How on earth did Taita do it? They had no diving equipment.' He grasped the niche and hovered there for a moment, un-

decided if he should risk going further. He knew
he was almost at his physical limit. Already he
was hunting for air, his chest beginning to con-
vulse involuntarily.

'What about one more for the hell of it!' He
was beginning to feel light-headed, and a strange
glow of euphoria came over him. He recognized
the danger signs, and looked down at his own
body. Through the murk he saw that his skin
was wrinkled and folded by the pressure of
water. There were over two atmospheres' weight
bearing down upon him, crushing in his chest.
His brain was becoming starved of oxygen, and
he felt reckless and invulnerable.

'Once more into the breach, dear friends,' he
thought drunkenly, and went on down.

'Number eight, and the doctor's at the gate.'
He felt the eighth niche under his fingers. He
was thinking in gibberish now: 'Number eight,
and I'll have her on a plate.'

He turned to go up again, and his feet touched
bottom. 'Fifty feet deep,' he realized even
through his fuddled state. 'I have left it too
late. Got to get back. Got to breathe.'

He was bracing himself to push off from the
bottom when something grabbed his legs and
dragged him hard against the rock wall.

'Octopus!' he thought, remembering the line
from Taita's stele, *Her vagina is an octopus that
has swallowed up a king.*

He tried to kick out, but his legs were bound
as if by the arms of a sea monster; some cold,

insidious embrace held him captive. 'Taita's octopus. My oath! He meant it literally. It's got me.'

He was pinned against the wall, crushed, helpless. Terror seized him, and the rush of it through his blood flushed away the hallucinations of his oxygen-impoverished brain. He realized what had happened to him.

'No octopus. This is water pressure.' He had experienced the same phenomenon once before. On an army training exercise, while diving near the inlet to the turbines of the generators in Loch Arran, his buddy diver who was roped to him had drifted into their terrible suction. His companion had been sucked against the grille of the intake and his body had been crushed so that the splinters of his ribs had been driven through the flesh of his chest and had come out through the black neoprene rubber of his suit like daggers.

Nicholas had narrowly escaped the same fate. The fact that he was a few feet to one side of his buddy had meant that he escaped the full brunt of the rush of water into the turbine intake. Nevertheless, one of his legs was broken, and it had taken the strength of two other army divers to prise him out of the grip of the current.

This time he was at the limit of his air, and there was no other diver to assist him. He was being sucked into a narrow opening in the rock, the mouth of an underwater tunnel, a subaqueous shaft that bored into the rock wall.

His upper body was free of the baleful influence of the rushing flood, but his legs were being drawn inexorably into it. He was aware that the surrounds of the opening were sharply demarcated, as straight and as square as a lintel hewn by a mason. He was being dragged over and around this lintel. Spreading out his arms, he resisted with all his strength, but his hooked fingers slid over the polished, slimy surface of the rock.

'This is the big one,' he thought. 'This is the one punch that you can't duck.' He hooked his fingers, and felt his nails tear and break as they rasped against the rock. Then suddenly they locked into the last niche in the wall above the sink-hole which was sucking him under.

Now at least he had an anchor point. With both hands he clung to the niche, and fought the pull of the water. He fought it with all his remaining strength and all his heart, but he was near the end of his store of both. He strained until he felt the muscles in both arms popping, until the sinews in his neck stood out in steely cords and he felt something in his head must burst. But he had halted the insidious slide of his body into the sink-hole.

'One more,' he thought. 'Just one more try.' And he knew that was all he had left within him. His air was all used up, and so were his courage and his resolve. His mind swirled, and dark shapes clouded his vision.

From somewhere deep inside himself he drew

out the last reserves, and pulled until the darkness in his head exploded in sheets of bright colours, shooting stars and Catherine wheels that dazzled him. But he kept on pulling. He felt his legs coming out of it, the grip of the waters weakening, and he pulled once more with strength that he had never realized he possessed.

Then suddenly he was free and shooting towards the surface, but it was too late. The darkness filled his head and in his ears was a sound like the roaring of the waterfall in the abyss. He was drowning. He was all used up. He had no knowledge of where he was, how much further he had to go to the surface, but he knew only that he was not going to make it. He was finished.

When he came out through the surface, he did not know that he had done so, and he did not have enough strength left to lift his face out of the water and to breathe. He wallowed there like a waterlogged carcass, face down and dying. Then he felt Royan's fingers lock into the hair in the back of his head, and the cold air on his face as she lifted it clear.

'Nicky!' she screamed at him. 'Breathe, Nicky, breathe!'

He opened his mouth and let out a spray of water and saliva and stale air, and then gagged and gasped.

'You're still alive! Oh, thank God. You were down for so long. I thought you had drowned.'

As he coughed and fought for air and his senses

returned, he realized in a vague way that she must have dropped out of the sling seat and come to his aid.

'You were under for so long. I could not believe it.' She held his head up, clinging with her free hand to the niche in the wall. 'You are going to be all right now. I have got you. Just take it easy for a while. It's going to be all right.'

It was amazing how much her voice encouraged him. The air tasted good and sweet and he felt his strength slowly returning.

'We have to get you up,' she told him. 'A few minutes more to get yourself together, and then I will help you into the sling.'

She swam with him across to the dangling sling and signalled to the men at the top of the cliff to lower it into the water. Then she held the folds of canvas open so that he could slip his legs into them.

'Are you all right, Nicky?' she demanded anxiously. 'Hang on until you get to the top.' She placed his hands on the side ropes of the harness. 'Hold tight!'

'Can't leave you down here,' he blurted groggily.

'I'll be fine,' she assured him. 'Just have Aly send the seat down again for me.'

When he was halfway up he looked down and saw her head bobbing in the dark waters. She looked very small and lonely, and her face pale and pathetic.

'Guts!' His voice was so weak and hoarse that he did not recognize it. 'You've got real guts.' But already he was too high for the words to carry down to her.

Once they had got Royan safely up out of the ravine, Nicholas ordered Aly to dismantle the gantry and hide the sections in the thorn scrub. From the helicopter it would be highly visible and he did not wish to stir Jake Helm's curiosity.

He was in no shape to give the men a hand, but lay in the shade of one of the thorn trees with Royan tending to him. He was dismayed to find how much his near-drowning had taken out of him. He had a blinding headache, caused by oxygen starvation. His chest was very painful and stabbed him every time he breathed: in his struggles he must have torn or sprained something.

He was impressed with Royan's forbearance. She made no attempt to question him about his discoveries in the bottom of the gorge, and seemed genuinely more concerned with his wellbeing than with the progress of their exploration.

When she helped him to his feet and they started back towards camp, he moved like an old man, lame and stiff. Every muscle and sinew in his body ached. He knew that the lactic acid and nitrogen that had built up in his tissues would take some time to be reabsorbed and dispersed.

Once they reached camp Royan led him to his hut and fussed over him as she settled him under the mosquito net. By this time he was feeling a lot better, but he neglected to inform her of this fact. It was pleasant to have a woman caring for him again. She brought him a couple of aspirin tablets and a steaming mug of tea, stiff with sugar. He was putting it on a little when he asked weakly for a second mugful.

Sitting beside his bed, she solicitously watched him drink it. 'Better?' she asked, when he had finished.

'The odds are two to one that I will survive,' he told her, and she smiled.

'I can see that you are better. Your cheek is showing again. You gave me an awful scare, you know.'

'Anything to get your attention.'

'Now that we have decided that you will live, tell me what happened. What sort of trouble did you run into down there in the pool?'

'What you really want to know is what I found down there. Am I correct?'

'That too,' she admitted.

Then he told her everything that he had discovered and how he had been caught in the inflow of the underwater sink-hole. She listened without interruption, and even when he had finished speaking she said nothing for a while, but frowned with concentrated thought.

At last she looked up at him. 'You mean that Taita was able to take those stone niches right down to the very bottom of the pool, fifty feet below the surface?' and when he nodded, she was silent again. Then she said, 'How on earth did he accomplish that? What are your thoughts on the subject?'

'Four thousand years ago the water level may have been lower. There may have been a drought year when the river dried up, and enabled him to get in there. How am I doing?'

'Not a bad try,' she admitted, 'but then why go to all the trouble of building a scaffold? Why not just use the dry river bed as an access? Then again, surely the attraction of the spot for Taita was the river. If it was dry, then it would be just like a thousand other places in this gorge. No, I have a feeling that the fact that it was so inaccessible was the main, if not the only, reason he chose to work there.'

'I suspect that you are correct,' he agreed.

'So if the river was running, even at its lowest level as it is now, how on earth did he manage to carve those niches below the surface? And what would be the point in having scaffolding under water?'

'Beats me. I have no idea,' he admitted.

'All right, let's leave that for the moment. Now let's go over your description of the sink-hole that almost sucked you in. Did you form any estimate of the size of the opening?'

He shook his head. 'It is almost totally dark down there. I could not see more than two or three feet in front of me.'

'Was the entrance directly between the two rows of niches?'

'No, not directly,' he said thoughtfully. 'It was slightly to one side. I hit the bottom of the pool with my feet, and was just about to push off when it grabbed me.'

'So it must be at the very bottom of the pool, and slightly downstream from the scaffolding. You say that the entrance seemed to have a square coping?'

'I am not absolutely sure of that — remember that I could see very little. But that was the impression I received.'

'It may have been another man-made structure, then — perhaps some type of adit shaft driven into the side of the pool?'

'It's possible,' he agreed reluctantly. 'But on the other hand it could just as easily be a natural fault in the strata that the river is draining into.'

She stood up to leave, and he demanded, 'Where are you going?'

'I won't be long. I am going to my hut to fetch my notes, and the material from the stele. Back in a moment.'

When she returned she sat on the floor beside his bed, with her legs drawn up under her in that double-jointed feminine fashion. As she spread her papers around her, he pulled up the edge of the mosquito net and looked down at what she was doing.

'Yesterday, while you were busy building the gantry, I was able to decipher most of the rest of the "spring" face of the stele.' She moved her notebook so that he was able to overlook the pages she had opened. 'These are my preliminary notes. You will see where I have inserted a number of question marks — here and here, for instance. That is where I am uncertain of the translation, or where Taita has used a new and strange symbol. I will have to give more time and consideration to those later.'

'I follow you,' he said, and she went on.

'These sections that I have highlighted with green are quotations from the standard version of the *Book of the Dead*. Take this one here: *"The universe is drawn in circles, the disc of the sun god, Ra. The life of man is a circle that begins in the womb and ends in the tomb. The circle of the chariot wheel foreshadows the death of the serpent that it crushes beneath its rim."* '

'Yes, I recognize the quotation,' he said.

'On the other hand, these parts of the text that I have highlighted in yellow are original Taita writings, or at least are not quotations from the *Book of the Dead* or any other source that I am aware of. This paragraph here in particular is the one that I wanted to bring to your attention.'

She traced a section with her forefinger as she read it aloud, ' *"The daughter of the goddess has conceived. She has been impregnated by the*

353

one who is without seed. She has begotten her own twin sister. The foetus lies for ever coiled in her own womb. Her twin shall never be born. She will never see the light of Ra. She will live for ever in the darkness. In the womb of the sister her bridegroom claims her in eternal marriage. The unborn twin becomes the bride of the god, who was a man. Their destinies are intertwined. They shall live for ever. They shall not perish." '

She looked up from the notebook. 'When I first read it, I was satisfied that the daughter of the goddess was the Dandera river, as we had already agreed. I was also pretty sure that the god that was once a man must be Pharaoh. Mamose was only deified on his ascension to the throne of Egypt. Before that he was a man.'

Nicholas nodded. 'The seedless one is obviously Taita himself. He makes repeated references to the fact that he was a eunuch. But now,' he suggested, 'if you have some new ideas about the mysterious twin sister, let's hear them.'

'The twin of the river would most likely be a branch, or a fork of the stream, wouldn't it?'

'Ah, I see what you are driving at. You are suggesting that the sink-hole is the twin. Down there in the gorge it will never see the light of Ra. Taita, the seedless one, claims paternity, so he is telling us that he is the architect.'

'Exactly, and he has married the twin of the river to Pharaoh Mamose for all eternity. Putting that all together, I have come to the conclusion that we will never find the location of Pharaoh Mamose's tomb until we explore thoroughly that sink-hole that nearly drowned you.'

'How do you suggest we do that?' he asked, and she shrugged.

'I am not the engineer, Nicky. I leave that to you to arrange. All I know is that Taita devised some way of doing it — not only of getting there but of working down there. If our interpretation of the stele is correct, then he carried out extensive mining operations at the bottom of the pool. If he could do it, then there is no reason why you can't do it also.'

'Ah!' he demurred. 'Taita was a genius. He says so repeatedly. I am just an old plodder.'

'I have got all my bets on you, Nicky. You won't let me down, will you?'

There was no call for intensive bushcraft to follow this spoor. His quarry had taken very few anti-tracking precautions. Quite openly they were following the main trail down the Abbay gorge, heading directly westwards towards the Sudanese border. Mek Nimmur was on his way back to his own stronghold.

Boris estimated that he had between fifteen and twenty men with him. It was difficult to be certain, for the tracks on the pathway overlapped each other, and of course he would have scouts on the point ahead of him and sweeping his flanks. There would also be a rearguard dragging the trail behind him.

They were making good time, but such a large party would not be able to outpace a single pursuer. He was sure he was gaining on them. He reckoned that he had started four hours behind them, but judging by recent signs he was now less than two hours adrift.

Without breaking his trot, he stooped to pick something up from the path. As he ran on he examined it. It was a twig, the soft tip shoot of a kusagga-sagga plant that grew beside the track. One of the men ahead of him had brushed against it as he passed, and snapped it off the main branch. It gave Boris a fairly accurate gauge of how far he was behind. Even in the heat of the gorge, the tender shoot had barely begun to wilt. He was even closer than he had estimated.

He slowed down a little as he considered his next move. He knew this part of the valley fairly well. The previous year he had hunted over much of this terrain with an American client, who had been looking for a trophy Walia ibex. They had spent almost a month combing these same gullies and wooded ravines before they had brought down a huge old ram, black with age and carrying a pair of curled, back-sweeping horns that ranked as the tenth largest ever in the *Rowland Ward* record book.

He knew that two or three miles ahead the Nile began another oxbow loop out to the south, and that it then doubled back upon itself. The main trail followed the river, because a series of sheer and formidable cliffs guarded the high ground in the centre of the loop of the river. It was, however, possible to cut the corner. Boris had done it before, while following the wounded ibex.

The American hunter had not killed cleanly — his bullet had struck the ram too far back, missing the heart-lung cavity and piercing the gut. The stricken wild goat had taken to the high ground, following one of its secret paths up amongst the crags. Boris and the American had followed it up and over the mountain. Boris remembered how dangerous and treacherous the path had been, but when it descended the far side of the mountain it had cut off nearly ten miles.

If he could find the beginning of the goat path again, there was every chance that he would be able to get ahead of Mek Nimmur and be lying in wait for him on the far side. That would give him an enormous advantage. The guerrilla leader would be expecting pursuit, not ambush. He would be covering his back trail, and it was highly unlikely that Boris would be able to slip past the rearguard without alerting his intended victims. On the other hand, once he was ahead of them he would be in control. Then he could choose his own killing ground.

As the trail and the main flow of the Nile started to turn away towards the south, he kept watching the high ground above it, seeking a familiar landmark. He had not gone another half-mile before he found it. Here there was a break in the line of dark cliffs, a heavily forested re-entrant, that cut into the wall of basalt.

He stopped and mopped the sweat from his face and neck. 'Too much vodka,' he grunted, 'you are getting soft.' His shirt was as sodden as though he had plunged in the river.

He changed the sling of the rifle to his other shoulder, lifted his binoculars and swept the sides of the wooded gully. They appeared sheer and unscalable, but then he picked out the stunted shape of a small tree that grew out of a narrow crack in the face. It looked like a Japanese bonsai, with a twisted, malformed trunk and tortured branches.

The Walia ibex had been standing on the ledge just above that tree when the American had fired. In his mind's eye Boris could still see the way in which the wild goat had hunched its back as the bullet struck, and then spun around and raced away up the cliff. He panned the glasses upwards gently, and could just make out the inclination of the narrow ledge as it angled up the face.

'*Da, da*. This is the spot.' He was thinking in his mother tongue again. It was a relief after these last days of having to struggle in French and English.

Before he began the climb, he left the trail and scrambled down the boulder-strewn slope to the river. He knelt at the edge of the Nile and splashed double handfuls over himself, soaking his cropped head and sluicing the sweat from his face and neck. He drained and refilled his water bottle, then drank until his belly was painfully full. Then he rinsed out the bottle and refilled it. There was no water on the mountain. Finally he dipped his bush hat in the river and placed it back on his head, sodden and streaming water down his neck and face.

He climbed back to the main trail and followed it for another hundred paces, moving slowly and studying the ground. At one place there was a rock boulder almost blocking the path. The men ahead of him had been forced to step over this obstruction, on to a patch of talcum-fine dust beyond it. They had left perfect impressions of their footprints for him to read.

Most of the men were wearing Israeli-style para boots with a zigzag-patterned sole, and those coming up from behind had overtrodden the spoor of the leaders. He had to go down on one knee to examine the signs minutely before he could pick out the imprint of a much smaller and more delicately formed foot, a lighter, unmistakably feminine tread. It was partially obliterated by other larger masculine footprints, but the outline of the toe was clear, and the pattern was that of a smooth rubber-soled Bata tennis shoe. He would have recognized it from ten thousand others.

He was relieved to find that Tessay was still

with the group, and that she and her lover had not left and taken another path. Mek Nimmur was a sly one, and cunning. He had escaped from Boris's clutches once before. But not this time! The Russian shook his head vehemently: not this time.

He gave his full attention to the female footprint once again. It gave him a pang to look at it. His anger returned in full force. He did not consider his feelings for the woman. Love and desire did not enter into the equation. She was his chattel, and she had been stolen from him. It was only the insult that had significance for him. She had rejected and humiliated him, and for that she was going to die.

He felt the old thrill run through his blood at the thought of the kill. Killing had always been his trade and his vocation, but no matter how often he exercised his craft the thrill was never blunted, the pleasure never satiated. Perhaps it was the only true pleasure left to him, pure and unjaded — not even the vodka could weaken and dilute it as it had the physical act of copulation. He would enjoy killing her even more than he had once enjoyed coupling with her.

These past few years he had hunted only the lower animals, but he had never forgotten what it was like to hunt down and to kill a human being, more especially a woman. He wanted Mek Nimmur, but he wanted the woman more.

In the days of President Mengistu, when he

had been the head of counter-intelligence, his men had known his tastes and had picked the pretty ones for him. He had only one regret now, and that was that this time he would have to do it swiftly. There could be no question of drawing it out and savouring the pleasure. Not like some of the other experiences, which had lasted for hours, sometimes for days.

'Bitch,' he mouthed, and kicked at the dust, stamping on the faint outline of her footprint, obliterating it just as he would do to her. 'Black fornicating bitch.'

He ran now with fresh strength and determination as he left the trail and climbed up towards the deformed tree and the beginning of the goat track up the cliff.

Exactly where he expected it, he found the start of the track and followed it upwards. The higher he climbed, the steeper it became. Often he had to use both hands to haul himself up a gradient, or to work his way along a narrow traverse.

The first time he had climbed this mountain he had been following the blood spoor of the wounded ibex, but now he did not have those splattered droplets to guide him, and twice he missed the path and found himself in a dead end on the cliff face. He was forced to edge back from the drop and retrace his footsteps until he found the correct turning. Each time he did so he was aware that he was losing time, and that Mek Nimmur might pass before he was able to intercept him.

Once he startled a small troop of wild goats which were lying on a ledge halfway up the cliff. They went bounding away up the rock face, more like birds than animals bound by the laws of gravity. They were led by a huge male with a streaming beard and long spiral horns, which in its flight showed Boris a direct route to the top of the cliff.

He tore the skin off his fingertips dragging himself up the last steep pitch, but finally he reached the top and wormed his way over the skyline, never lifting his head. A human form silhouetted against the clear, eggshell-blue sky would be visible from miles around. He moved along behind the crest until he found a small clump of sanseveria to give him cover, and used the erect, spiny leaves to break up the outline of his head as he surveyed the valley a thousand feet below through the binoculars.

From this height the Nile was a broad, glittering serpent uncoiling into the first bend of the oxbow, its surface ruffled by rapids and rocky reefs. The high ground on either bank formed standing waves of upthrust basalt, turbulent and chopped into confusion like a storm sea in a tropical typhoon. The whole danced and shimmered in the heat and the sun beat down with the blows of an executioner's axe, pounding this universe of red rock into heat-exhausted submission.

Though the air danced and trembled with the

mirage in the lenses of his binoculars, Boris traced out the rough trail beside the river, and followed it down the valley to the point where it was hidden by the bend. It was deserted, with no sign of human presence, and he knew that his quarry had moved on out of sight. He had no way of telling how far down the trail they had travelled — he knew only that he must hurry on if he were to cut them off on the far side of the mountain.

For the first time since he had left the river, he drank sparingly from the water bottle. He realized how the heat and the exertion of the climb had dehydrated him. In these conditions a man without water might be dead in hours. It was not in the least surprising that there was so little permanent human habitation down here in the gorge.

When he backed off the skyline he felt rejuvenated, and set out to cross the saddle of the mountain. It was less than a mile across, and without warning he came out on the top of the cliffs on the far side. One more unwary pace and he would have stepped off into space and plunged down a thousand feet. Once again he moved along the crest until he found a concealed vantage point from which to spy the terrain below.

The river was the same — a wide and confused expanse of white-ruffled rapids, running back towards him as it turned through the leg of the oxbow. The trail followed the near bank, except where it was forced to detour inland by the rugged bluffs and stone needles which rose out of the Nile waters.

In the great desolation of the gorge he could pick out no movement other than the run of wild waters and the ceaseless dance of the heat mirage. He knew it was not possible that Mek Nimmur had moved fast enough to have passed completely ahead of him; therefore he must still be coming around the bend of the oxbow.

Boris drank again, and rested for almost half an hour. At the end of that time he felt strong and fully recovered. He debated with himself whether to descend immediately and stake out an ambush on the trail, but in the end decided to keep to the high ground until he had his quarry in sight.

He checked his rifle carefully, making sure that the telescopic sight had not been bumped out of alignment during the climb, and then emptied the magazine and examined the five cartridges. The brass case of one of them was dented and discoloured, so he discarded it and reloaded with another from his belt. He chambered a round and set the safety-catch.

He set the weapon aside while he changed his sweat-dampened socks with a fresh dry pair from his pack and retied his bootlaces with care. Only a novice would risk blistered feet in these conditions, for within hours they would be infected and festering.

He drank once more, and then stood up and

slung the 30/06 on his shoulder. Ready now for anything that the goddess of the chase could send his way, he moved off along the crest to intercept the war party.

From every vantage point along the rim he glassed the valley below, each time without spying his quarry, and the afternoon passed swiftly. He was just beginning to worry that Mek Nimmur had somehow managed to slip past him unseen, that he had crossed the river at some secret ford or taken another path through a hidden valley, when there came a plaintive and querulous cry on the heat-hushed air. He looked up. A pair of kites were circling over one particular clump of thorn scrub on the river bank.

The yellow-billed kite is one of the most ubiquitous scavengers in Africa. It exists in close symbiotic association with man, feeding off his rubbish, picking up his leavings, soaring and circling over his villages or his temporary campsites, watching for his scraps or waiting patiently for him to squat in the bushes and then dropping down immediately he has finished his private business, acting as a universal sewage disposal agent.

Boris studied this pair of birds through his binoculars as they sailed idly in the heated air, always circling directly over that same patch of riverine bush. They had a distinctive manner of steering with their long bifurcated tails, twisting them from side to side as they flirted with the breeze. Their bright yellow beaks showed clearly as they turned their heads to look down at something in the scrub.

He smiled coldly to himself. '*Da!* Nimmur has gone into camp early. Perhaps the heat and the pace are too fierce for his new woman, or perhaps he has stopped to play with her a little.'

He moved on along the rim until he could look down directly into the patch of bush. He studied it through the binoculars, but without picking out any signs of human presence. After almost two hours he was becoming uncertain of his original assumption. The only thing that retained his attention was the pair of kites, which had settled in a treetop overlooking the patch of scrub. He had to trust that they were watching the men hidden in the scrub.

He glanced at the sun anxiously. It was sliding down towards the horizon at last and losing its furious heat. Then he looked down into the valley again.

Directly below the patch of bush was an indentation in the river bank that formed a backwater, almost a small lagoon. When the river was in flood it would be inundated, but now there was a small strip of gravel bank exposed. On this bank stood a number of boulders that had tumbled down from the cliff above. Some of them were lying on the beach, while others had rolled into the river and were half-submerged. The largest was the size of a cottage, a great round mass of dark rock.

As he watched, a man emerged unexpectedly

from the scrub. Boris's pulse quickened as he watched him scramble down on to one of the smaller boulders and jump from there on to the gravel bank. He knelt at the water's edge and filled a canvas bucket with water, then climbed back and disappeared into the bush again.

'Ah! The heat is too much even for them. They must drink, and that gives them away. If it had not been for the birds I would never have known that they were there.' He clucked softly with reluctant admiration. 'Nimmur is a careful man. No wonder he has survived so long. He keeps tight control. But even he must have water.'

Boris kept watching through the glasses as he tried to guess what Mek Nimmur would do next. 'He has lost much time here by sheltering from the heat. He will march again as soon as it is cooler. He will make a night march,' he decided, as he looked at the sun again. 'Three hours until dark. I must make my move before then. Once it is dark it will be difficult to pick my targets.'

Before he stood up he wriggled back from the skyline. He retraced his steps back along the mountainside until a bluff shielded him from the eyes of Mek Nimmur's sentries. Then he started down. There was no goat track here and he had to make his own going, but after a few false starts he discovered an inclined rock shelf that afforded him a fairly easy path down the face. When he reached the bottom of the gorge, he took careful stock of the lie and run of the stratum so as to be able to find it again in an emergency. It was a good escape route, and he knew that he might soon be under pursuit and duress.

It had taken him over an hour to negotiate the descent, and he knew that he was running out of time. He reached the trail at the water's edge, and started back along it towards Mek Nimmur's camp. He was in a hurry now, but even then he was careful to take anti-tracking precautions. He walked on the edge of the trail, stepping only on the stony ground, careful to leave no sign of his passing. But despite his caution, he nearly walked right into them.

He had not covered the first two hundred metres when in the back of his mind he registered the low, mournful whistle of a pale-winged starling, and almost ignored it until alarm bells sounded in his mind. The timing was all wrong. The starling only gave that particular call at dawn when it left its nesting site high up in the cliffs. This was late afternoon down in the heated depths of the gorge. He guessed that it was a signal from one of the scouts coming up the trail towards him. Mek Nimmur's party was on the move.

Boris reacted instantly. He slipped off the trail, and ran back the way he had come until he reached the beginning of the pathway along which he had descended the cliff. He climbed just high enough to be able to overlook the trail.

However, he realized that he had lost much of the advantage that he had built up by cutting across the mountain. This was not the ideal ambush position, and his escape route was exposed to enemy fire from below — he would be lucky to make it to the top. But the idea of abandoning his vengeance never occurred to him. As soon as his targets were in his sights, he would shoot from this stance.

However, he acknowledged to himself that Mek Nimmur had taken him by surprise. Boris had not anticipated that he would move before the sun had set. He had expected to be able to take up a position above the camp in the thorn patch and to be able to get off two careful, well-aimed shots before he was forced to run.

It was also part of his calculations that, once he had dropped Mek Nimmur, his men would not be eager to follow up with too much despatch. Boris planned to make a running retreat, stopping at every defensible strong point to fire a few shots, knock down one or two of them, and keep the pursuit circumspect and cautious until they eventually lost their taste for the game and let him go.

However, all that had now changed. He would have to take the first opportunity that presented itself — almost certainly a moving target — and as soon as he had fired he would be exposed on the path up the cliff face. His one advantage here was that his hunting rifle was a superbly accurate piece, whereas Mek Nimmur's men were all armed with AK-47 assault rifles, rapid-firing but notoriously wild at longer range, and more especially in the hands of these *shufta*. With proper training, the fighting tribesmen of Africa made some of the finest troops in the world. They possessed all the necessary skills, with one exception — they were notoriously poor marksmen.

He lay flat on the ledge, and the rock under him was so hot from the direct sunlight that it burned painfully even through his clothing. He pulled the pack from his back and set it up in front of him, settling the forestock of the rifle over it to give himself a dead rest. He peered through the telescope, wriggling into a comfortable position, sighting on a small rock beside the main trail and then swinging the barrel from side to side to make certain that he had a clear arc of fire.

Satisfied that this was the best stance he could find in the short time left to him, he set the rifle aside and picked up a handful of dirt. He rubbed this gently into his face, and the sweat turned it to mud that coated his pale skin and dulled the shine that an alert scout might pick out at long range. His last concern was to check the angle of the sun, and to satisfy himself that it was not reflecting off the lens of his scope or off any of the metal parts of the rifle. He reached over and pulled at the branch of the shrub beside him so that it cast its shadow over the weapon.

At last he settled down behind the rifle and cuddled the butt into his shoulder, regulating his breathing to a deep slow rhythm, dropping his pulse rate and steadying his hands. He did not have long to wait. He heard the bird-call again, but this time much nearer at hand. It was answered immediately from the far side of the trail, down closer to the river bank.

'The flankers will be having difficulty maintaining station over this terrain.' He grinned without humour, a death's-head grimace. 'They will be bunching and straggling.' As he thought it, a man came into view around the bend of the trail, about five hundred metres dead ahead.

Boris picked him up in the magnified field of the lens. He was a typical African guerrilla, a *shufta* dressed in a tattered and faded motley of camouflage and civilian clothing, festooned with pack and water bottle, ammunition and grenades, carrying his AK at high port. He halted the moment he came through the turn, and crouched into cover behind a boulder at the side of the trail.

For a long minute he surveyed the lie of the land ahead of him, his head turning slowly from side to side. At one point he seemed to be staring directly at Boris, who held his breath and lay as still as the rock beside him. But finally the *shufta* straightened up and gave a hand signal to those out of sight behind him. Then he came on down the trail at a trot. When he had covered fifty metres the rest of the party began to appear, keeping their intervals as precisely as beads on a string. It would not be possible to enfilade this line even with an RPD from a prepared position.

'Good!' Boris approved. 'These are crack troops. Mek must have hand-picked them.' He watched them through the lens, examining the features of each man as he came into view, searching for Mek Nimmur. There were seven of them spread out down the trail now, but still no sign of their leader. The man on the point drew level with Boris's position and then went on past him. A pair of flankers passed directly beneath where he lay, rustling softly by in the scrub not more than a dozen paces from him. He lay like a stone and let them go. The rest of them passed his position, well spaced and moving swiftly. For some minutes after the last of them had gone, the gorge seemed deserted and devoid of all human presence. Then there was another stealthy movement out there.

'The rearguard,' Boris grunted softly. 'Mek is keeping the woman at the rear. His new plaything. He is taking great care of her.'

He slipped the safety-catch on the rifle gently, making certain that no alien metallic sound fell on the heated and hushed air.

'Now let them come,' he breathed. 'I will take Mek first. Nothing fancy, no head shots. Squarely in the centre of the chest. The woman will freeze when he goes down. She does not have the reflexes of a warrior. She will give me a second unhurried shot. At this range there will be no question of a miss. Right between those pretty little black tits of hers.' He became sexually charged by the image of blood and violent death set opposite Tessay's loveliness and grace. 'I might even have a chance to get one of the others. But I can't bank on that. These men are good. More likely that they will dive into cover before I have even had time to kill the woman.'

He watched the faces of the rearguard as, one at a time, carefully spaced, they came into view. Each time he felt his heart trip with disappointment. In the end there were three of them on the path, moving past him at a steady, businesslike jog-trot. But no sign of Mek and the woman. The rearguard disappeared down the path, and the small sounds of their progress dwindled into silence. Boris lay alone on the ledge, his heart thumping and the sour taste of disappointment in the back of his throat.

'Where are they?' he thought bitterly. 'Where the hell is Mek?' And the obvious answer to his own question occurred to him immediately. They had taken a different trail. Mek had used this patrol as a decoy to lure him away.

He lay quietly for a measured five minutes by his wrist-watch, just in case there might be more men coming up the trail. His mind was racing. His last definite placing of Tessay had been the glimpse of her footprint on the trail at the far bend of the oxbow.

That was several hours ago, and if she and Mek had given him the slip they could be anywhere by now. Mek might have won himself a start of a full day or more — it might take Boris that long to work the spoor through. Feeling waves of anger overwhelm him, he had to close his eyes and fight it off in order to keep his sense of reason from being swamped. He had to think clearly now, not go rushing at the problem like a wounded buffalo. He knew that this was one of his weaknesses: he had to keep tight control of himself.

When he opened his eyes again, his anger had become cold and functional. He knew precisely what he had to do and the order in which he must do it. The very first task was to sweep and check the back trail. He had to establish the point at which Mek had left the main detachment of *shufta*.

He slipped down off the ledge and through the scrub to the open trail. Still anti-tracking, but moving swiftly, he made his way upstream, back towards the patch of thorn scrub where the party of *shufta* had lain up in the heat of the day. The first thing he noticed was that the pair of kites had gone. But he did not take this as proof that the bush was deserted, and began to circle it carefully. First he worked the incoming trail on the far side of the patch of bush. Although several hours old now, it was still clear enough to read.

Suddenly he stopped in the centre of the trail and felt the hair rise on his forearms and down the back of his neck as he stared at the sign in the dust of the path. He realized that he had walked into Mek's trap. There lay the distinctive imprint of a Bata tennis shoe.

Mek and the woman had gone into the patch of scrub and had not come out again. They were still in there, and Boris was seized by the strong premonition that Mek was watching him even at that moment, over the open sights of his AK. While he was out in the open like this, stooped over the spoor, Boris was completely vulnerable.

Hurling himself sideways off the path, he landed like a cat in the wire grass beside it, with the rifle at the ready. It took many minutes for his heartbeats to return to normal, and then he rose again into a stealthy crouch and began circling the patch of scrub very cautiously. His nerves were as taut as guitar strings, and his pale eyes darted from side to side. His finger lay upon the trigger of the 30/06 and he kept the muzzle weaving slowly, like the head of a cobra ready to strike in any direction.

He moved down towards the bank of the river, where the noise of the rapids would mask any sound he might make. But when he had almost reached the shelter of the house-sized boulder that he had noticed from the mountain crest he froze again. He had heard a sound that carried over the sound of Nile waters — a sound so incongruous in this place and at this time that for a moment he doubted his own hearing. It was the sound of a woman's laughter, sweet and clear as the tinkle of a crystal chandelier swinging in the breeze.

The sound came from below him, from the river bank beyond the tumbled boulder. He crept towards the boulder, determined to use it for cover and as a vantage point from which he could cover the bank beyond it. But before he reached it he heard the splash of some heavy object striking the surface of the river, and an excited female squeal, both playful and provocative.

Reaching the side of the boulder, and keeping close in under its protective bulk, he stole towards the corner, from which he could overlook the gravel bank beyond. Then, peeping cautiously around the angle of the boulder, he stared in amazement. He could barely believe what he was seeing. He could not credit this kind of stupidity from a man like Mek Nimmur. This was the hard man, the seasoned warrior and survivor of twenty years of bloody bush war acting like a love-sick teenage booby.

Mek Nimmur had sent his men away so that he could be alone to frolic with his new paramour. Boris took time to make absolutely certain that this was not some elaborate trap that had been set for him. It seemed too fortuitous, too heaven-sent to be really true. He searched every inch of the bank in both directions for hidden gunmen before he smiled his cold little smile.

'Of course they are alone. Mek would never let one of his men see Tessay naked like this.' His smile grew broader as he recognized the full extent of his luck. 'He must have gone crazy. Did he not realize that I would follow him? Did he think he was far enough ahead to be able to indulge himself like this? Is there anything in this world as stupid and as short-sighted as a standing prick?' Boris was gloating delightedly now.

The couple had stripped off their clothes and left them in a pile on the beach of grey basalt gravel in the shade of the tall boulder. They were splashing together in the slack water of the river at the edge of the main current. Both of them were stark mother-naked. Mek Nimmur was broad-shouldered, with a heavily muscled back and hard, tight buttocks. Beside him Tessay was slim as a river reed, her waist tiny and her hips narrow. Her skin was the colour of wild honey. They were completely absorbed in each other, without eyes or ears for anything else in this world.

'He must have left men guarding his back trail.' Boris gave Mek the benefit of some sense. 'He never expected me to be ahead of him on the trail. He thinks they are completely secure. Look at the fool,' he gloated, as Mek chased the girl and she let herself be caught. They fell into the shallow water locked in each other's embrace, mouths seeking each other as they surfaced again, laughing as the water streamed down their darkly beautiful faces, the epitome of handsome masculinity and lovely womanhood, the image of an African Adam and Eve captured for a moment in their own little carefree paradise.

Boris tore his eyes from them, and looked to where their clothing had been abandoned on the gravel bar. Mek's AK rifle lay carelessly on top of his camouflage jacket, within a few paces of where Boris stood. He crossed the open gravel bar with a few quick strides, picked up the AK, unclipped the curved magazine and dropped it into his pocket, ejected the round from the chamber and let it fly away into the gravel, replaced the unloaded rifle on the jacket, and rapidly returned to the lee of the boulder. Both Mek and Tessay remained utterly oblivious to what had happened.

Boris stood there quietly in the shadow of the rock, watching them at play in the river. They were almost childlike in their love and their complete preoccupation with each other.

Tessay at last broke from Mek's embrace and left the water. She came up the gravel bar, running long-legged and coltish, her wet silken breasts swinging and jostling each other at each stride as she looked back at him over her shoulder in open invitation. Mek followed her out, the water glistening in the dense curls of his barrel chest, his genitals weighty and puissant.

He caught her before she could reach her clothing and she struggled playfully for a while in his arms, until his mouth clamped down over hers. Then she gave herself up to him completely. While he kissed her his hands ran down her back and over her wet glistening buttocks. Pressing herself against him she moved her feet apart and spread her thighs, inviting him to explore the secrets of her body. She groaned with desire as his hand cupped her sex gently.

Boris felt his anger mingle with the perverse voyeuristic thrill of watching his own wife being taken by another man. A devil's brew of emotions bubbled up inside him. He felt his loins engorging and stiffening almost painfully with excitement, but at the same time his rage shook him like the branch of a tree in a gale of wind.

The lovers sank down on to their knees. Still locked together, Tessay fell backwards and pulled him over on top of herself.

Boris called out loudly, 'By God, Mek Nimmur, you will never know how ridiculous you look with your bare backside in the air like that.'

Mek reacted as swiftly as a leopard surprised on his kill. With a blur of movement he flipped over and reached for the AK-47. Although Boris was ready for him, covering him with the 30/06, aiming at the back of his neck when he shouted to him, Mek was so quick that he had swept up the AK from where it lay and had it pointed at Boris's belly before he could move. Mek pressed the trigger in the same instant as the muzzle came to bear.

The firing pin fell on the empty chamber with a futile click, and the two men stared at each other across the gravel beach, both with their weapons levelled. Tessay was curled naked where Mek had left her, her dark eyes liquid with pain and horror as she watched her husband and realized that Mek was about to die.

Boris chuckled softly, throatily. 'Where do you want it, Mek? How about I shoot the head off that filthy black tool of yours, while it is still standing up in the air like that?'

Mek Nimmur's eyes darted away from his adversary's face, back towards the mountain, and Boris realized that his guess had been correct. Mek had some of his men up there, but they were keeping out of view of the beach while their commander indulged himself.

'Don't worry about them. You will both be dead long before your chimps can get down here to save you.' Boris chuckled again. 'I am enjoying this. You and I had an appointment once before, but you broke it. Never mind — this is going to be even more fun.' He knew that it was not wise to delay with a man like this. Mek had made one mistake, and it was highly unlikely that he would make another. He should blow his head off now, and that would give him a few minutes more to deal with Tessay. But the temptation to gloat over him was too strong.

'I have good news for you, Mek. You will live a few seconds longer. I am going to kill the whore first, and I am going to let you watch. I hope you enjoy it as much as I am going to.' He sidled away from the shelter of the boulder, edging towards where Tessay lay curled on the gravel beach. She was turned half away from him, trying to cover her breasts and her pubic area with hands too small and delicate for the job. Even as he approached the woman, Boris was watching Mek with his full attention. Mek was the danger, and he never took his eyes off him. It was a mistake. He had underestimated the woman.

While pretending to turn away from him modestly, Tessay had reached down between her thighs and found a round, water-worn stone that fitted neatly into her small fist. Suddenly she uncoiled her lithe body and used all the strength of it to hurl the stone at his head. Boris caught the movement from the corner of his eye and flung up his arm to shield his head.

The stone, flying with surprising force at close range, never struck its target. Instead it caught the point of Boris's upraised elbow. His sleeves were rolled up high around his biceps, and there was no padding to cushion the impact of the stone; his arm was bent and flexed, the thin covering of skin drawn tightly over the bone of the joint. The head of the ulna cracked like glass, and Boris howled at the excruciating agony. His hand opened involuntarily, and his forefinger jerked away from the trigger without the strength to fire the shot he was aiming at Mek's belly.

Mek rolled to his feet, and before Boris could change the rifle to his other hand he disappeared behind the angle of the giant boulder.

With his left hand Boris swung the butt of the rifle at Tessay's head, knocking her backwards into the sand. Then he thrust the muzzle into her throat, pinning her there while he shouted angrily. 'I am going to kill her, you black bastard! If you want your whore, you'd better come fetch her!' The pain of the shattered elbow rendered his voice hoarse and brutish.

From somewhere behind the boulder Mek Nimmur's voice rang out strongly and clearly, calling a single word in Amharic that echoed along the cliffs. Then he spoke in English, 'My men will be here in a moment. Leave the woman and I will spare you. Harm her and I will make you plead for death.'

Boris stooped over Tessay and dragged her to her feet with his good arm locked around her throat. He held the rifle in the same hand, pointing it over her shoulder. The hand of his injured arm had recovered sufficiently from the first shock to be able to hold the pistol grip and to manipulate the trigger.

'She will be dead long before your men get here,' he shouted back as he started to drag her away from the boulder. 'Come and get her yourself, Mek. She is here if you want her.'

He tightened his lock around her throat, choking her until she struggled and gasped, tearing at his arm with her nails and leaving long red welts across the tanned skin.

'Listen to her! I am crushing this pretty neck. Listen to her choking.' He tightened his grip, forcing the sounds of distress out of her.

Boris was watching the corner of the boulder where Mek had disappeared. At the same time he was backing away from it, giving himself space in which to work. His mind was racing, for he knew that he could not escape. His right arm was barely usable, and there were too many of Mek's *shufta* companions. He had the woman, but he wanted the man as well. That was the best trade that he could hope for — both of them, he had to have both of them.

He heard a shout, a strange voice from higher up the slope. Mek's men were on their way. He was desperate now. Mek was not going to be drawn; he had not heard him speak or move for almost two minutes. He had lost him — by this time he could be anywhere.

'Too late,' Boris realized. 'I am not going to get him. Only the woman. But I must do it now.' He forced her to her knees and stooped over her, shifting the lock of his arm around her throat.

'Goodbye, Tessay,' he grated in her ear. He tightened his arm muscles and felt the vertebrae in her neck arched to breaking point. It needed only an ounce more pressure.

'It's all over for you,' he whispered, and began the final pressure. He knew from long experience the sound that the vertebrae would make as they gave, and he tensed himself for it, poised for that crackle like the breaking of a green branch, and the slack weight of her corpse in his grip.

Then something crashed into his back with a force that seemed to drive in his backbone and crush his ribs. Both the strength and the direction were entirely unexpected. It did not seem possible that Mek Nimmur could have moved so far and so swiftly. He must have left the shelter of the boulder and circled out through the scrub. Now he had come at Boris from behind.

His attack was so savage that the arm that Boris had wound around Tessay's neck opened. She drew in a wheezing, strangled breath and twisted out of his grip. Boris tried to turn and swing the rifle around, but Mek was on him again, seizing the rifle and trying to wrest it from Boris's hands.

The Russian's finger was still on the trigger, and a shot went off while the muzzle was level with Mek's face. The detonation stunned him for an instant, and he released the rifle and staggered backwards with his ears ringing.

Boris backed away from him, struggling with the weapon, trying to open the bolt and crank another cartridge into the chamber, but his crippled right arm made his movements clumsy and awkward. Mek gathered himself and charged head down across the gravel beach. He drove into Boris with all his weight, and the rifle flew out of the Russian's hands. Locked chest to chest the two of them spun around in a macabre waltz, trying to throw each other, wrestling for the advantage, until they tripped and went over backwards into the river.

They came to the surface still grappling and rolling over each other, first one on top and then the other, a fearful parody of the love-making which Boris had watched a few minutes earlier. Punching and straining and tripping each other, they struggled in the shallows. But every time they fell back into the water the slope of the bank beneath their feet forced them further out, until, when they were waist-deep, the main current of the Nile suddenly picked them up and swept them away downstream. They were still locked together, their heads bobbing in the tumble of waters, their arms thrashing the water white around them, bellowing at each other in primeval rage.

Tessay heard the men that Mek had called coming down through the scrub at the run. She snatched up her *shamma* and pulled it over her head as she ran to meet them. As the first of them burst on to the gravel bar with his AK cocked, she shouted to him in Amharic.

'There! Mek is in the water. He is fighting the Russian. Help him!' She ran with them along the bank. As they drew level with the two men in midstream one of the men stopped and levelled his AK, but Tessay rushed at him and struck up the barrel.

'You fool!' she shouted angrily. 'You will hit Mek.'

Jumping to the top of one of the riverside boulders, she shaded her eyes against the dazzling reflection of the low sun off the water. With a sick feeling in the pit of her stomach she saw that Boris had managed to get behind Mek and had a half nelson hold around his throat. He was forcing Mek's head under the surface. Mek was struggling like a hooked salmon in his grip as they were swept into a long chute of white water.

Tessay jumped down from the rock and ran on down the bank to the next point, from which she could only watch helplessly.

Boris was still holding Mek's head under water as they were borne together into the head of the chute. Fangs of black rock flashed by them on each side as they gathered speed. Mek was a powerful man and Boris had to exert every last ounce of his own strength to hold him, and he knew he could not do so much longer. Suddenly Mek reared back, and for a moment his head came out. He sucked a quick breath of air before Boris could force him under again, but that breath seemed to have renewed his strength.

Desperately Boris looked ahead to the tail of the chute as they sped towards it. There were more rocks there. Boris picked out one great black slab over which the waters poured in a standing wave three feet high. He steered for it, kicking and hauling Mek's body around with the last of his strength.

They flew down the slope of racing water with the rock slab waiting for them at the end like a lurking sea-monster. Boris continued to wrestle with Mek, until he had turned him into a position ahead of him. He planned to steer him into a head-on collision with the rock and use Mek's body to cushion his own impact.

At the very last moment before they struck Mek dragged his head out from the surface, and as he grabbed a precious lungful of air he saw the rock and realized the danger. With a single violent effort he ducked forward below the surface again and rolled over head-first. It was so powerful and unexpected that Boris was unable to resist. Instinctively he maintained his lock around Mek's neck and was carried forward over his back until their positions were reversed. Now Mek had managed to interpose Boris between himself and the rock, so that when they slammed into it it was the Russian who bore the full brunt of the impact.

Boris's right shoulder crunched like a walnut in the jaws of a steel cracker. Although his head was still under water he screamed at the brutal agony of it, and his lungs filled with water. He relinquished his grip and was flung clear of Mek. When he came to the surface he was floundering like a drowned insect, his right arm shattered in two places, his good arm flailing weakly, and his sodden lungs wheezing and pumping.

Mek exploded through the surface only a few yards behind him. Looking around quickly as he strained for air, he spotted Boris's bobbing head almost immediately and with a few powerful overarm strokes came up behind him.

Boris was so far gone that he was not aware of Mek's intentions until he seized his shirt collar from behind and twisted it like a strangler's garotte. With his other hand, below the surface, Mek secured a grip on the back of Boris's wide leather belt and used it like the helm of a rudder to steer him towards the next reef of rocks that was boiling the water ahead of them.

Through his waterlogged lungs Boris was trying to shout invective at him. 'Bastard! Black swine! Filthy —' But his voice was barely audible above the rush of the waters and the growl of the rocky spur that lay across their path. Mek rode him head-first into the rock and he felt the impact transferred through Boris's skull to jolt the straining muscles of his forearms. Instantly Boris went slack in his grip, his head lolled and his limbs became as limp and soft as strands of kelp washing in the surf.

As they tumbled into the next run of open water, Mek used his grip on the back of Boris's collar to lift the Russian's face above the surface. For a moment even he was struck with horror at the injury that he had inflicted. Boris's forehead was staved in. The skin was unbroken, but there was a deep indentation in his skull into which Mek could have thrust his thumb. And Boris's eyes bulged, pushed out of their sockets like those of a battered doll.

Mek swung the inert carcass around in the water, and stared at the broken head from a distance of only a few inches. He reached up and touched the depressed area of the skull with his fingertips, and felt the shards of splintered bone grate and give beneath the skin.

Once again he thrust the shattered head below the surface and held it there, while he crabbed sideways across the current towards the bank. There was no resistance from Boris, but Mek kept his head submerged for the rest of that long tortuous swim across the Nile.

'How do you kill a monster?' he thought grimly. 'I should bury him at a crossroads with a stake through his heart.' But instead he drowned him fifty times over, and at the next bend of the river they were washed into the bank.

Mek's men were waiting for him there. They supported him when his legs sagged under him, and they helped him up the bank. When they started to drag Boris's corpse out of the river, Mek stopped them abruptly.

'Leave him for the crocodiles. After what he has done to our country and our people, he deserves nothing better.' But even in his anger and his hatred he did not want Tessay to have to look at that mutilated head. She had been unable to keep pace with the men, but she was coming along the bank towards him now.

One of his men pushed Boris's corpse back into the current, and as it floated away he un-slung his AK rifle from his shoulder and let off a burst of automatic fire. The bullets chopped up the surface around Boris's head, and socked heavily into his back. They tore holes in his wet shirt and kicked out lumps of raw flesh. The other men on the bank shouted with laughter and joined in the fusillade, emptying their magazines into the lifeless body. Mek did not attempt to prevent them. Some of their close relatives had died most horribly under the Russian's care. The corpse rolled over in a pink cloud of its own blood, and for a moment Boris's pale bulging eyes stared at the sky. Then he sank away beneath the surface.

Mek stood up slowly and went to meet Tessay. He took her in his arms, and as he held her to his chest he whispered to her softly.

'It's all right. He won't ever hurt you again. It's all over. You are my woman now — for ever!'

Since Boris and Tessay had left the camp there was no longer any reason to maintain security, and Nicholas and Royan were no longer obliged to skulk in Royan's hut when they discussed their search for the tomb.

Nicholas transferred their headquarters into the dining hut, and had the camp staff build another large table on which they could spread the satellite photographs and all the other maps and material that they had accumulated. The chef sent a steady supply of coffee from the kitchen, while they pored over the papers and discussed their discoveries in Taita's pool and every theory that either of them dreamed up, no matter how far-fetched.

'We will never be certain if that shaft was made by Taita, or whether it was a natural sinkhole, until we can get back in there with the right equipment.'

'What type of equipment are you talking about?' she wanted to know.

'Scuba, not oxygen rebreathers. Although the navy rebreathing outfits are much lighter and more compact, you cannot use them below a depth of thirty-three feet, the equivalent of one atmosphere of water. After that pure oxygen becomes lethal. Have you ever used an aqualung?'

She nodded. 'When Duraid and I were on honeymoon at a resort on the Red Sea. I had a few lessons and made three or four open-water dives, but let me hasten to add that I am no expert.'

'I promise not to send you down there,' he smiled, 'but I think we can safely say that we have found enough evidence both in Tanus's tomb and Taita's pool to make it imperative that we mount the second phase of this operation.'

She nodded agreement. 'We will have to return with a much more extensive range of equipment, and some expert help. But you are not going to be able to pose as a tourist sportsman next time around. What possible excuse are we going to find for returning that will not set off all the alarm bells in the minds of Ethiopian bureaucracy?'

'You are speaking to the man who has paid unofficial and uninvited visits to both those charming lads Gadaffi and Saddam. Ethiopia should be a Sunday-school picnic in comparison.'

'When do the big rains start up in the mountains?' she asked suddenly.

'Yes!' His expression became serious. 'That is the jackpot question. You only have to look at the high-water mark on the walls of Taita's pool to have some idea what it must be like in there when the river is in full flood.' He flipped over the pages of his pocket diary. 'Luckily, we still have a bit of time — not a great deal, but enough. We will need to move pretty smartly. We have to get back home before I can start work on planning phase two.'

'We should pack up right away, then.'

'Yes, we should. But it seems a damned shame not to take full advantage of every moment we are here, having come all this way. I think we can spare just a few more days to sound out some ideas that I have about Taita's pool and the sink-hole, to try to arrive at some sort of informed guess about what we will need when we return.'

'You are the boss.'

'My word, how pleasant to hear a lady say that.'

She smiled sweetly. 'Enjoy the moment,' she counselled him, 'it may never happen again.' And then she became serious again. 'What are these ideas that you have?'

'What goes up must come down, what goes in must come out,' he said mysteriously. 'The water going into the sink-hole under such pressure must be going somewhere. Unless it joins a subterranean water system and makes its way into the Nile that way, then it should come to the surface where we can find it.'

'Go on,' she invited.

'One thing is certain. Nobody is going to get into the sink-hole from the pool. The pressure is lethal. But if we can find the outlet, we may be able to explore it from the other end.'

'That's a fascinating possibility.' She looked impressed, and turned to the satellite photograph. Nicholas had identified the monastery and ringed it on the photograph. He had marked in the approximate course of the river through the chasm, although the gorge itself was too narrow and covered with bush to show up on the small-scale picture, even under the high-powered magnifying lens.

'Here is the point where the river enters the chasm.' She pointed it out to him. 'And here is the side valley down which the trail detours. Okay?'

'Okay,' he nodded. 'What are you driving at?'

'On our approach march, we remarked that this valley might at one time have been the original course of the Dandera river, and that it seemed to have cut a new bed for itself through the chasm.'

'That's right,' Nicholas agreed. 'I am still listening.'

'The fall of the land towards the Nile is very steep at this point, isn't it? Well, do you recall we crossed another smaller, but still pretty substantial, stream on our way down the dry valley? That stream seemed to emerge from somewhere on the eastern side of the valley.'

'All right, I am with you now. You are suggesting that this may be the overflow from the sink-hole. Clever little devil, aren't you?'

'Just capitalizing on your genius.' She cast down her eyes modestly, and looked up at him from under her lashes. She was clowning, but her lashes were long and dense and curling, and her eyes were the colour of burnt honey with tiny golden highlights in their depths. At this close range he found them disturbing.

He stood up and suggested, 'Why don't we go and take a look?'

Nicholas went to fetch his camera bag and the light day-pack from his hut, and when he returned he found Royan ready to go. But she was not alone.

'I see that you are bringing your chaperon with you,' he remarked with resignation.

'Unless you are tough enough to send him away.' Royan smiled encouragement at Tamre who stood at her side, grinning and bobbing and hugging his shoulders in the ecstasy of being in the presence of his idol.

'Oh, very well.' Nicholas gave in without a struggle. 'Let the little devil come along.'

Tamre lolloped away up the path ahead of them, his grubby *shamma* flapping around his long skinny legs, chanting the repetitive chorus of an Amharic psalm, and every few minutes looking back to make certain that Royan was still following him. It was a hard pull up the valley, and the noonday heat was debilitating. Although Tamre seemed totally unaffected, the other two were both sweating in dark patches through their shirts by the time they reached the point where the stream debouched into the valley. Gratefully, they sought the shade of a patch of acacia trees, and while they rested Nicholas glassed the side of the valley through his binoculars.

'How are they after the dunking I gave them?' she asked.

'Waterproof,' he grunted, 'full marks to Herr Zeiss.'

'What do you see up there?'

'Not much. The bush is too thick. We will have to foot-slog up the side. Sorry.'

They left the shade and made their way up the side of the valley in the direct burning sunlight. The stream tumbled down a series of cascades, each with a pool at its foot. The bush crowded the banks, lush and green where the roots had been able to reach the water. Clouds of black and yellow butterflies danced over the pools, and a black and white wagtail patrolled the moss-green rocks along the edge, its long tail gyrating back and forth like the needle of a metronome.

Halfway up the slope they paused beside one of the pools to rest, and Nicholas used his hat like a fly-swatter to stun a brown and yellow grasshopper. He tossed the insect on to the surface of the pool, and as it kicked weakly and floated towards the exit a long dark shadow rose from the bottom. There was a swirl and a mirrorlike flash of a scaly silver belly, and the grasshopper disappeared.

'Ten-pounder,' Nicholas lamented. 'Why didn't I bring my rod?'

Tamre was crouched near Nicholas on the pool bank, and suddenly he lifted his hand and held it out. Almost at once one of the circling butterflies settled upon his finger. It perched there with its velvety black and yellow wings fanning gently. They stared at him in astonishment, for it was as though the insect had come to his bidding. Tamre giggled and offered the butterfly to Royan. When she held out her hand, he gently transferred the gorgeous insect to her palm.

'Thank you, Tamre. That is a wonderful gift. Now my gift to you is to set it free again.' She pursed her lips and blew it softly into flight. They watched the butterfly climb high above the pool, and Tamre clapped his hands and laughed with delight.

'Strange,' Nicholas murmured. 'He seems to have a special empathy with all the creatures of the wilderness. I think that Jali Hora, the abbot, does not try to control him, but lets him do very much as his simple fancy dictates. Special treatment for a fey soul, one that hears a different tune and dances to it. I must admit that, despite myself, I am becoming quite fond of the lad.'

It was only another fifty feet higher that they came to the source. There was a low cliff of red sandstone, from a grotto at whose foot the stream gushed. The entrance was screened by a heavy growth of ferns, and Nicholas went down on his knees to pull them aside and peer into the low opening.

'What can you see?' Royan demanded behind him.

'Not much. It's dark in there, but it seems to go in for quite some way.'

'You are too big to get in there. You had better let me go in.'

'Good place for water cobra,' he remarked.

'Lots of frogs for them to eat. Are you sure you want to go?'

'I never said that I wanted to.' She sat on the bank while she unlaced her shoes, then lowered herself into the stream. It came halfway up her thighs, and she waded forward against the flow with difficulty.

She was forced to bend almost double to creep under the overhanging roof of the grotto. As she moved deeper in, her voice came back to him.

'The roof gets lower.'

'Be careful, dear girl. Don't take any chances.'

'I do wish you wouldn't call me "dear girl".' Her voice resonated strangely from the cave entrance.

'Well, you are both those things, a girl and dear. How about if I call you "young lady"?'

'Not that either. My name is Royan.' There was silence for a while, then she called again. 'This is as far as I can go. It all narrows down into a shaft of some sort.'

'A shaft?' he demanded.

'Well, at least a roughly rectangular opening.'

'Do you think it is the work of humans?'

'Impossible to tell. The water is coming out of it like the spout of a bath tap. A solid jet.'

'No evidence of any excavation? No marks of tools on the rock?'

'Nothing. It's slick and water-worn, covered with moss and algae.'

'Could a man get into the opening, I mean

if it were not for the water pressure?'

'If he was a pygmy or a dwarf.'

'Or a child?' he suggested.

'Or a child,' she agreed. 'But who would send a child in there?'

'The ancients often used child-slaves. Taita might have done the same.'

'Don't suggest it. You are destroying my high opinion of Taita,' she told him as she backed out of the entrance of the grotto. There were pieces of fern and moss in her hair, and she was soaked from the waist downwards. He gave her a hand and boosted her back on to the bank. The curve of her bottom was clearly visible through her wet trousers. He forced himself not to dwell upon the view.

'So we have to conclude that the shaft is a natural flaw in the limstone, and not a man-made tunnel?'

'I didn't say that. No. I said that I couldn't be sure. You might be correct. Children might have been used to dig it. After all, they were used in the coalmines during the industrial revolution.'

'But there is no way that we would be able to explore the tunnel from this end?'

'Impossible.' She was vehement. 'The water is pouring out under enormous pressure. I tried to push my arm up the shaft, but I did not have the strength.'

'Pity! I was hoping for some more irrefutable evidence, or at least another lead.' He sat down beside her on the bank, and ferreted in his pack. She looked at him quizzically when he brought out a small black anodized instrument and opened the lid.

'Aneroid barometer,' he explained. 'Every good navigator should have one.' He studied it for a moment and then made a note of the reading.

'Explain,' she invited.

'I want to know if this spring is below the level of the entrance to the sink-hole in Taita's pool. If it is not, then we can cross it off our list of possibilities.'

He stood up. 'If you are ready, we can move on.'

'Where to?'

'Why, Taita's pool, of course. We need a reading up there to establish the difference in altitude between the two points.'

Once Tamre knew where they were headed he showed them a short-cut, so it took them just under two hours from the fountain head to the top of the cliff face above Taita's pool.

While they rested, Royan remarked, 'Tamre seems to spend most of his days wandering around in the bush. He knows every path and game trail. He is an excellent guide.'

'Better than Boris, at least,' Nicholas agreed,

as he fished out his barometer and took another reading.

'You look particularly pleased with yourself.' Royan watched his face as he studied the instrument.

'Every reason to be,' he told her. 'Allowing one hundred and eighty feet for the height of the cliff below us, and another fifty feet for the depth of the pool, the entrance to the sinkhole is still over a hundred feet higher than your outlet through the fern grotto on the other side of the ridge.'

'Which means?'

'Which means that there is a distinct possibility that the streams are one and the same. The inflow is here in Taita's pool and the outflow is from your grotto.'

'How on earth did Taita do it?' she puzzled. 'How did he get to the bottom of the pool? You are the engineering marvel. Tell me how you would do it.'

He shrugged, but she persisted. 'I mean, there must be some established way of doing things like that, of working under water. How do they build the piers of a bridge, or the foundations of a dam, or — or — or how did Taita himself build the shaft below the level of the Nile to measure the flow of the river? You remember the description that he gives of his hydrograph in *River God*?'

'The accepted technique is to build a coffer dam,' Nicholas said casually, and then broke off and stared at her. 'My oath, you really are a corker. A dam! What if that old ruffian, Taita, dammed the whole flipping river!'

'Would that have been possible?'

'I am beginning to believe that with Taita anything is possible. He certainly had unlimited manpower at his disposal, and if he could build the hydrograph on the Nile at Aswan, then he understood very clearly the principles of hydrodynamics. After all, the old Egyptians' lives were completely bound up with the seasonal inundations of the river and the management of the floods. From what we have gathered about the old man, it certainly seems possible.'

'How could we prove it?'

'By finding the remains of his dam. It had to be a hell of a work to hold the Dandera river. There is a good chance that some evidence of it remains.'

'Where would he have built the dam?' she asked excitedly. 'Or let me put it another way, where would you site the dam if you had to do it?'

'There is one natural place for it,' he answered promptly. 'The spot where the trail leaves the river and detours down the valley, and the river falls into the chasm.' They both turned their heads in unison and looked upstream.

'What are we waiting for?' she asked, and sprang to her feet. 'Let's go look-see!'

Their excitement was infectious, and Tamre giggled and danced ahead of them along the trail through the thorns and then up the valley to the point where it rejoined the river. The sun had lost the worst of its heat by the time they stood once again above the falls where the Dandera river plunged into the mouth of the chasm, and began its last lap in the race to join the Nile.

'If Taita had thrown a dam across here —' Nicholas made a sweep of his arms across the mouth of the gorge, '— he could have diverted the river down the side valley here.'

'It looks possible,' she laughed. Tamre giggled in sympathy, not understanding a word of what they were saying, but enjoying himself immensely.

'I would need a dumpy level to take some shots of the actual fall of the land. It can be very deceptive, but with the naked eye it does look possible, as you say.' He shaded his eyes and looked up the bluffs on each side of the waterfall. They formed two craggy portals of limestone, between which the river roared as it plunged over the lip.

'I would like to climb up there to get a clearer picture of the layout of the terrain. Are you game?'

'Try and stop me,' she challenged him, and led the climb. It was a heavy scramble, and in some places the limestone was rotten and crumbling dangerously. However, when they came out on the summit of the eastern portal they were rewarded with a splendid overall view of the ground below.

Directly to the north, the escarpment rose like a sheer wall with its battlements crenellated and serrated. Above and beyond it there was a dream of further mountains, the high peaks of the Choke, blue as a heron's plumage against the clearer distant blue of the African sky.

All around them were the badlands of the gorge, a vast confusion of ridges and spines and reefs of rock of fifty different hues, some ash-grey and white, others black as the hide of a bull buffalo, or red as his heart blood. The riverine bush was green, the poisonous vivid green of the mamba in the treetop, while further from the water the scrub was grey and sear, and along the spines of the broken kopjes stood the stark outlines of ancient drought-struck trees, their tortured limbs twisted and black against the sky.

'The picture of devastation,' Royan whispered as she looked around her, 'untamed and untamable. No wonder Taita chose this place. It repels all intruders.'

They were both silent for a while, awed by the wild grandeur of the scene, but as soon as they had recovered from the exertion of the climb their enthusiasm resurfaced.

'Now you can get a good picture of it.' Nicholas pointed down into the valley below them. 'There is a clear divide at the fork of the valley. You can see the natural fall of the ground. There, from that side of the gorge to that point below us, is the narrowest part. It is a neck where the river squeezes through — the natural site for a dam.' He swivelled and pointed down to the left of where they sat. 'It would not take much to spill the river into the valley. Once he had finished whatever he was up to in the chasm, it would take even less to break down the wall of the dam and let the river resume its natural course again.'

Tamre watched their faces eagerly, turning his head to each speaker in turn, uncomprehending, but aping Royan's expression like a mirror. If she nodded he nodded, when she frowned he did the same, and when she smiled he giggled happily.

'It's a big river.' Royan shook her head, while Tamre wagged his from side to side in sympathy and looked wise. 'What method would he have used? An earthen dam? Surely not?'

'The Egyptians used earthen canals and dams for a great many of their irrigation works,' Nicholas mused. 'On the other hand, when they had rock available to work with they used it extensively. They were expert masons. You have stood in the quarries at Aswan.'

'Not much topsoil here in the gorge,' she pointed out. 'But on the other hand, there is plenty of rock. It's like a geological museum. Every type of rock that you could wish for.'

'I agree,' he said. 'Rather than an earthen wall, Taita would most probably have used a masonry and rock fill. That is the type of dam the ancients built in Egypt, long before his time.

405

If that is the case, there is a chance that traces of it have survived.'

'Okay. Let's work on that hypothesis. Taita built a dam of rock slabs, and then he breached it again. Where would we find the remains of it?'

'We would have to start searching on the actual site,' he answered. 'There at the neck of the gorge. Then we would have to search downstream from there.'

They scrambled down the slope again, with Tamre picking out the easiest route for Royan, stopping to beckon her whenever she faltered or paused for breath. They came out in the neck of the valley and stood on the rocky bank of the river, looking about them.

'How high would the wall have been?' Royan asked.

'Not too high. Again, I can't give you a precise answer until I have shot the levels.' He climbed a little way up the side of the wall. There he squatted and turned his head back and forth, looking first down the length of the valley and then towards the lip of the waterfall that dropped into the mouth of the chasm.

Three times he changed his position, on each occasion moving a few paces higher up the slope. The cliff became steeper the higher he climbed. In the end he was clinging precariously to the side of it, but he seemed satisfied. Then he called down to her.

'I would say this is about it, where I am now.

This would be the height of the dam wall. It looks about fifteen feet high to me.'

Royan was still standing on the bank, and now she turned and stared across at the far bank of the river, estimating the distance to the limestone cliff rising above it.

'Roughly a hundred feet across,' she shouted up to him.

'About that,' he agreed. 'A lot of work, but not impossible.'

'Taita was never one to be daunted by size or difficulty.' She cupped her hands around her mouth to shout up to him. 'While you are up there, can you see any sign of works? Taita would have had to pin the dam wall into the cliff.'

He scrambled along the cliff, keeping to the same level, until he was almost directly above the falls and could go no further. Then he slid down to where Royan and Tamre waited.

'Nothing?' she anticipated, and he shook his head.

'No, but you can't really expect that there would be anything left after nearly four thousand years. These cliffs have been exposed to wind and weather for all that time. I think our best bet will be to look for any surviving blocks from the dam wall that might have been carried away when Taita breached it to flood the chasm again.'

They started down the valley, where Royan came upon a chunk of stone that seemed to be of a different type from the surrounding country rock. It was the size of an old-fashioned cabin trunk. Although it was half-covered by undergrowth, the uppermost end — the one that was exposed — had a definite right-angled corner to it. She called Nicholas across to her.

'Look at that.' Royan patted it proudly. 'What do you think of that?'

He climbed down beside her and ran his hands over the exposed surface of the slab. 'Possible,' he repeated. 'But to be certain we would have to find the chisel marks where the old masons started the fracture. As you know, they chiselled a hole into the stone, and then wedged it open until it split.'

Both of them went over the exposed surface carefully, and although Royan found an indentation that she declared was a weathered chisel mark, Nicholas gave her only four out of ten on the scale of probability.

'We are running out of time,' he said, enticing her away from her find, 'and we still have a lot of ground to cover.'

They searched the valley floor for half a kilometre further, and then Nicholas called it off. 'Even in the heaviest flood it is unlikely that any blocks would have been carried down this far. Let's go back and see if anything was washed over the falls into the mouth of the chasm.'

They returned to the bank of the Dandera and worked their way down as far as the falls.

Nicholas peered over.

'It's not as deep here as it is further down,' he estimated. 'I would guess that it is less than a hundred feet.'

'Do you think you could get down there?' she asked dubiously. Spray blew back out of the depths into their faces, and they had to shout at each other to make themselves heard over the thunder of the waters.

'Not without a rope, and some muscle men to haul me back out of there.' He perched himself on the brink and focused the binoculars down into the bowl. There was a jumble of loose rock down there — small, rounded boulders, and one or two very much larger. Some of them were angular, and some with a little imagination could be called retangular. However, their surfaces had been smoothed by the rushing waters, and were gleaming wet. All of them seemed partially submerged or obscured by spray.

'I don't think we can decide anything from up here, and to tell the truth I don't fancy going down there — not this evening anyway.'

Royan sat down beside him and hugged her knees to her chest. She was dispirited. 'So there is nothing we can be certain about. Did Taita dam the river, or didn't he?'

Quite naturally he placed his arm around her shoulders to console her, and after a moment she relaxed and leaned against him. They stared down into the chasm in silence. At last she drew back from him gently, and stood up.

'I suppose we should start back to camp. How long will it take us?'

'At least three hours.' He stood up beside her. 'You are right. It will be dark before we get back, and there is no moon tonight.'

'Funny how tired you feel after a disappointment,' she said, and stretched. 'I could lie down and sleep right here on one of Taita's stone blocks.' She broke off and stared at him. 'Nicky, where did he get them?'

'Where did he get what?' He looked puzzled.

'Don't you see! We are going at it from the wrong end. We have been trying to find out what happened to the blocks. This morning you mentioned the quarries at Aswan. Shouldn't we consider where Taita found the blocks for his dam, rather than what happened to them afterwards?'

'The quarry!' Nicholas exclaimed. 'My word, you are right. The beginning, not the end. We should be looking for the quarry, not the remnants of the dam wall.'

'Where do we start?'

'I hoped you were going to tell me.' He laughed out loud, and immediately Tamre bubbled with sympathetic laughter. They both looked at the boy.

'I think we should start with Tamre, our faithful guide,' she said, and took his hand. 'Listen to me, Tamre. Listen very carefully!' Obediently he cocked his head and stared at her face, summoning all his errant concentration.

'We are looking for a place where the square stones come from.' He looked mystified, so she tried again. 'Long ago there were men who cut the rock from the mountains. Somewhere near here, they left a big hole. Perhaps there are still square blocks of stone lying in the hole?'

Suddenly the boy's face cleared and split into a beatific smile. 'The Jesus stone!' he cried happily.

He sprang to his feet without relinquishing his grip on her hand. 'I show you my Jesus stone.' He dragged her after him as he bounded away down the valley.

'Wait, Tamre!' she pleaded. 'Not so fast.' But in vain. Tamre kept up the pace and burst into an Amharic hymn as he ran. Nicholas followed at a more sedate pace, and caught up with them a quarter of a mile down the valley.

There he found Tamre on his knees, pressing his forehead against the rock wall of the valley, his eyes shut tightly as he prayed. He had dragged Royan down beside him.

'What on earth are you doing?' Nicholas demanded, as he came up.

'We are praying,' she told him primly. 'Tamre's instructions. We have to pray before we can go to the Jesus stone.'

She turned away from Nicholas, closed her eyes and clasped her hands in front of her eyes, then began to pray softly.

Nicholas found a seat on a boulder a little

411

way from them. 'I don't suppose it can do any harm,' he consoled himself, as he settled down to wait.

Abruptly Tamre sprang to his feet and performed a giddy little dance, flapping his arms and whirling around until he raised the dust. Then he stopped and chanted. 'It is done. We can go in to the Jesus stone.'

Once again he seized Royan's hand and led her to the rock wall. In front of Nicholas's eyes the two of them seemed to vanish, and he stood up in mild alarm.

'Royan!' he called. 'Where are you? What's going on?'

'This way, Nicky. Come this way!'

He went to the wall and exclaimed with astonishment, 'My oath! We would never have found this in a year of searching.'

The cliff face was folded back upon itself, forming a concealed entrance. He walked through the opening, gazing up the vertical sides, and within thirty paces came out into an open amphitheatre that was at least a hundred yards across and open to the sky. The walls were of solid rock, and he could see at a glance that it was the same micaceous schist as the block which Royan had found lying on the floor of the valley.

It was apparent that the bowl had been quarried out of the living rock, leaving tiers rising up to the top of the walls. The recesses from which the blocks had been hacked were still plain to see and had left deep steps with right-angled profiles. Some scrub and undergrowth had found a precarious foothold in the cracks, but the open quarry was not choked with this growth and Nicholas could see that a stockpile of finished granite blocks remained scattered about the bottom of the excavation. He was so awed by the discovery that he could find no words to express himself. He stood just inside the entrance, his head slowly turning from side to side as he tried to take it all in.

Tamre had led Royan to the centre of the quarry where one large slab lay on its own. It was obvious that the ancients had been on the point of removing it and transporting it up the valley, for it was finished and dressed into a perfect rectangle.

'The Jesus stone!' Tamre chanted, kneeling before the slab and pulling Royan down beside him. 'Jesus led me here. The first time I came here I saw him standing on the stone. He had a long white beard and eyes that were kind and sad.' He crossed himself and began to recite one of the psalms, swaying and bobbing to the rhythm.

As Nicholas moved up quietly behind them he saw the evidence that Tamre had visited this sacred place of his regularly. The Jesus stone was his own private altar, and his pathetic little offerings were lying where he had laid them. There were old *tej* flasks and baked clay pots, most of them cracked and broken. In them stood bunches of wild flowers that had long ago wilted and dried out. There were other treasures that he had gathered and placed upon his altar — tortoise shells and porcupine quills, a cross that had been hand-carved from wood and decorated with scraps of coloured cloth, necklaces of lucky beans, and models of animals and birds moulded from blue river clay.

Nicholas stood and watched the two of them kneeling and praying together in front of the primitive altar. He felt deeply moved by this evidence of the boy's faith, and by his childlike trust in bringing them to this place.

At last Royan stood up and came to join him. Together she and Nicholas began to make a slow circuit of the quarry floor. They spoke little, and then only in whispers as though they were in a cathedral or some holy place. She touched his arm and pointed. A number of the square blocks still lay in their original positions in the quarry walls. They had not been completely freed from the mother rock, like a foetus attached by an umbilical cord which had never been severed by the ancient masons.

It was a perfect illustration of the quarrying methods used by the ancients. Work could be seen in progress in all the various stages, from the marking out of the blocks by the master craftsman, the drilling of the tap holes, the wedging of the cleavage lines, right up to the finished product lifted out of the wall and ready for transport to the dam site.

The sun had set and it was almost dark by the time they came round to the entrance of the quarry again. They sat together on one of the finished blocks, with Tamre sitting at their feet like a puppy, looking up at Royan's face.

'If he had a tail he would wag it,' Nicholas smiled.

'We can never betray his trust, and desecrate this place in any way. He has made it his own temple. I don't think he has ever brought another living soul here. Will you promise me that we will always respect it, no matter what?'

'That is the very least I can do,' he agreed. Then, turning to Tamre, he said, 'You have done a very good thing by bringing us here to your Jesus stone. I am very pleased with you. The lady is very pleased with you.'

'We should start back to camp now,' Royan suggested, looking up at the patch of sky above them. Already it was purple and indigo, shot through with the last rays of the sunset.

'I don't think that would be very wise,' he disagreed. 'Because it is a moonless night one of us could very easily break a leg in the dark. That is something not to be recommended out here. It might take a week to get back to any adequate medical attention.'

'You plan to sleep here?' she asked, with surprise.

'Why not? I can whip up a fire in no time and I also have a pack of survival rations for dinner — I have done this kind of thing before,

415

you know! And you have your chaperon with you, so your honour is safe. So why not?'

'Why not, indeed?' she laughed. 'We will be able to make a more detailed inspection of the quarry tomorrow early.'

He stood up to start gathering firewood, but then stopped and looked up at the sky. She heard it too, that now familiar fluttering whistle in the air.

'The Pegasus helicopter once again,' he said unnecessarily. 'I wonder what the hell they are up to at this time of day?'

They both stared up into the gathering darkness and watched the navigational lights of the aircraft pass a thousand feet overhead, flashing red and green and white as it headed southwards in the direction of the monastery.

Nicholas built a small fire in the corner of the quarry nearest the entrance, and as they sat around it he divided the pack of dry survival rations into three parts. They nibbled them, and washed down the sweet and sticky concentrated tablets with water from his bottle.

The fire threw ghostly reflections up the side of the quarry wall, and enhanced the moving shadows. When a nightjar uttered its warbling cry from a niche high up the wall, it was so eerie and evocative that Royan shivered and moved a little closer to Nicholas.

'I wonder if somewhere on the other side Taita is aware of our progress,' she said. 'I get the feeling that we have him a little worried by now. We have untangled the first part of the conundrum that he set for us, and I'll bet he never expected anybody to do that well.'

'The next step will be to get to the bottom of his pool. That will be really one up on the old devil. What do you hope we might find down there?'

'I hesitate to put it into words,' she replied. 'I might talk it away, and put a jinx on us.'

'I am not superstitious. Well, not much anyway. Shall I say it for you?' he offered, and she laughed and nodded. He went on, 'We hope to find the entrance to the tomb of Pharaoh Mamose. No more hints and riddles and red herrings. The veritable tomb.'

She crossed her fingers. 'From your lips to God's ear!' Then she grew serious. 'What do you think of our chances? I mean of finding the tomb intact?'

He shrugged. 'I will answer that once we get to the bottom of the pool.'

'How are we going to do that? You have ruled out the use of an aqualung.'

'I don't know,' he confessed. 'At this stage I just don't know. Perhaps we might be able to get in there with full-helmeted diving suits.'

She was silent as she considered the seeming impossibility of the task ahead.

'Cheer up!' He put his arm around her shoulders, and she made no move to pull away from him. 'There is one consolation. If Taita has made it so tough for us, he has also made it tough for anyone else to have got in there ahead of us. I think that if the tomb is really down there, no other grave robbers have beaten us to it.'

'If the entrance to the tomb is at the bottom of the pool, then his descriptions in the scrolls are deliberately misleading. The information that has come down to us has been garbled by Taita, then by Duraid, and finally by Wilbur Smith. We are faced with the task of finding our way through this labyrinth of deliberate misinformation.'

They were silent again for a while and then Royan smiled in the firelight, her face lighting up with anticipation.

'Oh, Nicky! It is such an exciting challenge.' Then her voice descended an octave. 'But is there a way? Is it possible to get in there?'

'We will find out.'

'When?'

'In due course. I haven't thought it out fully as yet. All I am certain of is that it is going to take a prodigious amount of planning and hard work.'

'You are still committed, then?' She wanted his assurance. She knew that she could never do it alone. 'You aren't daunted by the project?'

Nicholas chuckled. 'I will admit that I never expected Taita to lead us on such a merry chase. I imagined simply breaking open a stone gateway and finding it all waiting for us there, like Howard Carter walking into the tomb of Tutankhamen. However, to answer your question, yes, I am daunted by what it's going to involve — but hell, nothing could stop me now! I have the smell of glory in my nostrils and the gleam of gold in my eye.'

While they talked, Tamre curled up in the dust on the other side of the fire, and pulled his *shamma* over his head. His rest must have been interrupted by dreams and fantasies, for he burbled and squeaked and giggled in his sleep.

'I wonder what goes on in that poor demented head, and what visions he sees,' Royan whispered. 'He says he saw Jesus here in the quarry, and I am sure that he really believes that he did.'

Their voices became softer and drowsier as the fire burned down, and Royan murmured, just before she fell asleep on Nicholas's shoulder, 'If the tomb of Pharaoh Mamose is below the level of the river, then surely the contents will be water-damaged?'

'I can't believe that Taita would have built his dam and spent fifteen years working on the tomb, as he says that he did in the scrolls, only to flood it deliberately and despoil the mummy of his king and ruin his treasure,' Nicholas murmured, with her hair tickling his cheek. 'No, that would have precluded Pharaoh's resurrection in the other world, and brought all his work to nothing. I think Taita has taken all that into his calculations.'

She snuggled closer, and sighed with satisfaction.

A little while later he said softly, 'Goodnight, Royan,' but she did not reply and her breathing was deep and even. He smiled to himself, and gently kissed the top of her head.

N icholas was not certain what had woken him. He took a few moments to place himself, and then he realized that he was still in the quarry. There was no moon but the stars hung down close to the earth, as big and fat as bunches of ripe grapes. By their light he saw that Royan had slipped down and was lying flat on the ground beside him.

He stood up carefully, so as not to disturb her, and moved well away from the dead fire to empty his bladder. The night was deathly quiet. No night bird called, nor was there the sound of any of the other nocturnal creatures. The rocks around him still radiated the heat of the previous day's sunlight.

Suddenly the sound that had woken him was repeated. It was a faint and distant susurration that echoed along the cliffs, so that he could form no judgement as to the direction from which it came. But he was in no doubt what the sound was. He had heard it so often before.

It was the sound of faraway automatic gunfire, almost certainly an AK-47 assault rifle firing, not long ragged bursts, but short taps of three rounds, an art that took expertise and practice. He was sure that the person doing the shooting was a trained professional.

He tilted his wrist so that the luminescent dial of his watch caught the starlight, and he saw that it was a few minutes after three o'clock in the morning.

He stood listening for a long time, but the firing was not repeated. At last he returned to where Royan lay and settled down beside her again. However, he slept only shallowly and intermittently, and kept starting awake listening for more gunfire in the night.

Royan began to stir at the first lemon and orange flush of dawn in the eastern sky, and while they ate the remains of the survival rations for their breakfast he told her about the noise that had woken him during the night.

'Do you think it could have been Boris?' she asked. 'He may have caught up with Mek and Tessay.'

'I doubt that very much. Boris has already been gone several days. He should be well out of earshot by now, even beyond the sound range of the heaviest weapons.'

'Who do you suppose it was, then?'

'I have no idea. But I don't like it. We should start back to camp as soon as we have had another look around the quarry. After that there is nothing further that we can do at this stage. We should make tracks for home and mother.'

As soon as the light was strong enough, Nicholas shot a spool of film to make a record of the quarry. For comparison of scale, Royan posed beside the wall in which the embryonic blocks still lay. As she warmed to her role as a model she started to clown for him. She climbed on to the biggest of the slabs and hammed it up for the camera, pouting with one hand behind her head in the style of Marilyn Monroe.

When, finally, they went off down the valley towards the monastery they were both exultant and garrulous after their success. Their discussion was animated as they bounced ideas back and forth, and laid their plans for the further exploitation of these wonderful discoveries. By the time they reached the pink cliffs at the lower end of the chasm it was late morning. There they met a small party of monks from the monastery coming up the trail.

Even from a distance it was obvious that something dreadful had happened during their absence: the sorrowful ululations of the monks sent chills down Royan's spine. It was the universal African sound of mourning, the harbinger of death and disaster. As they approached they saw that the monks were picking up handfuls of dust from the track and pouring it over their heads as they wailed and lamented.

'What is it, Tamre?' Royan asked the boy. 'Go and find out for us!' Tamre ran ahead to meet his brother monks. They stopped in the middle of the path and fell into a high-pitched discussion, weeping and gesticulating. Then Tamre ran back to them.

'Our people at the camp. Something terrible has happened. Bad men came in the night. Many of the servants are dead,' he screamed.

Nicholas grabbed Royan's hand. 'Come on!' he snapped, 'let's find out what is going on here.'

They ran the last mile to the camp, and arrived to find another circle of monks gathered around something in front of the kitchen hut. Nicholas pushed them aside and elbowed his way to the front. There he stopped and stared with a sinking feeling in his gut, and the sweat on his face turned cold with horror. Under a buzzing blue pall of flies lay the blood-splattered corpse of the cook and three other camp servants. Their hands had been bound behind their backs, and then they had been forced to kneel before being shot in the back of the head at close range.

'Don't look!' Nicholas warned Royan as she came up. 'It's not very pretty.'

But she ignored his advice and came to stand beside him. 'Oh, sweet heavens. They have been slaughtered like cattle in an abattoir.' She gagged.

'This explains the sound of gunfire that I heard last night,' he answered grimly. He went forward to identify the dead men. 'Aly and Kif are not here. Where are they?' He raised his voice and called in Arabic, turning to face the crowd. 'Aly, where are you?'

The tracker pushed his way forward. 'I am here, *effendi*.' His voice was shaky and his face was haggard. There was blood on the front of his shirt.

'How did this happen?' Nicholas seized his arm and steadied him.

'Men came in the night with the guns. *Shufta.* They shot into the huts where we were sleeping. They gave us no warning. They just started shooting.'

'How many of them? Who were they?' Nicholas demanded.

'I do not know how many of them there were. It was dark. I was asleep. I ran away when the shooting began. They were *shufta*, bandits, killers. They were hyenas and jackals — there was no reason for what they have done. These men were my brothers, my friends.' He began to sob, and the tears streamed down his face.

Royan turned away, sickened and horrified. She went to her hut and stopped in the doorway. It had been ransacked. Her bags had been turned out on to the floor. Her bedding had been stripped, and the mattress thrown into the corner. As though she were a sleep-walker in a nightmare, she crossed the floor and picked up the canvas folder in which she kept her papers. She turned it upside down and shook it. It was empty. The satellite photographs and the maps, all her rubbings of the stele, the Polaroids that Nicholas had taken in Tanus's tomb — everything was gone.

Royan picked up the bed and set it the right way up. She sat down on it, and tried to gather her thoughts. She felt confused and shaken. The image of those bloody, bullet-ripped corpses laid out in front of the kitchen haunted her, and she found it difficult to concentrate and to think clearly.

Nicholas burst into her hut and looked around quickly. 'They did the same thing to me. Ransacked the place. My rifle has gone, and all my papers. But at least I had the passports and travellers' cheques in my day-pack —' He broke off as he saw the empty canvas folder lying at her feet. 'Have they taken the —'

'Yes!' she forestalled his question. 'They have cleaned out all our research material, even the Polaroids. Thank God you had the undeveloped rolls of film with you. It's the same as happened to Duraid and me all over again. We aren't safe from them, even here, even out in the remotest part of the bush.' There was the edge of hysteria in her voice. She jumped up from the bed and ran to him.

'Oh, Nicky, what would have happened if we

had been in camp last night?' She threw her arms around him, and clung to him. 'We would be lying out there in the sun now, all bloody and covered with flies.'

'Steady on, my dear. Let's not jump to any conclusions. This could just be a chance raid by bandits.'

'Then why did they steal our papers? What value would ordinary *shufta* place on rubbings and Polaroids? Where was the Pegasus helicopter heading just before the raid? They were after us, Nicky. I feel it so strongly. They wanted to kill us just as they did Duraid. They could return at any time, and now we are unarmed and helpless.'

'All right, I agree with you that we are pretty vulnerable here. It would be wise to get out as soon as possible. There isn't any point in staying on here anyway. There's nothing more we can do at this stage.' He hugged her and shook her gently. 'Brace up! We will salvage what we can from this mess, and then get moving back to the vehicles right away.'

'What about the dead men?' She stood back, and with an effort forced back her tears and brought herself under control. 'How many of our people survived?'

'Aly, Salin and Kif escaped. They dived out of their huts and ran off into the darkness as soon as the shooting started. I have told them to get ready to leave right away. I have spoken to one of the senior priests. They will take care of the burial of the dead, and will report to the authorities as soon as they are able. But they agree that the attack was aimed at us, and that we are still in danger, and that we should get away as soon as possible.'

Within the hour they were ready to start. Nicholas had decided to leave all the camping equipment and Boris's personal gear in the charge of Jali Hora. The mules were lightly loaded, and he planned to make a forced march out of the gorge.

The abbot had given them an escort of monks to accompany them to the top of the escarpment. 'Only a truly Godless man would attack you while you are under the protection of the cross,' he explained.

Nicholas found the dried hide and head of the striped dik-dik still in the skinning shed. He rolled it into a bundle and strapped it on to the load atop one of the mules, and then gave the order for the attenuated caravan to move out.

Tamre had insinuated himself into the group of monks who were escorting the party. He kept close behind Royan as they set off up the trail, with the lamentations and farewells of the monastic community following them for the first mile.

It was hot in this brutal midday. There was no movement of air to bring relief, and the stone walls of the valley sucked up the heat of that awful sun and spewed it back over them as they toiled up the steep gradients. It dried their sweat even as it oozed through their pores, leaving patterns of white salt crystals on their skins and clothing. The muleteers, spurred on by fear, set a killing pace, trotting behind their beasts and prodding their testicles with a sharpened stick to keep them moving at their best pace.

By mid-afternoon they had retraced the morning's travel and once more reached the putative site of Taita's dam wall. Nicholas and Royan took a few minutes' breather to dip their heads in the river and sluice the salt and sweat from their faces and necks. Then they stood together above the falls and took a brief farewell of the chasm in which lay all their hopes and dreams.

'How long until we return?' she asked.

'We cannot afford to leave it too long,' he told her. 'Big rains are due soon, and the hyenas have got the scent and are crowding in. From now on every day will be precious, and every hour we lose may be crucial.'

She stared down into the chasm and said softly, 'You haven't won yet, Taita. The game is still afoot.'

They turned away together and followed the mules up the trail towards the escarpment wall. That evening they did not stop at the traditional campsite beside the river, but pressed on several miles further until darkness forced a halt. There was no attempt to build a comfortable camp. They dined on cakes of *injera* bread dipped in the *wat* pot that the monks had carried with them. Then Nicholas and Royan spread their bedrolls side by side on the stony earth and, using the mule packs as pillows, fell into exhausted, dreamless sleep.

The next morning, while the mules were being loaded in the pre-dawn darkness, they drank a bowl of strong bitter black Ethiopian coffee. Then they started out along the trail again.

As the rising sun lit the sheer walls of the escarpment ahead of them they seemed close enough to touch, and Nicholas remarked to Royan, as she swung along long-legged beside him, 'At this pace we should reach the foot of the escarpment this afternoon, and there is a good chance that we might sleep tonight in the cavern behind the waterfall.'

'That means we could cut a couple of days off the journey and reach the trucks some time tomorrow.'

'Possibly,' he said. 'I'll be glad to get out of here.'

'It feels like a trap,' Royan agreed, looking at the rocky, broken ground that rose on either hand, hemming them into the narrow bottom of the Dandera river. 'I have been doing a bit of thinking, Nicky.'

'Let's hear your conclusions.'

'No conclusions, only some disturbing thoughts. Suppose somebody at Pegasus who can understand them is now in possession of our rubbings and Polaroids. What will their reaction be if they know how much progress we have made in the search?'

'Not very happy thoughts,' he agreed. 'But on the other hand there is not much we can do about any of that until we get back to civilization, except keep our eyes wide open and our wits about us. Hell, I haven't even got the little Rigby rifle. We are a flock of sitting ducks.'

Aly, the muleteers and the monks seemed to be of the same opinion, for they never slackened the pace. It was midday before they called the first brief halt to brew coffee and to water the mules. While the men lit fires, Nicholas took his binoculars from the mule pack and began to climb the rock slope. He had not covered much ground before he glanced back and saw Royan climbing after him. He waited for her to catch up.

'You should have taken the chance to rest,' he told her severely. 'Heat exhaustion is a real danger.'

'I don't trust you going off on your own. I want to know what you are up to.'

'Just a little recce. We should have scouts out ahead, not just go charging blindly along the trail like this. If I remember correctly from the inward march, some of the worst ground lies just ahead of us. Lord knows what we may run into.'

They went on upwards, but it was not possible to reach the crest for a sheet of unscalable vertical cliff barred their way. Nicholas chose the best vantage point below this barrier, and glassed both slopes of the valley ahead of them. The terrain was as he had remembered it. They were approaching the foot of the escarpment wall and the ground was becoming more rugged and severe, like the swell of the open ocean sensing the land and rising up in alarm before breaking in confusion upon the shore. The trail followed the river closely. The cliffs hung over the narrow aisle of ground that made up the bank, sculpted by wind and weather into strange, menacing shapes, like the battlements of a wicked witch's castle in an old Disney cartoon. At one point a buttress of red sandstone overhung the trail, forcing the river to detour around it, and the trail was reduced so much that it would be difficult for a laden mule to negotiate without being pushed off the bank into the river.

Nicholas studied the bottom of the valley carefully through the lens. He could pick out nothing that seemed suspicious or untoward, so he raised his head and swept the cliffs and their tops.

At that moment Aly's voice came up from the valley below, echoing along the slope as he shouted, 'Hurry, *effendi!* The mules are ready to go on!'

Nicholas waved down to him, but then lifted

the binoculars for one more sweep of the ground ahead. A wink of bright light caught his eye — a brief ephemeral stab of brilliance like the signal of a heliograph. He switched his whole attention to the spot on the cliff from which it had emanated.

'What is it? What have you seen?' Royan demanded.

'I am not sure. Probably nothing,' he replied, without lowering the binoculars. It may have been a reflection from a polished metal surface, or from the lens of another pair of binoculars, or from the barrel of a sniper's rifle, he thought. On the other hand, a chip of mica or a pebble of rock crystal could reflect sunlight the same way, and even some of the aloes and other succulent plants have shiny leaves. He watched the spot carefully for a few more minutes, and then Aly's voice floated up to them again.

'Hurry, *effendi!* The mule-drivers will not wait!'

He stood up. 'All right. Nothing. Let's go.' He took Royan's arm to help her over the rough footing, and they started down. At that moment he heard the rattle of stones from further up the slope, and he stopped her and held her arm to keep her quiet. They waited, watching the skyline.

Abruptly a pair of long curling horns appeared over the crest, and under them the head of an old kudu bull, his trumpet-shaped ears pricked forward and the fringe of his dewlap blowing in the hot, light breeze. He stopped on the edge of the cliff just above where they crouched, but he had not seen them. The kudu turned his head and stared back in the direction from which he had come. The sunlight glinted in his nearest eye, and the set of his head and the alert, tense stance made it clear that something had disturbed him.

For a long moment he stood poised like that, and then, still without being aware of the presence of Nicholas and Royan, he snorted and abruptly leaped away in full flight. He vanished from their sight behind the ridge and the sound of his run dwindled into silence.

'Something scared the living daylights out of him.'

'What?' enquired Royan.

'Could have been anything — a leopard, perhaps,' he replied, and he hesitated as he looked down the slope. The caravan of mules and monks had set off already and was following the trail up along the river bank.

'What should we do?' Royan asked.

'We should reconnoitre the ground ahead — that is if we had the men, which we haven't.' The caravan was pulling away swiftly. Unless they went down immediately they would be left behind alone, unarmed. He had nothing concrete to act upon, and yet he had to make an immediate decision.

'Come on!' He took her hand again, and they slid and scrambled down the slope. Once they reached the trail they had to break into a run to catch up with the tail of the caravan.

Now that they were again part of the column, Nicholas could turn his attention to searching the skyline above them more thoroughly. The cliffs loomed over them, blocking out half the sky. The river on their left hand washed out any other sounds with its noisy, burbling current.

Nicholas was not really alarmed. He prided himself on being able to sense trouble in advance, a sixth sense that had saved his life more than once before. He thought of it as his early-warning system, but now it was sending no messages. There were any number of possible explanations for the reflection he had picked up from the crest of the cliff, and for the behaviour of the bull kudu.

However, he was still a little on edge, and he was giving the high ground above them all his attention. He saw a speck flick over the top of the cliff, twisting and falling — a dead leaf on the warm, wayward breeze. It was too small and insignificant to be of any danger, but nevertheless he followed the movement with his eye, his interest idle.

The brown leaf spiralled and looped, and finally touched lightly against his cheek. He lifted his hand as a reflex, and caught it. He rubbed the brown scrap between his fingers, expecting it to crackle and crumble. Instead it was soft and supple, with a fine, almost greasy texture.

He opened his hand and studied it more closely. It was no leaf, he saw at once, but a torn scrap of greased paper, brown and translucent. Suddenly all his early-warning bells jangled. It was not just the incongruity of manufactured paper suddenly materializing in this remote setting. He recognized the quality and texture of that particular type of paper. He lifted it to his nose and sniffed it. The sharp, nitrous odour prickled the back of his throat.

'Gelly!' he exclaimed aloud. He knew the smell instantly.

Blasting gelignite was seldom employed for military purposes in this age of Semtex and plastic explosives, but was still widely used in the mining industry and in mineral exploration. Usually the sticks of nitrogelatine in a wood pulp and sodium nitrate base was wrapped in that distinctive brown greased paper. Before the detonator was placed in the head of the stick, it was common practice to tear off the corner of the paper wrapper to expose the treacle-brown explosive beneath. He had used it often enough in the old days never to forget the odour of it.

His mind was racing now. If somebody was expecting them and had mined the cliff with gelignite, then the reflection he had picked up could have been from the coils of copper wiring strung between the explosive in the rock, or it could have been from some other item of equipment. If that was so, then the operator

435

might even at this moment be lying concealed up there, ready to press the plunger on the circuit box. The kudu bull might have been fleeing from the concealed human presence.

'Aly!' he bellowed down to the head of the caravan, 'Stop them! Turn them back!'

He started to run forward towards the head of the caravan, but in his heart he knew it was already too late. If there was somebody up there on the cliff, he was watching every move that Nicholas made. Nicholas could never hope to reach the head of the column and turn the mules around on the narrow trail, and get them back to safety before . . . He came up short and looked back at Royan. Her safety was his main concern. He turned and ran back to grab her arm.

'Come on! We have to get off the track.'

'What is it, Nicky? What are you doing?' She was resisting him, pulling back against his grip on her arm.

'I'll explain later,' he snapped at her brusquely. 'Just trust me now.' He dragged her a couple of paces before she gave in and began to run with him, back in the direction from which they had come.

They had not covered fifty yards before the cliff face blew. A vast disruption of air swept over them with a force that made them stagger. It clapped painfully in their skulls and threatened to implode the delicate membranes of their ear-drums. Then the main force of the blast swept over them, not a single blast but a long, rolling detonation like thunder breaking directly overhead. It stunned and battered them so that they reeled into each other and lost the direction of their flight.

Nicholas seized her in a steadying embrace, and looked back. He saw a series of explosions leap from the crest of the cliff. Tall, dancing fountains of dirt and dust and rubble, pirouetting one after the other in strict choreography, like a chorus-line of hellish ballerinas.

Even in the terror of the moment he could appreciate the expertise with which the gelignite had been laid. This was a master bomber at work. The leaping columns of rubble subsided upon themselves, leaving the fine, tawny mist of dust drifting and spiralling against the clear blue of the sky, and for a moment longer it seemed that the destruction was complete. Then the silhouette of the cliff began to alter.

Slowly at first the wall of rock started to lean outwards. He saw great cracks appear in the face, opening like leering mouths. Sheets of rock collapsed and in slow motion slithered down upon themselves like the silken skirts of a curtseying giantess. The rock groaned and crackled and rumbled as the entire cliff began to fall into the river far below.

Nicholas was mesmerized by the awful sight, and his brain seemed to have been numbed by the explosion. It took a huge effort to force himself to think and to act. He saw that the centre of the explosion had occurred further down the trail, near the head of the mule caravan. Tamre was up there, beside Aly. He and Royan were at the tail of the caravan. The bomber up on the cliff had obviously been waiting for them to come directly into the epicentre of his explosive trap, but had been forced to trigger it when he saw them running back down the trail and realized that they had been alerted and were about to escape.

Yet they were not clear — they were about to catch the peripheral force of the landslide that was developing above them. Still holding Royan, Nicholas stared up the falling cliff face and made a desperate calculation.

He watched in petrified fascination as the vast tide of falling rock swept over the trail ahead of him, picking up men and mules and carrying them with it over the edge and down into the river bed. It swallowed them, lapping them up like the tongue of some fearsome monster and chewing them to pulp with razor fangs of red rock. Even above the rumbling roar of the rock tide he heard the terrified screams of men and animals as they were ploughed under.

The wave of destruction spread towards where he and Royan stood upon the trail. If they had been directly under the explosion they would have stood as little chance as those others, but as it ran down the cliff its destructive momentum was dissipating. On the other hand, Nicholas realized that there was no hope that they would be able to outrun it, and what was about to fall upon them would still be devastating.

There was no time to explain to Royan what they had to do — he had only seconds left in which to act. Sweeping her up in his arms, he leaped over the bank towards the river. He lost his footing almost immediately and they went down together, rolling end over end, but thirty feet down there was a spur of rock the size of a house. As they came up against the upper side of it, it broke their fall.

They were half-stunned, but Nicholas dragged Royan to her feet and guided her into the lee of the rock wall. There was a cut-back here, and they crept into it and crouched flat. Pressing themselves hard against the wall, they both held their breath as the first chunk of cliff came bounding and bouncing down towards them like a gigantic rubber ball, picking up speed with gravity, until it smashed into their shelter with a force that made the solid rock against which they were cringing vibrate and resound like a cathedral bell, and the hurtling missile leaped high over their heads, spinning massively in flight before it dropped into the river. It raised a tidal wave from the surface that broke like storm surf on both banks.

This was merely the forerunner of the maelstrom that now poured over them. It seemed that half the mountain was falling upon them. As each slab crashed into their shelter daggers and splinters burst from its leading edges, filling the air they breathed with fine white dust and the sulphurous stink of sparking flint. This immense cascade flew over their heads or piled up in front of their shelter, and loose chips and pebbles rained down upon them.

Nicholas crawled over the top of Royan, and covered her with his body. A stone struck the side of his head a glancing blow that made his ears ring, but he gritted his teeth and fought the impulse to lift his head and look up. He felt something warm and ticklish snaking through the short hairs behind his right ear. It crept down his cheek like a living thing, and it was only when it reached the corner of his mouth and he tasted the metallic salt that he realized it was a trickle of blood.

The fine talcum dust powdered them and irritated their throats, so that they coughed and choked in the uproar. The dust seeped into their eyes, and they were forced to clench their lids and keep them tightly shut.

One mass of rock the size of a wagon sprang high in the air and then fell back close beside where they lay. The impact made the earth jump so violently that Royan, with Nicholas's weight on top of her, was struck in the belly and diaphragm with a force that drove the wind from her lungs, and she thought that her ribs had been crushed.

Then gradually the downpouring of earth and rock began to subside. The breath-stopping impact of great boulders into their shelter became less frequent. The fine dust they were breathing began to settle. The rumbling and roaring let up gradually, until the only sound was the slip and slide of settling earth and rock and the burble of the river below them.

Warily, Nicholas at last lifted his head and tried to blink the dust off his eyelashes. Royan stirred under him, and he crawled back to let her sit up. They stared at each other. Their faces were caked into kabuki masks with the antimony-white dust, and their hair was powdered like the wigs of eighteenth-century French aristocrats.

'You are bleeding,' Royan whispered, her voice husky with dust and terror.

Nicholas lifted his hand to his face and it came away covered with a paste of dust and blood. 'It's just a nick,' he said. 'How are you?'

'I think I may have twisted my knee. I felt something give when we fell. I don't think it's serious. There is very little pain.'

'Then we have both been ridiculously lucky,' he told her. 'Nobody deserved to survive that.'

She made an effort to stand, but he restrained her with a hand on her shoulder. 'Wait! The entire slope above us is broken and unstable. Give it time. There will be loose rocks coming down for a while yet.' He untied the Paisley bandana from around his throat and handed it to her. 'Besides which, we don't want —' But he changed his mind and did not finish his sentence.

441

While she wiped her face she asked shakily, 'You were going to say, besides which — ?'

'Besides which, we don't want to give those bastards up there any idea that we have survived their little party. Otherwise we will have them down here finishing the job, cutting throats. Much better they believe that we snuffed it, as intended.'

She stared at him. 'Do you think they are still up there, watching us?'

'Count on it,' he answered grimly. 'They must be pretty chuffed with the fact that they have at last succeeded in getting rid of you. We don't want to pop our heads up right now and spoil it for them.'

'How did you know what was going to happen?' she asked. 'If you hadn't grabbed me —' Her voice petered out.

In a few words he explained about the scrap of gelignite wrapping. 'Simplest thing in the world to pick one of the narrowest sections of the trail and mine the cliff —' He broke off as, faintly but unmistakably, there came the sound of an aircraft engine and the flutter of rotors in full, fine pitch for take-off.

'Quickly,' he snapped at her. 'Get in as close as you can to the overhang.' He pushed her back against the sheltering boulder. 'Lie flat!' When she obeyed without question, he lay beside her and piled loose rubble over them both.

'Lie still. Don't move, whatever you do.'

They lay and listened to the sound of the

helicopter approaching, and circling overhead. It moved up and down the valley, flying a few feet above the surface of the river. At one point it was directly above the ledge on which they lay, and they were buffeted by the down-draught of the rotors.

'Looking for survivors,' said Nicholas grimly. 'Don't move. They haven't spotted us yet.'

'If they were watching us before the blast, they should have been able to come directly to where we are,' she whispered. 'They seem confused.'

'They must have lost us in the dust of the avalanche and the break-up of the cliff face. They aren't sure where we are lying.' The sound of the helicopter moved off slowly along the river, and Nicholas told her, 'I am going to risk a peep, to make sure it's the Pegasus job — not that there can be many other choppers in this area. Keep your head down!'

He lifted his head slowly and cautiously, and one glance was sufficient to confirm all his spec-ulations. Half a mile upstream, the Pegasus Jet Ranger hovered over the river. It was moving slowly away from him, so that from this angle Nicholas was unable to see through the wind-screen into the cockpit. But at that moment the engine beat changed as the pilot changed pitch and pulled on the collective.

As the aircraft rose vertically and turned northwards, Nicholas caught a glimpse of the passengers. Jake Helm sat in the front seat beside the pilot, and Colonel Nogo was in the seat behind him. They were both staring down into the river valley, but in seconds the helicopter lifted them away and the machine disappeared beyond the ridge, flying in the direction of the escarpment, and the sound of its engines dwindled into silence. Nicholas crawled out from beneath the boulder and pulled Royan to her feet.

'No more doubts. We know who we are dealing with now. That was Helm and Nogo in the chopper. Helm almost certainly laid the gelly, and Nogo probably led the men who hit our camp last night. Each of them doing the job he does best,' Nicholas told her. 'So that confirms it. Whoever owns Pegasus is the ugly behind all this. Helm and Nogo are merely the stooges.'

'But Nogo is an officer in the Ethiopian army,' she protested.

'Welcome to Africa.' He did not smile as he said it. 'Here everything is for sale at a price, including government officials and army officers.' Now he scowled so that the caked dust on his face was dislodged and filtered down in a fine powdering. 'Now, however, our main concern is to get out of the gorge and back to civilization.'

He looked up the slope. The trail above them had been obliterated beneath the rock fall. 'We can't get back that way,' he told her, and took her hand. But when he lifted her to her feet she gasped and quickly shifted her weight to her right leg.

'My knee!' Then she smiled bravely. 'It will be all right.'

However, she was limping heavily as they scrambled down to the river, terrified that their movements would set off another rock slide. They ended up waist-deep in the water under the bank.

Royan stood behind Nicholas and washed the blood and dust from the wound in his scalp. 'Not too bad,' she told him. 'Doesn't need a stitch.'

'I have a tube of Betadyne in my pack,' he said. He fished it out, and she smeared the wound with the yellow-brown ointment before binding it up with the Paisley bandana.

'That will do.' She patted his shoulder.

'Thank the Lord for my bum-bag,' Nicholas remarked as he zipped it closed. 'At least we have a few essentials with us. Now our next job is to look for any other survivors.'

'Tamre!' she exclaimed.

They floundered along the bank. The river was clogged with loose rock and earth that had fallen from the cliff. In the deeper places they were forced in up to their armpits, and Nicholas carried his pack at arm's length above his head. The loose rock was treacherous, and gave way under them when they tried to scramble out of the water to search for the other members of the caravan.

They found the bodies of two of the monks, both of them crushed and half-buried. They did not even attempt to dig them free. One of the mules lay with one leg in the air and the rest of its body completely covered with broken rock. The pack that it had carried had burst open and the contents were scattered about. The rolled skin and trophies of the dik-dik had been churned into the muck. Nicholas rescued them and strapped them on to his bum-bag.

'More to carry,' Royan warned him.

'Only a pound or two, but worth it,' he replied.

They made their way towards the point below the trail where they had last seen Tamre and Aly. But though they searched for almost an hour they found no sign of either of them. The slope above them was devastated: raw ravaged earth, great rocks shattered, bushes and trees uprooted and smashed to kindling.

Royan climbed as high as her injured leg enabled her, then cupped her hands around her mouth and shouted, 'Tamre! Tamre! Tamre!' The echoes took her cry and flung it from wall to valley wall.

'I think he is done for. The poor little devil has been buried,' Nicholas called up to her. 'We have been at it an hour now. We cannot afford more time, if we are to get out ourselves. We will have to leave him.'

She ignored him and worked her way along the rock-slide, loose scree rolling under her feet, and he could see that the knee was giving her pain.

'Tamre! Answer me,' she called in Arabic. 'Tamre! Where are you?'

'Royan! That's enough. You are going to damage that knee even more. You are putting both of us at risk now. Give it up!'

At that moment they both heard a soft groan from higher up the slope. Royan scrambled up towards the sound, slipping and sliding back almost as far as she climbed, but at last she gave a cry of horror. Nicholas dumped his pack and went up after her. When he reached her side, he too dropped to his knees.

Tamre was pinned down in the rubble. His face was barely recognizable. It was torn and lacerated, with half the skin ripped off. Royan had lifted his head into her lap, and was using her sleeve to wipe the filth out of his nostrils to allow him to breathe more freely. Blood was oozing from the corner of his mouth, and when he groaned again it welled up in a fresh flood. Royan dabbed at it, smearing it across his chin.

His lower body was buried, and Nicholas tried to clear the broken rock; but almost immediately he realized the futility of it. A lump of raw rock the size of a billiard table lay across him. It weighed many tons, and must certainly have crushed his spine and pelvis. No single man would be able to move that massive weight unaided. Even if it were possible, the grinding action of any movement would inevitably aggravate the terrible injuries that Tamre had already sustained.

'Do something, Nicky,' Royan whispered. 'We have to do something for him.'

Nicholas looked at her and shook his head. Royan's eyes flooded with tears, and they broke over her lower lids and scattered like raindrops into Tamre's upturned face, diluting the blood to the pink of rose wine.

'We can't just sit here and let him die,' she protested, and at the sound of her voice Tamre opened his eyes and looked into her face.

He smiled through the blood, and that smile lit his dusty, broken face. 'Ummee!' he whispered. 'You are my mother. You are so kind. I love you, my mother.'

The words were bitten off and a spasm stiffened his body. His face contorted with agony and he gave a soft, strangled cry, and then slumped. The rigidity went out of his shoulders and his head rolled to one side.

Royan sat for a long time holding his head and weeping softly, but bitterly, until Nicholas touched her hand and said gently, 'He is dead, Royan.'

She nodded. 'I know. He held on just long enough to say goodbye to me.'

He let her mourn a little longer, and then he told her softly, 'We must go, my dear.'

'You are right. But it is so hard to leave him here. He never had anybody. He was so alone. He called me mother. I think he truly loved me.'

'I know he did,' Nicholas assured her, lifting the boy's dead head from her lap and helping her to her feet. 'Go down and wait for me. I will cover him the best I can.'

Nicholas crossed Tamre's hands upon his chest, and folded his fingers around the silver crucifix that hung around his neck. Then he piled loose rock carefully over him, covering his head so that the crows and vultures could not reach him.

He slid down to where she waited in the water, and slung his pack over one shoulder.

'We must go on,' he told Royan.

She wiped away the tears with the back of her hand and nodded. 'I am ready now.'

They waded upstream, pushing hard against the current. The rock-slide had blocked half the river bed and the waters squeezed through the gap that was left. When at last they reached the point on the bank above the avalanche, they climbed out of the river and picked their way up the steep bank until at last they could crawl out on to the intact section of the pathway.

They took a moment to recover and looked back. The river below the rock-slide was running red-brown with mud. Even if the monks at the monastery downstream had not heard the explosions, they would be alarmed by that flood of discoloured water and would come to investigate. They would find the bodies and take them down for decent burial. That thought comforted Royan a little as they struck out along the trail, with two days' hard travel still ahead of them.

Royan was limping heavily now, but each time Nicholas tried to help her she brushed his hand away. 'I am all right. It's just a bit stiff.' She would not allow him to inspect the knee, but kept on stubbornly along the trail ahead of him.

They marched mostly in silence for the rest of that day. Nicholas respected her grief and was grateful for her reticence. This ability to be quiet and yet not give out a sense of alienation and withdrawal to those around her was one of the qualities he admired in her. They spoke briefly late that afternoon while they paused to rest beside the path.

'The only consolation is that now Pegasus will believe that we are safely buried under the rockslide and they won't bother to come looking for us again. We can push on without wasting time scouting the trail ahead,' Nicholas told her.

They camped that night below the escarpment, just before the path began the climb up the vertical wall. Nicholas led her well off the path, into a heavily wooded gully, and built a small screened fire that could not be seen from the trail.

Here at last she relented and allowed him to examine her knee. It was bruised and swollen, and hot to the touch. 'You shouldn't be walking on this,' he told her.

'Do I have any option?' she asked, and he had no reply. He wetted his bandana from the water bottle and bound up her leg as

450

tightly as he dared without cutting off the circulation. Then he found a phial of Brufen in his bum-bag and made her take two of these anti-inflammatories.

'It feels better already,' she told him.

They shared the last bar of survival rations from his pack, sitting hunched up over the fire and talking quietly, still subdued and shaken by their experiences.

'What will happen when we reach the top?' Royan asked. 'Will the trucks still be parked where we left them? Will the men that Boris left to guard them still be there? What will happen if we run into the men from Pegasus again?'

'I can't give you any answers. We will just have to face each problem as it comes up.'

'One thing I am looking forward to when we reach Addis Ababa — reporting the massacre of Tamre and the others to the Ethiopian police. I want Helm and his gang to pay for what they have done.'

He was quiet for a while before he replied. 'I don't know if that is the wisest thing to do,' he ventured at last.

'What do you mean? We were witnesses to murder. We cannot let them get away with it.'

'Just remember that we want to return to Ethiopia. If we make a huge fuss now, we will have the entire valley swarming with troops and police. It may put an end to our further attempts to solve Taita's riddle, and to trace the tomb of Mamose.'

'I hadn't thought of that,' she said thought-fully. 'But still, it was murder, and Tamre —'

'I know, I know,' he soothed her. 'But there are more certain ways of wreaking vengeance on Pegasus than trying to turn them over to Ethiopian justice. Consider for the moment the fact that Nogo is working with Helm. We saw him in the helicopter. If Pegasus have an army colonel in their pay, who else is working for them? The police? The head of the army? Members of the cabinet? We just don't know at this stage.'

'I hadn't thought about that either,' she admitted.

'Let's begin to think African from here on, and take a leaf out of Taita's scrolls. Like him we must be devious and cunning. We don't go rushing in shouting accusations. If we could just sneak out of the country, leaving everybody to believe that we are buried under the avalanche, that might be ideal. It would make our return to the gorge that much easier. Unfortunately I don't think we will be able to get away with that. But from now on, we should be as cagey and careful as circumstances permit.'

She stared into the dancing flames for a long while, then sighed and asked, 'You said there is a better vengeance to be had on Pegasus. What did you have in mind?'

'Why, simply whisking Mamose's treasure out from under their noses.'

She laughed for the first time that long cruel

day. 'You are right, of course. Whoever owns Pegasus wants it desperately enough to kill for it. We must hope that depriving him of it will hurt him almost as badly as he has hurt us.'

Both of them were so tired that it was already half-light when they woke the next morning. As soon as Royan tried to stand she groaned and sank back. He went to her immediately, and she made no protest when he placed her bare leg across his lap.

He unwrapped the bandana, and frowned as he saw the knee. It was nearly twice its normal girth, and the bruising was plum and ripe grape. He wet the bandana again, and rewrapped the knee. He made her take the last two Brufen from the phial, and then helped her to her feet.

'How does it feel?' he asked anxiously, and she hobbled a few paces and smiled at him bravely.

'It will be all right as soon as I walk the stiffness out of it, I'm sure.'

He looked up the escarpment. So close in under the wall, the height was foreshortened, but he recalled every tortuous step of the way. It had taken them a full day to come down.

'Of course it will.' He smiled encouragement at her, and took her arm. 'Lean on me. It'll be a stroll in the park.'

They toiled upwards all that morning. The

trail seemed to rise more steeply with every pace they took. She never complained, but she was ashen pale and sweating with the pain. By midday they had not yet reached the waterfall, and Nicholas made her stop to rest. They had nothing to eat, but she drank thirstily from the water bottle. He did not try to ration her, but limited himself to a single mouthful.

When she tried to rise, and go on, she gasped and staggered so violently that she might have fallen if he had not steadied her.

'Damn! Damn! Damn!' she swore bitterly. 'It's stiffened up on me.'

'Never mind,' he said cheerfully, and stripped his bum-bag of all but the most crucial items of equipment. He kept the dik-dik skin, however, rolling it into a tight ball and stuffing it into the bag. Then he rebuckled it around his waist, and grinned at her cheerfully. 'Skinny little thing like you. Hop on my back.'

'You can't carry me up there.' She looked up the trail, steep as a ladderway, and was aghast.

'It's the only train leaving from this station,' he told her, and offered her his back. She crawled up on to it.

'Don't you think you should dump the dik-dik skin?' she asked.

'Perish the thought!' he said, and started up.

It was slow and heavy-going. After a while he had nothing left over for talking, and he trudged upwards in dogged silence. Sweat drenched his shirt, but she found neither the wet warmth of it that permeated her blouse on to her own skin, nor the strong masculine odour of it offensive. Instead, it was comforting and reassuring.

Every half-hour he stopped and lowered her to the ground, and lay quietly with his eyes closed until his breathing became regular and even again. Then he opened his eyes and grinned at her.

'Hi ho, Silver!' He pushed himself to his feet, and bowed his back for her to scramble aboard.

As the day wore on, his jokes became more forced and feeble. By late afternoon the pace was down to an exhausted plod, and at the more difficult places he had to pause and gather himself before stepping up. She tried to help him by climbing down from his back, and supporting herself on his shoulder as they struggled over the more arduous pitches, but even with this respite she knew that he was burning up the very last of his strength.

Neither of them could truly credit their achievement when they reeled around another corner of the track and saw before them the waterfall, spilling down like a white lacy curtain across the trail. Nicholas staggered into the cavern behind the sheet of falling water and lowered her to the floor. Then he collapsed and lay like a dead man.

It was dark when he had at last recovered sufficiently to open his eyes and sit up. While he was resting Royan had gathered some wood from the monks' stockpile and managed to get a small fire going.

'Good girl,' he told her. 'If ever you want a job as a housekeeper —'

'Don't tempt me.' She hobbled over to him, and examined the cut in his scalp. 'Nice healthy scab,' she told him, and then suddenly and impulsively she hugged his head to her bosom and stroked his dusty, sweat-stiff hair off his forehead.

'Oh, Nicky! How can I ever repay you for what you did for me today?'

A flippant reply rose to his lips, but even in his weakened state he had the good sense to bite it back. He was in no state to attempt any further intimacy. So he lay in her embrace, enjoying the feel of her body against his, but not taking the risk of scaring her off with a move of his own.

At last she released him gently, and sat back. 'I very much regret, sir, that the housekeeper cannot offer you smoked salmon and champagne for your dinner. How about a mug of mountain water, pure and nourishing?'

'I think we can do better than that.' He took the dry-cell torch from his bum-bag, and by its beam selected a round, fist-sized stone from the floor of the cavern. With this in his right hand he turned the light upwards, and played it over the cavern roof. Immediately there was a rustling of wings and the alarmed cooing of

456

the rock pigeons that were roosting on the ledges. Nicholas manoeuvred into position below them, dazzling them with the torchbeam.

With his first throw he brought down a brace of them, fluttering and squawking to the cavern floor, while the rest of the flock exploded out into the night in a great clattering uproar of frantic wings. Nicholas pounced on the downed birds and with a practised flick of the wrist wrung their necks.

'How do you fancy a juicy slice of roast pigeon?' he asked her.

She lay propped on one elbow, and he sat cross-legged facing her, each of them plucking the vinous-maroon and grey feathers from one of the pigeon carcasses. Even when it came to drawing the bird, she was not squeamish, as many other women might have been faced with the same task. This, together with her stoical performance during the day's struggle up the mountain, enhanced his opinion of her. She had repeatedly proved to him how game and plucky she was. His feelings towards her were strengthening and maturing every day.

Concentrating on removing the fine bristles from the puckered breast skin of the bird, she said, 'It is beyond all doubt now that the material stolen in the raid on our camp is in Pegasus hands.'

'I was thinking the same thing,' Nicholas nodded, 'and we know from the antennae at their base camp above the falls that they have satellite communications. We can place a pretty certain bet that Jake Helm has already telefaxed it through to the big man, whoever he may be.'

'So he has all the details of the stele in Tanus's tomb. We know that he already has the seventh scroll in his possession. If he isn't an expert Egyptologist himself, he must have somebody in his pay who is. Wouldn't you agree with that?'

'I would guess that he can read hieroglyphics himself. I would think that he must be an avid collector. I know the type. It is an obsession with them.'

'I know the type as well.' She smiled at him. 'There is one sitting not a thousand miles away from me at this very moment.'

'Touché!' he laughed, and held up his hands in surrender. 'But I have only been lightly bitten by the bug, compared to others I could name. Those other two on Duraid's list, for instance.'

'Peter Walsh and Gotthold von Schiller,' she reeled off the names.

'Those two are homicidal collectors,' he confirmed. 'I am sure neither of them would hesitate to kill for the chance of having Pharaoh Mamose's treasure to themselves.'

'But from what I know about them, both of them are billionaires, at least in dollar terms.'

'Money has nothing to do with it, don't you see. If they laid hands upon it, they would never ever dream of selling a single artefact from the hoard. They would lock it all away in some deep vault, and not let another living soul lay eyes upon it. They would gloat on it in private — it's a bizarre, masturbatory passion.'

'What an odd word to describe it,' she protested.

'But accurate, I assure you. It's a sexual thing, a compulsion, like that of a serial killer.'

'I love all things Egyptian, but I don't think I can even imagine a craving that intense.'

'You must remember that these are not ordinary men whom we are considering. Their wealth allows them to pander to any appetite. All the normal, natural human appetites soon become jaded and satiated. They can have anything they want. Any man or any woman. Any thing, any perversion, whether legal or not. In the end they have to find something that no one else can ever have. It's the only thing that can still give them the old thrill.'

'So in whoever is behind Pegasus we are dealing with a madman?' she asked softly.

'Much more than that,' he corrected her. 'We are dealing with an enormously wealthy and powerful maniac, who in his disease will stop at nothing.'

They picked the cold carcasses of the roasted pigeons for their breakfast. Then, while the other one tactfully went to the back of the cavern and averted his or her gaze, they took turns

459

to strip naked and bathe under the waterfall.

After the heat of the gorge the water was icy cold. It battered them with the force of a fire hose. Royan hopped on her good leg, gasping and whimpering under the torrent, and emerged covered in goose-pimples and shuddering blue with cold. However, it refreshed her, and even in her filthy, sweat-stinking clothes it gave her heart to start out on the last bitter climb to the summit.

Before leaving the cavern they examined each other's injuries again. Nicholas's scalp wound was healing cleanly, but Royan's knee was no better than the previous day. The bruises were starting to turn a virulent puce, the colour of decomposing liver, and the swelling was un-abated. There was very little he could do for it, other than strapping it again with the bandana.

At last Nicholas admitted defeat, and abandoned his bum-bag and the roll of dik-dik skin. He knew that he was reaching the limit of his physical reserves, and he realized that, light as these items were, every extra pound that he carried today might mean the difference between reaching the summit or breaking down on the trail. He retained only the three rolls of un-developed film, each in its plastic capsule. These were their only record of the hieroglyphics on the stele in Tanus's tomb. He dared not risk losing them, so he buttoned them into the breast pocket of his khaki shirt. He tucked both the bag and the skin into a crack in the wall at the back of the cavern, determined to retrieve them at some later date.

And so they started out on the last but most onerous leg of the trail. To begin with Royan was on her own two feet, but leaning heavily on his shoulder. However, before the first hour was over her knee could no longer take the strain, and she subsided on to a rock on the edge of the pathway.

'I am being an awful nuisance, aren't I?'

'Come on board, lady. Always room for a small one.'

With Royan perched on Nicholas's back, her injured leg sticking out stiffly in front of her, they toiled upwards, but their progress was even slower than it had been the day before. Nicholas was forced to pause and rest at shorter and shorter intervals. On the easier pitches she dismounted and hopped along on one leg beside him, steadying herself with one hand on his shoulder. Then she would collapse, and he had to lift her to her feet and pull her up on to his back once again.

The journey descended into nightmare, and both of them lost all sense of the passage of time. Hours blended with hours into a single unremitting agony. At one stage they lay beside each other on the path, sick and nauseated with thirst and exhaustion and pain. They had emptied the water bottle an hour ago, and there was no more on this section of the path —

nothing to drink until they reached the summit and were reunited with the Dandera river.

'Go on and leave me here,' she whispered hoarsely.

He sat up immediately and stared at her aghast. 'Don't be silly. I need you for ballast.'

'It can't be much further to the top,' she insisted. 'You can come back with some of Boris's men to help carry me.'

'If they are still there, and if Pegasus doesn't find you first.' He stood up a little unsteadily. 'Forget it. You are coming along on this ride, all the way.' And he hoisted her to her feet.

He made her count aloud every step he took, and at every hundredth he paused and rested. Then he started the next hundred, with her counting softly in his ear, clinging with both arms around his neck. The whole universe seemed to shrink in upon them to the ground directly at his feet. They no longer saw the rock cliff on one side nor the deep void of space on the other. When he lurched or jolted her and the pain shot through her knee, she closed her eyes and tried not to let her voice betray it to him as she kept counting.

When he rested, he had to lean against the cliff face, not trusting his legs to get him up again if he lay down. He dared not lower her to the ground. The effort of lifting her again would be too much. He no longer had the strength for it.

'It's almost dark,' she whispered in his ear.

'You must stop here for the night. It's enough for one day. You are killing yourself, Nicky.'

'Another hundred,' he mumbled.

'No, Nicky. Put me down!'

For answer he pushed off from the rock wall with his shoulder and staggered on upwards.

'Count!' he ordered.

'Fifty-one, fifty-two,' she obeyed. Suddenly the gradient altered so sharply under his feet that he almost fell. The path had levelled out, and like a drunkard he reached up for a step that wasn't there.

He staggered and then caught his balance. He stood teetering on the brink of the precipice and peered into the dusk ahead of him, at first unable to credit what he was seeing. There were lights in the gloom, and he thought that he had begun to hallucinate. Then he heard men's voices, and he shook his head to clear it and bring himself back to reality.

'Oh, dear God. You have made it. We are at the top, Nicky. There are the vehicles. You did it, Nicky. You did it!'

He tried to speak, but his throat had closed up and no words came. He reeled forward towards the lights, and Royan cried out weakly on his back.

'Help us here. Please help us.' First in English and then in Arabic. 'Please help us.'

There were startled cries and the sounds of running men. Nicholas sank down slowly into the fine highland grass and let Royan slide off his back. Dark figures gathered around them, chattering in Amharic, and friendly hands seized them and half-carried, half-dragged them towards the lights. Then a torch was shone into Nicholas's face and a very English voice said, 'Hello, Nicky. Nice surprise. I came down from Addis to look for your corpse. Heard you were dead. Bit premature, what?'

'Hello, Geoffrey. Good of you to take the trouble.'

'I dare say you could use a cup of tea. You look a bit done in,' said Geoffrey Tennant. 'Never realized that your beard had ginger and grey bits in it. Designer stubble. Fashionable. Suits you actually.'

Nicholas realized what a picture he must present, ragged and unshaven, filthy and haggard with exhaustion.

'You remember Dr Al Simma? She has a bit of a dicky knee. Wonder if you would mind taking care of her?'

Then his legs gave way under him, and Geoffrey Tennant caught him before he fell.

'Steady on, old boy.' He led him to a canvas-backed camp chair, and seated him solicitously. Another chair was brought for Royan.

'*Letta chai hapa!*' Geoffrey gave the universal call of an Englishman in Africa, and minutes later thrust mugs of steaming over-sweetened tea into their hands.

Nicholas saluted Royan with his mug. 'Here's to us. There's none like us!'

They both drank deeply, scalding their tongues, but the caffeine and sugar hit their bloodstreams like a charge of electricity.

'Now I know I am going to live,' Nicholas sighed.

'Don't want to be pushy, Nicky, but do you mind telling me what the hell is going on here?' Geoffrey asked.

'Why don't you tell me?' Nicholas countered. He needed time to evaluate the situation. What did Geoffrey know and who had told him? Geoffrey obliged immediately.

'First thing we heard was that white hunter chappie of yours, Brusilov, had been fished out of the river near the Sudanese border, absolutely riddled with bullet holes. The crocs and catfish had snacked on his face, so the border police identified him by the documents in his money belt.'

Nicholas glanced across at Royan and cautioned her with a frown.

'Last time we saw him, he went off on a scouting expedition on his own,' Nicholas explained. 'He probably ran into the same bunch of *shufta* who raided our camp four nights ago.'

'Yes, we heard about that too. Colonel Nogo here radioed in a report to Addis.'

Neither of them had recognized Nogo in the crowd of men. It was only when he stepped forward into the light of the camp lanterns that Royan stiffened, and such an expression of loathing flashed across her face that Nicholas reached

465

across surreptitiously and took her hand to re-strain her from any indiscretion. After a moment she relaxed and composed her features.

'I am very relieved to see you, Sir Quenton-Harper. You have given us all a very worrying few days,' said Nogo.

'I do apologize,' said Nicholas smoothly.

'Please, sir, I meant no offence. It is just that we had a report from the Pegasus Exploration Company that you and Dr Al Simma had been caught up in a blasting accident. I was present when Mr Helm of the exploration company warned you that they were conducting blasting in the gorge.'

'But you —' Royan flared bitterly, and Nicholas squeezed her hand hard to stop her going on.

'It was probably our own carelessness, as you suggest. Nevertheless, Dr Al Simma has been injured and we are both badly shaken up by the accident. More important than that, however, is the fact that a number of other people, camp staff and monks from the monastery, have been killed in the *shufta* raid and in the blasting accident. As soon as we get back to Addis I will make a full statement to the authorities.'

'I do hope that you don't think any blame attaches —' Nogo started, but Nicholas cut him short.

'Of course not. Not your fault at all. You warned us about the danger of *shufta* in the gorge. You were not present, so what could you have done to prevent any of this? I would say that you have done your duty in the most exemplary fashion.'

Nogo looked relieved. 'You are most gracious to say so, Sir Quenton-Harper.'

Nicholas studied him for a moment longer. He seemed the most amiable of young men behind the metal-rimmed spectacles, so concerned and eager to please. For a moment Nicholas almost believed that he had been mistaken, and that it had been somebody else that he had seen in the Jet Ranger, hovering over the avalanche site like a vulture, searching for their dead bodies.

Nicholas forced himself to smile in his most friendly manner. 'I would be most grateful if you could do me a favour, Colonel.'

'Of course,' Nogo agreed readily. 'Anything at all.'

'I left a bag and one of my hunting trophies in the cavern under the Dandera waterfall. The bag contains our passports and travellers' cheques. Very grateful if you could send one of your men down to bring it up for me.'

While giving Nogo directions on how to find his possessions, he derived a perverse enjoyment from sending his would-be assassin on such a trivial errand. Then he turned back to his friend so that Nogo would not pick up the vindictive glint in his eyes. 'How did you get here, Geoffrey?'

'Light plane to Debra Maryam. There is an emergency landing field there. Colonel Nogo met us, and brought us the rest of the way by army jeep,' Geoffrey explained. 'The pilot and the aircraft are waiting for us at Debra Maryam.'

Geoffrey broke off and spoke to the camp staff in execrable Amharic, before turning back to Nicholas. 'I have just arranged a hot bath for you and Dr Al Simma. After that, a meal and a good night's sleep should work wonders. Tomorrow we can fly back to Addis. No reason why we shouldn't be there by tomorrow evening at the latest.'

He patted Royan's shoulder, disguising his carnal interest in her behind a benign avuncular smile. 'I must say I am rather pleased not to have to go traipsing down into the Abbay gorge looking for the pair of you. I hear that it's a pretty beastly part of the world.'

D o you mind, Dr Al Simma, if I sit in front? Terribly rude of me, but I am inclined to suffer from mal de air. Ha ha!' Geoffrey explained to Royan as they waited for three small boys to chase the goats off the emergency airfield at Debra Maryam. In the meantime Nicholas was stuffing the roll of dik-dik skin under the rear passenger seat. One of Nogo's sergeants had made a night descent of the escarpment, and had delivered both his bag and the skin while they were breakfasting that morning.

Nogo gave them a smart salute as they taxied out in a cloud of dust. Nicholas waved and smiled at him through the side window, murmuring, 'Screw you, Nogo, screw you very much indeed.'

When at last the pilot lifted the little Cessna 260 off the rough grass strip, the horizon over the Abbay gorge resembled a field of cosmic mushrooms, vast thunderheads reaching up into the stratosphere. The air beneath them was turbulent as a storm sea and they were thrown about mercilessly in the rear seats. Up in front Geoffrey seemed to be faring no better. He was very quiet and took no interest in their conversation.

There had been no opportunity for them to talk privately the previous evening, what with either Geoffrey or Nogo hovering within earshot at all times. Now with their heads close together, the engine beat covering their voices and Geoffrey occupied with his own queasy thoughts, they were able to concoct their story.

Geoffrey had made it clear that the British Ambassador in Addis was less than delighted with the inconvenience they had caused him. Apparently there had been a string of faxes from Whitehall since they had been reported missing. Added to that, the Ethiopian Commissioner of Police was anxious to question them. They had to make sure that they did not implicate Mek Nimmur in the killing of Boris Brusilov, and at the same time they must not alert or alarm Pegasus in any way. They realized that the reaction from that quarter would be swift and probably lethal if they gave the least suspicion that they knew who the other players were in Taita's game.

Most of all they must avoid antagonizing the Ethiopian authorities, or give them any cause to cancel their visas and declare them to be undesirable immigrants. They agreed to feign ignorance and play the role of innocents caught up in affairs which they had not precipitated and which they did not understand.

By the time that they landed at Addis Ababa they had prepared their story and rehearsed it thoroughly. As soon as the Cessna pulled on to the hardstand in front of the airport buildings and the pilot cut the engine, Geoffrey came back to life again, only a little green around the gills, and handed Royan down the aircraft steps with a flourish.

'Of course, you will stay at the residence,' he told them. 'The hotels in town are too dreadful to contemplate, and HE has a half-decent chef and a passable wine cellar. I will rustle up some togs for both of you. My missus is about the same size as you, Dr Al Simma, and Nicky will fit into my gear at a pinch. Thank God, I have a spare dinner jacket. HE is a bit of a stickler for form.'

The British Ambassador's residence had been built during the reign of the old Emperor, Haile Selassie, before Mussolini's invasion in the 1930s. Set on the outskirts of the town, it was an example of the better colonial architecture, with a thatched roof and wide verandas. The lawns, tended by a host of gardeners, were wide and green, contrasting with the brilliant crimson of the poinsettia. The mansion had survived both the revolution and the war of liberation that followed.

At the front entrance Geoffrey handed them over to an Ethiopian butler in a long, spotlessly white *shamma*, who showed them to adjoining bedrooms on the second floor. Nicholas heard the bathwater running in Royan's suite next door as he lay in his own brimming bath, sipping a whisky and soda and twiddling the taps with his big toe. Then there was the murmur of the doctor's voice from next door as he attended to Royan's knee.

Geoffrey's dinner jacket was loose round his waist and too short in the arms and legs, and his shoes pinched, added to which Nicholas was in need of a haircut, he realized, as he surveyed himself in the mirror.

'No help for it, now,' he decided with resignation, and went to knock on Royan's door.

'I say!' he exclaimed as she opened it. Sylvia

471

Tennant had loaned her a lime-green cocktail dress that set off Royan's olive skin marvellously well. Royan had washed her hair and left it loose on her shoulders. He felt his pulse accelerate like a teenager on his first date, and laughed at himself.

'You look absolutely scrumptious,' he told her, and meant it.

'Thank you, sir,' she laughed back at him, 'and you look very dashing yourself. May I take your arm?'

'I was hoping to carry you. Addictive activity.'

'Those days are over,' she told him, and brandished the carved ebony walking-stick with which the butler had provided her. She used it on her bad side. As they started down the long corridor, she asked in a whisper, 'What is the name of our host?'

'Her Britannic Majesty's Ambassador, Sir Oliver Bradford KCMG.'

'Which stands for Knight Commander of St Michael and St George, right?' she asked.

'No,' he corrected her, 'it stands for Kindly Call Me God.'

'You are impossible!' She giggled, and then became serious. 'Did you manage to send the fax to Mrs Street?'

'It went through at the first attempt and she acknowledged. Sends you her salaams, and promises to have some information about Pegasus double pronto.'

It was a mild evening and Sir Oliver was waiting to greet them on the veranda. Geoffrey hurried forward to make the introductions. The Ambassador had a bush of white hair and a red face. Geoffrey had warned them about him and his view on troublesome tourists, but his hostile frown started to fade as soon as he laid eyes on Royan.

There were a dozen other guests for dinner apart from Geoffrey and Sylvia Tennant, and Sir Oliver took Royan's arm and led her around the group introducing her. Nicholas trailed along behind them, resigned by now to the fact that Royan had that effect on most men.

'May I present General Obeid, the Commissioner of Police,' Sir Oliver said. The head of the Ethiopian police force was tall and very dark-complexioned, suave and elegant in his blue mess uniform. He bowed over Royan's hand.

'I believe that we have an appointment to meet tomorrow morning. I look forward to that with the keenest pleasure.'

Royan glanced at Sir Oliver uncertainly. She had been told nothing of this.

'General Obeid wants to know from you and Sir Nicholas a little more about this business in the Abbay gorge,' Sir Oliver explained. 'I took the liberty of having my secretary make the appointment.'

'Just a routine interview, I assure you both, Dr Al Simma and Sir Nicholas. I will take up very little of your time, I promise you that.'

'Of course we will do everything that we can

to assist you,' Nicholas told him politely. 'What time are we coming to see you?'

'I believe we are meeting at eleven in the morning, if that suits you.'

'A most civilized hour,' Nicholas agreed.

'My driver will pick you up at ten-thirty, and take you down to police headquarters,' Sir Oliver promised.

At the dinner table Royan was seated between Sir Oliver and General Obeid. She was pretty and charming, and both men were attentive. Nicholas realized that he would have to become accustomed to sharing her company with other men; he had had her to himself for much too long.

For his own part, Nicholas found Lady Bradford at the other end of the table rather heavy-going. She was a second wife, thirty years younger than her husband, with a pronounced London accent and an even more pronounced common streak, with a mane of dyed blonde hair and an improbable bust which overflowed her sequined *décolletage*. An old man's folly, Nicholas concluded. It appeared that she had made herself an expert on the genealogy of the English aristocracy — in other words she was an arrant snob. She questioned him closely on his antecedents, insisting on going back several generations.

In the end she called to her husband down the table, 'Sir Nicholas owns Quenton Park. Did you know that, dear?' And then she turned back to Nicholas. 'My husband is a very keen shot.'

Sir Oliver looked suitably impressed by his wife's intelligence. 'Quenton Park, hey? I read an article in the *Shooting Times* the other day. You have a drive there called the "High Beeches". Is that right?'

'The "High Larches",' Nicholas corrected him.

'Some of the best birds in Britain. That's what they said,' Sir Oliver enthused, looking eager and expectant.

'I don't know about that,' Nicholas protested modestly. 'But we are rather proud of them. You must come and have a shot at them next time you are home — as my guest, of course.'

From that moment Sir Oliver's attitude towards Nicholas altered dramatically. He became affable and solicitous, even going so far as to send the butler to fetch a bottle of the 1954 Lafite.

'You have made a good impression,' Geoffrey murmured wryly. 'HE doesn't waste the 1954 on anybody but the chosen few.'

It was after midnight when Nicholas was at last able to escape from his hostess and rescue Royan from Sir Oliver and General Obeid. He led her away, supporting her as she limped along fetchingly at his side, avoiding Geoffrey Tennant's knowing and speculative gaze until they had negotiated the first landing of the staircase.

'Well, you were definitely the star of the evening,' he told her.

'You had Lady Bradford purring like a cat,' she counter-attacked, and he was delighted to hear the faint tone of possessive jealousy in her voice. He had not been the only one.

At her door she solved any problems by offering him her cheek, and he kissed it chastely.

'Those bosoms!' she murmured. 'Don't have nightmares about them.' And she closed the door behind her.

He felt quite jaunty as he went to his own room, but as he opened the door he saw the envelope lying at the threshold. During dinner, one of the servants must have pushed it under the door. Quickly he tore open the flap of the envelope and unfolded the pages that it contained. His expression changed as he scanned through them, and he left the bedroom and went back to tap on Royan's door.

After a moment she opened it a crack, and peeped out at him. He saw the confusion in her eyes, and he hurried to allay her suspicions.

'Reply to my fax.' He showed her the sheaf of papers. 'Are you decent?'

'One moment.' She closed the door, and opened it again only seconds later. 'Come in,' she said.

She indicated the decanter on the cabinet. 'Would you like a nightcap?'

'I think I need one. We know who runs Pegasus now.'

'Tell me!' she ordered, but he took his time

pouring a Scotch, and then smiled at her over his shoulder. 'How about a soda water for you?'

'Damn you, Nicholas Quenton-Harper.' She stamped her stockinged foot. 'Don't you dare torment me. Who is it?'

'When I first met you, you were a dutiful little Arab girl. One who realized the superiority of the male species. Listen to you now. I think I have spoiled you.'

'I think I should warn you that you are flirting with disaster.' She tried to suppress her smile. 'Tell me, please, Nicky.'

'Sit down,' he ordered, and took the armchair facing her. He unfolded the fax and then looked up at her. 'Mrs Street has worked fast. In my fax, I suggested that she rang my stockbroker in the city. We are three hours ahead of Greenwich Mean Time, so it seems that she must have caught him before he left his office. Anyway, she has all the information I asked for.'

'Stop it, Nicky, or I will tear my bodice and scream and cause a scandal. Tell me!'

He rustled the pages, and then read. 'Pegasus Exploration is registered on the Sydney Stock Exchange in Australia with a share capital of twenty million —'

'Don't go through all the details,' she pleaded. 'Just name the man.'

'Sixty-five per cent of the shares in Pegasus are owned by Valhalla Mining Company,' he continued imperturbably, 'and the remaining thirty-five per cent are owned by Anaconda Metals of Austria.'

She had given up pleading with him and sat forward in her chair, watching him with a fixed gaze.

'Both Valhalla and Anaconda are fully-owned subsidiaries of HMI, Hamburg Manufacturing Industries. All the shares in HMI are owned by the von Schiller family trust, the sole trustees of which are Gotthold Ernst von Schiller and his wife, Ingemar.'

'Von Schiller,' she repeated softly, still staring at him. 'Duraid had him on his list of possible sponsors. He must have read the Wilbur Smith book — I know it has been translated into German. He probably contacted Duraid just the way that you did. But he was not put off as easily as you were by Duraid's denials.'

'That's the way I read it also,' Nicholas nodded. 'It would have been easy to sniff around the Cairo museum, and find that Duraid and you were working on something big. The rest of it we know only too well.'

'But how did he move Pegasus into Ethiopia so quickly?' she demanded.

'That must have been a stroke of luck on von Schiller's side — the luck of the devil. Geoffrey tells me that Pegasus obtained a concession to prospect for copper from President Mengistu five years ago, just before he was ousted. Von Schiller was already in place, even before he heard about the scrolls. All it involved was moving the base camp down from the north where they were working and relocating it on the escarpment of the Abbay gorge, to be ready to take advantage of any fresh developments. We will probably find that Jake Helm is one of his heavies, his dirty tricks specialist that he sends to any of his trouble spots around the world. It's apparent that he has Nogo in his pocket. We waltzed right into their arms.'

Royan looked thoughtful. 'It all makes sense. As soon as Helm reported our arrival to his master, von Schiller must have ordered him to set up the *shufta* raid on our camp. Oh, sweet heaven, I hate him. I have never laid eyes on him, but I hate him more than I thought I was capable of hating anything or anybody.'

'Well, at least we know now who we are dealing with.'

'Not altogether,' she demurred. 'Von Schiller must have had a man in Cairo. Somebody on the inside there.'

'What is the name of your minister?' Nicholas wanted to know.

'No,' she denied it instantly. 'Not Atalan Abou Sin. I have known him all my life. He is a tower of integrity.'

'It's amazing what effect a bribe of a hundred thousand dollars or so can have on the foundations of even the best-constructed tower,' Nicholas observed quietly, and she looked stricken.

They were the only two at breakfast. Sir Oliver had left for his office an hour earlier, and Lady Bradford had not yet risen to greet the clear, cool highland morning.

'I hardly slept last night, thinking about Atalan. Oh, Nicky, I can't bear even the suspicion that he might be involved in Duraid's murder.'

'Sorry if I gave you a rough night, but we have to consider all the angles,' he tried to soothe her, and then changed the subject. 'We have wasted enough time here. Pegasus have got a clear run of the field at the moment. I want to get back home, and start putting together our own expeditionary force for the return.'

'Would you like me to get on to the airline and make our reservations?' She stood up immediately. 'I will go off and find a phone.'

'Finish your breakfast first.'

'I have had all I want.' She made for the door, and he called after her.

'No wonder you are so skinny. They tell me anorexia nervosa is a rotten way to go.' And he helped himself to another slice of toast and marmalade.

She was back within fifteen minutes. 'Tomorrow afternoon at three-thirty. Kenya Airways to Nairobi, connecting the same evening with British Airways to Heathrow.'

'Well done.' He wiped his mouth on his napkin, and stood up. 'Our car is waiting to take us down to police headquarters to speak to your new admirer, General Obeid. Let's go.'

There was a police officer waiting to meet them and usher them into the headquarters building, through the private entrance. He introduced himself as Inspector Galla and treated them with the greatest deference as he led them through to the Commissioner's suite.

General Obeid rose to his feet as soon as they entered his office, and came around his desk to greet them. He was charming and affable, fussing over Royan as he led them through to his private sitting room. Once they were seated, Inspector Galla poured the inevitable tiny bowls of bitter black coffee.

After a polite interval of small talk the general came directly to the business in hand. 'As I promised, I won't detain you longer than is absolutely necessary. Inspector Galla here will be recording your statements. Firstly I would like to deal with the disappearance and death of Major Brusilov. I presume you are aware that he was formerly an officer in the Russian KGB?'

The interview lasted much longer than they had expected. General Obeid was thorough, but unfailingly polite. Finally he had their statements typed out by a police stenographer, and after they had read and signed them, the general walked with them as far as the entrance where their car was waiting. Nicholas recognized this

481

as a mark of special favour.

'If there is anything I can do for you, anything that you need, please do not hesitate to call upon me. It has been a great pleasure meeting you, Dr Al Simma. You must come back to Ethiopia and visit us again soon.'

'Despite our little misadventure, I have thoroughly enjoyed your beautiful country,' she told him sweetly. 'You may see us again sooner than you expect.'

'What a charming man,' she remarked, as they settled into the back seat of Sir Oliver's Rolls. 'I really like him.'

'It would seem to be mutual,' said Nicholas.

R oyan's words were prophetic. There were identical envelopes addressed to each of them lying at their places on the dining-room table the next morning when they came down to breakfast.

Nicholas opened his as he ordered coffee from the waiter in his ankle-length *shamma,* and his expression changed as he read the note.

'Hello!' he exclaimed. 'We made an even bigger impression on the boys in blue than we realized. General Obeid wants to see me again.' He read aloud from the note, ' "You are ordered to present yourself at police headquarters at or before noon." ' Nicholas whistled softly. 'Strong language. No please or thank you.'

'Mine is identical.' Royan glanced at the note on an official police letterhead. 'What on earth do you suppose it means?'

'We will find out soon enough,' Nicholas promised her. 'But it sounds a little ominous. Methinks the love affair is over.'

This morning, when they arrived at police headquarters, there was no reception committee to welcome them. The guard at the private entrance sent them around to the general charge office, where they were involved in a long, confused discussion with the desk officer, who had only a rudimentary knowledge of English. From previous experience in Africa Nicholas knew better than to lose his temper, or even to let his irritation show. Finally the desk officer held a long whispered telephone conversation with some unknown person, at the end of which he waved them airily towards a hard wooden bench against the far wall.

'You wait. Man come soon.'

For the next forty minutes they shared their seat with a colourful selection of other supplicants, applicants, complainants and petty criminals. One or two of them were bleeding copiously from assault by persons unknown, and yet others were in manacles.

'It seems our star is on the wane,' Nicholas remarked as he held a handkerchief to his nose. It was obvious that some of his neighbours had not had a close acquaintance with soap and water for some time. 'No more VIP treatment.'

At the end of forty minutes Inspector Galla, he who had treated them so deferentially the day before, looked over the partition and beckoned to them in a high-handed fashion.

He ignored Nicholas's outstretched right hand and led them through to one of the back rooms. There he did not offer them a seat but addressed Nicholas coldly. 'You are responsible for the loss of a firearm that was in your possession.'

'That is correct. As I explained to you in my statement yesterday —'

Inspector Galla cut him off. 'The loss of a firearm due to negligence is a very serious offence,' he said severely.

'There was no negligence on my part,' Nicholas denied.

'You left the firearm unguarded. You made no attempt to lock it in a steel safe. That is negligence.'

'With respect, Inspector, there is a notable dearth of steel safes in the Abbay gorge.'

'Negligence,' Galla repeated. 'Criminal negligence. How are we to know that the weapon has not fallen into the hands of elements opposed to the government?'

'You mean some unknown person may overthrow the government with a 275 Rigby?' Nicholas smiled.

Inspector Galla ignored the sally, and produced two documents from the drawer of his desk. 'It is my duty to serve these deportation orders on both you and Dr Al Simma. You have twenty-four hours to leave Ethiopia, and thereafter you will be considered to be prohibited immigrants, both of you.'

'Dr Al Simma has not lost any weapons,' Nicholas pointed out mildly. 'In fact as far as I am aware, she has never been even mildly negligent in her entire life.' And again his comment was ignored.

'Please sign here to acknowledge that you have received and understood the orders.'

'I would like to speak to General Obeid, the Commissioner of Police,' said Nicholas.

'General Obeid left this morning for an inspection tour of the northern frontier districts. He will not return to Addis Ababa for some weeks.'

'By which time we will be safely back in England?'

'Exactly.' Inspector Galla smiled for the first time, a thin, wintry smirk. 'Please sign here, and here.'

'What happened?' Royan demanded, as the driver opened the door of the Rolls for her and she settled into the seat beside Nicholas. 'It was all so sudden and unexpected. One moment everybody loved us, and the next we are being booted down the stairs.'

'Do you want my guess?' Nicholas asked, and then went on without waiting for her reply. 'Nogo is not the only one in Pegasus's back pocket. Overnight Obeid has been in contact with von Schiller, and received his orders.'

485

'Do you realize what this means, Nicky? It means that we will not be able to return to Ethiopia. That puts the tomb of Mamose beyond our grasp.' She stared at him with large dark eyes full of dismay.

'When Duraid and I visited Iraq and Libya, neither of us had letters of invitation from either Saddam or Gadaffi, as I recall.'

'You look delighted at the prospect of breaking the law,' she accused. 'You are smirking all over your face.'

'After all, it is only Ethiopian law,' he pointed out virtuously. 'Not to be taken too seriously.'

'And it will be an Ethiopian prison they toss you into. That you can take seriously.'

'You too,' he grinned, 'if they catch us.'

You can be certain that HE has already registered a formal complaint with the President's office,' Geoffrey told them as he drove them to the airport the next day. 'He is most upset at the whole business, I can tell you. Deportation orders and all that rot. Never heard the likes.'

'Don't fuss yourself, old boy,' Nicholas told him. 'As it is, neither of us intends coming back here again. No harm done.'

'It's the principle of the thing. Prominent British subject being treated like a common criminal. No respect shown.' He sighed. 'Sometimes I wish I had been born a hundred years ago. We wouldn't have to put up with this sort of nonsense. Just send a gunboat.'

'Quite so, Geoffrey, but please don't let it upset you.'

Geoffrey hovered around them like a cat with kittens while they checked in at the Kenya Airways counter. They had only their hand luggage, two small cheap nylon holdalls that they had bought that morning at a street market. Nicholas had rolled his dik-dik skin into a ball and wrapped it in an embroidered *shamma* that he had purchased in the same market.

Geoffrey waited with them until their flight was called and waved to them after they passed through the barrier, aiming this affectionate display more at Royan than Nicholas.

They had been allocated seats behind the wing, and Royan was beside the window. The Kenya Airways plane started its engines and began to taxi slowly past the airport buildings. Nicholas was arguing with a stewardess who wanted him to stow his precious dik-dik skin in its purple nylon bag in the overhead locker, while Royan peered out of the porthole beside her for her last glimpse of Addis during take-off.

Suddenly Royan stiffened in her seat, and while still gazing out of the window reached across and seized Nicholas's arm.

'Look!' she hissed with such venom in her tone that he leaned across her to see what had excited her.

'Pegasus!' she exclaimed, and pointed to the Falcon executive jet that had just taxied in and parked at the far end of the airport buildings. The small, sleek aircraft was painted green and on its tall tail fin the scarlet horse reared on its hind legs in that stylized pose. While they watched through the window, the door in the fuselage of the green Falcon was lowered, and a small reception committee waiting on the tarmac pressed forward expectantly to greet the passengers as they appeared in the doorway of the jet.

The first of these was a small man, neatly dressed in a cream tropical suit and a white panama straw hat. Despite his size he exuded an air of confidence and command, that special aura of power. His face was pale, as though he had come from a northern winter, and it looked incongruous in this setting. His jaw was firm and stubborn, his nose prominent and his gaze beneath dark beetling eyebrows penetrating.

Nicholas recognized him immediately. He had seen him often enough on the auction floors at Sotheby's and Christie's. This man was not the type of person whom anyone would forget in a hurry.

'Von Schiller!' he exclaimed, as the German surveyed with an imperial gaze the men who waited on the tarmac below him.

'He looks like a bantam rooster,' Royan murmured, 'or a standing cobra.'

Von Schiller raised his panama hat and ran down the steps of the Falcon with a light, athletic tread, and Nicholas said quietly, 'You wouldn't think that he is almost seventy.'

'He moves like a man of forty,' Royan agreed. 'He must dye his hair and eyebrows — see how dark they are.'

'My oath!' Nicholas was startled. 'Look who is here to greet him.'

There was the glint of sunlight on decorations and regimental insignia. A tall figure in blue uniform detached itself from the welcoming group and touched the shiny patent-leather brim of his cap in a respectful salute, before taking von Schiller's hand and shaking it cordially.

'Your erstwhile admirer, General Obeid. No wonder he could not meet us yesterday. He was much too busy.'

'Look, Nicky,' Royan gasped. She was no longer watching the pair at the foot of the steps, who were still clasping hands as they chatted with animation. Her whole attention was focused on the top of the steps of the Falcon jet, where another, younger, man had appeared. He was bare-headed, and Nicholas had the impression of sallow skin and dense, dark, wavy hair.

'Never seen him in my life before. Who is he?' Nicholas asked her.

'Nahoot Guddabi. Duraid's assistant from the museum. The man who now has his job.'

As Nahoot started down the steps of the Falcon their own aircraft trundled on down the tarmac, then swung out on to the main taxi-way and blocked any further view of the gathering beside the Pegasus jet. Both of them fell back in their seats and stared at each other for a long moment. Nicholas recovered his voice first.

'A witches' sabbath. A convocation of the ugly ones. We were lucky to witness it. There are no more secrets now. We know very clearly who the opposition is.'

'Von Schiller is the puppet-master,' she agreed, breathless with anger and horror. 'But Nahoot Guddabi is his hunting dog. Nahoot must be the one who hired the killers in Cairo and turned them loose on us. Oh God, Nicky, you should have heard him at the funeral, going on about how much he admired and respected Duraid. The filthy, murderous hypocrite!'

They were both silent until the aircraft had taken off and climbed to cruise altitude, then Royan said quietly, 'Of course, you were right about Obeid. He is deep in von Schiller's pocket also.'

'He may simply have been acting as the representative of the Ethiopian government, paying respect to a major foreign concession-holder, somebody who they hope is going to discover fabulous copper deposits in their poverty-stricken country and make them all rich.'

She shook her head firmly. 'If it was as simple as that, it would be one of the cabinet ministers meeting him, not the chief of police. No, Obeid has the stink of treachery on him, just the same as Nahoot.'

Seeing her husband's killers in the flesh had reopened the half-healed wounds of Royan's grief and mourning. These bitter emotions were a flame that was burning her up, like the bushfire in the trunk of a hollow forest tree, consuming her from within. Nicholas knew that he could not quench that flame, that he could only hope to distract her for a while. He talked to her quietly, turning her dark thoughts away from death and vengeance to the challenge of Taita's game and the riddle of the lost tomb.

By the time that they had changed planes at Nairobi and landed at Heathrow the following morning, the two of them had sketched out a plan of action for their return to the Nile gorge and the exploration of Taita's pool in the chasm. But although now Royan appeared on the surface to be her usual calm and cheerful self once again, Nicholas knew that the pain of her loss was still there beneath the surface.

They landed at Heathrow so early that they walked through the immigration gates without running into a queue, and since they had no bags in the hold they did not have to play the customary game of roulette at the luggage carousel — will they arrive or won't they?

Carrying the dik-dik skin in the nylon bag

491

under his arm, and with Royan limping on her cane on his other arm, Nicholas sauntered through the green channel of HM Customs, as innocent as a cherub from the roof of the Sistine Chapel.

'You are so brazen,' she whispered to him once they were through and clear. 'If you can lie so convincingly to Customs, how can I ever trust you again?'

Their luck held. There was no queue at the taxi rank, and in a little over an hour after touch-down the taxi deposited them on the pavement outside Nicholas's town house in Knightsbridge. It was only eight-thirty on a Monday morning.

While Royan showered, Nicholas went down to the corner shop under an umbrella to fetch some groceries. Then they shared the task of cooking breakfast, Royan taking care of the toast while Nicholas whipped up his speciality, a herb omelette.

'Surely you're going to need expert help when we go back to the Abbay gorge?' Royan observed, as she let the butter melt into the hot toast.

'I already have the right man in mind. I have worked with him before,' he told her. 'Ex-Royal Engineers. Expert in diving and underwater construction. Retired and living in a little cottage in Devon. I suspect he is a little short of the ready, and bored out of his considerable mind. I expect him to jump at any opportunity to alleviate either condition.'

As soon as they had finished breakfast, Nicholas told her, 'I will do the dishes. You take the films of the stele to be developed. There is a one-hour service at the branch of Boots opposite Harrods.'

'That's what I call a fair distribution of labour,' she remarked with a long-suffering air. 'You have a dishwasher, and it's raining again outside.'

'All right,' he laughed. 'To sweeten the pill, I'll lend you my raincoat. While you are waiting for the films to be developed you can go shopping to replace the togs you lost in the rock-fall. I have some crucial phone calls to make.'

As soon as she had left, Nicholas settled at his desk with a notepad at one hand and the telephone at the other. His first call was to Quenton Park, where Mrs Street tried not to show how delighted she was to have him home.

'Your desk is about two feet deep with mail awaiting your return. It's mostly bills.'

'Cheerful, aren't we?'

'The lawyers have been pestering me, and Mr Markham from Lloyd's has been ringing every day.'

'Don't tell any of them that I am back, there's a good girl.' Nicholas knew exactly what they wanted from him — the same thing that persistent callers always wanted: money. In this case it was not simply five hundred guineas for an overdue tailor's bill, but two and a half million pounds. 'It's probably better if I stay in York, rather than at Quenton,' he told Mrs Street. 'They won't be able to find me at the flat.'

He pushed his debts to the back of his mind, and concentrated on the task at hand. 'Have you got your pencil and notepad ready? All right, here's what I want you to do.'

It took him ten minutes to finish his dictation, and then Mrs Street read it back to him. 'Okay. Get on with it, will you. We'll be back this evening. Dr Al Simma will be staying indefinitely. Ask the housekeeper to prepare the second bedroom for her at the flat.'

Next he rang the number in Devon, and while the phone rang he imagined the converted coastguard's cottage on top of the cliffs overlooking a grey, storm-whipped winter sea. Daniel Webb was probably in his workshop in the back garden, either tinkering with his 1935 Jaguar, the great love of his life, or tying salmon flies. Fishing was his other passion, the one that had originally brought them together.

'Hello?' Daniel's voice was guarded and suspicious. Nicholas could imagine him, his bald head freckled like a plover's egg, gripping the telephone with a hairy, work-scarred fist.

'Sapper, I have a job for you. Are you a starter?'

'Where are we headed, Major?' Although it had been three years, he recognized Nicholas's voice instantly.

'Sunny climes and dancing girls. Same pay as the last time.'

'I'm a starter. Where do we meet?'

'At the flat. You remember it from last time. Tomorrow. Bring your slide rule.' Nicholas knew that Danny put no store by these new-fangled pocket computers.

'The Jag is still in good nick. I'll leave early and be there for lunch tomorrow.'

Nicholas hung up, and then made two more calls: one to his Jersey bank, and the other to the Cayman Islands. The funds in both his emergency accounts were running low. His budget for the expedition that he had worked out with Royan on the flight was two hundred and thirty thousand. Like all budgets, he knew that it was optimistic.

'Always add fifty per cent,' he warned himself. 'Which means that the cupboard will be bare by the time we are finished. Let's hope and pray that you are not pulling our legs, Taita.'

He gave the passwords to the respective bank accountants and instructed them to make transfers into his holding accounts, ready to draw on immediately.

There were two more calls he had to make before they left for York. The fate of all their plans hung on them, and the contacts that he had for both of them were at the best tenuous, and at the worst chimerical.

The first number was engaged. He rang it five times more, and on each occasion got the irritating high-pitched busy tone in his ear. He tried one last time and was answered by a reassuring west country accent.

'Good afternoon. British Embassy. How may I help you?' Nicholas glanced at his wrist-watch. There was a three-hour time difference. Of course, it would be afternoon in Addis.

'This is Sir Nicholas Quenton-Harper calling from the UK. Is Mr Geoffrey Tennant, your military attaché, available, please?'

Geoffrey came on the line almost immediately. 'My dear boy. So you made it all the way home. Lucky you.'

'Just thought I would set your mind at rest. Knew you would be losing sleep.'

'How is the charming Dr Al Simma?'

'She sends her love.'

'I wish I could believe you.' Geoffrey sighed dramatically.

'Big favour, Geoff. Do you know a Colonel Maryam Kidane at the Ministry of Defence?'

'First-rate chap,' Geoffrey affirmed immediately. 'Know him well. Played tennis with him last Saturday, actually. Demon back-hand.'

'Please ask him to contact me urgently.' He gave Geoffrey the telephone number of the flat in York. 'Tell him it's in connection with a rare breed of Ethiopian swallow for the museum collection.'

'Up to your shenanigans again, Nicky. Not enough that you get slung out of Ethiopia on your ear. Now you are trading in rare birds.

Probably CITES Schedule One. Endangered species.'

'Will you do it for me, Geoff?'

'Of course. Serve to Lead, old boy. Always the sucker.'

'I owe you one.'

'More than one. Half a dozen, more like it.'

He had less success with his next call. International Enquiries gave him a number in Malta. On his first attempt he received an encouraging ringing tone.

'Pick it up, Jannie,' he pleaded in a whisper, but on the sixth ring an answering machine cut in.

'You have reached the head office of Africair Services. There is nobody available to take your call at the moment. Please leave your name and number and a short message after the tone. We will get back to you as soon as possible. Thank you.' Jannie Badenhorst's rich South African accent was unmistakable.

'Jannie. This is Nicholas Quenton-Harper. Is that broken-down old Herc of yours still airworthy? This job should be a lark. What's more, the money is good. Call me at the flat in the UK. No hurry. Yesterday, or the day before, will do just fine.'

Royan rang the doorbell a minute after he finished the last call, and he ran down the stairs.

'Your timing is impeccable,' he told her as she came in with the end of her nose pink with cold, shaking the raindrops off the coat he had lent her. 'Did you get the films developed?'

She pulled the yellow packet out of the coat pocket and brandished it triumphantly.

'You are a master photographer,' she told him. 'They have turned out perfectly. I can read every character on the stele with the naked eye. We are back in Taita's game again.'

They spread the glossy photographs across his desktop and gloated over them.

'You have had duplicates made? A set for each of us. Excellent,' Nicholas approved. 'The negatives will go into the safe deposit box at my bank. We won't take a chance on losing them the second time around.'

Using his large magnifying glass, Royan studied each of the prints in turn, and she picked out the clearest shot of each of the four sides of the stele.

'These will be our working copies. I don't think we are really going to miss the rubbings that we lifted from the stone. These should suffice.' She read aloud a snippet from one of the blocks of hieroglyphics. ' "*The cobra uncoils and lifts his jewelled hood. The stars of morning shine within his eyes. Three times his black and slippery tongue kisses the air.*" ' She was flushed with excitement. 'I wonder what Taita is telling us with that verse. Oh, Nicky, it's so exciting to be unravelling the mysteries again!'

'Leave it alone now,' he ordered sternly. 'I know you. Once you start, we'll be here all night. Let's get the Range Rover packed up.

It's a long, hard haul up to York, and there is an AA warning of black ice on the motorway. A bit of a change from the weather in the Abbay gorge.'

She straightened up and shuffled the prints into a neat pile. 'You are right. Sometimes I do tend to get carried away.' She stood up. 'Before we go, may I make a phone call home?'

'By home, I take it that you mean Cairo?'

'Sorry. Yes, to Cairo. Duraid's family —'

'Please! No need to explain. There is the phone. Help yourself. I'll be waiting downstairs in the kitchen when you are finished. We both need a cup of tea before we get going.'

She came down into the kitchen half an hour later looking guilty, and told him directly, 'I am afraid that I am going to be a nuisance again. I have a confession to make.'

'Spit it out,' he invited.

'I have to go back home to Cairo,' she said, and he looked at her startled. 'Just for a few days,' she qualified hurriedly. 'I was speaking to Duraid's brother. There are some of Duraid's affairs that I have to see to.'

'I don't like you going back there on your own,' he shook his head, 'after your last experiences.'

'If our theory is correct, and Nahoot Guddabi was the danger, then he is in Ethiopia now. I should be quite safe.'

'Still, I don't like it. You are the key to Taita's game.'

'Thank you kindly, sir,' she said with mock outrage. 'Is that the only reason you don't want me bumped off?'

'If forced into a corner, I may admit that I have also grown rather partial to having you around.'

'I'll be back before you know I've even gone. Besides which, you will have plenty to keep you busy while I am away.'

'I don't suppose that I can stop you,' he grumbled. 'When do you plan to leave?'

'There's a flight at eight this evening.'

'A bit sudden. I mean, we have only just arrived.' He made one last feeble protest, then capitulated. 'I will run you out to the airport.'

'No, Nicky. Heathrow is out of your way. I can catch the train.'

'I insist.'

On a Monday evening the traffic was reasonably light and, once they had cleared the main built-up area, they made good time. The journey was further lightened by their animated discussion as he related the contents of the phone calls he had made in her absence.

'Through Maryam Kidane, I hope to be in contact with Mek Nimmur again pretty soon. Mek is the kingpin of the whole plan. Without him we can't even make the first move on Taita's bao board.'

He dropped her off at the departures entrance at Heathrow. 'Phone me tomorrow morning from Cairo to let me know you are all right, and when you are coming back. I'll be at the flat.'

'Reversed charges,' she warned him as she offered him her cheek to kiss. Then she slid across the seat and slammed the door behind her.

He watched her waiflike figure in the rearview mirror as he pulled away, and he was filled with melancholy and a sense of loss. Then quite suddenly he was aware of a new sensation of disquiet. His early-warning bells were jangling. Something unpleasant was afoot. Something nasty was about to happen when she reached Egypt. Another dangerous beast had escaped from its cage and was prowling the darkness waiting its opportunity to pounce, but it was still too early for him to discern its colour or shape.

'Please don't let anything happen to her,' he spoke aloud, but he did not know to whom his plea was addressed. He thought of turning back and making her stay with him, but he had no rights in the matter, and he knew she would not obey him. Short of physical force, there was no way he could impose his will upon her. He had to let her go.

'But I don't like it one little bit,' he reaffirmed.

His private secretary, and the other men who worked for him, knew exactly what he expected of them. Everything was as he required it. Gotthold von Schiller looked around the interior of the Quonset hut with approval. Helm had done well in the time that he had been given to prepare the base for his boss's arrival.

His own private quarters occupied half the long portable building. They were spartan, but sterilely clean and neat. His clothes hung in the cupboard and his cosmetics and medicines were set out in the bathroom cabinet. His private kitchen was fully equipped and stocked with provisions. His own Chinese chef had flown out in the Falcon with him, bringing everything with him that he needed to provide the meals that his master demanded.

Von Schiller was a vegetarian, a non-smoker and a teetotaller. Twenty years ago he had been a famous trencherman who loved the hearty food of the Black Forest, the wines of the Rhine valley and the rich dark tobaccos of Cuba. In those days he had been obese, with rolls of chin sagging over his collar. Now, despite his age, he was as lean and fit and vital as a racing greyhound.

In the autumn of his life, the pleasures were of the mind and the emotions, more than of the physical senses. He placed a higher value on inanimate objects than on living creatures, either human or animal. A piece of stone carved by masons who had been dead for thousands of years could excite him more than the soft warm body of the most lovely young woman. He loved order and control. Power over men and events sustained him more than did the taste of food. Power and the possession of beautiful and unique objects were his passions, now that his body was running down and his animal appetites were losing their zest.

Every item of all that vast and priceless collection of ancient treasures that he had already assembled had been discovered by other men. This was his chance, his very last chance to make his own discovery, to break the seals on the door of a Pharaoh's tomb and be the first man in four thousand years to gaze upon the contents. Perhaps that was his real hope for immortality, and there was no price in gold and human life he was not fully prepared to pay for it. Already men had died in this passion of his, and he cared not that there would be other sacrifices. No price was too high.

He checked his image in the full-length mirror that hung on the wall opposite his bed. He smoothed the thick, coarse, dark hair. Of course it was dyed, but that was one of his few remaining conceits. Then he crossed the uncarpeted wooden floor of his own quarters, and opened the door into the long conference room which would be his headquarters over the days to come.

The persons seated there rose to their feet immediately, their attitudes servile and their expressions obsequious. Von Schiller strode to the head of the long table and stepped up on to the block of wood covered with carpeting that his private secretary had placed there for him.

This block went everywhere with him. It was nine inches high. From this elevation von Schiller looked down upon the men and one woman who waited for him. He looked them over unhurriedly, letting them stand a while. From the vantage point of his block, he was taller than any of them.

First he looked at Helm. The Texan had worked for him for over a decade. Completely reliable, he was strong both physically and mentally and would follow orders without question or qualms. Von Schiller had come to rely on him. He could send him anywhere in the world, from Zaïre to Queensland, from the Arctic Circle to the steaming equatorial forests, and Helm would get the job done with the minimum of fuss and with very few unpleasant consequences. He was ruthless but discreet, and like a good hunting dog he knew his master.

From Helm he looked at the woman. Utte Kemper was his private secretary. She ordered and directed the details of his life, from his food to his block, from his medicine to his social calendar. No man or woman was ever received into his presence without her prior arrangement. She was also his communications expert. The mass of electronic equipment that occupied one wall of the hut was her preserve. Utte was able to find her way through the ether with the infallible instinct of a homing pigeon. From the archaic art of the keyboard and Morse code to burst transmissions and random switching he had never known another person, male or female, who could match her wizardry. She was at that perfect age for a woman, forty, slim and blonde, with slanting green eyes over high cheekbones, resembling the young Dietrich.

Von Schiller's own wife, Ingemar, had been an invalid for the last twenty years, and Utte Kemper had stepped into the void she had left in his life. Yet she was more than either secretary or wife to him.

When he had first met Utte, she had been holding a very senior position in the technical section of the German national telecommunications network, and moonlighting as a pornographic actress — not for the money but for love of the job. Copies of the videos she had made at that time were amongst von Schiller's most precious possessions, after his collection of Egyptian antiquities. Like Helm, she had no qualms. There was nothing she would not do to him, or allow him to do to her, to fulfil his most bizarre fantasies. When he watched her videos and she did some of these things to him, she was the only woman who could still bring him to orgasm. Yet even this happened less frequently with every month that passed, and each time the spasms of sexual release she could evoke from his aging body were less intense.

Utte had her recording equipment set up before her on the table. It was part of her multifarious duties to keep accurate and complete records of every meeting and conversation. Then von Schiller looked past these two trusted employees to the two other men standing at the table.

Colonel Nogo he had met for the first time that morning, as he stepped down from the Jet Ranger helicopter that had flown them down from Addis Ababa to the base camp here on the summit of the escarpment of the Nile gorge. He knew very little about him, except that Helm had selected him, and was so far satisfied with his performance. Von Schiller himself was not equally impressed. There had already been some bungling. Nogo had allowed Quenton-Harper and the Egyptian woman to slip through his clutches. After a lifetime of operating in Africa, von Schiller placed little trust or store in blacks and preferred to work with Europeans. However, he realized that for the time being Nogo's services were indispensable. He was, after all, the military commander of the southern Gojam. No doubt once he had served his purpose he could be taken care of. Helm would see to that. He would not have to bother himself with the details.

Von Schiller looked now at the last man at the table. Here was another who was indispensable for the time being. Nahoot Guddabi was the one who had brought the existence of the seventh scroll to his attention. Apparently some English author had written a fictionalized version of the scrolls, but von Schiller never read fiction of any sort, either in German or in any of the four foreign languages in which he was fluent. Without Nahoot bringing the existence of the Taita scrolls to his notice, he might have overlooked this opportunity of his lifetime.

The Egyptian had come to him as soon as the original translation of the scrolls had been completed by Duraid Al Simma, and the existence of an unrecorded Pharaoh and his tomb had been mooted. Since then they had been in constant contact, and when the time came that Al Simma and his wife had started to make too much headway with their investigations, von Schiller had employed Nahoot to get rid of them and to bring the seventh scroll to him.

The scroll was now the shining star of his collection, safely housed with his other ancient treasures in the steel and concrete vaults below the Schloss in the mountains that was his private retreat, his Eagle's Nest.

Despite this, the choice of Nahoot to undertake the more sensitive work of ridding him of Al Simma and his wife had proved to be a mistake. He should have sent a professional to take care of them, but Nahoot had argued that he was capable of seeing it through, and he had been well paid for the work that he had mismanaged so ineptly. He too would be disposable in time, but right now von Schiller still needed him.

There was no question that Nahoot's understanding of Egyptology and hieroglyphics was far in advance of von Schiller's own. After all, Nahoot had spent most of his life studying them, while von Schiller was an amateur and only a comparatively recent enthusiast. Nahoot was able to read the scrolls and this new material that they had acquired as though they were letters from a friend, whereas von Schiller was obliged to puzzle over each symbol and resort frequently to his reference books. Even then, he was not capable of picking up the finer nuances of meaning in the text. Without Nahoot's assistance he could not hope to solve the riddles which confronted him in the search for Mamose's tomb.

This was the team who were now assembled beneath him, waiting for him to start the proceedings. 'Sit down, please, Fräulein Kemper,' he said at last. 'You too, gentlemen. Let us get started.'

Von Schiller remained standing on his block at the head of the table. He enjoyed the feeling of superior height. His short stature had been a source of humiliation ever since his schooldays when he had been nicknamed 'Pippa' by his peers.

'Fräulein Kemper will be recording everything which is said here this afternoon. She will also issue each of you with a folder of documents which she will collect from you again at the end of this meeting. I want to make it very clear that none of this material will ever leave this room. It is of the most confidential nature, and belongs to me alone. I will take a most stringent view of any breach of this instruction.'

As Utte handed out the folders, von Schiller looked at each recipient in turn. His expression made it clear what the penalty would be for any contravention of his instructions.

Then von Schiller opened the dossier that lay on the tabletop in front of him. He stood over it, leaning forward on his bunched fists.

'In your folders you will find copies of the Polaroid photographs that were recovered from Quenton-Harper's camp. Please look at these now.'

Each of them opened their own folder.

'Since our arrival Dr Nahoot has had an opportunity to study these, and he is of the opinion that they are genuine, and that the stele in the photographs is an authentic artefect of ancient Egyptian origin, almost certainly dating from the Second Intermediate Period, circa 1790 BC. Is there anything you wish to add to that, Doctor?'

'Thank you, Herr von Schiller.' Nahoot smiled oleaginously, but his dark eyes were nervous. There was something cold and dispassionate about the old German that terrified him. He had displayed no emotion whatsoever as he ordered Nahoot to arrange the death of Duraid Al Simma and his wife. Nahoot knew that he would be equally unmoved if he were to order Nahoot's own murder. He realized that he was riding the tiger's back. 'I would just like to qualify that statement. I said that the stele pictured in these prints appeared to be genuine. Of course, I would not be able to give you a definite opinion until I was able to examine the actual stone at first hand.'

'I note your qualification,' von Schiller nodded, 'and we are assembled here to find the means to obtain the stele for your examination and verdict.' He picked up the glossy print that Utte had made from the original that morning in the laboratory darkroom in the adjoining hut. Photography was not the least of her many talents and skills, and she had done a very competent job. The copies of the Polaroids that Helm had transmitted to him in Hamburg had been blurred and distorted, but still they had been sufficient to bring him rushing across the continents in all this haste. Now he held these clear likenesses in full colour, and his excitement threatened to suffocate him.

While they were all silent, he caressed the print as lovingly as if it had been the actual object that it portrayed. If this were genuine, as he knew instinctively that it was, then it alone would be well worth the considerable cost in time and money and human life that he had already paid. It was a marvellous treasure, to match even the original seventh scroll which was already in his collection. The condition and state of preservation of the stele after four thousand years seemed to be extraordinary. He lusted for it as he had for few things in his long life. It required an effort to set aside this pervasive longing, and to apply his mind to the task ahead of him.

'If, however, the stele is genuine, Doctor, can you tell us, or rather, can you suggest to us where it may be situated, and where we should direct our search?'

'I believe that we should not consider the stele in isolation, Herr von Schiller. We should look at the other Polaroids that Colonel Nogo was able to recover for us, and which Fräulein Kemper has so ingeniously copied.' Nahoot set aside the one print, and selected another from the pile in the folder in front of him. 'This one, for example.'

The others riffled through their own folders and selected the same print as he was displaying.

'If you study the background of this copy, you will see that in the shadows behind the stele there appears to be the wall of some type of cave or cavern.' He looked up at von Schiller, who nodded encouragement. 'There also appears to be some type of barred doorway.' Nahoot set the print aside and selected another. 'Now, see here. This is a photograph taken of another subject. It is, I believe, of a mural decoration painted upon either a plastered wall or the bare rock of a cave, possibly an excavated tomb. It seems to have been taken through the grille of the gate which I pointed out to you in the first photograph of the stele. This mural is almost certainly Egyptian in style and influence. In fact it very strongly reminds me of those murals that decorated the tomb of Queen Lostris in Upper Egypt in which the original Taita scrolls were uncovered.'

'Yes. Yes. Go on!' von Schiller encouraged him.

'Very well, then. Using the barred gate as the connecting factor, there is every reason to believe that both stele and murals are located in the same cave or tomb.'

'If that is so, what indications do we have as to where Quenton-Harper photographed these Polaroids?' Von Schiller was still frowning angrily as he looked at each of them in turn. They all tried to avoid his blue, penetrating scrutiny.

'Colonel Nogo,' von Schiller singled him out, 'this is your country. You know the terrain intimately. Let's hear your thoughts on the subject.'

Colonel Nogo shook his head. 'This man, this Egyptian —' he used the epithet disparagingly, 'is mistaken. This is not an Egyptian tomb in the photographs.'

'Why do you say that?' Nahoot challenged him angrily. 'What do you know about Egyptology? I have spent twenty-five years —'

'Wait,' von Schiller silenced him peremptorily. 'Let him finish.' He looked at Nogo. 'Go on, colonel.'

'I agree that I don't know anything about

Egyptian tombs, but these photographs were taken in a Christian church.'

'What makes you so sure?' Nahoot demanded bitterly, his authority challenged.

'Let me explain to you that I was ordained as a priest fifteen years ago. Later, I became disillusioned with Christianity and all other religions, and left the Church to become a soldier. I tell you this so that you may believe that I know what I am talking about.' He smiled with supercilious malice at Nahoot, before going on. 'Look at this first print again, and you will be able to make out on the wall in the background, near the corner of the grille gate, the outline of a human hand and the stylized picture of a fish. Those are symbols of the Coptic Church. You can see them reproduced in any church or cathedral in the land.'

Each of them peered at their own copy of the same print, but none of them ventured an opinion until von Schiller had given his.

'You are right,' von Schiller said softly. 'There is, as you say, the hand and the fish.'

'But I assure you the hieroglyphics on the stele and the murals and the wooden coffin are all Egyptian,' Nahoot defended himself stoutly. 'I would stake my life on it.'

Nogo shook his head, and began to argue. 'I know what I am saying —'

Von Schiller held up his hand to silence them both while he considered the problem. At last he came to some decision.

'Colonel Nogo, show me on the satellite photograph the site of Quenton-Harper's camp where you obtained these Polaroids.'

Nogo stood up, and came around the table to stand beside von Schiller. He leaned over the satellite photograph and prodded his forefinger at the spot near where the Dandera river joined the Nile. The photograph had once been in the possession of Quenton-Harper, and had been captured in the raid on his camp. There were numerous markings in coloured marker pen on the copy, which Nogo presumed had been placed there by the Englishman.

'It was here, sir. You can see that Quenton-Harper has marked the spot with a green circle.'

'Now show me where the nearest Coptic church is situated.'

'Why, Herr von Schiller, it's right here. Again Quenton-Harper has marked it with red ink. It is situated only a mile from the campsite. The monastery of St Frumentius.'

'There is your answer, then.' Von Schiller was still frowning. 'Coptic and Egyptian symbols together. The monastery.'

They stared at him, none of them daring to question his conclusion.

'I want that monastery searched,' he said softly. 'I want every room and every inch of every wall examined.' He turned back to Nogo. 'Can you get your men in there?'

'Of course, Herr von Schiller. I already have one of my reliable men in the monastery —

one of the monks is in my pay. Added to that, there is still martial law in force here in Gojam. I am the military commander. I am fully empowered to search for rebels and dissidents and bandits wherever I suspect they may be sheltering.'

'Will your men enter a church to perform their duty?' Helm wanted to know. 'Do you personally have any religious scruples? It may be necessary to — how can I put it — desecrate hallowed premises.'

'I have already explained to you that I have renounced religion for other more worldly beliefs. I would take pleasure in destroying such superstitious and dangerous symbols as will certainly be found in the monastery of St Frumentius. As for my men, I will select only Moslems or Animists who are hostile to the cross, and all it stands for. I will lead them personally. I assure you that there will be no difficulty in that respect.'

'How will you explain this to your superiors in Addis Ababa? I do not want to be associated in any way with your actions at the monastery,' von Schiller said.

'I have been ordered by the high command in Addis to take all possible steps against the dissident rebels that are operating in the Abbay gorge. I will be completely able to justify any search of the monastery.'

'I want that stele. I want it at any cost. Do you understand me, colonel?'

'I understand you perfectly, Herr von Schiller.'

'As you already know, I am a generous man to those who serve me well. Bring it to me in good condition and you will be well rewarded. You may call on Mr Helm for any assistance that he can give you, including the use of Pegasus equipment and personnel.'

'If we are able to use your helicopter, it will save a great deal of time. I can take my men down there tomorrow, and if the stone is in the monastery I will be able to deliver it to you by tomorrow evening.'

'Excellent. You will take Dr Guddabi with you. He must search the area for other valuables and translate any inscriptions or engravings that you find in the monastery. Please provide him with military uniform. He must appear to be one of your troopers. I do not want to become involved in recriminations at a later date.'

'We will leave as soon as it is light enough to take off tomorrow morning. I will commence the arrangements immediately.' Tuma Nogo saluted von Schiller and strode eagerly from the hut.

Although Colonel Nogo had never entered either the *qiddist* or the *maqdas*, he had often visited the monastery of St Frumentius. He was therefore fully aware of the magnitude of the task ahead of him, and the likely reaction of the monks and the congregation to his forced entry to their premises. In addition, he was familiar with numerous similar rock cathedrals in other parts of the country. In fact he had been ordained in the famous cathedral of Lalibelela, so he knew just how labyrinthine one of these subterranean warrens could be.

He estimated that he would need at least twenty men to secure and search the monastery, and to fend off the outraged retaliation of the abbot and his monks. He selected his best men personally. None of them was squeamish.

Two hours before dawn he paraded them within the security of the Pegasus compound, under the glare of the floodlights, and briefed them carefully. At the end of the briefing he made each man step from the ranks in turn and recite his orders to ensure there was no misunderstanding. Then he inspected their arms and equipment meticulously.

Tuma Nogo was painfully conscious of his own culpability in allowing the Englishman and the Egyptian woman to escape, and he could sense the danger in Herr von Schiller's attitude towards him. He had few illusions about the consequences if he were to fail again. In the short time since he had made the acquaintance of Gotthold von Schiller, Nogo had come to fear him as he had never feared God or the Devil in the days of his priesthood. He realized that this raid was an opportunity to reinstate himself with the formidable little German.

The Jet Ranger was standing by, the pilot at the controls, the engines running and the rotors turning lazily, but it could not carry such a large number of fully equipped men. It would need four round trips to ferry them all down to the assembly point in the gorge. Nogo flew with the first flight, and took Nahoot Guddabi with him. The helicopter dropped them three miles from the monastery, in a clearing on the banks of the Dandera river, the same drop area as they had used for the raid on Quenton-Harper's camp.

The drop area was just far enough from the monastery for the engine noise of the Jet Ranger not to alarm the monks. Even if they did hear it, Nogo was banking on the probability that they were by this time thoroughly conditioned to the frequent sorties of the machine, and would not associate it with any threat to themselves.

The men waited in the darkness, warned to silence and not even allowed by Nogo to smoke, while the Jet Ranger ferried in the remaining troopers. When the last flight came in Nogo ordered his detachment to fall in, and led them in single file down the path beside the river. They were all trained bush fighters in top physical condition, and they moved swiftly and purposefully through the night. Only Nahoot was a soft urbanite, and within half a mile he was wheezing and whining for a chance to rest. Nogo smiled vindictively to himself as he listened to

Nahoot's pathetic whispered pleas for mercy as he was prodded along by the men behind him.

Nogo had timed his arrival at the monastery to coincide with the hour of matins and lauds, the break of day. He led his contingent down the cliff staircase at a trot. Their weapons were at high port, all the equipment was carefully muted so as not to clatter or creak, and their rubber-soled paratrooper boots made little noise on the stone paving as they hurried along the deserted cloisters to the entrance of the underground cathedral.

From the interior echoed the monotonous chanting and drumming of the ceremony, punctuated at intervals by the higher treble descant of the abbot leading the service. Colonel Nogo paused outside the doors, and his men drew up in double ranks behind him. There was no need for orders, for his briefing had covered every aspect of the raid. He looked the men over for a moment, then nodded at his lieutenant.

The outer chamber of the church was empty, as the monks were gathered in the middle chamber, the *qiddist*. Nogo crossed the outer nave swiftly, with his detachment moving up close behind him. Then he ran up the steps to the wooden doors of the *qiddist*, which stood open. As he entered, his men fanned out in two files behind him and swiftly took up their positions along the side walls of the *qiddist*, their assault rifles cocked and locked, and with bayonets fixed, covering the kneeling congregation.

It was done so silently and swiftly that it was some minutes before the monks gradually became aware of this alien presence in their holy place. The chanting and drumming died away, and the dark faces turned apprehensively towards the ranks of armed men. Only Jali Hora, the ancient abbot, was unaware of anything untoward happening. Completely absorbed in his devotions, he continued kneeling before the doors of the *maqdas*, the Holy of Holies, his quavering voice the lonely cry of a lost soul.

In the silence Colonel Nogo marched down the centre of the nave, kicking the kneeling monks out of his way. When he came up behind Jali Hora he seized him by his skinny black shoulder and threw him roughly to the ground. The tinsel crown flew from his silvered pate and rolled across the slabs with a brassy clatter.

Nogo left him sprawling and turned to face the rows of monks in their white *shammas*, addressing them imperiously in Amharic.

'I am here to search this church and the other buildings of this monastery, on suspicion that there are dissident rebels and other bandits harboured here.' He paused and surveyed the cowering holy men haughtily and threateningly. 'I must warn you that any attempt to prevent my men performing their duties will be regarded as an act of banditry and provocation. It will be met with force.'

Jali Hora crawled to his knees and then, using

one of the embroidered hangings for support, slowly hoisted himself to his feet. Still clinging to the tapestry of the Virgin and child, he gathered himself with an effort.

'These are hallowed precincts,' he cried, in a surprisingly clear and strong voice. 'We are dedicated to the service and worship of almighty God, the Father, the Son and the Holy Ghost.'

'Silence!' Nogo bellowed at him. He unbuckled the flap of the webbing holster on his hip and placed his hand threateningly on the grip of the Tokarev pistol it contained.

Jali Hora ignored the threat. 'We are holy men in a place of God. There are no *shufta* here. There are no law-breakers amongst us. In the name of God the most high, I call upon you to be gone, to leave us to our prayers and our worship, and not to desecrate —'

Nogo drew the pistol and in the same movement swung the black steel barrel into the abbot's face with a vicious back-handed blow. Jali Hora's mouth burst open like the rind of a ripe pomegranate; the red juice burst from his crushed lips and flooded down the front of his tattered velvet vestments. A low moan of horror went up from the ranks of squatting monks.

Still clinging to the tapestry, Jali Hora kept his feet, but he was swaying and teetering wildly. He opened his shattered mouth to speak again, but the only sound that came from it was a high-pitched cawing, like that of a dying crow, and the blood splattered in bright droplets from his lips.

Nogo laughed and kicked his legs from under him. Jali Hora collapsed like a heap of dirty laundry and lay on the paving, groaning in his own blood and spittle.

'Where is your God now, you old baboon? Bleat to him as loud as you will, and he will never answer you,' Nogo chuckled.

With the pistol he gestured to his lieutenant across the church. He left six of his men guarding the monks, four at the doorway and one at each side wall. The others bunched up and followed him to the entrance to the *maqdas*.

The doors were locked. Nogo rattled the ancient padlock impatiently. 'Open this immediately, you old crow!' he shouted at Jali Hora who still lay in a bundle, moaning and sobbing.

'He is too far gone in senility,' the lieutenant shook his head. 'His mind has gone, colonel. He does not understand the command.'

'Break it open, then,' Nogo ordered. 'No, don't waste any more time. Shoot the lock away. The wood is rotten.'

Obediently the lieutenant stepped up to the door, and gestured his men to stand well clear. He aimed his AK-47 into the wood of the door lintel and fired a long, continuous burst.

Dust and chips of wood and stone flew in a cloud, and fresh yellow splinters splattered the paving. The noise of gunfire and the whine of ricochets was deafening in the echoing hall of the *qiddist,* and the monks wailed and howled and covered their ears and their eyes where they knelt. The lieutenant stepped back from the shattered door. The black wrought-iron hasp and staple hung at an angle, the supporting woodwork almost shot through.

'Break it down now!' Nogo ordered, and five of his men ran forward and put their shoulders to the sagging door. At their combined thrust there was a crackling, rending sound, and now the monks were screaming. Some of them had covered their heads with the skirts of their *shammas* so as not to have to witness this sacrilege; others were tearing at their faces with their fingernails, leaving long bloody gouges down their own cheeks.

'Again!' roared Nogo, and his men rushed the door once more, using their shoulders in unison. The lock was ripped away from its fastenings, and they pushed the massive door fully open and peered into the dim recesses of the *maqdas* beyond. The chamber was lit only by a few smoky oil lamps.

Now suddenly even these non-Christians were reluctant to cross that threshold into the holy place. They all hung back, even Tuma Nogo, despite his defiant protestations of non-belief.

'Nahoot!' He looked back over his shoulder at the bedraggled and still sweating Egyptian. 'This is your job now. Herr von Schiller has ordered you to find the things we want. Come here.'

As Nahoot came forward, Nogo seized his arm and thrust him through the doorway. 'Get in there, oh follower of the Prophet. The Trinity of Christian gods cannot harm you.'

He stepped into the *maqdas* immediately after Nahoot and shone his torch around the low chamber. The beam of light danced over the shelves of votive offerings, sparkling on the glass and precious stones, on the brass and gold and silver. It stopped on the high cedarwood altar, lighting the Epiphany crown and the chalices, reflected from the communion plate and the tall silver Coptic cross.

'Beyond the altar,' Nahoot cried out with excitement. 'The barred gateway! This is the place where the Polaroids were taken.'

He broke away from the group in the doorway and ran wildly across the chamber. Gripping the bars of the gate in his clenched fists, he peered between them like a prisoner sentenced to life imprisonment.

'This is the tomb. Bring the light!' His voice was a high-pitched and frantic scream.

Nogo ran to join him, brushing past the damask-covered *tabot* stone. He shone the torch through the bars of the gate.

'By the sweet compassion of God, and the eternal breath of his Prophet,' Nahoot's voice sank from a scream to a whisper, 'these are the murals of the ancient scribe. This is the work of the slave Taita.' As Royan had done, he recognized the style and the execution immediately.

Taita's brush was so distinctive, and his talent had outlasted the ages.

'Open this gate!' Nahoot's tone rose again, becoming strident and impatient.

'Here, you men!' Nogo responded, and they crowded around the ancient structure, trying at first to rip it from the cavern wall by main strength. Almost at once it became apparent that this was a futile effort, and Nogo stopped them.

'Search the monks' quarters!' he ordered his lieutenant. 'Find me tools to do the job.'

The junior officer hurried from the chamber, taking most of the troopers with him. Nogo turned from the gate and studied the rest of the interior of the *maqdas*.

'The stele!' he rasped. 'Herr von Schiller wants the stone above everything else.' He played the torchbeam around the chamber. 'From what angle was the Polaroid taken —'

He broke off abruptly, and held the light on the damask-covered *tabot* stone, on which the velvet-cloaked tabernacle stood.

'Yes,' cried Nahoot at his shoulder. 'That is it.'

Tuma Nogo crossed to the pillar with half a dozen strides and seized the gold-tasselled border of the tabernacle cloth. He pulled it away. The tabernacle was a simple chest carved from olive wood, glowing with the patina that priestly hands had imparted to the wood over the centuries.

'Primitive superstitions,' Nogo muttered contemptuously and, picking it up in both hands, hurled it against the cavern wall. The wood splintered and the lid of the chest burst open. A stack of inscribed clay tablets spilled out on to the cavern paving slabs, but neither Nogo nor Nahoot took any notice of these sacred items.

'Uncover it,' Nahoot encouraged him. 'Uncover the stone.'

Nogo tugged at the corner of the damask cloth, but it caught on the angle of the pillar beneath it. Impatiently he heaved at it with all his strength, and the old and rotten material tore with a soft ripping sound.

Taita's stone testament, the carved stele, was revealed. Even Nogo was impressed by the discovery. He backed away from it with the torn covering cloth in his hand.

'It is the stone in the photograph,' he whispered. 'This is what Herr von Schiller ordered us to find. We are rich men.'

His words of avarice broke the spell. Nahoot ran forward, and threw himself on his knees in front of the stele. He clasped it with both arms, like a lover too long deprived. He sobbed softly, and with amazement Nogo saw tears streaming unashamedly down his cheeks. Nogo himself had considered only the value of the reward that it would bring. He had never thought that any man could long so deeply for an inanimate object, especially something so mundane as this pillar of ordinary stone.

They were still posed like this, Nahoot kneeling at the stele like a worshipper and Nogo standing silently behind him, when the lieutenant ran back into the cavern. Somewhere he had found a rusty mattock with a raw timber handle.

His arrival roused both men from their trance, and Nogo ordered him, 'Break open the gate!'

Although the gate was antique and the wood brittle, it took the efforts of several men working in relays to rip the stanchions out of their foundations in the rock of the cavern wall.

At last, however, the heavy gate sagged forward. As the workers jumped aside it fell with a shattering crash to the slabs, raising a mist of red dust that dimmed the light of the lamps and the electric torch.

Nahoot was the first one into the tomb. He ran through the veil of swirling dust and once again threw himself to his knees beside the ancient crumbling wooden coffin.

'Bring the light,' he shouted impatiently. Nogo stepped up behind him and shone the torchlight on the coffin.

The portraits of the man were three dimensional, not only on the sides, but on the lid too. Clearly the artist was the same as the one who had executed the murals. The upper portrait was in excellent condition. It depicted a man in the prime of life with a strong, proud face, that of a farmer or a soldier with a calm and unruffled gaze. He was a handsome man, with thick blond tresses, skilfully painted as if by someone who had known him well and loved him. The artist seemed to have captured his character, and then eulogized his salient virtues.

Nahoot looked up from the portrait to the inscription on the wall of the tomb above it. He read it aloud, and then, with tears still backing up behind his eyelids, he looked down again at the coffin and read the cartouche that was painted below the portrait of the blond general.

'Tanus, Lord Harrab.' His voice choked up with emotion, and he swallowed noisily and cleared his throat. 'This follows exactly the description in the seventh scroll. We have the stele and the coffin. They are great and priceless treasures. Herr von Schiller will be delighted.'

'I wish I could believe what you say,' Nogo told him dubiously. 'Herr von Schiller is a dangerous man.'

'You have done well so far,' Nahoot assured him. 'It remains only for you to move the stele and the coffin out of this monastery to where the helicopter can fly them to the Pegasus camp. If you can do that, you will be a very rich man. Richer than you ever believed was possible.'

This spur was enough for Nogo. He stood over his men as they laboured around the base of the stele, digging in clouds of dust, levering the paving slabs out of their mooring. Finally they freed the foundation of the stele and between them lifted the stone out of the position in which it had stood for nearly four thousand years.

Only once it was free did they realize the weight of the stone. Although slender, it was a solid half-ton weight. Nahoot went back into the *qiddist*, and, ignoring the rows of squatting monks, pulled down a dozen of the thick woollen tapestries from the walls and had the troopers carry them back into the *maqdas*.

He wrapped both the stele and the coffin in the heavy folds of coarse-spun wool. It was tough as canvas, and afforded the men who were to carry it a secure handhold. Ten of the burly troopers were able to lift and carry the stele, while three men were able to handle the wooden coffin and its desiccated contents. This left seven armed men free to provide an escort. Then the heavily burdened procession moved out through the ruined doorway of the Holy of Holies into the crowded central *qiddist*.

As soon as the assembled monks realized what they were carrying away with them, a shocked babble of voices, of lamentations and exhortations, rose from the squatting ranks of holy men.

'Quiet!' Nogo roared. 'Silence! Keep these fools quiet.'

The guards waded forward into the mass of humanity, clearing a passage for the treasures they were plundering, laying about them with boot and rifle butt, shouting at the monks to give way and to let the staggering porters through. The hubbub rose louder, the monks encouraging each other with their howls of protest, whipping themselves into a frenzy of religious outrage. Some of them leaped to their feet, defying the commands bellowed at them to remain seated. They crowded closer and closer to the armed troopers, clutching at their uniforms, chanting and whirling about them in a challenging display of mounting hostility.

In the midst of this uproar, suddenly the spectral figure of Jali Hora reappeared. His beard and robes were stained with blood, his eyes were crazy, bloodshot and staring. From his battered lips and ruined mouth issued a long, sustained shriek. The ranks of dancing monks opened to let him through, and he rushed like an animated scarecrow with his skirts flapping around his thin legs straight at Colonel Nogo.

'Get back, you old maniac!' Nogo warned him, and lifted the muzzle of his assault rifle to fend him away.

Jali Hora was far past any earthly restraint. He did not even check, but ran straight on to the point of the bayonet that Nogo was aiming at his belly.

The needle-pointed steel stabbed through his gaudy robes and ran into the flesh beneath them as easily as a gaff into the body of a struggling fish. The point of the bayonet emerged from the middle of his back, pricking through the velvet cloak, all pinkly smeared with the old man's blood. Spitted upon the steel, Jali Hora wriggled and contorted, a dreadful squeal bursting from his bloody lips.

Nogo tried to pull the bayonet free, but the wet clinging suction of the abbot's guts held the steel fast, and when Nogo jerked harder, Jali Hora was tossed about like a puppet, his arms flapping and his legs kicking and dancing comically.

There was only one way to free the blade of a bayonet that was trapped like this. Nogo slipped the rate-of-fire selector on the AK-47 to 'Single Shot'. He fired once.

The detonation of the shot was muffled by Jali Hora's body, but was yet so thunderous that for a moment it stilled the outcry of the monks. The high-velocity bullet tore down the entry track of the blade. It was moving at three times the speed of sound, creating a wave of hydrostatic shock behind it that turned the old man's bowels to jelly and liquidized his flesh. The suction that had held the bayonet was broken, and the blast of shot hurled Jali Hora's carcass off the point of the blade, flinging it into the arms of the monks who were crowding close behind him.

For a moment longer the strained, unnatural silence persisted, and then it was shattered by a higher, more angry chorus of horror from the monks. It was as though they were compelled by a single mind, a single instinct. Like a flock of white birds they flew at the band of armed men in their midst and descended upon them, intent on retribution for murder. They counted no cost to themselves, but with their bare hands they tore at them, hooked fingers clawing for their eyes, seizing the barrels of the levelled rifles. Some of them even grasped the blades of the bayonets with their naked hands, and the razor steel sliced through flesh and tendons.

For a short while it seemed that the soldiers would be overwhelmed and smothered by the sheer weight of numbers, but then those troopers carrying the stele and the coffin dropped their loads and unslung their weapons.

The monks crowded them too closely for them to swing the rifles, and they were forced to hack and stab with the bayonets to clear a space around them in which to do their work. They did not need much room, for the AK-47 has a short barrel and compact action. Their first burst of fully automatic fire, aimed into the monks at belly height and point-blank range, scythed a windrow through them. Every bullet told, and the full metal jacket ball whipped through one man's torso with almost no check, going on to kill the man behind him.

By now all the troopers were firing from the hip, traversing back and forth, spraying the packed ranks of monks like gardeners hosing a bed of white pansies. As one magazine of twenty-eight rounds emptied they snapped it off and replaced it with another, fully loaded.

Nahoot cowered behind the fallen pillar, using it as a shield. The roar of gunfire deafened and confused him. He stared around him and could not credit the carnage he was witnessing. At such close range the 7.62 round is a terrible missile, which can blow off an arm or a leg as efficiently as an axe-stroke, but more messily. Taken in the belly, it can gut a man like a fish.

Nahoot saw one of the monks hit in the forehead. His skull erupted in a cloud of blood and brain tissue, and the gunman who had shot him laughed as he fired. They were all caught up in the madness of the moment. Like a pack of wild dogs that had run down their prey, they kept on firing and reloading and firing again.

The monks in the front rows turned to flee and ran into those behind. They struggled together, howling with agony and terror, until the storm of bullets swept over them, killing and maiming, and they fell upon the heaps of dead and dying. The floor of the chamber was carpeted with the dead and the wounded. Trying to escape the hail of bullets the monks blocked the doorway, plugging it tight with their struggling white-clad bodies, and now the troopers standing clear in the centre of the *qiddist* turned their guns upon this trapped mass of humanity. The bullets socked into them and they heaved and tossed like the trees of the forest in a gale of wind. Now there was very little screaming; the guns were the only voices that still clamoured.

It was some minutes before the guns stuttered into silence, and then the only sound was the groans and the weeping of the wounded. The chamber was filled with a blue mist of gunsmoke and the stink of burned powder. Even the laughter of the soldiers was silenced as they stared around them, and realized the enormity of the slaughter. The entire floor was carpeted with bodies, their *shammas* splashed and speckled with gouts of scarlet, and the stone paving beneath them was awash with sheets of fresh blood in which the empty brass cartridge cases sparkled like jewels.

'Cease firing!' Nogo gave the belated order. 'Shoulder arms! Pick up the load! Forward march!'

His voice roused them, and they slung their weapons and stooped to lift their heavy, tapestry-wrapped burdens. Then they staggered forward, their boots squelching in the blood, tripping over the corpses, stepping on bodies that either convulsed or lay inert. Gagging in the stench of gunsmoke and blood, of bowels and guts ripped wide open by the bullets, they crossed the chamber.

When they reached the doorway and staggered down the steps into the deserted outer chamber of the church, Nahoot saw the relief on the faces of even these battle-hardened veterans as they escaped from the reeking charnel-house. For Nahoot it was too much. Never in his worst nightmares had he seen sights such as these.

He tottered to the side wall of the chamber and clung to one of the woollen hangings for support; then, heaving and retching, he brought up a mouthful of bitter bile. When he looked around him again, he was alone except for a wounded monk who was dragging himself across the flags towards him, his spine shot through and his paralysed legs slithering behind him, leaving a slimy snail's trail of blood across the stone floor.

Nahoot screamed and backed away from the wounded monk, then whirled and fled from the church, along the cloisters above the gorge of the Nile, following the group of soldiers as they carried their burdens up the stone staircase. He was so wild with horror that he did not even hear the approach of the helicopter until it was hovering directly overhead on the glistening silver disc of its spinning rotor.

Gotthold von Schiller stood outside the front door of the Quonset hut, with Utte Kemper waiting a pace behind him. The pilot had radioed ahead while the Jet Ranger was in flight, so all was in readiness to receive the precious cargo it was carrying. The helicopter raised a cloud of pale dust from the landing circle as it sank down to the earth. The long tapestry-covered load it carried had not been able to fit into the cabin, and was strapped across the landing skids of the aircraft. The instant that the skids kissed the ground and the pilot cut back the throttle, Jake Helm led out a team of a dozen men to loosen the nylon retaining straps and lift the heavy bundle down. Between them the gang of overall-clad workers carried the stele to the hut and eased it through the door. Helm hovered close at hand, issuing terse orders.

A space had been cleared in the centre of the conference room, the long table pushed back against the wall. With extreme care the stele was laid there, and minutes later the coffin of Tanus, the Great Lion of Egypt, was laid beside it.

Brusquely Helm dismissed the gang and closed and bolted the door behind them as they left. Only the four of them remained in the room. Nahoot and Helm crouched beside the stele, ready to unwrap the woollen tapestry. Von Schiller stood at the head of it, with Utte at his side.

'Shall we begin?' Helm asked softly, watching von Schiller's face the way a faithful dog watches its master.

'Carefully,' von Schiller warned him in strangled tones. 'Do not damage anything.' He was sweating in a sheen across his forehead, and his face was very pale. Utte edged protectively closer to him, but he did not glance in her direction. He was staring fixedly at the treasure that lay at his feet.

Helm opened his clasp-knife and cut away the tasselled cords that secured the covering. As he watched, von Schiller's breathing became louder. It rasped in his throat like a man in the terminal stages of emphysema.

'Yes,' he whispered hoarsely, 'that's the way to do it.' Utte Kemper watched his face. He was always like this when he made another significant addition to his collection of antiquities. He seemed on the verge of a seizure, of a massive heart attack, but she knew he had the heart of an ox.

Helm came to the top end of the pillar and carefully opened a small slit in the cloth. He eased the point of the blade into this opening, and then ran it slowly down towards the base, like a zip fastener. The blade was razor-sharp and the cloth fell away to reveal the inscribed stone beneath it.

The sweat burst out like a heavy dew on von Schiller's skin. It dripped from his chin on to the front of his khaki bush jacket. He made a small moaning sound as he saw the carved hieroglyphics. Utte watched him, her own excitement mounting. She knew what to expect of him, when he was caught up in this paroxysm of emotion.

'See here, Herr von Schiller.' Nahoot knelt beside the obelisk and traced the outline of a broken-winged hawk with his finger. 'This is the signature of the slave, Taita.'

'Is it genuine?' Von Schiller's voice was that of a very sick man, wheezing and gusty.

'It is genuine. I will guarantee it with my life.'

'It may come to that,' von Schiller warned him. His eyes were glittering with the hard brilliance of pale sapphires.

'This column was carved nearly four thousand years ago,' Nahoot repeated stoutly. 'This is the veritable seal of the scribe.' He translated glibly and easily from the blocks of figures, his face shining with an almost religious rapture: ' *"Anubis, the jackal-headed, the god of the cemeteries, holds in his paws the blood and the viscera, the bones and the lungs and the heart that are my separate parts. He moves them like the stones of the bao board, my limbs serve him as counters, my head is the great bull of the long board"* —'

'Enough!' von Schiller commanded. 'There will be time for more later. Go now. Leave me alone. Do not return until I send for you.'

Nahoot looked startled and scrambled to his feet uncertainly. He had not expected to be dismissed so abruptly in the moment of his triumph. Helm beckoned him, and the two of them went quickly to the door of the hut.

'Helm,' von Schiller called thickly after him, 'make certain that nobody disturbs me.'

'Of course, Herr von Schiller.' He glanced enquiringly at Utte Kemper.

'No,' said von Schiller. 'She stays.'

The two men left the room, and Helm shut the door carefully behind them. Utte crossed the room and turned the key. Then she faced von Schiller with her hands behind her and her back pressed to the door.

Her breasts were thrust forward, firm and pointed. The nipples showed clearly through the thin cotton blouse, hard as marbles.

'The costume?' she asked. 'Do you want the costume?' Her own voice was tight and strained. She enjoyed this game almost as much as he did.

'Yes, the costume,' he whispered.

She crossed the room and disappeared through the door into his private quarters. As soon as she was gone von Schiller began to undress. When he stood mother-naked in the centre of the room, he threw his clothing in a heap into one corner and turned to face the door through which she would return.

Suddenly she stood in the doorway, and he gasped at the transformation. She wore the wig of tight Egyptian braids and over it the *uraeus*, the golden circlet with the hooded cobra standing erect above her forehead. The crown was genuine, as old as the ages — von Schiller had paid five million Deutschmarks for it.

'I am the reincarnation of the ancient Egyptian Queen Lostris,' she purred. 'My soul is immortal. My flesh is incorruptible.' She wore golden sandals from the tomb of a princess, and bracelets and finger rings and earrings from the same tomb. All were authentic royal relics.

'Yes.' His voice was choking, his face as pale as death.

'Nothing can destroy me. I will live for ever,' she said. Her skirt was diaphanous yellow silk, belted with gold and precious stones.

'For ever,' he repeated.

She was naked above the waist. Her breasts were big and white as milk. She cupped them in her own hands.

'These have been young and smooth for four thousand years,' she purred. 'I offer them to you.'

She stepped out of the open golden sandals and her feet were slim and neat. She parted the frontal split in the yellow skirts and held it so that her lower body was exposed. All her movements were slow and calculated. She was a clever actress.

'This is the promise of eternal life.' She placed her right hand on her dense honey-coloured pubic bush. 'I offer it to you.'

He groaned softly and blinked the streaming sweat out of his eyes, watching her avidly.

She undulated her hips, slowly and lewdly as an uncoiling cobra. She moved her feet apart and opened her thighs. With her fingers she spread the lips of her vulva.

'This is the gateway to eternity. I open it for you.'

Von Schiller groaned aloud. No matter how often repeated, the ritual never failed. Like a man in a trance he moved towards her. His body was thin, dried out like a thousand-year-old mummy. His chest hair was a silver fuzz, the skin of his sunken belly was folded and wrinkled, but his pubic hair was dark and thick as the hair on his head. His penis was huge, out of all proportion to the skinny old frame from which it dangled. As she moved slowly to meet him it filled out and hung at a different angle, and of its own accord the wizened foreskin peeled back to reveal the massive purple head beneath it.

'On the stele,' he grunted. 'Quickly! On the stone.'

She turned her back to him and knelt upon the stone, watching him over her shoulder as he came up behind her. Her buttocks were round and white as a pair of ostrich eggs.

Helm and his men worked late that night in the Pegasus workshop, making the wooden crates to house both the stele and the coffin securely. At dawn the next day they were loaded on to one of the heavy trucks, cushioned with thick rubber matting and strapped down on to specially fitted cradles.

At his own suggestion Nahoot rode in the back of the truck, which would take just over thirty hours to cover the long and arduous journey to Addis Ababa. The Pegasus Falcon was standing on the airport tarmac when the dusty truck trundled out through the security gates and parked beside it.

Von Schiller and Utte Kemper had made the journey in the company helicopter. General

Obeid was with them. He had come to wish them *au revoir* and Godspeed.

While the wooden crates were loaded into the jet, Obeid spoke to the waiting Customs officer. He stamped the documents clearing the two cases of 'Geological Samples' for export, and then discreetly retired.

'Loaded and ready to start engines, Herr von Schiller,' said the uniformed Pegasus chief pilot, saluting.

Von Schiller shook hands with Obeid and clambered up the boarding ladder. Utte and Nahoot Guddabi followed him. The rings under Nahoot's eyes were even darker and deeper than usual. The journey had come close to exhausting him entirely, but he would not let the wooden cases out of his sight.

The Falcon climbed up into a bright clear sky over the mountains and headed northwards. A few moments after the pilot extinguished the Seat Belt panel, Utte Kemper thrust her lovely blonde head through the cockpit door and asked the chief pilot, 'Herr von Schiller would like to know our ETA.'

'I expect to touch down at Frankfurt at 2100 hours. Please inform Herr von Schiller that I have already radioed head office to give instructions for transport to be awaiting our arrival at the airport.'

The Falcon landed a few minutes ahead of schedule and taxied to the private hangar. The senior Customs and Immigration officials who were waiting for them were old acquaintances who were always on hand when the Falcon carried a special cargo. After they had completed the formalities they drank a schnapps with Gotthold von Schiller at the Falcon's tiny fitted bar, and discreetly pocketed the envelopes that lay on the bar counter beside each crystal glass.

The drive up into the mountains took most of the rest of the night. Von Schiller's chauffeur followed the covered Pegasus truck along the icy winding mountain road, never letting it and its cargo out of sight. At five in the morning they drove through the stone gate of the Schloss, where the snow lay half a metre deep in the deer park. The castle itself, with its dark stone battlements and arrow-slit windows, looked like something from Bram Stoker's novel. However, even at this hour the butler and all his staff were on hand to welcome the master.

Herr Reeper, the custodian of von Schiller's collection, and his most trusted assistants were also waiting, ready to move the two wooden cases down into the vault. Reverently they loaded them on to the forklift and rode down with them in the specially installed elevator.

While they unpacked the crates, von Schiller returned to his suite in the north tower. He bathed and ate a light breakfast, prepared by the Chinese chef. When he had eaten, he went to his wife's bedroom. She was even frailer than she had been when last he had seen her. Her hair was now completely white, her face pinched and waxy. He sent the nurse away, and kissed his wife's forehead tenderly. The cancer was eating her away slowly, but she was the mother of his two sons, and in his own peculiar way he still loved her.

He spent an hour with her, and then went to his own bedroom and slept for four hours. At his age he never needed more sleep than that, no matter how tired he might be. He worked until mid-afternoon with Utte and two other secretaries, and then the custodian called on the house intercom to tell him that they were ready for him in the vault.

Von Schiller and Utte rode down together in the elevator, and when the door slid open both Herr Reeper and Nahoot were waiting for them. One look at their faces told von Schiller that they were beside themselves with excitement, bubbling over with news for him.

'Are the X-rays completed?' von Schiller demanded as they hurried after him down the subterranean passageway to the vault.

'The technicians have completed their work,' Reeper told him. 'They have done a fine job. The plates are wonderful. *Ja, wunderbar!*'

Von Schiller had endowed the clinic, so any request of his was treated as a royal command. The director had sent down his most modern portable X-ray equipment and two technicians to photograph the mummy of Lord Harrab, and a senior radiologist to interpret the plates.

Reeper inserted his plastic pass card into the

lock of the steel vault door, and with a soft pneumatic hiss it slid open. They all stood aside for von Schiller to enter first. He paused in the doorway, and looked around the great vault. The pleasure never palled. On the contrary, it seemed to grow more intense every time he entered this place.

The walls were enclosed in two metres of steel and concrete, and were guarded by every electronic device that genius could devise. But this was not apparent when he viewed the softly lit and elegantly appointed main display room. It had been planned and decorated by one of Europe's foremost interior designers. The theme colour was blue. Each item of the collection was housed in its own case, and each of these was cunningly arranged to show it to its best advantage.

Everywhere was the soft glimmer of gold and precious gems nestling on midnight-blue velvet cushions. Artfully concealed spotlights illuminated the lustre of lovingly polished alabaster and stone, the glow of ivory and obsidian. There were marvellous statues. The pantheon of the old gods were here assembled: Thoth and Anubis, Hapi and Seth, and the glorious trinity of Osiris and Isis and Horus, the son. They gazed out with those inscrutable eyes which had looked upon the procession of the ages.

On its temporary plinth in the centre of the room, in pride of place, stood the latest addition to this extraordinary hoard, the tall, graceful stone testament of Taita. Von Schiller stopped beside it to caress the polished stone before he passed on into the second room.

Here the coffin of Tanus, Lord Harrab, lay across a pair of trestles. A white-coated radiologist hovered over her back-lit display board on which the X-ray plates were clipped. Von Schiller went directly to the display and peered at the shadowy pictures upon it. Within the outline of the wooden coffin, the reclining human shape with hands crossed over its chest was very clear. It reminded him of a carved effigy atop the sarcophagus of an old knight in the precincts of a medieval cathedral.

'What can you tell me about this body?' he asked the radiologist without looking at her.

'Male,' she said crisply. 'Late middle age. Over fifty and under sixty-five at death. Short stature.' All the listeners winced and glanced at von Schiller. He seemed not to have noticed this solecism. 'Five teeth missing. One front upper, one eye tooth and three molars. Wisdom teeth impacted. Extensive caries in most surviving teeth. Evidence of chronic bilharzia infection. Possible poliomyelitis in infancy, withering in left leg.' She recited her findings for five minutes, and then ended, 'Probable cause of death was a puncture wound in upper right thorax. Lance or arrow. Extrapolating from the entry angle, the head of the lance or arrow would have transfixed the right lung.'

'Anything else?' von Schiller asked when she

fell silent. The radiologist hesitated, and then went on.

'Herr von Schiller, you will recall that I have examined several mummies for you. In this instance, the incisions through which the viscera were removed appear to have been made with more skill and finesse than those of the other cadavers. The operator seems to have been a trained physician.'

'Thank you.' Von Schiller turned from her to Nahoot. 'Do you have any comments, at this stage?'

'Only that these descriptions do not fit those given in the seventh scroll for Tanus, Lord Harrab, at the time of his death.'

'In what way?'

'Tanus was a tall man. Much younger. See the portraits on the coffin lid.'

'Go on,' von Schiller invited.

Nahoot stepped up to the display of X-ray plates and pointed out several solid dark objects, all of them with clean outlines, that adorned the body.

'Jewellery,' he said. 'Amulets. Bracelets. Pectorals. Several necklaces. Rings and earrings. But, most significant,' Nahoot touched the dark circle around the dead brow, 'the *uraeus* crown. The outline of the sacred serpent is quite unmistakable, beneath the bandages.'

'What does that indicate?' Von Schiller was puzzled.

'This was not the body of a commoner, or

even of a noble. The extent of ornamentation is too extensive. But most significant, the *uraeus* crown. The sacred cobra. That was only worn by royalty. I believe that what we have here is a royal mummy.'

'Impossible,' snapped von Schiller. 'Look at the inscription on the coffin. Those that were painted on the walls of the tomb. Clearly this is the mummy of an Egyptian general.'

'With respect, Herr von Schiller. There is a possible explanation. In the book written by the Englishman, *River God*, there is an interesting suggestion that the slave Taita swopped the two mummies, that of Pharaoh Mamose and his good friend, Tanus.'

'For what earthly reason would he do that?' Von Schiller looked incredulous.

'Not for any earthly reason, but for a spiritual and supernatural reason. Taita wished his friend to have the use and ownership of all Pharaoh's treasure in the after-world. It was his last gift to a friend.'

'Do you believe that?'

'I do not disbelieve it. There is one other fact that tends to support this theory. It is quite obvious from the X-rays that the coffin is too large for the body within. To me, it seems obvious that it was designed to accommodate a larger man. Yes, Herr von Schiller, I do believe that there is an excellent chance that this is a royal mummy.'

Von Schiller had gone ashen pale as he listened. Sweat beaded upon his forehead, and his voice was hoarse and chesty as he asked,

'A royal mummy?'

'It may very well be so.'

Slowly von Schiller moved closer to the sealed coffin on its trestle, until he was staring down at the portrait of the dead man upon its lid.

'The golden *uraeus* of Mamose. The personal jewellery of a pharaoh.' His hand was shaking as he laid it on the coffin lid. 'If that is so, then this find exceeds our most extravagant hopes.'

Von Schiller drew a deep steadying breath. 'Open the coffin. Unwrap the mummy of the Pharaoh Mamose.'

It was painstaking work. Nahoot had performed the same task many times before, yet never on the earthly remains of such an illustrious personage as an Egyptian pharaoh.

Nahoot first had to establish where the joint of the lid lay beneath the paint. Once he had done this, he could whittle away at the ancient varnish and glues that secured the lid in place. Great care had to be taken to inflict as little damage as possible: the fragile coffin in itself was a priceless treasure. This work took the greater part of two days.

When the lid was free and ready to be lifted, Nahoot sent a message to von Schiller, who was in an executive meeting with his sons and the other directors of his company in the library upstairs. Von Schiller had refused to go into the city for this meeting: he could not bear to be separated from his latest treasure. Immediately he heard from Nahoot he adjourned the meeting until the following Monday, and dismissed his directors and his offspring unceremoniously. Then, without waiting to see them into their waiting limousines, he hurried down to the vaults.

Nahoot and Reeper had rigged a light scaffold over the coffin, from which hung two sets of block and tackle. As soon as von Schiller entered the vault, Reeper sent away his assistants. Only the three of them would be present to witness the opening of the coffin.

Reeper brought him the carpet-covered block for him to stand on and positioned it at the head of the coffin, so that von Schiller would be able to see inside as they worked. From this eminence the old man nodded to them to proceed. The ratchets of the two blocks clicked, one pawl at a time, as both Reeper and Nahoot gently put pressure on the tackle. There was a faint crackling and tearing sound, at which von Schiller winced.

'It is only the last shreds of glue holding the lid,' Nahoot reassured him.

'Go on!' von Schiller ordered, and they lifted the lid another six inches until it hung suspended over the body of the coffin. The scaffolding was on nylon castors which rolled smoothly over the tiled floor. They wheeled away the entire structure, with the coffin lid still suspended from it.

Von Schiller peered into the open coffin. His expression changed to one of astonishment. He had expected to see the neatly swathed human form lying serenely in the traditional funereal pose. Instead, the interior of the coffin was stuffed untidily with loose linen bandages that entirely hid the body from view.

'What on earth —' von Schiller exclaimed with astonishment. He reached out to take a handful of the old discoloured wrappings, but Nahoot stopped him.

'No! Don't touch it,' he cried out excitedly, and then was immediately apologetic. 'Forgive me, Herr von Schiller, but this is fascinating. It strongly supports the theory of an exchange of bodies. I think we should study it, before we proceed with the unwrapping. With your permission of course, Herr von Schiller.'

Von Schiller hesitated. He was anxious to discover what lay beneath this rat's nest of old rags, but he realized the virtue of caution and prudence now. A hasty move might do irreparable damage. He straightened up and stepped down from his block.

'Very well,' he grunted. He pulled a handkerchief from the breast pocket of his dark blue double-breasted suit jacket, and mopped the heavy sweat from his face. His voice was shaky as he asked, 'Is it possible? Could this be Mamose himself?'

Stuffing the handkerchief back into his trouser pocket, he discovered with mild surprise that he had a painful erection. With his hand in his pocket he rearranged it to lie flat against his stomach. 'Remove the loose wrappings.'

'With your permission, Herr von Schiller, we should take the photographs first,' Reeper suggested tactfully.

'Of course,' von Schiller agreed at once. 'We are scientists, archaeologists, not common looters. Take the photographs.'

They worked slowly, and von Schiller found the delay tantalizing. There was no sense of the passage of time down here in the vault, but at one stage von Schiller, now in his shirtsleeves, glanced at his gold wrist-watch and was surprised to see that it was past nine o'clock at night. He unknotted his necktie, threw it on the bench where his jacket already lay, and re-applied himself to the task.

Gradually the shape of a human body emerged from under the compacted mass of ancient bindings, but it was after midnight when at last Nahoot teased away the last untidy clump of old cloth from the mummy's torso. They blinked at the glimpse of gold just visible through the neat layers of bandages laid upon the corpse by the meticulous and skilful hands of the embalmers.

'Originally, of course, there would have been

several massive outer coffins. These are missing, as are the masks. Those must still be in Pharaoh's original sarcophagus, covering the body of Tanus in the royal tomb that still awaits discovery. What we have left here is only the inner dressing of the royal mummy.'

With long forceps he peeled away the top layer of bandage as von Schiller, perched on his block, grunted and shuffled his feet.

'The pectoral medallion of the royal house of Mamose,' Nahoot whispered reverently. The great jewel blazed under the arc light. Resplendent in blue lapis lazuli and red carnelian and gold, it covered the entire chest of the mummy. The central motif was of a vulture in flight, soaring on wide pinions, and in its talons it clutched the golden cartouche of the king. The craftsmanship was marvellous, the design splendid.

'There is no doubt now,' von Schiller whispered. 'The cartouche proves the identity of the body.'

Next they unwrapped the king's hands, clasped over the great medallion. The fingers were long and sensitive, each of them loaded with circle after circle of magnificent rings. Clasped in his dead hands were the flail and sceptre of majesty, and Nahoot exulted when they saw them.

'The symbols of kingship. Proof on proof that this is Mamose the Eighth, ruler of the Upper and Lower Kingdoms of ancient Egypt.'

He moved up to the king's still veiled head, but von Schiller stopped him. 'Leave that until last!' he ordered. 'I am not yet ready to look upon the face of Pharaoh.'

So Nahoot and Reeper transferred their attention to the king's lower body. As they lifted away each layer of linen, so were revealed scores of amulets that the embalmers had placed beneath the bandages as charms to protect the dead man. They were of gold and carved jewels and ceramic in glowing colours and marvellous shapes — all the birds of the air and the creatures of the land and the fish of the Nile waters. They photographed each amulet *in situ* before working it free and placing it into a numbered slot in the trays that had been set out upon the workbench.

Pharaoh's feet were as small and delicate as his hands, and each toe was laden with precious rings. Only his head was still covered, and both men looked enquiringly at von Schiller. 'It is very late, Herr von Schiller,' Reeper said, 'if you wish to rest —'

'Continue!' he ordered brusquely. So they moved up on each side of the mummy's head, while von Schiller remained on his stand between them.

Gradually the king's face was exposed to the light, for the first time in nearly four thousand years. His hair was thin and wispy, still red with the henna dye he had used in his lifetime. His skin had been cured with aromatic resins until it was hard as polished amber. His nose was thin and beaked. His lips were drawn back in a soft, almost dreamy smile which exposed the gap in his front teeth.

The resin coated his eyelashes, so that they seemed wet with tears and the lids only half-shut. Life seemed to gleam there still, and only when von Schiller leaned closer did he realize that the light in those ancient sockets was the reflection from the white porcelain discs that the undertakers had placed in the empty sockets during the embalming.

On his brow the Pharaoh wore the sacred *uraeus* crown. Every detail of the cobra head was still perfect. There was no wearing or abrading of the soft metal. The serpent's fangs were sharp and recurved, and the long forked tongue curled between them. The eyes were of shining blue glass. On the band of gold beneath the hooded asp was engraved the royal cartouche of Mamose.

'I want that crown.' Von Schiller's voice was choking with passion. 'Remove it, so that I can hold it in my own hands.'

'We may not be able to lift it without damaging the head of the royal mummy,' Nahoot protested.

'Do not argue with me. Do as I tell you.'

'Immediately, Herr von Schiller,' Nahoot capitulated. 'But it will take time to free it. If Herr von Schiller wishes to rest now, we will inform you when we have loosened the crown and have it ready for you.'

The circle of gold had adhered to the resin-soaked skin of the king's forehead. In order to remove it Nahoot and Reeper first had to lift the complete body out of the coffin and lay it on the stainless steel mortuary stretcher which already waited to receive it. Then the resin had to be softened and removed with specially prepared solvents. The whole process took as long as Nahoot had predicted, but finally it was completed.

They laid the golden *uraeus* upon a blue velvet cushion, as if for a coronation ceremony. They dimmed all the other lights in the main chamber of the vault, and arranged a single spot to fall upon the crown. Then they both went upstairs to inform von Schiller.

He would not let the two archaeologists accompany him when he returned to the vaults to view the crown. Only Utte Kemper was with him when he keyed the lock to the armoured door of the vault, and the heavy door slid open.

The first thing that caught von Schiller's eye as he entered the vault was the glittering crown in its velvet nest.

Immediately he began to wheeze for air like an asthmatic, and he seized her hand and squeezed until her knuckles crackled with the pressure and she whimpered with pain. But the pain excited her. Von Schiller undressed her, placed the golden crown upon her head and laid her naked in the open coffin.

'I am the promise of life,' she whispered from the ancient coffin. 'Mine is the shining face of immortality.'

He did not touch her. Naked, he stood over the coffin with his inflamed and swollen rod thrusting from the base of his belly like a creature with separate life.

She ran her hands slowly down her own body, and as they reached her mons Veneris, she intoned gravely, 'May you live for ever!'

The wondrous efficacy of the crown of Mamose was proven beyond any doubt. Nothing before had produced this effect upon Gotthold von Schiller. For at her words, the purple head of his penis erupted of its own accord and glistening silver strings of his semen dribbled down and splattered upon her soft white belly.

In the open coffin Utte Kemper arched her back, and writhed in her own consuming orgasm.

It seemed to Royan that she had been away from Egypt for years instead of weeks. She realized just how much she had missed the crowded and bustling streets of the city, the wondrous smells of spices and food and perfume in the bazaars, and the wailing voice of the muezzin calling the faithful to prayer from the turrets of the mosques.

That very first morning she left her flat in

Giza while it was still dark, and since her injured knee was still swollen and painful she used her stick as she limped along the banks of the Nile. She watched the dawn cobble the river waters with a pathway of gold and copper and set the triangular sails of the feluccas ablaze.

This was a different Nile from the one she had encountered in Ethiopia. This was not the Abbay, but the true Nile. It was broader and slower, and the muddy stink of it was familiar and well beloved. This was her river and her land. She found that her resolve to do what she had come home to do was reinforced. Her doubts were set at rest, her conscience soothed. As she turned away from it she felt strong and sure of herself and the course that she must take.

She visited Duraid's family. She had to make amends to them for her sudden departure and her long, unexplained absence. At first her brother-in-law was cool and stiff towards her; but after his wife had wept and embraced Royan and the children had clambered all over her — she was always their favourite *ammah* — he warmed to her and relented sufficiently to offer to drive her out to the oasis. When she explained that she wanted to be alone when she visited the cemetery, he unbent so far as to lend her his beloved Citroën.

As she stood beside Duraid's grave the smell of the desert filled her nostrils and the hot breeze fidgeted with her hair. Duraid had loved the desert. She was glad for him that from now onwards he would always be close to it. The headstone was simple and traditional: just his name and dates under the outline of the cross. She knelt beside it and tidied the grave, renewing the wilted and dried bouquets of flowers with those that she had brought with her from Cairo.

Then she sat quietly beside him for a long while. She made no rehearsed speeches, but simply ran over in her mind so many of the good quiet times they had passed together. She remembered his kindness and his understanding, and the security and warmth of his love for her. She regretted that she had never been able to return it in the same measure, but she knew that he had accepted and understood that.

She hoped that he also understood why she had come back now. This was a leave-taking. She had come to say goodbye. She had mourned him and, although she would always remember him and he would always be a part of her, it was time for her to move on. It was time for him to let her go. When at last she left the cemetery, she walked away without looking back.

She took the long road around the south side of the lake to avoid having to pass the burnt-out villa; she did not wish to be reminded of that night of horror on which Duraid had died there. It was therefore after dark when she returned to the city, and the family were relieved to see her. Her brother-in-law walked three times around the Citroën, checking for damage to the paintwork, before ushering her into the house where his wife had set a feast for them.

A talan Abou Sin, the minister whom Royan had come specifically to see, was out of Cairo on an official visit to Paris. She had three days to wait for his return, and because she knew that Nahoot Guddabi was no longer in Cairo, she felt safe and able to spend much of that time at the museum. She had many friends there, and they were delighted to see her and to bring her up to date with all that had happened during the time that she had been away.

The rest of the time she spent in the museum reading room, going over the microfilm of the Taita scrolls, searching for any clues that she might have missed in her previous readings. There was a section of the second scroll which she read carefully and from which she made extensive notes. Now that the prospect of finding the tomb of Pharaoh Mamose intact had become real and credible, her interest in what that tomb might contain had been stimulated.

The section of the scroll upon which she concentrated was a description that the scribe, Taita, had given of a royal visit by the Pharaoh to the workshops of the necropolis, where his funerary treasure was being manufactured and assembled within the walls of the great temple that he had built for his own embalming. According to Taita they had visited the separate workshops, first the armoury with its collection of accoutrements of the battlefield and the chase, and then the furniture workshop, home of exquisite workmanship. In the studio of the sculptors, Taita described the work on the statues of the gods and the life-sized images of the king in every different activity of his life that would line the long causeway from the necropolis to the tomb in the Valley of the Kings. In this workshop the masons were also hard at work on the massive granite sarcophagus which would house the king's mummy over the ages. However, according to Taita's later account history had cheated Pharaoh Mamose of this part of his treasure, and all these heavy and unwieldy items of stone had been abandoned and left behind in the Valley of the Kings when the Egyptians fled south along the Nile to the land they called Cush, to escape the Hyksos invasion that overwhelmed their homeland.

As Royan turned with more attention to the scribe's description of the studio of the goldsmiths, the phrase which he used to describe the golden death-mask of the Pharaoh struck her forcibly. *'This was the peak and the zenith. All the unborn ages might one day marvel at its splendour.'* Royan looked up dreamily from the microfilm and wondered if those words of the ancient scribe were not prophetic. Was she destined to be one of those who would marvel at the splendour of the golden death-mask? Might she be the first to do so in almost four thousand years? Might she touch this wonder, take it up in her hands and at last do with it as her conscience dictated?

Reading Taita's account left Royan with a sense of ancient suffering, and a feeling of compassion for the people of those times. They were, after all — no matter how far removed in time — her own people. As a Coptic Egyptian, she was one of their direct descendants. Perhaps this empathy was the main reason why, even as a child, she had originally determined to make her life's work a study of these people and the old ways.

However, she had much else to think of during those days of waiting for the return of Atalan Abou Sin. Not least of these were her feelings for Nicholas Quenton-Harper. Since she had visited the little cemetery at the oasis and made her peace with Duraid's memory, her thoughts of Nicholas had taken on a new poignancy. There was so much she was still uncertain of, and there were so many difficult choices to make. It was not possible to fulfil all her plans and desires without sacrificing others almost equally demanding.

When at last the hour of her appointment to see Atalan came around, she had difficulty bringing herself to go to him. Like somebody in a trance she limped through the bazaars, using her stick to protect her injured knee, hardly hearing the merchants calling their wares to her. From her skin tone and European clothing they presumed she must be a tourist.

She hesitated so long over taking this irrevocable step that she was almost an hour late for the appointment. Fortunately this was Egypt, and Atalan was an Arab to whom time did not have the same significance as it did to the Western part of Royan's make-up.

He was his usual urbane and charming self. Today, in the privacy of his own office, he was comfortably dressed in a white *disdasha* and a headcloth. He shook hands with her warmly. If this had been London he might have kissed her cheek, but not here in the East where a man never kissed any woman but his wife and then only in the privacy of their home.

He led her through to his private sitting room, where his male secretary served them small cups of tar-thick coffee and lingered to preserve the propriety of this meeting. After an exchange of compliments and the obligatory interval of polite small-talk, Royan could come obliquely to the main reason for her visit.

'I have spent much of the last few days at the museum, working in the reading room. I managed to see many of my old colleagues there, and I was surprised to hear that Nahoot had withdrawn his application for the post of director.'

Atalan sighed, 'My nephew is a headstrong boy at times. The job was his, but at the very last moment he came to tell me that he had been offered another in Germany. I tried to dissuade him. I told him that he would not enjoy the northern climate after being brought up in the Nile valley. I told him that there are many things in life such as country and family that no amount of money can recompense. But —' Atalan spread his hands in an eloquent gesture.

'So who have you chosen to fill the post of director?' she asked with an innocence that did not deceive him.

'We have not yet made any permanent appointment. Nobody automatically comes to mind, now that Nahoot has withdrawn. Perhaps we will be forced to advertise internationally. I for one would be very sad to see it go to a foreigner, no matter how well qualified.'

'Your excellency, may I speak to you in private?' Royan asked, and glanced significantly at the male secretary hovering at the doorway. Atalan hesitated only a moment.

'Of course.' He gestured to the secretary to leave the room, and when he had withdrawn and closed the door behind him Atalan leaned towards her and dropped his voice slightly. 'What is it that you wish to discuss, my dear lady?'

It was an hour later that Royan left him. He walked with her as far as the lift outside his suite of offices.

As he shook hands his voice was low and mellifluous, 'We will meet again soon, inshallah.'

When the Egyptair flight landed at Heathrow and Royan left the airport arrivals hall for a place in the queue at the taxi rank outside, it seemed that the temperature difference from Cairo was at least fifteen degrees. Her train arrived at York in the damp misty cold of late afternoon. From the railway station she phoned the number that Nicholas had given her.

'You silly girl,' he scolded her. 'Why didn't you let me know you were on your way? I would have met you at the airport.'

She was surprised at how pleased she was to see him, and at how much she had missed him, as she watched him step out of the Range Rover and come striding towards her on those long legs. He was bare-headed and obviously had not subjected himself to a haircut since she had last seen him. His dark hair was rumpled and wind-tossed and the silver wings fluffed over his ears.

'How's the knee?' he greeted her. 'Do you still need to be carried?'

'Almost better now. Nearly time to throw away the stick.' She felt a sudden urge to throw her arms around his neck, but at the last moment she prevented herself from making a display and merely offered him a cold, rosy brown cheek to kiss. He smelt good — of leather and some spicy aftershave, and of clean virile manhood.

In the driver's seat he delayed starting the engine for a moment, and studied her face in the street light that streamed in through the side window.

'You look mighty pleased with yourself, madam. Cat been at the cream?'

'Just pleased to see old friends,' she smiled, 'but I must admit Cairo is always a tonic.'

'No supper laid on. Thought we would stop at a pub. Do you fancy steak and kidney pud?'

'I want to see my mother. I feel so guilty. I don't even know how her leg is mending.'

'Popped in to see her day before yesterday. She's doing fine. Loving the new puppy. Named it Taita, would you believe?'

'You are really a very kind person — I mean, taking the trouble to visit her.'

'I like her. One of the good old ones. They don't build them like that any more. I suggest we have a bite to eat, and then I will pick up a bottle of Laphroaig and we will go and see her.'

It was after midnight when they left Georgina's cottage. She had dispensed rough frontier justice to the malt whisky that Nicholas had brought and now she waved them off, standing in the kitchen doorway, clutching her new puppy to her ample bosom and teetering slightly on her plaster-cast leg.

'You are a bad influence on my mother,' Royan told him.

'Who's a bad influence on whom?' he protested. 'Some of those jokes of hers turned the Stilton a richer shade of blue.'

'You should have let me stay with her.'

'She has Taita to keep her company now. Besides, I need you close at hand. Plenty of work to do. I can't wait to show you what I have been up to since you went swanning off to Egypt.'

The Quenton Park housekeeper had prepared her a bedroom in the flat in the lanes behind York Minster.

As Nicholas carried her bags up the stairs rip-saw snoring came from behind the door of the bedroom on the second landing, and she looked at Nicholas enquiringly.

'Sapper Webb,' he told her. 'Latest addition to the team. Our own engineer. You will meet him tomorrow, and I think you will like him. He is a fisherman.'

'What's that got to do with me liking him?'

'All the best people are fishermen.'

'Present company excluded,' she laughed. 'Are you staying at Quenton Park?'

'Giving the house a wide berth, for the time being.' He shook his head. 'Don't want it bruited about that I am back in England. There are some fellows from Lloyd's that I would rather not speak to at the moment. I will be in the small bedroom on the top floor. Call if you need me.'

When she was alone she looked around the tiny chintzy room with its own doll's house bathroom, and the double bed that took up most of the floor area. She remembered his remark about calling if she needed him, and she looked up at the ceiling just as she heard him drop one of his shoes on the floor.

'Don't tempt me,' she whispered. The smell of him lingered in her nostrils, and she remembered the feel of his lean hard body, moist with sweat, pressed against hers as he had carried her up out of the Abbay gorge. Hunger and need were two words she had not thought of for many years. They were starting to loom too large in her existence.

'Enough of that, my girl,' she chided herself, and went to run a bath.

Nicholas pounded on her door the next morning on his way downstairs.

'Come along, Royan. Life is real. Life is urgent.'

It was still pitch dark outside, and she groaned softly and asked, 'What time is it?' But he was gone, and faintly she could hear him whistling 'The Big Rock Candy Mountain' somewhere downstairs.

She checked her watch and groaned again. 'Whistling at six-thirty, after what he and Mummy did to the Laphroaig last night. I don't believe it. The man is truly a monster.'

Twenty minutes later she found him in a dark

blue fisherman's sweater and jeans and a butcher's apron, working in the kitchen.

'Slice toast for three, there's a love.' He gestured towards the brown loaf that lay beside the electric toaster. 'Omelettes coming up in five minutes.'

She looked at the other man in the room. He was middle-aged, with wide shoulders and sleeves rolled up high around muscular biceps, and he was as bald as a cannonball.

'Hello,' she said, 'I am Royan Al Simma.'

'Sorry.' Nicholas waved the egg-whisk. 'This is Danny — Daniel Webb, known as Sapper to his friends.'

Danny stood up with a cup of coffee in his big competent-looking fist. 'Pleased to meet you, Miss Al Simma. May I pour you a cup of coffee?' The top of his head was freckled, and she noticed how blue his eyes were.

'Dr Al Simma,' Nicholas corrected him.

'But please call me Royan,' she cut in quickly, 'and yes, I'd love a cup.'

There was no mention of Ethiopia or Taita's game during breakfast, and Royan ate her omelette and listened respectfully to a passionate dissertation on how to catch sail fish on a fly rod from Sapper, while Nicholas heckled him mercilessly, calling into question almost every statement he made. Very obviously they had a good relationship, and she supposed she would become accustomed to all the angling jargon.

As soon as breakfast was over, Nicholas stood

up with the coffee pot in one hand. 'Bring your mugs, and follow me.'

He led Royan to the front sitting room. 'I have a surprise for you. My people up at the museum worked round the clock to get it ready for you.'

He threw open the door of the sitting room, with an imitation of a trumpet flourish, 'Tarantara!'

On the centre table stood a fully mounted model of the striped dik-dik, crowned with the pricked horns and clad in the skin that Nicholas had smuggled back from Africa. It was so realistic that for a moment she expected it to leap off the table and dash away as she walked towards it.

'Oh, Nicky. It's beautifully done!' She circled it appraisingly. 'The artist has captured it exactly.'

The model brought back to her vividly the heat and smell of the bush in the gorge, and she felt a twinge of nostalgia and sadness for the delicate, beautiful creature. Its glass eyes were deceptively lifelike and bright, and the end of its proboscis looked wet and gleaming as though it was about to wiggle it and sniff the air.

'I think it's splendid. Glad you agree with me.' He stroked the soft, smooth hide. She felt this was not the moment to spoil his boyish pleasure. 'As soon as we have sorted out Taita's puzzle, I intend writing a paper on it for the

Natural History Museum, the same lads that called Great-grandpapa a liar. Restore the family honour.' He laughed and spread a dust-sheet over the model. Carefully he lifted it down from the table and placed it safely in a corner of the room where it was out of harm's way.

'That was the first surprise I had saved up for you. But now for the big one.' He pointed to a sofa against one wall. 'Take a seat. I don't want you to be bowled over by this.'

She smiled at his nonsense, but went obediently to the furthest end of the sofa and curled her legs under her as she settled there. Sapper Webb came to sit awkwardly at the other end, obviously uncomfortable at being so close to her.

'Let's talk about how we are going to get into the chasm on the Dandera river,' Nicholas suggested. 'Sapper and I have talked about nothing else the whole time that you have been away.'

'That and catching fish, I'll warrant.' She grinned at him, and he looked guilty.

'Well, both subjects involve water. That is my justification.' His expression became serious. 'You recall that we discussed the idea of exploring the depths of Taita's pool with scuba gear, and I explained the difficulties.'

'I remember,' she agreed. 'You said the pressure into the underwater opening was too great, and that we would have to find another method of getting in there.'

'Correct.' Nicholas smiled mysteriously. 'Well, Sapper here has already earned the exorbitant fee that I have promised him — promised, I emphasize, not yet paid. He has come up with the alternative method.'

Now she too became serious and unfolded her legs. She placed both feet on the floor and leaned forward attentively, with her elbows on her knees and her chin cupped in her hands.

'It must have been all those brains of his that pushed out his hair. I mean, it's very neat thinking. Although it was staring us both in the face, neither you nor I thought of it.'

'Stop it, Nicky,' she told him ominously, 'you are doing it again.'

'I am going to give you a clue.' He ignored the warning and went on teasing her blithely. 'Sometimes the old ways are the best. That's the clue.'

'If you are so clever, how come you aren't famous?' she began, and then broke off as the solution occurred to her. 'The old ways? You mean, the same way as Taita did it? The same way he reached the bottom of the pool without the benefit of diving equipment?'

'By George! I think she's got it!' Nicholas put on a convincing Rex Harrison imitation.

'A dam.' Royan clapped her hands. 'You propose to redam the river at the same place where Taita built his dam four thousand years ago.'

'She's got it!' Nicholas laughed. 'No flies on our girl! Show her your drawings, Sapper.'

Sapper Webb made no attempt to disguise his self-satisfaction as he went to the board that stood against the facing wall. Royan had noticed it, but had paid no attention to it, until now he pulled away the cover and proudly displayed the illustrations that were pegged to it.

She recognized immediately the enlargements of the photographs that Nicholas had taken at the putative site of Taita's dam on the Dandera river, and others that he had taken in the ancient quarry that Tamre had shown them. These had been liberally adorned with calculations and lines in thick black marker pen.

'The major has provided me with estimates of the dimensions of the river bed at this point, and he has also calculated the height that we will have to raise the wall to induce a flow down the former course. I have, of course, allowed for errors in these calculations. Even if these errors are in the region of thirty per cent, I believe that the project is still feasible with the very limited equipment we will have available to us.'

'If the ancient Egyptians could do it, it will be a breeze for you, Sapper.'

'Kind of you to say so, major, but "breeze" is not the word I would have chosen.'

He turned to the drawings pegged beside the photographs on the board, and Royan saw that they were plans and elevations of the project based upon the photographs and Nicholas's estimates.

'There are a number of different methods of dam construction, but these days most of them presuppose the availability of reinforced concrete and heavy earth-moving equipment. I understand that we will not have the benefit of these modern aids.'

'Remember Taita,' Nicholas exhorted him. 'He did it without bulldozers.'

'On the other hand, the Egyptians probably had unlimited numbers of slaves at their disposal.'

'Slaves I can promise you. Or the modern equivalent thereof. Unlimited numbers? Well, perhaps not.'

'The more labour you can provide, the sooner I can divert the flow of the river for you. We are agreed that this has to be done before the onset of the rainy season.'

'We have two months at the most.' Nicholas dropped his flippant attitude. 'As regards the provision of labour, I will be relying on enlisting the aid of the monastic community at St Frumentius. I am still working out a sound theological reason that might convince them to take part in the building of the dam. I don't think they will fall for the idea that we have discovered the site of the Holy Sepulchre in Ethiopia and not in Jerusalem.'

'You find me the labour, and I will build your dam,' Sapper grunted. 'As you said earlier, the old ways are the best. It is almost certain that the ancients would have used a system of gabions and coffer dams to lay the foundations of the original dam.'

'Sorry,' Royan interrupted. 'Gabions? I don't have an engineering degree.'

'I am the one who must apologize.' Sapper made a clumsy attempt at chivalry. 'Let me show you my drawings.' He turned to the board. 'What this fellow Taita probably did was to weave huge bamboo baskets, which he placed in the river and filled with rock and stone. These are what we call gabions.' He indicated the plans on the board. 'After that he would have used rough-cut timber to build circular walls between the gabions — the coffer dams. These he would also have filled with stone and earth.'

'I get the general idea,' Royan said, sounding dubious, 'but then it is not really necessary for me to understand all the details.'

'Right you are!' Sapper agreed heartily. 'Although the major assures me that there is all the timber we will need on the site, I plan to use wire mesh for the construction of the gabions and human labour for the filling of the mesh nets with stone and aggregate.'

'Wire mesh?' Royan demanded. 'Where do you hope to find that in the Abbay valley?'

Sapper began to reply, but Nicholas forestalled him. 'I will come to that in a moment. Let Sapper finish his lecture. Don't spoil his fun. Tell Royan about the stone from the quarry. She will enjoy that.'

'Although I have designed the dam as a temporary structure, we have to make certain that it is capable of holding back the river long enough to enable the members of our team to enter the underwater tunnel in the downstream pool safely —'

'We call it Taita's pool,' Nicholas told him, and Sapper nodded.

'We have to make sure that the dam does not burst while people are in there. You can imagine the consequences, should that happen.'

He was silent for a moment while he let them dwell upon the possibility. Royan shuddered slightly and hugged her own arms.

'Not very pleasant,' Nicholas agreed. 'So you plan to use the blocks?' he prompted Sapper.

'That's right. I have studied the photographs taken in the quarry. I have picked out over a hundred and fifty granite blocks lying there completed or almost completed, and I calculate that if we use these in combination with the steel mesh gabions and the timber coffer walls, this would give us a firm foundation for the main dam wall.'

'Those blocks must weigh many tons each,' Royan pointed out. 'How will you move them?' Then, as Sapper opened his mouth to explain, she changed her mind. 'No! don't tell me. If you say it's possible, I will take your word for it.'

'It's possible,' Sapper assured her.

'Taita did it,' Nicholas said. 'We will be doing it all his way. That should please you. After all, he is a relative of yours.'

'You know, you are right. In a strange sort

of way, it does give me pleasure.' She smiled at him. 'I think it's a good omen. When does all this happen?'

'It's happening already,' Nicholas told her. 'Sapper and I have already ordered all the stores and equipment that we will be taking with us. Even the mesh for the gabions has been precut to size by a small engineering firm near here. Thanks to the recession, they had machines standing idle.'

'I have been down there at their workshop every day, supervising the cutting and packing,' Sapper butted in. 'Half the shipment is already on its way. The rest of it will follow before the weekend.'

'Sapper is leaving this afternoon to take charge and get it all loaded. You and I have some last-minute arrangements to see to, and then we will follow him at the end of the week. You must remember I was not expecting you back from Cairo so soon,' Nicholas said. 'If I had known, I could have arranged for us all to fly down to Valletta together.'

'Valletta?' Royan looked mystified. 'As in Malta? I thought we were going to Ethiopia.'

'Malta is where Jannie Badenhorst has his base.'

'Jannie who?'

'Badenhorst. Africair.'

'Now you have really lost me.'

'Africair is an air transport company that owns one old ex-RAF Hercules, flown by Jannie and his son Fred. They use Malta as their base. It's a stable and pragmatic little country — no African politics, no corruption — and yet it is the door to most of the destinations in the Middle East and in the northern half of Africa where Jannie and Fred do most of their work. His main employment is smuggling booze into the Islamic countries, where of course it is prohibited. He's the Al Capone of the Mediterranean. Bootlegging is big business in that part of the world, but he does take on other work. Duraid and I flew into Libya from there with Jannie on our little jaunt to the Tibesti Massif. Jannie will be taking us down to the Abbay.'

'Nicky, I don't want to be a killjoy, but you and I are now undesirable immigrants to Ethiopia. Had you overlooked that little fact? How do you propose to get back in there?'

'Through the back door,' Nicholas grinned, 'and my old pal Mek Nimmur is the gatekeeper.'

'You have been in contact with Mek?'

'With Tessay. It seems that she is now his go-between. I imagine it's very convenient for Mek to have her on board. She has all the right connections, and she can slip in and out of Khartoum or Addis or places where it might be awkward or even dangerous for him to be seen.'

'Well, well!' Royan looked impressed. 'You have been busy.'

'Not all of us can afford a holiday in Cairo whenever the fancy takes us,' he told her tartly.

'One more little question.' She ignored the

jibe, although she realized that despite his easy smile her absence must have irked him. 'Does Mek know about Taita's game?'

'Not in detail.' Nicholas shook his head. 'But he has some suspicions, and anyway I know I can rely on him.' He hesitated, and then went on. 'Tessay was very cagey when I spoke to her on the phone, but it seems that there has been some sort of attack on St Frumentius monastery. Jali Hora and thirty or forty of his monks were massacred, and most of the sacred relics from the church were stolen.'

'Oh, dear God, no!' Royan looked stricken. 'Who would do a thing like that?'

'The same people who murdered Duraid, and made three attempts to wipe you out.'

'Pegasus.'

'Von Schiller,' he agreed.

'Then we are directly responsible,' Royan whispered. 'We led them to the monastery. The Polaroids they captured from us when they raided our camp would have shown them the stele and the tomb of Tanus. Von Schiller wouldn't have to be a clairvoyant to guess where we had taken them. Now there is more blood on our hands.'

'Hell, Royan, how can you take responsibility for von Schiller's madness? I am not going to let you punish yourself for that.' Nicholas's tone was sharp and angry.

'We started this whole thing.'

'I don't agree with that, but I admit that von

Schiller is the one who must have cleaned out the *maqdas* of St Frumentius and that the stele and the coffin are now almost certainly part of his collection.'

'Oh, Nicky, I feel so guilty. I never realized what a danger we were to those simple devout Christians.'

'Do you want to call off the whole thing?' he asked cruelly.

She thought about it seriously for a while, then shook her head.

'No. Perhaps when we go back we will be able to compensate the monks for their losses with what we find in the bottom of Taita's pool.'

'I hope so,' he agreed fervently. 'I do hope so.'

The giant Hercules C-Mk1 four-engined turbo-prop aircraft was painted a dusty nondescript brown, and the identification lettering on the fuselage was faded and indistinct. There was no Africair legend displayed anywhere on the machine, and it had a tired and scruffy appearance that spoke eloquently of the fact that it was almost forty years old and had flown well over half a million hours even before it had fallen into Jannie Badenhorst's hands.

'Does that thing still fly?' Royan asked, as she looked at it standing forlornly in a back corner of the Valletta airfield. Its drooping belly gave it the air of a sad old street-walker who had been put out of business by an unexpected and unlooked-for pregnancy.

'Jannie keeps it looking that way deliberately,' Nicholas assured her. 'The places that he flies to, it's best not to draw envious eyes.'

'He certainly succeeds.'

'But both Jannie and Fred are first-rate aero-engineers. Between them they keep Big Dolly perfect under her engine cowlings.'

'Big Dolly?'

'Dolly Parton. Jannie is an avid fan.' The taxi dropped them and their meagre luggage outside the side door of the hangar, and Nicholas paid the driver while Royan thrust her hands into the pockets of her anorak and shivered in the cold wind off the Mediterranean.

'There's Jannie now.' Nicholas pointed to the bulky figure in greasy brown overalls coming down the loading ramp of the Hercules. He saw them and jumped down off the ramp.

'Hello, man! I was beginning to give up on you,' he said as he came shambling across the tarmac. He looked like a rugby player, as he had been in his youth, and the slight limp was from an old playing-field injury.

'We were late leaving Heathrow. Strike by French air traffic control. The joys of international travel,' Nicholas told him, and then introduced Royan.

'Come and meet my new secretary,' Jannie

581

invited. 'She may even give you a cup of coffee.'

He led them through a wicket in the main hangar door and into the cavernous interior. There was a small office cubicle beside the entrance with a sign over the door saying 'Africair' and the company logo of a winged battleaxe. Mara, Jannie's new secretary, was a Maltese lady only a few years younger than himself. What she lacked in youth and beauty she fully made up for across the chest.

'Jannie likes them mature and with plenty of top hamper,' Nicholas murmured to Royan from the side of his mouth.

Mara gave them coffee, while Jannie went over his flight plan with Nicholas.

'It's a little complicated,' he apologized. 'As you can imagine, we will have to do a bit of ducking and diving. Muammar Gadaffi is not wallowing in affection for me at the moment, so I'd rather not overfly any of his territory. We will be going in through Egypt, but without landing there.' He pointed out their flight path on the maps spread over his desk.

'Bit of a problem over the Sudan. They are having a little civil war there.' He winked at Nicholas. 'However, the northern government are not equipped with the most up-to-date radar in the world. Lot of old Russian reject stuff. It's an enormous bit of country, and Fred and I have worked out their blank spots. We will be keeping well clear of their main military installations.'

'What's our flying time?' Nicholas wanted to know.

Jannie pulled a face. 'Big Dolly is no sprinter, and as I have just told you we will not be taking any short-cuts.'

'How long?' Nicholas insisted.

'Fred and I have rigged up bunks and a kitchen, so that during the flight you will have all the comforts of home.' He lifted his cap and scratched his head before he admitted, 'Fifteen hours.'

'Has Big Dolly got that sort of endurance?' Nicholas wanted to know.

'Extra tanks. Seventy-one thousand kilos of fuel. Even with the load you have given us, we can get there and back without refuelling.' He was interrupted by the huge hangar doors rolling open, and a heavy truck being driven through. 'That will be Fred and Sapper now.' Jannie swigged the last of his coffee and hugged Mara. She giggled, and her bosom quivered like a snowfield on the point of an avalanche.

The truck parked at the far end of the hangar, where an array of equipment and stores was already neatly stacked, ready for loading. When Fred climbed down from the cab, Jannie introduced him to Royan. He was a younger version of the father, already beginning to spread around the waist, and with an open bucolic face, more like a Karroo sheep farmer than a commercial pilot.

'That's the last truckload.' Sapper came

around the front of the truck and shook Nicholas's hand. 'All set to begin loading.'

'I want to take off before four o'clock tomorrow morning. That will get us into our rendezvous at the optimum time tomorrow evening,' Jannie cut in. 'We have a bit of work to do, if we are going to get some sleep before we leave.' He gestured to the pallets waiting to be loaded. 'I wanted to get some of the local lads to give a hand with the loading, but Sapper wouldn't hear of it.'

'Quite right,' Nicholas agreed. 'The fewer who are in on this, the merrier. Let's get cracking.'

The cargo had been prepacked on the steel pallets, secured with heavy nylon strapping and covered with cargo netting. There were thirty-six loaded pallets, and the canvas packs containing the parachutes formed an integral part of each load. This huge cargo would require two separate flights to ferry it all across to Africa.

Royan called out the contents of each pallet from the typed manifest, while Nicholas checked it against the actual load. Nicholas and Sapper had worked out the loads carefully to ensure that the items that would be required first were on the initial flight. Only when he was certain that each pallet was complete in every detail did he signal to Fred, who was operating the forklift. Fred ran the arms into the slots of the pallet and lifted it, then he drove it out of the hangar and up the ramp of the Hercules.

In the hold of the enormous aircraft, Jannie

and Sapper helped Fred to position each pallet precisely on the rollers and then strap it down securely. The last part of the cargo to go aboard was the small front-end-loading tractor. Sapper had found this in a secondhand yard in York, and after testing it exhaustively declared it to be a 'steal'. Now he drove this up the ramp under its own power, and lovingly strapped it down to the rollers.

The tractor made up almost a third of the total weight of the entire shipment, but it was the one item that Sapper considered essential if they were to complete the earthworks for the dam in the time that Nicholas had stipulated. He had calculated that it would require a cluster of five cargo parachutes to get the heavy tractor back to earth without damage. Fuel for it would of course present a problem, and the bulk of the second cargo would be made up of dieseline in special nylon tanks that could withstand the impact of an airdrop.

It was after midnight before the aircraft was loaded with the first shipment. The remaining pallets were still stacked against the hangar wall awaiting Big Dolly's return for the second flight. Now they could turn their full attention to the farewell banquet of island specialities that Mara had laid out for them in the tiny Africair office.

'Yes,' Jannie assured them, 'she's also a good cook,' and gave Mara a loving squeeze as she rested her bosom on his shoulder, leaning over him to refill his plate with calamari.

'Happy landings!' Nicholas gave them the toast in red Chianti.

'Eight hours between the throttle and the bottle,' Jannie apologized, as he drank the toast in Coca-Cola.

They lay down in their clothes to get a few hours' sleep on the bunks bolted to the bulkhead behind the flight deck, but it seemed to Royan that she was woken only a few minutes later by the quiet voices of the two pilots completing their pre-take-off checks, and the whine of the starters on the huge turbo-prop engines. As Jannie spoke on the radio to the control tower, and Fred taxied out to the holding point, the three passengers climbed out of their bunks and strapped themselves into the folding seats down the side of the main cabin. Big Dolly climbed into the night sky and the lights of the island dwindled and were swiftly lost behind them. Then there was only the dark sea below and the bright pricking of the stars above. Royan turned her head to smile at Nicholas in the dim overhead lights of the cabin.

'Well, Taita, we are back on court for the final set.' Her voice was tight with excitement.

'The one good thing about being forced to sneak about like this is that Pegasus may take a while to find out that we are back in the Abbay gorge.' Nicholas looked complacent.

'Let's hope that you are right.' Royan held up her right hand and crossed her fingers. 'We will have enough to worry about with what Taita has in store for us, without Pegasus muscling in on us again just yet.'

They are on their way back to Ethiopia,' said von Schiller with utter certainty.

'How can we be certain of that, Herr von Schiller?' Nahoot asked.

Von Schiller glared at him. The Egyptian irritated him intensely, and he was beginning to regret having employed him. Nahoot had made very little headway in deciphering the meaning of the engravings on the stele that they had taken from the monastery.

The actual translation had offered no insurmountable problems. Von Schiller was convinced that he could have done this work himself, without Nahoot's assistance, given time and the use of his extensive library of reference works. It comprised, for the most part, nonsensical rhymes and extraneous couplets out of place and context. One face of the stele was almost completely covered by columns of letters and figures that bore no relation whatsoever to the text on the other three faces of the column.

But although Nahoot would not admit it, it was clear that the underlying meaning behind most of this had eluded him. Von Schiller's patience was almost exhausted. He was tired of listening to Nahoot's excuses, and to promises that were never fulfilled. Everything about him, from his oily ingratiating tone of voice to his sad eyes in their deep lined sockets, had begun to annoy him. But especially he had come to detest his exasperating habit of questioning the statements that he, Gotthold von Schiller, made.

'General Obeid was able to inform me of their exact flight arrangements when they left Addis Ababa. It was very simple to have my security men at the airport when they arrived in England. Neither Harper nor the woman are the kind of people that are easily overlooked, even in a crowd. My men followed the woman to Cairo —'

'Excuse me, Herr von Schiller, but why did you not have her taken care of if you were aware of her movements?'

'*Dummkopf!*' von Schiller snapped at him. 'Because it now seems that she is much more likely to lead me to the tomb than you are.'

'But, sir, I have done —' Nahoot protested.

'You have done nothing but make up excuses for your own failure. Thanks to you, the stele is still an enigma,' von Schiller interrupted him contemptuously.

'It is very difficult —'

'Of course it is difficult. That's why I am paying you a great deal of money. If it were easy I would have done it myself. If it is indeed the instruction to find the tomb of Mamose, then the scribe Taita meant it to be difficult.'

'If I am allowed a little more time, I think

I am very near to establishing the key —'

'You have no more time. Did you not hear what I have just told you? Harper is on his way back to the Abbay gorge. They flew from Malta last night in a chartered aircraft that was heavily loaded with cargo. My men were not able to establish the nature of that cargo, except that it included some earth-moving equipment, a front-end-loading tractor. To me, this can mean only one thing. They have located the tomb, and they are returning to begin excavating it.'

'You will be able to get rid of them as soon as they reach the monastery.' Nahoot relished the thought. 'Colonel Nogo will —'

'Why do I have to keep repeating myself?' Von Schiller's voice turned shrill and he slapped his hand down on the tabletop. 'They are now our best chance of finding the tomb of Mamose. The very last thing that I want to happen is that any harm should come to them.' He glared at Nahoot. 'I am sending you back to Ethiopia immediately. Perhaps you will be of some use to me there. You are certainly no use here.'

Nahoot looked disgruntled, but he had better sense than to argue again. He sat sullenly as von Schiller went on, 'You will go to the base camp and place yourself under the command of Helm. You will take your orders from him. Treat them as if they come directly from me. Do you understand?'

'Yes, Herr von Schiller,' Nahoot muttered sulkily.

'Do not interfere in any way with Harper and the woman. They must not even know that you are at the base camp. The Pegasus geological team will carry on its normal duties.' He paused and smiled bleakly, then went on, 'It is most fortunate that Helm has actually discovered very promising evidence of large deposits of galena, which as you may know is the ore from which lead is obtained. He will continue the exploratory work on these deposits, and if they bear out their promise they will make the entire operation highly profitable.'

'What exactly will be my duties?' Nahoot wanted to know.

'You will be playing the waiting game. I want you there ready to take advantage of any progress that Harper makes. However, you are to give him plenty of elbow room. You will not alert him by any overflights with the helicopter, or by approaching his camp. No more midnight raids. Every move that you make must be cleared with me before, I repeat before, you take any action.'

'If I am to operate under these restrictions, how will I know if Harper and the woman have made any progress?'

'Colonel Nogo already has a reliable man, a spy, in the monastery. He will inform us of every move that Harper makes.'

'But what about me? What will be my work?'

'You will evaluate the intelligence that Nogo collects. You are familiar with archaeological methods. You will be able to judge what Harper is trying to achieve, and you will be able to tell what success he is enjoying.'

'I see,' Nahoot muttered.

'If it were possible I would have gone back to the Abbay gorge myself. However, this is not possible. It may take time, months perhaps, before Harper makes any important progress. You know as well as anybody that these things take time.'

'Howard Carter worked for ten years at Thebes before he found the tomb of Tutankhamen,' Nahoot pointed out maliciously.

'I hope that it will not take that long,' said von Schiller coldly. 'If it does, it is very unlikely that you will still be involved with the search. As for myself, I have a series of very important negotiations coming up here in Germany, as well as the annual general meeting of the company. These I cannot miss.'

'You will not be coming back to Ethiopia at all, then?' Nahoot perked up at the prospect of escaping from von Schiller's malignant influence.

'I will come as soon as there is something for me there. I will be relying on you to decide when my presence is needed.'

'What about the stele? I should —'

'You will continue to work on the translation.' Von Schiller forestalled his objections. 'You will take a full set of photographs with you to Ethiopia, and you will continue your work while

591

you are there. I shall expect you to report to me by satellite, at least once a week, on your progress.'

'When do you want me to leave?'

'Immediately. Today if that is possible. Speak to Fräulein Kemper. She will make your travel arrangements.'

For the first time during the interview Nahoot looked happy.

Big Dolly droned on steadily south-eastwards, and there was very little to relieve the boredom of the flight. The dawn was just breaking when they crossed the African coast at a remote and lonely desert beach that Jannie had chosen for just this reason. Once they were over the land there was as little of interest to see as there had been over the sea. The desert stretched away, bleak and brown and featureless in every direction.

At irregular intervals they heard Jannie in the cockpit speaking to air traffic control, but as they were able to hear only half the conversation they had no idea as to the identity or the nationality of the station. Occasionally Jannie dropped the heavily accented English he was affecting and broke into Arabic. Royan was surprised by Jannie's fluency in the language, but then as an Afrikaner the guttural sounds came naturally to him. He was even able to mimic the different accents and dialects of Libyan and Egyptian convincingly as he lied his way across the desert.

For the first few hours Sapper pored over his dam drawings; then, unable to proceed further until he had the exact measurements of the site, he curled up on his bunk with a paperback novel. The unfortunate author was unable to hold his attention for long. The open book sagged down over his face, and the pages fluttered every time he emitted a long grinding snore.

Nicholas and Royan huddled on her bunk with the chessboard between them, until hunger overtook them and they moved to the makeshift galley. Here Royan took the subservient role of bread-slicer and coffee-maker, while Nicholas demonstrated his artistry in creating a range of Dagwood sandwiches. They shared the food with Jannie and Fred, perched up behind the pilots' seats in the cockpit.

'Are we still over Egyptian territory?' Royan asked.

With his mouth full, Jannie pointed out over the port wingtip of Big Dolly. 'Fifty nautical miles out there is Wadi Halfia. My father was killed there in 1943. He was with the Sixth South African Division. They called it Wadi Hellfire.' He took another monstrous bite of sandwich. 'I never knew the old man. Fred and I landed there once. Tried to find his grave.' He shrugged eloquently. 'It's a hell of a big piece of country.

Lots of graves. Very few of them marked.'

Nobody spoke for a while. They chewed their sandwiches, thinking their own thoughts. Nicholas's father had also fought in the desert against Rommel. He had been more fortunate than Jannie's father.

Nicholas glanced across at Royan. She was staring out of the window at her homeland, and there was something so passionate and fraught in her gaze that Nicholas was startled. The temptation to think of her as an English girl, like her mother, was at most times irresistible. It was only in odd moments such as these that he became intensely aware of the other facets of her being.

She seemed unaware of his scrutiny. Her preoccupation was total. He wondered what she was thinking — what dark and mysterious thoughts were smouldering there. He remembered how she had seized the very first opportunity on their return from Ethiopia to hurry back to Cairo, and once again a feeling of disquiet came over him. He wondered if other emotional ties of which he was unaware might not transcend those loyalties which he had taken for granted. He realized with something of a shock that they had been together for only a few short weeks, and despite the strong attraction that she exerted over him he knew very little about her.

At that moment she started and looked round at him quickly. Crowded as they were at the portside window, they stared into each other's eyes from a distance of only a foot or so. It was only for a few seconds but what he saw in her eyes, the dark shadows of guilt or some other emotion, did nothing to allay his misgivings.

She turned back to Jannie, leaning over his shoulder to ask, 'When will we cross the Nile?'

'On the other side of the border. The Sudanese government concentrate all their attentions on the rebels in the far south. There are some stretches of the river here in the north that are completely deserted. Pretty soon now we will be going down right on the deck, to get under the radar pings from the Sudanese stations around Khartoum. We will slip through one of the gaps.'

Jannie lifted the aeronautical map on its clipboard from his lap, and held it so she could see it. With one thick, stubby finger he showed Royan their intended route. It was drawn in with blue wax pencil, 'Big Dolly has taken this route so often that she could fly it without my hands on the stick, couldn't you, old girl?' He patted the instrument panel affectionately.

Two hours later, when Nicholas and Royan were back at the chessboard in the main cabin, Jannie called them on the PA, 'Okay, folks. No need to panic. We are going to lose some altitude now. Come up front and watch the show.'

Strapped into fold-down seats in the back of the flight deck, they were treated to a superb exhibition of low flying by Fred. The descent was so rapid that Royan felt they were about to fall out of the sky, and that she had left her stomach back there somewhere at thirty thousand feet. Fred levelled Big Dolly out only feet above the desert floor, so low that it was like riding in a high-speed bus rather than flying. Fred lifted her delicately over each undulation of the tawny, sun-scorched terrain, skimming the black rock ridges and standing on a wingtip to swerve around the occasional wind-blasted hill.

'Nile crossing in seven and a half minutes.' Jannie punched the stopwatch fixed to the control wheel in front of him. 'And unless my navigation has gone all to hell there should be an island shaped like a shark directly under us as we cross.'

As the needle of the stopwatch came up to the mark, the broad, glittering expanse of the river flashed beneath them. Royan caught a brief glimpse of a green island with a few thatched huts on the tip, and a dozen dugout canoes lying on the narrow beach.

'Well, the old man hasn't lost his touch yet,' Fred remarked. 'Still good for a few thousand miles before we trade him in.'

'Not so much of the old man stuff, you little squirt. I have some tricks up my sleeve that I haven't even used yet.'

'Ask Mara.' Fred grinned affectionately at his father as he banked on to a new southwesterly heading, and with his wingtip so close to the ground that he scattered a herd of camels feeding in the sparse thorn scrub. They lumbered away across the plain, each trailing a wisp of white dust like a wedding train.

'Another three hours' flying time to the rendezvous.' Jannie looked up from the map. 'Spot on! We should land forty minutes before sunset. Couldn't be better.'

'I'd better go and change into my hiking gear, then.' Royan went back into the main cabin, pulled her bag from under the bunk and disappeared into the lavatory. When she emerged twenty minutes later she wore khaki culottes and a cotton top.

'These boots were made for walking.' She stamped them on the deck.

'That's fine.' Nicholas watched her from the bunk. 'But how about that knee?'

'It will get me there,' she said, defensively.

'You mean I am to be deprived of the pleasure of back-packing you again?'

The Ethiopian mountains came up so subtly on the eastern horizon that Royan was not aware of them until Nicholas pointed out to her the faint blue outline against the brighter blue of the African sky.

'Almost there.' He glanced at his wrist-watch. 'Let's go up to the flight deck.'

Looking forward through the windshield there was no landmark ahead of them — just the vast brown savannah, speckled with the black dots of acacia trees.

'Ten minutes to go,' Jannie intoned. 'Anyone see anything?' There was no reply, and they all stared ahead.

'Five minutes.'

'Over there!' Nicholas pointed over his shoulder. 'That's the course of the Blue Nile.' A denser grove of thorn trees formed a dark line far ahead. 'And there is the smokestack of the derelict sugar-mill on the river bank. Mek Nimmur says that the airstrip is about three miles from the mill.'

'Well, if it is, it's not shown on the chart,' Jannie grumbled. 'One minute before we are on the coordinates.' The minute ticked off slowly on the stopwatch.

'Still nothing —' Fred broke off as a red flare shot up from the earth directly ahead and flashed past Big Dolly's nose. Everyone in the cockpit smiled and relaxed with relief.

'Right on the nose.' Nicholas patted Jannie's shoulder in congratulations. 'Couldn't have done better myself.'

Fred climbed a few hundred feet and came round in a one-eighty turn. Now there were two signal fires burning out there on the plain — one with black smoke, the other sending a column of white straight up into the still evening sky. It was only when they were a kilometre out that they were able to make out the faint outline of the overgrown and long-disused landing strip. Roseires airstrip had been built twenty years before by a company that tried to grow sugar cane under irrigation from the Blue Nile. But Africa had won again and the company had passed into oblivion, leaving this feeble scrape mark on the plain as its epitaph. Mek Nimmur had chosen this remote and deserted place for the rendezvous.

'No sign of a reception committee,' Jannie grunted. 'What do you want me to do?'

'Continue your approach,' Nicholas told him. 'There should be another flare — ah, there it is!' The ball of fire shot up from a clump of thorn trees at the far end of the runway, and for the first time they were able to make out human figures in the bleak landscape. They had stayed hidden until the very last moment.

'That's Mek, all right! Go ahead and land.'

As Big Dolly finished her roll-out and the end of the rough and pitted runway came up ahead, a figure in camouflage fatigues popped up ahead of them. With a pair of paddles it signalled them to taxi into the space between two of the tallest thorn trees.

Jannie cut the engines and grinned at them over his shoulder. 'Well, boys and girls, looks like we pulled off another lucky one!'

Even from the height of Big Dolly's cockpit there was no mistaking the commanding figure of Mek Nimmur as he emerged from the cover of the clump of acacia trees. Only now

599

did they realize that the trees had been shrouded with camouflage netting; this was why they had not been able to spot any sign of human presence from the air. As soon as the loading ramp was lowered, Mek Nimmur came striding up it.

'Nicholas!' They embraced and, after Mek had kissed him noisily on each cheek, he held Nicholas at arm's length and studied his face, delighted to see him again. 'So I was right! You are up to your old tricks. Not simply a dik-dik shoot, was it?'

'How can I lie to an old friend?' Nicholas shrugged.

'It always came easy to you,' Mek laughed, 'but I am glad we are going to have some fun together. Life has been very boring recently.'

'I bet!' Nicholas punched his shoulder affectionately.

A slim, graceful figure followed Mek up the ramp. In the olive-green fatigues Nicholas hardly recognized Tessay until she spoke. She wore canvas para boots and a cloth cap that made her look like a boy.

'Nicholas! Royan! Welcome back!' Tessay cried. The two women embraced as enthusiastically as the men had done.

'Come on, you Ous!' Jannie protested. 'This isn't Woodstock. I have to get back to Malta tonight. I want to take off before dark.'

Swiftly Mek took charge of the offloading. His men swarmed aboard and manhandled the pallets forward on the rollers, while Sapper started up his beloved front-end-loader and used it to run the cargo down the ramp and stack it in the acacia grove under the camouflage netting. With so many hands to help it went swiftly, and Big Dolly's hold was emptied just as the sun settled wearily on to the horizon, and the short African twilight bled all colour from the landscape.

Jannie and Nicholas had one last hurried discussion in the cockpit while Fred completed his flight checks. They went over the plans and radio procedures one last time.

'Four days from today,' Jannie agreed, as they shook hands briefly.

'Let the man go, Nicholas,' Mek bellowed from below. 'We must get across the border before dawn.'

They watched Big Dolly taxi down to the end of the strip and swing around. The engine beat crescendoed as she came tearing back in a long rolling shroud of dust and lifted off over their heads. Jannie waggled his wings in farewell and, without navigation lights showing, the great aircraft blended like a black bat into the darkening sky and disappeared almost immediately.

'Come here.' Nicholas led Royan to a seat under the acacia. 'I don't want that knee to play up again.' He pushed her culottes halfway up her thigh and strapped the knee with an elastic bandage, trying not to make his pleasure in this task too apparent. He was pleased to see that the bruising had almost faded and there

601

was no longer any swelling.

He palpated it gently. Her skin was velvety and the flesh beneath it firm and warm to the touch. He looked up, and from the expression on her face realized that she was enjoying this intimacy as much as he was. As he caught her eye she flushed slightly, and quickly smoothed down her culottes.

She jumped up and said, 'Tessay and I have a lot of catching up to do,' and hurried across to join her.

'I am leaving a full combat platoon to guard your stores here,' Mek explained to Nicholas as Tessay led Royan away. 'We will travel in a very small party as far as the border. I don't expect any trouble. There is very little enemy activity in this sector at the moment. Lots of fighting in the south, but we are quiet here. That is why I chose this rendezvous.'

'How far to the Ethiopian border?' Nicholas wanted to know.

'Five hours' march,' Mek told him. 'We will slip through one of our pipelines after the moon has set. The rest of my men are waiting in the entrance to the Abbay gorge. We should rendezvous with them before dawn tomorrow.'

'And from there to the monastery?'

'Another two days' march,' Mek replied. 'We will be there just in time to receive the drop from your fat friend in the fat plane.'

He turned away and gave his last orders to the platoon commander who would remain at

Roseires to guard the stores. Then he assembled the party of six men who would form their escort across the border. Mek divided up the loads between them. The most important single item was the radio, a modern military lightweight model which Nicholas carried himself.

'Those bags of yours are too difficult to carry. You will have to repack them,' Mek told Nicholas and Royan. So they emptied their bags and stuffed the contents into the two canvas haversacks that Mek had ready for them. Two of his men slung the haversacks over their shoulders and disappeared into the darkness.

'He is not taking that!' Mek stared aghast at the bulky legs of the theodolite that Sapper had retrieved from one of the pallets. Sapper spoke no Arabic, so Nicholas had to translate.

'Sapper says that it is a delicate instrument. He cannot allow it to be dropped from the aircraft. He says that if it is damaged he will not be able to do the work he was hired for.'

'Who is going to carry it?' Mek demanded. 'My men will mutiny if I try to make them do it.'

'Tell the cantankerous bugger that I will carry it myself.' Sapper drew himself up with dignity. 'I wouldn't let one of his great clumsy oafs lay a finger on it.' He picked up the bundle, placed it over his shoulder and stalked away with a stiff back.

Mek let the advance guard have a five-minute start, and then he nodded. 'We can go now.'

Thirty minutes after Big Dolly had taken off, they left the airfield and set out across the dark and silent plain, headed into the east. Mek set a hard pace. He and Nicholas seemed to have the eyes of a pair of cats, Royan thought, as she followed close behind them. They could see in the darkness, and only a whispered warning from one of them prevented her falling into a hole or tripping over a pile of rocks in the darkness. When she did stumble, Nicholas seemed always to be there, reaching back to steady her with a strong, firm grip.

They marched in complete and disciplined silence. It was only every hour, when they rested for five minutes, that Nicholas and Mek sat close together, and from the few quiet words she picked up Royan realized that Nicholas was explaining to him the full reasons for their return to the Abbay gorge. She heard Nicholas repeat the names 'Mamose' and 'Taita' often, and Mek's deep voice questioning him at length. Then they would be up again and moving forward in the night.

After a while she lost all sense of the distance they had travelled. Only the hourly rest periods orientated her to the passage of time. Fatigue crept over her slowly, until it required an effort to lift her foot for each pace. Despite her boast, her knee was beginning to ache. Now and then she felt Nicholas touch her arm, guiding her over the rough places. At other times they would stop abruptly at some whispered warning from up front. Then they would stand quietly waiting in the darkness, nerves tensed, until at another whisper they would move on again at the same pressing pace. Once she smelt the cool muddy effluvium of the river on the dry warm night air, and she knew that they must be very close to the Nile. Without a word being spoken she sensed the nervous tension in the men ahead of her, and was aware of the alertness in the way they carried themselves and their weapons.

'Crossing the border now,' Nicholas breathed close to her face, and the tension was infectious. She forgot her tiredness, and heard her pulse beating in her own ears.

This time they did not stop for the usual rest break, but continued for another hour until slowly she felt the mood of the men changing. Someone laughed softly, and there was a lightness in their pace as they swung on towards the luminescence in the eastern sky. Abruptly the moon thrust its crescent horns above the dark silhouette of far-off mountain ranges.

'All clear. We are through,' Nicholas told her in his normal voice. 'Welcome back to Ethiopia. How are you feeling?'

'I'm okay.'

'I am tired too.' He grinned at her in the moonlight. 'Pretty soon we will camp and rest. Not much further.'

He was lying, of course: the march went on and on until she wanted to weep. And then suddenly she heard the sound of the river again, the soft rushing flow of the Nile in the dawn. Up ahead she heard Mek talking to the men who were waiting for them, and then Nicholas guided her off the path and made her sit while he knelt in front of her and unlaced her boots.

'You did well. I am proud of you,' he told her, as he stripped off her socks and examined her feet for blisters. Then he unbandaged the knee. It was slightly swollen, and he massaged it with a skilled and tender touch.

She sighed softly, 'Don't stop. That feels good.'

'I'll give you a Brufen for the inflammation.' He dug the pills out of his pack and then spread his padded jacket for her to lie on. 'Sorry, the sleeping bags are with our other gear. Have to rough it until Jannie makes his air drop.'

He passed her the water bottle, and while she swallowed the pill he pulled the tab on a pack of emergency rations. 'Not exactly gourmet fare.' He sniffed the contents. 'In the army we call them rat packs.' She fell asleep with her mouth still half-filled with tasteless meat loaf and plastic cheese.

When Nicholas woke her with a mug of hot sweet tea, she saw it was already late afternoon. He sat beside her and sipped at his own mug, noisily blowing away the steam between each mouthful.

'You will be pleased to know that Mek is now fully in the picture. He has agreed to help us.'

'What have you told him?'

'Just enough to keep him interested.' Nicholas grinned. 'The theory of progressive disclosure. Never tell everything all at once, feed it to them a little at a time. He knows what we are looking for, and that we are going to dam a river.'

'What about men to work on the dam?'

'The monks at St Frumentius will do whatever he tells them. He is a great hero.'

'What have you promised him in return?'

'We haven't got round to that yet. I told him that we have no idea what we are going to find, and he laughed and said he would trust me.'

'Silly boy, isn't he?'

'Not exacly how I would describe Mek Nimmur,' he murmured. 'I think when the time is ripe he will let us know what the price of his cooperation is.' He looked up at that moment. 'We were just talking about you, Mek.'

Mek strode up to them, and then squatted on his haunches beside Nicholas.

'What were you saying about me?'

'Royan says you are a hard bastard, pushing her on a forced march all night.'

'Nicholas is spoiling you. I have been watching him fussing over you,' he chuckled. 'What I say is, treat them rough. Women love it.' Then he grew serious. 'I am sorry, Royan. The border is always a bad place. You will find me less of a monster now we are on home ground.'

'We are very grateful for all you are doing.'

He inclined his head gravely, 'Nicholas is an

old friend, and I hope that you are a new friend.'

'I have been terribly distressed. Tessay told me last night that there had been trouble at the monastery.'

Mek scowled and tugged at his short beard, pulling a tuft of hair from his own chin with the force of his anger. 'Nogo and his killers. This is just a sample of what we are fighting against. We have been rescued from the tyranny of Mengistu, only to be plunged into fresh horror.'

'What happened, Mek?'

Speaking tersely but vividly, he described the massacre and the plunder of the monastery's treasures. 'There was no doubt it was Nogo. Every one of the monks that escaped knows him well.'

His anger was too fierce for him to contain, and he stood up abruptly. 'The monastery means much to all the people of the Gojam. I was christened there, by Jali Hora himself. The murder of the abbot and the desecration of the church is a terrible outrage.' He jammed his cap down on his head. 'And now we must get on. The road ahead is steep and difficult.'

Now that they were clear of the border, it was safe to move in daylight. The second day's march carried them into the depths of the gorge. There were no foothills: it was like

608

entering through the keep of a vast castle. The walls of the great central massif rose up almost four thousand feet on either hand, and the river snaked along in the depths, its entire length churned by rapids and breaking white water. At noon Mek broke the march to rest in a grove of trees beside the river. There was a beach below them, sheltered by massive boulders which must have rolled down from the cliffs that hung like a rampart above them.

The five of them sat a little apart from each other. Sapper was still smarting from his altercation over the theodolite with Mek, and keeping himself aloof. He placed the heavy instrument in a conspicuous position and sat ostentatiously close to it. Mek and Tessay seemed strangely quiet and withdrawn, until suddenly Tessay reached out and grasped Mek's hand.

'I want to tell them,' she blurted out impulsively.

Mek looked away at the river for a moment before he nodded. 'Why not?' he shrugged at last.

'I want them to know,' Tessay insisted. 'They knew Boris. They will understand.'

'Do you want me to tell them?' Mek asked softly, and he was still holding her hand.

'Yes,' she nodded, 'it is best that it comes from you.'

Mek was silent for a while, gathering his words, and then he started in that low rumbling voice, not looking at them, but watching

Tessay's face. 'The very first moment I looked upon this woman, I knew that she was the one that God had sent my way.'

Tessay moved closer to him.

'Tessay and I said our vows together on the night of Timkat and asked for God's forgiveness, and then I took her away as my woman.'

She laid her head upon his great muscular shoulder.

'The Russian followed us. He found us here, on this very spot. He tried to kill us both.'

Tessay looked down at the beach upon which she and Mek had so nearly died, and she shuddered at the memory.

'We fought,' he said simply, 'and when he was dead, I sent his body floating away down the river.'

'We knew he was dead,' Royan told them. 'We heard from the people at the embassy that the police found his body downstream, near the border. We didn't know how it had happened.'

They were all quiet for a while, and then Nicholas broke the silence, 'I wish I had been there to watch. It must have been one hell of a fight.' He shook his head in awe.

'The Russian was good. I am glad I don't have to fight him again,' Mek admitted, and stood up. 'We can reach the monastery before dark, if we start now.'

Mai Metemma, the newly elected abbot of St Frumentius, met them on the terrace of the monastery overlooking the river. He was only a little younger than Jali Hora had been, tall and with a dignified silver head, and today he was wearing the blue crown in honour of such a distinguished guest as Mek Nimmur.

After the visitors had bathed and rested for an hour in the cells that had been set aside for them, the monks came to lead them to the welcome feast that had been prepared. When the *tej* flasks had been refilled for the third time, and the mood of the abbot and of his monks had mellowed, Mek began to whisper into the old man's ear.

'You recall the history of St Frumentius — how God cast him up on our shore from the storm-tossed sea, so that he might bring the true faith to us?'

The abbot's eyes filled with tears. 'His holy body was entombed here, in our *maqdas*. The barbarians came and stole the relic away from us. We are children without a father. The reason for the building of this church and monastery has been taken away,' he lamented. 'No longer will the pilgrims come from every corner of Ethiopia to pray at his shrine. We will be forgotten by the Church. We are undone. Our monastery will perish and our monks will be blown away like dead leaves on the wind.'

'When St Frumentius came to Ethiopia he was not alone. Another Christian came with him from the High Church in Byzantium,' Mek reminded him in a soft, soothing rumble.

'St Antonia.' The abbot reached for his *tej* flask to allay the intensity of his sorrow.

'St Antonia,' Mek agreed. 'He died before St Frumentius, but he was no less holy than his brother.'

'St Antonia was also a great and holy man, deserving of our love and veneration.' The abbot took a long swallow from the flask.

'The ways of God are mysterious, are they not?' Mek shook his head at the wonder of the workings of the universe.

'His ways are deep and not for us to question or understand.'

'And yet he is compassionate, and he rewards the devout.'

'He is all-compassionate.' The abbot's tears overflowed and ran down his cheeks.

'You and your monastery have suffered a grievous loss. The sacred relic of St Frumentius has been taken from you — alas, never to be recovered. But what if God were to send you another? What if he were to send you the sacred body of St Antonia?'

The abbot looked up through his tears, his expression suddenly calculating. 'That would be a miracle indeed.'

Mek Nimmur placed his arm around the old

man's shoulders and whispered quietly in his ear, and Mai Metemma stopped weeping and listened intently.

I have obtained your workers for you,' Mek told Nicholas as they began the march up the valley the next morning. 'Mai Metemma has promised to give us a hundred men within two days and another five hundred to follow them within the next week. He is handing out indulgences to all those who volunteer to work on the dam. They will be spared the fires of purgatory if they take part in such a glorious project as the recovery of the holy relic of St Antonia.'

Both the women stopped in their tracks and stared at him.

'What did you promise the poor old man?' Tessay demanded.

'A body to replace the one that Nogo plundered from the church. If we do discover the tomb, then the monastery's share will be the mummy of Mamose.'

'That's a mean thing to do,' Royan exploded. 'You will cheat him into helping us.'

'It is not a cheat.' Mek's dark eyes flashed at the accusation. 'The relic that they lost was not the veritable body of St Frumentius, and yet for hundreds of years it served the purpose of uniting the community of monks and drawing

Christians from all over this land. Now that it is gone, the very existence of the monastery is threatened. They have lost their reason for continuing.'

'So you are tempting them with a false promise!' Royan was still angry.

'The body of Mamose is every bit as authentic as the one they lost. What does it matter if it is the body of an ancient Egyptian rather than that of an ancient Christian, just as long as it serves as a focus for the faith and if it is the means by which the monastery might survive for another five hundred years?'

'I think Mek is making sense.' Nicholas gave his opinion.

'Since when have you been an expert in Christianity? You are an atheist,' Royan flashed at him, and he held up his hands as if to ward off a blow.

'You are right. What do I know about it anyway? You argue it out with Mek. I am going to discuss the theory of dam-building with Sapper Webb.' He sauntered up to the head of the file of men and fell in beside his engineer.

From time to time he heard heated voices raised behind him, and he grinned. He knew Mek, but he was also beginning to understand the lady. It would be fascinating to see who would win this argument.

They reached the head of the chasm in the middle of the afternoon, and while Mek searched out a campsite Nicholas took Sapper immediately to the narrow neck of the river just above where it plunged over the waterfall. While Sapper set up the theodolite, Nicholas took the graduated levelling staff. Sapper ordered him up and down the face of the cliff with peremptory hand signals, all the while peering into the lens of the theodolite, while Nicholas teetered on insecure footing and tried to keep the staff upright for Sapper to take his sightings.

'Okay!' Sapper bellowed, after taking his twentieth shot. 'Now I want you on the other side of the river.'

'Fine!' Nicholas bellowed back. 'Do you want me to fly or swim?'

Nicholas hiked three miles upstream to the ford where the trail crossed the Dandera river, and then fought his way back through the tangled riverine undergrowth to the point on the bank opposite which Sapper lay in the shade smoking a soothing cigarette.

'Don't rupture yourself, will you?' Nicholas yelled across the water at him.

It was almost dark before Sapper had made all the shots he wanted, and Nicholas was still faced with the long return trip over the ford. He covered the last mile in almost total darkness, guided only by the flicker of the campfires. Wearily he stumbled into the camp and flung down the levelling staff.

'You had better tell me that it was worth it,' he growled at Sapper, who did not look up from his slide rule. He was working over his revised drawings by the glaring light of a small butane lantern.

'You weren't too far out in your estimates,' he congratulated Nicholas. 'The river is forty-one yards wide at the critical point above the falls, where I want to site the structure.'

'All I want to know is if you will be able to throw a dam across it.'

Sapper grinned and laid his finger down the side of his nose, 'You get me my ruddy front-ender, and I'll dam the bleeding Nile itself.'

After they had eaten their dinner — another of the rat packs — Royan glanced across the fire at Nicholas. When she caught his eye she inclined her head in invitation. Then she stood up and casually drifted out of camp, looking back once to make sure he was following her. Nicholas lighted the path with his torch as they picked their way back to the dam site and found a boulder overlooking the water on which to sit.

He switched off the torch and they were silent for a while as their eyes adjusted to the starlight, and then Royan whispered, 'There were times that I thought we would never return here — that it was all a dream, and that Taita's pool never existed.'

'For us perhaps it never will, without the help of the monks from the monastery.' There was a note of enquiry in his voice.

'You and Mek Nimmur win,' she chuckled softly. 'Of course we have to accept their help. Mek's arguments were very convincing.'

'So you agree that their reward should be the mummy of Mamose?'

'I agree that they may take whatever mummy we discover, if we discover one at all,' she qualified. 'For all we know, the true mummy of Mamose may be the one that Nogo stole.'

Quite naturally he slipped his arm around her shoulders, and after a moment she relaxed against him.

'Oh, Nicky, I am afraid and excited. Afraid that all our hopes are vain, and excited that we might have found the key to Taita's game.' She turned her face to his, and he felt her breath on his lips.

He kissed her, tenderly. Then he drew back with the warmth of her lingering on his lips and studied her face in the starlight. She made no movement to pull away from him. Instead she swayed towards him, and kissed him back. At first it was a staid sisterly kiss, with her mouth tightly closed. He brought his right hand up behind her head and weaved his fingers into her hair, holding her face to his. He opened his mouth over hers, and she made a little sound of dissent through her closed lips.

Slowly, voluptuously, he worked her lips apart, and her protests died away as he probed her mouth deeply with his tongue. She was making a contented little mewling sound now, like a kitten nursing on the teat, and her arms went around him. She kneaded his back with strong supple fingers, her mouth wide open to his kiss, her tongue sinuous and slippery as it twined around his.

He slid his other hand up between their bodies and unhooked the buttons of her shirt down as low as her belt. She leaned back slightly in his embrace to make it easier for him. With a delicious shock he discovered that her breasts were naked under the thin cotton shirt. He cupped one of them in his hand: it was small and firm, only just filling his hand. When he pinched the nipple gently, it stiffened between his fingers like a tiny ripe strawberry.

He broke off the kiss and bowed his head to her bosom. She moaned softly, and with one hand guided him down. When he sucked her nipple into his mouth she gasped and hooked the nails of her other hand into his back, like a cat responding to a caress. Her whole body undulated in his embrace, and after a while she pulled his mouth away. He thought for a moment that she was rejecting him, but then she moved his head across and placed her other nipple in his mouth. Once again she gasped as he sucked it in.

Her movements became more abandoned, keeping pace with his own arousal. He could restrain himself no longer and he reached up under her khaki culottes and laid his hand on the plump mound of her sex. Then with one swift lithe movement she broke away and sprang to her feet. She stood back from him, smoothing down her culottes and buttoning her shirt with fingers that trembled.

'I am so sorry, Nicky. I want to, oh God, you will never know how much I want to. But —' she shook her head and she was panting wildly, 'not yet. Please, Nicky, forgive me. I am caught between two worlds. One half of me wants this so very much, but the other half will not allow me —'

He stood up and kissed her chastely. 'There is no hurry. Good things are worth waiting for,' he told her with his mouth just touching hers. 'Come! I will take you home now.'

While it was still dark the next morning, the first levy of priests that Mai Metemma had promised came filing up the valley. Their chanting awoke the camp, and everyone came sleepily out of their thatched lean-to shelters to welcome the long column of holy men.

'Sweet heavens,' Nicholas yawned, 'it looks

619

as though we have started another crusade. They must have left the monastery in the middle of the night to get here at this hour.' He went to find Tessay, and when he did he told her, 'You are hereby appointed official translator. Sapper speaks not a word of either Arabic or Amharic. Stick close to him.'

As soon as it was fully light, Mek and Nicholas left camp to reconnoitre a drop site. By noon they had agreed that there was only one possibility: they would have to use the valley itself. Compared to the rocky ridges that surrounded them, the floor of the valley was level and fairly free of obstructions. It was imperative that the drop should take place as close to the dam site as possible, for every mile that the stores must be manhandled would add immeasurably to the time and effort needed for the work.

'Time is the major factor,' Nicholas told Mek as they stood in the chosen drop zone the following morning. 'Every day counts from now until the rains break.'

Mek looked up at the sky. 'Pray God for late rains.'

They marked out their drop site a mile down from the river, along the stretch where the valley was widest and there was a clear approach through a gap in the hills. Jannie would need to fly straight and level for five miles under full flap and with the loading ramp down.

'Cutting it fine,' Mek remarked, as they surveyed the rugged slopes and frowning peaks that surrounded them. 'Can your fat friend fly?'

'Fly? He is half-bird,' Nicholas told him.

They moved down the valley to check the placement of the flares and the markers. The markers consisted of crosses of quartz stones laid out down the centre of the valley floor, and they would be highly visible from the air. Sapper was up at the head of the valley. They could see him there on the skyline as he moved around, setting out his smoke flares to mark the approach to the drop zone.

When Nicholas turned around and looked in the opposite direction, he could see the two women sitting on a rock together at the far end of the valley. Sapper had already helped them to set up their flares. These would mark the far limit of the zone, and give Jannie a mark for his climb out of the valley.

Nicholas then turned his attention back to Mek's men as they finished laying out the stark white quartz markers. Once these were all in place, Mek ordered the area to be cleared. Then, lugging the radio, they climbed up to join Sapper on the high ground at the head of the valley. Mek helped Nicholas string out the aerial. Then Nicholas switched on and adjusted the gain carefully before he thumbed the microphone.

'Big Dolly. Come in, Big Dolly!' Nicholas invited, but the static hummed and whined.

'They must be running late.' Nicholas tried not to let his disquiet show. 'Jannie will be coming straight in from Malta on this run. After the first drop he will go back to your base at Roseires and pick up the second load. With luck, both loads should all be dropped before noon tomorrow.'

'If the fat man comes at all,' Mek remarked.

'Jannie is a pro,' Nicholas grunted. 'He will come.' He held the microphone to his lips, 'Big Dolly. Do you read? Over.'

Every ten minutes he called out into the empty echoing silence. Each time his call went unanswered he had visions of Sudanese MiG interceptors racing in with their missiles cocked and locked, and the old Hercules plunging earthwards in flames.

'Come in, Big Dolly!' he pleaded, and at last a thin, scratchy voice floated into his headset. 'Pharaoh. This is Big Dolly. ETA forty-five minutes. Standing by.' Jannie's transmission was terse. He was too much of an old hand at the smuggling game to give a hostile listener time to fix his position.

'Big Dolly. Understand four five. Pharaoh standing by.' Nicholas grinned at Mek. 'Looks like we are in business after all.'

Mek heard it first. His ear was battle-tuned. In this land, if you wanted to go on living it paid to pick up any aircraft long before it arrived. Nicholas was out of training, so it was almost five minutes later that he picked up the distinctive drone of the multi-props echoing weirdly off the cliffs of the gorge. It was impossible to be certain of the direction, but they shaded their eyes and stared into the west.

'There she is.' Nicholas redeemed himself as he spotted the tiny dark speck, so low as almost to blend into the background of the escarpment wall. He nodded at Sapper.

Sapper ran out to his flares and fussed over them briefly. When he backed away they bloomed into clouds of dense marigold-yellow smoke that drifted out sluggishly on the light breeze. The smoke would give Jannie the strength and direction of the wind, as well as his orientation for the drop zone.

Nicholas lifted his binoculars and gazed towards the other end of the narrow valley. He saw that Royan and Tessay were busy with their flares. Suddenly crimson smoke billowed from them, and the women ran back to their original position and stood staring up at the sky.

Nicholas called softly into the microphone. 'Big Dolly. Smoke is up. Do you have it visual?'

'Affirmative. You are visual. For what you are about to receive may you be truly thankful.' Jannie's South African accent was unmistakable as he uttered the cheerful blasphemy.

They watched the aircraft grow in size until its wings seemed to fill half the sky, and then its profile altered as the great wing flaps dropped and the ramp below its belly drooped open. Big Dolly slowed her flight so dramatically that she seemed to hang suspended on an invisible thread from the high African sun. Slowly she came around, banking steeply as Jannie lined her up on the smoke flares, dropping lower and still lower, headed directly at where they stood.

With a savage roar that made all three of them duck, she passed so low over their heads that it seemed she would wipe them off the crest. Nicholas had a glimpse of Jannie peering down at him from the cockpit, a fat smile on his face and one hand raised in a laconic wave, and then he was past.

Nicholas straightened up and watched Big Dolly sweep majestically down the centre of the valley. The first pallet dropped out of her and plunged earthwards, until at the last moment its parachutes burst open like a bride's bouquet. The fall of the heavy container was arrested abruptly. It dangled and swung, and seconds later struck the floor of the valley in a cloud of yellow dust and with a crash they could hear up on the ridge. Then two more loads dropped from her, and they too hung for a moment on their chutes before they slammed in.

Big Dolly's engines howled under full throttle and her nose lifted as she bored for height while she passed over the crimson smoke clouds, and then climbed out of the deadly trap of the valley. She came round in another wide turn and lined up for the second run. Once again the pallets dropped out of her as she roared over the quartz markers and then climbed out over the end wall of the valley, skimming the rocky spikes that would have clawed her down.

Six times Jannie repeated the dangerous

manoeuvre, and each time he dropped three of the heavy rectangular loads. They lay strewn down the length of the valley, shrouded by the tumbled white silk of their own parachutes.

As Jannie climbed away from the last pass, his voice echoed in Nicholas's earphones. 'Don't go away, Pharaoh! I will be back.' Then Big Dolly lifted her belly ramp like an old lady hoisting her knickers and headed away westwards.

Nicholas and Mek ran down into the valley, where the monks were already jabbering and laughing around the pallets. Quickly the two of them took control, sorting the men into gangs and directing them as they broke down the loads and carried them away.

Nicholas and Sapper had planned that the pallets should be dropped in the order that their contents would be needed. The first pallet contained canned and dried food, all their personal effects and camping equipment, along with those other little creature comforts that Nicholas had allowed, including mosquito nets and a case of malt whisky. He was relieved to see that there was no leakage from the precious case: not one of the bottles had been broken in the drop.

Sapper took charge of the building material and heavy equipment. With Tessay relaying his orders, it was dragged and manhandled away to the ancient quarry where it would be packed and stored until needed on site. Darkness fell with more than half the pallets still not unpacked, lying where they had fallen. Mek placed an armed guard over them, and they all traipsed wearily back up the valley to the camp.

That night, with a dram of whisky and a decent meal warming his belly, a mosquito net over his head and a thick foam mattress under him, Nicholas drifted off to sleep with a smile on his face. They were off to a good start.

The chanting of the monks at their matins woke him, 'We won't need an alarm clock here,' he groaned, and staggered down to the river to wash and shave.

As the sun gilded the battlements of the escarpment, he and Mek were already at their post on the heights, searching the western sky. The plan had been for Jannie to spend the night at Roseires, while Mek's men assisted him with the loading of the cargo they had stored there on their first flight out from Malta. This was one of the vulnerable stages of the operation. Although Mek had assured them that there was little military presence in the area at the moment, it needed only a stray Sudanese government patrol to stumble on Big Dolly while she was on the ground to plunge them all into disaster. So it was with a leap of the heart that they heard the familiar drone of the turbo-props reverberating off the cliffs.

Big Dolly lined up again for her first pass down the valley, and as she flew over the quartz crosses the huge yellow front-end loader tumbled out of her hold. Instinctively Nicholas held his breath as he watched it come hurtling down and then jerk up short on the parachute shrouds. It swayed wildly all over the sky, yoyoing on the nylon ropes, and the monks howled with amazement and excitement as they watched it drop in. It struck in a cloud of dust.

Sapper was standing next to Nicholas, groaning and covering his eyes so that he did not have to watch the cloud of dust rising into the air. 'Shit!' he said in a hollow voice.

'Is that a command, or merely a request?' Nicholas asked, but he wasn't really amused.

As the last pallet dropped, and the aircraft climbed away under full power, Nicholas called Jannie on the radio.

'Many thanks, Big Dolly. Safe flight home.'

'Inshallah! If God wills!' Jannie called back.

'I will call you when I need a lift back.'

'I'll be waiting.' Big Dolly trundled away. 'Break a leg!'

'Well now.' Nicholas slapped Sapper's back. 'Let's go down and see if you still have a front-ender.'

The battered yellow machine lay on its side with oil pouring out of her, like blood from a heart-shot dinosaur.

'You can push off. Just leave me a dozen of these black guys to help me,' Sapper told them as sorrowfully as if he was standing at the grave-side of his beloved.

Sapper did not return to camp for dinner, so Tessay sent a bowl of *wat* and some *injera* bread down to him to eat while he worked.

Nicholas considered going down to offer his help with repairing the damaged tractor, but thought better of it. From bitter experience he knew that at certain times Sapper wanted to be left alone, and that this was one of those times.

In the small dark hours of the morning the camp was lit up by the blaze of headlights and the hills reverberated to the roar of a diesel engine. With even his bald head covered with grease and dust, hollow-eyed but triumphant, Sapper drove the yellow tractor into the camp and shouted at them from the high driver's seat.

'Okay, knaves and nymphs! Drop your cocks and grab your socks. Let's go build a dam.'

It took them another two full days to gather in all the pallets that lay strewn down the valley and to carry the stores into the ancient quarry. There they stacked them carefully in accordance with the manifest that Nicholas and Sapper had drawn up in England. It was essential that they knew where every item was stored, and that they had immediate access to it when needed. In the meantime Sapper was at work on the dam site, laying out his foundations, driving numbered wooden pegs into the banks of the river, and taking his final measurements with the long steel surveyor's tape.

During this preliminary work Nicholas was watching the performance of the monks, and getting to know them individually. He was able to pick out the natural leaders and the most intelligent and willing men amongst them. He was also able to identify those who spoke Arabic or a little English. The most promising of these was a monk named Hansith Sherif, whom Nicholas made his personal assistant and interpreter.

Once they were settled into the camp, and had worked out a relationship with the monks, Mek Nimmur took Nicholas aside out of earshot of the two women.

'From now on, my work will be the security of the site. We will have to be ready to prevent another raid like the one on your camp, and the slaughter at St Frumentius. Nogo and his thugs are still out there. It won't take long for him to hear that you are back in the gorge. When he comes, I will be waiting for him.'

'You are better with an AK-47 than with a pickaxe,' Nicholas agreed. 'Just leave Tessay here with me. I need her.'

'So do I.' Mek smiled and shook his head ruefully. 'I am only just learning how much. Look after her for me. I will be back every night to check on her.'

Mek took his men into the bush and deployed them in defensive positions along the trail and around the camp. When Nicholas looked up from his own work he could often make out the figure of one of Mek's sentries on the high ground above the camp. It was reassuring to know that they were there.

However, as he had promised, Mek was back in camp most evenings, and often in the night Nicholas heard, coming from the shelter he shared with Tessay, his deep rumbling laughter blending with her sweet silvery tones. Then Nicholas lay awake and thought about Royan in the hut so close, but yet so far away from where he lay.

On the fifth day the second draft of three hundred labourers that Mai Metemma had conscripted for them arrived, and Nicholas was astonished. Things seldom worked that way in Africa. Nothing ever happened ahead of the promised time. He wondered what exactly Mek had told the abbot, but then decided that he didn't really want to know, for now the main construction work could begin.

These men were not monks, for St Frumentius had already given its all to the sacred labour, but villagers who lived up on the highlands of the escarpment. Mai Metemma had coerced them with promises of religious indulgences and threats of hellfire.

Nicholas and Sapper divided this workforce into gangs of thirty men each, and set one of the picked monks as foreman over each gang. They were careful to grade the men by their physical appearance, so that the big strapping specimens were all grouped together as the project stormtroopers, while the smaller, more wiry men could be reserved for the tasks in which brute strength was not a necessity.

Nicholas dreamed up a name for each gang — the Buffaloes, the Lions, the Axes and so on. It taxed his powers of invention, but he wanted to inspire in them a sense of pride and, to his own particular advantage, to encourage the gangs to compete with one another. He paraded them in the quarry, each group headed by its newly appointed ecclesiastical foreman. Using one of the ancient stone blocks as a platform, and with Tessay interpreting for him, he harangued them heartily and then told them that they would be paid in silver Maria Theresa dollars. He set their wages at three times the going rate.

Up to this stage the men had listened to him with a sullen air of resignation, but now a remarkable transformation came over them. None of them had expected to be paid for the work, and most of them were wondering how soon they could desert and go home. Now Nicholas was promising them not only money, but silver dollars. In Ethiopia for the past two hundred years the Maria Theresa dollar had been regarded as the only true coinage. For this reason they were still minted with the original date of 1780 and the portrait of the old Empress, with her double chin and her *décolletage* exposing half her great bust. One of these coins was more prized than a sackful of the worthless paper birr issued by the regime in Addis. To pay his labour bills, Nicholas had included a chest of these silver coins in the first pallet load that Jannie had dropped.

Celestial grins bloomed as they listened, and white teeth sparkled in their ebony faces. Someone began to sing, and they all stamped and danced and cheered Nicholas as they trooped off to queue for their tools. With mattocks and shovels at the slope they filed off up the valley to the dam site, still singing and prancing.

'St Nicholas,' Tessay laughed. 'Father Christmas. They will never forget you now.'

'They may even enshrine you and build a monastery over you,' Royan suggested sweetly.

'What they don't know is that they are going to earn every single dollar, the hard way.'

From then onwards the work began as soon as it was light enough to see, and stopped only when it was too dark to continue. The men came back to their temporary compound each night by the light of grass torches, too weary to sing. However, Nicholas had contracted with the headmen from the highland villages to supply a slaughter beast every day. Each morning the women came down the trail driving the animal before them, and with huge pots of *tej* balanced on their heads.

Over the days that followed, there were no deserters from Nicholas's little army of workers.

Mounted on the high seat of the front-ender, Sapper lifted the first filled mesh gabion in the hydraulic arms. The mesh-bound parcel of boulders weighed several tons, and all work on the site came to a halt as the men crowded the banks of the Dandera river to watch. A hum of astonishment went up as Sapper eased the yellow tractor down the steep bank and, with the gabion held high, drove the vehicle into the water. The current, affronted by this invasion, swirled angrily around the high rear wheels, but Sapper pushed in deeper.

The crowds lining the bank began to chant and clap encouragement as the water reached as high as the belly of the machine, and clouds of steam hissed from the hot steel of the sump. Sapper locked the brakes, and then lowered the heavy gabion into the flood before reversing back up the bank. The men cheered him wildly, even though the first gabion was instantly submerged and only a whirlpool on the river's surface marked its position. Another filled gabion lay ready. The front-ender waddled up to it, lowered its steel arms and picked it up as tenderly as a mother gathering up her infant.

Nicholas shouted at the foremen to get their gangs back to work. The long lines of men came up the valley, naked except for their brief white loincloths. Sweating heavily in the heat of the gorge, their skin glistened like anthracite freshly cut from the coal face. Each of them carried on his head a basket of stone aggregate, which he dumped into the mouth of the waiting gabion. Then he returned with his empty basket down the hill to the quarry. As each gabion was filled, another team fitted the mesh lid and laced it closed with heavy eight-gauge wire.

'Twenty dollars bonus to the team with the most baskets filled today!' Nicholas bellowed. They shouted with glee and redoubled their efforts, but they were unable to keep up with Sapper on the front-ender. He laid his stone piers artfully, working out from the shallow water alongside the bank so that each gabion lay against its neighbour, keying into the wall to give mutual support.

At first there was little evident progress, but as a solid reef was built up beneath the surface the river began to react savagely. The voice of the water changed from a low rustle to a dull roar as it tore at Sapper's wall.

Soon the top of the wall of gabions thrust its head above the surface, and the river was constricted to half its former width. Now its mood was truculent. It poured through the gap in a solid green torrent, and crept almost imperceptibly up the banks as it was forced to back up behind the barrier. The river worried the foundations of the dam, clawing at it to find its weak spots, and the progress of the work slowed down as the waters rose higher.

Up in the riverine forests along the banks the axemen were at work, and Nicholas winced each time one of the great trees toppled, groaning and shrieking like a living creature. He liked to think of himself as a conservationist, and some of these trees had taken centuries to reach this girth.

'Do you want your bleeding dam, or your pretty trees?' Sapper demanded ferociously, when Nicholas lamented in his hearing. Nicholas turned away without replying.

They were all becoming tired with the unremitting labour. Their nerves were stretching towards snapping point, and tempers were mercurial. Already there had been a number of murderous fights amongst the workmen, and each time Nicholas had been forced to duck in under the swinging steel mattocks to break it up and separate the combatants.

Slowly they squeezed the river in its bed as the pier crept out from the bank, and the time came when they had to transfer their efforts to the far bank. It required the combined efforts of their entire labour force to build a new road along the bank as far as the ford. There they manhandled the front-ender into the water, and, with a hundred men hauling on the tow ropes and her tall lugged rear wheels spinning and churning the surface to a froth, they dragged her across.

Then they had to build another road back along the far bank to reach the dam site. They cut out the treetrunks that obstructed them and levered the boulders out of the way to get the tractor through. Once they had her back at the dam site they could begin the same process of laying out gabions from the far bank.

Gradually, a few metres each day, the two walls crept closer to each other, and as the gap between them narrowed the water rose higher and became more raucous, making the work more difficult.

In the meanwhile, two hundred metres upstream of the dam site, the Falcons and the Scorpions were at work. These two teams were building the raft of treetrunks that they had hacked from the forest. The timbers were lashed together to form a grating. Over this was laid heavy PVC sheeting to make it waterproof; then a second grating of treetrunks went over this to form a gigantic sandwich. It was all lashed together with heavy baling wire. Finally, one end of the grating was ballasted with boulders.

Sapper arranged the ballast of boulders to make the raft one-side heavy, so that it would float almost vertically in the water, with one end of it scraping the bottom of the river and the other sticking up above the surface. The dimensions of the completed raft were carefully related to the gap between the two buttresses of the dam. And while the work on the raft and the wall continued Sapper built up a stockpile of filled gabions, which he stacked on both banks below the dam.

Three other full work teams, the Elephants, the Buffaloes and the Rhinos, comprising the biggest and strongest men in the force, laboured at the head of the valley. They were digging out a deep canal into which the river could be diverted.

'Your hot-shot engineer, Taita, never thought of that little refinement,' Sapper gloated to Royan as they stood on the lip of the trench. 'What it means is that we only have to raise the level of the river another six feet before it will start flowing down the canal and into the valley. Without it we would have had to lift the water almost twenty feet to divert it.'

'Perhaps the river levels were different four thousand years ago.' Royan felt a strange loyalty to the long-dead Egyptian, and she defended him. 'Or perhaps he dug a canal but all traces of it have been obliterated.'

'Not bleeding likely,' Sapper grunted. 'The little perisher just plain didn't think of it.' His expression was smug and self-satisfied. 'One up on Mr Taita, I think.'

Royan smiled to herself. It was strange how even the practical and down-to-earth Sapper felt that this was a direct personal challenge from down the ages. He too had been caught up in Taita's game.

By dint of neither threat nor heavenly reward could the monks be inveigled into working on Sundays. Each Saturday evening they knocked off an hour earlier and trooped away down the valley on the trail to the monastery, so as to be in time for Holy Communion the next day. Although Nicholas grumbled and scowled at their desertion, secretly he was as relieved as any of them for the chance to rest. They were all exhausted, and for once there would be no chanting of matins to wake them at four o'clock the next morning.

So on Saturday night they all swore to each other that they would sleep late the next morning, but from force of habit Nicholas found himself awake and fully alert at that same iniquitous hour. He could not stay in his camp bed, and when he came back from his ablutions at the riverside he found that Royan was also awake and dressed.

'Coffee?' She lifted the pot off the fire and poured a mugful for him.

'I slept terribly badly last night,' she admitted. 'I had the most ridiculous dreams. I found myself in Mamose's tomb, lost in a labyrinth of passages. I was searching for the burial chamber, opening doors, but there were always people in the rooms that I looked into. Duraid was working in one room and he looked up and said, "Remember the protocol of the four bulls. Start at the beginning." He was so real and alive. I wanted to go to him but the door closed in my face, and I knew I would never see him again.' Tears filled her eyes and glistened in the light of the campfire.

Nicholas sought to distract her from the painful memory. 'Who were in the other rooms?' he asked.

'In the next room was Nahoot Guddabi. He laughed spitefully and said, "The jackal chases the sun," and his head changed into the head of Anubis, the jackal god of the cemetery, and he yelped and barked. I was so frightened that I ran.'

She sipped her coffee. 'It was all meaningless and silly, but von Schiller was in the next room, and he rose in the air and flapped his wings and said, "The vulture rises, and the stone falls." I hated him so much I wanted to strike him, but then he was gone.'

'And then you woke up?' Nicholas suggested.

'No. There was one other room.'

'Who was in it?'

She dropped her eyes, and her voice was small, 'You were,' she said.

'Me? What did I say?' He smiled.

'You didn't say anything,' she whispered, and blushed so suddenly and fiercely that he was instantly intrigued.

'What did I do then?' He was still smiling.

'Nothing. I mean, I can't tell you.' The dream returned to her, vivid and real as life, every detail of his naked body, even the smell and the feel of him. She forced herself to stop thinking about it. She felt vulnerable as she had been in the dream.

'Tell me about it,' he insisted.

'No!' She stood up quickly, confused and still blushing, trying to thrust the images from her.

Last night had been the first time in her life that she had ever dreamed of a man in that way, the first time she had ever experienced a full orgasm in her sleep. This morning, when she awoke, she found that she had soaked right through her pyjamas bottoms.

'We have a full day ahead of us with no work to do,' she blurted — the first thought that came into her mind.

'On the contrary.' He stood up with her. 'We still have to make the arrangements for getting out of here. When the time comes, we will probably be in something of a hurry.'

'Mind if I tag along?' she asked.

Two teams, the Buffaloes and the Elephants, with only their foremen missing, were waiting for them at the quarry. They comprised sixty of the strongest men in the labour force. Nicholas unpacked the inflatable Avon rafts from one of the pallets. Each raft was deflated and folded into a neat pack, with the paddles strapped along the sides. These craft had been specifically designed for river-running in turbulent water, and each was capable of carrying sixteen crew and a ton of cargo.

Nicholas directed them to strap the heavy packs on to the carrying poles that they had cut for that purpose. Five men on each end of the long poles, with the bundle of the boat slung in the centre, made light of the load. They set off at a cracking pace down the trail, and as soon as one team tired the next was ready to take over. They made the exchange without even stopping, the new porters slipping their shoulders under the pole on the run while the exhausted team dropped out.

Nicholas carried the radio in its shockproof and waterproof fibreglass case. He would not trust such a precious instrument to one of the porters. He and Royan trotted along behind the caravan, joining in the chorus of the work chant that the porters sang as they carried their loads down to the monastery.

Mai Metemma was waiting on the terrace outside the church of St Frumentius to welcome them. He led them down the staircase hewn out of the rock of the cliff, two hundred feet to the very water's edge. There was a narrow rocky ledge against which the Nile waters dashed, and the spray from the high waterfalls drifted over them like a perpetual drizzle of rain. After the heat and the bright sunlight above, it was cold and gloomy and dank down here in the depths of the gorge. The black cliffs ran with water, and the ledge on which they stood was wet and slippery underfoot.

Royan shivered as she watched the river racing by, forming a great spinning vortex as it swirled around the deep rock bowl and then raced out through the narrow throat of the gorge on its long hectic journey towards Egypt and the north.

'If only I had known that this was the road you were planning on taking home —' she eyed the river dubiously.

'If you would prefer to walk, it's okay by me,' Nicholas told her. 'With luck we will be carrying some extra baggage. The river is the logical escape route.'

'I suppose it makes sense, but still it's not terribly inviting.' She broke off a piece of driftwood from a stranded tangle that lay trapped upon the ledge and tossed it into the river. It was whipped away, and raced over the standing wave where some submerged obstacle forced the surface to bulge up.

'What speed is that current?' she asked in a subdued voice as the splinter of driftwood was sucked below the surface.

'Oh, not much more than eight or nine knots,' he told her offhandedly, 'but that's nothing. The river is still very low. Just wait until it starts raining up in the mountains, then you will really see some water passing through here. It will be great fun. Lots of people would pay good money for the chance to run a river like this. You are going to love it.'

'Thanks,' she said drily. 'I can't wait.'

Fifty feet above the ledge, out of reach of the Nile's highest water level, was a small cavern — the Epiphany shrine. Long ago the monks had cut this passage deeply into the rock face, and it ended in a spacious, candle-lit chamber that housed a life-sized statue of the Virgin, dressed in faded velvet robes, with the infant in her arms. Mai Metemma gave them his sanction to store the rafts in the shrine, and they stacked them against a side wall. When the porters had left, Nicholas showed Royan how to operate the quick-release handles on the packs, and the CO_2 cylinders which would inflate the rafts within minutes. He wrapped the radio case and his small emergency pack in a sheet of plastic and stowed them in one of the boat packs, where he could lay his hands on them again in a hurry.

'You do intend coming along on this joy ride?' she asked anxiously. 'You aren't planning on sending me down on my ownsome?'

'It is best that you know how it all works,' he told her. 'If things start to get a little hairy when the time comes to leave here, I may need your help in launching the rafts.'

When they climbed back up the staircase into the warmth and the sunlight, Royan's uncertain mood had changed. 'It's not yet noon, and we have the rest of the day to ourselves. Let's go back to Taita's pool again,' she suggested, and he shrugged indulgently.

The Buffaloes and the Elephants accompanied them as far as the branch in the trail. Here the teams headed back towards the dam, and shouted and hallooed their farewells after Nicholas and Royan.

Even in the short time since their last visit, the path through the undergrowth had become overgrown. Nicholas was forced to use his machete to hack a way through, and they ducked under the trailing thorn branches. It was mid-afternoon when they eventually crossed the high ridge and stood once again on the cliff directly above Taita's pool.

'It looks as though we were the last ones here.' Nicholas's tone was relieved. 'No signs of any other visitors since us.'

'Were you expecting any?'

'You never know. Von Schiller is a formidable character, and he has some charming lads working for him. Helm is one that worries me, and I had a nasty feeling that he might have been snooping around here. I am going to take a closer look.'

He worked quickly around the entire area, casting widely for any sign of intruders. Then came back to where she sat on the lip of the abyss and dropped down beside her.

'Nothing,' he admitted. 'We have still got the

running to ourselves.'

'Once Sapper stops the river upstream, this is going to be our main area of operations, isn't it?' she asked.

'Yes, but even before Sapper closes the dam I want to open a fly camp here, and move all the gear and equipment we will need from the quarry to have it handy when we start the exploration of the pool.'

'How are we going to get down into the pool? Down the river bed, once it is dry?'

'I suppose we could use the dry river bed as a road, and come down it from below the dam or up from the monastery end, through the pink cliffs.'

'But that is not the way you are planning to get in, is it?' she guessed.

'Even with no water in it, the river bed will be a long way round. It's a three- or four-mile haul from either end of the abyss, added to which it will be a pretty rough road to travel.' He grinned ruefully. 'You are speaking to an expert on the subject. I went down it the hard way, and I wouldn't want to do it again. There are at least five chutes and rock jams that I can remember being thrown over.'

'What is your better idea, then?' she asked.

'It's not my idea,' he contradicted her. 'It's Taita's idea really.'

She peered over the edge. 'You mean to build a scaffold down the cliff, just the way he did it?'

'What's good enough for Taita is good enough for me,' he acknowledged. 'The old boy probably had a good look at the alternative of using the river bed as an access road, and abandoned the idea.'

'When will you start work on the scaffold, then?'

'One of our teams is already cutting bamboo poles higher up the gorge. Tomorrow we will begin carrying them up here, and stacking them. We can't waste a day. Once the dam is closed, we have to get into the dry pool as soon as possible.'

As if to add weight to his words there came a far-off mutter of thunder, and they both craned their heads to peer up with trepidation at the escarpment. Probably a hundred miles to the north, faintly washed as a sepia print superimposed upon the razor-edged blue silhouette of the escarpment wall, rose high tumbled towers of cumulo-nimbus clouds. Neither of them spoke about it, but both were aware of how ominously the storm clouds were settling on the distant mountains.

Nicholas glanced at his wrist-watch and stood up. 'Time to start back if we are to get into camp before dark.'

He gave her his hand and lifted her to her feet. She dusted off her clothes and then stepped right to the very lip of the canyon.

'Wake up, Taita. We are hot on your tracks,' she called down into the shadows.

'Don't challenge him.' Nicholas took her arm and drew her back. 'The old ruffian has given us enough trouble already.'

The axemen had left the stumps of several great trees standing on the banks of the Dandera upstream from the dam. Sapper used these as anchor points for the heavy cables that he strung across the river. Through the cables he had rigged a cunning series of pulley blocks. The main cable was run back and connected to the tow hitch on the front-ender. Two other cables were laid out, one to each bank, where the Buffaloes and the Elephants stood ready to handle them. One team was under the direction of Nicholas, and the other under Mek Nimmur. For this crucial part of the construction, Mek had come down from the hills to lend a hand.

The grating of massive treetrunks lay on the river verge, already half in the water. Heavily weighted with boulders, it was an unwieldy structure that would require all their combined efforts to manoeuvre into position. Sapper slitted his eyes as he studied the layout, and then looked downstream to the partially completed dam. The two walls of gabions stretched out from either bank, but the gap in the middle of the river was twenty feet across and the whole volume of the river roared through it.

'The one thing we don't want is to let the

bleeding plug run away from us and slam into the ruddy wall,' he warned Nicholas and Mek. 'Otherwise we are going to lose a big chunk of what we have done so far. I want to cuddle her in there, nice and softly, and let her sit snug in the gap. Any questions? This is your last chance to ask. You all know the signals.'

Sapper took one last drag on his cigarette, and flicked the stub into the river. Then, looking lugubrious, he said, 'Okay, gents. The last one in the water is a sissy.'

Compared to their men, Nicholas and Mek were overdressed in their khaki shorts. The others were all stark naked. When the order was given they trooped waist-deep into the river and took up their stations along the cables.

Before he followed them into the river, Nicholas took one last look round. At breakfast that morning Royan had innocently asked to borrow his binoculars. Now he knew why. She and Tessay were perched up on top of the slope high above the gorge. Even as Nicholas watched, he saw Royan pass the binoculars to Tessay. They were not missing a moment of this fateful operation.

Nicholas looked back from the ridge to the rows of big naked men, pulled a face and muttered, 'My oath, there are some prize specimens around here. I just hope that Royan isn't making comparisons.'

Sapper climbed up on to the yellow tractor, and with a roar and a cloud of diesel smoke the engine burst into life. He raised one hand above his head with the fist clenched, and Nicholas relayed the order to his team: 'Take the strain.'

The foremen repeated it in Amharic, and the men leaned back against the cables. Sapper threw the tractor into extra low, and eased her forward. The belly straightened in the lines, the sheave wheels squealed, and the timber grating slid ponderously down the bank into the river. The weighted end of the grating sank immediately and bumped along the bottom, while the lighter end floated high. Slowly they hauled it out into midstream, until it was hanging vertically in the water.

The current seized it and began to bear it away, straight at the wall of gabions. It picked up speed alarmingly. The tractor bellowed and blew out clouds of black smoke as Sapper threw her into reverse and backed up on the cables. The teams of naked black men heaved and chanted — some of them had already been dragged in neck-deep as they hauled on the lines.

The grating steadied across the current, and they let it fall away at a more sedate pace, down towards the open gap in the wall. As it began to slew towards one bank, Sapper lifted his right arm and windmilled it. Obediently, Mek's team on the far bank paid out rope and Nicholas's team on the near bank picked it up. Once again the grating was lined up on the gap.

'Rock and roll. Close the hole,' bellowed Sapper, and now the full current was too powerful to resist. It dragged both teams into the river until some of them were in over their heads, losing their hold on the lines and floundering and swimming. However, those men who still had their footing managed to slow the rush of the grating just enough to prevent it smashing out of control into the dam. It settled firmly across the gap, like a mammoth plug in the outlet of a giant's bathtub, and instantly the current was cut off.

While the men in the water struggled ashore, their bodies wet and gleaming in the sunlight, Sapper threw off the cables from his tow hitch and roared along the bank with the front-ender in its highest gear. As it passed him, Nicholas grabbed a handhold and swung himself up on to the footplate behind Sapper's seat.

'Got to shore up now, before the grating bursts,' Sapper yelled.

From his vantage point, clinging to the rear of the tall machine, Nicholas had a moment to assess the position. The dam was holding, but only just. Numerous jets of water spurted through every gap between the grating and the gabions. The pressure of water against the sheets of PVC in the grating was enormous. It was taking the full thrust of the river, flexing and bowing before it like a castle portcullis attacked with a battering ram.

Sapper picked up one of the gabions that were standing ready on the bank and drove down into the river bed below the dam. The flow of the water had shrivelled to a mere knee-deep trickle. Jets of water squirted through every chink in the wall, and the gabions were not impermeable; water was finding its way through the tightly packed stones.

As the front-ender churned and lurched over the rough bed at the back of the wall, Nicholas and Sapper were drenched by the jets spurting over them. It was like working under a cold shower. Sapper drove in close behind the straining grating and placed the heavy gabion against it. He threw the tractor into reverse and climbed up the bank to pick up another gabion. Slowly he built up a retaining wall behind the grating, placing the gabions in sloping ranks, until this revetment was as strong as the side piers.

Nicholas jumped down from the tractor and left Sapper to it while he ran back upstream to the canal that the teams had dug at the head of the valley. Most of the workers had gathered along the banks of this cutting already, and Nicholas saw both Royan and Tessay in the front row of the excited crowd.

Nicholas pushed his way through to Royan's side, and she grabbed his hand. 'It's working, Nicky. The dam wall is holding.'

Even as they watched they could see the level of the trapped waters rising up the wall of grating and gabions. While the men chattered and laughed and urged it on, the river lapped at the entrance of the canal.

Fifty men seized their tools and jumped down

into the bottom of the canal. Dust flew in clouds as they shovelled the broken earth aside to lead the first trickle of water into the mouth of the canal. The men on the banks above them whooped and chanted to encourage them, and a thin snake of river water found its way into the mouth of the canal. The men with the mattocks and shovels ran ahead of it, enticing it on down the cutting. Every time it met any obstruction and faltered, they fell upon the blockage and tore it away.

At last the thin trickle of water felt the gradient fall away as the valley opened before it. The trickle increased to a freshet, and then to a torrent. With its new strength it gouged out the canal and burst through with the full flow of the river behind it.

The men in the bottom of the cutting yelled with fright at the suddenness and ferocity of it, and scrambled up the sides of the canal. But some of them were not quick enough and were swept away, struggling and screaming for help. The men on the banks ran alongside them, throwing ropes and dragging them sodden and muddy from the flood.

Now the river roared through the canal and tore on down the valley, rediscovering the ancient course that it had not followed for thousands of years. For almost an hour they stood upon the bank watching it, for it exercised over them the particular spell that turbulent waters always have over men. They were forced to retreat step by step as the river cut the banks out from under their feet.

At last Nicholas roused himself, and went back to where Sapper was still shoring up the dam wall. By now he had erected a sloping revetment on the downstream side of the dam wall, with four rows of gabions on the bottom course gradually narrowing as it reached the top of the retaining wall. For the time being the dam was secure, the vulnerable grating had been shored up with the heavy, stone-filled mesh baskets, and the overflow through the canal into the valley had relieved much of the pressure upon it.

'Do you think it will hold?' Royan eyed the structure with suspicion.

'Until the rains come, we hope.' Nicholas drew her away. 'We don't want to waste any more time here. Time to go on downstream to begin work at Taita's pool.'

They followed the banks of the new river that they had created, down the length of the long valley. At places they were forced to detour higher up the slope because the overflow from the dam had cut away and submerged the old trail. Eventually they reached the confluence of the stream that had as its source the butterfly fountain that they had explored with Tamre. They paused on the bank, and Nicholas and Royan looked at each other wordlessly. The stream had dried up.

Turning aside, they followed the empty stream bed up the hills and at last scrambled out on to the ledge from which the butterfly fountain had poured. The cave was still surrounded by lush green ferns, but it was like the eye socket in a skull, dark and empty.

'The spring has dried up!' Royan whispered. 'The dam has shrivelled it. That's the proof that the fountain was fed from Taita's pool. Now we have diverted the river we have killed the fountain.' Her eyes were bright and sparkling with excitement. 'Come on. Let's waste no more time here. Let's get on up to Taita's pool.'

Nicholas was the first one down into Taita's pool. This time he had a bosun's chair to sit in and a properly rigged block and tackle to lower him over the cliff. As he swung down around the overhang of the cliff, the chair swung awkwardly against the rock and the thumb of his right hand was trapped between the wooden seat of the chair and the wall. He exclaimed with the pain and, when he wrenched it free, he found that the skin had been torn from the knuckle and that blood was oozing up and dripping down his legs. It was painful but not serious, and he sucked the wound clean. It was still weeping drops of blood, but he had no time to attend to the injury now.

He was around the overhang, and the abyss opened under him, sombre and repellent. His eye was drawn irresistibly to the engraving on the wall, etched between the vertical rows of niches. Now that he knew what to look for, he could make out the outline of the maimed hawk. It cheered and encouraged him. Since their flight from the gorge over a month previously he had often been haunted by the feeling that they had imagined it all, that the cartouche of Taita was a hallucination, and that when they returned they would find the cliff wall smooth and unblemished. But there it was, the signpost and the promise.

He peered down past his own feet to the bottom of the gorge, and saw at once that the waterfall above the pool had been reduced to a trickle. The water still coming down the smooth black chute of polished rock was that which was filtering through the gaps and chinks in the dam wall upstream and the last drainage from the sandbanks and the pools higher up the gorge.

The level of the great pool under him had fallen drastically. He could make out the high-water level by the wet markings on the rock cliff. Fifty feet of the wall that had previously been submerged was now exposed. Another eight pairs of chiselled niches were visible in the face. Where once he had been forced to swim down to them, they were now high and dry.

However, the pool was not completely drained. It was dished below the level of the downstream outlet, so that it was unable to empty itself by gravitational flow. There was still a puddle of black water trapped in the centre, with a narrow ledge surrounding it. Nicholas landed on this ledge and stepped out of the bosun's chair. It was strange to stand on firm rock down here where last he had struggled for his life and very nearly been sucked under and drowned.

He looked up to where beams of sunlight penetrated the upper levels of the chasm. It was like being in the bottom of a mineshaft, and he shuddered at the feel of the clammy air on his bare arms and the eerie sensation in the pit of his stomach. He tugged on the line to send the rope chair back to the surface, and then edged his way along the slippery rock ledge towards the cliff face where the rows of dark niches stood out clearly against the lighter stone.

Now he could make out the shape of the opening in the wall that had so nearly sucked him down into its dark and slimy throat. It was almost completely submerged in a deeper corner where the pool flowed back against the cliff. All that was visible above the surface was the top arch of an irregular entrance at the foot of the descending rows of niches. The rest of it was still submerged.

The ledge narrowed as he worked his way along the foot of the cliff until he had his back to the rock and was moving sideways with his toes in the water. Eventually he could go no further without actually stepping down into the water. He had no way of judging the depth of the waters, which were turbid and uninviting.

Still trying to keep his feet dry, he squatted down on the narrow ledge and leaned out so far that his balance was threatened. He steadied himself with one hand against the wall, and with the other reached out towards the partially submerged opening.

The lip of the hole was smooth, as he had remembered it, and once again it seemed to him that it was too square and straight to be anything other than man-made. As he rolled up his sleeve he noticed that his injured thumb was still bleeding, but he ignored it and thrust his arm down below the surface of the pool. He groped downwards, trying to trace the sill of the opening. He felt what seemed to be blocks of roughly dressed masonry, and reached down further until the water reached halfway up his biceps.

Suddenly some living creature, swift and weighty, swirled in the dark waters right in front of his face, and as an immediate reflex he jerked his arm out of the water. The thing followed his arm up to the surface, slashing at his bare flesh with long, needle-sharp fangs, and he had a glimpse of a head as evil and villainous as that of a barracuda. He realized instinctively that it must have been attracted by the smell of the blood from his injured thumb.

He leaped to his feet and teetered on the narrow ledge, clutching his arm. Only one of the creature's frontal fangs had touched him, but it had opened the skin like a razor cut, a long shallow wound across the back of his right hand from which fresh blood dribbled and splattered into the pool at his feet.

Instantly the black waters seemed to come alive, roiling and seething with frenzied writhing aquatic shapes. Nicholas, his back flattened against the rock wall, stared down at them with loathing and horror. He could vaguely make out the shape of them, sinuous and ribbonlike, some of them as thick as his calf, black and gleaming.

One of them thrust its head out on to the ledge and snapped its jaws. Its eyes were huge and glistening and its snout was elongated, the long jaws lined with fangs that overlapped its thin lips. The body behind the head was six feet long, and lashed like a whip as it drove itself high up on to the ledge, reaching out for Nicholas's bare legs. He shouted with revulsion and leaped back, stumbling and splashing on to safer footing. Clutching his bleeding hand, he stared back. The evil head had disappeared, but the surface of the pool was still agitated by the lithe ophidian shapes.

'Eels!' he realized. 'Giant tropical eels.'

Of course the blood had excited them. The fall in the water-level had trapped them in the pool, congregated them in such numbers that they had probably already devoured the fish that they depended upon for food. Now they were ravenous. Probably all the pools of water that remained in the abyss were infested with these fearsome creatures. He was thankful that during his last swim in this pool he had not bled into the water.

He unwound the cotton kerchief from his neck and wrapped it round his wounded hand. The eels were a deadly threat to any attempt to explore the opening in the cliff. But already he was considering ways of ridding the pool of them and of gaining access to the underwater opening.

Slowly the frenzy in the pool quietened and its surface grew still again. Nicholas looked up to see the bosun's chair descending, with Royan's slim, shapely legs dangling below the wooden seat.

'What have you found?' she called down to him excitedly. 'Is there a tunnel —' then she broke off suddenly as she saw the blood on his clothing, and the bandage swathing his hand.

'Oh dear God,' she exclaimed. 'What have you done? You are hurt. How badly?' Her feet touched the ledge beside him and she slid from the chair and took his injured hand gently. 'What have you done to yourself?'

'It's not as bad as it looks,' he assured her. 'Lots of blood but not deep.'

'How did you do it?' she insisted.

For an answer he tore a corner off the blood-stained kerchief. 'Watch!' he instructed her, wadding it into a ball and tossing it out into the pool.

Royan screamed with horror as the waters boiled with the long fleeting shapes. One of them wriggled half its monstrous length out on to the ledge, before flopping back. It left a shining trail of silver slime across the black stones.

'Taita has left his guard dogs to see us off,' Nicholas remarked. 'We are going to have to take care of those beauties before we can explore the entrance below the surface.'

The bamboo scaffolding that Sapper and Nicholas had built down the cliff was anchored in the niches that had been cut into the rock nearly four thousand years before. Taita had probably lashed his framework together with bark rope, but Sapper had used heavy-gauge galvanized wire, and the structure was strong enough to bear the weight of many men. The Buffaloes formed a living chain and passed all the material and equipment down the scaffolding from hand to hand.

The very first piece of equipment to reach the floor of the cavern was the portable Honda EM500 generator. Sapper connected it up to the lights that he had rigged along the foot of the cliff. The small petrol engine ran smoothly and quietly, but the amount of power it put out was impressive. The floodlights chased the shadows from the furthest corners of the cavern, and lit the deep rock bowl like a stage.

Immediately the mood changed. Everybody became more cheerful and confident. There was laughter and excited chatter from the chain of men on the scaffolding as Royan climbed down to join Sapper and Nicholas at the side of the pool.

'Now that we know that they are working, switch off those lights,' Nicholas ordered.

'It's so dark and gloomy without them,' Royan protested.

'Saving fuel,' Nicholas explained. 'No filling station on the corner. We only have two hundred litres in reserve, and although the little Honda is pretty economical we have to be careful. We don't know how long we are going to need it in the tunnel.'

Royan shrugged with resignation, and when Sapper cut the generator the cavern was plunged once more into gloom and shadow. She looked at the dark pool and pulled a face.

'What are you going to do about those horrid pets of yours?' she demanded, glancing at Nicholas's bandaged right hand.

'Sapper and I have worked out a plan. We thought of trying to empty the pool completely, using a bucket chain. But the amount of water still coming down the river bed makes that a poor choice.'

'We would be lucky to hold our own against that flow, even working around the clock with

661

buckets,' Sapper grunted. 'If only the major had thought to bring along a high-speed water pump —'

'Even I can't think of everything, Sapper. What we are going to do is to build a small coffer dam around the underwater opening, and bale that out with buckets.'

Royan stood back and watched the preparations. Half a dozen of the empty mesh gabions were carried down the scaffolding and placed at the edge of the pool. Here they were partially filled with boulders that the men gathered up from the river bed. However, the gabions were not filled so full that they became too heavy to handle. There was no front-ender down here to move them around, and they would be forced to rely on old-fashioned manpower. There was just sufficient of the yellow PVC sheeting left over to wrap around each gabion and render it waterproof.

'What about your eels?' Royan was fascinated by these loathsome creatures, and she hung well back from the edge of the pool. 'You can't send any of your men in there!'

'Watch and learn.' Nicholas grinned at her. 'I have a little treat in store for your favourite fish.'

Once all the preparations for the construction of the coffer were complete, Nicholas cleared the cavern, sending Royan and Sapper and all of the men up the scaffolding. He alone remained at the edge of the pool, with the bag of fragmentation grenades that he had begged from Mek Nimmur slung over his shoulder.

With a grenade in each hand, he hesitated. 'Seven-second delay,' he reminded himself. 'Quenton-Harper dry flies. More effective than the Royal Coachman!'

He pulled the pins from each of the grenades and then lobbed them out into the middle of the pool. Quickly he turned away and hurried to the furthest corner of the cavern. He knelt with his face to the rock wall and covered his ears with both hands.

Squeezing his eyes shut, he braced himself. The rock floor jumped under him and the double shock waves from the explosions swept over him in quick succession, with a savage power that drove in his chest and stopped his breath. In the confines of the chasm the detonations were thunderous, but his ears were protected and the deep water of the pool absorbed much of the blast. A twin fountain of water shot high into the air and splashed against the cliff above his head. It poured down in a sheet over him, soaking his clothing.

As the echoes died away, he stood up. His hearing had not been adversely affected, and he had suffered no injury other than the shower of cold water. Back at the edge of the pool the water shimmered with movement. Scores of the great eels flopped and writhed on the surface, flashing their white bellies as they twisted. Many of them were dead, their bellies burst open, floating inert, while others were merely stunned by the blast. Knowing how tenaciously they clung to life he suspected that they would soon recover, but for the time being they were no longer a danger.

He bellowed up toward the top of the cliff. 'All clear, Sapper. Send them down.'

The men came swarming down the scaffolding, amazed by the carnage that the grenades had wreaked in the pool. They lined the bank and began to fish out the bodies of the dead eels.

'You eat them?' Nicholas demanded of one of the monks.

'Very good!' The monk rubbed his belly in anticipation.

'Enough of that, you greedy perishers.' Sapper drove them back to work. 'Let's get those gabions in place before they wake up and start eating you.'

With a bamboo pole Nicholas sounded the depth of the water that covered the entrance to the shaft, and found that it was well over the height of a man's head. They were forced to roll the gabions down into it, and complete the filling once they were in position. It was difficult and taxing work, and took almost two days to complete, but at last they had built a half-moon-shaped weir around the underwater entrance, walling it off from the main body of water in the pool.

Using leather buckets and clay *tej* pots the

Buffaloes began to bale out the coffer and scoop the water over the wall into the main pool. Nicholas and Royan watched with silent trepidation as the level in the coffer fell and the opening in the cliff was gradually revealed.

Very soon they were able to see that it was almost rectangular, about three metres wide by two metres high. The sides and the roof had been eroded by the rush of water through the opening, but as the level fell lower they could see the remains of shaped stone blocks that had probably once sealed the opening. Four courses of them still stood where the ancient masons had placed them across the threshold of the opening, but the others had been torn out by thousands of years of flood seasons and thrown into the tunnel behind, partially blocking it.

Eagerly Nicholas climbed down into the coffer. It was not yet empty, but he could not control his impatience. The water was knee-deep as he crawled forward into the opening, and with his bare hands tried to shift some of the rock debris that choked it.

'It's definitely some sort of shaft,' he shouted back, and Royan could not restrain herself either. She came slithering and sloshing down into the coffer, and pushed into the opening beside him.

'There's an obstruction,' she cried in disappointment. 'Did Taita do that deliberately?'

'Might have,' Nicholas gave his opinion. 'Hard to tell. A lot of this rubble and flotsam has been sucked in from the main flow of the river, but he might have filled the tunnel behind him as he pulled out.'

'It's going to take a tremendous amount of work just to clear it enough to find out where this passage leads to.' Royan's voice had lost its ring of excitement.

'I am afraid it is,' Nicholas agreed. 'We are going to have to clear every bit of this rubbish by hand, and there won't be time for the niceties of formal archaeological excavation. We are just going to rip it out.' He clambered back out of the coffer, and reached back to hand her up the bank. 'Well, at least we have the flood-lights,' he added. 'We can keep the men working in shifts, night and day, until we get through.'

They have dammed the Dandera river,' said Nahoot Guddabi, and Gotthold von Schiller stared at him in astonishment.

'Dammed the river? Are you certain?' he demanded.

'Yes, Herr von Schiller. We have a report from our spy in Harper's camp. He has over three hundred men working in the gorge. That is not all. He has air-dropped huge amounts of equipment and supplies. It is like a military operation. Our spy tells us that he even has an earth-moving machine, some sort of tractor, which he has brought in.'

Von Schiller looked across the table at Jake Helm for confirmation, and Helm nodded. 'Yes, Herr von Schiller. That is true. Harper must have spent a large amount of money. The air charter alone could have cost him fifty grand.'

Von Schiller felt the first stirrings of real passion since the urgent satellite message had summoned him from Frankfurt. He had flown directly to Addis Ababa, where the Jet Ranger had been waiting to carry him to the Pegasus base camp on the escarpment above the Abbay gorge.

If this was true, and he did not doubt Helm's word, then Harper was on to something of enormous importance. He looked out of the window of the Quonset hut to where the Dandera flowed down the valley below the base camp. It was a large river. To dam that volume of water would be an expensive and difficult project in this remote and primitive situation — not a project to be taken on lightly without the prospect of substantial reward.

He felt a reluctant admiration for the Englishman's achievement. 'Show me where he has placed his dam!' he ordered, and Helm came around the table to stand beside him. Von Schiller was standing on his block, and their eyes were on the same level.

Helm bent over the satellite photograph and carefully marked in the site of the dam. They both studied it for a minute, and then von Schiller asked, 'What do you make of it, Helm?'

Helm shook his head, hunching it down on his bull-like shoulders. 'I can only guess.'

'Guess then,' said von Schiller, but still Helm hesitated.

'Go on!'

'Either he wants to move the water to another area downstream, to use it for washing out a deposit, gold nuggets or artefacts made of precious metals, perhaps even to use it for hosing the overburden off the site of the tomb —'

'Highly unlikely!' von Schiller interjected. 'That would be an inefficient and expensive manner of excavation.'

'I agree that it is far-fetched.' Nahoot obsequiously followed von Schiller's lead, but no one even looked at him.

'What is your other supposition?' Von Schiller glared at Helm.

'The only other reason for damming the river, that I can think of, would be to reach something that has been covered by the water. Something lying in the bed of the river.'

'That is more logical,' von Schiller mused, and turned his attention back to the photograph. 'What is there below this dam site?'

'The river enters a deep and narrow ravine here.' Helm pointed at the spot. 'Just below his dam. The ravine stretches about eight miles, down to this point, just above the monastery. I have flown over it in the helicopter, and it seems to be impassable, and yet —' he broke off.

'Yes, go on! And yet — what?'

'On one flight over the area, we found Harper and the woman on the high ground above the ravine. They were at this spot here.' He touched the photograph, and von Schiller leaned forward to peer at it.

'What were they doing there?' he demanded, without looking up.

'Nothing. They were merely sitting on the top of the cliff above the ravine.'

'But they were aware of your presence?'

'Of course. We were in the helicopter. They heard our approach. They were watching us, and Harper even waved.'

'And so they would have ceased whatever activity they were engaged in when they became aware of your approach?'

Von Schiller was silent for so long that they began to fidget uncomfortably and exchange glances. When he spoke it was so unexpected that Nahoot started.

'Harper obviously has reason to believe that the tomb lies in the gorge below the dam. When and how do you make contact with your spy that you have in Harper's camp?'

'Harper is receiving some of his supplies from the villages here on the escarpment. The women are driving down slaughter cattle to feed his men, and carrying down pots of *tej*. Our man sends back his reports with the women when they return.'

'Very well. Very well!' Von Schiller waved

him to silence. 'I don't need to know his life history. All I want to know is if Harper is working in the ravine below his dam. How soon can you find this out?'

'By the day after tomorrow at the latest,' Helm promised him.

Von Schiller turned to Colonel Nogo at the far end of the conference table. So far he had not spoken, but had watched and listened quietly to the others.

'How many men have you deployed in this area?' von Schiller asked.

'Three full companies, over three hundred men. All well trained. Many are battle-hardened veterans.'

'Where are they? Show me on the map.'

The colonel came to stand beside him. 'One company here, another billeted at the village of Debra Maryam, and the third company at the foot of the escarpment, ready to move forward and attack Harper's camp.'

'I think you should attack them now. Wipe them out, before they can uncover the tomb —' Nahoot came in again.

'Shut your mouth,' von Schiller snapped without looking up at Nahoot. 'I will ask for your opinion when I need it.'

He considered the map for a while longer, then asked Nogo, 'How many men has this guerrilla commander, what is his name, the one who has allied himself to Harper?'

'Mek Nimmur is not a guerrilla. He is a bandit, and notorious *shufta* terrorist,' Nogo corrected him hotly.

'One man's freedom fighter is the next man's terrorist,' von Schiller remarked drily. 'How many men has he under his command?'

'Not many. Fewer than a hundred, perhaps no more than fifty. He has them all guarding Harper's camp, and the dam.'

Von Schiller nodded to himself, plucking at the lobe of his ear. 'How did Harper and his gang return to Ethiopia?' he mused. 'I know he flew from Malta, but it is not possible that the aircraft could have landed down there in the gorge.'

He hopped down off his block and strutted to the window of the hut through which he had a panoramic view spread below him. He stared down into the depths of the gorge, a vista of cliffs and broken hilltops and wild tablelands, smoked blue with distance.

'How did they get in without being discovered by the authorities? Did he parachute in, the same way as he dropped his supplies?'

'No,' said Nogo. 'My informer tells us that he marched in with Mek Nimmur, some days before the supplies were dropped to him.'

'So from where did he march?' von Schiller pondered. 'Where is the nearest airfield where a heavy aircraft could land?'

'If he came in with Mek Nimmur, then they almost certainly came in from the Sudan. That is where Nimmur operates from. There are many old abandoned airfields near the border. The war,' Nogo shrugged expressively, 'the armies are always on the move, that war has been going on for twenty years.'

'From the Sudan?' Von Schiller picked out the border on the map. 'So they must have trekked in along the river.'

'Almost certainly,' Nogo agreed.

'Then just as certainly Harper plans to escape the same way. I want you to move the company of men that you have at Debra Maryam and deploy them here and here. On both banks of the river, below the monastery. They must be in a position to prevent Harper reaching the Sudanese border, if he should try to make a run for it.'

'Yes. Good! I understand. That is good tactics,' Nogo nodded gloatingly, his eyes bright behind the lenses of his spectacles.

'Then I want your remaining men moved down to the foot of the escarpment. Tell them to avoid contact with Mek Nimmur's men, but to be in a position to move forward very quickly and seize the dam area, and to block off the ravine below the dam as soon as I give you the word.'

'When will that be?' Nogo asked.

'We will continue to watch him carefully. If he makes a discovery, he will start moving the artefacts out. Many of them will be too large to conceal. Your informer will know about it. That is when we will move in on him.'

'You should move in now, Herr von Schiller,' Nahoot advised him, 'before he gets a chance to open the tomb.'

'Don't be an idiot,' von Schiller snarled at him. 'If we strike too soon, we might never discover what he obviously has learned about the whereabouts of the tomb.'

'We could force him —'

'If I have learned anything in my life, it is that you cannot force a man like Harper. There is a certain type of Englishman — I remember during the last war with them —' He broke off and frowned. 'No. They are very difficult people. We must not rush it now. When Harper makes a discovery in the ravine, that will be the time to pounce.' The frown faded and he smiled a small, cold smile. 'The waiting game. In the meantime, we play the waiting game.'

The debris that filled the shaft was not so tightly packed that it completely blocked the flow of water through it. If it had done so, Nicholas would never have been sucked in by the current, as he had been on his first dive into the pool. There were still gaps in the blockage where the larger boulders had lodged or where a treetrunk had been sucked in and jammed sideways across the width of the tunnel. Through these sections the water had found the weak spots and kept them open.

Nevertheless, the debris had taken centuries to wedge itself in, and it required back-breaking effort to prise it apart. The clearing operation was further hampered by the lack of working space in the shaft. Only three or four of the big men from the Buffaloes were able to work in the shaft at any one time. The rest of the team were employed in passing back the rubble as it was levered out.

Nicholas changed the shifts every hour. They had more labour than they needed, and changing them often meant that the men at the face were always rested and strong, and eager to earn the bonus of silver dollars that Nicholas promised them for their progress along the shaft. At each change of shift, Nicholas disappeared into the mouth of the tunnel with Sapper's steel tape and measured the advance.

'One hundred and twenty feet! Well done, the Buffaloes,' he told Hansith Sherif, the fore-man monk, and then watched the water trickling past his feet. The floor of the tunnel was still sloping downwards at a constant angle. He looked back along it towards the pool, and now in the floodlights the rectangular shape of the walls was very clear to see. It was obvious that the tunnel had been designed and surveyed by an engineer.

He transferred his attention back to the floor of the tunnel and watched the run of water, trying to judge how deep they were below the original river level.

'Eighty or ninety feet,' he estimated. 'No wonder the pressure in the mouth of the tunnel almost crushed me —' he broke off as an unusually shaped fragment in the muck at his feet caught his eye. He stooped and picked it up. Then took it to one of the floodlamps and by its light examined it closely. As he rubbed it clean between finger and thumb, he began to grin.

Sloshing back along the tunnel, he yelled, 'Royan!' Triumphantly brandishing the fragment, he demanded, 'What do you make of that, then?'

She was sitting on the wall of the coffer, and reached down and snatched the object out of his grasp.

'Oh, sweet Mary! Where did you find this, Nicky?'

'Lying in the mud. Right there in the adit, where it's been for the last four thousand years. Where one of Taita's workmen dropped and broke it, probably while he was sneaking a sup of wine behind the slave driver's back.'

Eagerly Royan held the broken shard of pottery up to the lamplight. 'You are right, Nicky,' she exclaimed. 'It's part of a wine vessel. Look at the flared neck and belled lip. But if there was any doubt, which there isn't, the black firing around the rim dates it perfectly in our period. No older than 2000 BC.'

Still clutching the fragment of broken pottery, she jumped down into the mud and slush of the coffer and flung both arms around his neck.

'Further proof, Nicky. We are on Taita's tracks. Can't you get them to clear any faster? We are breathing down the back of the old rogue's neck.'

Halfway through the next shift an excited yelling echoed out of the mouth of the tunnel, and Nicholas hurried back down to the face.

'What is it, Hansith?' he demanded in Arabic of the foreman monk. 'What are you shouting about?'

'We have broken through, *effendi.*' Hansith Sherif grinned at him, his teeth gleaming in his black and mud-smeared face. Nicholas eagerly pushed his way through the workmen. They had levered a huge round boulder out of the pack, and beyond it lay an opening. He shone his electric torch through this window in the wall, but could make out very little except empty black space.

Stepping back, he slapped the monk on the back. 'Well done, Hansith. A dollar bonus for every man in the team. But keep them working! Clear away all this rubbish.' But it was not as easily done as he had ordered. The shifts changed twice more before the shaft was cleared completely of the last of the extraneous rubble and broken rock. Only then could Nicholas and Royan stand in the threshold of the cavern beyond the tunnel.

'What has happened here? What has caused this?' Royan's voice was puzzled as Nicholas

676

played his torch out into the void.

'I think this is a cave-in area. There was probably a fault in the rock strata running through here and here.' He picked out the cracks in the roof of the cavern.

'You think the flow of the water through the shaft has scoured it out?' she asked.

'I would say so, yes.' Nicholas turned the beam of light downwards. 'The floor has fallen out of the shaft also.'

The rock had subsided in front of them, leaving a deep hole. Ten feet below where they stood the hole was filled with water, forming a large circular pool with vertical rock sides. Overhead the roof had fallen in and was now a high dome of irregular rock, and the far side of the pool was shrouded in shadows a hundred feet or more in front of them.

There was no apparent way around this obstacle without entering the water. Nicholas shouted to Hansith to bring one of the long bamboo poles that they had used for the scaffolding. The pole was thirty feet long and they had to manoeuvre its length down the tunnel. Nicholas sounded the pool with the bamboo, probing it down into the turbid water as deeply as he could reach.

'No bottom.' He shook his head. 'Do you know what I think?' He retrieved the pole and passed it back to Hansith.

'Tell me,' Royan invited.

'I think that this is the natural fault that leads

the water away to the other side of the hills, and comes to the surface again at the butterfly fountain. The river has carved its own path.'

'Why hasn't it drained, then?' Royan looked down dubiously in the pool below them.

'A U-bend in the shaft, probably. Water still trapped in the top of the shaft like the bowl of a lavatory.'

He probed the waters of the pool with the beam of his torch, and Royan exclaimed with horror and disgust as one of the giant eels came racing to the surface, attracted by the light.

'The filthy creatures!' She stepped back involuntarily. 'The whole river must be infested with them.'

The long dark shape circled the pool swiftly and then disappeared back into the depths as suddenly as it had appeared.

'If you are right, and a section of Taita's adit has collapsed, then the continuation of his tunnel should be on the far side of this.' She pointed across the pool, and Nicholas lifted the beam of the torch and shone it in the direction she indicated.

'Look, Nicky!' she cried. 'There it is.'

The dark rectangular opening yawned at them from across the pool.

'How do we get across there?' Royan asked, disconsolate.

'The answer to that is, not very easily. Dammit to hell!' Nicholas swore heartily. 'This is going to cost us another couple of days that we can ill afford. We are going to have to build some sort of bridge across it.'

'What kind of bridge?'

'Get Sapper down here. This is his department.'

Sapper stood at the brink of the sink-hole and glared across at the far bank.

'Pontoons,' he grunted. 'How many of those inflatable rafts have you got squirrelled away?'

'Forget it, Sapper!' Nicholas shook his head. 'You are not getting those dirty great paws of yours on my rafts.'

'Suit yourself.' Sapper spread his hands in resignation. 'It would be the easiest and quickest way of doing it. Anchor a raft in the middle and build a catwalk over the top of it. I need something that floats high —'

'Baobab.' Nicholas snapped his fingers. 'That should do the trick very nicely. When it's dried out, baobab wood is as light as balsa. Floats just as well as one of my inflatable rafts.'

'Plenty of baobabs growing along the hills,' Sapper agreed. 'Every second tree in this valley seems to be a ruddy baobab.'

Three hundred yards from the top of the cliff grew a massive specimen of *Adansonia digitata*. Its smooth bark resembled the skin of one of the great reptiles from the age of the dinosaurs. Its girth was tremendous — twenty men with outstretched arms could not have encircled it. The upper branches were bare and twisted, and it looked as though it had been dead for a hundred years. Only the heavy velvet-covered pods proved that it still lived; they hung thickly from the high branches, bursting open to spill the black seeds which were coated thickly with white cream of tartar.

'The Zulus say that the Nkulu Kulu, the Great Spirit, planted the baobab upside down with its roots in the air to punish it,' Nicholas told Royan as they looked up at the enormous spread of its branches.

'Why would he want to do that?' she wanted to know. 'What did the poor old baobab do that was so bad?'

'It boasted that it was the tallest and thickest tree of the forest, and so the Nkulu Kulu decided to teach it a little lesson in humility.'

One of the gigantic branches had snapped off under its own weight, and lay on the rocky ground beneath the trunk. The wood was white and fibrous, light as cork. Under Nicholas's direction the axemen cut it into manageable lengths. Once they had been carried down the adit shaft to the sink-hole, Sapper stapled the logs together and floated them across the pool to form a causeway. He anchored this to the rock face at either end, and then over it he laid a catwalk of bamboo poles. The bridge of baobab logs floated high, and although it bobbed and swayed, it could easily support the weight of a dozen men at a time.

Nicholas was the first one across the sink-hole. He placed a roughly made ladder against the high vertical bank, and scrambled up into the mouth of the adit on the far side of the pool. Royan was close behind him.

The two of them stood in the entrance to this continuation of the shaft, and as soon as Nicholas shone his torch into it they realized that the nature of the construction had changed. This section had not been so heavily scoured out and eroded by the rush of river water through it. The main flow must have drained away through the sink-hole. The dimensions were the same, three metres wide by two high, but the rectangular shape was more precise and although the walls and roof were rough, like those of a mine, the marks of the tools that had shaped it were now clearly visible. The footing of the tunnel was roughly paved with slabs of crudely dressed stone.

This whole length of the tunnel had also been submerged, for it lay below the natural level of the river before it had been dammed. The paving under their feet was wet and covered with a slime that had not yet had time to dry out since it had been exposed by the receding waters. The roof and walls of the tunnel ran with moisture, and the air was dank and cold and smelled of mud and rot.

They waited for Sapper to string the cables for the lights across the causeway. He set up the lamps and switched them on. At once they were aware that ahead of them the shaft had begun to rise at an angle of about twenty degrees.

'You can see what the old devil Taita was up to here. He has taken us down well below water level to flood the tunnel to a length and depth that nobody would be able to swim along. Now he is angling up again,' Nicholas pointed out to Royan. They started forward, moving slowly up the ascending shaft, and Nicholas counted aloud each pace he took.

'One hundred and eight, one hundred and nine, one hundred and ten —' suddenly they came to the recent low river level. It was clearly marked as a dry line on the walls of the tunnel. The paving under their feet was also dry and free of the slippery coating of slime. Fifty paces further on they passed the high flood level of the river, which was just as clearly etched on the rock floor and the walls. Beyond that the tunnel had never been immersed, and the walls were in the same condition as the Egyptian slave workmen had left them four thousand years earlier. The marks of the bronze chisels were as pristine as if they had been inflicted just days before.

Only ten feet beyond the highest point that the river waters had ever reached, they came out upon a stone landing. Here the floor levelled out, and then the tunnel turned sharply back upon itself.

'Let's spare a minute just to think about this

as a feat of engineering.' Nicholas took Royan's arm and pointed back down the tunnel. 'Taita has placed this landing on which we are standing precisely above the high-water mark of the river. How did he work it out so exactly? He had no dumpy level, and only the crudest measuring equipment. And yet he calculated it as accurately as this. It's a hell of a piece of work.'

'Well, he tells us repeatedly in the scrolls that he is a genius. I suppose we will have to believe him now.' She pulled against his grip. 'Let's go on. I must see what lies around this corner,' she urged.

Side by side they turned through the one hundred and eighty degree corner and Nicholas held the hand lamp high, with the electrical cable trailing back down the shaft behind him. As he lit the way ahead, Royan exclaimed aloud and seized Nicholas's free hand. Both of them froze with astonishment.

Taita had designed the turning of the ascending ramp for dramatic effect. The lower section of the shaft through which they had passed was crudely constructed, the walls irregular and undressed, the roof lumpy and cracked. Taita had calculated his levels so finely that he had known that the lower levels of the shaft would be submerged and damaged by the water. He had wasted no effort on beautifying them.

Now before them rose a wide stairway. The angle of its ascent was such that, from where they stood on the landing, the top of it was hidden from their view. Each step stretched the full width of the tunnel, and rose a hand's breadth. The treads were cut from slabs of mottled gneiss, polished and fitted to each other so precisely that the joints between them were barely visible. The roof of the tunnel was three times as high as it had been in the lower reaches of the tunnel, perfectly domed and proportioned. The walls and the curved roof were of beautifully dressed blue granite blocks, keyed into each other with marvellous precision and symmetry. The whole was a masterpiece of the mason's art, majestic and portentous. There was both a promise and a menace in this vestibule to the unknown. Its simplicity and lack of ornamentation made it even more impressive.

Royan tugged softly at Nicholas's hand and together they stepped on to the first tread of the stairway. It was carpeted with a fine layer of dust, soft and white as talcum powder. The dust rose in soft eddies and wisps around their knees and then subsided as they passed on upwards. It muted the harsh glare of the electric lamp that Nicholas carried high in his right hand.

Gradually, as they went on upwards, the top of the staircase came into view ahead of them. Royan dug her fingernails into the palm of Nicholas's hand as she saw what lay ahead. The staircase ended on another level landing, across which a rectangular doorway faced them. They stepped up on to the landing and stood before the doorway. Neither of them had words to express this supreme moment: they stood in silence for what seemed like an eternity, holding each other's hand with a fierce and possessive grip.

Finally Nicholas tore his eyes off the gateway, and looked down at Royan. He saw his own feelings mirrored in her face, her eyes shone as though lit from within by an incandescent passion. There was no other person alive with whom he would wish to share this moment. He wanted it to last for ever.

She turned her head and looked at him. They stared deeply and solemnly into each other's eyes. Both of them were aware that this was a high tide in their lives, one that could never be repeated. She tightened her grip on his hand, and looked back to the doorway facing them. It had been plastered over with white river clay, a surface that had mellowed to the shade of ivory. There was no crack or blemish in its smooth expanse, like the flawless skin of a beautiful virgin.

Their eyes fastened avidly on the two embossed seals in the centre of the expanse of white clay. The upper one was in the shape of the royal cartouche, the rectangular knot surmounted by the scarab, the horned beetle that signified the great circle of eternity.

Royan's lips formed the words as she read them from the hieroglyphics, but she uttered no sound. ' "*The Almighty. The Divine. Ruler of the Upper and Lower Kingdoms of Egypt. Familiar of the god, Horus. Beloved of Osiris and* of Isis. *Mamose, may he live for ever!*" '

Below this magnificent royal seal was a smaller, simpler design in the shape of a hawk, with one broken wing drooping across its barred breast, and the legend: '*I, Taita the slave, have obeyed your command, divine Pharaoh.*' Underneath the maimed hawk was a single column of hieroglyphics that spelled out the stern warning: '*Stranger! The gods are watching. Disturb the king's eternal rest at your peril!*'

Breaking the seals on the doorway was a momentous act, and despite the fact that the time before the onset of the rains was fast running out, neither of them was prepared to undertake it lightly. They had to make every effort to keep permanent records of everything they discovered, and to inflict as little damage as possible while gaining access.

They spent one of their precious remaining days preparing for the break-in to the tomb. Naturally, Nicholas's first concern was the security of the tomb area. He asked Mek Nimmur to place an armed guard on the causeway over the sink-hole in the approach tunnel, and access beyond this point was restricted. Only Nicholas, Royan, Sapper, Mek, Tessay and four of the monks whom Nicholas had selected were allowed across the bridge.

Hansith Sherif had proved himself repeatedly

during the clearing of the lower tunnel. Physically strong, willing and intelligent, he had become Nicholas's principal assistant. It was Hansith who carried the tripod and spare camera equipment while Nicholas photographed the approach tunnel and the sealed doorway. He shot three rolls of high-speed film to make certain that they had a complete record of the unbroken seals and the doorway surrounds. Only when the filming was completed would Nicholas allow Hansith and the other three monks to bring up the tools needed for the break-in.

Sapper moved the Honda generator up as far as the sink-hole, to reduce the voltage drop over the distance that the current had to travel down the cable. Then he set up the floodlights on the upper landing of the staircase and focused them on the white expanse of the plastered doorway.

When they assembled at the threshold they were all in a sober mood. Despite the fact that the tomb was thousands of years old, it was still an act of desecration that they were about to perpetrate. Royan had translated the hieroglyphic warning on the sealed doorway to Sapper, Mek and Tessay, and none of them was prepared to take it lightly.

Nicholas marked out the square opening he intended cutting through the plaster covering. This was large enough to afford access, but it also enclosed the royal cartouche and Tatia's maimed hawk seal. He intended lifting these out in one piece, and preserving them intact. In his imagination, he could already see them displayed in a prominent position in the museum at Quenton Park.

Nicholas began on the right-hand upper corner of the opening. First he used a long, needle-sharp awl as a probe. He pressed and twisted the needle point through the dried clay in an attempt to determine exactly what lay beneath the surface. Very soon he found out that the plaster had been laid over laths of finely interwoven reeds.

'That makes it a lot easier,' he told Royan. 'The reed mat will help to hold the plaster together and prevent it cracking and breaking up.'

He kept working the point of the awl deeper, until suddenly the resistance gave way and the blade ran in its full length.

'Six inches,' he said, measuring the thickness of the door off the blade. 'Taita never skimps, does he? It's a heavy bit of work.'

Still using the awl, Nicholas drilled all four corners of the square opening he intended cutting. Then he stepped back and gestured for Hansith to bring up the heavy four-inch gimlet to enlarge them. This was the type of drill that fishermen use for cutting through lake ice in winter.

As soon as the gimlet broke through, Nicholas impatiently pulled Hansith aside and peered into the hole. Beyond the opening all was completely dark, but he caught a whiff of the faint breath of ancient air that washed through the opening. The odour was dry and dead and austere, the smell of the ages long past.

'What do you see?' Royan demanded at his elbow.

'The light! Give me the light!' he ordered, and when Sapper handed it to him, he held it to the opening.

'Tell me!' Royan was dancing beside him with impatience. 'What do you see now?'

'Colours!' he whispered. 'The most marvellous, indescribable colours.' He stepped back and, lifting her around the waist, held her so that she could look into the aperture.

'Beautiful!' she cried. 'It's so beautiful.'

Sapper rigged up the heavy-duty electric blower fan which would circulate the air in the shaft, while Nicholas prepared the chain-saw. When he was ready, Nicholas handed Royan a pair of goggles and a dust mask and helped her to adjust them. Then he made her fit a pair of wax ear plugs.

Before he started the chain-saw, he sent the rest of them back down the tunnel as far as the causeway over the sink-hole. In the confined space the exhaust fumes from the chain-saw and the dust, together with the noise of the petrol engine, would be overpowering, but apart from that he wanted only Royan with him at the moment of the break-in.

When they were alone, Nicholas switched the blower fan to its highest speed, then donned his own mask and goggles and plugged his ears. He pulled the starter cord of the chain-saw motor and it burst into life in a cloud of blue exhaust smoke.

Nicholas braced himself and pressed the spinning chain blade into the gimlet hole in the plastered doorway. It cut through the thick white plaster and the laths beneath it like a knife through the icing on a wedding cake. Carefully he ran the cutting edge down the line he had marked out.

A cloud of flying white plaster dust filled the air. Within seconds they could see only a few feet in front of their eyes. Doggedly Nicholas kept the cut going, down the right-hand side, across the bottom, then up the left side. Finally he made the last cut across the top, and when the square trapdoor began to sag forward under its own weight he killed the engine of the chain-saw and set it aside.

Royan jumped forwards to help him, and together in the eddies of dust and smoke they steadied the square of plaster and prevented it from crashing to the paving and shattering into a thousand pieces. Gently they lifted it out of the opening and, with the seals still intact, laid it against the side wall of the landing.

The open hatchway they had cut through the

plaster was a dark square. Nicholas adjusted the floodlight to shine through it, but the dust was still too dense for them to be able to see much of the interior. Nicholas climbed through the hatch into the space beyond. All was obscured by a dense fog of dust that not even the lamps could penetrate.

He did not attempt to explore further, but immediately turned back to help Royan through the opening after him. He recognized her right to share every moment of this discovery. Beyond the wall they stood quietly together, waiting for the blower fan to clear the air. Slowly the dust fog began to dissipate, and the first thing they became aware of was the floor beneath their feet.

No longer made of stone slabs, it was covered with tiles of yellow agate that had been polished to a gloss and fitted together so cunningly that no joints were visible. It was like a single sheet of lovely opaque glass, dulled only by the film of fine talcum dust that had settled upon it. Where their feet had disturbed the layer of dust the agate sparkled through it, catching the light of the floodlamp.

Then the fog of dust that surrounded them thinned, and gradually a miraculous blaze of colours and shapes began to appear through the murk. Royan lifted the dust mask from her face and let it drop to the agate floor. Nicholas followed her example, and took a breath of the stagnant air. No draught had disturbed it for thousands of years and it had the odour of great antiquity, the musty smell of the linen bandages of an embalmed corpse.

Now the miasma of dust faded away and before them opened a long straight passageway, the end of which was hidden in shadow and darkness. Nicholas turned back to the opening in the sealed door behind them, and reached through it to bring in the floodlight on its stand. Quickly he arranged it to illuminate the full length of the passageway ahead of them.

As they started forward, the images of the old gods hovered around them. They glowered at the intruders from the walls and hung over them, watching them with huge and hostile eyes from the ceiling high overhead. Nicholas and Royan passed on slowly. Their footfalls on the agate tiles were muted by the thin carpet of dust, and the dust that still hung in the air reflected the light and cast over them a luminous net that had an ethereal, dreamlike quality.

Inscriptions covered every inch of space upon the walls and the high roof. There were long quotations from all the mystical writings, from the *Book of Breathings*, the *Book of the Pylons* and the *Book of Wisdom*. Other blocks of hieroglyphics recited the history of Pharaoh Mamose's existence on this earth, and extolled those virtues that made the gods love him.

Further along they came to the first of eight shrines set into the walls of the long funeral gallery. This one was the shrine of Osiris. It was a circular chamber, the curved wall decorated with texts in praise of the god, and in its niche a small statue of Osiris in his tall feathered head-dress, with eyes of onyx and rock crystal which stared at them so implacably that Royan shivered. Nicholas reached out and touched the foot of the god.

He said one word, 'Gold!'

Then he looked up at the towering mural that covered the wall and half the domed ceiling above and around the shrine. It was another gigantic figure of the father Osiris, god of the Underworld, with his green face and false beard, his arms crossed upon his chest, holding the flail and the crook, wearing his tall feathered head-dress and with the erect cobra on his brow. They gazed up at him with a sense of awe. As the lamplight wavered in the shifting dust cloud the god seemed to become imbued with life, and to move and sway before their eyes.

They did not linger at the first shrine, for beyond it the gallery ran on, straight as the flight of an arrow to its target. They followed it. The next shrine set into the wall was dedicated to the goddess. The golden figure of Isis sat in her niche, upon the throne that was her symbol. The infant Horus suckled at her breast. Her eyes were ivory and blue lapis lazuli.

Her murals covered the walls around her niche. There she was, the mother with great kohl-lined eyes as black as night, wearing the sun disc and the horns of the sacred cow upon her head. All around her, hieroglyphic symbols covered the wall, so bright that they glowed like a cloud of fireflies; for she possessed a hundred diverse names. Amongst these were Ast and Net and Bast. She was also Ptah and Seker and Mersekert and Rennut. Each of these names was a word of power, for her sanctity and her benevolent aura had lived on where most of the old gods had withered away for lack of worshippers to repeat and keep alive these mystic names.

In ancient Byzantium and later in Christian Egypt they had bestowed the old goddess's virtues and attributes upon the Virgin Mary. The image of her suckling the infant Horus had been perpetuated in the icons of the Madonna and child. Thus Royan responded to the goddess in all her entities, the mingled blood of Royan's forefathers in her veins acknowledging both Isis and Mary, heresy and truth mingling inextricably in her heart, so that she felt at once both guilt and religious elation.

In the next shrine was a golden figure of Horus, the falcon-headed, the last of the holy trinity. In his right hand he held the war-bow and in his left the *ankh,* for life and death were his to dispense. His eyes were red carnelians.

Portraits of his other entities surrounded the statue: Horus the infant, suckling at the breast of Isis, Horus as the divine youth Harpocrates, proud and lithe and beautiful, one finger touching his chin in the ritual gesture, striding out on sandalled feet under his short, stiff kilt. Then

Horus the falcon-headed, sometimes with the body of a lion and then with the body of a young warrior, wearing the great crown of the south and the north united. Beneath him was the inscription: *'Great God and Lord of Heaven, of manifest Power, Mighty one amongst all the gods, whose strength has vanquished the foes of his divine father, Osiris.'*

In the fourth shrine stood Seth, the arch-fiend, the god of violence and discord. His body was gold, but his head was the head of a black hyena.

In the fifth shrine stood the god of the dead and of the cemeteries, Anubis the jackal-headed. It was he who officiated at the embalming, and whose duty it was to examine the tongue of the great balance when the heart of the deceased was weighed. If the beam of the scales were exactly horizontal, then the dead man was declared worthy, but if the balance tipped against him Anubis threw the heart to the crocodile monster and it was devoured.

The sixth shrine was dedicated to the god of writing, Thoth. He had the head of a sacred ibis and his stylus was in his hand. In the seventh shrine the sacred cow Hathor stood squarely on all four hooves, her piebald body spotted black and white, her face benignly human but with huge, trumpet-shaped ears. The eighth shrine was the largest and most splendid of all, for it belonged to Amon-Ra, father of all creation. He was the sun, an enormous golden disc from which the slanting golden rays emanated.

Nicholas paused here and looked back down the long gallery. Those eight sacred statues comprised a treasure that matched anything that Howard Carter and Lord Carnarvon had discovered in the tomb of Tutankhamen. He felt in his heart that it was crass even to consider their monetary value. However, the simple truth was that even one of these extraordinary works of art would be sufficient to pay off all his debts many times over. But he thrust the thought aside and turned once more to face the commodious chamber at the far end of the gallery.

'The burial chamber,' Royan murmured with awe. 'The tomb.'

As they walked towards it the shadows retreated before them, like the ghost of the long-dead pharaoh scurrying back to its final resting place. Now they could see into the tomb. Its walls were aflame with still more magnificent murals. Though they had gazed upon so many of these already, their eyes and their senses were not yet jaded or wearied by such profusion.

A single elongated figure rose up the far wall, and then stooped across the ceiling. It was the supple, sinuous body of the goddess Nut, giving birth to the sun. The golden rays poured forth from her open womb, suffusing the sarcophagus of the pharaoh and endowing the dead king with new life.

The royal sarcophagus stood in the centre of the chamber, a massive coffin hewn from a solid granite block. How many slaves must have laboured to bring this mass of stone along the subterranean passages, Nicholas wondered. He could imagine their sweating bodies gleaming in the lamplight, and hear the grating squeal of the wooden rollers under the immense weight of the coffin.

Then Nicholas looked down into the coffin, and felt the plunge of his spirits as he realized that the sarcophagus was empty. The massive granite lid had been lifted from its seat, and flung aside with such violence that it had cracked across its width and now lay in two pieces on the floor beside the coffin.

They moved forward slowly, the bitter taste of disappointment mingling with the dust upon their tongues, until they could look down into the open sarcophagus. It contained only the shattered fragments of the four canopic jars. These vessels had been carved from alabaster to contain the entrails, liver and other internal organs of the king. The broken lids were decorated with the heads of gods and fabulous creatures from beyond the grave.

'Empty!' whispered Royan. 'The body of the king has gone.'

Over the following days, while they photographed the murals and packed the statues of the eight gods and goddesses from the funeral gallery, Royan and Nicholas discussed and argued the disappearance of the royal mummy from its sarcophagus.

'The seals on the gate of the tomb were intact,' Royan pointed out repeatedly.

'There is probably an explanation for that,' Nicholas told her. 'Taita himself might have removed the treasure and the body. Many times in the writing of the seventh scroll he laments the waste of such treasure. He points out that it could have been much better spent in protecting and nurturing the nation and its people.'

'No, it does not make sense,' Royan argued, 'to go to such lengths as to dam the river and tunnel under the pool, to build this elaborate tomb, and then to remove and destroy the king's mummy. Taita was always a logical person. In his own way he revered the gods of Egypt. It shows in all his writings. He would never have flouted the religious traditions in which he believed so strongly. Something about this tomb does not ring true for me — the mysterious and almost offhanded disappearance of the body, even the paintings and the inscriptions upon the walls.'

'I agree with you about the missing corpse, but what do you find illogical about the decorations?' Nicholas wanted to know.

'Well, the paintings first.' She indicated the image of Isis with a wave of her hand. 'They are lovely, and they are the work of a competent classical artist, but they are hackneyed and stylized in form and choice of colour. The figures are stiff and wooden — they do not move and dance. They lack that spark of genius that we were shown in the tomb of Queen Lostris where the original scrolls in their alabaster jars were hidden.'

Nicholas considered the murals thoughtfully. 'I see what you mean. Even the murals in the tomb of Tanus at the monastery are in a different class from these.'

'Exactly!' she said forcefully. 'Those were the paintings of Taita himself. These are not. They were done by one of his hacks.'

'What else is there about the inscriptions that you don't like?'

'Have you ever heard of another tomb that did not have the text of the *Book of the Dead* inscribed upon its walls, or that did not depict the dead person's journey through the seven pylons to reach the paradise beyond?'

Nicholas looked startled; he had never considered that fact. Without replying he left her and went back down the long gallery, ostensibly to supervise the packing of the sacred statues, but in reality to give himself more time to consider what she had said.

Before leaving England Nicholas had seen to it that all of the more vulnerable and breakable equipment that they had air-freighted into the gorge had been packed in sturdy metal ammunition crates. All these crates had waterproof rubber seals and strong lever fastenings. The original contents had been padded and protected with polystyrene packing. When they left Ethiopia the equipment would be abandoned, but the crates, together with the packing material, had been carefully preserved for transporting the treasures that they might find in the tomb.

While six of the sacred statues fitted neatly into the crates, the images of Hathor the cow and satanic Seth were too large. However, Nicholas discovered that these had been carved in separate parts. The heads were detachable, and the hoofed legs of Hathor were held into the body by wooden pins that were rotted to dust. Broken down into their separate parts, even these two larger statues could also be packed into the metal cases.

Nicholas watched Hansith packing Seth's ferocious head of ebony and black resin into one of the crates. Then after a while he went back to where Royan was working on the inscriptions on the wall above the empty sarcophagus.

'Very well. I agree. You are right about the lack of inscriptions from the *Book of the Dead*. It does seem strange. But what can we do about it, other than accepting it as a mystery which we can never unravel?'

'Nicky, there is something more here. This is not everything. I feel it in every fibre of my being. We are missing something.'

'Who am I, a mere male, to question the veracity of a woman's instincts.'

'Stop being superior,' she snapped. 'How long

do I have to work over the inscriptions from the stele?'

'A week or two at the most. I have to set up an RV with Jannie. We have to be there at Roseires airstrip when he comes in to pick us up. That's one date we dare not break.'

'Good Lord. I thought you would have arranged that long ago. How will you contact Jannie from here?'

'Quite simple really.' Nicholas smiled. 'There is a public telephone at the post office in Debra Maryam. Tessay can move freely anywhere in the Gojam. She will go up the escarpment with an escort of monks and telephone Geoffrey Tennant at the British Embassy in Addis. I have already arranged it with Geoffrey. He will relay a message on to Jannie.'

'Will Tessay do it for you?'

He nodded. 'She has agreed to go up to Debra Maryam tomorrow. Jannie must have as much notice as possible to get himself prepared for the flight out from Malta. It's going to need some fine timing for all of us to arrive at the airstrip simultaneously. It will be asking for trouble for one party to sit around waiting at Roseires for the others to arrive.'

Dawn on the first of April,' Nicholas gave Tessay the message. 'Tell Jannie we will be there on April Fools' Day! A nice easy one to remember.'

They watched Tessay set off along the trail with her escort of monks and Royan asked Mek Nimmur quietly, 'Don't you worry about her going off like this on her own?'

'She is a very competent person, and she is well known and liked throughout the Gojam. She is as safe as any person can be in a dangerous land.' Mek watched Tessay's slim figure in shamma and jodhpur pants becoming smaller with distance. 'I wish I could go with her, but —' Mek shrugged.

Suddenly Royan exclaimed, 'There is something that I forgot to ask her.' She left Nicholas and Mek standing, and ran down the trail calling after the other woman. Her voice floated back to where Nicholas stood watching her.

'Tessay! Wait! Come back!'

Tessay turned and waited for Royan to catch up with her. While the two women stood talking together, Nicholas lost interest and turned to study the distant silhouette of the escarpment. With a sinking feeling in the pit of his stomach he saw that the thunderheads on the mountain tops were denser and more ominous than they had been only days before. The rains were building up swiftly now. He wondered if they really had as long as they hoped before the dam was threatened and they were driven out of the gorge by the rising waters.

He looked back down the path just in time to see Royan pass something to Tessay, who nodded and pushed it into the pocket of her jodhpurs. Then at last the two women embraced warmly, and Tessay turned away. Royan stood in the middle of the trail, watching until a bend in the valley hid Tessay from her. Then she walked slowly back to where Nicholas waited.

'What was all that about?' he wanted to know, and she smiled mysteriously.

'Girls' secrets. There are some things that it's best you brutish males don't know about.' But when Nicholas raised an eyebrow at her, she relented and told him, 'Tessay will ask Geoffrey Tennant to send a message to Mummy, just to let her know that I am all right. I don't want her to worry about me.'

As they climbed back down the scaffolding to where the fly camp had been set up on the rock ledge beside Taita's pool, Nicholas thought how fortuitous it was that Royan had her mother's phone number already written down to hand to Tessay, and he wondered at this sudden urge of Royan's to report her whereabouts to her mother. 'I wonder what she is really up to?' he mused. 'I will try and wheedle it out of Tessay when she returns.'

Royan would have preferred to camp in the tomb itself, so as to be in the midst of the inscriptions on which she was working, but Nicholas had insisted that they sleep in the open air, and the ledge was as close as they could get to their workplace. 'The musty air in the tomb is very probably unhealthy,' he told her. 'Cave disease is a real danger in these old enclosed places. They say that is what killed some of Howard Carter's people working in the tomb of Tutankhamen.'

'The fungus spores that cause cave disease breed in bat dung,' she pointed out. 'There are no bats in Mamose's tomb. Taita sealed it up too tightly.'

'Humour me,' he begged. 'You cannot work in there for days on end. I want you at least to get out of the tomb for a few hours each day.'

She shrugged. 'Only as a special favour to you,' she agreed, but as they reached the foot of the scaffolding she gave her new sleeping quarters only a perfunctory glance and then headed for the coffer dam and the entrance to the approach tunnel.

They had converted the landing at the top of the staircase, outside the plaster-sealed entrance to the tomb, into their workshop. Royan spread her drawings and photographs and reference books on the rough table of hand-hewn planks that Hansith made for her. Sapper had placed one of the floodlamps above this crude desk so that she had good light to work by. Against one wall of the landing they had stacked the ammunition crates which contained the eight sacred statues. Nicholas had insisted on storing all their discoveries where he could safeguard them adequately. Mek's armed men still kept a twenty-four-hour guard on the causeway over the sink-hole.

While Nicholas completed his photographic record of the walls of the long gallery and the empty burial chamber, Royan sat at her table and pored over her papers for hours at a time, scribbling notes and calculations from them into her notebooks. Now and then she would jump up from her desk and dart through the hatch in the white plaster doorway into the long gallery to study a detail on the decorated walls.

Whenever this happened, Nicholas straightened up from his camera tripod and watched her with a fond and indulgent expression. So intent was she that she seemed completely oblivious of him and everybody else about her. Nicholas had never seen her in this mood, and the depth of her powers of concentration impressed him.

When she had worked for fifteen hours without a break he went out on to the landing to rescue her and to lead her, protesting, back down the tunnel to the pool where there was a hot meal waiting for them. After she had eaten he led her to her hut and insisted that she lie down on her inflatable mattress.

'You are going to sleep now, Royan,' he ordered.

He woke to hear her creeping stealthily out of the hut next door to his, back along the ledge to the entrance to the tomb. He checked his watch and grunted with disbelief when he realized that they had slept for only three and a half hours. He shaved quickly and bolted back a slab of toasted *injera* bread and a cup of tea before following her into the tomb.

He found her standing in the long gallery before the empty niche in the shrine where the statuette of Osiris had stood. She was so preoccupied that she did not hear him come up behind her, and she started violently when he touched her arm.

'You startled me,' she scolded him.

'What are you staring at?' he asked. 'What have you discovered?'

'Nothing,' she denied swiftly, and then after a moment, 'I don't know. It's just an idea.'

'Come on! What are you up to?'

'It's easier for me to show you.' She led him back to her table on the stone landing, and rearranged her notebooks carefully before she spoke again.

'What I have been doing these last few days is going through the material on the stele of Tanus's tomb, picking out all the quotations that I recognize from the classical books of mystery, the *Book of Breathings*, the *Book of the Pylons* and the *Book of Thoth*, and setting those on one side.' She showed him fifteen pages in her neat small script. 'All this is ancient material, none of it original compositions by Taita. I have discarded it for the time being.'

She set the first notebook aside and picked up the next. 'All this is from the fourth face of the stele. It's nothing that I recognize, but seems to be only long lists of numbers and figures. Some sort of code, perhaps? I am not sure, but I do have some ideas on it that I will come to later.

'Now this here,' she showed him the next book, 'this is all fresh material that I don't remember reading in any of the ancient classics. Much of it, if not all of it, must be original Taita writings. If he has left any more clues for us, I believe they will be here, in these sections.'

He grinned, 'Like that marvellous quotation describing the pink and private parts of the goddess. Is that what you are referring to?'

'Trust you not to forget that.' She flushed lightly and refused to look up from her notebook. 'Look at this quotation from the head of the third face of the stele, the side Taita has headed *"autumn"*. It's the very first one that caught my attention.'

Nicholas leaned forward and read the hieroglyphics aloud: ' *"The great god Osiris makes the opening coup with deference to the protocol of the four bulls. At the first pylon he bears full testimony to the immutable law of the board."* ' He looked up at her. 'Yes, I remember that quotation. Taita is referring to bao, the game that the old devil loved so passionately.'

'That's right.' Royan looked slightly embarrassed. 'But do you also remember that I told you about a dream that I had in which I saw

Duraid again in one of the chambers of the tomb?'

'I remember.' He chuckled at her discomfort. 'He said something to you about the protocol of the four bulls. Now we are going into the realm of divination by dreams, are we?'

She looked annoyed by his levity. 'All I am suggesting is that my subconscious had been digesting the quotation and come up with an answer, which it put into the mouth of Duraid in the dream. Can't you be serious just for one moment?'

'Sorry.' He was contrite. 'Remind me what you heard Duraid say.'

'In the dream he told me, *"Remember the protocol of the four bulls — Start at the beginning."* '

'I am no expert on the game of bao. What did he mean?'

'The rules and subtleties of the game have been lost in the mists of antiquity. But as you know, we have found examples of the bao board amongst the grave goods in the tombs of the eleventh to the seventeenth dynasties, and we can only guess that it was an early form of chess.' She began to sketch for him on one of the blank pages at the back of her notebook.

'The wooden board was laid out like a chessboard, eight rows of cups wide and eight rows deep. Like this.' She drew it in with quick, deft strokes of her ballpoint pen. 'The pieces were coloured stones that moved in a prescribed fashion. I won't go into all the details, but the protocol of the four bulls was an opening gambit in the game favoured by grand masters of Taita's calibre. It consisted of making sacrifices to mass the highest-ranking stones in the first cup from where they could dominate the important central files of the board.'

'I am not sure where we are going, but lead on. I am listening.' Nicholas tried not to look too mystified.

'The first cup of the board.' She indicated it on her sketch, as though instructing a backward child. 'The beginning. Duraid said, *"Start at the beginning."* Taita said, *"The great god Osiris makes the opening coup."*'

'I still don't follow you.' Nicholas shook his head.

'Come with me.' Carrying the notebooks, she led him through the hatch in the white plaster doorway and stood beside him at the shrine of Osiris. 'The opening coup. The beginning.'

She turned and faced down the gallery. 'This is the first shrine. How many shrines are there altogether?'

'Three for the trinity, then Seth, Thoth, Anubis, Hathor and Ra,' he listed. 'Eight altogether.'

'Glory be!' She laughed. 'The lad can count! How many cups in the files of the bao board?'

'Eight across, and eight down —' he broke off and stared at her. 'You think — ?'

She did not answer, but opened the notebook.

'All of these numbers and extraneous symbols — they spell no coherent words. They do not relate to each other in any way, except that no number in the list is greater than eight.'

'I thought I had caught up with you, but I just lost you again.'

'If somebody were to read the notations of a game of chess four thousand years from now, what would he make of it?' she asked. 'Wouldn't it just be lists of numbers and extraneous symbols to him? You really are being extremely dense, aren't you? This is like pulling teeth.'

'Oh, Lordy, Lordy!' His face cleared. 'You clever lady! Taita is playing the game of bao with us.'

'And this is the first pylon, where it starts.' She gestured to the shrine. 'This is where the great god Osiris makes the opening coup. This is where we must start at the beginning of the sacred bao board. This is where we counter his opening move.'

They both looked around the shrine for a while, studying the curved walls and the high domed roof, and then Nicholas broke the silence. 'At the risk of being called extremely dense and having my teeth pulled, may I ask a question? How the hell do we play a game when we don't even know the rules?'

Colonel Nogo exuded confidence and self-importance as he swaggered into the conference room to answer von Schiller's summons. Nahoot Guddabi bustled along behind him, determined not to be excluded from any of the proceedings. He too tried to look confident and important, but in truth he felt his position was very insecure and that he needed to justify himself to his master.

Von Schiller was dictating correspondence to Utte Kemper, but as soon as they entered the room he stood up quickly and stepped on to the carpeted block.

'You promised that you would have a report for me yesterday,' he snapped at Nogo, ignoring Nahoot. 'Have you not heard anything from this informer of yours in the gorge?'

'I apologize for keeping you waiting like this, Herr von Schiller.' Nogo was immediately deflated by this sharp attack, and he became restless and uneasy. The German frightened him. 'The women were a day late returning from Harper's camp. They are very unreliable, these country people. Time means very little to them.'

'Yes, yes.' Von Schiller was impatient. 'I know the failings of your black brethren, and I might add you are not completely innocent of these yourself, Nogo. But tell me what news you have for me.'

'Harper finished work on the dam seven days ago, and immediately he moved his camp downstream, to a new place on the hills above the ravine. He then built some sort of bamboo ladder down into the ravine. My informer tells me that they are clearing a hole at the bottom of the empty pool —'

'A hole? What kind of hole?' Von Schiller turned pale as he listened, and began sweating in a light sheen across his forehead.

'Are you all right, Herr von Schiller?' Nogo was alarmed. The German looked very ill, as if he were about to collapse.

'I am perfectly well,' von Schiller shouted at him. 'What hole was this? Describe it to me.'

'The woman bringing the message is a stupid peasant.' Nogo was uncomfortable, squirming under von Schiller's grilling. 'She says only that when the river water fell, there was a hole in the bottom that was filled with rock and rubbish and that they have cleared this out.'

'A tunnel!' Nahoot could contain himself no longer. 'It must be the entrance tunnel to the tomb.'

'Be quiet!' Von Schiller turned on him furiously. 'You have no facts to back up that supposition. Let Nogo finish.' He turned back to the colonel. 'Go on. Give me the rest of it.'

'The woman says that there is a cave at the end of the hole. Like a rock shrine, with pictures on the walls —'

'Pictures? What pictures?'

'The woman said they were pictures of the saints.' Nogo made a deprecating gesture. 'She is a very uneducated woman. Stupid —'

'Christian saints?' von Schiller demanded.

Nahoot interjected, 'That is not possible, Herr von Schiller. I tell you that Harper has discovered the tomb of Mamose. You must act swiftly now.'

'I will not warn you again, you miserable little man,' von Schiller snarled at him. 'Keep quiet.'

He turned back to Nogo. 'Was there anything else in the cavern? Tell me everything the woman said.'

'Pictures and statues of the saints.' Nogo spread his hands. 'I am sorry, Herr von Schiller, that's what she said. I know this is all nonsense, but that is what the woman told me.'

'I will judge what is and what is not nonsense,' von Schiller told him. 'What did she say happened to these statues of the saints?'

'Harper has packed them in boxes.'

'Has he removed them from the shrine?'

'I do not know, Herr von Schiller. The woman did not say.'

Von Schiller stepped down from his block. He began to pace up and down the length of the hut, muttering to himself distractedly.

'Herr von Schiller —' Nahoot began, but the German waved him to silence. At last he stopped in front of Nogo and stared up at him.

'Did they find a mummy, a body, in the shrine?' he demanded.

'I do not know, Herr von Schiller. The woman did not say.'

'Where is she?' Von Schiller was so agitated that he clutched the front of Nogo's uniform jacket and stood on tiptoe to thrust his face up close to his. 'Where is this woman? Have you let her go?' Tiny droplets of spittle flew into Nogo's face and he blinked and tried to duck, but von Schiller had him in a death grip.

'No, sir. She is still here. I did not want to bring her to you —'

'You fool. All you are telling me is second-hand. Bring her in here immediately. I want to question her face to face.' He shoved Nogo away from him. 'Go and fetch her.'

Nogo returned minutes later dragging the woman into the room by one arm. She was young, and despite the blue tattoos across her cheeks and chin she was pretty. She wore the long black robes and head-covering of a married woman, and carried an infant on her hip.

As soon as Nogo released her arm she sank to the floor and whimpered with terror. The child she carried whined in sympathy. Its nostrils were plugged with white crusts of dried snot. The woman opened the top of her robe with a shaking hand, fished out one of her milk-swollen breasts and thrust the nipple into the child's mouth. Infant and mother stared at von Schiller with terrified eyes.

'Ask her if there was a coffin or body of the saint in the shrine,' von Schiller ordered, eyeing

714

the woman with distaste.

Nogo questioned her for a minute and then shook his head. 'She does not know anything about a body. She is very stupid. She does not understand very well.'

'Ask her about the statues of the saints. What has Harper done with them? Where are they now? Has he removed them from the shrine?'

After another long exchange with the woman, Nogo shook his head. 'No. She says that the statues are still in the shrine. The white man has packed them into boxes and the soldiers are guarding them.'

'Soldiers? What soldiers?'

'Soldiers of Mek Nimmur, the *shufta* commander that I told you about. He is still with Harper.'

'How many boxes are there?' In his impatience von Schiller went up to where the woman sat and prodded her with the toe of his boot. 'How many statues are there?'

The woman wailed with terror and shrank away from him. Von Schiller recoiled from her at the same time, with an expression of disgust.

'Gott im Himmel!' He pulled a handkerchief from his pocket and patted his mouth and nose with it. 'She stinks like an animal. Ask her how many boxes.'

'Not many,' Nogo translated, 'perhaps five, not more than ten. She is not sure.'

'What size? How big are they?'

When Nogo put the question to her, the

715

woman indicated the length of her arm. Von Schiller's disappointment registered clearly in his face.

'So few pieces, and so insignificant.' He turned away from the woman and went to stare out of the south-facing window of the hut, down over the escarpment rim into the wilderness of the gorge. 'If what this creature says is true, then Harper has not yet discovered the treasure of Mamose. There should be more, much more.'

Nogo was talking rapidly to the woman again, and now he turned back to von Schiller. 'She says that one of Harper's party has left the camp in the gorge, and gone to Debra Maryam.'

Von Schiller spun away from the window and stared at him. 'One of his party? Who? Which one?'

'She is an Ethiopian woman. The concubine of Mek Nimmur. A woman she calls Woizero Tessay. I know of her. She was married to the Russian hunter, before she became Mek Nimmur's whore.'

Von Schiller rushed across the room and seized the woman by the front of her robe. He hauled her to her feet with such violence that the infant was jerked from her grip and fell howling to the floor.

'Ask her where the woman is now,' he instructed Nogo.

The mother pulled free from his grip and grovelled on the floor, trying to pick up and console her screaming infant. Nogo grabbed her and slapped her face resoundingly to get her attention. She clasped her baby to her breast and gabbled out a reply.

'She does not know,' Nogo admitted. 'She thinks she is still at Debra Maryam.'

'Get that filthy bitch out of here!' Von Schiller jerked his head at the woman and her child. Nogo dragged them from the hut.

'What else do you know of this woman of Mek Nimmur's?' he asked in milder tones when Nogo returned.

'She is from one of the noble families in Addis Ababa, a blood relative of Ras Tafari Makonnen, the old Emperor Haile Selassie.'

'If she is Mek Nimmur's woman, and has come directly from Harper's camp, then she will be able to answer the questions that this other creature could not.'

'That is true, Herr von Schiller. But she may not wish to tell us.'

'I want her,' von Schiller said. 'Bring her here. Helm will speak to her. I am sure he will be able to make her see reason.'

'She is an important person. Her family has much influence.' Nogo thought about it for a moment. 'But on the other hand, she has been consorting with a notorious bandit. That is all the reason I need for bringing her in. I will send a detachment of my men, under one of my most trusted officers, to arrest her immediately.' He hesitated. 'If the woman is questioned severely, it would be as well that she were not allowed to return to her friends in Addis. They could make trouble for all of us. Even for you, Herr von Schiller.'

'What do you propose?' von Schiller wanted to know.

'When she has answered your questions, there will have to be a little accident,' Nogo suggested.

'Do what is necessary,' von Schiller ordered. 'I will leave the details to you, but make sure that if it is necessary to dispose of the woman it is done properly. I have had enough bungling.' As he spoke these words he looked across at Nahoot Guddabi, who lowered his gaze and flushed angrily.

They had spent almost two full days at the shrine of Osiris in the long gallery. No ancient worshipper had ever studied the texts upon those walls more avidly than Nicholas and Royan, or examined the flamboyant murals of the great god with more minute attention.

They took it in turn to recite aloud the extracts from the stele of Tanus that Royan had picked out and recorded in her notebooks, repeating them until they knew each quotation by heart. While one read aloud, the other concentrated his or her full attention upon the walls, trying to discover some connecting link.

' "*My love is a flask of cold water in the desert. My love is a banner unfurling in the breeze. My*

love is the first shout of the newborn infant," '
Nicholas read.

Royan looked up at him from where she squatted attentively before the shrine, and smiled. 'At times Taita was really rather cute, wasn't he?' she said. 'Such a romantic.'

'Concentrate, for heaven's sake. This isn't a poetry appreciation class. We are doing serious business here.'

'Barbarian!' she muttered under her breath, but turned back to the wall of inscriptions.

'Try this one again,' Nicholas ordered, and read out, ' *"We lie in the vale of a thousand joinings, of infant to mother, of man to woman, of friend to friend, of teacher to pupil, of sex to sex."* '

'That's the third time you have picked out that particular quotation this morning. What is there about it that appeals to you so strongly?' She did not look up at him, but the back of her neck turned a ruddier shade of brown.

'Sorry! Thought you might find that one as romantic as the other,' he mumbled. 'Let's try this one then. *"I have suffered and loved. I have withstood the wind and the storm. The arrow pierced my flesh but did not harm me. I have eschewed the false path that lies straight before me. I have taken the hidden stairway to the seat of the gods."* '

Royan rocked back on her heels and glanced down the long gallery. 'Something there perhaps. *"The false path that lies straight before me. The hidden stairway"*?'

'We are straining a bit now. Snapping at gnats like a hungry trout.

She stood up and pushed the tendrils of sweaty hair off her forehead. 'Oh, Nicky. It's so discouraging. We don't even know where to begin.'

'Courage, lassie.' He feigned the cheerfulness he did not feel. 'We begin at the beginning like your friend Taita said we must. Let me try you with this one again.' He placed his hand over his heart like a Victorian actor and emoted, ' *"The vulture rises on mighty pinions to greet the sun"* —'

She laughed softly at his clowning, and then her eyes wandered from his face and passed over his shoulder. Suddenly she started.

'The vulture!' she blurted, and pointed at the wall behind him.

He spun around and stared in the direction she was indicating.

There was the vulture, a magnificent image of the bird, the fierce eyes glaring and the yellow beak hooked and pointed. Its wings were spread wide, with each feather outlined in jewel-like colours. It stood as tall as Nicholas, but its wingspread covered half the wall. They stared at it together, and then Royan lifted her eyes to the ceiling high above where they stood. She touched his arm and motioned him to do the same.

'The sun!' she whispered. The golden sun disc of Ra was painted in the highest portion of the roof. Its warmth seemed to illuminate the shadows. Its rays spread out in every direction, but one of these beams followed the curve of the wall and descended to envelop the vulture image in its spreading luminosity.

' "*The vulture rises to greet the sun*",' she repeated. 'Does Taita mean it literally?'

He moved closer to the mural and examined it minutely, running his hands over the wings and down its belly to the cruel curved talons. Beneath the paint the plastered wall was smooth. There was no projection or any irregularity.

'The head, Nicky. Look at the head of the bird!' She jumped up and tried to reach it, but her fingers fell short and she turned to him with a desperate edge to her voice. 'You do it — you are much taller than I am.'

Only then did he see the slight shadow down one side of the bird's head where the floodlamp caught it, and as he touched it he realized that the head was in relief, standing slightly above the level of the surrounding wall. He ran his fingers over the raised head and found that the beak was part of the relief.

'Can you feel any joint in the plaster?' Royan demanded.

He shook his head. 'No. It's smooth. It all seems to be part of the main wall.'

' "*The vulture rises to greet the sun*",' she insisted. 'Can't you detect any movement? Try pushing the head upwards towards the sun painting.'

He placed the heel of his hand under the bulge

of the head and pushed upwards. 'Nothing!' he grunted.

'It's been there for almost four thousand years.' She was hopping from one foot to the other with frustration. 'Dammit, Nicky, if there is a moving part, it will be stiff. Harder! Push harder!'

He shifted his feet to get well under it and placed both hands under the projection of the head. Slowly he brought all his strength to bear. The cords in his neck stood out and blood flooded his face, turning it a deep, angry red.

'Harder!' she implored him, but at last he dropped his arms to his sides and stood back.

'No.' His voice was hoarse and strained with the effort. 'It's solid. Won't budge.'

'Lift me up. Let me look.'

'With the greatest of pleasure. Any excuse to lay lascivious hands on you.' He stepped behind her and placed both arms around her waist, then lifted her until she was able to touch the bird's head.

Quickly she explored it with her fingertips, and then she let out a small cry of triumph.

'Nicky! You have started something. The paint is cracked all around the outline of the head. I can feel it. Lift me higher!'

He grunted with the effort but raised her another foot off the floor.

'Yes, definitely!' she exclaimed. 'Something has moved. There is a hairline crack in the wall above the head, as well. You have a look!'

He fetched one of the empty ammunition crates from the landing outside the entrance and placed it below the vulture image. When he stepped up on to it he was on a level with the vulture's eye.

His expression changed. Quickly he groped in his pocket and brought out his clasp knife. He opened the blade and probed carefully around the outline of the head. Tiny specks of dried paint and plaster filtered down as he worked.

'It does look as though the head is a separate detached piece,' he admitted.

'Look on top of it, higher up the wall. There along the edge of the sunbeam. Can't you see a vertical crack in the plaster?'

'You are right, you know,' he admitted. 'But if I try to open that crack I am going to damage the mural. Do you want me to do that?'

She hesitated only a moment. 'This tomb is going to be reflooded when the river rises, so we are going to lose it again anyway. It's worth the risk. Do it, Nicky!'

He pressed the point of the knife-blade into the fine crack and twisted it gently. A slab of painted plaster the size of his spread hand fell out of the wall and splattered into the dust on the agate tiles of the floor.

He peered into the cavity that it had left in the wall.

'It looks like some kind of slot or groove in the wall,' he said. 'I am going to clear its full length.' Carefully he worked at the cavity he had opened, and more loose plaster rained down.

Royan sneezed in the dust, but would not retreat. Particles of debris lodged in her hair like confetti.

'Yes,' he said at last. 'There is a vertical groove running up here.'

'Chip the plaster away from the crack around the vulture's head,' she ordered, and he wiped the blade against his trouser leg and attacked the wall again.

'It's free,' he said at last. 'It looks as though the head will travel up the groove. Anyway, I am going to try it. Stand back and give me room to work.'

He placed the heels of both hands under the head of the vulture, and heaved upwards against it. Royan bunched her hands into fists and screwed up her face in sympathy with his effort.

There was a soft grating sound, and the head began to move jerkily up the exposed groove in the wall. It reached the top of the slot and Nicholas jumped down from the crate. They both stared expectantly at the disembodied head, now disfigured by the chipped and damaged plaster.

After a long, breathless wait, Royan whispered dejectedly, 'Nothing! It hasn't changed anything.'

'The rest of the quotation from the stele,' he reminded her. 'There was more to it than just the vulture and the sun.'

'You are right.' She looked around the rest of the wall eagerly. ' "*The jackal howls and turns upon his tail.*" '

She pointed with a trembling finger at the small, almost insignificant figure of Anubis, the jackal-headed god of the graveyards, on the wall opposite the vulture that they had mutilated. Standing at the foot of the huge, towering painting of Osiris, he was only a little larger in size than the ringed and bejewelled big toe of the husband of Isis and father of Horus.

Royan ran to the wall, and the moment she touched Anubis she felt that his image too was raised. She flung all her strength against the tiny figure, trying to twist it first one way and then the other.

' "*The jackal turns upon his tail*",' she panted as she wrestled with him. 'He must turn!'

'Here, let me do that.' Gently Nicholas pulled her away, and knelt before the black-headed god image. Once again he used the blade of his clasp knife to chip away the plaster and the thick layer of paint from around the outline.

'It seems to be carved in some sort of hard wood and then it's been plastered over,' he told her, as he tested the construction of the figure with the point of the blade.

When at last he had chipped it clear he tried to twist it in a clockwise direction, and grunted with the effort.

'No!' He gave up at last.

'They had no clock dials in ancient Egypt,'

she reminded him agitatedly. 'The other way. Turn it the other way.'

When he tried to turn it counter-clockwise, there was another rasping, gritty sound from behind the wall panel. The tiny figure revolved slowly in his hands, until the black head pointed down towards the yellow tiles.

They both stood well back from the wall, looking expectantly at it, but after another long wait even Nicholas was disheartened.

'I don't know what to expect, but whatever it is, it isn't happening,' he grunted with disgust.

'There is still the last part of the quotation,' Royan whispered. ' *"The river flows towards the earth. Beware, you violators of the sacred places, lest the wrath of all the gods descend upon you!"* '

'The river?' Nicholas asked. 'As Sapper might say, I don't see no perishing river.'

Royan did not even smile at the cockney accent. Instead she searched the profusion of writing and images that covered all the walls around them. Then she saw it.

'Hapi!' Her voice was shrill with excitement. 'The god of the Nile! The river!'

High up the wall, on a level with the head of the great god Osiris, the god of the river looked down upon them. Hapi was a hermaphrodite, with the breasts of a woman and the genitals of a man protruding from under the pendulous belly. The mouth in his hippopotamus head gaped wide to display the great curved tusks that lined his cavernous jaws.

Standing on a pile of ammunition boxes, Nicholas was able to reach the Hapi image at the full stretch of his arms. As he touched it he exulted, 'This one is raised also.'

' "*The river flows towards the earth,*" ' she called up to him. 'It must move downwards. Try it, Nicky.'

'Give me a chance to clear the edges.' He used the point of the blade to chip the outline of the god free, and then he probed the plaster beneath it and found another vertical slot running towards the floor.

'Ready to give it a go now.' He folded the knife and tucked it back into his pocket. 'Hold your breath and say a little prayer for me,' he instructed.

He settled both hands on the image of the god and began to pull steadily downwards. Gradually he brought more pressure to bear upon it, until he was hanging all his weight on it. Nothing moved.

'It's not working,' he grunted.

'Wait!' she ordered. 'I am coming up.'

She scrambled up on to the boxes behind him and placed both arms around his neck. 'Hang on tight,' she ordered.

'Every little bit helps, I suppose,' he agreed, as she lifted her feet and hung her full weight on his shoulders.

'It's moving!' he shouted. Suddenly the image of Hapi gave way under his hands, and with

727

a sharp grating sound travelled down to the bottom end of the groove in the wall.

Nicholas lost his grip on the smoothly rounded shape as it came up hard against the end of its slot. The stack of boxes under them toppled, and both he and Royan dropped back to the floor of the gallery. She was still hanging around his neck, and he lost his balance as she pulled him over backwards. The two of them sprawled on the agate floor in an untidy tangle of arms and legs. Nicholas scrambled to his feet and pulled her up beside him.

'What has happened?' she gasped, looking up wildly at the damaged Hapi figure and then around the walls of the gallery.

'Nothing,' he said. 'Nothing has moved.'

'Perhaps there is another —' she began, but broke off at a sound from the roof above them. They both stared upwards, startled and filled with sudden trepidation. There was a ponderous movement from above the high plastered ceiling.

'What is that?' Royan whispered. 'There is something up there. It sounds like a living thing.'

A giant was moving, coming awake after slumbering for thousands of years, stretching and turning as he awoke.

'Is it — ?' She could not finish the question. She had an image in her mind of the great god himself stirring in a hidden chamber in the rock, opening those baleful, slanted eyes, rising on one elbow to discover who had disturbed him from his eternal sleep.

Then there was another sound, a creaking and rumbling as though the arm of a mighty balance was swinging slowly across, as its equilibrium altered. Softly at first, then louder, the movement gathered momentum, like the beginning of a mountain avalanche. Then there was a report like the shot of a cannon.

A crack appeared in the high ceiling, running the length of the gallery. Dust smoked from the jagged opening, and then, slowly as a nightmare, the roof began to sag down over where they stood. Both of them were paralysed with superstitious horror, unable to tear their gaze from the slow, inexorable collapse of the ceiling upon them. Then a chunk of plaster struck Nicholas's upturned face, slamming into his cheek, tearing the skin and sending him staggering backwards against the wall. The shock and pain aroused him at last.

'The warning!' he blurted. 'Taita's warning. The wrath of the gods.' He sprang to her side and grabbed her hand, 'Run!' He pulled her after him. 'Taita has booby-trapped the roof!'

They raced back along the gallery towards the opening in the sealed entrance. Lumps of stone and plaster began to rain down and dust filled the passageway, half-blinding them. The dull rumble overhead became a rising roar as progressively the roof collapsed. They did not dare to look back as the thunder of falling masonry swept towards them, threatening to overtake and overwhelm them before they were able to reach the entrance.

A jagged piece of rock as large as her head struck Royan a glancing blow on her shoulder, and her legs sagged under her. She would have gone down if he had not flung one arm around her and held her upright, dragging her along the gallery. The dust obscured the passage ahead of them, so that the square opening that offered their only chance of escape receded in the choking fog.

'Keep going!' he yelled at her. 'Almost there.' As he spoke, a thick sheet of plaster came crashing down and smashed into the tripod stand of the floodlamp. Instantly the gallery was plunged into utter darkness.

Completely unsighted, Nicholas's first instinct was to come up short and try to orientate himself. But all around him the rubble of the roof was falling heavier and faster. He knew that at any second the entire roof would come down on top of them, burying and crushing them. Running on without a check, he dragged Royan along behind him in the darkness. He reached the end wall at full tilt, and the impact knocked the breath out of him. Now, through the swirling dust cloud, he was just able to make out the rectangular opening in the plaster wall in front of him, back-lit by the lamps on the landing at the head of the staircase outside.

As he reeled backwards he seized Royan around the waist and lifted her bodily off her feet. He hurled her through the opening and heard her cry out as she fell heavily on the far side. Another piece of rubble struck him on the back of his head and knocked him to his knees. He felt himself teetering on the very brink of consciousness, but crawled forward, groping frantically until he touched the jagged edge of the opening. With this handhold he was able to drag himself over the sill, just as the full weight of the roof came thundering down along the entire gallery.

Here on the upper landing of the staircase Royan was crouching on her knees. She crawled towards him, guided once more by the lamp-light.

'Are you all right?' she panted. A trickle of blood snaked down her cheek from a wound in her scalp line. It cut a dark glistening runnel through the caked white dust that powdered her face.

He did not answer, but dragged himself to his feet and pulled Royan up beside him. 'Can't stay here,' he croaked, just as a thick white breath of dust blew through the mouth of the opening and swept over them, choking them and dimming the floodlamps to a faint glimmer.

'Not safe.' He pulled her away from the opening. 'The whole thing might cave in.' His voice was rough, his throat closing with the dust.

He dragged her to the head of the steps and they staggered down together, stumbling against each other, their feet sliding under them as they came on to the algae-slippery footing. Through the dust mist ahead of them loomed the broad square figure of Sapper.

'What the ruddy hell is going on?' he bellowed with relief as he saw them.

'Give me a hand here,' Nicholas yelled back at him. Sapper lifted Royan in his arms and together they ran back down the tunnel, only stopping to draw breath when they reached the causeway over the sink-hole.

The post office in the village of Debra Maryam was a small building in the dusty street behind the church. Its walls were of un-plastered unburnt and unpainted brick, and its galvanized iron roof glared like a mirror in the high mountain sunlight. The public telephone should have been in its booth outside the front door. However, the instrument had long since vanished — stolen, vandalized or, more likely, removed by the military to prevent it being used by political dissidents and rebels.

Tessay had expected this, and hardly glanced into the booth before she strode into the small room which was the main post office. It was filled with a motley crowd of peasants and vil-lagers, queuing to conduct their leisurely busi-ness with the elderly postmaster, the only person behind the barred counter. Some of the cus-tomers had spread their cloaks on the floor and settled in for a long wait, chatting and smoking while their children romped and crawled around them.

Most of the patient crowd recognized Tessay as soon as she entered the room. Even those who had waited most of the morning in the lines at the counter greeted her respectfully and stood aside to allow her to go to the head of the queue. Despite two decades of African socialism, the feudal instincts of the rural population were still strong. Tessay was a noblewoman and she was entitled to this preference.

'Thank you, my friends.' She smiled at them and shook her head. 'You are kind, but I will wait my turn.'

They were embarrassed by her refusal, and when the old postmaster leaned over his counter top and added his insistence to the others, one of the older women seized Tessay's arm and forcefully propelled her forward.

'Jesus and all the saints bless you, Woizero Tessay.' The postmaster clapped his hands in respectful greeting. 'Welcome back to Debra Maryam. What is it that your ladyship desires?'

The entire clientele of the post office crowded around Tessay so as not to miss a detail of her transaction.

'I want to make a telephone call to Addis,' she told the postmaster and there was a hum of comment and discussion. This was unusual and important business indeed.

'I will take you to the telephone exchange,' the postmaster told her importantly, and donned his official blue cap for the occasion. He came around the counter shouting and hectoring the other customers, pushing them aside to make way for Lady Sun. Then he ushered her through to the back room of the building, where the telephone exchange occupied a cubicle the size of a small lavatory.

Tessay, the postmaster and as many of the other customers who could find standing room pushed their way into the tiny room. The exchange operator was almost overcome by the honour being accorded him by the beautiful Tessay, and he shouted into his headset like a sergeant major commanding a flag party.

'Soon now!' he beamed at Tessay. 'Only small delay. Then you speak to British Embassy in Addis.'

Tessay, who knew well what a small delay constituted, retired to the front veranda of the post office and sent for food and flasks to be brought from the village *tej* shop. She treated her escort of monks, together with half the population of Debra Maryam, to a happy picnic while she waited for her call to be patched through half a dozen antiquated village exchanges to the capital. Thanks to the *tej*, spirits were high amongst her entourage when finally, an hour later, the postmaster rushed out to tell her proudly that they had succeeded and that her party was awaiting her on the line in the back room.

Tessay, the monks and fifty villagers followed

the postmaster back into the exchange and crowded, jabbering, into the cubicle. The overflow backed up into the main post hall.

'Geoffrey Tennant speaking.' The upper-class English accent was tinny with distance and static.

'Mr Tennant, this is Woizero Tessay.'

'I was expecting your call.' Geoffrey's voice lightened as he realized that he was talking to a pretty girl. 'How are you, my dear?'

Tessay passed Nicholas's message to him.

'Tell Nicky it's as good as done,' Geoffrey acknowledged, and hung up.

'Now,' Tessay addressed the postmaster, 'I want to place another call to Addis — to the Egyptian Embassy.'

There was a buzz of delight from her audience when they realized that the entertainment was not yet over for the day. Everybody repaired to the veranda for more *tej* and conversation.

The second call took even longer to connect, and it was after five o'clock when Tessay was at last put in contact with the Egyptian cultural attaché. Had she not once met him at one of those ubiquitous cocktail parties on the diplomatic circuit in Addis, and made a profound impression on him then, he would probably not have accepted her call now.

'You are very lucky to have reached me so late,' he told her. 'We usually close at four-thirty, but there is a meeting of the Organization of African Unity on at the moment and I am working late. Anyway, how may I help you, Woizero Tessay?'

As soon as she told him the name and rank of the person in Cairo to whom Royan's message was addressed, his superior and condescending attitude altered dramatically and he became effusive and eager to please. He wrote down everything she said in detail, asking her to repeat and spell the names of people and places. Finally he read his notes back to her for confirmation.

At the end of the long conversation, he dropped his voice to an intimate level and told her, 'I was greatly saddened to hear of your recent bereavement, Lady Sun. Colonel Brusilov was a man I held in high regard. Perhaps when you return to Addis you would do me the honour of dining with me one evening.'

'How kind and thoughtful of you.' Tessay's tones were honeyed. 'I would so much enjoy meeting your charming wife again.' She hung up while he was still making confused noises of assent and denial.

By this time the sun was already setting behind the sky castles of cumulo-nimbus, and there was the smell of rain in the air. It was too late to start the journey back down the escarpment that evening, so Tessay was relieved when the headman of Debra Maryam village sent one of his teenage daughters to invite her to spend the night as a guest in his home.

The headman's house was the finest in the village, not one of the circular *tukul*s, but a square brick building with an iron roof. His wife and daughters had prepared a banquet in Tessay's honour, and all the village notables, including the priests from the church, had been invited. It was therefore after midnight before Tessay was able to escape to the principal bedroom, which the headman and his wife had vacated for her.

Just before Tessay fell asleep she heard the heavy raindrops rattling on the corrugated iron roof over her head. It was a comforting sound, but she thought briefly of the dam further downstream in the gorge, and hoped that this shower was merely the harbinger and not the true onset of the big rains.

When she started awake much later the rain had passed. Beyond her uncurtained window the night was moonless and silent, except for the howling of a pariah-dog down in the village. She wondered what had woken her, and was filled suddenly with a premonition of impending disaster, a legacy from the Mengistu days, when any sound in the night might warn of the arrival of the security police. So strong was this feeling that she could not get to sleep again. Creeping quietly out of her bed, she began dressing in the dark. She had decided to call her monks and start back along the trail in the darkness. Only when she was at Mek Nimmur's side once again would she feel secure.

She had just pulled on her jodhpurs and was searching beneath the bed for her sandals when she heard the sound of a truck engine in the distance. She went to the window and listened. The air had been cooled by the rain and she felt the chill on her naked arms and chest.

The truck sounded as though it was approaching the village from the south, up the track that followed the river bank. It was coming fast, and her sense of unease sharpened. The villagers had spoken to the monks, and it was now common knowledge that she was Mek Nimmur's woman. Mek was a wanted man. Suddenly she felt very vulnerable and alone.

Quickly she pulled the woollen *shamma* over her head and thrust her feet into her sandals. As she crept from the room she heard the headman snoring in the front room where he and his wife had moved to make room for her. She turned down the short passage to the kitchen. The fire in the hearth had burned down, but she could make out the shapes of the sleeping monks on the mud floor. They lay with their *shamma*s pulled over their heads, completely covered, like a row of bodies on mortuary tables. She knelt beside the nearest of them and shook him, but obviously he had enjoyed the *tej* at dinner because he was difficult to rouse.

The sound of the approaching truck was much louder and closer by now, and she felt her uneasiness take on a tinge of panic. Realizing that in an emergency the monks would probably be of little real help to her, she stood up and groped her way quickly towards the back door.

The truck was right outside the front of the

house now. The headlights flashed across the front windows and were briefly reflected down the passageway. Abruptly the engine roar sank to a burble as the driver decelerated, and she heard the squeal of brakes and the crunch of tyres in the gravel outside. Then there was shouting and the trampling of many feet as men jumped down from the back of the stationary truck.

Tessay froze halfway across the small kitchen, her head cocked to listen. Suddenly there was a loud banging on the flimsy front door, and chillingly familiar shouts of, 'Open up here! Central Intelligence! Open the door! Nobody leave the house!'

Tessay ran for the back door, but in the darkness she tripped over a low table covered with dirty dishes from the previous evening's meal. She fell heavily and the bowls and *tej* flasks crashed to the floor and shattered. Instantly the men at the front door put their shoulders to it, tearing it off its hinges. They burst into the house, shouting and breaking furniture, torches flashing as they searched the front rooms. There was a confused babble of alarm as the headman and his family struggled awake, and then the sound of heavy blows with club and rifle butt, followed by shrieks of pain and terror.

Tessay reached the back door and struggled to open it. The sound of strange men rampaging through the house made her fingers clumsy. She struggled with the lock. All the while she could hear other men outside running through the yard to surround the house completely. At last she got the door open. It was dark and the area was unfamiliar so she did not know in which direction to run, but she heard the river close by in the night.

'If I can only reach the bank,' she thought, and started across the yard.

As she did so the beam of an electric torch blinded her, and a coarse voice bellowed, 'There she is!'

Any doubt that she was the prey was instantly dispelled, and she fled like a startled hare in the beam of the light. They bayed behind her like a pack of hounds. She reached the bank of the river and spun off to the right, downstream. A pistol cracked out behind her and she ducked as a shot fluted past her head.

'Don't shoot, you baboons!' a voice roared in commanding tones. 'We want her for questioning.'

In the torchbeam her white *shamma* flashed like the wings of a moth flitting around the candle flame.

'Stop her!' shouted the officer behind her. 'Don't let her get away.'

But she was fleet as a gazelle, and her lightly sandalled feet flew across the rough terrain while the heavily equipped soldiers blundered along behind her. Her spirits soared as she realized that she was pulling away from them.

The sound of the pursuit dwindled behind

her and she had reached the limit of the effective range of the torchbeam when she ran into a fence of rusty barbed wire. Three wire strands whipped across her lower body, at the level of her knees, her hips and her diaphragm. The top strand drove the breath from her lungs, and the barbs tore through the wool of her clothing and into her flesh. They snagged her like a fish in the mesh of a net, and she hung there struggling helplessly. Rough hands seized her and dragged her off the wire, and she sobbed with despair and with the pain of the sharp wire spurs tearing her skin. One of the soldiers grabbed her wrist and twisted it up between her shoulder-blades, laughing with sadistic relish when she cried out at the pain.

The officer came up panting over the rough ground. He was overweight, and even in the cold night air he was sweating heavily. It greased his fat cheeks and glistened in the light of the torch.

'Do not hurt her, you oaf,' he gasped. 'She is not a criminal. She is a high-bred lady. Bring her to the truck, but treat her with respect.'

With a man on each arm they marched her to the truck, holding her so that her feet barely touched the rough ground, and then shoved her up into the cab on to the seat beside the uniformed driver. The plump officer climbed in heavily after her, and she found herself wedged in firmly between the two men. The soldiers scrambled up into the rear of the truck, and the driver revved the engine and let out the clutch.

Tessay was sobbing softly, and the officer glanced sideways at her. She saw in the reflection of the headlights that his expression was gentle and sympathetic, completely at odds with his actions.

'Where are you taking me?' she asked softly, stifling her sobs. 'What have I done wrong?'

'I have been ordered to take you to Colonel Nogo, the district commander, for questioning in connection with *shufta* activities in the Gojam,' he told her, as they jolted and bounced down the rough track.

They were both silent for a while, and then the officer said quietly in English, 'The driver speaks only Amharic. I wanted to tell you that I knew your father, Alto Zemen. He was a good man. I am sorry for what is happening here tonight, but I am only a lieutenant. I have to follow my orders.'

'I understand that it is not your choice, or your blame.'

'My name is Hammed. If I can, I will help you. For Alto Zemen's sake.'

'Thank you, Lieutenant Hammed. I need friends now.'

While they waited for the dust of the cave-in to settle, and for any loose hanging rock to fall or stabilize, Nicholas dressed the minor injuries that Royan had sustained. The cut over her temple was not deep, barely more than a scratch. Nicholas saw that it did not require a stitch. He disinfected it and covered it with a Band Aid. However, her shoulder, which the falling rock had struck, was badly bruised. He massaged it with arnica cream.

His own bruises he treated less ceremoniously. Within an hour of the cave-in he was ready to go back up the tunnel. He ordered Royan and Sapper to remain on the causeway over the sink-hole while he returned to the landing at the top of the stairs alone. He carried a bamboo pole and a hand lamp connected to the Honda generator.

Nicholas proceeded with the utmost caution, probing the roof of the tunnel for weakness as he went. When he reached the landing he saw at once that the rock fall had smashed down what remained of the white plaster door that had originally sealed the entrance to the tomb. The ammunition crates, eight of which contained the statues from the shrines, had been knocked about and scattered, and some of them were partially buried under the fallen rubble. He retrieved them and opened each of the packed crates in turn to check the contents. With immense relief he discovered that the stout metal containers had withstood the rough treatment and there was no damage to the precious statues they held. One at a time he carried them back down the tunnel as far as the causeway and handed them into Sapper's care.

When he returned to the landing outside the tomb, Royan insisted on accompanying him. Even his lurid descriptions of the danger of a further rock-fall could not dissuade her. Her dismay when she stood outside the shattered gallery was overwhelming.

'It's totally destroyed,' she whispered. 'All those marvellous works of art. I cannot believe that Taita wanted this to happen.'

'No,' Nicholas agreed ruefully. 'His plan was to give us a big send-off along the road past the seven pylons to the happy hunting grounds. And he damned nigh succeeded.'

'It's going to take a lot of hard work to clear up this mess,' she said.

'What on earth are you talking about?' He turned on her in genuine alarm. 'We have saved the statues, and that's all we can hope for. Now I think it's time to cut our losses and get out of here.'

'Get out of here? Are you crazy?' She rounded on him furiously. 'Are you out of your mind?'

'At least the statues will pay our costs,' he explained, 'and there might even be something left over to divvy up between us, in accordance with our agreement.'

'You aren't dreaming of giving up now, when we are so close?' Her voice rose sharply with agitation.

'The gallery is destroyed —' he began in more reasonable tones, but she stamped her foot with agitation and shouted him down.

'The tomb is still there. Dammit, Nicky, Taita would not have gone to those lengths if it were not. We are getting too close now — that is why he fired that warning shot across our bows. Don't you see? We have him really worried now. We can't give up with the prize almost in sight.'

'Royan, be reasonable.'

'No! No! You be reasonable.' She refused to listen. 'You have to start clearing the gallery right away. I know the entrance is open now. All we have to do is clear this mess, and I am certain that we will find the true entrance to the tomb behind the rubble that Taita deliberately dropped on us.'

'I think that bang on your head has loosened a couple of nuts and bolts.' He threw up his hands in resignation. 'But what's the use arguing with a crazy woman? We will clear just enough of the scree to prove to you that there is nothing more to discover in there.'

'The dust is going to be our big problem.' Sapper eyed the blocked gallery entrance when they told him what they intended. 'As soon as we touch that rubble there is going to be clouds of it — more than our little blower fan can handle.'

'Right,' Nicholas agreed briskly. 'We will have to wet it all down. Two lines of men back down the tunnel to the sink-hole. One chain passing up water buckets, and the other chain passing back the rubble from the cave-in.'

'It's going to take a lot of work.' Sapper sucked his bottom lip lugubriously.

'You signed on to be tough,' Nicholas reminded him. 'No time to start whinging now.'

The monks, still convinced that they were engaged on the Lord's work, accepted this new task cheerfully. They sang as they passed the chunks of broken plaster and rock in one direction and the clay pots of water from the sinkhole in the other. Nicholas worked at the rock-fall with the gang of Buffaloes, led by Hansith. It was hard, messy and dangerous work, for each piece of rubble had to be doused with water before it could be levered out of the pack and passed down the chain. The staircase was soon running with muddy water and the steps were treacherous underfoot. The fallen rock was loose and unstable, and there was always the danger of a secondary collapse.

So many men working in the confined spaces of the gallery and tunnel taxed the ability of the little blower fan to recirculate the air, and it was hot and oppressive. The men stripped to loincloths and their bodies glistened with sweat. The rubble passed back down the tunnel was dumped into the sink-hole. Even that large volume of material made no difference to the level of the black waters. It was simply swallowed up into the depths without trace.

Nicholas found the crowded workings so humid and claustrophobic that at the change of the first shift he had to escape into the open air, if only for a few minutes. Even the dark and forbidding chasm of Taita's pool was a relief after the close confines of the underground workings. Mek Nimmur was waiting for him when he climbed out over the wall of the coffer dam on to the ledge beside the pool.

'Nicholas!' Mek's handsome dark face was grave. 'Has Tessay returned from Debra Maryam yet? She should have been back yesterday.'

'I have not seen her, Mek. I thought she was with you.'

Mek shook his head. 'I wanted to make certain that she had not returned without my men seeing her, before I send a patrol up the trail to search for her.'

'I am sorry, Mek. I did not anticipate any danger in sending her up the escarpment.' Nicholas felt a stab of guilt.

'If I had thought there was any danger, I would not have allowed her to go,' Mek agreed. 'I have sent men to search for her.'

But Tessay's absence was another worry for Nicholas. It lurked at the edge of his mind during the days that followed, as the clearing of the long funeral gallery proceeded too slowly for his satisfaction.

Royan spent as much time at the face as Nicholas did, and both of them were as filthy with mud and dirt as the Buffaloes who were labouring there beside them. She mourned over each fragment of the shattered murals. Before they were carried away to be thrown into the sink-hole, she tried to retrieve those on which significant portions of the paintings were still intact. There was one jagged piece of plaster on which the lovely head of Isis was still in one piece, and another on which the entire figure of Thoth, the god of writing, was preserved. However, most of the paintings were destroyed beyond any hope of ever restoring them, and sadly they were consigned to the pit.

There was no sense of time in the long gallery, and they could not tell night from day. It was always a surprise to leave the precincts of the tomb and find that the stars were shining in the narrow strip of sky that showed above Taita's pool, or to find the bright African sun burning hotly down out of the cloudless blue. They ate and slept only when their bodies demanded it, not according to the passage of the hours.

Re-entering the tomb after a few hours' sleep in their shelters beside the pool, they were crossing the causeway over the sink-hole when a wild cry reverberated down the shaft ahead of them. Immediately there was a hullabaloo of query and answer, and excited shouts from the men working in the upper levels of the tunnel.

'Hansith has found something,' Royan cried. 'Dammit, Nicky, I knew we should have stayed —' She began to run, and he hurried after her.

They came out on the landing in front of the gallery to find it crowded with chattering, gesticulating, half-naked workmen. Nicholas forced his way through them with Royan on his heels. They realized that Hansith had cleared the gallery as far as where the shrine of Osiris had once stood. The roof above them was jagged and broken, and lying amongst the rubbish on the ruined agate tiles of the floor Nicholas made out the remains of the mechanism which Taita had placed in the roof, and which they had brought crashing down when they had activated the device. The main part of this was an enormous stone wheel, resembling a mill wheel and weighing many tons. Nicholas stopped to give it a cursory examination.

'When you read *River God*, you realize that Taita had an obsession with the wheel,' he told Royan. 'Chariot wheels, water wheels, and now this must have been the balance wheel of his booby-trap. When we moved the levers, we toppled the wedges that held this monstrosity in place. Once it started rolling, it tumbled all the drop-stones that he had stacked above the ceiling of the gallery.' He glanced up at the shattered roof.

'Not now, Nicky!' Royan was hopping with impatience. 'Time for your lectures later. Taita's death-trap is not what has excited Hansith. He has found something else. Come on!'

They pushed their way through the pack of workmen until they reached Hansith's tall figure.

'What is it?' Nicholas shouted over the heads

749

of the others. 'What have you found, Hansith?'

'Here, *effendi*,' Hansith shouted back. 'Come quickly.'

They pushed their way to the face, and stopped beside the monk at the end of the blocked gallery.

'There!' Hansith pointed proudly.

Nicholas went down on one knee in the shattered remains of the shrine. Small pieces of the painted plaster still adhered to the fractured rock wall. Hansith pulled a slab out of the collapsed face, and pointed into the space it had left. Nicholas peered into it and felt his pulse begin to race. There was an opening in the side of the gallery. Even at first glance he realized that it was the mouth of another tunnel leading off at right-angles from the long gallery. It had been concealed behind the plaster-covered image of the great god.

As he stared into it with awe, he felt Royan's hand on his arm and her warm breath on his cheek. 'This is it, Nicky. The entrance to the true tomb of Mamose. This gallery was a bluff. Taita's red herring. This is the veritable tomb.'

'Hansith!' Nicholas called to him in a voice that was hoarse with emotion. 'Get your men to clear this doorway.'

As the workmen moved the rocks Nicholas and Royan hovered close behind them, so that they were able to watch the shape of the doorway as it was fully revealed. It proved to be a dark rectangle, of the same dimensions as the tunnel leading up from the sink-hole, three metres wide by two high. The lintel and the door jambs were of beautifully cut and dressed stone, and when Nicholas shone his lamp into the opening he saw a flight of stone steps rising before him.

They moved the cables and the lights into the gallery and arranged them at the entrance to this new doorway, but when Nicholas set foot on the first step he found Royan at his side.

'I am coming with you,' she told him firmly.

'It's probably booby-trapped,' he warned her. 'Taita is lying in wait for you around the first bend.'

'Don't try that. It just won't work, mister! I am coming.'

They went slowly up the steep steps, pausing on each one to survey the walls and the way ahead. Twenty steps from the bottom they reached another landing. A pair of doorways led off it, one on either side. However, the staircase continued climbing directly ahead of them.

'Which way?' Nicholas asked.

'Keep going up,' Royan urged him. 'We can explore these side passages later.'

Cautiously, they continued climbing. After twenty more steps they came out on an identical landing, with a doorway on each side and the stairway in front of them.

'Keep going up,' Royan ordered, without waiting for him to ask.

Twenty more steps and there was another

landing, with the familiar openings on either side and the stairway straight ahead.

'This isn't making sense,' Nicholas protested, but she prodded him in the back.

'We should keep going on upwards,' she told him, and he did not protest further. They passed another landing and then yet another, each of them the exact image of those that they had passed lower down.

'At last!' Nicholas exclaimed when they came out at the top of the staircase, with the expected doorway on each side but now a blank wall in front of them. 'This is as far as it goes.'

'How many landings are there?' she asked. 'How many altogether?'

'Eight,' he answered.

'Eight,' she agreed. 'Isn't that a familiar number by now?'

He turned to stare down at her in the lamplight. 'You mean —'

'I mean the eight shrines in the long gallery, these eight landings, and the eight cups of the bao board.'

They stood silent and undecided on the top landing and looked about them.

'Okay,' he said at last, 'if you are so damned clever, tell me which way to go now.'

'Eeny-meeny-miny-moe,' she recited. 'Let's try the right-hand doorway.'

They followed the right-hand passage only a short distance before they were confronted by a T-junction — a blank wall with identical twin passageways on each side.

'Take the right one again,' she counselled, and they followed it. But when they came to the next T-junction Nicholas stopped and faced her.

'You know what is happening here, don't you?' he demanded. 'This is another one of Taita's tricks. He has led us into a maze. If it were not for the cable, we would be lost already.'

With a bemused expression she looked back the way they had come, and then down the unexplored passages to their right and left.

'When he built this, Taita could not have anticipated the age of electricity. He expected any grave robber to be equipped the same way he was. Imagine being caught in here without the electric cable to follow back the way we have come,' Nicholas said softly. 'Imagine having only an oil lamp for light. Imagine what would happen to you when the oil burnt out and you were lost in here in the utter darkness.'

Royan shivered and gripped his arm. 'It's scaring!' she whispered.

'Taita is beginning to play rough,' Nicholas said softly. 'I was developing rather a soft spot for the old boy. But now I am beginning to change my mind.'

She shuddered again. 'Let's go back,' she whispered, 'We should never have rushed in here like this. We must go back and work it out carefully. We are unprepared. I have the feeling that we are in danger — I mean real danger, the same as we were in the long gallery.'

As they started back through the twists and turns, picking up the electric cable as they retreated down the stone passageways, the temptation to break into a run became stronger with each step. Royan hung tightly to Nicholas's arm. It seemed to both of them that some intelligent and malignant presence lurked behind them in the darkness, following them, watching them and biding its time.

The army truck carrying Tessay drove back through the village of Debra Maryam, and then turned off on to the track that followed the Dandera river downstream towards the escarpment of the Abbay gorge.

'This is not the way to army headquarters,' Tessay told Lieutenant Hammed, and he shifted awkwardly on the seat beside her.

'Colonel Nogo is not at his headquarters. I have orders to take you to another location.'

'There is only one other place in this direction,' she said. 'The base camp of the foreign prospecting company, Pegasus.'

'Colonel Nogo is using that as a forward base in his campaign against the *shufta* in the valley,' he explained. 'I have orders to take you to him there.'

Neither of them spoke again during the long,

754

bumpy ride over the rough track. It was almost noon when at last they reached the edge of the escarpment and turned off on to the fork that brought them at last to the Pegasus camp. The camouflage-clad guards at the gate saluted when they recognized Hammed. The truck drove through the gates, and parked in front of one of the long Quonset huts within the compound.

'Please wait here.' Hammed got down and went into the hut, but was gone for only a few minutes.

'Please come with me, Lady Sun.' He looked awkward and embarrassed, and could not meet her eyes as he helped her down from the cab. He led her to the door of the hut, and stood aside to let her enter first.

She looked around the sparsely furnished room, and realized that it must be the company's administration centre. A conference table ran almost the full length of the room, and there were filing cabinets and two desks set against the side walls. A map of the area and a few technical charts were the only decorations on the bare walls. Two men sat at the table, and she recognized both of them immediately.

Colonel Nogo looked up at her, and his eyes were cold behind his metal-framed spectacles. As always, his long, thin body was immaculately uniformed; but his head was bare. His maroon beret lay on the table in front of him. Jake Helm leaned back in his chair with his arms folded. At first glance, his short-cropped hair

755

made him look like a boy. Only when she looked closer did she see how his skin was weathered, and notice the crows' feet at the corners of his eyes. He wore an open-necked shirt and blue jeans that were bleached almost white. His belt buckle was of ornate Indian silver, the shape of a wild mustang's head. The sleeves of his cotton shirt were rolled high around his lumpy biceps. He chewed upon the dead butt of a cheap Dutch cheroot, and the smell of the strong tobacco was rank and offensive.

'Very well, lieutenant,' Nogo dismissed Hammed in Amharic. 'Wait outside. I will call you when I need you.'

Once Hammed had left the room, Tessay demanded, 'Why have I been arrested, Colonel Nogo?'

Neither man acknowledged the question. They both regarded her expressionlessly.

'I demand to know the reason for this high-handed treatment,' she persisted.

'You have been consorting with a band of notorious terrorists,' said Nogo softly. 'Your actions have made you one of them, a *shufta*.'

'That is not true.'

'You have trespassed in a mineral concession in the Abbay valley,' said Helm. 'And you and your accomplices have begun mining operations in the area which belongs to this company.'

'There are no mining operations,' she protested.

'We have other information. We have evi-

756

dence that you have built a dam across the Dandera river —'

'That is nothing to do with me.'

'So you do not deny that there is a dam?'

'It is nothing to do with me,' she repeated. 'I am not a member of any terrorist group, and I have not taken part in any mining operations.'

They were both silent again. Nogo made an entry in the notebook in front of him. Helm stood up and sauntered across to the window behind her right shoulder. The silence drew out until she could bear it no longer. Even though she knew it was part of the campaign of nerves they were waging against her, she had to break it.

'I have travelled most of the night in an army truck,' she said. 'I am tired, and I need to go to a lavatory.'

'If what you need to do is urgent you can do it where you are standing. Neither Mr Helm nor I will be offended.' Nogo tittered in a surprisingly girlish manner, but did not look up from his book.

She looked over her shoulder at the door, but Helm crossed to it and turned the key in the lock, slipping the key into his pocket. She knew she must show no weakness in front of these two, and, though she was tired and afraid and her bladder ached, she feigned an air of confidence and assurance and crossed to the nearest chair. She pulled it from the table and sat down in it easily.

Nogo looked up at her and frowned. He had not expected her to react this way.

'You know the *shufta* bandit Mek Nimmur,' he accused abruptly.

'No,' she said coldly. 'I know the patriot and democratic leader Mek Nimmur. He is no *shufta*.'

'You are his concubine, his whore. Of course, you will say this.'

She looked away from him with disdain, and his voice rose shrilly. 'Where is Mek Nimmur? How many men does he have with him?' Her composure was beginning to rattle him.

She ignored the question, and Nogo scowled at her furiously. 'If you do not cooperate with us, I will have to use stronger methods to make you answer my questions,' he warned.

She turned in her chair and stared out of the window. In the long silence that followed, Jake Helm crossed the room and went to the door behind Nogo that led through to the rooms at the rear of the hut. He disappeared through it, and closed it behind him. The walls of the hut were thin, and Tessay made out the murmur of voices from the room beyond. The cadence and inflection were neither English nor Amharic. They were using a foreign language in there. She guessed that Helm was receiving instructions from a superior, who did not want her to be able to recognize him at some later date.

After a few minutes Helm re-emerged and closed the door behind him without locking it.

He nodded to Nogo, who at once stood up. They both came across to stand in front of Tessay.

'I think that it will be better for all of us if we finish this business as quickly as possible,' said Helm softly. 'Then you can go to the bathroom, and I can go to my breakfast.'

She raised her chin and stared at him defiantly, but did not answer him.

'Colonel Nogo has tried to be reasonable. He is bound by certain niceties of his official position. Fortunately I do not have the same restraints. I am going to ask you the same questions that he did, but this time you will answer them.'

He took the dead cheroot from his mouth and examined the tip. Then he threw the butt into a corner of the room and took a flat tin from his hip pocket. From it he selected a fresh cheroot, long and black, and lit it carefully, holding the match to it until it was drawing evenly. Then, amid a cloud of pungent tobacco smoke, he waved the match to extinction and asked,

'Where is Mek Nimmur?'

She shrugged and looked away, out of the side window of the hut.

Abruptly, without signalling the blow in any way, he hit her open-handed across her face. It was a savage blow, delivered with a force that snapped her head around. Then, before she could recover, he swung back again and slammed his knuckles across her jawline. Her head was thrown back violently in the opposite direction and she was knocked flying from her chair.

Nogo stooped over her and seized her arms, twisting them up behind her back. He lifted her back into the seat and stood behind her. He held her in such a surprisingly powerful grip that she could feel the skin of her upper arms bruising beneath his fingers.

'I have no more time to waste,' Helm said quietly, taking the burning cheroot from his lips to inspect the glowing tip. 'Let us start again. Where is Mek Nimmur?'

Tessay's left eardrum felt as if it had burst with the ferocity of those blows. Her hearing buzzed and sang. Her teeth had been driven halfway through the flesh of her cheek, and her mouth filled slowly with her own blood.

'Where is Mek Nimmur?' Helm repeated, leaning his face closer to hers. 'What are your friends doing with the dam in the Dandera river?'

She gathered the blood and saliva in her mouth, and suddenly and explosively spat it into his face.

He recoiled violently and wiped the bloody mess from his eyes with the palm of his hand.

'Hold her!' he said to Nogo, and seized the front of her blouse. With one heave he ripped it open down to her waist, and Nogo giggled and leaned forward over her shoulder to look at her breasts. He giggled again as Helm took one of them in his hand and squeezed out the nipple between his finger and thumb. It was the dark purple colour of a ripe mulberry.

He held her like that, pinching her flesh with his nails until the skin tore and a droplet of blood welled up and trickled over his thumb. Then with his other hand he took the burning cheroot from his lips and blew on the top until it glowed hotly.

'Where is Mek Nimmur?' he asked, and lowered the cheroot towards her breast. 'What are they doing in the Dandera river?'

She stared down in horror as he brought the burning cheroot closer, and tried to wriggle away from him. But Nogo held her firmly from behind. She screamed once, on an agonized drawn-out note, as the glowing coal touched the tip of her nipple and the delicate skin began to blister.

W inter,' said Royan, spreading the enlargement of the fourth face of the stele from Tanus's tomb under the bright glare of the floodlamp. 'This is the side that contains Taita's notations, which I am postulating are those of the bao board. I don't understand all of them, but by a process of elimination I have determined that the first symbol denotes one of the four sides, or as he terms them the castles of the board.'

She showed him the pages of her notebook on which she had made her calculations.

'See here, the seated baboon is the north castle, the bee is the south, the bird is the west and the scorpion the east.' She pointed out to him the same symbols on the photograph of the stele. 'Then the second and third figures are numbers — I believe that they designate the file and the cup. With these we can follow the moves of his imaginary red stones. The reds are the highest-ranking colours on the board.'

'What about the verses between each set of notations?' Nicholas asked. 'Such as this one here, about the north wind and the storm?'

'I am not sure about those. Probably merely smokescreens, if I know Taita. He is never one to make life too easy for us. Perhaps they do have significance, but we can only hope to un-ravel them as we work through the moves of our stones.'

Nicholas studied her figures a while, then grinned ruefully. 'Just think how remote was the possibility that anybody would ever be able to decipher the clues he left behind. The first requirement is that the searcher must have access to both chronicles, the seventh scroll and the stele of Tanus, before he had any chance of understanding the key to the tomb.'

She laughed — a throaty, well-satisfied sound. 'Yes, he must have believed that he was perfectly safe. Well, we will see now, Master Taita. We will see just how clever you really were.' Then, sober and businesslike once more, she looked up the stone staircase that led to Taita's maze.

'Now we have to see if my figures and theories fit into the hard stones and walls of Taita's architecture. But where do we start?'

'At the beginning,' Nicholas suggested, 'the god plays the first coup. That's what Taita told us. If we start here in the shrine of Osiris, at the foot of the staircase, then perhaps that will give us the alignment of his imaginary bao board.'

'I had the same idea,' she agreed immediately. 'Let's postulate that this is the north castle of Taita's board. Then we work the protocol of the four bulls from here.'

It was slow and painstaking work, trying to work their way into the mind of the ancient scribe by probing the labyrinth of passages and tunnels that he had built four thousand years previously. This time they moved into the maze with more circumspection. Nicholas had filled his pockets with lumps of dried white river clay, and he used these like a schoolmaster's stick of chalk to write on the stone walls at each branch and fork of the tunnels, setting out the notations from the winter face of the stele and marking a signpost to enable them not only to find their way through the maze but to relate it to the model that Royan was drawing up in her notebook.

They found that their first assumption that the shrine of Osiris was the north castle of the board seemed to be correct, and they happily believed that with this as the key it would be a simple matter to follow the moves of play to their conclusion. But these hopes were soon dashed as they realized that Taita was not thinking in the simple two dimensions of the conventional board. He had added the third dimension to the equation.

The stairway leading up from the shrine of Osiris was not the only link between the eight landings. Each of the passages leading off from it was subtly angled either upwards or downwards. As they followed the twists and turns of one of these tunnels they did not detect the fact that they were changing levels. Then suddenly they re-emerged on to the central staircase, but on a landing higher than the one they had entered from.

They stood there and stared at each other in horrified disbelief.

Royan spoke first. 'I didn't even have the feeling that we were ascending,' she whispered. 'The whole thing is infinitely more complex than I first assumed.'

'It must be constructed like one of those nuclear models of some complicated carbon atom,' Nicholas agreed with awe. 'It interlinks on all eight planes. Quite frankly, it's terrifying.'

'Now I have some inkling what those extraneous symbols signify,' Royan muttered. 'They set out the levels. We are going to have to rethink the entire concept.'

'Three-dimensional bao, played to enigmatic rules. What chance have we got against him?'

Nicholas shook his head ruefully. 'What we really need is a computer. Taita wasn't puffing his own virtues without good reason. The old hooligan really was a mathematical genius.' He shone the lamp back down the tunnel from which they had come. 'Even when you know it's there you cannot actually see the fall in the floor level. He designed and built it without even a slide rule or a spirit level in his back pocket. This maze is an extraordinary piece of engineering.'

'You can form your fan club later,' she suggested. 'But right now let's start grinding those numbers again.'

'I am going to move the lights and the desks up here, on to this central landing of the staircase.' Nicholas agreed, 'I think we should work from the centre of the board. It may help us to visualize it. Right now he has got me thoroughly confused.'

The only sound in the room was the soft sobbing of the woman who lay curled on the floor in a puddle of her own blood and urine.

Tuma Nogo sat at the long conference table and lit a cigarette. His hands trembled slightly, and he looked sickened. He was a soldier, and he had lived through the Mengistu terror. He was a hard man and accustomed to violence and cruelty, but he was shaken with what he had just witnessed. He knew now why von Schiller placed such reliance on Helm. The man was barely human.

Across the room Jake Helm was washing his hands in the small basin. He dried them fastidiously and then dabbed at the stains on his clothing with the towel as he came back and stood over Tessay.

'I don't think there is anything else she can tell us,' he said calmly. 'I don't think she held anything back.'

Nogo glanced down at the woman, and saw the livid burns that spotted her chest and her cheeks like the running ulcerations of some dreadful smallpox. Her eyes were closed, and her lashes were frizzled away. She had held out well. It was only when Helm had touched her eyelids with the burning cheroot that she had at last capitulated, and gabbled out the answers to his questions.

Nogo felt queasy, but he was relieved that it had not been necessary to hold her lids open, as Helm had ordered, and to watch as he quenched the flame of the cheroot against her weeping eyeballs.

'Watch her,' Helm ordered, as he rolled down his sleeves. 'She is a tough one. Don't take any chances with her.'

Helm walked past him, and went to the door in the far end of the hut. He left the door open, and Nogo could hear their voices, but they were speaking in German so he could not understand what they were saying. He understood now why von Schiller had chosen not to be present during the questioning. He obviously knew how Helm worked.

Helm came back into the room, and nodded at Nogo. 'Very well. We are finished with her. You know what to do.'

Nogo stood up nervously and placed his hand on the webbing holster at his side.

'Here?' he asked. 'Now?'

'Don't be a bloody fool,' Helm snapped. 'Take her away. Far away. Then get somebody in here to clean up this mess.' Helm turned on his heel and went back into the rear room.

Nogo roused himself and then went to the door of the hut. He walked wide of where Tessay lay, so as not to soil his canvas paratrooper boots.

'Lieutenant Hammed!' he called through the door.

Hammed and Nogo lifted Tessay to her feet. Neither of them spoke and they were subdued, almost chastened, as they helped her into her torn and bloodied clothing. Hammed averted his eyes from her naked body and the burns and other injuries that marred her glossy amber skin. He draped the *shamma* over her shoulders, and led her towards the door. When she stumbled he caught her before she fell and supported her with a hand under her elbow. He led her down the steps to the truck, and she moved slowly, like a very old woman. She sat in the passenger seat with her burned and swollen face in her cupped hands.

Nogo summoned Hammed with a jerk of his head, and led him aside. He spoke quietly to him, and Hammed's expression became stricken as he listened to his orders. At one point he started to protest, but Nogo snarled at him savagely and he chewed his lower lip in silence.

'Remember!' Nogo repeated. 'Well away from any of the villages. Make certain that there are no witnesses. Report back to me immediately.'

Hammed straightened his shoulders and saluted before he marched back to the truck and climbed up into the seat beside Tessay. He gave the driver a curt order and they drove out of the camp, following the track back towards Debra Maryam.

Tessay was so confused and in such pain that she had lost all sense of time. Only half-conscious, she lurched about in the seat when the truck hit a particularly rough stretch of the track, and her head rolled loosely on her shoulders. Her face was so swollen that it required an effort to force her eyelids apart, and when she did she thought that her vision was failing and that she was going blind. Then she realized that the sun had set and darkness had fallen. She must have spent the whole day in the hut with Helm.

She felt a mild lift of relief that the burns on her eyelids had not done more damage. At least she was still able to see. She peered out through the windscreen, and found that in the headlights the road was unfamiliar.

'Where are you taking me?' she mumbled. 'This is not the way back to the village.'

Lieutenant Hammed sat slumped beside her in the seat and would not answer. She relapsed into a daze of pain and exhaustion.

She was jerked awake when the truck braked abruptly and the driver switched off the ignition. Rude hands dragged her out of the cab and into the glare of the headlights. Her hands were jerked behind her back and her wrists were bound together with a raw-hide thong.

'You are hurting me,' she whimpered. 'You are cutting my wrists.' She had used up the last of her strength and courage. She felt beaten and pathetic, with no fight left in her.

One of the soldiers yanked on her bound wrists and shoved her off the road. Two others followed, each carrying trenching tools. There was enough of a moon for her to see a grove of eucalyptus trees about a hundred metres from the side of the road, and they led her there. They pushed her down at the base of one of the trees and the man who had tied her wrists stood over her, holding his rifle casually aimed down at her and smoking a cigarette with his free hand. The others stacked their rifles and began digging. They seemed to take no interest in her at all, but were discussing the All Africa Soccer Championships that were being held in Lusaka, and the Ethiopian team's chances of reaching the finals.

It was only after a while that it began to sink into Tessay's befuddled mind that they were digging a grave for her. The saliva in her injured mouth dried up and she looked around desperately for Lieutenant Hammed. But he had stayed with the truck.

'Please,' she whispered to her guard, but before she could say more he kicked her painfully in the belly.

'Keep quiet!' he used the derogatory term of address only applied to an animal or a person of the lowest order, and as she lay doubled up on the ground she realized the futility of appealing to them. A feeling of weakness and resignation overwhelmed her and she found herself weeping softly and hopelessly in the darkness.

When she looked up again through her swollen lids, there was sufficient moonlight for her to see that the grave was now so deep that the two men still digging in it were out of her line of sight. Spadefuls of dirt flew over the lip of the hole and splattered on to the growing pile. Her guard left her side for a moment and sauntered over to the edge of the hole. He looked down in it and then grunted.

'Good. That is deep enough. Call the lieutenant.'

The two soldiers scrambled up out of the grave, then gathered up their tools and weapons and traipsed off into the darkness of the grove. Chatting amicably amongst themselves they headed back towards where the truck was parked, leaving Tessay and her guard.

She lay there shivering with the cold and with terror, while her guard squatted at the lip of her grave and puffed on his cigarette. She thought that if she could get to her feet she could kick him into the hole and make a run for it, back through the trees. But when she tried to sit up her movements were stiff and slow, and she had no feeling in her hands or feet. She tried to force herself to move, but at that moment she heard Lieutenant Hammed coming from the truck and she slumped back in despair.

Hammed was carrying an electric torch. He flashed it down into the grave.

'Good,' he said loudly. 'That is deep enough.'

He switched off the torch and said to the man guarding her, 'No witnesses. Go back and wait at the truck. When you hear the shots, come back with the others to help me fill the hole.'

The guard slung his rifle over his shoulder and disappeared amongst the trees. Hammed waited until the man was well out of earshot, then he came to Tessay and hoisted her to her feet. He pushed her to the edge of the grave, and then she felt him fumbling with her clothing. She tried to lash out at him, but her arms were still bound behind her.

'I want your *shamma*.' He pulled the white woollen cloak off over her shoulders, and then went with it to the edge of the grave. He jumped down into the hole and she heard him scuffling about in the bottom.

His voice came back to her, speaking softly. 'They must see something here. A body —'

He climbed back beside her, puffing with the exertion, and stepped behind her. She felt the touch of cold metal on the inside of her wrists, and then he was sawing at the leather thong. She felt her bonds fall away, and she gasped at the pain as the blood poured back into her numb hands.

'What are you doing?' she whispered in confusion. She looked down into the grave and saw the pale *shamma* arranged to look like a human body. 'Are you going —'

'Please don't talk,' he instructed her softly, as he took her by the shoulder and led her back amongst the trees.

'Lie here.' He pushed her down and made her lie flat, with her face to the ground. He began piling dead leaves and fallen branches over her.

'Stay here! Do not try to run. Don't move or speak until we are gone.'

He flashed the torch briefly over the mound of dead branches to make certain she was covered, then he left her and hurried back to the graveside, unbuckling the flap of his pistol holster as he went. Two spaced pistol shots cracked out in the night, so loud and unexpectedly that she jumped and her heart raced wildly.

Then she heard Hammed shout, 'Come, you

men. Let's get this thing finished.'

They trooped back into the grove, and she heard the sound of their spades and the thump of earth clods falling into the grave.

'I cannot see what I am doing, lieutenant,' a voice complained. 'Where is your torchlight?'

'You don't need a light to fill a hole,' Hammed snarled. 'Get on with your work. Tramp that loose soil down. I don't want anybody stumbling on this place.'

She lay quietly, trying to stop the wild tremors that shook her body. At last the sound of the shovels let up, and she heard Hammed's voice again.

'That will do. Make certain you leave nothing here. Back to the truck!'

Their footsteps and their voices died away. At a distance she heard the truck engine whirl and fire. The headlights shone through the trees as the truck backed and filled, turning in the direction from which they had come.

Long after the sound of the engine had died away completely, she continued to lie under the pile of dead branches. She was still shaking with the cold and weeping softly and silently with exhaustion and pain and relief. Then slowly she pushed the branches off herself and crawled to the trunk of the nearest tree. She used it to pull herself up to her feet, and then stood there, swaying weakly in the darkness.

It was only then that guilt overwhelmed her. 'I have betrayed Mek,' she thought sickeningly.

'I have told everything to his enemies. I must warn him. I must get back to him and warn him.'

She pushed herself away from the treetrunk and blundered back through the darkness towards the track.

The only means of ascertaining if they had solved Taita's codes correctly was to play out the moves he had listed. They went very carefully through the tunnels of the maze, stepping out the moves that he had noted and marking them on the walls in white chalk figures.

There were eighteen moves set out on the winter face of the stele. Using Royan's first interpretation of the symbols, they were able to advance through twelve of these. Then they found themselves at a dead end, confronted by a blank stone wall and unable to make the next move.

'Damnation!' Nicholas kicked the wall, and when this had no effect he hurled the chunk of white chalk at it. 'I wish I could get my hands on that old devil. Castration would be the least of his worries.'

'Sorry.' Royan scraped the hair back out of her eyes. 'I thought I had it right. It must be the figures in the second column. We will have to invert them.'

'We will have to start again,' Nicholas groaned.

'Right at the very beginning,' she agreed.

'How do we know when we have finally got it right?' he wanted to know.

'If by following the clues we arrive at one of the winning combinations, a bao equivalent of checkmate, on precisely the eighteenth move. There will be no logical move after that, and we can assume we have worked through it correctly.'

'And what will we find if we ever reach that position?'

'I will tell you when we get there.' She smiled at him sweetly. 'Cheer up, Nicky. It's only just starting to hurt.'

Royan inverted the values of the second and third numbers of Taita's notations, taking the first as the cup value and the second as the file value. This time they completed only five moves before they were stymied and could proceed no further.

'Perhaps our assumption about the third symbol being the change of level is incorrect?' Nicholas suggested. 'Let's start again and give that the second value.'

'Nicky, do you realize just how many possible combinations there are, given the three variables?' She was at last starting to waver. 'Taita has assumed an intimate knowledge of the game. We have only the sketchiest notions of how it was played. It's like a grand master trying to explain to a novice the intricacies of the King's Indian Defence.'

'In Russian!' Nicholas embroidered the simile. 'At this rate we are getting nowhere in a hurry. There must be some other way of approaching it. Let's go over the epigrams Taita stuck in between the notations again.'

'All right. I'll read and you listen.' She hunched over her notes. 'The trouble is that a subtle variation of the translation might change the sense. Taita loved puns, and a pun can rely on a single word for effect. One wrong twist or slant to a word and we have lost it.'

'Try anyway,' Nicholas encouraged her. 'Remember that even Taita had never played bao in three dimensions before. If he left a clue it would have to be at the very beginning of the stele. Concentrate on the first couple of notations and the epigrams that separate them.'

'We'll try it that way,' Royan agreed. 'The first notation is the bee followed by the numbers five and seven and the sistrum.'

Nicholas grinned. 'Okay, I have heard that so often already that I will never forget it. What follows?'

'The first quotation.' She ran her finger over the hieroglyphics. ' "*What can be given a name can be known. What is nameless can only be felt. I sail with the tide behind me and the wind in my face. O, my beloved, the taste of you is sweet upon my lips.*" '

'Is that all?' he asked.

'Yes, then the next notation. The scorpion and the number two and three and the sistrum again.'

'Slowly! Slowly! First things first. What can we make out of the *"sailing"* and the *"beloved"*?'

So they riddled and wrestled with the text of the stele, until their eyes burned and they had lost track of day or night. They were eventually recalled to reality by Sapper's voice echoing up the staircase. Nicholas stood up from the desk and stretched before he looked at his watch.

'Eight o'clock. But I'm not sure if that is morning or evening.'

Then he started as Sapper came up the staircase, and saw that his bald head was shining with moisture and his shirt was soaked.

'What happened to you?' Nicholas demanded. 'Did you fall into the sink-hole?'

Sapper wiped his face with the palm of his hand. 'Didn't anybody tell you? It's pissing with rain outside.'

They both stared at him in horror.

'So soon?' Royan whispered. 'It wasn't supposed to start for weeks yet.'

Sapper shrugged. 'Somebody forgot to tell the weatherman.'

'Has it set in?' Nicholas asked. 'What's the state of the river? Has the level started to rise yet?'

'That's what I came to tell you. I am going up to the dam, taking the Buffaloes with me.

I want to keep an eye on it. As soon as it gets unsafe I will send a runner down to you. When I do that, don't stop to argue. Get out of here fast. It will mean that I expect the dam to burst at any moment.'

'Don't take Hansith with you,' Nicholas ordered. 'I need him here.'

When Sapper had gone, taking most of the workers from the tunnel with him, Royan and Nicholas looked at each other seriously.

'We are running out of time fast, and Taita still has us in a tangle,' Nicholas said. 'One thing I must warn you. When the river starts to rise —'

She did not let him finish. 'The river!' she cried. 'Not the sea! I was mistaken in the translation. I read it as *"tide"*. I assumed Taita was referring to the sea, but it should have been *"current"*. The Egyptians made no distinction between the two words.'

They both rushed back to the desk and her notebooks. ' *"The current behind me and the wind in my face"*,' Nicholas changed the quotation.

'On the Nile,' Royan exulted, 'the prevailing wind is always from the north, and the current always from the south. Taita was facing north. The north castle.'

'We assumed the symbol for the north was the baboon,' he reminded her.

'No! I was wrong.' Her face was alight with the fires of inspiration. ' *"O, my beloved, the taste of you is sweet upon my lips."* Honey! The bee! I had the symbols for the north and south inverted.'

'What about east and west? What can we find there?' He turned back to the texts with fresh enthusiasm. ' "*My sins are red as carnelians. They bind me like chains of bronze. They prick my heart with fire, and I turn my eyes towards the evening star.*" '

'I don't see —'

' "*Prick*" is the wrong translation,' he stuttered eagerly. 'It should be "*sting*". The scorpion looking towards the evening star. The evening star is always in the west. The scorpion is the western castle, not the eastern castle.'

'We had the board inverted.' She jumped up excitedly. 'Let's play it that way!'

'We still have not determined the levels,' he objected. 'Is the sistrum the upper level, or is it the three swords?'

'Now that we have made this breakthrough, that is the only variable. We are either right or wrong. We will play the sistrum first as the upper level, and if that doesn't work we can play it the other way round.'

It was so much easier now. The intricacies of the maze had become less forbidding with familiarity. There were the large white chalk signs in Nicholas's handwriting on each corner and at each fork and T-junction of the tunnels. They moved swiftly through the complex twists and turns, their excitement rising sharply as they followed each notation and found the way still clear before them.

'The eighteenth move.' Royan's voice trembled. 'Hold both thumbs. If it takes us into one of the open files that threaten the opponent's south castle, then that will be the check coup.' She drew a deep breath and read it aloud to him. 'The bird. The numbers three and five. With the lower level symbol of the three swords.'

They paced it out and passed the five junctions into the lowest level of the maze, reading their position from the chalk marks on the stone blocks of the walls at each fork.

'This is it!' Nicholas told her, and they stood together and looked about them.

'There is nothing outstanding about this spot.' Disappointment was bitter in Royan's tone. 'We have passed over it fifty times before. It is just like any of the other turns.'

'That is exactly what Taita would have wanted. Hell! He wouldn't have put up a signpost saying "X marks the spot", would he now?'

'So what do we do?' She looked at him, for once at a loss.

'Read the last epigram from the stele.'

She had her notebook in her hand. ' "*From the black and holy earth of this very Egypt the harvest is abundant. I whip the flanks of my donkey, and the wooden spike of the plough breaks new ground. I plant the seed, and reap the grape and the ears of corn. In time I drink the wine and eat the loaf. I follow the rhythm of the seasons, and tend the earth." '*

She looked up at him. 'The rhythm of the seasons? Is he referring us to the four faces of the stele? The earth?' she asked and looked down at the slabs beneath their feet. 'The promise of reward from the earth? Under our feet, perhaps?' she asked.

He stamped his foot on the slabs, but the sound was dull and solid. 'Only one way to find out.' He raised his voice and it echoed weirdly through the labyrinth. 'Hansith! Come down here!'

Sapper sat on the high seat of his yellow front-end loader in the rain and cheerfully cursed his gang of Buffaloes, secure in the knowledge that they understood not a word of his insults. The rain swept over them in intermittent gusts off the high mountains. It was not yet the solid, drenching downpour of the true wet season. However, the river was rising sullenly, turning dirty blue-grey with the mud and sediment that it was bringing down.

He knew that the flood had not yet begun in earnest. The thunder that growled ominously along the mountain peaks like a pride of hunting lions was only the prelude to the vast celestial onslaught which would soon follow. Although the river was lapping the top course of gabions of Sapper's dam, and was roaring through the bypass that he had cut into the side valley, he was still holding it at bay.

His Buffaloes were packing more baskets with aggregate, using up the last of the steel mesh from the stores in the quarry. As soon as each of these was filled and wired closed, Sapper picked it up in the front bucket of the tractor and drove it down the bank of the Dandera. He reinforced all the weak spots in the dam wall, and then he began raising it another course. Sapper was fully aware of the overturning effect that the river would exert once it began to pour over the top of the wall. Nothing would be able to withstand its power once this happened. It would carry away a rock-filled gabion as if it were the branch of a baobab tree. It needed only a single breach in the wall to bring the entire structure tumbling and rolling down. He had no illusions as to just how swiftly the river could do its fatal work.

He knew that he dared not wait for the first breach to develop in the wall before he warned Nicholas and Royan in the chasm downstream. The river could easily outrun any messenger he sent, and once the wall began to go it would already be too late. It would be a matter of fine judgement, and he slitted his eyes against another gust of slanting rain that blew into his face. His instinct was to call them out of the chasm now — there was already less than twelve inches of free-board at the top of the wall.

However, he knew that Nicholas would be

furious if he was made to evacuate the workings prematurely, and in so doing aborted all their efforts. Sapper was fully aware of the extreme risks that Nicholas had taken and of the crippling expenditure he had made to reach this stage. Before they had left England, he had hinted to Sapper of the straitened circumstances in which he found himself. Although Sapper did not understand the intricacies or the responsibilities of being a 'Name' at Lloyd's, there had been so much publicity in the British press that he could not but realize that, if their venture here failed, the next stop for Nicholas would be the bankruptcy courts — and Nicholas was his friend.

The squall of rain blew over, and a bright hot sun burst through the low cloud banks. The flow of the river seemed undiminished, but at least the water level on the dam wall was no longer rising.

'I'll give it another hour,' he grunted, engaging the gears of the tractor and easing her down the bank to place another gabion in position.

Nicholas worked shoulder to shoulder with Hansith's gang as they began to strip the paving slabs from the floor of the lowest level of the maze. The joints between the slabs were so tight that, even using crowbars, they had difficulty prising them apart. In order to save time, Nicholas made the hard choice of going into a destructive search. He put four of the strongest men in the team to work with home-made sledgehammers, lumps of ironstone on wooden shafts, to break up the slabs so that they could be more readily levered out of the floor. He felt guilty about the damage they were causing to the site, but the work went ahead very much faster.

The high spirits and enthusiasm of the men were at last beginning to wane. They had worked too long in the oppressive confines of the maze, and every one of them was fully aware of the rising level of the river at the head of the gorge, and of the mortal threat behind those waters. Their expressions were surly and there was little laughter or banter. But more worrying for Nicholas was the fact that at the beginning of this shift Hansith had reported the first desertions. Sixteen of his men had failed to report for duty. They had quietly rolled their blankets during the night, picked up whatever items of value or utility they found lying around the camp, and crept away into the darkness.

Nicholas knew that it was no use sending any-one after them — they had too much of a start, and would be halfway up the escarpment al-ready. This was Africa, and Nicholas was certain that now that the rot had started it would spread very quickly.

He joked and jollied them along, not allowing

them to sense his true feelings. He worked shoulder to shoulder and sweated along with them in the excavation in an attempt to hold them. But he knew that, unless they made another discovery under these slabs to keep their interest and expectations alight, he might wake up tomorrow to find that even the monks and the faithful Hansith were gone.

He had started lifting the slabs in the angle of the corner of the maze, and they worked out from there in both directions down the arms of the tunnel. His heart sank as they broke up each paving slab with the hammers only to find beneath it the solid stratum of the country rock with no indication of any joint or opening.

'It doesn't look very hopeful,' he muttered to Royan as he took a short break to drink from one of the water flasks.

She too was looking unhappy as she poured water from the flask into his cupped hands, so that he could wash the sweat and grime from his face.

'I may have got the symbols for the levels wrong,' she suggested. 'It is just the kind of trick Taita would play, to work out combinations which would both give a logical solution.' She hesitated before she appealed to him for guidance. 'Do you think I should start working back the other combination —'

Her question was interrupted by a bellow from Hansith. 'In the name of the Blessed Virgin, *effendi*, come quickly!'

They spun around together. In her haste Royan dropped the flask, which shattered at her feet. She did not seem to notice that it had drenched her legs, but ran back to where Hansith was standing with the hammer poised for another stroke.

'What is it —' she broke off as they both saw that beneath the paving slabs Hansith had uncovered another layer of dressed stone sills.

These were laid neatly across the floor of the tunnel from wall to wall, recessed into the surrounding rock, with knife-edge joints between them. Their sides were smooth and plain, without engravings or markings upon them.

'What is it, Nicky?' Royan demanded.

'Either it's another layer of paving, or it's a cover over an opening in the floor,' he told her eagerly. 'We won't know until we lift one of them.'

The stone sills were too thick and heavy to be cracked with the primitive hammers, although Hansith tried his best. In the end they were forced to dig around the first of them and lever it free. It took five men to raise the end of it and lift it off its foundation.

'There is an opening under it.' Royan went down on her knees to peer into the space that it had left. 'Some kind of open shaft!'

Once the first sill was removed it was easier to get a purchase on the others that blocked the rectangular opening. When they had cleared them all away, Nicholas shone the lamp down into the dark shaft that was revealed. It stretched from wall to wall of the tunnel, and the head room was sufficient for even Nicholas to stand up to his full height on the steps that led down at a forty-five degree angle.

'Another stairway,' he exulted. 'Surely this must be it. Even Taita must have exhausted all the false leads by now.'

The workmen were crowding up behind them, their sullen mood evaporating at this fresh discovery and the certainty of additional bonuses in silver dollars that they had earned.

'Are we going down?' Royan asked. 'I know we should be careful and check it for traps, but we are running out of time, Nicky.'

'You are right, as always. The time has come when we have to press on regardless.'

'Caution thrown to the winds.' She took his hand, laughing. 'Let's go down together.'

They descended side by side, one cautious step at a time, with the lamp held head high and the shadows retreating before them.

'There is a chamber at the bottom,' Royan exclaimed.

'Looks like a store room — what are all those objects stacked along the walls? There must be hundreds of them. Are they coffins, sarcophaguses?' The dark shapes were almost human, standing shoulder to shoulder, rank after rank, around the walls of the square chamber.

'No, I think those are corn baskets on one side,' she said, recognizing them. 'Those on the other side look like wine amphorae. Probably some sort of offering to the dead.'

'If this is one of the funeral store rooms,' said Nicholas in a voice tight with excitement, 'then we are getting very close to the tomb now.'

'Yes!' she cried. 'Look — there is another doorway on the far side of this store room. Shine the light over there.'

The beam picked out the square opening facing them across this lower chamber. It was inviting, beckoning them almost seductively. They almost ran down the last few steps into the chamber lined with the reed baskets and pottery wine jars. But as they reached the level floor of the store room they ran into an invisible barrier that stopped both of them dead and sent them reeling backwards.

'God!' Nicholas clutched at his throat, his voice a strangled choke. 'Get back. Got to get back.'

Royan was sinking to her knees, also gasping and hunting for breath.

'Nicky!' she tried to scream, but her breath was trapped in her lungs. She felt that a steel noose had encircled her chest and, as it tightened, the breath was being forced out of her.

'Nicky! Help me!' She was strangling, like a fish thrown up on the bank. The strength drained from her limbs, and her vision began to break up and fade. She did not have the strength to stand.

He stooped over her and tried to lift her, but he was almost as weak. He felt his own legs buckling, no longer able to support even his own weight.

'Four minutes,' he thought desperately as he suffocated. 'That's all we have got. Four minutes to brain death and oblivion. We have to get air.'

From behind her, he slipped his arms under her armpits and locked his hands together over her breasts. Again he tried to lift her, but his strength was gone. He began to walk backwards towards the stairs down which they had run so lightly, and every pace required a huge effort. She was already unconscious, lying inert in the circle of his arms. Her limp legs trailed across the stone floor as he dragged her back.

The lowest step caught his heels and he almost toppled over backwards. With an effort he regained his balance and lugged her back up the steps, her feet sliding and bumping loosely over the treads. He wanted to shout to Hansith for help, but he did not have the air in his lungs to utter a sound.

'If you drop her now, she's dead,' he told himself, and he struggled up another five steps, his lungs hunting for precious air and finding none. His strength oozed out of him a drop at a time as his vision slid and wobbled and distorted.

'Let me breathe,' he pleaded. 'Please God, let me breathe.'

Miraculously, like a direct answer to his prayer, he felt the precious oxygen slide down his panting throat and swell his lungs. At once his strength began flooding back and he tightened his grip around Royan's chest and lifted her bodily. He staggered up the remaining steps with her body in his arms and sprawled out of the mouth of the shaft on to the slabs of the tunnel at Hansith's feet.

'What is is, *effendi?* What has happened to you and the lady?'

Nicholas had no breath to answer him. He laid Royan in the position for mouth-to-mouth resuscitation, and slapped her cheeks.

'Come on!' he pleaded with her. 'Speak! Talk to me!'

There was no response, so he knelt over her, covered her open mouth with his own and blew down her throat, until from the corner of his eye he saw her chest swelling and inflating.

He sat back for a count of three. 'Please, my darling, please breathe!' There was no colour in her yellow, corpse-like face.

He bent over her and covered her mouth again, and as he filled her lungs with his own breath he felt her stir under him.

'That's it, my darling,' he told her. 'Breathe! Breathe for me.'

At the next breath she pushed him away and sat up groggily, staring round at the circle of faces that hovered over her anxiously. She picked out Nicholas's pale face amongst the black faces of the men.

'Nicky! What happened?'

'I am not sure — but whatever it was, it almost got both of us. How are you feeling now?'

'It was as though an invisible hand had me by the throat, and was strangling me. I couldn't breathe, and then I passed out.'

'It must be some kind of gas filling the lower levels of the passage. You were only out for less than two minutes,' he reassured her. 'It takes four minutes of oxygen starvation to kill the brain.'

'I have a terrible headache.' She pressed her fingers to her temples. 'I heard your voice calling me back. You called me "my darling".' She dropped her eyes.

'Just a little slip of the tongue.' He lifted her to her feet and for a moment she swayed against him, her breasts soft and warm against his chest.

'Thank you once again, Nicky. I am so deeply in your debt already, I will never be able to repay you.'

'I am sure we will be able to work something out.'

She was suddenly aware of the men's eyes watching her and drew away from him. 'What kind of gas? And how did it get there? Was it another of Taita's tricks, do you think, Nicky?'

'One of the gases of decay, most probably,' was his opinion. 'Because it is trapped in the lower part of the passage, it must be a heavier-than-air type. I would guess that it is probably carbon dioxide, although it could be something like methane. I think methane is heavier than air, isn't it?'

'Did Taita do it deliberately?' The colour was returning to her cheeks, and she was recovering swiftly.

'I don't know, but those baskets and jars are suspicious. I will be able to answer that question when we have had a chance to examine their contents.' He touched her cheek tenderly. 'How are you feeling? How is your headache?'

'Better. What do we do now?'

'Clear the gas from the chamber,' he told her, 'and as soon as possible.'

He used a candle from his emergency pack to test for the gas level in the shaft. With it burning in his right hand he went back down the steps, holding it low to the floor, descending a step at a time. The candle flame burned brightly, dancing to the movement of air as he went down. Then, abruptly on the sixth step above the floor level of the chamber, the flame turned yellow and snuffed out.

He marked the level on the wall in white chalk, and called up to Royan at the head of the shaft, 'Well, at least it's not methane. I am still here. Must be carbon dioxide.'

'Pretty conclusive test,' she laughed. 'If it goes boom, it's methane.'

'Hansith, bring down the blower fan,' Nicholas shouted to the big monk.

Holding his breath as though he were

snorkelling under water, Nicholas carried the fan down the lower steps and set it up on the floor of the chamber. He set the fan speed at 'High' and immediately retreated up the shaft, drawing a huge breath as soon as he was above the chalk mark on the wall.

'How long will it take to clear the gas?' Royan asked anxiously, looking at her wrist-watch.

'I will test with the candle every fifteen minutes.'

It was an hour before the gas had dispersed enough to enable him to reach the floor of the chamber again, and breathe the air down there. Then Nicholas ordered Hansith to bring down a bundle of firewood and build a fire in the centre of the stone floor, to heat and circulate the air more rapidly.

While he was doing this, Nicholas and Royan examined one of the baskets that stood against the wall.

'The crafty old ruffian!' Nicholas muttered half in exasperation and half in admiration. 'It looks like a mixture of manure and grass and dead leaves, the same as a compost heap.'

They crossed the chamber, turned one of the pottery jars on its side, and studied the powder that spilled out of it. Nicholas took up a handful and rubbed it between his fingers, then sniffed it warily.

'Crushed limestone!' he muttered. 'Although it has long ago dried out and lost any odour, Taita probably soaked it with some form of acid.

Vinegar, perhaps, or even urine would have done the trick. As it broke down the limestone, it formed carbon dioxide.'

'So it was another deliberate trap,' Royan exclaimed.

'Even so many thousands of years ago, Taita must have understood the processes of decay. He knew what gases those mixtures would produce. Amongst all the other accomplishments he boasts of, he must also have been a nifty chemist.'

'Furthermore, he must have known that without a draught or any movement of air, these heavy inert gases would hang here in the bottom of the chamber indefinitely,' she agreed. 'I expect that this shaft is designed like a U-trap. I bet that the passage rises again —' she pointed at the mysterious doorway in the far wall, 'in fact I can see the first steps even from here.'

'We will soon find out if you are right,' he told her, 'because that's exactly where we are heading right now — up those steps.'

Sapper had placed cairns of stones at the water's edge to monitor the river level. He watched them the way a stockbroker watches his ticker tape.

It had been six hours since the last rain squall had passed. The clouds over the valley had burned away in the hot, bright sunlight, although they still hung densely over the northern horizon. Their great dun-coloured thunderheads reared to the heavens, menacing and ominous, forming their own mighty ranges that dwarfed the mountains beneath them. At any time the downpour might begin up there in the highlands. Once that happened, Sapper wondered how long it would take the flood waters to reach them here in the Abbay gorge.

He dismounted stiffly from the tractor, and went down the bank to inspect his stone markers. The water level had fallen almost a foot in the past hour. He forced himself not to let his optimism bubble over — after all, it had taken only fifteen minutes for the river to rise the same amount. The final outcome was inevitable. The rains would come. The river would spate. The dam would burst. He looked downstream at the dam wall, and shook his head with resignation.

He had done as much as possible to delay that moment. He had raised the level of the dam wall almost four feet, and packed in another buttress behind the wall to strengthen it. There was nothing further for him to do, and he could only wait.

Climbing up the bank, he leaned wearily against the yellow steel of his machine and looked across at his team of Buffaloes, strewn along the bank like casualties on a battlefield. They had worked for two days to hold back the waters, and now they were exhausted. He knew that he could not call on them for another effort; the next time the river attacked, it would overwhelm them.

He saw some of the men stir and sit up, and their faces turned upstream. He heard their voices faint on the wind. Something was exciting their interest. He climbed up on to the tractor and shaded his eyes. The unmistakable figure of Mek Nimmur was coming down the trail from the direction of the escarpment, stocky and powerful in his camo fatigues, his gait determined. He was accompanied by two of his company commanders.

Mek hailed Sapper from a distance. 'How is your dam holding?' he called in Arabic, which Sapper did not understand. 'Soon it will rain on the mountains. You won't be able to hold out here much longer.' But his gestures towards sky and river were immediately intelligible to Sapper.

Sapper jumped down from the machine to greet him, and they shook hands cordially. They had recognized in each other the qualities of strength and professionalism that they both admired.

Mek seized his company commander, who spoke English, by the arm, and the man fell into his by now familiar role of interpreter.

'It is not only the weather that troubles me,' Mek confided in a low voice, and the interpreter relayed the information to Sapper. 'I have reports that the government troops are moving into position to attack us. My intelligence is that they have a full battalion moving down this way from Debra Maryam, and another force below the monastery at St Frumentius, moving up the Abbay river.'

'Pincer movement, hey?' said Sapper.

Mek listened to the translation and nodded gravely. 'I am heavily outnumbered and I don't know how long I will be able to hold them when they attack. My men are guerrillas. It is not our role to fight set-piece battles. It is the war of the flea for us. Hit and run. I came to warn you to be ready to pull out at short notice.'

'Don't worry too much about me,' Sapper grunted. 'I am a sprinter. Hundred yards dash is my speciality. It's Nicholas and Royan you should be thinking of, them in that ruddy rabbit warren of theirs.'

'I am on my way to them now, but I wanted to arrange a fall-back position. If we get cut off from each other in the fighting, Nicholas has cached the boats at the monastery. That is where we will assemble.'

'Okay, Mek —' Sapper stopped speaking and all three of them looked up the trail, where there was a fresh disturbance amongst the men along the bank. 'What's going on?'

'One of my patrols coming in,' Mek narrowed his eyes. 'There must be some new development.' He stopped speaking as he realized that Sapper could not understand him, and then his expression changed as he recognized the small, slim figure that was being carried on a rough litter by the men of his patrol.

Tessay saw him running towards her and sat up weakly on the litter. The men lowered her to the ground and Mek went down on his knees beside the litter and placed both his arms around her. They held each other in silence for a long moment. Then Mek gently cupped her face in his hands and examined her swollen and scarred features. Some of the burns had become infected, and her eyes were slits beneath the bloated lids.

'Who did this to you?' he asked softly.

She mumbled incoherently through her black-scabbed lips. 'They made me —'

'No! Don't try to talk.' He changed his mind as her lower lip cracked open and a droplet of fresh blood welled up and glistened like a ruby on her skin.

'I have to tell you,' she insisted in a broken whisper. 'They made me tell them everything. The numbers of your men. What you and Nicholas are doing here. Everything. I am sorry, Mek. I betrayed you.'

'Who was it? Who did this to you?'

'Nogo and the American, Helm,' she said, and although he embraced her as gently as a father with his infant in his arms, his eyes were terrible.

The lower chamber of the tunnel was cleared of gas at last. Hansith's fire burned bright and steady in the middle of the floor, the rising hot air wafting away the noxious vapours and dispersing them through the upper levels of the maze, where they mingled with the cleaner oxygen-rich air and lost their toxicity. By this time Royan had fully recovered from the physical effects of the gassing, but her confidence was shaken, and she allowed Nicholas to lead the way up the steps that rose from the far side of the chamber.

'It's the perfect gas trap,' Nicholas pointed out to her as they climbed cautiously. 'No doubt at all that Taita knew exactly what he was doing when he built this section of the tunnel.'

'Surely he must have expected any interloper of his period to have either succumbed to his hellish devices, lost his way in the maze, or given up and turned back by now,' she reasoned.

'Are you trying to convince me that this was Taita's last line of defence, and that he has no more tricks in store for us? Is that it?' Nicholas asked as he took another step upwards.

'No. Actually I was trying to convince myself, and not having much success. I just don't trust him one little bit any more. I have come to expect the worst from him. I expect the roof to collapse on me at any moment, or the floor to open and drop us into a fiery furnace or something worse.'

They had descended forty steps down into the chamber, and the staircase they were now climbing was a mirror image of that. It rose at the same angle and the tread of each step was the same depth and width. As their heads rose above the fortieth step, Nicholas played the beam of the lamp down the spacious, level arcade that opened before them, and they were dazzled by a riot of colour and pattern, bright and lovely as a field of desert blooms after rain. The paintings covered the walls and ceiling of the arcade, stunning in their profusion, wondrous in their execution.

'Taita!' Royan cried in a voice that quivered and broke. 'These are his paintings. There is no other artist like him, I could never mistake it. I would know his work anywhere.'

They stood on the top step and gazed around in wonder. When compared to these, the murals in the long gallery seemed pale and stilted, the tawdry sham that they really were. This was the work of a great master, a timeless genius, whose art could enchant and enrapture now just as readily as it had four thousand years ago.

They moved forward slowly, almost involuntarily, down the arcade. It was lined on each side with small chambers, like the stalls in an oriental bazaar. The entrance to each was guarded by tall columns that reached up to the roof. Each column was a carved statue of one member of the pantheon of gods. Between them they held the high-vaulted ceiling suspended.

As they drew level with the first two stalls, Nicholas stopped and squeezed her arm.

'The treasure chambers of Pharaoh,' he whispered.

The stalls were packed from floor to ceiling with wonderful and beautiful things.

'The furniture store.' Royan's voice was as reverential as his as she recognized the shapes of chairs and stools and beds and divans. She went to the nearest chamber and touched a royal throne. The arms were twining serpents of bronze and lapis lazuli. The legs were those of lions with claws of gold. The seat and back were chased with scenes of the hunt, and wings of gold surmounted the high back.

Stacked behind the throne was a great profusion of other furniture. They recognized a screened divan, its sides enclosed in an exquisite lacework of ebony and ivory. But there were dozens of other items besides, most of them broken down into their separate parts so that it was not possible to guess what they were. They gleamed with precious metals and coloured stones in such confusion and variety that it was too much to take in in a single glance. Both the alcoves on either side of the arcade were stuffed with these marvellous collections. Royan shook her head in wonder, and Nicholas led her on. The walls that separated the alcoves were decorated with panels illustrating the *Book of the Dead*, and the journey of Pharaoh through the pylons, the dangers and the trials, the demons and the monsters that awaited him along the way.

'These are the paintings that were missing from the mock tomb in the long gallery,' Royan told him. 'But just look upon the face of the king. You can see he was a real person. Those are perfect royal portraits.'

The mural beside them depicted the great god Osiris leading Pharaoh by the hand, protecting him from the monsters that crowded close on either hand, waiting their chance to devour him. It showed the face of the king as he must truly have been, a man with a kind and gentle, if rather weak, face.

'Look at the figures,' Nicholas agreed. 'They are not stiff wooden dolls always stepping forward with the right foot. These are real men and women. They are anatomically correct. The artist understood perspective and had studied the human body.'

They came to the next pair of alcoves, and paused to peer into them.

'Weapons,' said Nicholas. 'Just look at that chariot!'

The panels of the chariot were covered with a skin of gold leaf, so that it dazzled the eye. The harness and traces seemed only to await the horses that would draw it into battle, and the quivers strapped to the side panels behind each tall wheel bulged with arrows and javelins.

The cartouche of Mamose was emblazoned on the side panels.

Piled beside this magnificent vehicle were war bows whose stocks were bound with wire of electrum and bronze and gold. There were arrays of daggers with ivory handles and swords with blades of glistening bronze. There were racks of spears and pikes. There were shields of bronze, the targets decorated with scenes of war and the name of the divine Mamose. There were helmets and breastplates made from the skin of the crocodile, and the uniforms and regalia of the famous regiments of Egypt dressed the life-sized wooden statues of the king that stood in rows against the walls of the alcoves.

They walked on down the aisle, between more paintings and murals depicting the life and the death of the king. They saw him playing with his daughters and dandling his infant son. They saw him fishing and hunting and hawking, in council with his ministers and his nomarches, dallying with his wives and concubines, and feasting with the priests of the temple.

'What a chronicle of life in ancient times,' Royan breathed with awe. 'There has never been a discovery remotely like this before.'

Each of the persons in the panels had obviously been drawn from life. They were real breathing living men and women, every face and every expression different, captured with the keen eye, the humour and the great humanity of the artist.

'That must be Taita himself.' Royan pointed out the self-portrait of the eunuch in one of the central panels. 'I wonder if he took poetic licence, or was he truly so noble and beautiful?'

They paused to admire the face of Taita, their adversary, and looked into his searching, intelligent eyes. Such was the skill of the artist that he watched them as keenly as they studied him. A small, enigmatic smile played on Taita's lips. The painting had been varnished, so that it was perfectly preserved, as if it had been painted the day before. Taita's lips seemed moist and his eyes gleamed softly with life.

'His complexion is fair and his eyes are blue!' Royan exclaimed. 'Although that red hair is almost certainly dyed with henna.'

'It is weird to think that, although he lived so long ago, he almost succeeded in killing us,' Nicholas said softly.

'In what land was he born? He never tells us that in the scrolls. Was it Greece or Italy? Was he from one of the Germanic tribes, or was he of Viking stock? We will never know, for he himself probably did not know his own origins.'

'There he is again in the next panel.' Nicholas pointed down the arcade to where the unmistakable face of the eunuch appeared in the throng that knelt in homage before the throne on which sat Pharaoh and his queen. 'Like Hitchcock, he seems to like to appear in his own creations.'

They went on past the treasure stalls in which

were stored plates and goblets and bowls of alabaster and bronze chased with silver and gold, polished bronze mirrors and rolls of precious silk and linen and woollen cloth that had long ago rotted to shaggy black amorphous heaps. On the walls that divided these from the next set of stalls they saw re-enacted the battle with the Hyksos in which Pharaoh had been struck down, the arrow shot by the Hyksos king lodged in his breast. Then in the next panel Taita, the surgeon, bent over him with the surgical instruments in his hands, removing the blood-smeared barb from deep in his flesh.

Now they came to alcoves in which were stacked hundreds of cedarwood chests. The boxes were painted with the royal cartouche of Mamose, and with scenes of the king at his toilet: lining his eyes with kohl, painting his face with white antimony and scarlet rouge, being shaved by his barbers and dressed by his valets.

'Some of those chests will contain the royal cosmetics,' Royan murmured, 'and some of them will be Pharaoh's wardrobes of clothing. There will be costumes in them for every occasion in his after-life. I long to be able to unpack and examine them.'

The next set of wall panels showed the marriage of the king to the young virgin, Taita's mistress. The face of Queen Lostris was rendered with loving detail. The artist gloated on her beauty and exaggerated it, his brush strokes caressing her naked breasts and lingering on all

her virtues until they epitomized feminine perfection.

'How much Taita loved her,' Royan murmured, and there was envy in her voice. 'You
can see it in every line he drew.'

Nicholas smiled softly and put his arms around
her shoulders.

There were hundreds more wooden chests
stacked in the next alcoves. Painted on the lids
were miniatures of the king decked in all his
jewellery: his fingers and toes were thick with
rings and his chest was covered with pectoral
medallions, while bangles of gold adorned his
arms and bracelets his wrists. In one portrait
he wore the double crown of the two kingdoms
of Egypt united, the red crown and the white
with the heads of the vulture and the cobra
on his brow. In another he wore the blue war
crown, and on a third the Nemes crown with
gold and lapis wings that covered his ears.

'If each of those chests contains the treasures
depicted on its lid —' Nicholas broke off, unable
to continue the thought. The possibility of such
riches was daunting, and the imagination balked
at the magnitude of it.

'Do you remember what Taita wrote in the
scrolls? *"I cannot believe that such a treasure was
ever before accumulated in one place at one time"*?'
Royan asked him. 'It seems that it is all still
here, every single gem and grain of gold. The
treasure of Mamose is intact.'

Beyond the treasury there was another alcove

lined with shelves on which stood the *ushabti* figures: dolls made of green glazed porcelain or carved from cedarwood. They were an army of tiny figures, men and women from all the trades and professions. There were priests and scribes and lawyers and physicians, gardeners and farmers, bakers and brewers, handmaidens and dancing girls, seamstresses and laundry-maids, soldiers and barbers, and common labourers. Each of them carried the tools and accoutrements of his or her trade. They would accompany the king to the after-world and there would work for Pharaoh, and would go forward in his place if he were ever called upon to perform a service for the other gods.

At last Nicholas and Royan came to the end of this fabulous arcade, and found their way closed off by a series of tall, free-standing screens, tabernacles that had been once fine white linen mesh but were now decayed and rotted into ribbons and streamers, dirty and shabby as old cobwebs. And yet the stars and rosettes of shining gold that decorated these curtains were still hanging in the mesh like fish in a fisherman's net. Through this ethereal web of silken wisps and golden stars they could make out the shape of another gateway beyond.

'That must be the entrance to the actual tomb,' Royan whispered. 'There is only a thin veil between us and the king now.'

They hesitated at the threshold, gripped by a strange reluctance to take the final step.

As an old warrior, Mek Nimmur had seen and treated most of the injuries that a man might sustain on the battlefield. His little guerrilla group did not have a doctor, or even a medical orderly. Mek himself treated most of his casualties, and he always had a medical kit close at hand.

He had the men carry Tessay to one of the huts near the quarry, where, screened by the grass walls, he stripped her of her tattered clothing and treated her injuries. He cleaned her burns and abrasions with disinfectant, and covered the worst of them with clean field dressings. Then he rolled her gently on to her stomach and snapped the glass phial off the needle of the disposable syringe which was preloaded with a broad-spectrum antibiotic.

She winced at the sting of the needle, and he said, 'I am not a very good doctor.'

'I would have no other. Oh, Mek! I thought I would never see you again. I did not fear death as much as I feared that.'

He helped her dress in the spare clothing from his pack, a sweatshirt and fatigues that were many sizes too large for her. He rolled up the cuffs for her, and his touch was gentle. His hands were those of a lover, not a soldier.

'I must look so ugly,' she whispered through her swollen, black-scabbed lips.

'You are beautiful,' he denied it. 'To me you will always be beautiful.' He touched her cheek carefully, so as not to harm the raw burns that covered it.

At that moment they heard the gunfire. It was still faint with distance, borne down from the north on the rain winds.

Mek stood up immediately. 'It has begun. Nogo is attacking at last.'

'It's all my fault. I told him —'

'No,' he told her firmly. 'It is not your fault. You did what you had to do. If you had not, they would have hurt you even worse than this. They would have attacked us, even if you had told them nothing.'

He picked up his webbing belt and strapped it around his waist. From far off they heard the crumping detonation of exploding mortar shells.

'I have to go now,' he told her.

'I know. Do not worry about me.'

'I will always worry about you. These men will carry you down to the monastery. That is the assembly point. Wait for me there. I cannot hope to hold Nogo for long. He is too strong. I will come to you soon.'

'I love you,' she whispered. 'I will wait for you for ever.'

'You are my woman,' he told her in his deep, soft voice, and then he ducked through the doorway of the hut and was gone.

When Nicholas touched the frame of the screen, fragments of the mesh veil tore free with even that tiny movement and fell to the tiles of the floor. The golden rosettes trapped in their folds tinkled on the stones. Now there was an opening in the curtain large enough for them to step through. They found themselves before the inner doorway. It was guarded on one side by a massive statue of the great god Osiris with his hands crossed over his chest, clutching the crook and the flail. Opposite stood his wife Isis, with the lunar crown and horns on her head. Their blank eyes stared out into eternity, and their expressions were serene. Nicholas and Royan passed between these twelve-foot-high statues and found themselves at last in the veritable tomb of Mamose.

The roof was vaulted, and the quality of the murals that covered it and the walls was different — formal and classical. The colours were of a deeper, more sombre hue, and the patterns more intricate. The chamber was smaller than they had anticipated; just large enough to accommodate the huge granite sarcophagus of the divine Pharaoh Mamose.

The sarcophagus stood chest-high. Its side panels were engraved in bas-relief with scenes of Pharaoh and the other gods. The stone lid was in the shape of a full-length effigy of the supine figure of the king. They saw at once that it was still in its original position, and that the clay seals of the priests of Osiris which secured the lid were intact. The tomb had never been violated. The mummy had lain within it undisturbed through the millennia.

But this was not what amazed them. There were two extraneous items within the otherwise classically correct tomb. On the lid of the sarcophagus lay a magnificent war bow. Almost as long as Nicholas was tall, the entire length of its stock was bound with coils of shining electrum wire, that alloy of gold and silver whose formula has been lost in antiquity.

The other item that should never have been placed in a royal tomb stood at the foot of the sarcophagus. It was a small human figure, one of the *ushabti* dolls. A glance confirmed the superior quality of the carving of this effigy, and both of them recognized the features instantly. Only minutes before, they had seen that face painted upon the walls of the arcade, outside the tomb.

The words of Taita, from the scrolls, seemed to reverberate within the confines of the tomb, and hang like fireflies in the air above the sarcophagus:

When I stood for the very last time beside the royal sarcophagus, I sent all the workmen away. I would be the very last to leave the

811

tomb, and after me the entrance would be sealed.

When I was alone I opened the bundle I carried. From it I took the long bow, Lanata. Tanus had named it after my mistress, for Lanata had been her baby name. I had made the bow for him. It was the last gift from the two of us. I placed it upon the sealed stone lid of his coffin.

There was one other item in my bundle. It was the wooden ushabti *figure that I had carved. I placed it at the foot of the sarcophagus. While I carved it, I had set up three copper mirrors so that I could study my own features from every angle and reproduce them faithfully. The doll was a miniature Taita.*

Upon the base I had inscribed the words —

Royan knelt at the foot of the coffin and picked up the *ushabti* figure. Reverently she turned it in her hands and studied the hieroglyphics carved into the base of the figure.

Nicholas knelt beside her. 'Read it to me,' he said.

Softly she obeyed. ' *"My name is Taita. I am a physician and a poet. I am an architect and a philosopher. I am your friend. I will answer for you."* '

'So it's all true,' Nicholas whispered.

Royan replaced the *ushabti* exactly as she had found it and, still on her knees, turned

812

her face to his.

'I have never known another moment like this,' she whispered. 'I want it never to end.'

'It will never end, my darling,' he answered her. 'You and I are only just beginning.'

Mek Nimmur watched them coming, skirting the bottom slope of the hill. It took the trained eye of a bush-fighter to pick them out as they moved through the thick scrub and thorn. As he evaluated them he felt a twinge of dismay. These were crack troops, seasoned during long years of war. He had once fought with them against the Mengistu tyranny, and he had probably trained many of those men down there. Now they were coming against him. Such was the cycle of war and violence in this racked continent, where the endless struggles were fuelled and nurtured by the age-old tribal enmities and the greed and corruption of the new-age politicians and their outmoded ideologies.

But this was not the moment for dialectics, he thought bitterly, and focused his mind on the tactics of the battlefield beneath him. Yes! These men were good. He could see it in the way they advanced, like wraiths through the scrub. For every one of them he picked out, he knew there were a dozen others that remained unseen.

'Company strength,' he thought, and glanced around at his own small force. Fourteen men amongst the rocks, they could only hope to hit their adversary hard while they still had the advantage of surprise, and then pull back before Nogo ranged his mortars in on the hilltop where they lay.

He looked up at the sky and wondered whether Nogo would call in an air strike. Thirty-five minutes' flying time for a stick of those Soviet-built Tupolevs from the air base at Addis, and he could almost smell the sweet stench of napalm on the humid wind, and see the rolling cloud of flame sweeping towards them. That was the only thing his men really feared. But there would be no air strike — not this time, he decided. Nogo and his paymaster, the German von Schiller, wanted the spoils from the tomb that Nicholas Quenton-Harper had discovered in the gorge. They did not want to share any of it with those political fat cats in Addis. They would not want to draw any government attention to themselves and this little private campaign of theirs in the Abbay gorge.

He looked back down the slope. The enemy was moving in nicely, swinging around the hillside to intersect the trail along the Dandera river. Soon they must send a patrol up here to secure their flank before they could sweep on. Yes, there they were. Eight, no, ten men detaching from the main advance, and moving cautiously up the slope beneath him.

'I will let them get in close,' he decided. 'I would like to get them all, but that is too much to hope for. I would settle for four or five of them, and it would be good to leave a few squealers in the scrub.' He grinned cruelly. 'Nothing like a man screaming with a belly wound to take the fire out of his comrades, and make them keep their heads down.'

He looked across the rock-strewn slope, and saw that his RPD light machine gun was perfectly sited to enfilade their advance up the slope. Salim, his machine gunner, was an artist with that weapon. Perhaps, after all, he could hope to put down more than five of them.

'We will see,' thought Mek, 'but I must time it right.'

He saw that there was a gap in the ridge of rock just below him.

'They will not want to expose themselves by crossing the open ridge,' he judged. 'They will tend to bunch up and sneak through the gap. That will be the moment.'

He looked back at the RPD. Salim was watching him, waiting for his signal. Mek looked back down the slope.

'Yes,' he thought. 'Their line is bunching. The big one on the left is already out of position. Those two inside him are angling across towards the gap.'

Nogo's men's camouflage blended perfectly with the scrub, and the barrels of their weapons were wrapped with rags and scraps of camouflage netting so that they threw no sunlight reflections. They were almost invisible in the bush; it was only their movements and the skin tones that betrayed them. They were so close now that Mek caught the occasional gleam of one of their eyeballs but he still could not pick out their machine gunner.

He must silence the gun with his first burst. 'Ah, yes,' he thought with relief. 'There he is. On the right flank. I nearly missed him.'

The man was short and thick-set, with heavy shoulders and long arms, simian, carrying the gun easily on his hip. It was a Soviet-made 7.62mm RPD. The wink of brass from the cartridges in the ammunition belts festooned over those great shoulders had given him away.

Mek eased himself down and inched around the base of the rock that covered him. He slipped the rate-of-fire selector on his AKM to rapid, and laid his cheek on the wooden butt. It was his personal weapon. A gunsmith in Addis had trued the action and lapped the barrel for him, as well as glass-bedding the barrel into the stock. All this had been done to improve the accuracy of this notoriously inaccurate assault rifle. It was still no sniper's weapon, but with these modifications he could expect to place all his shots within a two-inch circle at a hundred metres.

The man carrying the RPD up the slope was now only fifty metres below where he lay. Mek glanced to his right to make sure that the three others were moving into the gap where Salim could take them out with a single burst; then he settled the pip of his foresight in the centre of the RPD machine gunner's belly, using his belt buckle as an aiming mark, and fired a tap of three.

The AKM rode up viciously and the triple detonation stung his eardrums, but Mek saw his bullets strike, stitching a row up the man's torso. One hit low in the belly, the second in the diaphragm and the third at the base of his throat. He spun around, his arms flinging out and jerking, and then crashed over backwards, out of sight in the underbrush.

All around Mek his men were firing. He wondered how many of them Salim had taken with that first burst, but there was no longer anything to see. The enemy were all down in cover. A faint haze of gunsmoke blued the air as they returned fire, and the scrub trembled and shook to the recoil and the muzzle blast of their weapons.

Then, in the uproar of fire, in the whine and wail of ricochets off the rocks, one of them began to scream.

'I am hit. In Allah's name, help me.' His cries rang eerily across the hillside, and the enemy fire slackened perceptibly. Mek clipped a fresh magazine on to the AKM.

'Sing, little bird. Sing!' he muttered grimly.

It required the combined strength of Nicholas, Hansith and eight other men to lift the lid off the stone sarcophagus. Staggering under its weight, they laid it carefully against the wall of the tomb. Then Royan and Nicholas stood on the plinth of the sarcophagus to look down into the interior.

Fitted neatly into the stone receptacle was an enormous wooden coffin. Its lid too was in the form of the reclining Pharaoh. He was in the posture of death with his hands crossed at his breast, clutching the flail and the crook. The coffin was gilded and encrusted with semi-precious stones. The expression on the face of the king's effigy was serene.

They lifted the coffin out of the sarcophagus, and its weight was less than that of the stone lid. Carefully Nicholas split the golden seals and the layer of hard dried resin that held the lid of the coffin in place. Within it they found another coffin, fitted perfectly, and when they opened that yet another coffin was revealed. It was like a nest of Russian dolls, one within the other, becoming smaller with each revelation.

In the end there were seven coffins, each of them progressively more ornate and richly decorated than the previous one. The seventh coffin was only slightly larger than a man, and it was made of gold. The polished metal caught the light of the lamps like a thousand mirrors and threw bright arrows and darts into every recess of the tomb.

When at last they opened the golden inner coffin they found that it was filled with flowers. The blooms had dried and faded, so their colour was sepia. Their scent had long ago evaporated, so that only the musky aroma of great age wafted up from the coffin. The petals were so dry and papery that they crumbled at the first touch. Beneath the faded blooms was a layer of the finest linen; once it must have been snowy white, but now it was brown with age and the stain of the juices from the flowers. Through the soft folds they saw once again the gleam of gold.

Standing on either side of the coffin, Nicholas and Royan peeled back the linen mesh. It crackled softly and tore like tissue paper under their fingers, but as it came away they both involuntarily gasped with wonder as the death-mask of Pharaoh was revealed. It was only fractionally larger than the head of a man, but it was a perfect image in every detail. Pharaoh's features had been preserved for all eternity in this extraordinary work of art. They stared in silent wonder into the obsidian and rock crystal eyes of Pharaoh, and Pharaoh gazed back at them sadly, almost accusingly.

It was a long time before either of them could summon the courage and presumption to lift it away from the head of the mummy. But when they did so, they found further evidence that in antiquity the body of the king and that of his general, Tanus, had been changed. The mummy that lay before them was obviously too large for the coffin that contained it. It had been partially unwrapped, and cramped into the interior.

'A royal mummy would have had hundreds of charms and amulets placed beneath the wrappings,' Royan whispered. 'This is the plainly dressed corpse of a nobleman and not that of the king.'

Nicholas gently lifted the inner layer of bandage away from the dead head and a thick coil of braided hair was revealed.

'The portraits of Pharaoh Mamose on the walls of the arcade show that his head hair was dyed with henna,' Nicholas murmured. 'Look at this.'

The braid was the colour of the winter grasses of the African savannah, gold and silver.

'There can be no doubt now. This is the body of Tanus. The friend of Taita and the lover of the queen.'

'Yes,' Royan agreed, her eyes soft with tears. 'He is the true father of Lostris's son, who became in his time the Pharaoh Tamose and the forefather of a great line of kings. So this is the man whose blood runs through the history of ancient Egypt.'

'In his way he was as great as any Pharaoh,' Nicholas said quietly.

It was Royan who roused herself first. 'The river!' she cried, with a razor edge to her voice. 'We cannot let all this go again, when the river rises.'

'Neither can we hope to save all of it. There is too much. A great mass of treasure. Our time here has almost run out, so we must pick out the most beautiful and important pieces and pack them into the crates. Lord alone knows if we even have time for that.'

So they worked in a frenzy in the short time that was left to them. They could not even think about saving the statues and the murals, the furniture and the weapons, the banqueting utensils and the wardrobes of costumes. The great golden chariot must stand where it had stood for four thousand years.

They removed the golden death-mask from over Tanus's head, but they left his mummy in the innermost of the golden coffins. Then Nicholas sent for Mai Metemma. The old abbot came with twenty of his monks to receive the holy relic of the ancient saint that he had been promised as his reward. Reverentially, chanting deep and slow, they bore Tanus's coffin away to its new resting place in the *maqdas* of the monastery.

'At least the old hero will be treated with respect,' Royan said softly. Then she looked around the tomb. 'We cannot leave the site like this, with the coffins thrown about and the lids discarded,' Royan protested. 'It looks as though grave-robbers have been at work here.'

'Grave-robbers is exactly what we are.' Nicholas smiled at her.

'No, we are archaeologists,' she denied hotly, 'and we must try to act like it.'

So they replaced the six remaining coffins one within the other, laid them back in the great sarcophagus, and finally replaced the massive stone lid. Only then did Royan allow them to begin selecting and packing the treasures they would take with them.

The death-mask was without any doubt the premier item in the entire tomb. It fitted neatly into one of the crates, with the wooden *ushabti* of Taita laid alongside it, packed with Styrofoam until it was firmly secured. Royan scribbled on the lid in waterproof wax crayon: 'Mask & Taita Ushabti'.

Their final selection was, perforce, hurried and superficial. They could not rip open every one of the cedarwood chests that were piled high in the alcoves of the arcade. The painted and gilded chests themselves were priceless artefacts, and should be treated with respect. So they allowed themselves to be guided by the illustrations on the lid of each. They discovered immediately that these were indeed an accurate inventory and catalogue of the contents. In the chest which showed Pharaoh decked in the blue war crown, they found the actual crown laid on gilded leather pillows that had been moulded to fit it exactly and to protect it.

Even in the short time left to them they became almost surfeited by the magnificence of the items they uncovered as they selected and opened the cedarwood chests. Not only the blue crown, but the red and white crown of the kingdoms united was there, and the splendid Nemes crown, all three in such a miraculous state of preservation that they might have been lifted from Pharaoh's brow that morning.

From the very outset it had to be a prerequisite that any artefact must be small enough to fit into one of the ammunition crates. If it were too large, no matter what its value or historical significance, then it had to be rejected and left in the tomb. Fortunately, many of the cedarwood chests containing the royal jewellery fitted snugly into the metal crates, so that not only the contents but also the chests themselves could be saved. However, the larger items, the crowns and the huge jewelled gold pectoral medallions, had to be repacked.

As the ammunition crates were filled, they carried them down and stacked them on the landing outside the sealed doorway, ready to be carried out. Including the crates that contained the eight statuettes of the gods from the long gallery, they had packed and catalogued forty-eight crates when they heard Sapper's unmistakable accents floating up the staircase.

'Major, where the hell are you? You can't bugger about in here any longer. Come on, man! Get your hairy arse out of here. The river is in full spate, and the dam is going to burst at any minute.'

Sapper came bounding up the staircase, but even he stopped in wonder and awe as he looked for the first time upon the splendours of the funeral arcade of Pharaoh Mamose. It took some minutes for him to recover from the shock and to revert to his old prosaic self again.

'I mean it, major! It's a matter of minutes, not hours. That ruddy dam is going to go. Apart from that, Mek is fighting in the hills at the head of the chasm. You can hear the gunfire even at the bottom of the cliff in Taita's pool. You and Royan have to get out and fast, I kid you not!'

'Okay, Sapper. We are on our way. Get back to the chamber at the bottom of those stairs. You saw those ammunition crates down there?' Sapper nodded, and Nicholas went on quickly, 'Have the men lug those crates out of here. Get them down to the monastery. I want you to supervise that part of it. We will follow you down the trail with the rest of them.'

'Don't mess around, major. Your life isn't worth a pile of old junk like this. Get moving now.'

'Get on with it, Sapper. But don't let Royan hear you call it a pile of old junk. You could be in really serious trouble.'

Sapper shrugged. 'Don't say I didn't warn you.' He turned and started back down the staircase.

'You know where the boats are stashed,' Nicholas shouted after him. 'If you get there before me, get them inflated and the crates lashed down. We will be right behind you.'

The moment Sapper was gone, Nicholas raced back down the arcade to where Royan was still at work in the treasury.

'That's it!' he shouted at her. 'No more time. Let's get out.'

'Nicky, we can't leave this —'

'Out!' He grabbed her arm. 'We are getting out now. Unless you want to share Tanus's tomb with him on a permanent basis.'

'Can't I just —'

'No, you crazy woman! Now! The dam will go at any moment.'

She broke away from him, snatched up some handfuls of left-over jewellery from the open chest at her feet, and began stuffing them into her pockets.

'I can't leave these.'

He seized her around the waist and swung her over his shoulder. 'I told you I meant it,' he said grimly, and ran with her down the arcade.

'Nicky! Put me down.' She kicked with outrage, but he continued running down into the chamber at the foot of the staircase.

Hansith and his men were carrying the last

few packed ammunition crates up the staircase on the far side of the chamber. They balanced the crates easily on their heads and went up the steps with alacrity.

Here Nicholas set Royan down on her own feet again. 'Will you promise to behave now? We aren't playing games. This is deadly serious — I mean deadly, if we get trapped down here.'

'I know.' She looked contrite. 'I just couldn't bear to leave the rest of it.'

'Enough of that. Let's go.' Nicholas grabbed her hand and dragged her after him. After the first few steps she shook her hand free and started to run in earnest, outstripping him and reaching the top of the staircase a few paces ahead of him.

Even under their burdens the porters were making good time. Caught up in the long hurrying column, Nicholas and Royan wound their way back through the maze, grateful for the signposts at each corner, and made it down the central staircase into the ruined long gallery without taking a wrong turning. Sapper was waiting for them at the ruins of the sealed doorway, and grunted with relief when he saw them amongst the porters.

'I thought I told you to go on ahead and get the boats ready,' Nicholas shouted at him.

'Couldn't trust you not to be bloody stupid.' Sapper looked miserable. 'Wanted to make sure you didn't hang about in there.'

'I am touched, Sapper.' Nicholas punched his

shoulder, and then they ran down the approach tunnel and clattered over the bridge across the sink-hole.

'Where is Mek?' Nicholas panted at Sapper's back as he jogged in front of him. 'Have you seen Tessay?'

'Tessay is back. She had a nasty experience. She was in a terrible mess. Seems she got badly knocked about.'

'What has happened to her?' Nicholas was appalled. 'Where is she?'

'It looks like she fell into the hands of von Schiller's gorillas and they beat the hell out of her. Mek's men are taking her down to the monastery. She will wait for us at the boats.'

'Thank God for that,' Nicholas muttered, and then louder, 'What about Mek?'

'He is trying to hold off Nogo's attack. I have been hearing rifle fire and grenades and mortar shells all morning. He too is going to fall back and wait for us at the boats.'

They ran the last few yards down the tunnel ankle-deep in slush and water, and at last crawled over the wall of the coffer dam on to the rocky ledge around Taita's pool. Nicholas looked up to see Hansith's porters scrambling up the bamboo scaffolding ladder towards the top of the cliff, each of them hauling up one of the ammunition crates.

At that moment he caught a sound that he recognized instantly. He cocked his head to listen and then told Royan grimly, 'Gunfire! Mek is fighting it out, but it's pretty darned close.'

'My bag!' Royan started towards her thatched shelter at the foot of the cliff. 'I must get my kit.'

'You won't need your makeup or your pyjamas, and I've got your passport.' He seized her arm and turned her back towards the foot of the ladder. 'In fact the only thing you need now is plenty of space between you and Colonel Nogo. Come along, Royan!'

They swarmed up the bamboo scaffolding and when they reached the cliff top Royan was surprised to discover that, although the earth was wet underfoot from the recent rain squalls, the sun was high and hot. She had lost all sense of time in the cold, gloomy passages of the tomb, and now she held up her face to the sunlight and drank it in gratefully for a moment while Nicholas checked the porters and made certain that they were all out of the chasm.

Sapper set off at the head of the column along the trail through the thorn forest, with the file of porters strung out behind him. Nicholas and Royan waited until all the men were on the pathway before they themselves brought up the rear of the column. The sound of the fighting was frighteningly close now. It seemed to be almost at the brink of the chasm close behind them, less than half a mile away. The crackle of automatic fire gave a spring and a lift to the feet of the porters, and the entire party raced back through the forest to reach the main trail down to the monastery before they were cut off by Nogo's advance.

Before they reached the junction of the paths, they ran into a party of stretcher-bearers carrying a litter. They too were headed down towards the monastery. Nicholas thought the person they were carrying was one of the wounded guerrillas of Mek's force. But even when he caught up with them it took a moment for him to recognize Tessay's swollen and burned face.

'Tessay!' He stooped over her. 'Who did this to you?'

She looked up at him with the huge dark eyes of a wounded child, and told him in halting, broken words.

'Helm!' Nicholas blurted. 'I'd love to get my hands on that bastard.' At that moment Royan caught up with them, and she let out a small cry of horror as she saw Tessay's face. Then immediately she took charge of her.

Nicholas spoke quickly to one of the stretcher-bearers whom he recognized.

'Mezra, what is happening out there?'

'Nogo moved a force in from the east of the gorge. They outflanked us, and we are pulling out. This is not our kind of fighting.'

'I know,' Nicholas remarked grimly. 'Guerrillas must keep moving. Where is Mek Nimmur?'

'He is retreating down the eastern bank of the chasm.' As Mezra replied, they heard a renewed outburst of firing behind them. 'That is him!' Mezra nodded. 'Nogo is pushing him hard.'

'What are your orders?'

'To take Lady Sun to the boats and wait for Mek Nimmur there.'

'Good!' Nicholas told him. 'We will go with you.'

The Jet Ranger was flying low, hugging the contours of the land, never cresting the high ground. Helm knew that Mek Nimmur's *shufta* were armed with RPGs, rocket-launchers. In the hands of a trained man, these were deadly weapons against a slow-flying, unarmoured aircraft such as the Jet Ranger. The pilot's defence was to use the terrain as cover, weaving and twisting up the valleys so as to deny the rocketeers a clear shot.

Although the rain clouds were slumping down the escarpment into the Abbay gorge, the helicopter was keeping well below them. However, the sudden squalls of wind rocked the machine dangerously and splatterings of heavy raindrops rattled against the windshield. The pilot sat forward in the seat, leaning against his shoulder-straps as he concentrated on this dangerous low flying in these unpleasant conditions. Helm sat in the right-hand seat, beside the pilot. Von Schiller and Nahoot Guddabi were together in the rear passenger seat, both of them craning nervously to peer out of the side windows as the heavily wooded slopes of the valley streamed past, seemingly close enough to touch.

Every few minutes the radio crackled into life, and they could hear the terse transmissions of Nogo's men on the ground calling for mortar support or reporting objectives attained. The pilot translated the radio gabble for them, twisting round in his seat to tell von Schiller, 'There is a sharp fire-fight going on along the top of the chasm, but the *shufta* are on the run. Nogo is handling his force well. They have just dislodged a strong force from the hillside to the east of us,' he pointed out of the left-hand port, 'and they are hammering the *shufta* with mortars as they run.'

'Have they reached the spot in the chasm where Quenton-Harper was working?'

'It isn't clear. All a bit confused.' The pilot listened to the next burst of Arabic on the radio. 'I think that was Nogo himself speaking just then.'

'Call him up!' von Schiller ordered Helm, leaning over the back of his seat. 'Ask him if they have secured the tomb site yet.'

Helm reached across and lifted the microphone off its hook below the instrument panel. 'Rose Petal, this is Bismarck. Do you copy?'

There was a pause filled with static, and then Nogo's voice speaking English. 'Go ahead, Bismarck.'

'Have you secured the primary objective? Over.'

'Affirmative, Bismarck. All secured. All opposition suppressed. I am sending men down the ladder to clear the workings.'

Helm swivelled in his seat to look back at von Schiller. 'Nogo has men in the chasm already. We can go in and land.'

'Tell him not to let any of his men into the workings before I arrive,' von Schiller ordered sternly, but his expression was triumphant. 'I must be the first in there. Make him understand that.'

While Helm relayed his orders to Nogo, von Schiller tapped the pilot on the shoulder. 'How long to the objective?'

'About five minutes' flying time, sir.'

'Circle the site when you arrive. Don't land until we are sure Nogo has it under his control.'

The pilot lifted the collective and the sound of the rotors altered as they changed pitch. The helicopter slowed and then hovered in midair, while the pilot pointed down.

'What is it?' von Schiller followed his gesture. 'What do you see?'

'The dam,' Helm answered. 'Quenton-Harper's dam. He did a load of work down there.'

The wide body of trapped water gleamed grey and sullen under the rain clouds, tainted with the run-off from the highlands. The water diverted into the side canal boiled white and angrily down into the long valley.

'Deserted!' Helm commented. 'All Harper's men have pulled out.'

'What is that yellow object on the bank?' von Schiller wanted to know.

'That's the earth-moving machine. You remember? My informer told us about it.'

'Don't waste any more time,' von Schiller ordered. 'Nothing more to see here. Let's get on!'

Helm tapped the pilot's shoulder, and gestured downstream.

Sapper was waiting for them to catch up at the junction of the trail, where the diverted river was roaring down the valley in a torrent and had washed out a long section of the original track. The porters, strung out in a long line down the valley, each with an ammunition crate balanced on his head, were picking their way along the higher ground above the water.

Tessay's litter was near the rear of the column, with Royan and Nicholas trotting on each side of it and steadying it over the rough and uneven sections of the path.

'Where is Hansith?' Nicholas shouted at Sapper, shading his eyes to check the men ahead of him, and trying to pick out the big monk's distinctive form from amongst the others in the caravan.

'I thought he was with you,' Sapper shouted back. 'I haven't seen him since we left the chasm.'

Nicholas turned and stared back the way they had come, along the footpath through the thorn forest.

'Damn the man,' he grunted. 'We can't go back to look for him. He will have to make his own way down to the monastery.'

At that moment they heard the faint but familiar flutter of rotors in the hot, humid air below the lowering cloud masses.

'The Pegasus chopper! Sounds as though von Schiller is heading directly for Taita's pool. He must have known all along exactly where we were working,' said Nicholas bitterly. 'Not wasting any time. Like a vulture coming in to a fresh carcass.'

Royan was also looking up at the sound, trying to pick out the shape of the aircraft against the dark clouds. Her face was flushed from the run, the tendrils of sweat-damp hair dangled down her cheeks. 'If those swine are allowed to enter our tomb it will be a dreadful desecration of a sacred place,' she said angrily.

Suddenly Nicholas reached across the litter and took her arm. His expression was stern and determined. 'You are right. Go on down to the monastery with Tessay. I will follow you later.' Before she could protest or question him, he strode across to Sapper.

'I am putting the two women in your care,

Sapper. Look after them.'

'Where are you going, Nicky?' Royan had come up behind him, and overheard his orders to Sapper. 'What are you going to do?'

'One little chore. Won't take me long.'

'You aren't going back there?' She was horrified. 'You will get yourself killed or worse. You saw what Helm did to Tessay —'

'Don't fuss yourself, my love,' he laughed, and before she realized what he intended he kissed her full on the lips. While she was still flustered and confused by this display in front of so many men, he pushed her gently away.

'Take care of Tessay. I will meet you at the boats.'

Before she could protest further, he turned and struck out up the valley at a long-legged lope which carried him over the rough terrain so swiftly that she had no further chance to prevent him.

'Nicky!' she screamed after him despairingly, but he pretended not to hear and kept going, following the diverted river upstream, back towards the dam.

The Jet Ranger followed the convoluted course of the river below the dam. At moments they could look directly down into the narrow gap between the high cliffs, into the shaded depths of the chasm, almost dry now, with only the occasional gleam of the shrunken and still pools.

'There they are!' Helm pointed dead ahead. There was a small cluster of men on the brink of the chasm.

'Make sure they aren't *shufta!*' There was fear in von Schiller's voice.

'No!' Helm reassured him loudly. 'I recognize Nogo, and that tall one beside him in the white *shamma* is the monk Hansith Sherif, our informer.' He shouted above the engine beat at the pilot, 'You can go in and land. There! Nogo is waving you in!'

The moment the skids of the helicopter touched the ground, both Nogo and Hansith ran forward. Between them they helped von Schiller down from the passenger cabin and hustled him clear of the spinning rotors.

'My men have secured the area,' Nogo assured him. 'We have driven the *shufta* down the valley towards the river. This man is Hansith Sherif, who has been working beside Harper in the tomb. He knows every inch of the tunnels.'

'Does he speak English?' Von Schiller looked up at the tall monk eagerly.

'A little bit,' Hansith answered for himself.

'Good! Good!' Von Schiller beamed at him. 'Show me the way. I will follow you. Come on, Guddabi, it's about time you did some work for the money I am paying you.'

Hansith led them quickly to the head of the scaffolding, where von Schiller paused and looked down nervously into the gloomy depths of the chasm. The bamboo framework seemed flimsy and rickety, the drop deep and terrifying. Von Schiller was on the point of protesting when Nahoot Guddabi whimpered behind him.

'He does not expect us to climb down there, does he?'

His terror bolstered von Schiller immediately, and he turned on Nahoot with relish. 'It is the only access to the tomb. Follow the man down. I will be close behind you.'

When Nahoot still hesitated, Helm put a calloused hand in the small of his back and shoved him forward.

'Get on with it. You are wasting time.'

Reluctantly Nahoot started down the scaffolding after the monk, and von Schiller followed him. The framework of bamboo shook and swayed under their combined weight and the drop to the rocks below sucked at them, but at last they reached the ledge beside Taita's pool. There they stood in a small group, staring about them in awe and wonder.

'Where is the tunnel?' von Schiller demanded as soon as he had regained his breath, and Hansith beckoned to him to follow him to the wall of the small coffer dam.

Here von Schiller paused and looked around at Helm and Nogo. 'I want you to remain on guard here. I will enter the tomb with Guddabi and this monk. I will send for you when you are needed.'

'I would feel happier to be with you, to protect you, Herr von Schiller —' Helm began, but the old man frowned at him.

'Do as I tell you!' And with Hansith steadying him he climbed stiffly down the wall of the coffer dam into the mouth of the tunnel. Nahoot Guddabi followed him closely.

'The lights? Where does the power come from?' von Schiller wanted to know.

'There is a machine,' Hansith explained, and at that moment they heard the soft burble of the generator ahead of them. None of them spoke again as they moved down the entrance tunnel after Hansith, until they reached the bridge over the dark waters of the sink-hole.

'This is very rough construction,' Nahoot muttered, his uneasiness at last giving way to professional interest. 'It does not remind me of any other Egyptian tomb I have ever inspected. I think we may have been misled. It is probably some native Ethiopian workings.'

'You are making a premature judgement,' von Schiller admonished him. 'Wait until we have seen the rest of what this man has to show us.'

Von Schiller steadied himself with a hand on Hansith's shoulder as they crossed the bobbing pontoons of baobab wood, and he scrambled ashore on the far side with relief. They started up the rising section of the tunnel and passed the high-water mark.

As soon as the construction of the walls

changed to packed and dressed stone, Nahoot remarked on it. 'Ah! I was disappointed at first. I thought we had been duped, but now one can see the Egyptian influence.'

They reached the landing outside the ruined gallery on which stood the Honda generator. By now both von Schiller and Nahoot were sweating with exertion and trembling with excitement.

'This looks more and more promising. It may very well be a royal tomb,' Nahoot exulted. Von Schiller pointed to the plaster seals stacked against the side wall where Nicholas and Royan had abandoned them. Nahoot fell to his knees beside them and examined them eagerly, his voice trembling as he cried out.

'The cartouche of Mamose, and the seal of the scribe Taita!' He looked up at von Schiller with shining eyes, 'There can be no doubts now. I have led you to the tomb as I promised you I would.'

For a moment von Schiller stared at him, speechless in the face of such bare-faced arrogance. Then he snorted with disgust and stooped to peer through the open doorway into the long gallery.

'This has been destroyed!' he cried in horror. 'The tomb has been annihilated.'

'No, no!' Hansith assured him. 'Come this way. There is another tunnel beyond.'

As they picked their way through the rubble and wreckage, Hansith told them in halting, broken English how the roof of the gallery had collapsed, and how he, Hansith, had found the true entrance under the ruins.

Nahoot stopped every few paces to examine and exclaim over the scraps of painted plaster that had survived the fall of the roof. 'These must have been magnificent. Classical work of the highest order —'

'There is more to show you. Much more,' Hansith promised them, and von Schiller snarled at Nahoot.

'Leave these damaged sections now. Time is running out on us. We must hurry on directly to the burial chamber.'

Hansith led them up the hidden staircase into the maze of the bao, and then through the twists and turns to the lowest level.

'How did Harper and the woman ever find their way through this?' von Schiller marvelled. 'It's a rabbit warren.'

'Another concealed staircase!' Nahoot was amazed, and stuttered with excitement as they descended into the gas trap where the ranks of amphorae had stood undisturbed for thousands of years, and then climbed the last flight of stairs to the beginning of the funeral arcade.

Now both of them were stunned by the splendour of the murals and the majesty of the great god images that guarded the length of the arcade. They stood side by side unable to move, frozen with awe as they gazed about them.

'I never expected anything like this,' von

Schiller whispered. 'This exceeds anything that I ever hoped for.'

'The rooms on each side are filled with treasures.' Hansith pointed down the arcade. 'There are such things as you have never dreamed. Harper was able to take very little with him — a few small boxes. He has left piles of goods, stacks of chests.'

'Where is the coffin? Where is the body that was in the tomb?' von Schiller demanded.

'Harper has given the body, in its golden coffin, to the abbot. They have taken it away to the monastery.'

'Nogo will soon fetch it back for us. You need not worry about that, Herr von Schiller,' Nahoot assured him.

As though the spell that held them was shattered by this promise, they started forward together, slowly at first, and then both of them began to run. Von Schiller tottered into the nearest store room on his old, stiff legs, and giggled like a child on Christmas morning as he gazed upon the piled treasures. 'Incredible!'

He dragged down one of the cedarwood chests from the nearest stack, and ripped off the lid with trembling fingers. When he saw the contents he was struck speechless. He knelt over the chest and began to weep softly with emotion too overwhelming to express in words.

Nicholas was banking on the fact that Nogo's men would be driving along the cliff tops to reach Taita's pool, and that he would have a free run up the course of the diverted stream to the dam site. He took no precautions against running into them, other than to pause every few minutes to listen and peer ahead. He knew that he had little time left to him. He could not expect the rest of the party to wait for him at the boats and endanger themselves for this whimsy of his.

Twice he heard automatic gunfire in the distance, coming from the direction of the chasm, down towards the pool. However, the chance he took paid off, and he reached the dam site without running into any of Nogo's forces. He did not, however, push his luck too far. Before approaching the dam openly, he climbed the hillside above it and surveyed the area. It gave him time to recover from the hard run up the valley, and to check that Nogo had not left men to guard the dam, although he considered this unlikely.

He could see that the yellow front-loader tractor was still parked on the bank high above the wall where Sapper had left it. He could also see no sign of any human presence, no armed Ethiopian army guards. He grunted with relief and wiped the sweat out of his eyes with his shirtsleeve.

Even with his naked eye he could see that the water was lapping the top of the wall and squirting through the gaps and chinks between the gabions. Yet from where he stood the wall still seemed to be holding well, and it would need another foot rise in the level of the backed-up river to overturn it.

'Well done, Sapper,' he thought, grinning. 'You did a hell of a job.'

Nicholas studied the level of the river and the condition of the waters that were being held back by the wall. The flow down from the mountains was much stronger than when he had last been here. The river bed was brimming from bank to bank, and some of the trees and bushes at the edge were already partially submerged, bowing and nodding as the swift current tugged at them. The flood was a sullen grey colour, fast and hostile, swirling into the pond of the dam before finding the outlet into the side channel and tearing down it, growling like a wild animal released from its cage, brimming into spume and white water as it felt the sharp fall into the valley.

Next he looked towards the escarpment of the gorge. It was blotted out by banks of dark, menacing cloud that obscured the northern horizon. At that moment a squall of wind swept over him, cold with the threat of rain. He needed no further urging and started down the slope towards the dam, slipping and sliding in his haste. Before he reached the bottom, the squall of wind had turned to cold rain. It flung needles into his face and plastered his shirt to his body.

He reached the tractor and scrambled up into the driver's seat. There was a moment of panic when he thought that Sapper might have removed the key from its hiding-place under the seat. He scrabbled for it for a few seconds until his fingers closed over it, and then let out a sigh of relief.

'Sapper, for a moment there you were very close to death. I would have broken your neck with my own hands.'

He thrust the key into the ignition lock and turned it to the preheat position, waiting for the coil light on the dashboard to turn from red to green.

'Come on!' he muttered impatiently. Those few seconds of delay seemed like a lifetime. Then the green light flashed and he twisted the key to start.

The engine fired at the first turn and Nicholas hooted, 'Full marks, Sapper. All is forgiven.'

He gave the machine time to warm up to optimum operating temperature, slitting his eyes against the rain as he waited and looking around at the hills above him, fearful that the sound of the engine might bring Nogo's gorillas swarming down on him. However, there was no sign of life on the rainswept heights.

He eased the tractor into her lowest gear and turned her down the bank. Below the dam wall the water that was finding its way through the gaps was less than hub-deep. The tractor bounced and ground its way through the boulder-strewn watercourse. Nicholas stopped the machine in the middle of the river bed while he studied the downstream face of the dam wall for its weakest section. Then he lined up below the centre of the wall, at the point where Sapper had shored up the raft of logs with rows of gabions.

'Sorry for all your hard work,' he apologized to Sapper, as he manoeuvred the steel scoop of the tractor to the right height and angle before attacking the wall. He worried the gabion he had selected out of its niche in the row, reversing and thrusting at it until he could get the scoop under it and drag it free. He pulled away and dropped the heavy wire mesh basket over the waterfall, then drove back and renewed the attack.

It was slow work. The pressure of the water had wedged in the gabions, keying them into the wall so it took almost ten minutes to free the second basket. As he dropped that one over the waterfall, he glanced for the first time at the fuel gauge on the dashboard of the tractor and his heart sank. It was registering empty. Sapper must have neglected to refuel it: either he had exhausted the fuel supply or he had not expected ever to use the machine again when he abandoned it.

Even as Nicholas thought about it the engine

stuttered as it starved. He reversed it sharply, changing the angle of inclination so that the remaining fuel in the tank could slosh forward. The engine caught and cleared, running smoothly and strongly once again. Quickly he changed gear and ran back at the wall.

'No more time for finesse,' he told himself grimly. 'From here on in it's brute force and muscle.'

By removing two of the gabions he had exposed a corner of the log raft behind them. This was the vulnerable part of the wall. He worked the hydraulic controls and lifted the scoop to its highest travel. Then he lowered it carefully, an inch at a time, until it hooked over the end of the thickest log in the jam. He locked the hydraulics and thrust the tractor into reverse, gradually pouring on full power until the engine was roaring and blowing out a cloud of thick blue diesel smoke.

Nothing gave. The log was jammed solidly and the wall was held together by the keying of the gabions into each other and the enormous pressure of water behind them. Despairingly, Nicholas kept the throttle wide open. The lugged tyres spun and skidded on the boulders under them, throwing a tall shower of spray high into the air and churning out loose rock and gravel.

'Come on!' Nicholas pleaded with the machine. 'Come on! You can do it.'

The engine beat faltered again as she starved

for fuel. She spluttered and coughed, and almost stalled.

'Please!' Nicholas begged her aloud. 'One more try.'

Almost as if it had heard him, the engine fired again, ran unevenly for a few moments, and then abruptly bellowed at full power again.

'That's it, my beauty,' Nicholas yelled, as it lurched and hammered against the wall.

With a sound like a cannon shot the log snapped and the top end of it flew out of the wall, leaving a long, deep hole through which the river poured triumphantly, a thick, solid column of dirty grey water.

'Thar she blows!' Nicholas shouted, jumping down from the driver's seat. He knew there was not enough time left for him to drive the tractor out of the river bed. He could move more quickly on his own feet.

The current seized his legs, trying to pull them out from under him. It was like one of those childhood nightmares when monsters were pursuing him and, despite his every effort, his legs would only move in slow motion. He glanced back over his shoulder, and at that instant he saw the central section of the dam wall burst, blowing outward in a violent eruption of furious waters. He struggled on another few paces towards the bank before the deep and turbulent tide picked him up. He was helpless in its grip. It swept him away, over the waterfall and down, down into the hungry maw of the chasm.

'These are the royal crook and sceptre of the Pharaoh,' cried von Schiller in a voice that was gusty and faint with emotion as he lifted them out of the cedarwood chest.

'And this is his false beard and his ceremonial pectoral emblem.' Nahoot knelt beside him on the floor of the tomb under the great statue of Osiris. All the ill feelings between them were forgotten in the wonder of the moment as they examined the fabulous treasures of Egypt.

'This is the greatest archaeological discovery of all time,' von Schiller whispered, his voice tremulous. He pulled his handkerchief from his pocket and dabbed at the perspiration of excitement that trickled down his cheeks.

'There is years of work here,' Nahoot told him seriously. 'This incredible collection will have to be catalogued and evaluated. It will be known for ever as the von Schiller hoard. Your name will be perpetuated for all time. It is like the Egyptian dream of immortality. You will never be forgotten. You will live for ever.'

A rapturous expression crossed von Schiller's features. He had not considered that possibility. Up until this moment he had not considered sharing this treasure with anybody, except in his particular way with Utte Kemper, but Nahoot's words had awakened in him the old impossible dream of eternity. Perhaps he might make arrangements for it to be made accessible to the public — but only after his own death, naturally.

Then he thrust the temptation aside. He would not debase this treasure by making it available to the common rabble. It had been assembled for the funeral of a pharaoh. Von Schiller saw himself as the modern equivalent of a pharaoh.

'No!' he told Nahoot violently. 'This is mine, all mine. When I die it will go with me, all of it. I have made the arrangements already, in my will. My sons know what to do. This will all be with me in my own grave. My royal grave.'

Nahoot stared at him aghast. He had not realized until that moment that the old man was mad, that his obsessions had driven him over the edge of sanity. But the Egyptian knew that there was no point in arguing with him now — later he would find a way to save this marvellous treasure from the oblivion of another tomb. So he bowed his head in mock acquiescence.

'You are right, Herr von Schiller. That is the only fitting manner to dispose of it. You deserve that form of burial. However, our main concern now must be to get all of it to safety. Helm has warned us about the danger of the river, of the dam bursting. We must call him and Nogo. Nogo's men must clear out the tomb. We can ferry the treasure in the helicopter up to the Pegasus camp, where I can pack it securely for the journey to Germany.'

'Yes. Yes.' Von Schiller scrambled to his feet, suddenly terrified at the prospect of being deprived of this wondrous hoard by the flooded river. 'Send the monk, what is his name, Hansith, send him to call Helm. He must come at once.'

Nahoot jumped up to his feet. 'Hansith!' he shouted. 'Where are you?'

The monk had been waiting at the entrance to the burial chamber, kneeling in prayer before the empty sarcophagus which had contained the body of the saint. He was torn now between religious conviction and greed. When he heard his name called he genuflected deeply, and then rose and hurried back to join von Schiller and Nahoot.

'You must go back to the pool where we left the others —' Nahoot started to relay the orders, but suddenly a strange, distracted expression crossed Hansith's darkly handsome features and he held up his hand for silence.

'What is it?' Nahoot demanded angrily. 'What is it that you can hear?'

Hansith shook his head. 'Be quiet! Listen! Can't you hear it?'

'There is nothing —' Nahoot began, but then broke off suddenly, and wild terror filled his dark eyes.

There was the softest sound, gentle as the sigh of a summer zephyr, lulling and low.

'What do you hear?' von Schiller demanded.

His hearing had long ago deteriorated, and the sound was far beyond the range of his old ears.

'Water!' whispered Nahoot. 'Running water!'

'The river!' shouted Hansith. 'The tunnel is flooding!' He whirled round and went bounding down the funeral arcade with long, lithe strides.

'We will be trapped in here!' screamed Nahoot, and raced after him.

'Wait for me,' von Schiller yelled, and tried to follow. But he soon fell behind the two much younger men.

The monk, however, was far ahead of both of them as he took the flight of stairs up from the gas trap two at a time.

'Hansith! Come back! I order you,' Nahoot cried despairingly in his wake, but he caught only a flash of the monk's white robe as he darted into the first twist of the labyrinth.

'Guddabi, where are you?' von Schiller's voice quavered and echoed through the stone corridors. But Nahoot did not reply as he ran on in the direction which he thought the monk had taken, passing the first turn in the maze without even glancing at the chalk marks on the wall. He thought he heard Hansith's racing footsteps ahead of him, but by the time he had turned the third corner he knew he was lost.

He stopped with his heart racing savagely and the bitter gall of terror in the back of his throat.

'Hansith! Where are you?' he screamed wildly.

Von Schiller's voice came back to him, ringing weirdly down the passageways, 'Guddabi!

851

Guddabi! Don't leave me here.'

'Shut up!' he screamed. 'Keep quiet, you old fool!'

Panting heavily, the blood pounding in his ears, he tried to listen for the sound of Hansith's feet. But he heard only the sound of the river. The gentle susurration seemed to emanate from the very walls around him.

'No! Don't leave me here,' he screamed, and began to run without direction, panic-stricken, through the maze.

Hansith took each twist and turn unerringly, with the terror of dreadful death driving his feet. But at the head of the central staircase his ankle twisted under him and he fell heavily. He tumbled down the steeply inclined shaft, bumping and rolling the full length, gathering speed as he went until he reached the bottom and lay sprawled on the agate tiles of the long gallery.

He dragged himself to his feet, bruised and shaken by the fall, and tried to run on. But his leg gave way under him again, and he fell in a tangle. His ankle was badly sprained and would not carry his weight. Nevertheless he dragged himself up a second time and hobbled down the gallery, supporting himself with one hand on the shattered wall.

When he reached the doorway and crawled

through it on to the landing beside the generator the sound of the water came up the tunnel. It was much louder now — a low, reverberating growl which almost blotted out the soft, discreet hum of the generator.

'Sweet loving Christ and the Virgin, save me!' he pleaded as he staggered and lurched down the tunnel, falling twice more before he reached the lower level.

On his knees he peered ahead, and in the glare of the electric lights strung along the roof of the tunnel he could make out the sink-hole below him. He did not at first recognize it, for it had all changed. The water level was no longer lower than the paved floor on which he sprawled. It was brimming, a great swirling maelstrom, and the water pouring into it was being sucked away through the hidden outlet almost as fast as it entered from the tunnel mouth on the far side. The pontoon bridge was tangled and half-submerged, bobbing and canting and rearing as it fought its retaining cables like an unbroken horse on a tether.

From Taita's pool a roaring river of water was boring down the far branch of the tunnel across the sink-hole. The tunnel was flooding rapidly, the water already reaching halfway up the walls, but he knew that it was the only escape route from the tomb. Every moment he delayed, the flood became stronger.

'I have to get out through there.' He pushed himself to his feet again.

He reached the first pontoon of the bridge, but it was careering about so madly that he dared not attempt to remain upright upon it. He dropped to his hands and knees, crawled out on to the flimsy structure and managed to drag himself forward from one pontoon to the next.

'Please God and St Michael help me. Don't let me die like this,' he prayed aloud. He reached the far side of the sink-hole and groped for a handhold on the roughly hewn walls of the tunnel.

He found a hold with his fingertips and pulled himself into the mouth of the tunnel, but now the full force of the water pouring down the shaft struck his lower body. He hung there for a moment, pinned by the raging waters, unable to move a pace forward. He knew that if his grip failed he would be swept back into the sink-hole and sucked down into those terrible black depths.

The electric bulbs strung along the roof of the tunnel ahead of him still burned brightly, so that he could see almost to the open basin of Taita's pool where the bamboo scaffolding would offer escape to the top of the chasm. It was only two hundred feet ahead of him. He gathered all his strength and pulled himself forward against the raging waters, reaching forward from one precarious handhold to the next. His fingernails tore and the flesh smeared from the tips of his fingers on the jagged rock, but he forced his way onwards.

At last he could see daylight ahead of him, filtering from Taita's pool. Only another forty feet to go, and he realized with a surge of relief and joy that he was going to make it out of the deadly trap of the shaft. Then he heard a fresh sound, a harsher, more brutal roar as the full flood of the burst dam poured down the waterfall into Taita's pool. It found the entrance to the tunnel and came down it in a solid wave, filling the passageway to the roof, ripping out the wiring of the lights and plunging Hansith into darkness.

It struck him with such force that it seemed to be not mere water but the solid rock of an avalanche, and he could not resist it. It tore him from his insecure perch and plucked him away, tossing him backwards, spinning him down the length of the shaft that he had gained with so much effort, and hurling him into the sink-hole beyond. He was swirled end over end by the crazed waters. In the darkness and wild confusion he did not know which direction was up and which down, but it made no difference for he could not swim against its power.

Then the sink-hole seized him full in its grip and sucked him swiftly and deeply down. The pressure of the water began to crush him. One of his eardrums burst, and as he opened his mouth to scream at the agony of it the water spurted down his throat and flooded his lungs. The last thing he ever felt was when he was flung against the side wall of the sink-hole, travelling as fast as the falling waters, and the bones of his right shoulder shattered. He could not scream again through his sodden lungs, but soon the pain faded into oblivion.

As his corpse was drawn swiftly through the subterranean shaft it became mangled and dismembered on the jagged rock sides, and was no longer recognizable as human by the time it was discharged through the butterfly fountain on the far side of the mountain. From there the torn fragments were washed down the diverted Dandera river to join, at last, the wider and more stately waters of the Blue Nile.

The waters pouring through the gap in the dam wall picked up the yellow front-loader and tumbled it over the waterfall into the chasm as though it were a child's toy. Nicholas had a glimpse of it in the air below him. Even as he fell himself, he realized that if he had stayed with the machine he would have been crushed beneath it. The huge machine struck the surface of the pool in a fountain of white spray and disappeared.

Nicholas followed it down, falling free, even managing to keep his head uppermost, feet foremost, as he swooped down the waterfall. The flood that carried him cushioned his fall, so that instead of being dashed against the exposed boulders at the bottom, he bounced and tumbled in the racing torrent. He came to the surface fifty yards downstream, tossed his wet hair out of his eyes and glanced around him quickly.

The tractor was gone, swallowed deep into the pool at the foot of the waterfall, but ahead of him was a small island of rock in the middle of the river. With a dozen overarm strokes he swam to it and clung to a rocky spur. From there he looked up at the sheer walls of the chasm and remembered the last time he had been trapped down here. The elation he had felt at the destruction of the dam and the flooding of Pharaoh's tomb evaporated.

He knew that he would not be able to climb those slick, water-smoothed cliffs that offered no handholds and which belled outwards in an overhang over his head. Instead he weighed the chances of working his way back upstream to the foot of the falls. From here it looked as though there was some sort of funnel or crevice up the east side of the chute which might offer a ladderway to the top, but it would be a hard and dangerous climb.

The volume of water coming over the falls was not as heavy as he had expected, considering the vast body of water that was being held back by the dam. He realized then that the greater part of the wall of gabions must still be in place and that this torrent was only the result of water escaping through the narrow gap he had torn in the centre of the wall. The remaining gabions must still be holding in place under their own weight. However, he realized that they could not hold much longer and that the river must soon plough them aside and burst through in full force. So he abandoned the idea of swimming back to the foot of the falls.

'Have to get out of its way,' he thought desperately, as he imagined being caught up in the terrible flood which would certainly come down at any moment. 'If I can reach the side somewhere, perhaps find a ledge, climb above the flood.' But he knew it was a forlorn hope. He had swum the length of the canyon once before without finding a handhold on the slick walls.

'Swim ahead of it?' he thought. 'A slim chance, but the only one I have.' He kicked off his boots, and gathered himself. He was about to push off from his temporary refuge, when he heard the rest of the dam wall high above him give way.

There was a rumbling roar, the crackle of logs snapping and breaking, the grating and grinding of heavy gabions being thrown around like empty rubbish cans, and then suddenly and terrifyingly a solid wave of grey water burst over the top of the falls, carrying with it a wall of trash and debris.

'Oh mother! Too late. Here comes the big one!'

He shoved off from his rock, turning downstream, and swam with all his strength, kicking and flailing his arms in a wild crawl stroke.

He heard the roar of the approaching wave and glanced back over his shoulder. It was over-hauling him swiftly, filling the chasm from wall to wall, fifteen feet high and curling at the top. He had a fleeting mental image from his youth, waiting to surf that notorious wave at Cape St Vincent, hanging on the line-up and seeing it humping up behind him, this great wall of water, so mountainous and so overwhelming.

'Ride it!' he told himself, judging the moment. 'Catch it like a slider.'

He clawed through the water, trying to get up speed to ride up the wall. He felt it seize him and lift him so violently that his guts swooped, and then he was on the crest of it. He arched his back and tucked his arms behind him in the classic body-surfer's position, hanging in the face of the wave, slightly head down, the front half of his body thrust clear of the water, steering with his legs. After the first few terrifying seconds he realized that he was riding her high and had some control; his panic abated and he was overcome by a sense of wild ex-hilaration.

'Twenty knots!' He estimated his speed by the giddy blur of the canyon walls passing him on either side. He steered away from the nearest wall, sliding across the face, taking up station in the centre of the wave. He was carried along by the wave and by the thrilling sensation of speed and danger.

The increased depth of water in the chasm

covered the dangerous, knife-sharp rocks, enabling him to ride clear of them. It smoothed out the waterfalls and the chutes, so that instead of dropping down them and plummeting below the surface of the pool beneath he slid down them with a smooth rush, holding his position in the face of the wave with a few quick overarm strokes or a kick of the legs.

'Hell! This is fun!' He laughed aloud. 'People would pay money to do this. Beats the hell out of bungee jumping.'

Within the first mile the wave began to lose its shape and impetus as it spread out down the canyon. Soon it would no longer have the power to hold him up in the surfing position, and he glanced around him swiftly. Floating near by, keeping pace with him in the flotsam of debris from the dam, was one of the treetrunks that had formed part of the raft with which Sapper had plugged the gap in the wall.

He steered across to this ponderous piece of timber. It was thirty feet long and floated low in the flood, its back showing like that of a whale. Its branches had been roughly hacked away by the axemen, and the spikes that remained provided secure handholds. Nicholas pulled himself up on to the treetrunk, lying on his belly, facing downstream, with his legs still dangling in the water. Swiftly he recovered his breath and felt his full strength returning.

Although it had smoothed out and lost its wave formation, the flood was still tearing down the chasm at a tremendous pace. 'Still not much under ten knots,' he estimated. 'When this lot hits Taita's pool, I pity von Schiller and any of his uglies who are in the tomb. They are going to stay in there for the next four thousand years.' He threw back his head and laughed triumphantly. 'It worked! Damn me to hell, if it didn't work just the way I planned it.'

He stopped laughing abruptly as he felt the treetrunk veer across the river towards one of the canyon walls.

'Oh, oh! More trouble.'

He rolled to one side of the treetrunk and kicked out strongly. His ungainly vessel responded, swinging heavily across the current. It was sluggish steering, not enough to avoid contact with the rock wall entirely, but instead of striking full-on it was merely a glancing collision that pushed him back again into the main flow of the current.

He was gaining confidence and expertise every moment, 'I can ride her all the way down to the monastery!' he exclaimed delightedly. 'At this rate of knots I might even get to the boats before Sapper and Royan.'

Looking ahead, he recognized this stretch of the chasm that he was hurtling through.

'This is the bend above Taita's pool. Be there in another minute or two. I expect the scaffolding has been washed away by now.'

He pulled himself as high on the log as he could without upsetting its balance, and peered ahead, blinking the water out of his eyes. He saw the head of the falls above Taita's pool racing towards him, and he braced himself for the drop.

The long, smooth chute of racing water opened ahead of him, and the moment before he flew down it he had a glimpse into the basin of rock below it. He saw at once that his expectations had been premature. The bamboo scaffolding had not been entirely washed away, although it was badly damaged. The lowest section was gone, but the upper part hung drunkenly down the rock cliff, just touching the surface of the racing waters. It was swaying and swinging loosely as the current snatched at it, and incredulously he realized that there were at least two men trapped on the flimsy structure, clinging desperately to the ladder-way of lurching, clattering poles. Both of them were trying to claw their way up it to the top of the cliff.

In that fraction of a second Nicholas saw a flash of steel-rimmed spectacles under a maroon beret, and realized that the man nearest the top of the cliff was Tuma Nogo. Then Nogo succeeded in reaching the top of the scaffolding and disappeared over the top of the cliff. That one glance was all Nicholas had time for before his log was plunged into the water-chute, gathering speed until it was tearing downwards at a steeply canted angle. The point dug in as it hit the surface of the pool at the bottom, and the log almost pole-vaulted end over end, but

Nicholas clung on to his handholds, and gradually it righted itself.

For a few moments the log was stalled in the vortex below the falls, but almost at once the current grabbed it again and it gathered speed, bearing away down the length of Taita's pool as ponderously as a wooden man-o'-war.

Nicholas had a second of respite in which to look around the basin of Taita's pool. He saw at once that the entrance tunnel to the tomb was entirely submerged and, judging by the water level up the cliff wall, it was already fifty feet or more beneath the surface. He felt a leap of triumph. The tomb was once more protected from the depredations of any other grave-robber.

Then he looked up the battered remnants of the bamboo scaffolding skewed down the cliff, torn half away from the ancient niches in the rock, and he saw the other man still clinging to the wreckage. He was twenty feet above the water level, and seemed frozen there like a cat in the high branches of a windswept tree.

At that moment Nicholas realized that his log was swinging in the grip of the river, curling in towards the dangling scaffold. He was about to try to steer it clear, when the man on the framework high above him turned his head and looked down at him. Nicholas saw that he was a white man, his face a pale blob in the gloom of the canyon, and a moment later he recognized him with a stab of hatred through the chest.

'Helm!' he exclaimed. 'Jake Helm.'

He had an image of Tamre, the epileptic boy, crushed beneath the rockfall, and of Tessay's burned and battered face. His outrage and hatred surged. Instead of steering the log away from the scaffold, he reversed his thrust and swung in towards the cliff. There was a breathless interval when Nicholas thought he might miss, but at the last moment the leading end of the log swung sharply and the point of it crashed into the trailing end of the bamboo, hooking on to it.

The log's weight and momentum were irresistible. The bamboo poles crackled and snapped like dry kindling, and then the whole rickety structure tore loose from the wall and came crashing down over the log. Helm swung out overhead, then released his grip and dropped feet first into the water close alongside the log. He went deep below the surface. While he was under, Nicholas pulled himself up to sit astride the log and grabbed a length of bamboo pole that had broken off the scaffolding and was floating alongside his perch.

The log was trapped in a back eddy of the swollen river, and now it began to spin slowly in the slack water outside the main current. Nicholas was still riding high on the log. He hefted the bamboo, swinging it back and forth like a baseball bat, to get the feel of it. Then he cocked it over his shoulder and waited for Helm to show himself.

A second later the Texan's head broke out, streaming water. His eyes were screwed closed, and he let out a gasp of water and air and tried to suck in a breath. Nicholas aimed the pole at his head and swung with all his strength, but just at that moment Helm opened his eyes and saw the blow coming.

He was as quick as a water snake, rolling his head under the swinging club so that it merely touched the side of his cropped blond head and then glanced away. Nicholas was thrown off balance by his own swing, and before he could recover Helm had drawn a quick breath and ducked below the surface again.

Nicholas poised the club, ready to strike a second time, peering down into the murky water, muttering angrily at himself for having missed the first blow while he still had the advantage of surprise. He had no illusions about what he was in for, now that Helm had been warned.

The seconds drew out with no sign of his adversary reappearing, and Nicholas looked behind him anxiously, trying to anticipate where he would come up again. For a long minute nothing happened. He lowered the club nervously, and changed his grip so as to be ready to stab in any direction with the sharp broken tip.

Suddenly his left ankle was seized in a crushing grip below the water and, before he could grab a handhold to resist, Nicholas was jerked from his seat on the log and went over backwards into the river. As he plunged beneath the water he felt Helm's fingers clawing at his face. He grabbed one of the fingers and wrenched it back, feeling it snap in his grasp as he forced it back towards its own wrist. But Helm was galvanized by the agony of the dislocated joint, and one of his long muscular arms whipped around Nicholas's neck like the tentacles of an octopus.

The two of them came to the surface for a moment, both of them drew one quick, harsh breath, then Helm forced Nicholas's head backwards and water flooded into his open mouth. The lock on his neck tightened, and he felt the tension on his vertebrae. It was a killer grip. If Helm had only had a solid purchase he could have exerted the last ounce of pressure which would have snapped his spine. But Nicholas kept rolling back in the direction of the thrust, giving with it, and preventing Helm from bringing all his strength to bear. As he went over he saw Helm's face in front of his, magnified and distorted through the tainted grey water. He looked monstrous and evil.

As Helm rolled over the top of him Nicholas locked both hands around his waist to hold him firmly, then brought up his right knee between Helm's legs, hard into his crotch, and felt the bone of his kneecap make contact. The bunch of genitals was full and rubbery; Helm contorted and his lock on Nicholas's neck eased. Nicholas used the slack to reach down and grab a handful of Helm's damaged testicles and twist them savagely. He saw the man's face inches in front of his own twist into a rictus of pain and Helm pulled away from him, releasing his lock on Nicholas's throat and reaching down to grab his wrist with both hands.

Again they came to the surface close alongside the floating log, and Nicholas realized that the current had taken hold of them again and was carrying them away through the outlet of Taita's pool into the full stream of the river. Nicholas released his grip on Helm's balls and with his other hand aimed a punch at his face, but they were too close to each other and the blow lacked power. It glanced off Helm's cheek, and Nicholas tried to lock his extended arm around his neck, going for a headlock himself. Helm hunched his head down on his shoulders, slipping under the hold. Then suddenly he reached forward fast as a striking adder and sank his teeth into Nicholas's chin.

The surprise was complete, and the pain was excruciating as his teeth locked into the flesh. Nicholas shouted and clawed at Helm's face, going for his eyes, trying to drive his fingernails through the lids. But Helm squeezed his eyes tight closed and his teeth cut in ever deeper, so that Nicholas's blood welled up and oozed from the corners of Helm's mouth.

The log was still floating beside them, inches from the back of Helm's head. Nicholas seized his ears, one in each hand, and twisted him around in the water. He could see over the top of Helm's head, while Helm's vision was blocked. There was a nub of raw wood sticking out of the tree trunk where an axe had hacked away a side branch. The cut was at an angle, leaving a sharp spike. Through tears of agony Nicholas lined up the spike with the back of Helm's head. He could feel Helm's teeth almost meeting in the flesh of his face. They had cut through the lower lip so that blood was starting to fill Nicholas's mouth. Helm was worrying him like a pit-bull in the arena, wrenching his head from side to side. Soon he would come away with a bloody mouthful of Nicholas's flesh.

With all the strength of pain and desperation, Nicholas hurled himself forward, and, using his upper body and his grip on the sides of Helm's head, drove him on to the sharp wooden spike. The point found the joint between the vertebrae of the spine and the base of Helm's skull, going in like a nail and partially severing the spinal cord. Helm's jaws sprang open as he went into spasm. Nicholas pulled away from him with a flap of loose flesh hanging from his chin, and blood streaming and spurting from the deep ragged wound.

Helm was impaled upon the spike, like a carcass on a butcher's hook. His limbs twitched and the muscles of his face convulsed, his eyelids shivered and jumped like those of an epileptic, and his eyeballs rolled back into his skull so that only the whites showed, flashing grotesquely in the gloom of the chasm.

Nicholas pulled himself up on to the log beside the Texan's body, and hung there panting and bleeding in gouts down his chin on to his chest. Slowly the log revolved under the eccentric weight distribution, and Helm began to slide off the spike. His skin tore with a sound like silk parting, and the vertebrae of his spine grated on wood. Then the corpse, at last quiescent, flopped face down into the water and began to sink.

Nicholas would not let him go so easily. 'Let's make sure of you, dear boy,' he grated through his swollen, bleeding mouth. He spat out a mouthful of blood and saliva as he stretched out and grabbed the back of Helm's collar, holding him face down in the water under the log. They picked up speed rapidly down the last stretch of the canyon, but Nicholas held on doggedly, drowning any last spark of life from Helm's carcass, until at last it was torn from his grip by the current and he watched it sink away into the grey, roiling waters.

'I'll give your love to Tessay,' Nicholas called after him as he disappeared. Then he gave all his concentration to balancing the log and staying aboard for the ride through the tumbling, racing current. At last he was spewed out through the pink rock portals into the bottom reach of the Dandera river. As he was swept beneath the rope suspension bridge he slid off the log and struck out for the western bank, very much aware of the terrible drop into the Nile that lay half a mile downstream.

Sitting on the bank, he tore a strip from the tail of his shirt. Then he bound up his wounded chin as best he could, strapping it around the back of his head. The blood soaked through the thin wet cotton, but he knotted it tighter and it began to staunch the flow.

He stood up unsteadily and pushed his way through the strip of thick riverine bush which bounded the river, until at last he struck the trail that led down to the monastery and hobbled down it on his bare feet. He only stopped once, and that was when he heard the sound of the helicopter taking off from the top of the cliff above the chasm far behind him.

He looked back. 'Sounds as though Tuma Nogo made it out of there, more's the pity. I wonder what happened to von Schiller and the Egyptian,' he muttered grimly, fingering his injured face. 'At least none of them are going to get into the tomb, not unless they dam the river again.' Suddenly a thought occurred to him.

'My God, what if von Schiller was already in there when the river hit?' He began to chuckle, and then shook his head. 'Too much to hope for. Justice is never that neat.' He shook his head again, but the movement started his wound aching brutally. He clutched his bandaged jaw with one hand and started down the trail again, breaking into a trot as he reached the paved causeway that led down to the monastery.

Nahoot Guddabi ran full into von Schiller around a corner of the maze, and in a peculiar way the old man's presence, even though he was of no conceivable value in this crisis, steadied him and kept at bay the panic that threatened at any moment to boil over and overwhelm him. Without Hansith the maze was a weird and lonely place. Any human company was a blessing. For a moment the two of them clung together like children lost in the forest.

Von Schiller still carried part of the treasure that they had been examining when Hansith had panicked and run. He had Pharaoh's golden crook in one hand and the ceremonial flail in the other.

'Where is the monk?' he screamed at Guddabi. 'Why did you run off and leave me? We have to find the way out of these tunnels, you idiot. Don't you realize the danger?'

'How do you expect me to know the way —' Nahoot began furiously, and then broke off as he noticed the chalk notations on the wall behind von Schiller's shoulder, and for the first time realized their significance.

'That's it!' he exclaimed with relief. 'Harper or the Al Simma woman have marked it out for us. Come on!' He started down the tunnel, following the signposting. However, by the time they came out on the central staircase almost an hour had passed since Hansith had left them. As they hurried down the staircase into the long gallery the sound of the river rose to a pervading hiss, like the breathing of a sleeping dragon.

Nahoot broke into a run and von Schiller staggered along behind him, his aged legs weakening with fear.

'Wait!' he shouted after Nahoot, who ignored his plea and ducked out through the opening in the plaster-sealed doorway. On the landing the generator was still running smoothly, and Nahoot did not even glance at it as he hurried down the inclined shaft in the bright dazzle of the light bulbs along the roof.

He turned the corner still at a run, and stopped dead as he realized that the tunnel below him was flooded, right back up to the level of the ancient high-water mark on the masonry blocks of the walls. There was no sign of the sink-hole or the pontoon bridge. They were submerged under fifty feet or more of water.

The Dandera river, guardian of the tomb down all the ages, had resumed its duty. Dark and implacable, it sealed the entrance to the tomb as it had done these four thousand years past.

'Allah!' whispered Nahoot. 'Allah have mercy on us.'

Von Schiller came around the corner of the tunnel and stopped beside Nahoot. The two of them stared in horror at the flooded shaft. Then slowly von Schiller sagged against the side wall.

'We are trapped,' he whispered, and at those words Nahoot whimpered softly and sank to his knees. He began to pray in a high, nasal sing-song. The sound infuriated von Schiller.

'That will not help us. Stop it!' He swung the golden flail in his right hand across Nahoot's bowed back. Nahoot cried out at the pain and crawled away from von Schiller.

'We must find a way out of here.' Von Schiller's voice steadied. He was accustomed to command, and now he took charge.

'There must be another way out of here,' he decided. 'We will search. If there is an opening to the outside then we should feel a draught of air.' His voice became firmer and more confident. 'Yes! That's what we will do. Switch off that fan, and we will try to detect any movement of air.'

Nahoot responded eagerly to his tone and authority, and hurried back to switch off the electric fan.

'You have your cigarette lighter,' von Schiller told him. 'We will light tapers from these.' He pointed at the papers and photographs that Royan had left lying on the trestle table by the doorway. 'We will use the smoke to detect any draught.'

For the next two hours they moved through all levels of the tomb, holding aloft the burning tapers, watching the movement of the smoke. At no point could they detect even the faintest movement of air in the tunnels, and in the end

873

they came back to the flooded shaft and stared despairingly at the pool of still black water that blocked it.

'That is the only way out,' von Schiller whispered.

'I wonder if the monk escaped that way,' said Nahoot as he slumped down the wall.

'There is no other way.'

They were silent for a while; it was difficult to judge the passage of time in the tomb. Now that the river had found its own level there was no movement of water in the shaft, and the faint and distant sound of the current running through the sink-hole seemed merely to enhance the silence. In it they could hear their own breathing.

Nahoot spoke at last. 'The fuel in the generator. It must be running low. I did not see any reserves —'

They thought about what would happen when the small fuel tank ran dry. They thought about the darkness to come.

Suddenly von Schiller screamed, 'You have to go out through the shaft to fetch help. I order you to do it.'

Nahoot stared at him in disbelief. 'It's over a hundred yards back through the tunnel to the outside, and the river is in flood.'

Von Schiller sprang to his feet and stood over Nahoot threateningly. 'The monk escaped that way. It's the only way. You must swim through the tunnel and reach Helm and Nogo. Helm will know what to do. He will make a plan to get me out of here.'

'You are mad.' Nahoot backed away from him, but von Schiller followed him.

'I order you to do it!'

'You crazy old man!' Nahoot tried to scramble to his feet, but von Schiller swung the heavy golden flail, a sudden unexpected blow in Nahoot's face that knocked him over backwards, splitting his lips and breaking off two of his front teeth.

'You are mad!' he wailed. 'You can't do this —' but von Schiller swung again and again, lacerating his face and shoulders, the heavy golden tails of the whip cutting through the thin cotton of his shirt.

'I will kill you,' von Schiller screamed, raining blows on him. 'If you don't obey me I will kill you.'

'Stop!' Nahoot whined. 'No, please, stop. I will do it, only stop.'

He crawled away from von Schiller, dragging himself along the floor of the tunnel until he sat waist-deep in the water.

'Give me time to prepare,' he pleaded.

'Go now!' Von Schiller menaced him, lifting the whip high. 'Very likely you will find air trapped in the tunnel. You will find your way through. Go!'

Nahoot scooped a double handful of water and dashed it into his own face, washing away the blood that poured from one of the deep cuts in his cheek.

'I have to take off my clothes, my shoes,' he whimpered, pleading for time, but von Schiller would not allow him to leave the water.

'Do it where you are standing,' he ordered, brandishing the heavy whip. In his other hand he held the heavy golden crook. Nahoot realized that a blow from that weapon could crack his skull.

Standing knee-deep at the water's edge, Nahoot hopped on one foot as he pulled off his shoes. Then, slowly and reluctantly, he stripped to his underpants. His shoulders were deeply scored by the lash of the flail, fresh blood welling up and slithering like scarlet serpents down his back.

He knew that he had to placate this crazy old madman. He would duck under the surface and swim a short way down the tunnel, hold on to the side wall down there for as long as his breath lasted, and then swim back again.

'Go!' von Schiller shouted at him. 'You are wasting time. Don't think that I will let you get out of this.'

Nahoot waded deeper into the shaft until the water covered his chest. He paused there for a few minutes as he drew a series of deep breaths. Then at last he held his breath and ducked below the surface. Von Schiller stood waiting at the edge of the pool, staring down into it but unable to see anything beneath the black and ominous surface. In the lamplight Nahoot's blood stained the surface.

A minute passed slowly, and then suddenly there was a heavy swirl beneath the waters, and a human arm rose through the dark surface, hand and fingers extended as though in supplication. Then slowly it sank out of sight again.

Von Schiller craned forward, 'Guddabi!' he called angrily. 'What are you playing at?'

There was another swirl below the water, and something flashed like a mirror in the depths.

'Guddabi!' von Schiller's voice rose petulantly.

Almost as if in response to the summons, Nahoot's head broke out through the surface. His skin was waxen yellow, drained of all blood, and his mouth gaped open in a dreadful, silent scream. The water around him boiled as though a shoal of great fish were feeding below. As von Schiller stared in incomprehension, a dark tide rose up around Nahoot's head and stained the surface a rose-petal red. For a moment von Schiller did not realize that it was Nahoot's blood.

Then he saw the long, sinuous shapes darting and twisting beneath the surface, surrounding Nahoot, feeding upon his flesh. Nahoot lifted his hand again and extended it towards von Schiller, pleadingly. The arm was half-devoured, mutilated by deep half-moon wounds where the flesh had been bitten away in chunks.

Von Schiller screamed in horror, backing away

from the pool. Nahoot's eyes were huge and dark and accusing. He stared at von Schiller and a wild cawing sound that was not human issued from his straining throat.

Even as von Schiller watched, one of the giant tropical eels thrust its head through the surface and its teeth gleamed like broken glass as it gaped wide, and then locked its jaws on to Nahoot's throat. Nahoot made no effort to tear the creature away. He was too far gone. He stared at von Schiller all the while that the eel, twisting and rolling into a gleaming ball of slimy coils, still hung from his throat.

Slowly Nahoot's head sank below the surface again. For long minutes the pool was agitated by the movements in its depth and the occasional gleam of one of the serpentine fish. Then gradually the surface settled as still and serene as a sheet of black glass.

Von Schiller turned and ran, back up the incline shaft, past the landing on which the generator still puttered quietly, blindly trying to get as far away as he could from that dreadful pool. He did not know where he was going, but followed any passageway that opened in front of him. At the foot of the central stairway he ran into the corner of the wall and stunned himself, falling to the agate tiles and lying there blubbering as a large purple lump rose on his forehead.

After a while he dragged himself to his feet and lurched up the stairs. He was confused and disorientated, his mind starting to break up in delirium, driven over the edge of sanity by horror and fear. He fell again, and crawled along the tunnel on his hands and knees to the next corner of the maze. Only then was he able to regain his feet to stagger onwards.

The steep shaft leading down into Taita's gas trap opened under his feet without him seeing it. He fell down the steps, jarring and bruising his legs and chest. Then he was on his feet again, reeling across the store room past the ranks of amphorae, up the far staircase and into the painted arcade that led to the tomb of Pharaoh Mamose.

He had tottered down half the length of it, dishevelled and wild-eyed and demented, when suddenly the lights dimmed for a moment, fading to a yellow glow. Then they brightened again as the generator sucked the last drops of fuel from the bottom of the tank. Von Schiller stopped in the centre of the arcade and looked up at the lights with despair. He knew what was coming. For another few minutes the bulbs burned on, bright and cheerfully, and then again they dimmed and faded.

The darkness settled over him like the heavy velvet folds of a funeral pall. It was so intense and complete that it seemed to have a physical weight and texture. He could taste the darkness in his mouth as it seemed to force its way into his body and suffocate him.

He ran again, wildly and blindly, losing all

sense of direction in the blackness. He crashed headlong into stone and fell again, stunned. He could feel the warm tickle of blood running down his face, and he could not breathe. He whimpered and gasped and slowly, lying on his side, he curled himself into a ball like a foetus in the womb.

He wondered how long it would take him to die, and his soul quailed as he knew that it might take days and even weeks. He moved slightly, cuddling in closer to the stone object with which he had collided. In the darkness he had no way of telling that it was the great sarcophagus of Mamose that sheltered him. Thus he lay in the darkness of the tomb, surrounded by the funeral treasures of an emperor, and waited for his own slow but inexorable death.

The monastery of St Frumentius was deserted. The monks had heard the gunfire and the sounds of battle echoing down the gorge, and had gathered up their treasures and fled.

Nicholas ran down the long, empty cloister, pausing to catch his breath at the head of the staircase that led down to the level of the Nile and the Epiphany shrine where he had stored the boats. Panting, he searched the gloom of the deep basin below him into which the sunlight seldom reached, but the moving clouds of silver spray from the twin waterfalls screened the depths. He had no way of telling if Sapper and Royan were down there waiting for him, or if they had run into trouble on the trail.

He adjusted the tattered and bloodstained bandage around his chin, and then started down. Then he heard her voice in the silver mist below him, calling his name, and she came pelting up the slippery, slime-covered stairs towards him.

'Nicholas! Oh, thank God! I thought you weren't coming.' She would have rushed into his embrace, but then she saw his bandaged and blood-smeared face, and she stopped and stared at him, appalled.

'Sweet Mary!' she whispered. 'What happened to you, Nicky?'

'A little tiff with Jake Helm. Just a scratch, but I am not much good at kissing right now,' he mumbled, trying to grin around the bandage. 'You will have to wait for later.'

He put one arm around her shoulders, almost swinging her off her feet, as he turned her to face down the stairs again.

'Where are the others?' He hurried her down.

'They are all here,' she told him. 'Sapper and Mek are pumping the boats and loading.'

'Tessay?'

'She's safe.'

They scrambled down the last flight of steps on to the jetty below the Epiphany shrine. The Nile had risen ten feet since Nicholas had last stood there. The river was full and angry, muddy and swift. He could barely make out the cliffs on the far bank through the drifting clouds of spray.

The five Avon boats were drawn up at the edge. Four of them were already fully inflated, and the last one was billowing and swelling as the air was released into it from the compressed air cylinder. Mek and Sapper were packing the ammunition crates into the ready boats and strapping them down under green nylon cargo nets.

Sapper looked up at Nicholas and a comical expression of astonishment spread over his bluff features, 'What the blue bleeding blazes happened to your face?'

'Tell you about it one day,' Nicholas promised, and turned to embrace Mek.

'Thank you, old friend,' he said sincerely. 'Your men fought well, and you waited for me.' Nicholas glanced at the row of wounded guerrillas that lay against the foot of the cliff. 'How many casualties?'

'Three dead, and these six wounded. It could have been much worse if Nogo's men had pushed us harder.'

'Still, it's too many,' said Nicholas.

'Even one is too many,' Mek agreed gruffly.

'Where are the rest of your men?'

'On the run for the border. Kept just enough of them with me to handle the boats.' Mek stripped the filthy bandage from Nicholas's chin. Royan gasped when she saw the injury, but Mek grinned.

'Looks as though you were chewed by a shark.'

'That's right, I was,' Nicholas agreed.

Mek shrugged. 'It needs at least a dozen stitches.' He shouted for one of his men to bring his pack.

'Sorry, no anaesthetic,' he warned Nicholas as he forced him to sit on the transom of one of the boats and poured antiseptic straight from the bottle.

Nicholas let out a gasp of pain. 'Burns, doesn't it?' Mek agreed complacently. 'But just wait until I start sewing.'

'This kindness will be written down against your name in the golden book,' Nicholas told him, and with an evil leer Mek broke the seal on a suture pack.

As Mek worked on the wound, pulling the edges together and tugging the thread tight, he spoke quietly so that Nicholas alone could hear. 'Nogo has at least a full company of men guarding the river downstream. My scouts tell me that he has placed them to cover the trails on both banks.'

'He doesn't know that we have boats to run the river, does he?' Nicholas asked through gritted teeth.

'I think it is unlikely, but he knows a great deal about our movements. Perhaps he had an informer amongst your workmen.' Mek paused as he pricked the needle into Nicholas's flesh, and then went on, 'And Nogo still has the helicopter. He will spot us on the river as soon as this cloud breaks.'

'The river is our only escape route. Let's pray that the weather stays socked in, like this.'

By the time Mek had tied off the last knot and covered Nicholas's chin with a Steri-Strip plaster, Sapper had finished inflating and loading the last boat.

Four of Mek's men carried Tessay's litter to one of the boats. Mek helped her aboard and settled her on the deck, making sure that she had one of the safety straps close at hand. Then he left her and hurried to where his wounded men lay in order to help them into the boats too. Most of them could walk, but two had to be carried.

After that he came back to Nicholas. 'I see you have found your radio,' he said, as he glanced at the fibreglass case that Nicholas had slung over his shoulder on its carrying strap.

'Without it we would be in big trouble.' Nicholas patted the case affectionately.

'I will take command of that boat, with Tessay.'

'Good!' Nicholas agreed. 'Royan will go with me in the lead boat.'

'You had better let me lead,' Mek said.

'What do you know about river running?' Nicholas asked him. 'I am the only one of us who has ever shot this river before.'

'That was twenty years ago,' Mek pointed out.

'I am an even better man now than I was then,' Nicholas grinned. 'Don't argue, Mek. You come next, and Sapper in the one behind you. Are there any of your men who know the river to command the other two boats?'

'All my men know the river,' Mek told him, and shouted his orders. Each of them hurried to the Avon he had been allocated. Nicholas gave Royan a boost over the gunwale of their boat, and then helped his men launch her down the rocky bank. As soon as the hull floated free they scrambled aboard and each man grabbed a paddle.

As they bent to their paddles, Nicholas saw at once that every man of his crew was indeed a riverman, as Mek had boasted. They pulled strongly but smoothly, and the light inflatable craft shot out into the main stream of the Nile.

The Avons were designed to accommodate sixteen, and were lightly loaded. The ammunition cases that held the grave goods from the tomb were bulky but weighed little, and there were not more than a dozen people in any one boat. They all floated high and handled well.

'Bad water ahead,' Nicholas told Royan grimly. 'All the way to the Sudanese border.' He stood at the steering sweep in the stern, from where he had a good forward view. Royan crouched at his feet, clinging to one of the safety straps and trying to keep out of the way of the oarsmen.

They cut across the current that was scouring

the great stone basin below the falls, and Nicholas lined up for the narrow heads through which the river was escaping to the west. He looked up at the sky and saw through the spray that the rain clouds were low and purple. They seemed to sag down upon the tops of the tall cliffs.

'Luck starting to run our way,' he told Royan. 'Even with the helicopter they won't be able to find us in this weather.'

He glanced at his Rolex and the spray was beading the glass. 'Couple of hours until nightfall. We should be able to put a few miles of river behind us before we are forced to stop for the night.'

He looked back over his stern and saw the rest of the little flotilla bobbing along behind him. The Avons were reflective yellow in colour and stood out brilliantly even in the mist and murk of the gorge. He lifted his clenched fist high in the signal to advance, and from the following boat Mek repeated the gesture and grinned at him through his beard.

The river grabbed them and they shot through its portals into the narrow, twisted gut of the Nile. The men at the oars stopped paddling, and let the river take them. All they could do now was to help Nicholas to steer her through any desperate moments, and they crouched ready along the gunwales.

The high water in the gorge had covered many of the reefs of rock, but their presence below the surface was clearly marked by the waters that humped up in standing waves or foamed white in the narrows between them. The flood reached up high on either bank, dashing against the cliffs of the sub-gorge. If an Avon overturned, or even if a crew member were thrown overboard, there would be no place on this river to heave-to and pick up survivors.

Nicholas stood high and craned ahead. He had to pick his route well in advance, and once committed he had to steer her through. It all depended on his ability to read the river and judge her moods. He was out of practice, and he had that tight, hard cannonball of fear in the pit of his belly as he put the long sweep over and steered for the first run of fast green water. They went swooping down it, Nicholas holding their bows into it with delicate touches of the sweep, and came out into the bottom of it with all the other boats following them down in sequence.

'Nothing to it!' Royan laughed up at him.

'Don't say it!' Nicholas pleaded with her. 'The bad angel is listening.' And he lined up for the head of the next set of rapids that raced towards them with terrifying speed.

Nicholas steered through the gap between two outcrops of rock and they shot the barrel, gaining speed down the chute. It was only when they were halfway down that he saw the tall standing wave below them over which the river leaped. He put the sweep across and tried to steer round it, but the river had them firmly in its grip.

Like a hunter taking a fence they shot up the front of the standing wave, and then with a sickening lurch plummeted down the far side into the deep trough. The Avon folded across the middle, the bows almost touching the stern as she tried to pull through the hole in the river surface.

The crew were tumbled over each other and Nicholas would have been catapulted overside if it had not been for his body line and his grip on the steering sweep. Royan flung herself flat on the deck and hung on to the safety strap with all her strength as the Avon's buoyancy exerted itself and the boat bounded high in the air, whipping back elastically into its original shape, then hovered a moment and almost capsized before it crashed back, right side up.

One of the crew had been hurled overboard and was floundering alongside, carried along at the same speed as the flying Avon, so his comrades were able to lean out and haul him back on board. The cargo of ammunition crates had tumbled and shifted, but the nets had prevented any of them from being lost over the side.

'What did you do that for?' Royan yelled at him. 'Just when I was beginning to trust you.'

'Just testing,' he yelled back. 'Wanted to see how tough you really are.'

'I admit it, I am a sissy,' she assured him. 'You really don't need to do it again.'

Looking back, Nicholas saw Mek's boat crash

through the trough just as they had, but the following craft had enough warning to steer clear and slip through the sides of the run.

He looked ahead again, and his whole existence became the wild waters of the river. His universe was contained within the tall cliffs of the sub-gorge as he battled to bring the racing Avon through. He did not know whether it was spray or rain that stung his cheeks and his wounded chin, and that flew horizontally into his eyes and half-blinded him. At times it was a mixture of the two.

An hour later Nicholas misjudged the rapids again, and they went in sideways and almost capsized. Two of his crew were hurled overboard. Steering fine and leaning outboard they managed to pull one of them from the river, but the other man struck a rock before they could reach him. He went under and did not rise again. None of them spoke or mourned him, for they were all too busy staying alive themselves.

Once Royan shouted up at Nicholas through the rattling spray and the thunder of the river all around them, 'Helicopter! Can you hear it?'

Half-deafened, he looked up at the lowering grey belly of the clouds that hung at the level of the cliffs, and faintly made out the whistle and flutter of the rotors.

'Above the cloud!' he shouted back, wiping the rain and the spray from his eyes with the back of his hand. 'They will never spot us in this.'

The onset of the African night was sped upon them by the low cloud. In the gathering darkness another hazard leaped upon them with no warning at all. One instant they were running hard and clear down a smooth stretch of the river, and the next the waters opened ahead of them and they were hurled out into space. It seemed that they fell for ever, although it was a drop of not more than thirty feet, before they hit the bottom and found themselves floating in a tangle of men and boats in the pool below the falls. Here the river was stalled for a moment, revolving upon itself while it gathered its strength for the next mad charge down the gorge.

One of the Avons had capsized and was floating belly up — even its highly stable hull had not been able to weather the drop down the falls. The crews of the other boats gathered themselves and then paddled across to drag the survivors from the water and to salvage the oars and other floating equipment. It took the combined efforts of all of them to right the overturned Avon, and then it was almost completely dark by the time they had it back on even keel.

'Count the crates!' Nicholas ordered. 'How many have we lost?'

He could hardly credit his good fortune when Sapper shouted back, 'Eleven still on board. All present and correct.' The cargo nets were holding well. But all of them, men and women, were exhausted and soaked through and shivering with the cold. Any attempt to go on in darkness would be suicidal. Nicholas looked across at Mek in the nearest boat and shook his head.

'There is a bit of slack water in the angle of the cliff.' Mek pointed towards the tail of the pool. 'We might be able to find moorings for the night.'

There was a stunted but tough little tree growing out of the vertical fissure in the rock, and they used this as a bollard and made a line fast to it. Then they lashed all the Avons together in a line down the cliff and settled in for the night. There was no chance of hot food or drink and they had to make do with some cold tinned rations eaten off the blade of a bayonet, and a few chunks of soggy *injera* bread.

Mek scrambled over from his own boat and huddled down close beside Nicholas with one arm over his shoulder and his lips close to his ear.

'I have made a roll call. Another man missing when we went over the falls. We won't find him now.'

'I am not doing too well,' Nicholas admitted. 'Perhaps you should lead tomorrow.'

'Not your fault.' Mek squeezed his shoulders. 'Nobody could have done better. It was this last waterfall —' he broke off and they listened to it thundering away in the darkness.

'How far have we come?' Nicholas asked. 'And how much further to go?'

'It's almost impossible to tell, but I guess we are halfway to the border. Should reach there some time tomorrow afternoon.'

They were silent for a while, and then Mek asked, 'What is the date today? I have lost count of the days.'

'So have I.' Nicholas tilted his wrist-watch so that he could read the luminous dial in the last of the light. 'Good God! It's the thirtieth already,' he said.

'Your pick-up aircraft is due at Roseires air-strip the day after tomorrow.'

'The first of April,' Nicholas agreed. 'Will we make it?'

'You answer that question for me.' Mek grinned in the night without humour. 'What chances of your fat friend being late?'

'Jannie is a pro. He is never late,' said Nicholas. Again a silence fell, and then Nicholas asked, 'When we reach Roseires, what do you want me to do with your share of the booty?' Nicholas kicked one of the ammunition crates. 'Do you want to take it with you?'

'After we see you off on the plane with your fat friend, we are going to be doing some hot-footed running from Nogo. I don't want to be carrying any extra luggage. You take my share with you. Sell it for me — I need the money to keep fighting here.'

'You trust me?'

'You are my friend.'

'Friends are the easiest to cheat — they never expect it,' Nicholas told him, and Mek punched his shoulder and chuckled.

'Get some sleep. We will have to do some hard paddling tomorrow.' Mek stood up in the Avon as she pitched and rolled gently to the push of the current. 'Sleep well, old friend,' he said, and climbed across to the boat alongside, where Tessay waited for him.

Nicholas braced his back against the soft pneumatic gunwale of the Avon and took Royan in his arms. She sat between his knees and leaned back against his chest, shivering in her sodden clothes.

After a while her shivering abated, and she murmured, 'You make a very good hot-water bottle.'

'That's one reason for keeping me around on a permanent basis,' he said, and stroked her wet hair. She did not answer him, but snuggled closer, and a short while afterwards her breathing slowed as she fell into an exhausted sleep.

Although he was cold and stiff and his shoulders ached and his palms were blistered from wrestling with the steering oar, he could not find sleep as readily as she had. Now that the prospect of reaching the airstrip at Roseires loomed closer, he was troubled by problems other than those of simply navigating the river and battling his way through Nogo's men. Those were enemies he could recognize and fight; but there was something more than that which he would soon have to face.

Royan stirred in his arms and muttered something he could not catch. She was dreaming and talking in her sleep.

He held her gently and she settled down again. He had started to drift off himself when she spoke again, this time quite clearly. 'I am sorry, Nicky. Don't hate me for it. I couldn't let you —' her words slurred and he could make no sense of the rest of it.

He was fully awake now, her words aggravating his doubts and misgivings. During the rest of that night he slept only intermittently, and his rest was troubled by dreams as distressing as hers must have been to her.

On the pre-dawn darkness he shook Royan gently. She moaned and came awake slowly and reluctantly.

They bolted down a few mouthfuls of the cold rations that remained from the previous night. Then, as dawn lit the gorge just enough for them to see the surface of the river and the obstacles ahead, they pushed off from their moorings and the yellow boats strung out down the current. The battle against the river began all over again.

The cloud cover was still low and unbroken, and the rain squalls swept over them at intervals.

They kept going all that morning, and slowly the mood of the river began to ameliorate. The current was not so swift and treacherous, and the banks not so high and rugged.

It was mid-afternoon and the clouds were still closed in solidly overhead as they entered a stretch where the river threaded itself through a series of bluffs and headlands, and they came upon another set of rapids. Perhaps Nicholas was more expert in his technique by now, for they swept through them without mishap, and it seemed to him that each stretch of white water was progressively less severe than the last.

'I think we are through the worst of it now,' he told Royan as she sat on the deck below him. 'The gradient and the fall of the river are definitely more gentle now. I think it is flattening out as we approach the plains of the Sudan.'

'How much further to Roseires?' she asked.

'I don't know, but the border can't be too far ahead now.'

Nicholas and Mek were keeping the flotilla closed up in line astern, so that orders could be shouted across the gaps between them and all the boats kept under their command.

Nicholas steered for the deeper water on the outside of the next wide bend, and as he came through it he saw that the stretch of river ahead seemed open and altogether free of rapids or shoals. He relaxed and smiled at Royan.

'How about lunch at the Dorchester grill next Sunday? Best roast beef trolley in London.'

He thought he saw a shadow pass across her eyes before she smiled brightly and replied, 'Sounds good to me.'

'And afterwards we can go back home and curl up in front of the telly and watch *Match of the Day*, or play our own little match.'

'You are rude,' she laughed, 'but it does sound tempting.'

He was about to stoop over her, and kiss her for the pleasure of watching her blush again, when he saw the dance of tiny white fountains spurting up from the surface of the river ahead of their bows, coming swiftly towards them. Then, moments later, he heard the crackle of automatic fire, the distinctive sound of a Soviet RPD.

He threw himself down over the top of Royan, covering her with his own body, and heard Mek bellowing from the boat behind them.

'Return fire! Keep their heads down.'

His men threw down their paddles and seized their weapons. They blazed away towards the inner curve of the bank from where the attack was coming.

The attackers were completely concealed amongst the rocks and scrub, and there was no definite target to shoot at. However, in an ambush like this it was essential to lay down as heavy a covering fire as possible, to keep the attackers' heads down and to upset their aim.

A bullet tore through the nylon skin of the

Avon close to Royan's head and went on to slam into one of the metal ammunition crates. The sides of their craft offered no protection at all from the heavy fusillade that lashed them. One of their crew was hit in the head. The bullet cut the top off his skull like the shell of a soft-boiled egg, and he was flung over the side. Royan screamed more with horror than with fear, while Nicholas snatched up the assault rifle that the dead man had dropped and emptied the magazine towards the bank, firing short taps of three and raking the scrub that concealed their attackers.

The Avon still raced downstream on the current, spiralling aimlessly as she lost direction without the steering oar. It took them less than a minute to be carried past the ambush and around the next bend of the river.

Nicholas dropped the empty rifle and shouted across at Mek, 'Are you all right?'

'One man hit here,' Mek yelled back. 'Not too bad.'

Each of the boats reported their casualties: a total of one dead and three wounded. None of the wounded was in a serious condition, and although three of the boats had been holed, the hulls were made up of watertight compartments and were all still floating high.

Mek steered his Avon alongside Nicholas's and called across. 'I was beginning to think we had given Nogo the slip.'

'We got off lightly that time,' Nicholas called

back. 'We probably took them by surprise. They weren't expecting us to be on the water.'

'Well, no more surprises for him now. You can bet they are on the radio already. Nogo knows exactly where we are and where we are headed.' He looked up at the cloud. 'We can only hope the cloud stays thick and low.'

'How much further to the Sudanese border?'

'Not sure, but it can't be more than another couple of hours.'

'Is the crossing guarded?' Nicholas asked.

'No. Nothing there. Just empty bush on both sides.'

'Let's hope it stays empty,' Nicholas muttered.

Within thirty minutes of the fire-fight, they heard the helicopter again. It was flying above the clouds, and as they listened it passed over- head, but out of sight, and headed on down- stream. Twenty minuies later they heard it again, coming back in the opposite direction, and shortly after that it flew downstream again, still above the cloud.

'What the hell is Nogo playing at?' Mek called across to Nicholas. 'Sounds as though he is pa- trolling the river, but he can't get under the cloud.'

'My guess is that he is ferrying men down- stream to cut us off. Now he knows we are using boats, he also knows that we can only head in one direction. Nogo isn't one to worry about international borders. He may even have realized by now that we are heading for Roseires. It's the nearest unmanned airstrip along the river. He could be waiting for us when we try to land.'

Mek steered his Avon closer and passed a line across, tying the two boats together so that they could talk in normal tones.

'I don't like it, Nicholas. We are going to walk right into them again. What do you suggest?'

Nicholas pondered for a long minute. 'Don't you recognize this part of the river? Don't you know precisely where we are yet?'

Mek shook his head. 'I always keep well away from the river when we cross the border, but I will recognize the old sugar-mill at Roseires when we get there. It's about three miles upstream from the airstrip.'

'Deserted?' Nicholas asked.

'Yes. Abandoned ever since the war began twenty years ago.'

'With this cloud cover, it will be dark in an hour,' Nicholas said. 'The river is slower now and not so dangerous. We can take a chance and keep on going after dark. Perhaps Nogo won't expect that. We might be able to give him the slip in the dark.'

'Is that the best you can do?' Mek chuckled. 'As a plan it sounds to me a bit like closing your eyes and hoping for the best.'

'Well, if somebody could tell me where the hell we are, and what time Jannie will arrive tomorrow, I might be able to come up with something a bit more specific.' Nicholas grinned back at him. 'Until that happens, I am flying by the seat of my pants.'

All of them were tense with strung-out nerves as they paddled on into the premature dusk beneath the thick blanket of cloud and rain. Even in the gathering darkness the crew kept their weapons cocked and locked, trained on either bank of the river, ready to return fire instantly.

'We must have crossed the border an hour ago,' Mek called to Nicholas. 'The old sugar mill can't be far ahead.'

'In the dark, how will you find it?'

'There is the remains of an old stone jetty on the bank, from which the riverboats taking the sugar down to Khartoum used to load.'

Night came down upon them abruptly, and Nicholas felt a sense of relief as the river banks receded into the murk and the darkness hid them from hostile eyes ashore. As soon as it was fully dark they lashed the boats together to prevent them becoming separated and then let the river carry them on silently, keeping so close in to the right-hand bank that they ran aground more than once, and some of the men had to slip over the side and push them out into deeper water.

The stone piers of the jetty at Roseires sprang out at them unexpectedly, and Nicholas's leading Avon slammed into them before he could steer clear. However, the crew were ready and they jumped over the side into chest-deep water and dragged the boat to the bank. Immediately Mek leaped ashore and, with twenty of his men, spread out into the overgrown canefields along the bank to secure the area and prevent a surprise attack by Nogo's men.

There was confusion and more noise than Nicholas felt was safe as the rest of the flotilla beached, and they began to bring the wounded ashore and unload the cargo of ammunition cases. Nicholas piggy-backed Royan to the bank and then waded back to fetch Tessay. She was much stronger by now. The enforced rest during the voyage downriver had given her a chance to recover, and she stood up unaided in the Avon and climbed on to Nicholas's shoulders to be brought ashore.

Once on dry ground he let her slide down on to her own feet and asked her quietly, 'How are you feeling?'

'I will be all right now, thank you, Nicholas.'

He supported her for a moment while she recovered her balance and said quickly, 'I did not have a chance to ask earlier. What about Royan's message that she asked you to telephone from Debra Maryam? Did you get it through for her?'

'Yes, of course,' Tessay replied guilelessly. 'I told Royan that I had given her message to Moussad at the Egyptian Embassy. Didn't she tell you?'

Nicholas winced as though he had taken a

low punch, but he smiled and kept his tone casual. 'It must have slipped her mind. Not important, anyway. But thanks nevertheless, Tessay.'

At that moment Mek came striding out of the darkness and spoke in a harsh whisper. 'This sounds like a camel market. Nogo will hear us from five miles away.' Quickly he took command and started to organize the shore party.

Once the last of the ammunition crates were unloaded, they dragged the boats into the canefields and unscrewed the valves that deflated the pontoons. Then they piled cane trash over them. Still working in the dark, they distributed the cargo of ammunition crates amongst Mek's men. Sapper took a case under each arm. Nicholas slung the radio over one shoulder and his emergency pack over the other, and balanced on his head the case that contained Pharaoh's golden death-mask and the Taita *ushabti*.

Mek sent his scouts forward to sweep the route out to the airstrip and make certain that they did not run into an ambush. Then he took the point and the rest of them strung out in Indian file along the rough, overgrown track behind him. Before they had covered a mile the clouds suddenly opened overhead, and the crescent moon and the stars showed through and gave them enough light to make out the chimneystack of the ruined mill against the night sky.

But even with this moonlight their progress was slow and broken by long pauses, for the

902

stretcher-bearers carrying the wounded had difficulty keeping up. By the time they reached the airstrip it was after three in the morning and the moon had set. They stacked the ammunition cases in the same grove of acacia trees at the end of the runway where they had cached the pallets of dam-building equipment and the yellow tractor on the inward journey.

Although they were all exhausted by this time, Mek set out his pickets around the camp. The two women tended the wounded, working by the light of a small screened fire as they used up the last of Mek's medical supplies.

Sapper used the one electric torch whose batteries still held a charge, and he gave Nicholas a discreet screened light while he set up the radio and strung the aerial. Nicholas's relief was intense when he opened the fibreglass case and found that, despite its dunking in the Nile, the rubber gasket that sealed the lid had kept the radio dry. When he switched on the power, the pilot light lit up. He tuned in to the short-wave frequency and picked up the early morning commercial transmission of Radio Nairobi.

Yvonne Chaka Chaka was singing; he liked her voice and her style. But he quickly switched off the set so as to conserve the battery, and settled back against the bole of the acacia tree to try and get a little rest before daylight broke. However, sleep eluded him — his sense of betrayal and anger were too strong.

Tuma Nogo watched the sun push its great fiery head out of the surface of the Nile ahead of them. They were flying only feet above the water to keep under the Sudanese military radar transmissions. He knew there was a radar station at Khartoum that might be able to pick them up, even at this range. Relations with the Sudanese were strained, and he could expect a quick and savage response if they discovered that he had violated their border.

Nogo was a confused and worried man. Since the debacle in the gorge of the Dandera river everything had run strongly against him. He had lost all his allies. Until they were gone he had not realized how heavily he had come to rely on both Helm and von Schiller. Now he was on his own and he had already made many mistakes.

But despite all this he was determined to pursue the fugitives, and to run them down no matter how far he had to intrude into Sudanese territory. Over the past weeks it had gradually dawned upon Nogo, mostly by eavesdropping on the conversations of von Schiller and the Egyptian, that Harper and Mek Nimmur were in possession of treasure of immense value. His imagination could barely grasp the enormity of it, but he had heard others speak of tens of millions of dollars. Even a million dollars was a sum so vast that his mind had difficulty assimilating it, but he had a vague inkling as to what it might mean in earthly terms, of the possessions and women and luxuries it could buy.

Equally slowly it had dawned upon him that, now that von Schiller and Helm were gone, this treasure could be his alone; there was no longer any other person to stand in his way, other than the fleeing *shufta* led by Mek Nimmur and the Englishman. And he had overwhelming force on his side and the helicopter at his command.

If only he could pin the fugitives down, Nogo was certain he could wipe them out. There must be no survivors, no one to carry tales to Addis. After Mek and the Englishman and all their followers were dead it would be a simple matter to spirit his booty out of the country in the helicopter. There was a man in Nairobi and another in Khartoum whom he had dealt with before; they had bought contraband ivory and hashish from him. They would know how to market the booty to best advantage, although they were both devious men. He had already decided that he would not trust it all to one person but would spread the risk, so that even if one of them betrayed and cheated him —

His mind raced off on another tack, and he savoured the thought of great riches and what they could buy for him. He would have fine clothes and motor cars, land and cattle and women — white women and black and brown, all the women he could use, a new one for every day of his life. He broke off his greedy day-

905

dreams. First he had to find where the runaways had vanished to.

He had not realized that Harper and Mek Nimmur had inflatable boats hidden somewhere near the monastery. Hansith had not informed him of that fact. He and Helm had expected them to try to escape on foot, and all the plans to head them off before they could reach the Sudanese border had been based on that assumption. On Helm's orders, he had even set up a reserve fuel dump near the border where they expected Mek Nimmur to cross, from which they could refuel the helicopter. Without those supplies of fuel he would long ago have been forced to give up the chase.

Nogo had placed his men to cover the trails leading along the river bank towards the west, and he had not even considered guarding the river itself. It was quite by chance that one of his patrols had been in a position to spot the flotilla of yellow boats as they came racing downstream. However, there had not been enough warning to enable them to set up an effective ambush, and they had been able to fire on the boats only briefly before they escaped. They had not inflicted serious damage on any of the boats — at least, not enough to stop them getting through.

Immediately the company commander had radioed his report of this contact with Mek Nimmur, Nogo had started ferrying men downstream to the Sudanese border to cut off the flotilla. Unfortunately, the Jet Ranger could carry no more than six fully armed men at a time, and transporting them had been a time-consuming business. He had only succeeded in bringing sixty of his men into position before night had fallen.

During the night he fretted that the flotilla was slipping past him, and with the dawn they were in the air again. Fortunately the cloud had broken up during the night. There was still some high cumulus overhead, but they were now able to fly low along the river and search for any sign of Mek Nimmur's flotilla.

They had first flown back along the river on the Ethiopian side of the border, as far as the point where Mek Nimmur and Harper had been fired upon. They had picked up no sign of the boats, so Nogo had forced the pilot to turn back, cross the border and search the Sudanese stretch of the Nile. But Nogo had only been able to persuade his pilot to penetrate sixty nautical miles along the Nile into the Sudan before the man had rebelled. Despite the Tokarev pistol that Nogo held to his head, he had banked the Jet Ranger into a 180-degree turn and headed back low along the river.

By now Nogo knew he had been defeated and outwitted. He brooded unhappily in the front seat of the helicopter beside the pilot, trying to fathom out what had happened to his quarry. He saw the tall smokestack of the abandoned sugar-mill at Roseires poking up into the early morning sky, and he glowered at it angrily. They had passed the mill only a short while before on their way downstream.

'Turn in towards the north bank,' he ordered the pilot, and the man hesitated and glanced at him before he obeyed.

They passed directly over the building, flying lower than the chimney. The factory was roofless and the windows were empty rectangles in the broken walls. The boilers and machinery had been removed twenty years previously, and Nogo could look into the empty shell. The pilot hovered the aircraft while Nogo peered down, but there was no place where anyone could hide, and Nogo shook his head.

'Nothing! We have lost them. Head back upstream.'

The pilot lifted the machine's nose and turned away towards the river, obeying the order with alacrity. As the aircraft banked steeply, Nogo was looking down directly into the overgrown canefields verging the river when a flash of bright yellow caught his eye.

'Wait!' he shouted into his mike. 'There is something there. Go back!'

The helicopter hovered over the field, and Nogo gestured urgently downwards. 'Down! Put us down.'

As soon as the skids touched the earth, the stick of six heavily armed troopers dived out of the rear cabin and raced out to take up defensive positions. Nogo clambered out of the front door and ran into the overgrown bed of tall cane. One look was all he needed. The yellow boats had been deflated and folded and hastily covered. The earth around them had been churned up by booted feet. The tracks led away inland. The men who had made them had been heavily laden, for they had trodden deeply into the soft, sandy earth.

Nogo ran back to the helicopter and thrust his head in through the open cabin door. 'Is there an airstrip near here?' he shouted at the pilot, who shook his head.

'There is nothing shown on the chart.'

'There must have been one. The sugar-mill would have had a strip.'

'If there was one, it must have been decommissioned years ago.'

'We will find it,' Nogo declared. 'Mek Nimmur's tracks will lead us to it.' He sobered immediately. 'But I will have to bring up more men. Judging by his spoor, Mek Nimmur has at least fifty of his *shufta* with him.'

He left his men at the sugar-mill and flew back to the border with an empty rear cabin to pick up the first load of reinforcements.

Big Dolly! Come in, Big Dolly. This is Pharaoh. Do you read?' Nicholas put out his first call an hour before sunrise.

'If I know the way Jannie's mind works, and

I should, he would plan to make his approach flight in darkness and arrive here as soon as there is enough light to pick up the strip and land.'

'If the Fat Man comes,' Mek Nimmur qualified.

'He will come,' said Nicholas confidently. 'Jannie has never let me down yet.' He thumbed the microphone and called again: 'Big Dolly! Come in, Big Dolly.'

The static hummed softly, and Nicholas retuned the set carefully. He called again every fifteen minutes as they huddled around the set in the dark under the acacia trees.

Suddenly Royan started to her feet and exclaimed excitedly, 'There he is. I can hear Big Dolly's engines. Listen!'

Nicholas and Mek ran out into the open, and turned their faces upwards, looking into the north.

'That's not the Hercules,' Nicholas exclaimed suddenly. 'That's another machine.' He turned and faced southwards, towards the river. 'Anyway, it's coming from the wrong direction.'

'You are right,' Mek agreed. 'That's a single engine, and it's not a fixed wing. You can hear the rotors.'

'The Pegasus helicopter!' Nicholas exclaimed bitterly. 'They are on to us again.'

As they listened, the sound of the rotors faded. Nicholas looked relieved. 'They missed us. They can't have spotted the Avons.'

They trooped back under the cover of the acacias, and Nicholas called again on the radio, but there was no reply from Jannie.

Twenty minutes later they heard the sound of the Jet Ranger returning, and they monitored it anxiously.

'Gone again,' said Nicholas after a while, but then twenty minutes later they heard it yet again.

'Nogo is up to something out there,' Mek said uneasily.

'What do you think it is?' Nicholas was infected by his mood. When Mek worried, there was usually a damned good reason to worry.

'I don't know,' Mek admitted. 'Perhaps Nogo has spotted the Avons and is bringing up more men before he comes after us.' He went out into the open and listened intently, then came back to where Nicholas crouched over the radio.

'Keep calling,' he said. 'I am going out to the perimeter to make certain my men are ready to hold Nogo off if he comes.'

The helicopter moved up and down the Nile at short intervals during the next three hours, but the lack of any further developments lulled them, and Nicholas barely looked up from the radio each time they heard the distant beat of the rotors. Suddenly the radio crackled, and Nicholas started violently at the shock.

'Pharaoh! This is Big Dolly. Do you read?'

Nicholas's voice bubbled over with relief as he replied, 'This is Pharaoh. Speak sweet words to me, Big Dolly.'

'ETA your position one hour thirty minutes.' Jannie's accent was unmistakable.

'You will be very welcome!' Nicholas promised him fervently.

He hung up the microphone and beamed at the two women, 'Jannie is on his way, and he will —'

He broke off and his smile shrivelled to an expression of dismay. From the direction of the river came the unmistakable rattle of AK-47 rapid fire, followed a few seconds later by the crump of an exploding grenade.

'Oh, dammit to hell!' he groaned. 'I thought it was too good to last. Nogo has arrived.'

He picked up the mike again and spoke into it expressionlessly. 'Big Dolly! The uglies have arrived on the scene. It's going to have to be a hot extraction.'

'Hang on to your crown, Pharaoh!' Jannie's voice floated back. 'I am on my way.'

During the next half-hour the sounds of the fighting along the river intensified until the rattle of small-arms fire was almost continuous, and gradually it crept closer to the far end of the airstrip. It was clear that Mek's men, spread out thinly along the river end of the strip, were falling back before the thrust of Nogo's men. And every twenty minutes or so there was the sound of the returning helicopter, as it ferried another stick of men to increase the pressure on Mek's scanty defence.

Nicholas and Sapper were the only able-bodied men left in the acacia grove, for all the others had gone out to defend the perimeter. The two of them moved the ammunition crates to the edge of the trees, where they could be loaded in haste once the Hercules landed.

Nicholas sorted out the cargo, reading the contents of each crate from the notations on the lids in Royan's handwriting. The crate containing the death-mask and the Taita *ushabti* would be the first to go aboard, followed by the three crowns: the blue war crown, the Nemes crown and the red and white crown of the united kingdoms of upper and lower Egypt. The value of those three crates probably exceeded that of all the rest of the treasure combined.

Once the cargo had been taken care of, Nicholas went down the row of wounded men and spoke to each of them in turn. First, he thanked them for their help and sacrifice, and then offered to take them out on the Hercules to where they could receive proper medical attention. He promised each of them that, if they accepted the offer, he would see to it that once they had recovered from their wounds they could return to Ethiopia.

Seven of them — those who were less seriously wounded and were able to walk — refused to leave Mek Nimmur. Their loyalty was a touching demonstration of the high regard in which Mek was held by his men. The others reluctantly agreed to be evacuated, but only after Tessay had intervened and added her assurances to Nicholas's. Then he and Sapper carried them to the point at the edge of the grove where Jannie would halt Big Dolly for the pick-up.

'What about you?' Nicholas asked Tessay. 'Are you coming out with us? You are still in pretty bad shape.'

Tessay laughed. 'While I can still stand on my two feet, I will never leave Mek Nimmur.'

'I can't understand what you see in that old rogue,' Nicholas laughed with her. 'I have spoken to Mek. He wants me to take his share of the booty with me. He won't be able to carry any extra luggage at the moment.'

'Yes, I know. Mek and I discussed it. We need the money to continue the struggle here.'

She broke off and ducked involuntarily, as a stunning explosion cracked in their eardrums and a tall column of dust leaped into the air close to the edge of the grove. Shrapnel whistled over their heads and twigs and leaves rained down on them.

'Sweet Mary! What was that?' Tessay cried.

'Two-inch mortar,' said Nicholas. He had not moved, nor made any attempt to take cover. 'More bark than bite. Nogo must have brought it in with his last flight.'

'When will the Hercules get here?'

'I'll give Jannie a call, and ask him.'

As Nicholas sauntered over to the radio set Tessay whispered to Royan, 'Are you English always so cool?'

914

'Don't ask me — I'm mostly Egyptian, and I am terrified.' Royan smiled easily and put her arm around Tessay. 'I am going to miss you, Lady Sun.'

'Perhaps we will meet again in happier times.' Tessay turned her head and kissed her impulsively, and Royan hugged her hard.

'I hope so. I hope so with all my heart.'

Nicholas spoke into the microphone. 'Big Dolly, this is Pharaoh. What is your position now?'

'Pharaoh, we are twenty minutes out, and hurrying. Did you have baked beans for dinner or is that mortar fire I hear in the background?'

'With your wit you should have gone on the stage,' Nicholas told him. 'The uglies have control of the south end of the strip. Make your approach from the north. The wind is westerly at about five knots. So any way you come in, it will be cross-wind.'

'Roger, Pharaoh. How many passengers and cargo do you have for me?'

'Passengers are six cas-evac plus three. Cargo is fifty-two crates, about a quarter of a ton weight.'

'Hardly worth coming all this way for so little, Pharaoh.'

'Big Dolly. Be advised, there is another aircraft in the circuit. A Jet Ranger helicopter. Colour green and red. It is a hostile, but unarmed.'

'Roger, Pharaoh. I will call again on finals.'

915

Nicholas went back to where the two women were waiting with the wounded.

'Not long now,' he told them cheerfully. He had to raise his voice to make himself heard above the din of mortar bursts and rapid small-arms fire.

'Just enough time for a cup of tea,' he said. He pushed a few twigs into the embers of the previous night's fire, then rummaged in his small emergency pack for the last of his tea bags while Sapper placed the smoke-blackened billycan back on the burgeoning flames.

They only had one mug between them. 'Girls first,' said Nicholas, passing it to Royan. She took a swallow and scalded her lips.

'Good!' she sighed, and then cocked her head. 'This time it is definitely Big Dolly I can hear.'

Nicholas listened and then nodded. 'I think you are right.' He stood up and went to the radio. 'Big Dolly. You are audible.'

'Five minutes to landing, Pharaoh.'

From where he stood, Nicholas looked down the long strip. Mek's men were retreating, flitting like smoke through the thorn scrub and firing back in the direction of the river. Nogo was pushing them hard now.

'Hurry along, Jannie,' he murmured, and then adjusted his expression as he turned back to the two women. 'Plenty of time to finish your tea. Don't waste it.'

The rumble of Big Dolly's engines was louder than the sound of gunfire now. Then suddenly she was in sight, coming in so low that she seemed to brush the tops of the thorn trees. She was enormous. Her wingspan reached from one side of the narrow overgrown strip to the other. Jannie touched her down short, and she blew out a long rolling cloud of brown dust behind her as he put the engines into reverse thrust.

Big Dolly went barrelling past the clump of acacia, and Jannie waved to them from the high cockpit. The moment he had bled off enough speed, he stood on his footbrakes and rudder bar. Big Dolly spun around in her own length and came roaring back down the strip towards them, her loading ramp beginning to drop open even before she reached them.

Fred was waiting in the open hatchway, and he ran down to help Sapper and Nicholas with the wounded men on the litters. It took only a few minutes to carry them up the ramp, and then they started loading the ammunition crates. Even Royan gave a hand, staggering up the ramp with one of the lighter crates clutched to her chest.

A mortar shell exploded a hundred and fifty yards beyond the parked Hercules, and then half a minute later a second shell fell a hundred yards short.

'Ranging shots,' Nicholas grunted, picking up a crate under each arm and running up the ramp.

'They have us in their sights now,' Fred shouted. 'We have to get out of here. Leave the rest of the cargo. Let's go! Go!'

There were only four crates still lying under the spreading branches of the acacia, and both Nicholas and Sapper ignored the order and ran back down the ramp. They snatched up a crate under each arm and raced back. The ramp was starting to rise and Big Dolly's engines roared as she began to taxi out. They hurled the crates over the tailboard of the rising ramp and then jumped up to grab a handhold and pull themselves aboard. Nicholas was the first up and reached down to haul Sapper in.

When he looked back, Tessay was a small, lonely figure under the acacias.

'Give Mek my love and thanks,' he bellowed at her.

'You know how to contact us,' she screamed back.

'Goodbye, Tessay.' Royan's voice was lost in the blast of the great engines, and the dust blew back in a sheet over Tessay so that she was forced to cover her face and turn away. The ramp hissed closed on its hydraulic rams, and cut out their last glimpse of her.

Nicholas put an arm around Royan's shoulders and hustled her down the length of the cavernous cargo hold and into one of the jump seats at the entrance to the cockpit.

'Strap yourself in!' he ordered, and ran up the steps to the cockpit.

'Thought you had decided to stay behind,' Jannie greeted him mildly, without looking up

918

from his controls. 'Hold tight! Here we go.'

Nicholas clung on to the back of the pilot's seat as Jannie and Fred between them pushed forward the bank of throttle levers to full power, and Big Dolly built up speed until she was careering down the strip.

Looking over Jannie's shoulder, Nicholas saw the vague shapes of men in camouflage battle-dress amongst the thorn scrub at the end of the runway. Some of them were firing at the huge aircraft as it raced towards them.

'Those popguns aren't going to hurt her much,' Jannie grunted. 'Big Dolly is a tough old lady.' And he lifted her into the air.

They flashed over the heads of the enemy troops on the ground, and Jannie set her nose high in the climb attitude.

'Welcome aboard, folks, thank you for flying Africair. Next stop Malta,' Jannie drawled, and then his voice rose sharply, 'Oh, oh! Where did this little piss-cat come from?'

Directly ahead of them the Jet Ranger rose out of the thick scrub on the banks of the Nile. The angle of the helicopter's climb meant that the approaching Hercules was hidden from the pilot's view, and he continued to rise directly into their path.

'Only five hundred feet and a hundred and ten knots on the clock,' Fred shouted a warning at his father from the right-hand seat. 'Too low to turn.'

The Jet Ranger was so close that Nicholas

could clearly see Tuma Nogo in the front seat, his spectacles reflecting the sunlight like the eyes of a blind man, and his face freezing into a rictus of terror as he suddenly saw the great machine bearing down on them. At the last possible moment the pilot put his aircraft over in a wild dive to try to clear the nose of the approaching Hercules. It seemed impossible to avoid the collision, but he managed to bank the lighter, more manoeuvrable machine over until it rolled almost on to its back. It slipped under the belly of the Hercules, and the men in the cockpit of Jannie's plane barely felt the light kiss of the two fuselages.

However, the helicopter was flung over on to its nose by the impact, until it was pointing straight down at the earth only four hundred feet below. While Big Dolly flew on, climbing away steadily on an even keel, the pilot of the Jet Ranger struggled to control his crazily plummeting machine. Two hundred feet above the earth the turbulence thrown out astern by the massive T56-A-15 turbo-prop engines of the Hercules, each rated at 4900 horsepower, struck the helicopter with the force of an avalanche.

Like a dead leaf in an autumn gale she was swept away, spinning end over end, and when she struck the ground her own engines were still squealing at full power. On impact the fuselage crumpled like a sheet of aluminium cooking foil, and Nogo was dead even before the fuel tanks exploded and a fireball engulfed the Jet Ranger.

As soon as Jannie reached safe manoeuvring altitude he brought Big Dolly around on her northerly heading, and they could look back over the wing at the Roseires airstrip falling away behind them. The column of black smoke from the burning helicopter was tar-thick as it drifted away on the light westerly wind.

'You did say they were the uglies?' Jannie asked. 'So rather them than us, then?'

Once Jannie had settled Big Dolly on her northerly heading, and they were sailing low over the open deserted Sudanese plains, Nicholas went back into the main hold.

'Let's get the wounded settled down comfortably,' he suggested. Sapper and Royan unbuckled their safety belts and went back with him to attend to the men lying where their litters had been dumped during the haste of the getaway from Roseires.

After a while Nicholas left them to it and went forward to the small, well-stocked galley behind the flight deck. He opened some canned soup and sliced hunks of fresh bread from the loaves he found in the refrigerator. While the tea water boiled, he found his small emergency pack, and took from it the nylon wallet which contained his medicines and drugs. From one of the vials he shook five white tablets into the palm of his hand.

In the galley he crushed the tablets to powder, and when he poured tea into two of the mugs he stirred the powder in with it. Royan had enough English blood in her veins never to be able to refuse a mug of hot tea.

After they had served soup and buttered toast to the wounded men, Royan accepted her mug from Nicholas gratefully. While she and Sapper sipped their tea, Nicholas went back to the flight deck and leaned over the back of Jannie's seat.

'What is our flying time to the Egyptian border?' he asked.

'Four hours twenty minutes,' Jannie told him.

'Is there any way that we can avoid flying into Egyptian air space?' Nicholas wanted to know.

Jannie swivelled around in his seat and stared at him with astonishment. 'I suppose we could make a turn out to the west, through Gadaffiland. Of course, it would mean an extra seven hours' flying time, and we would probably run out of fuel and end up making a forced landing somewhere out there in the Sahara.' He lifted an eyebrow at Nicholas. 'Tell me, my boy, what inspired that stupid question?'

'It was just a rare thought,' Nicholas said.

'Let it be not merely rare, but extinct,' Jannie advised. 'I don't want to hear it asked again, ever.'

Nicholas slapped his shoulder. 'Put it out of your mind.'

When he went back into the main hold, Sapper and Royan were sitting on two of the fold-down bunks that were bolted to the main bulkhead. Royan's empty tea mug stood on the deck at her feet. Nicholas sat down beside her, and she reached up and touched the bloodstained dressing that covered his chin.

'You had better let me see to that.' Her fingers were deft and cool on his hot inflamed skin as she cleaned the stitches with an alcohol swab and then placed a fresh plaster over them. Nicholas felt a strong twinge of guilt as he submitted to her ministrations.

However, it was Sapper who was the first to show the effects of the doped tea. He lay back gently and closed his eyes, then a soft snore vibrated his lips. Minutes later Royan sagged drowsily against Nicholas's shoulder. When she was fast asleep, he let her down gently and lifted her feet up on to the bunk. He spread a rug over her. She did not even stir, and he had a moment's doubt about the strength of the tablets.

Then he kissed her forehead softly. 'How could I ever hate you?' he asked her softly. 'Whatever you did.'

He went into the lavatory and locked the door. He had plenty of time. Sapper and Royan would not wake for hours yet, and Jannie and Fred were happily ensconced on the flight-deck, listening to Dolly Parton tapes on the audio system.

When at last he had finished, Nicholas glanced at his wrist-watch and realized that it had taken him almost two hours. He closed the toilet seat and washed his hands carefully. Then he took one last careful look around the tiny cabin and unlocked the door.

Sapper and Royan were still fast asleep on the fold-down bunks. He went forward to the flight-deck, and Fred pulled his earphones down around his neck and grinned at him.

'Nile water. It's poisonous. You have been locked in the loo for the last couple of hours. Surprised that there is anything left of you.'

Nicholas ignored the jibe and leaned over Jannie's seat back. 'Where are we?'

With a thick forefinger Jannie stabbed the chart that he was balancing on his protruding belly. 'Almost in the clear,' he said complacently. 'Egyptian border in one hour twelve minutes.'

Nicholas remained standing behind his seat until Jannie grunted and lifted the microphone. 'Time to go into my act.'

'Hallo, Abu Simbel Approach!' he said in a Gulf States accent. 'This is Zulu Whiskey Uniform Five Zero Zero.'

There was a long silence from the Egyptian controller. Jannie grunted. 'He probably has a bint in the tower with him. Got to give him time to get his pants back on.'

Abu Simbel Control answered on his fifth call.

Jannie launched into his tried and tested routine, feigning ignorance in fluent colloquial Arabic.

After five minutes, Abu Simbel cleared him to continue on northwards, with an instruction to 'call again abeam Aswan'.

They flew on serenely for another hour, but Nicholas's nerves were screwing up tighter every minute.

Suddenly, without the least warning, there was a silvery flash ahead of them as a fighter interceptor, coming from below them, pulled up steeply across their bows. Jannie shouted with surprise and anger as another two warplanes rocketed up from under them, so close that they were buffeted by the turbulence of their jet trails.

They all recognized the type. They were MiG21 'Fishbeds' sporting the Egyptian air force livery, and with air-to-air missiles hanging in menacing pods under their swept-back wings.

'Unidentified aircraft!' Jannie yelled into his mouthpiece. 'You are on collision course. State your call sign!'

They all craned their necks and stared up through the Perspex canopy over the flight-deck. High above them they could see the three MiG fighters in formation circling against the blue of the African sky.

'ZWU 500. This is Red Leader of the Egyptian people's air force. You will conform to my orders.'

Jannie looked back at Nicholas, his expression

forlorn. 'Something has gone wrong here. How the hell did they tumble to us?'

'You'd better do what the man says, Dad,' Fred advised miserably, 'otherwise he is going to blow us all over the sky.'

Jannie shrugged helplessly, and then spoke into his microphone mournfully. 'Red Leader. This is ZWU 500. We will cooperate. Please state your intentions.'

'Your new heading is 053. Execute immediately!'

Jannie brought Big Dolly around into the east and then glanced at his chart.

'Aswan!' he said dolefully. 'The Gyppos are taking us to Aswan. What the hell, I might as well warn Aswan tower that we have wounded on board.'

Nicholas went back to Royan's bunk and shook her awake. She was groggy and unsteady on her feet from the effects of the drug as she staggered to the lavatory. However, when she emerged again ten minutes later her hair was combed and she seemed alert and recovered from the mild draught that she had drunk in her tea.

There was the Nile ahead of them once more, and the town of Aswan on both banks, nestling below the first cataract and the impounded waters of the High Dam. Kitchener's Island swam like a green fish in the middle of the stream.

As the voice of the military controller at the Aswan airfield gave Jannie his orders, Big Dolly settled with unruffled dignity and lined up for the straight-in approach to the tarmac runway. The MiG fighters which had shepherded them in from the desert were no longer visible, but their presence high above was betrayed by their terse radio transmissions as they handed over their captive to the ground control.

Big Dolly sailed in over the perimeter fence and touched down, and the voice of the controller ordered them, 'Turn first taxi-way right.'

Jannie obeyed, and as he turned off the main runway there was a small vehicle with a sign on its roof which read, in both English and Arabic, 'FOLLOW ME'.

The vehicle led them to a row of camouflaged concrete hangars in front of which a ground crew in khaki overalls signalled them with paddles into a parking stand. As soon as Jannie applied his brakes and brought Big Dolly to a halt, a file of four armoured half-tracks raced out and surrounded the huge aircraft, training their turret weapons upon her.

Obedient to the instructions radioed by control, Jannie shut down his engines and lowered the tail ramp of the aircraft. No one on the flight-deck had spoken since they had landed. They stood crowded together, looking unhappy, peering out of the cockpit windows.

Suddenly a white Cadillac with an escort of armed motorcyclists, followed by a military ambulance and a three-ton transport truck, drove through the gate of the perimeter fence and came directly to the foot of the cargo ramp of the Hercules. The chauffeur jumped out and opened the door, and his passenger stepped out into the late afternoon sunshine. He was clearly a person of authority, dignified and composed. He wore a light tropical suit and white shoes, a panama hat and dark glasses. As he came up the ramp to where the five of them waited, he was followed by two male secretaries.

He removed his dark glasses and tucked them into his breast pocket. As he recognized Royan he smiled and lifted his hat, 'Dr Al Simma — Royan! You did it. Congratulations!' He took her hand and shook it warmly, not relinquishing his grip as he looked directly at Nicholas.

'You must be Sir Nicholas Quenton-Harper. I have been looking forward to meeting you immensely. Won't you please introduce us, Royan?'

Royan could not meet Nicholas's accusing scrutiny as she said, 'May I present His Excellency, Atalan Abou Sin, Minister of Culture and Tourism in the Egyptian government.'

'You may indeed,' said Nicholas coldly. 'What an unexpected pleasure, Minister.'

'I would like to express the thanks of the President and the people of Egypt for returning to this country these precious relics of our ancient but glorious history.' He made a gesture that encompassed the stack of ammunition crates.

'Please, think nothing of it,' said Nicholas, but he never took his eyes off Royan. She kept her face turned half-away from him.

'On the contrary, we think the world of what you have done, Sir Nicholas.' Abou Sin's smile was charming and urbane. 'We are fully aware of the expense to which you have been put, and we would not want you to be out of pocket in this extraordinarily generous gesture of yours. Dr Al Simma tells me that the expedition to recover these treasures for us has cost you a quarter of a million sterling.' He took an envelope from his inside pocket, and proffered it to Nicholas.

'This is a banker's draft drawn on the Central Bank of Egypt. It is irrevocable, and payable anywhere in the world. It is for the sum of £250,000.'

'Very generous of you, Your Excellency.' Nicholas's voice was heavy with irony as he slipped the envelope into his top pocket. 'I presume this was Dr Al Simma's suggestion?'

'Of course,' beamed Abou Sin. 'Royan holds you in the very highest regard.'

'Does she, now?' Nicholas murmured, still staring at her expressionlessly.

'However, this other small token of our appreciation was the suggestion of the President himself.' The minister snapped his fingers and one of his secretaries stepped forward with a leather-covered medal case, which he opened before he presented it to Abou Sin.

On a bed of red velvet nestled a magnificent decoration, a star encrusted with seed pearls and tiny pavé diamonds. In the centre of the star was a golden lion rampant.

Abou Sin lifted the star from its case and advanced on Nicholas. 'The Order of the Great Lion of Egypt, First Class,' he announced, placing the scarlet ribbon over his head. The star hung resplendent on Nicholas's grubby shirtfront, heavily stained with sweat and dust and Nile mud.

Then the minister stood aside and made a gesture to the army colonel who was standing to attention at the foot of the ramp. Immediately there was an orderly rush of uniformed men up the ramp. The detachment of soldiers obviously had their orders. First they picked up the litters on which the wounded Ethiopians lay.

'I am glad that your pilot had the good sense to radio ahead that you had wounded men on board. Rest assured that they will receive the best care available,' Atalan Abou Sin promised as they were carried down to the waiting ambulance.

Then the soldiers returned and began carrying the ammunition cases down the ramp. They were loaded neatly into the three-tonner. Within ten minutes Big Dolly's hold was bare and empty. A tarpaulin cover was roped down securely over the back of the loaded truck. An escort of heavily armed motorcyclists fell into formation around it, and then, with sirens wailing, the little convoy roared away.

'Well, Sir Nicholas.' Abou Sin held out his hand courteously, and Nicholas took it with an air of resignation. 'I am sorry to have taken you out of your way like this. I know that you will be anxious to continue on your journey, so I will not detain you further. Is there anything I can do for you before you leave? Do you have sufficient fuel?'

Nicholas glanced at Jannie, and he shrugged. 'We have plenty of juice. Thank you, sir.'

Abou Sin turned back to Nicholas, 'We are planning to build a special annexe to the museum at Luxor to house these artefacts of Pharaoh Mamose that you have returned to Egypt. In due course you will be receiving a personal invitation from President Mubarak to attend, as an honoured guest, the opening of that museum. Dr Al Simma, whom I am sure you know has been appointed the new Director of the Department of Antiquities, will be in charge of the museum. I am sure she will be delighted to review the exhibits with you when you come back.'

He bowed to Sapper and the two pilots.

'Go with God,' he said, and went down the ramp. Royan began to follow him, but Nicholas called softly after her.

931

'Royan!' She froze, and then turned her head slowly and reluctantly to meet his eyes for the first time since they had landed.

'I didn't deserve that,' he said, and then with a stab of emotion he realized that she was weeping softly. Her lips quivered and the tears ran slowly down her cheeks.

'I am sorry, Nicky,' she whispered, 'but you must have known that I am not a thief. It belongs to Egypt, not to us.'

'So everything that I thought there was between us was a lie?' he demanded remorselessly.

'No!' she said. 'I —' and then she broke off without finishing what she was going to say. She ran down the ramp into the sunlight to where the chauffeur was holding the back door of the limousine open for her. She slipped on to the seat beside Abou Sin without looking back, and the Cadillac pulled away and drove through the gate.

'Let's get the hell out of here, before these Gyppos change their minds,' said Jannie.

'What a splendid idea,' said Nicholas bitterly.

Once they were airborne again, Aswan Control cleared them for a direct flight northwards to the Mediterranean coast. The four of them, Jannie and Fred, Sapper and Nicholas, stayed together on the flight-deck and watched the long green snake of the Nile crawl along

932

their right wingtip.

They spoke very little during this long leg of the flight. Once Jannie said quietly, 'So I can kiss my fee goodbye, I suppose?'

'I didn't really come along for the money,' said Sapper, 'but it would have been nice to be paid. Baby needs new shoes.'

'Does anybody want a cup of tea?' Nicholas asked, as though he had not heard.

'That would be nice,' said Jannie. 'Not as nice as the sixty grand that you owe me, but nice anyway.'

They flew over the battlefield of El Alamein, and even from twenty thousand feet they could pick out the twin monuments to the Allied and German dead. Then the blue of the sea stretched ahead of them.

Nicholas waited until the Egyptian coast receded behind them and then he let out a long, soft sigh.

'O, ye of little faith,' he accused them. 'When did I ever let you down? Everybody gets paid in full.'

They all stared at him long and hard, and then Jannie voiced their doubts. 'How?' he asked.

'Give me a hand, Sapper,' Nicholas invited, and started down the staircase. Jannie could not control his curiosity and handed over the controls to Fred. He followed the two Englishmen down to the lavatory on the main deck.

Sapper and Jannie watched from the doorway

as Nicholas took the Leatherman tool from his pocket and lifted the cover of the chemical toilet. Jannie grinned as Nicholas started to work on the screws, holding the hidden panel in place. Big Dolly was a smugglers' aircraft, and these little modifications were evidence of the pains that Jannie and Fred had taken to adapt her to that role. There were a number of these hidey-holes cunningly built into the engine housings and other parts of the fuselage.

When they had flown back from Libya, the Hannibal bronzes had reposed in the secret compartment behind this panel. The location of the panel in the back of the toilet made it highly unlikely that any follower of Islam would want to investigate such an unclean area.

'So that's what you were doing in here for so long,' Jannie laughed as Nicholas lifted out the panel. His grin faded as Nicholas reached into the space beyond and carefully drew out an extraordinary object. 'My God, what is that?'

'The blue war crown of ancient Egypt,' said Nicholas. He handed it to Sapper. 'Lay it on the bunk, but treat it carefully.'

He reached into the compartment again, 'And this is the Nemes crown.' He handed it to Jannie.

'And this is the red and white crown of the two kingdoms. And this is the death-mask of Pharaoh Mamose. Last but not least, this is the *ushabti* of the scribe Taita.'

The relics lay on the fold-down bunk, and they stood and stared at them reverently.

934

'I have helped you bring out stone friezes and little bronze statues, said Jannie softly. 'But nothing like this before.'

'But,' Sapper shook his head, 'the ammunition crates the Gyppos offloaded at Aswan? What was in them?'

'Five one-gallon bottles of chemical for the toilet,' said Nicholas, 'plus half a dozen spare oxygen cylinders, just to make up weight.'

'You switched them.' Sapper beamed at him. 'But how the hell did you know that Royan was going to scupper us?'

'She was right when she said I must have known she was no thief. The whole lark was out of character for her. She is,' he searched for the correct description, 'much too upright and honest. Not at all like the present company.'

'Thanks for the compliment,' said Jannie drily, 'but she must have given you more reason than that to make you suspicious.'

'Yes, of course.' Nicholas turned to him. 'The first real inkling I had was when we came back from Ethiopia the first time, and she immediately pushed off to Cairo. I guessed she was up to something. But I was absolutely certain only when I learned that she had passed a message, through Tessay, to the Egyptian Embassy in Addis. It was clear then that she had alerted them to our return flight.'

'The perfidious little bitch,' Jannie guffawed.

'Careful there!' said Nicholas stiffly. 'She is

a decent, honest and patriotic young woman, warm-hearted and —'

'Well, well!' Jannie winked at Sapper. 'Please excuse my slip.'

Only two of the great crowns of ancient Egypt were set out on the polished walnut conference table. Nicholas had placed them on the heads of two genuine Roman marble busts that he had borrowed from a dealer with whom he did regular business here in Zurich. He had drawn the blinds over the tenth-storey windows, and arranged the lighting to show the crowns to the best effect. The private conference room that he had hired for the occasion was in the Bank Leu building on Bahnhofstrasse.

While he waited alone for the arrival of his invited guest, he reviewed his preparations and could find no fault with them. He went to the full-length mirror on one wall and tightened the knot of his old Sandhurst tie. The stitches had been removed from his chin. Mek Nimmur had done a first-rate job, and the scar was neat and clean. His suit had been made by his tailor in Savile Row, so it was in a muted chalk stripe and had been worn enough to have acquired just the right degree of casual bagginess. The only shiny items of his dress were the hand-made shoes from Lobb of St James's Street.

The intercom buzzed softly and Nicholas lifted the handset.

'There is a Mr Walsh to see you, Sir Nicholas,' said the receptionist at the desk in the bank lobby downstairs.

'Please ask him to come up.'

Nicholas opened the door at the first ring and Walsh glowered at him from the threshold.

'I hope you are not wasting my time, Harper. I have flown all the way from Fort Worth.' It was only thirty hours since Nicholas had telephoned him at his ranch in Texas. Walsh must have jumped into his executive jet almost immediately to have got here so soon.

'Not Harper. Quenton-Harper,' said Nicholas.

'Okay then, Quenton-Harper. But cut the crap,' Walsh said angrily. 'What have you got for me?'

'I am also delighted to see you again, Mr Walsh.' Nicholas stood aside. 'Do come in.'

Walsh strode into the room. He was tall and round-shouldered, his jowls drooping and wrinkled and his nose beaky. With his hands clasped behind his back he looked like a buzzard on a fence pole. *Forbes* magazine listed his net worth at 1.7 billion dollars.

Two men followed him into the room, and Nicholas recognized both of them. The antiquarian world was very small and incestuous. One of them was the professor of ancient history at Dallas University. Walsh had endowed the chair. The other was one of the most respected and knowledgeable antiques dealers in the United States.

Walsh stopped so suddenly that they both ran into him from behind, but he did not seem to notice.

'Son of a gun!' he said softly, and his eyes lit with the flames of fanaticism. 'Are those fakes?'

'As fake as the Hannibal bronzes and the Hammurabi bas-relief you bought from me,' said Nicholas.

Walsh approached the exhibits as though they were the cathedral communion plate and he the archbishop.

'These must be fresh,' he whispered. 'Otherwise I would have known about them.'

'Fresh out of the ground,' Nicholas confirmed. 'You are the first one to have seen them.'

'Mamose!' Walsh read the cartouche on the *uraeus* of the Nemes crown. 'Then the rumours are true. You have opened a new tomb.'

'If you can call nearly four thousand years old new.'

Walsh and his advisers gathered around the table, pale and speechless with shock.

'Leave us, Harper,' said Walsh. 'I will call you when I am ready to talk to you again.'

'Sir Nicholas,' he prompted the American. Nicholas knew that he had the upper hand now.

'Please leave us, Sir Nicholas,' Walsh pleaded.

An hour later Nicholas sauntered back into

the conference room. The three men were seated around the table as though they could not bear to be parted from the two great crowns. Walsh nodded at his minions and they stood up and obediently but reluctantly filed from the room.

As soon as the door closed, Walsh asked brusquely, 'How much?'

'Fifteen million US dollars,' Nicholas replied.

'That's seven and a half mill each.'

'No, that's fifteen mill each. Thirty million the two.'

Walsh reeled in his chair. 'Are you crazy, or something?'

'There are those who think so,' Nicholas smiled.

'Split the difference,' said Walsh. 'Twenty-two and a half.'

Nicholas shook his head. 'Not negotiable.'

'Be reasonable, Harper!'

'Reasonability has never been one of my vices. Sorry.'

Walsh stood up. 'I am sorry too. Perhaps next time, Harper.'

He clasped his hands behind his back and stalked to the door. As he opened it, Nicholas called after him.

'Mr Walsh!'

He turned back eagerly. 'Yes?'

'Next time you may call me Nicholas, and I shall call you Peter, as old friends.'

'Is that all you have to say?'

939

'Of course. What else is there?' Nicholas looked puzzled.

'Damn you,' said Walsh, and came back to the table. He dropped into his chair. 'Damn you to hell and back!'

He sighed and pursed his lips, and then asked, 'Okay. How do you want it?'

'Two irrevocable bank drafts. Each for fifteen million.'

Walsh picked up the intercom, and spoke into it. 'Please ask Monsieur Montfleuri, your chief accountant, to come up here,' he ordered dolefully.

Nicholas sat at his desk in his study at Quenton Park. He stared at the panelling that covered the wall facing him. Although the panelling had originally come from one of the Catholic abbeys dissolved by Henry VIII in 1536 and had been bought by his grandfather almost a hundred years ago, it was newly installed in this setting.

He reached under the top of his desk and pressed the hidden button of the electronic control. A section of the panelling slid smoothly and silently aside to reveal the armoured plate glass of the display cabinet built into the wall behind it. At the same time the spotlights in the ceiling lit automatically, and their beams fell on the contents of the cabinet. The spots had been placed so that there was no reflection from the glass window to distract the eye, and the beams brought out the full glory of the double crown and the golden death-mask of Mamose.

He poured whisky into a crystal glass, and while he sipped it he savoured the thrill of ownership. But after a while he knew there was something missing. He picked up the Taita *ushabti* from the desk in front of him, and spoke to it as though he were addressing the subject himself.

'You knew the real meaning of loneliness, didn't you?' he asked softly. 'You knew what it was like to love someone you could never have.'

He set down the statuette and picked up the telephone. He dialled an international number and it rang three times before a man answered in Arabic.

'This is the office of the Director of Antiquities. How may I help you?'

'Is Dr Al Simma available?' he asked in the same language.

'Please hold the line. I am putting you through!'

'Dr Al Simma.' Her voice sent an electric thrill down his spine.

'Royan,' he said, and he could sense her shock in the long silence that followed.

'You!' she whispered. 'I did not think I would ever hear from you again.'

941

'I just rang to congratulate you on your appointment.'

'You cheated me,' she said. 'You switched the contents of three of the crates.'

'As a wise man once said, friends are the easiest to cheat — they don't expect it. You, of all people, should know the truth of that, Royan.'

'You have sold them, of course. I have heard a rumour that Peter Walsh paid twenty million.'

'Thirty million,' Nicholas corrected her. 'But only for the blue and the Nemes. Even as I speak to you, the red and white crown and the death-mask repose before me.'

'So now you can pay off your Lloyd's insurance losses. You must be very relieved.'

'You won't believe this, but the Lloyd's syndicate on which I am a Name has come up with much better results than were forecast. I wasn't really broke after all.'

'As my mother would say, "Bully for you." '

'Half of it has already gone to Mek Nimmur and Tessay.'

'At least that is a good cause.' Her tone tingled with hostility. 'Is that all you called to tell me?'

'No. There's something else that might amuse you. Your favourite author, Wilbur Smith, has agreed to write the story of our discovery of the tomb. He is calling the book *The Seventh Scroll*. It should be published early next year. I will send you a signed copy.'

'I hope he gets his facts straight this time,' she said drily.

They were both silent for a while, before Royan broke it. 'I have a mountain of work in front of me. If there is nothing else on your mind —'

'As a matter of fact there is.'

'Yes?'

'I would like you to marry me.'

He heard her draw breath sharply, and then after a long pause she asked softly, 'Why would you want anything so unlikely?'

'Because I have come to realize how much I love you.'

She was silent again, and then she said in a small voice, 'All right.'

'What do you mean, "All right"?'

'I mean, all right, I will marry you.'

'Why would you agree to anything so unlikely?' he asked.

'Because I have come to realize, despite everything, how much I love you back.'

'There is an Air Egypt flight from Heathrow at 5.30 this afternoon. If I drive like fury, I may just make it. But it gets me into Cairo rather late.'

'I will be waiting at the airport, no matter how late.'

'I am on my way!' Nicholas hung up, and went to the door, but suddenly he turned back and picked up the Taita *ushabti* from the desk.

'Come on, you old rogue.' He laughed triumphantly. 'You are going home, as a wedding gift.'

EPILOGUE

They strolled along the corniche in the mauve evening. Below them the Nile ran on eternally green and slow and inscrutable, disposing of the secrets of the ages. At the point on the river bank, below the ruins of the temple of Ramesses at Luxor, where once the great barge of Pharaoh Mamose had docked with Taita and his beloved mistress upon her prow, they paused for a while and leaned upon the coping of the stone retaining wall. They gazed out to the darkening hills across the river.

Time had long since obliterated the funerary temple and the great causeway of Mamose, and other kings had built their own monuments over the foundations. No man had ever discovered the tomb that he had never occupied, but it must have been situated close to the secret opening in the rock through which Duraid Al Simma had entered the tomb of Lostris and discovered there the scrolls of Taita in their alabaster jars.

All four of them were silent in the gathering dusk, the shared silence of firm friendship. They watched a cruise boat pass, coming upriver with the tourists clustered upon her decks, still agog after ten days of voyaging from Cairo on these enigmatic waters, pointing out to each other the great pylons and engraved walls of Ramesses' temple, their excited voices small and inconsequential in the hush of the desert evening.

Then Royan slipped her arm through Tessay's and the two women walked on ahead. They made a lovely pair, slim and young and honey-skinned, their laughter gay and sweet, their dark heads ruffling in the sultry puffs of Saharan air off the desert. Nicholas and Mek Nimmur followed them, each watching his own woman fondly as they bantered.

'So now you are one of the fatcats in Addis, you, the hard man, the bush fighter, you are now a politician. I can hardly believe it, Mek.'

'There is a time to fight and a time to make peace.' Mek was serious for a moment, but Nicholas mocked him lightly.

'I see that now that you are a politician you have to practise your clichés and your platitudes.' Nicholas punched his arm lightly. 'But how did you swing it, Mek? From dirty *shufta* bandit to Minister of Defence in one mighty bound.'

'The money from the sale of the blue crown helped a little. It gave me the clout I needed,' Mek admitted, 'but they knew they could never hold a democratic election without me as a candidate. In the end they were eager to have me on board.'

'The only quibble I have with the deal is that you handed all that lovely hard-won lolly over to them,' Nicholas mourned. 'Hell, Mek, fifteen million iron men don't come along every day.'

'I didn't hand it to them,' Mek corrected him. 'It was paid into the state coffers, where I can keep an eye on what eventually happens to it.'

'Still, fifteen mill is a lot of bread,' Nicholas sighed. 'Try as I might, I cannot approve of such extravagance, but I must admit that I do approve of your choice of running mate in your bid for the Presidency in the coming elections.'

They both looked at Tessay's slim back and bush of springing black curls as she strode along ahead of them on shapely brown legs under the white skirt.

'I may not approve of you as Minister of Defence, but I can see that she makes a very charming Minister of Culture and Tourism in the interim government.'

'She will make an even more impressive Vice-President when we win next August,' Mek predicted easily, and at that moment Royan looked back over her shoulder at them.

'We'll cross the road here,' she called. Nicholas had been so engrossed that he had not realized they had come up opposite to the new annexe to the Luxor Museum of Antiquities. The two women waited for them to catch up and then they separated and each of them took the arm of her own husband.

As they crossed the wide boulevard, threading their way between the slow clip-clopping horse-drawn gharries, Nicholas leaned down and brushed her cheek with his lips. 'You are really quite delectable, Lady Quenton-Harper.'

'You make me blush, Sir Nicky,' she giggled. 'You know that I am still not used to being called that.'

They reached the other side of the thoroughfare and paused before the entrance to the museum annexe. The sloping roof was supported by tall hypostyle columns, miniature copies of those at the temple of Karnak. The walls were made of massive blocks of yellow sandstone, and the lines of the building were clean and simple. It was very impressive.

Royan led them to the entrance doors of the museum, which was not yet open to the public. The President was flying up on Monday for the official opening, and Mek and Tessay were to be the official representatives of the Ethiopian government at the opening ceremony. The guards at the door saluted Royan respectfully and hurried to open the heavy brass-bound doors to let them pass.

The interior was hushed and cool, the air conditioning carefully regulated to preserve the ancient exhibits. The display cases were built into the sandstone walls, and the lighting was subtle and artful. It showed off the wondrous treasures of the Mamose funerary hoard to full advantage. The exhibits, arranged in ascending order of beauty and archaeological importance, sparkled and glowed in their nests of blue satin, the royal blue of the Pharaoh Mamose.

The four visitors were quiet and reverential

as they passed, their voices soft and subdued as they asked questions of Royan. Wonder and amazement held them enthralled. They paused at the entrance of the final chamber, the one that housed the most extraordinary and valuable items in this glittering collection.

'To think that this is only a small part of what treasure still remains in Mamose's tomb, sealed by the waters of the Dandera river,' whispered Tessay. 'It's so exciting that I can hardly wait for the adventure to continue.'

'I forgot to tell you!' Mek exclaimed, and it was clear from his triumphant grin that he had not forgotten at all, but had been merely waiting for the appropriate moment to impart his news. 'The Smithsonian have confirmed their grant to redam the Dandera and reopen the tomb. It will be a joint venture between the Institution and the governments of our two countries, Egypt and Ethiopia.'

'That is wonderful news,' Royan exclaimed delightedly. 'The tomb itself will be one of the great archaeological sites of the world, and a huge source of tourist revenue for Ethiopia —'

'Not so fast,' Mek interrupted her. 'There is one condition that they stipulate.'

Royan looked crestfallen. 'What is their condition?'

'They insist that you, Royan, take on the job of director of the project.'

She clapped her hands with delight, and then put on a mock-serious expression. 'However,

I have my own condition before I accept,' she said.

'And what is that?' Mek demanded.

'That I am able to appoint my own assistant on the dig.'

Mek let out a roar of laughter. 'We all know who that will be.' And he clapped Nicholas on the back. 'Just make sure that none of the artefacts cling to his sticky little fingers!' he warned.

Royan hugged Nicholas around the waist. 'He has completely reformed, I will now give you final proof of that.' Still clinging to her husband, she led them into the last chamber.

Mek and Tessay stopped in the entrance, silent with awe as they stared at the contents of the free-standing display case of armoured glass in the centre of the room. The red and white crown of the united kingdoms of upper and lower Egypt stood side by side with the glistening golden death-mask of Pharaoh Mamose in the brilliant light of the overhead spotlights.

At last Mek Nimmur recovered from the shock. Advancing slowly to the front panel of the display case, he stooped to read aloud the brass plate fixed to the front of it: ' "The permanent loan of Sir Nicholas and Lady Quenton-Harper." '

He turned back to stare at Nicholas incredulously. 'And you were the one who picked on me for turning over the money from the sale of the blue crown!' he accused him. 'How could

949

you bring yourself to give up your share of the loot, Nicholas?'

'It wasn't easy,' Nicholas admitted with a sigh, 'but I was faced with a delicate ultimatum from a certain party who is not standing a million miles away from us at this very moment.'

'Don't feel too sorry for the poor boy,' Royan laughed. 'He still has a big lump of Peter Walsh's money tucked away in Switzerland, the proceeds of the sale of the Nemes crown. I was unable to talk him into handing everything over.'

'Enough of these public disclosures of my domestic affairs,' said Nicholas firmly. 'The sun is long gone, and it's whisky time. I think I saw a bottle of Laphroaig behind the bar at the hotel. Let's go and find out if I was mistaken.'

He took Royan's arm and led her away, and the other two followed closely, laughing delightedly at his discomfort.

We hope you have enjoyed this Large Print book. Other Thorndike Press or Chivers Press Large Print books are available at your library or directly from the publishers. For more information about current and upcoming titles, please call or write, without obligation, to:

Thorndike Press
P.O. Box 159
Thorndike, Maine 04986
USA
Tel. (800) 223-6121 (U.S. & Canada)
In Maine call collect: (207) 948-2962

OR

Chivers Press Limited
Windsor Bridge Road
Bath BA2 3AX
England
Tel. (0225) 335336

All our Large Print titles are designed for easy reading, and all our books are made to last.